A Cornwall Christmas

Battling Demons, Volume 6

Kris Morris

Published by Kris Morris, 2016.

This is a work of fiction. Similarities to real people, places, or events are entirely coincidental.

A CORNWALL CHRISTMAS

First edition. November 23, 2016.

Copyright © 2016 Kris Morris.

Written by Kris Morris.

This is an unauthorised work of fiction. All royalties paid to the author will be donated to TheHorseCourse, a children's charity in Dorset, England. Thank you for supporting the work they do with abused and neglected children!

Thank you to my dear husband for believing in me, my sons for inspiration, and my friends Carole, Abby, Janet, and Anneke for ceaseless encouragement and for tolerating my insecurities.

Special thanks to my dear friend Abby Bukofzer and my son Karl for assisting with editing. And to my talented husband, Tim, for designing my book covers.

Prologue

Some years are better than others, and for Dr. Martin Ellingham, this had not been one of the better ones. The seemingly auspicious beginning had brought what he and his wife, Louisa, had hoped would be an end to the tempestuous nature of their relationship.

The wedding day had been a smashing success—in that they ended the day husband and wife. The disastrous honeymoon night that followed was, perhaps, a portent of things to come.

Louisa struggled to reconcile her wish to return to her position as headmistress at Portwenn Primary, with her desire to be at home with her baby son. And when she saw her husband, her unusual but rock solid man, descend into a deep depression, she did what came naturally to her when the going got tough—she ran off.

One would think that Martin Ellingham had lived a charmed life. But growing up the only child of a successful surgeon and his socialite wife had only served to hide the emotional and physical abuse he had suffered at the hands of both of his parents. Leaving him now, as a new husband and father, with a surety that he was neither deserving nor capable of either role.

To keep from losing his wife and son, he sought out and received help from a gifted psychiatrist. Confronting his past had been excruciatingly difficult, but he was making progress. He and Louisa were making progress as a couple as well.

And then an automobile accident, which nearly took Martin's life, left him recovering from severely injured limbs and forced both of them into altered roles. Louisa became Martin's rock and caregiver. And he had to learn to trust her with both his physical and emotional well-being.

She had made him a promise—to never again leave him. And he had pinned his faith on that promise. One phone call would start a chain reaction of events that would test their resolve and force them to make a life changing decision.

Chapter 1

Martin groped around on the little table beside the bed until his hand landed on his phone. "Ellingham!" he answered sharply, annoyed at the middle-of-the-night intrusion.

"I need your help, Dr. Ellig-am!" a breathy voice on the other end said.

He sat up abruptly, trying to shake the fog from his head. "What's going on, Evan?"

"It's my dad! He's been"—the little boy pulled in several ragged gasps of air—*"he's angry, Dr. Ellig-am. I got away, but he's lookin'. He's gonna f-find me!"*

Louisa sat up and flipped the switch on the table lamp. "What is it, Martin?" she asked, covering her eyes as the light streamed into her still-dilated pupils.

He shook his head and put his hand up, silencing her, before pulling himself from the warmth of the blankets. "Where are you, Evan?"

"In my house!"

"*Where* in your house?"

"Under my bed. But he's gonna find me!" the child whispered stridently.

Stepping into the chilly air, a surge of adrenaline coursed through Martin's body as his feet touched the icy floor. Gathering his clothes together, he tried to extract more information from the child.

"Where's your mother, Evan? Is she in the house?"

"Uh-uh."

He struggled, trying to hold his mobile in one hand while attempting to work the legs of his trousers over the metal fixators holding his fractured bones in place. Louisa jumped from the bed and hurried over to help him.

"Is your sister with you, Evan?"

"Uh-uh. They don't live here anymore. But, Dr. Ellig-am ... he's really angry! Can you come and help?"

There was a loud crash in the background followed by slurred expletives. *"Dammit! Where are you ... you ... lil' brrat?"*

The creases in Martin's forehead deepened as Jim Hanley's voice grew louder.

"Can you get to your door ... lock it?" Martin asked, grunting as he tried to force his still-swollen foot into a shoe.

"N-no. It gots a lock, but my sister stuck a crayon in it, and now it's bugger—"

There was a loud bang followed by the tinkling of glass, and the little boy began to cry. *"He's breakin' stuff now! Can you hurry?"*

"I'm working on it, Evan."

Martin wagged his finger at Louisa, pointing to his shoes as he mouthed the words *help me*. He lowered the phone and leaned over to whisper into her ear as she knelt down in front of him.

"Louisa, call nine-nine-nine. Tell them they need to get someone out to the Hanley farm. Then call Joe Penhale. Tell him I need him to pick me up. Jim Hanley's been drinking, and he's going after the boy."

"Yeah ... yeah," she replied, tying the last bow before grabbing for her phone and stepping out of the room to make the calls.

Martin listened helplessly to the child's whimpers and the occasional sound of objects falling on to the floor as the drunken man raged through the house. An inebriated voice demanded the child come out from under the bed.

"Thought you could hide ... hide from me, did you? Ged outta there, ya lil ... lil ... bastard!"

A high-pitched shriek emanated from the mobile in Martin's hand. "Evan?" Static came through the speaker.

The boy could be heard in the background now, pleading with his father for the return of his phone. "Please! I didn't steal it! My friend gave it to me! It's special; please don't break it!"

"They're sending a Cornwall County officer out to the Hanley's," Louisa said as she stepped back into the bedroom.

"What about Penhale?"

"His phone went right to voicemail."

"Typical!" Air hissed from the doctor's nose. Although the village's affable, but marginally competent, police constable had been a regular source of frustration for Martin, he had his shining moments. Unfortunately, it appeared this would not be one of them.

"Well, try Jeremy, then!" he snapped back, a crack beginning to show in his controlled facade. He pressed the speakerphone icon on his mobile and tossed the device on to the bed. Then he pulled the shirt he had taken off a few hours earlier from the laundry hamper and worked the right sleeve over the metal supporting the bones in his fractured arm.

"I didn't steal it!" The child's impassioned voice overlaid thuds and grunts as sounds emanated from the phone.

Martin pushed his left arm through the opposite sleeve and reached for the device. "Evan? *Evan?*"

He looked over at his wife, waiting while she quickly explained the situation to Jeremy Portman, his former at-home nurse and current assistant in his surgical practice.

"How soon can you get here, then?" Louisa gave him a shake of her head. "Oh, gawd." she groaned. "Yep, yep, I'll tell 'im."

She looked worriedly at her husband. "He and Poppy are coming back from a concert in Truro. They just left the petrol station at St. Columb Major, so it'll be close to a half hour before he can get here."

"Bugger!" Martin grabbed for his crutch and headed towards the doorway. "Tell Jeremy to meet me at the Hanley's. And keep trying to get through to Penhale. Tell him to meet me there, too."

"What are you doing, Martin? You can't go out there in the middle of the night! You need to wait for Joe Penhale!"

"Louisa, just tell Jeremy to meet me there! Penhale, too!"

She passed the information on to the aide and then reached for her dressing gown before catching up with her husband on the landing. A hand went to her mouth as they heard the little boy cry out over the speaker. There was a sharp crack, and the line went dead.

Martin looked at the mobile in his hand. The connection had been lost. "Keep trying to reach Penhale," he said as he turned for the stairs.

"No, Martin! You can't go out there! You've just started driving again … and there's the storm!" she said, gesturing towards the rain pelted windows.

She followed after him, her pleas continuing. "Martin, you can't defend yourself against Jim Hanley right now. This is crazy. *And* you're sick. Let Joe and Jeremy handle this … *please*."

He whirled his head around as he reached the top step. "Louisa, I *have* to help him!"

She felt a blinding panic wash over her as she watched him descend the stairs. "Come back here, Martin!"

James Henry, awakened by the commotion, had begun to wail, but his cries went unnoticed by his mother.

"Martin, stop!"

"Louisa, I can't," he said, giving her an apologetic look before limping towards the kitchen.

Pulling his mac from the coat rack by the door, he grabbed the car keys from the basket on the counter. Then, stopping at his consulting room, he picked up his medical bag before heading for the front door.

Louisa took hold of his shirt sleeve and tried to pull him back as he stepped out over the threshold. "Don't do this, Martin!" she said, her panic quickly boiling over into anger.

He pulled away from her grasp, stumbling as he made his way down the slate terrace towards the street.

Clutching the door frame, her eyes followed him, her gut clenching. "Don't you *dare* leave, Martin! If you walk away from me now, James and I'll be gone when you get back!" she shrieked at him over the howling wind and the roar of the waves.

Turning, he looked up at her, the porch light illuminating the dismay on his face. He hesitated for a moment before dipping his head into the wind and continuing towards the car.

Louisa stepped out on to the terrace, her hands balled into fists as she watched him drop into the seat of the Lexus. The anger that she had felt just moments before, wilted quickly into heartache as she became aware of the last words she had uttered to her husband.

"Martin! I didn't mean that!" she shouted as a clap of thunder reverberated overhead, obscuring her words.

The vehicle moved down the hill, its taillights fading behind the sheets of rain. Swallowing back a sob, she became aware of the shivers running through her as the cold wind blowing in off the sea penetrated her dressing gown. She returned to the cottage, swinging the door shut behind her. Then, leaning back against it, she pulled in several ragged breaths.

Becoming aware of her son's cries for attention, she hurried up the stairs, and after shucking her damp dressing gown, she scooped the boy into her arms. "Shh, shh, shh, James. It's all right. It's all right," she said softly.

She sat down in the rocker and nestled him to her breast, finding some reassurance in his warm solid body.

She couldn't take back the words that had been prompted by fear for her husband's safety. It had been little more than three months since the automobile accident that nearly took his life and left him still recovering from internal injuries and multiple fractures.

The external metal frames, holding in place the long pins that penetrated his bones, were a constant reminder to her of how fragile he still was.

But Martin was a dedicated doctor, and seven-year-old Evan Hanley was a patient. Nothing could keep him from tending to the needs of those who had entrusted their care to him.

The child's alcoholic father had abused the boy in his drunken rages. And when the protections put in place by the Children's Services system failed the child, Martin had stepped in.

Louisa's concerns for her husband went beyond those for his physical welfare. His own childhood history of physical and emotional abuse had made it difficult for him to keep his usual professional detachment with the little boy. And Evan Hanley adored her husband, seeing past his gruff exterior to the warm and very tender man he kept well-hidden from most people.

When the boy called him that night, there was no question that Martin would heed his cries for help. This very scenario was her worst fear when he gave the child the mobile to use if he should need assistance.

The baby fell back to sleep quickly, and Louisa laid him in his cot before dialling Joe Penhale's number. Again, it went to voicemail.

Scrolling through her contacts, she pressed Al Large's number, praying that this call would meet with success. The young man was Martin's elderly aunt Ruth's assistant at her B&B, and the son of Bert Large, the village's local plumber turned restaurateur.

"Hullo," the sleepy male voice drawled.

"Al, it's Louisa. I need your help," she said, dropping on to the bed before explaining the situation to the young man.

"So can you go over to Joe's ... see if he's home? It just wouldn't be like him to leave the village unattended."

"Sure. Sure. I'll head right over there."

Louisa rang off. Al Large was both conscientious and competent. His involvement in the situation relieved some of her anxiety. She breathed out a heavy sigh and went around the bed, picking up her husband's dressing gown from the chair and wrapping herself in it.

She wiped her tears on the sleeve, and a slight smile crossed her face as she heard her husband's voice in her head. *That's what tissues are made for, Louisa. Microorganisms will persist on there for days now!*

A loud crack of thunder caused their little stone cottage, perched on the cliff above the harbour, to tremble, and she went to the window to peer out into the inky night. *Please be all right, Martin. And please remember what I promised before—I will never leave you again.*

As Louisa worried at home, Martin wound his way through the narrow lanes that defined Cornwall. The visibility was poor, and the wind buffeted the car, straining the bones in his arm as he gripped tightly to the steering wheel.

He tried to focus his thoughts on the matter at hand, and yet Louisa's ultimatum tore at him. It wouldn't be the first time she said something she didn't mean. But it wouldn't be the first time she took their son and left either.

He sighed, pulling into the gravel drive. As he expected, the yard was devoid of vehicles, aside from the old red pickup belonging to Jim Hanley.

The police force in the area was not known for its rapid response time. It had been Martin's experience that by the time the county law enforcement people arrived on scene of an emergency, the locals had often dealt with the matter on their own.

Removing his medical bag from the back seat, he hobbled towards the house, the trepidation he felt slowing his steps as he neared the porch. He hesitated, his hand on the doorknob, and then he entered the Hanley home.

The living room floor was littered with undisposed bags of rubbish, and the air was heavy with the odour of decomposing foodstuffs. "Good, gawd," he muttered, wrinkling his nose.

He set his bag down on the floor before proceeding across the room. A plank creaked as he put his foot down, sending his heart sprinting. Jim Hanley's slurred words could be heard coming from the second floor, and he made his way to the steps.

Squeezing past an overturned end table lying at the bottom of the stairs, he began a precarious ascent up the rickety passageway. The boards under his feet gave slightly as his weight settled on to them. And the handrail, worn smooth by many decades of use, tipped as he tried to grasp hold of it, throwing him off balance before he caught himself with his crutch.

He stopped halfway up when a gravelly bass voice broke into song.

"*Pass around the grog, me ... me boys, and never mind the score,*
Drink the good ol'... good ol' liquor down afore we call fer more.
Fer to see who will not merry, merry be
Shall never taste ... taste of joy,
See, see, the cape's in view
*And **forward**, my brave boy!*
Forward, my brave boy! Forward!" The drunk said as feet could be heard scuffling against the floor.

"Stop, you're hurtin' me!" Evan's small voice pleaded.

"Quit yer whinin'. What are you, a mouse? Thas wha ya are, innit. Yer a cowar-cowarly lil' mouse!"

Martin forced himself up the final step and on to the landing.

"Dr. Ellig-am!" Evan yelled as he pulled free of his father's grasp and ran the length of the hallway, not slowing until he collided with the doctor's legs.

Martin gave the boy a nervous smile and put his hand on his head. Levelling his gaze at the child's inebriated father, he said, "Mr. Hanley, you're drunk. Why don't you go and have a lie-down ... sleep it off? I can watch your son for you."

"I ... I'm not drunk! Don't be comin' in ta my ... in ta my 'ouse, tell-tellin' me what ta do!" the man said, taking several unsteady steps forward.

Leaning over, Martin spoke softly to Evan, "I want you to wait for me downstairs."

The child shook his head as he looked up at him, tears welling in his eyes. "I wanna stay with you!" he said, wrapping his arms tightly around his legs.

"Don't you tell 'im what ta do neither!" Mr. Hanley erupted. "You stay right where ya are, boy!" The man staggered towards his son and grabbed on to the back of his pyjama top. He yanked it tightly around the child's neck and he fell back against his father's legs.

Martin dropped his crutch to the floor, wrapping his fingers around Hanley's wrists as he wrenched his hands upward, forcing his fists open.

"Go downstairs *now*, Evan!" Martin said forcefully, giving the boy a warning look.

The child peered up fearfully at him before slipping out from under his father's clutches and scurrying down the steps.

Releasing his grip, Martin gestured down the hall. "Now, Mr. Hanley, go and lie down."

The drunk turned his back on the doctor and took a step towards the hall before whirling around suddenly, pulling a small glass whiskey flask from his pocket and swinging it wildly at Martin.

Martin ducked, but the flask cracked against the side of his head before the drunk reeled sideways and tumbled down the stairs.

Grimacing, Martin pulled his hand up, pressing it to the knot that now pulsed above his ear. He squeezed his eyes shut as he waited for the stars to clear from his eyes, and then he turned to head down the stairs. His breath caught in his chest as he gazed down at the man lying inert on the floor below.

He inched down the steps, keeping one hand on the wall. Hanley's eyes were fixed and unseeing when he reached him, and blood seeped from his nose and ears as well as from a large gash in his forehead. He noted the man's blown pupils as he lowered himself to the floor. He pressed his fingers to his neck; Jim Hanley was dead.

A wave of nausea caused Martin to lurch to the side, swallowing repeatedly as he tried to quell the miserable sensation set off by the haemophobia that had forced him from his surgical career. He closed his eyes and took in several deep breaths, waiting for the feeling to pass.

When he looked up, Evan was crouched down in front of his father, fear clearly written on his face as the lifeless form stared coldly back at him.

"Evan, come here," Martin said softly. The boy was unresponsive.

The doctor took hold of the newel post and pulled himself to his feet and then reached down to take the child by the arm. Evan jumped up and bolted for the door.

The fierce wind howled into the house as the boy ran out and across the porch, into the cold night.

"Evan, wait!" Martin yelled out as he started after him. The frequent flashes of lightning illuminated the surroundings periodically, and he could make out the child's small form as it moved past the Lexus and away from the warmth of the house.

He stopped briefly, pulling his mac from the backseat of his car and slipping it over his left arm and around his shoulders. Then he retrieved a torch from the glovebox. He considered going back for his crutch, but he knew he'd never find the boy if he lost sight of him.

His concern for Evan's safety was very real. He was dressed only in pyjamas, lacking a dressing gown or even slippers on his feet. The forecasted low temperature that night was thirty-eight degrees Fahrenheit. That temperature alone could quickly cause hypothermia in a child, but combined with the gales and the steady rain, Evan could succumb quickly.

Moving as fast as his legs would allow, Martin followed the small silhouette as it moved nimbly across the rocky soil. He tried to take note of landmarks, distorted by the periodic flashes of lightning and the murky air.

"Evan! Evan, stop!" he shouted above the storm. The boy kept up his pace.

The uneven footing caused the doctor's steps to fall sharply, resulting in jolts of pain that radiated through his legs. He called out again to the boy, and the small figure finally stopped moving.

As he approached him, Evan dropped to the ground in front of a large granite boulder, pulling his legs up to his chest. Martin said nothing but removed his mac and wrapped it around the child. Then, putting a hand against the rock, he dropped stiffly to the ground, groaning involuntarily as his still-bruised hip made contact with the rock beneath him.

They were somewhat sheltered from the wind and rain, and Martin took the opportunity to check the boy over using the light from his torch. The child's nose was crusted with blood and his wrist was bruised and swollen, but he was reasonably certain it wasn't fractured.

A shivering Evan climbed into the doctor's lap and pulled his feet under him before wrapping his arms around his chest.

Pulling out his mobile, Martin peered at the screen, displaying no signal bars, and he groaned. He dropped the phone back into his pocket as he felt a sudden, overwhelming fatigue descend on him. The child's small body relaxed against his, and he fought the urge to lean his head back against the rock and go to sleep.

"Evan, we need to get you warmed up. We have to go back!" he shouted over the wind whistling across the moor.

The boy looked up at him, his eyes wide. "I don't wanna go back!" he said, shaking his head vigorously.

"Just back to my car. It's okay," Martin said, giving the boy a weary smile and a nod of his head.

"Kay."

The two walked hand in hand for a short distance before Evan sat down and pulled his foot into his lap. Tears welled in his eyes as Martin shined the torch beam on him.

"What is it, Evan?" he asked.

"It hurts!" He extended his leg into the air.

Martin held on to the child's ankle, sighing heavily when he saw the ragged cut across the bottom of his foot. He glanced around them, taking note of a pile of rocks nearby and then reached down and took Evan's hand, pulling him to his feet.

"I'll carry you ... on my back," he said as he led the boy to the rocks. "Climb up there, then grab hold around my neck."

Evan wasn't a tall boy and he was slight of build, but Martin wasn't used to walking as far as he had, and the child's added weight quickly wore him down.

The landmarks he had noted as he followed the boy on to the moor were hard to spot now that he was seeing them from a different perspective. And his head had begun to pound, making it hard for him to think clearly.

He pushed himself to keep going, scanning the rocks and sparse trees ahead for anything familiar. When it became increasingly difficult to pull his legs forward, he stopped at a low rock ledge and set the boy down.

"Evan, you're going to have to walk. I can't carry you any farther."

The thermal conductive properties of the metal in his fixators caused heat to be drawn from his body, and Martin's limbs had begun to ache intensely.

And he could no longer blame the confusion he was experiencing on the change in perspective, the flashes of lightning, or his overall fatigue. Though he couldn't make sense of it, Martin knew that he needed to find a place where they could get some shelter from the wind and rain. Someplace to wait out the night.

The two kept walking, Evan holding tightly to the doctor's wrist. The boy was now shivering violently, but Martin could do nothing more than to keep him moving.

He could see a large outcropping of rocks ahead when the lightning illuminated the sky, and he pushed himself towards it, stumbling more and more frequently as the strength in his legs waned.

As they began to work their way down a slight hill, his right foot slipped on a moss-covered rock, throwing him on to the hard ground.

He landed on his right shoulder, feeling a sickening pop. The joint, loosened in the accident, was forced apart, his humeral head slipping from its socket. He clenched his jaw against the resulting agony and blinked back tears.

They were tantalisingly close to the shelter that might provide them with some relief from the storm, but Martin couldn't get himself to his feet.

The sharp rocks bit at his skin as he inched his way over to a scraggly tree, keeping his arm held protectively against his side.

He pulled himself upright. Evan's movements had grown sluggish, and Martin now had to drag him along. He led the boy around the pile of massive boulders to the lee side and tugged him into an opening between the rocks.

They found some relief from not only the wind, rain, and cold, but also from the noise of the storm.

"How are you doing, Evan?" Martin asked as he took hold of the child's wrist, feeling for his pulse. The boy was shivering so violently that he couldn't speak. He just shook his head.

Martin took the raincoat from around the child. It was now covered in mud from being dragged along the ground, but it would help to conserve the heat remaining in their bodies.

Pulling the boy into his lap, he covered them both with the muddy mac. After once again checking his mobile for a signal, Martin dropped the device back into his pocket and tipped his head back, letting his eyes drift shut.

Chapter 2

Al pulled his hood up over his head as he dodged puddles in front of the police station. He ducked under the awning and pounded on the door.

"Joe! Joe, you in there?" he called out. Stepping back out into the rain, he peered up as a light came on in an upstairs window.

The sash was thrown up, and the pyjama-clad constable looked down, rubbing his hand over his eyes. "It's goin' on one o'clock in the morning, Al! Do we need to have a friendly conversation about breach of the peace?"

"There's an emergency!" The young man's words were whipped away by the wind.

Joe wiped the raindrops from his face. "Yer gonna have ta speak up, I can't hear you with this wind!"

"Can you let me in? I'm freezin' out here!"

"Don't go anywhere, I'm comin' down!" Joe replied before slamming the window shut.

Al huddled under the awning until the door was pulled open. Then he dashed into the building, pushing the door shut behind him. "Bit of a hurly-burly, innit!" he said, giving a shudder as he flipped his hood back.

"Not the best night ta be out roaming the streets, you know. You'll catch yer death," the policeman said as he looked at him askance.

Al shot the man a black look, wiping the moisture from his face. "It's not a social call, Joe. The doc needs yer help, and *you* weren't answerin' your phone."

"Ah, a bit of a mishap there. It's ... out of commission at the moment," Joe said, giving the young man an oafish grin. Would'a got a new one, but nothing was open. Funny that, eh. I mean it's not like—"

"Doesn't matter, Joe. The doc needs you out at Jim Hanley's farm. He's been drinkin' and he's off his head."

Joe furrowed his brow. "I'm not surprised. He's not *used* to drinkin'. He should know better, him havin' a medical degree and all."

"Not the doc! Jim Hanley! He's going off on his boy. The doc's gone out there, but he needs yer help. You want me ta go with you?"

"Nope, you better stay here. I'm on it!" Joe said. "Don't want any innocent civilian's gettin' caught in the crossfire!" He disappeared past the top of the stairs.

"I don't think anyone's got a gun!" Al hollered before heading back out into the storm.

As Joe Penhale was driving up the hill leading out of the village, Jeremy and Poppy were arriving at the Hanley farm.

"You better wait here," Jeremy said as he leaned over and gave his girlfriend a kiss before jumping from the car.

He hurried up to the home and rapped loudly on the door, peering in the windows. Seeing no obvious signs of human activity, he took hold of the rusty old knob, cringing as it screeched gratingly.

Stepping into the house, he pulled off his raincoat, causing a shower of water droplets to rain down on to the plank flooring. He folded it up, tucking it under his arm as he surveyed the room.

He quickly spotted his boss's medical bag sitting on the floor just inside the door. "Martin?" he called out. "Martin, you in here?"

Wind whistled through a crack in one of the leaky living room windows. Rain seeped in, despite the bread bags that had been stuffed between the side jamb and the sash, running along the sill before following a brown vertical stain down the wall and puddling on the floor.

He rounded the corner and stopped in his tracks when the body of Jim Hanley came into view. "Blimey," he muttered. The wound to the man's head, his slack jaw, and clouded corneas were clear evidence of Mr. Hanley's unfortunate demise.

Jeremy slipped past the body and ascended the stairs. "Martin? You up here, mate?" he called out as he passed the crutch laying on the landing.

Searching the second story rooms, he found them empty. There was a land line phone on a table in what appeared to be Mr. and Mrs. Hanley's bedroom, and Jeremy used it to call nine-nine-nine, requesting a coroner. Then he headed back downstairs.

It concerned him that Martin had gone off without his crutch. The doctor's sense of balance was still unreliable, and it seemed odd that he would leave it behind.

He checked out the rest of the house. And then, finding it empty, he ventured back out into the storm. He looked around the farmyard, taking note of the barn that stood at the back of the property. Ducking his head, he dashed towards the old structure.

PC Penhale arrived at the Hanley's just behind a Cornwall County police officer. Parking his Land Rover next to Martin's Lexus, Joe stepped from his vehicle and hoisted up his tool belt.

A burly man approached the constable, extending his hand. "Officer Simon Alton," he said.

Joe eyed him imperiously before returning the gesture. "PC Joseph Penhale. I had a drunk and disorderly report, possibly accompanied by actual bodily harm to a minor."

"Any weapons involved?" Simon asked as he started for the house.

"That has yet to be ascertained. I suggest we proceed with caution," Penhale said before taking hold of the man's arm and locking eyes with him. "Just to be sure we're on the same page before we enter the premises ... this is *my* bea-*t*," he said with his trademark emphasis on the last phoneme. "That understood ... *Simon?*"

"Whatever you say, Constable. You lead the way," the policeman said as he followed Joe up to the porch.

Pushing open the door to the house, Joe stepped inside. "Smells suspiciously of death in here."

PC Alton kicked at one of the rubbish bags strewn around the room. "Or last week's leftovers."

"No, I definitely think it's death," Penhale said as he spotted Jim Hanley's lifeless body at the bottom of the stairs. He leaned over, wrinkling up his nose as he peered closely at the man's clouded eyes. Then he grunted and walked over to pick up an old wool blanket from the sofa before covering him.

"Doc?" he called out, listening for a response. "I'll check upstairs, you cordon off the area around the victim," he instructed the other constable.

Joe pulled his Taser from his tool belt and crept up the steps.

Simon Alton watched from below, his brow furrowing. "Did you hear something?"

Joe turned and said in an undertone, "You can't be too careful."

Alton shrugged his shoulders before heading back outside to get a roll of police tape from his cruiser.

"Doc? You up there?" Joe called out again. He stepped on to the landing, crouching down to examine the whiskey flask laying on its side near the steps, and then took note of Martin's crutch.

"Doc?" Wandering down the hallway, he stopped to look into the bedrooms. The last room on the left, decorated with drawings of animals taped to the walls, was in disarray. The bed pulled out into the middle of the floor, a lamp lying on its side—the bulb broken, and in the doorway, a mobile phone with a shattered display screen. He turned and retraced his steps.

Simon had police tape strung across the front door, and he was now crouched down, examining Jim Hanley's corpse. He looked up as Joe made his way down the stairs. "Anyone up there?"

"No, and I have a very uneasy feeling about this. It's not like the doc to go off and leave a body unattended."

Penhale heard the sound of stomping feet on the porch and hurried over to prevent the breaching of the possible crime scene.

Jeremy Portman stood on the opposite side of the tape, poised to enter the house.

"Gotta stop you there, Jeremy," Joe said as he reached out and pushed the young man back. "We have a fatality we're dealing with ... have to rule out homicide."

Jeremy brushed the policeman's hand from his chest. "Joe, I've searched the house, the barn, the yard ... I can't find Martin or the Hanley boy. Martin's car is still here, though, so they've got to be around. We need to do a search of the area; something's not right."

Penhale hooked a thumb over his tool belt as he scratched at his head with his other hand. "I agree. It does seem suspicious. Gotta take care of the little matter of the corpse in the living room first though."

Jeremy's brows drew together as he stared back at him. "He's not going to get any deader, Joe! Martin and Evan could be in trouble!"

A beam of light panned across the front of the house, and the aide turned, watching as the county coroner's vehicle pulled into the yard.

"Turn things over to him, Joe," Jeremy said, thrusting a thumb towards the man as he stepped from his van.

The coroner climbed the steps to the Hanley home and peered up from under his hood, giving an annoyed grunt. "Dr. Richards ... I'm here for a body," he clipped.

PC Penhale stepped aside as the man ducked under the crime scene tape. "You must be psychic; we just happen to have one."

"I called him before you arrived, Joe," Jeremy explained as he followed the coroner under the barrier. "Now, can we let Dr. Richards take it from here ... go find Martin and the boy?"

The constable glanced down at the doctor as he knelt by Jim Hanley's remains and pulled a stethoscope from his toolbox. "I need to debrief the man first, Jeremy."

The coroner looked up at Joe with a look of haughty disdain. "No you don't! I need to debrief *you*! What's happened here?" he demanded, gruffly.

"I actually arrived before PC Penhale and Officer— well, we haven't been introduced," Jeremy said, pointing a finger at Simon.

The policeman was leaning against the wall with his arms folded across his chest. "Officer Simon Alton. Looks like an accidental death to me."

"The man was reportedly intoxicated. I suspect he fell down the stairs. But that's your call," Jeremy said.

The young man looking anxiously towards the door. "Dr. Ellingham, the GP over in Portwenn, received a call from the victim's little boy. He came to check things out ... make sure the boy was okay. There's a history of abuse during the father's periods of imbibing."

"When I arrived, there was no sign of either Dr. Ellingham or the boy. They could be in need of assistance. Can you take it from here?" Jeremy looked pointedly at the coroner.

"I'll need some help getting the body on the gurney, but I can spare you til then," Richards replied, crisply.

As Jeremy, Joe, and Officer Alton searched the farmyard, Martin and Evan were trying to wait out the storm and the night.

The large granite boulders that sheltered them provided some heat from the previous day's sunshine. It had helped to slow their rate of heat loss, but Martin had begun to shiver uncontrollably, and Evan had curled up tightly against his chest, completely covered by the raincoat.

Martin tried to stay awake, but he checked his watch frequently and knew that there had been unaccounted for periods of time.

He reached under the mac and felt for the familiar steady throbbing in Evan's neck. The boy's pulse was slowing gradually, and Martin feared he may not survive until morning. He pulled the child closer to him and bent his stiffened legs as far as possible, maximising body contact with the boy.

An intense ache had spread through his fractured limbs, and the pain in his shoulder continued to intensify as the muscles spasmed around the injury. He shifted slightly to relieve the pressure on his back and ribcage, causing Evan to stir and begin to cry.

"I'm c-c-cold, D-Doctor Ell-ig-am."

"Mmm. Me too ... Evan." He tried to flatten his left hand against the boy's body, but his fingers refused to open. "Let's play ... erm, let's play ... play a game," he slurred. "I'll say a let ... letter. Then you tell me..." His head dropped back and hit against the rock behind him, jarring him awake again.

The boy peered up at him through the gap between the mac and doctor's chest. "W-What's the g-game, Dr. Elligam?"

Martin fought to focus his thoughts. "I say a letter ... and you say ... you say the name ... of an animal that begins ... begins with that letter. The first letter ... is *B*."

"Can I s-s-say more than one?" Evan's hand worked it's way up, coming to rest against Martin's neck.

"Mmm. That's fine."

The boy lay quietly for some time without responding.

"Evan? Can you think ... of an animal?" Martin asked.

"I kn-know lots of *B* ani-animals. I'm t-trying to decide which is m-my f-favourite. I think the b-basking shark and the beluga w-whale."

Martin's head had dropped forward, sleep reclaiming him.

The boy's hand patted against his throat causing him to stir. He blinked his eyes and looked down at the child. "Can you ... think of an animal?"

"I need a letter."

"I gave you one—*B*."

Evan pulled his hand back down under the raincoat and poked his finger into the doctor's chest. "You're n-not p-paying attention. I t-told you, basking shark and b-beluga whale."

"I see. How about *P?* The letter *P*."

"I gots a g-good one for *P*," the boy said, his mood momentarily brighter. "Potato."

"That's a vegetable, Evan."

"N-not that kind. The Iris sh-shredder kind!" the child said, referencing his elderly neighbour's potato-loving Irish setter. "You're v-very funny, Dr. Ellig-am."

"Mm, yes."

The child lay quietly for some time, and Martin's head had begun to nod again when he heard the boy's breathy voice.

"Dr. Ellig-am ... did m-my dad die?"

Martin's heart felt heavy as he tipped his head back and closed his eyes. "Yes, Evan, I'm afraid so."

The child pushed his feet against his thigh, hiking himself higher and dropping his head on to the doctor's injured shoulder.

A sharp cry slipped from Martin's mouth as he grabbed at the boy's shirt and pulled him quickly to the left. Searing pain radiated down his right arm which hung limply at his side, and he struggled to pull in a breath of air.

Evan lay perfectly still, aside from the occasional shudder that vibrated through his body. "It's my f-fault ... isn't it."

Martin pulled his hand up from under the mac and wiped the tears from his eyes, taking in a deep breath. "No, you ... just f-forgot, Evan. I'm all right now," he said as he moved his arm back down and held it tightly around the boy.

Evan peered up at him, then closed his eyes and fell asleep.

Jeremy and the two officers were returning to the farmhouse from their unsuccessful search when Chippy Miller, one of the local fishermen, and Al Large pulled up in Chippy's pickup. They emerged from the vehicle and ran for the porch, their hooded heads bowed low.

"What are you fellas doin' out here?" Joe asked as he ducked under the barrier tape to enter the home.

"Thought you might need some assistance with Hanley. He's a hard one ta handle when he's been on a bender," Al explained.

Joe stared back at him, the corners of his mouth pulling down slightly in the socially acceptable expression when announcing someone's death. "He won't be givin' anybody any trouble this time, I'm afraid. He's dead."

"Crikey! What happened?" Chippy asked as he craned his neck to see past the doorway.

"Don't know, the matter's ... *unresolved* at the moment. And the doc and the boy appear to be missing."

"You boys ready to help me get the body loaded up?" Dr. Richards asked as he snapped the clasps shut on his toolbox.

PC Penhale glanced anxiously at Jeremy. "I've never actually touched a dead person before."

"Lucky for you then that you don't have to actually touch this one," Richards said. "Just grab hold of his shirt and lift him on to the body bag."

Joe and Jeremy hoisted the man's torso as Dr. Richards handled his legs. Hanley's arms, which had been folded across his stomach, slipped down and the right hand brushed against Joe's. The constable screwed up his face before trying to discreetly wipe any possible contaminants on to his trousers.

"Well, I agree with *his* assessment of the situation," the doctor said as jerked his thumb in Jeremy's direction. "I think this is a straightforward case of accidental death."

Joe tipped his head to the side and quirked his mouth. "I'd prefer to collect and analyse all the evidence before jumping to any conclusions."

Richard's gave him a shrug of his shoulders before returning his attention to the task at hand.

The zip of the slider as the coroner sealed the bag gave a sense of finality to Jim Hanley's rather miserable life. The body was lifted on to the gurney and wheeled to the van.

Joe, Jeremy, and Officer Alton watched as the vehicle left the farmyard. Then they returned to the house.

"Can we come in now, Joe? It's really cold out here." Al shifted uncomfortably from one foot to the other.

"Yeah, I can hardly feel my toes anymore, Joe!" Chippy said.

Joe's shoulders drooped as he blew out an exasperated breath. "See that you keep yourselves confined to a two-foot perimeter around the doorway," he said authoritatively, ripping the tape away.

Turning, he put his hands on his hips. Scanning the room, he glanced down as he felt something bump his leg. "What's Buddy doin' here?" he asked as he quickly whisked Martin's aunt's little terrier into his arms. "He could contaminate the crime scene!" The constable cocked his head to the side. "Well ... *potential* crime scene."

"Sorry, Joe. The poor little blighter was sittin' outside the chippy when we drove by. I felt sorry for 'im bein' out in this storm and all," Al said as he blew warm air into his cupped hands.

The little dog raised his head suddenly, his nose working furiously. Then wriggling from the constable's arms, he bounded up the steps.

"Buddy, no!" Joe dropped his chin to his chest as his hands flapped at his sides. "Bugger."

"Buddy! Come back here," Al yelled.

The dog sniffed around the landing, giving Martin's crutch special attention, before scurrying back down the stairway and out the door.

Joe's eyes widened as he watched Buddy's small form move away from the house. "Al and Chippy, follow me!

Officer Alton, I'm leaving you in charge here. I have a citizen in need of assistance," he said as he dashed through the doorway.

He ran to his police vehicle, and pulling the door shut, he turned the key in the ignition before leading the way across the rocky expanse, following after the little terrier as he sprinted ahead of him.

Chapter 3

"Wait a minute!" Jeremy yelled as he veered away from Chippy and Al to head back towards the house. "I'm going to fetch some blankets!"

The aide ran into the Hanley home, stopping briefly at his car, pulling the door open and ducking his head inside.

The warmth that emanated from the idling vehicle felt comforting against his stinging cheeks, and Poppy's softly scented perfume contrasted with the pungent smell of wet earth and decaying vegetation which filled the moorland air.

"We're going to try to find Martin and the kid, Poppy. You better go on back to the village. It's hard to tell how long we could be," he said.

Poppy took his icy hand in hers. "What d'you mean, find them? What's happened?"

"I don't have time to talk. Just ... well, when you get back to the village, stop at the surgery and tell Louisa we have things under control with Jim Hanley. But we don't know where Martin and the boy are at the moment. We're heading out to find them. Buddy seems to be on their trail, so hopefully, he'll lead us to them."

"Why's the coroner here?" Poppy asked, taking an anxious glance at the old farmhouse as she pulled herself from the car. "Was that Jim Hanley?"

"We can talk later! Just tell Louisa I'll ring her up as soon as we find Martin and Evan, and I can get a call out."

Passing him on the way to the driver's seat, Poppy brushed a kiss on his cheek before he moved off. "Jeremy!" she hollered above the storm. Be careful...okay?"

"I will." He gave her a reassuring smile before dashing for the house.

After pulling several blankets from the upstairs beds, he ran back down the steps. Officer Alton glanced up from the report he was working on. The aide gave him a nod of his head and stooped to grab Martin's medical bag before running out the door.

Chippy and Al were waiting in the pickup when Jeremy threw the back door of the cab open. He tossed the blankets on to the seat before sliding in next to them, then Chippy shifted the truck into gear and headed towards the rapidly fading lights of the Land Rover.

The three men sat for a few moments before Al's voice broke the silence. "What d'you think is goin' on? Do you 'spose the doc couldn't find the kid and went lookin' for 'im?"

"Your guess is as good as mine, Al," Jeremy said, tugging a knit cap from his pocket and pulling it over his head. "I do know that it's damn cold, and Martin's probably not dressed for it. Don't know about the boy."

Chippy held tight to the wheel as they bounced over the rocks. "We'll find 'em lads. We'll find 'em."

When she arrived at the surgery a half hour later, Poppy tapped quietly on the kitchen door. She waited nervously, knowing that the message she was there to deliver would not be well-received.

As the Ellingham's childminder, she had been witness to the stress Louisa had been under for the last several months, and she hated being the bearer of more bad news.

The lights were on in the kitchen, but her first hesitant knocks proved ineffective. She rapped more vigorously and watched as Louisa passed by the window.

"Poppy! Oh, dear. Come in out of the rain!" she said, stepping back to let the girl through. "What are you doing here at this hour of—"

She took a step back and pulled in a ragged breath. "Oh, God. What's wrong, Poppy? Something's happened to Martin, hasn't it?"

Louisa's red-rimmed eyes betrayed her already emotional state, and Poppy attempted a nonchalant tone. "Oh, no. Jeremy just asked me to stop and tell you that they have things under control with Jim Hanley."

Louisa let out a heavy breath and dropped into a chair. "Oh, thank goodness!"

Poppy hesitated. "But they don't know where Dr. Ellingham and Evan are at the moment ... they're going to look for them."

"What do you mean they don't know where they are? Martin's at the Hanley's."

The young childminder filled the tea kettle and flicked her thumb over the switch. "Maybe we should have a cuppa ... or hot chocolate?" she said as she took two cups from the cupboard.

"I don't *want* a cup of tea, Poppy. I want to know where my husband is!" Louisa demanded, her eyes narrowing.

"I'm sorry, Mrs. Ellingham. All I know is what Jeremy told me—that things are under control with Mr. Hanley, but they don't know where Dr. Ellingham and the little boy are.

"When we got to the farm, Jeremy told me to wait in the car, so I really *don't* know what's going on."

Louisa wrapped her arms around herself before she began to fire questions at the young woman. "Well, what did you see?"

"Just people comin' and goin' from the house most—"

"People? Who all was out there?"

"I'm not sure who *everybody* was, but—"

"Well, did you see Martin's car?"

"Yeah, but—"

"Was Al Large able to find Joe Penhale? Was Joe out there?"

The tea kettle hissed its readiness, and Poppy pulled it from the heating element before pouring hot water into the cups. Then she set a canister of hot chocolate mix next to the basket of tea bags in the middle of the table before taking a seat.

"Okay, this is what I saw. When we arrived, there was an old red pickup and Dr. Ellingham's Lexus parked in the yard. Jeremy told me to wait in the car. He went into the house and was in there for a while. Then he came out and walked around to the barn. I didn't—"

"What was he doing in the barn?"

Poppy scooped some of the hot chocolate mix into Louisa's cup and stirred it in. "I didn't have time to talk to him, so I don't know *what* he was doin'."

"What do you mean you didn't have time to talk to him? Was he in that much of a rush?"

Poppy shrugged her shoulders and tried to downplay her words. "I just mean that he didn't stay at the car long, and then I left."

"*Then* what?" Louisa pressed impatiently, making frantic circles in the air as she gave her head an exaggerated nod. "What happened after Jeremy went to the barn?"

"Then a police car pulled up ... oh, Joe Penhale, too. So yeah, Al did find Joe."

Poppy sipped at her tea, peering over the top of her cup. "They went inside, and then I saw Jeremy come back from the barn, and he went up to the porch. Jeremy and Joe were talkin' in the doorway when the coron—" Poppy hesitated. "So, another vehicle pulled in, and that guy walked up to the house. Him and Jeremy went inside together."

Louisa tipped her head down, peering up with a furrowed brow. "Poppy, what were you going to say?"

The girl folded her arms across her chest, and her fingers fiddled with her shirt sleeves. "Well, erm ... well, I'm just afraid you'll think the worst, and I'm sure it's nothin'. It couldn't have been—"

"Poppy! Just tell me, *please!*"

"A coroner came. But I really don't think it's something for you to worry about," the childminder said as she watched her employer, wide-eyed.

"A coroner! How can I help but worry?" Louisa got up and went to the window, watching the lightning rippling through the clouds as it illuminated the churning sea.

She turned and Poppy glanced up uncomfortably. "I'm sorry Mrs. Ellingham. I wasn't thinking. I shouldn't have said anything about the coroner."

Pulling the tea towel from the hook on the end of the counter, Louisa picked a cup up from the draining rack by the sink and began to vigorously rub it dry of non-existent moisture. "It doesn't matter. Martin is fine!" She set the cup on the shelf in the cupboard and then turned, flinging the tea towel down on the kitchen table. "Okay, what else?"

"Well, Chippy Miller and Al Large showed up in Chippy's pickup. Then after they put the ... mm, well after they got done helping the coroner—"

"Oh for goodness' sake, Poppy! Just say what happened, or I *will* be thinking the worst!" Louisa dropped back into her chair and huffed out a breath. "I'm sorry. I'm a bit tense."

"It's okay. I am too, and he's just my boss. Well, he's not *just* my boss. I hope you know that. But you know what I mean ... right? I mean, if it were Jeremy, I'd be so worried!"

Louisa put her hands over her face and began to cry.

Poppy hurried around putting an arm across her shoulders. "Oh, I'm so horrible at this kind of thing! I was tryin' not to upset you and—and—"

She pulled a tissue from the box on the counter and handed it to Louisa.

"Mrs. Ellingham, I'm sure your husband will be all right. Jeremy, Al, Joe and Chippy all went out looking for them. Oh, and Buddy was there, and he went running off ahead of them. If anyone can find the doc, Buddy can. Right?" Poppy said, giving her a half-smile.

Sliding her hands away from her face, Louisa peeked over at the childminder. "This is so inappropriate of me to be telling to you about this. I mean, I'm your employer. It's just ... it's just that I said something horrible to Martin right before he left, and I didn't get a chance to apologise."

The girl shifted into the chair next to her and took hold of her hand. "I'm sure Dr. Ellingham's friends will find him. And we both know Buddy'll be at his side before you can say Jack Robinson, right?"

Louisa stared back at her before she gave a nervous giggle. "Buddy does seem to have a knack for tracking Martin down."

"Yeah! I'm sure they'll find him ... and the boy." Poppy rubbed her hand across Louisa's back and then went to the cupboard and took out a package of chocolate digestives.

"Let's have a biscuit," she said as she put two on a plate and set it on the table. "And think good thoughts."

While Louisa's thoughts were of Martin, his thoughts were of her last words to him. They replayed in his head, over and over, as he drifted between torpidity and sleep.

He coughed, trying to clear his airway of the increasing congestion that was making it hard for him to breathe. Evan had grown quiet, and Martin again reached under the mac, pressing his fingertips to the child's neck.

Leaning his head back against the rock, he cursed the situation he was in, second guessing his decision to come out to the Hanley farm on his own. If he had waited for Jeremy there would have been two of them to handle the inebriated Jim Hanley, possibly preventing the man's fall to his death. But what might have happened to Evan if he had waited?

And what about Louisa. She must be truly regretting the day she married him now. Especially after what she had endured in the last months.

*God, what was I thinking? You **don't** deserve her, Ellingham.*

"Asinine is ... what it was," Martin mumbled. "Asini ... asinine. Idiot!"

The vehemence of Martin's garbled words caused Evan to stir slightly, and the doctor peered down at him.

"Evan ... wake up. We need ... need to stay ... stay awake." The boy lay unmoving once again, and Martin's head bobbed before dropping back against his granite pillow.

Don't you dare walk away from me! His wife's words and images of her walking off with James in her arms frequented his dreams as he slept. They merged with his semi-conscious thoughts. His mind pulled together bits and bobs from his autobiographical memory, creating distorted, cold-induced confabulations that left him feeling utterly forsaken.

Less than a mile away, though, a whimsical search and rescue operation was underway. Buddy trotted along, stopping periodically to stick his nose into the air as he gathered the vital information needed to track down Martin and the little boy.

He worked his way from rock to rock and scraggly tree to scraggly tree as he followed the scent. Joe Penhale zigzagged back and forth behind him, and Chippy Miller's truck waited in the wings for the assemblage to move forward.

Buddy seemed to lose the trail at one point, searching furiously around a large granite boulder.

"What's Penhale doing now?" Chippy asked as he pressed his foot down on the brake pedal. The men watched as the Land Rover circled the rock like a horse on a roundabout, with the constable in close pursuit of the little terrier as he attempted to pick up the doctor's scent.

"Joe's got a funny style, fer sure," Al said as he rubbed at the back of his neck.

Jeremy fidgeted in the back seat, glancing at his watch again. He found the roar of the wind and the ostensibly laissez faire approach of the constable beginning to wear on him. And he knew that if Martin and Evan were exposed to the extremes of the storm, time was of the essence. He huffed out a long breath and rubbed his palm across his forehead.

Buddy stopped and pushed his nose under the lee side of the boulder, and his plumed tail began to wag furiously. The dog scampered off quickly, and Chippy moved the pickup forward again.

The truck undulated as they descended a short, rocky slope before the little terrier in charge of the operation bolted to the right suddenly and disappeared into a granite outcropping.

Martin ... I need you, Martin. James and I need you, his wife whispered softly, her breath warm and moist in his ear. He sensed her weight pressing against his chest.

She was lovely—the most exquisite thing he had ever seen. And she wanted him. *Martin,* she cooed. *I need you.* He felt her breath brush his face, the odour of it triggering the almost autonomic firing of his medical mind.

Halitosis, a symptom of any number of medical conditions ... or possibly just a result of poor dental hygiene. *No, that's not likely. She adheres to a strict grooming regimen. Smells like fish. Perhaps a dietary explanation,* he surmised. *Good God, man! Focus! You'll end up walking home if you're not careful!*

Her tongue began to stroke his lips, teasingly, and her hair tickled as it fell against his cheek. It was all wonderful ... until air spilled from her lungs once again and the odour proved overwhelming.

He pulled his hand up and pushed her face away, but her tongue reached for his eyes, his nose, and, *Oh gawd!* Her tongue worked its way into his ear. *For God's sake, Louisa! Stop that!* Her cold, wet nose pushed into the crook of his neck, waking him from his fitful slumber.

"Martin! Can you hear me, mate?"

"Louisa?"

"Hate to disappoint you. It's me, Jeremy."

The young man's voice began to penetrate the mental fog, and he forced his eyes open. Buddy lay on his chest, his haunches nestled against Evan's head. The animal stared back at him before again nuzzling his nose into his neck. Martin was helpless, unable to resist his advances.

"You need to let go of the boy, Martin."

"He needs ... he *needs* to go to hos ... hospital."

The aide pulled firmly at the doctor's arm, trying to loosen his grip on the child. "We're *going* to take him to hospital. Try to relax your arm, mate. Let go of him."

His grudging muscles gave as Jeremy moved his arm to the side, and the heaviness in his chest eased slightly as the boy was pulled free.

Chippy took Evan from Jeremy's arms, tucking his limp body under his raincoat before hurrying to the Land Rover. "Jeremy says to get his clothes off 'im ... his pants, too. Then wrap 'im in a blanket."

"What about the doc? He okay?" Joe asked as he pulled the back doors of the vehicle open.

"Don't know yet. Jeremy's workin' with 'im." Chippy laid the boy down on the floor of the Land Rover. "Soon as you have 'im stripped down, move 'im to the front seat. We're gonna put the doc in the back. And turn the heat up as high as it'll go," he instructed before returning to help Al and the aide.

Jeremy rattled off quick instructions. "Chippy, you hang on to his shirt. Keep his head from hitting anything when we pull him out. Al, you and I'll grab on to his trousers." The aide reached under the rock shelter and pulled Martin's right arm up across his stomach. He groaned loudly, and Jeremy's hand went immediately to the likely source of his patient's pain.

The tell-tale deformation was obvious. "He's dislocated his right shoulder, so be careful with it, Chippy."

Martin tried to comprehend what was happening, but the movement of his body caused his head to spin, making him nauseous. He closed his eyes and allowed his rescuers to take control.

He felt himself being lifted from the cold earth as rain spattered his face, reviving him to a temporary semi-lucid state.

He was lowered to the doorway of the PC's vehicle. Chippy and Al supported him in a sitting position as his own trauma shears were used to cut his shirt and vest from his body before a blanket was pulled around him. The fuzzy image of the roof overhead slipped by as the men tipped him back and pulled him into the Land Rover.

Martin's thoughts turned to Evan, and he struggled to sit up, only to find himself being held down by strong arms. "Let go of ... me!" he protested. "The boy ... boy needs a doctor."

Al put a hand on his chest. "Jeremy's gone up front. He's gonna move the kid back here, Doc. Just so's you can keep an eye on 'im. Try ta relax," he said, giving him a smile.

Martin's eyes rolled back, and his head dropped to the floor with a thunk. Al pulled off his mac, rolling the wet exterior inside before lifting the doctor's head on to the makeshift pillow.

The back doors opened again, and Buddy slipped lithely inside the vehicle, curling up by Martin's head. Chippy passed Evan to Al and the young man dropped into one of the side seats. "I'll go pick Louiser up ... bring her over ta Truro," the fisherman said, jumping from the vehicle before slamming the doors shut behind him.

Jeremy pressed his fingers to the little boy's neck. "Okay, let's go, Joe."

The Land Rover lurched forward as the aide reached over to check Martin's pulse. "Keep the ride as smooth as you can, Joe. Jostling can cause cardiac arrhythmias in hypothermic patients."

"These *A*-rrhythmias—I take it that's something we want to avoid then?" the constable asked.

"Well, of course it is!" Jeremy snapped back. It's *not* a good thing, so go easy until we get on to the tarmac."

"Roger that." Joe held his thumb up as he peered into the rear-view mirror.

The aide pulled the stethoscope from around his neck and placed it against Martin's chest, worry etching his brow as he listened to the rattle in his patient's lungs. But aside from securing Martin's arm to his body to prevent any further injury to his shoulder, there wasn't a lot that Jeremy could do for him.

He moved between his two patients, monitoring their blood pressure and heart rate. The warmed IV fluids and other therapeutic measures that needed to be taken would have to wait until they reached Truro.

Buddy whined softly, his button eyes flitting from Martin to Jeremy and back again. Jeremy reached out and tousled the little terrier's furry head. "You did great, Buddy," he said softly.

The aide pulled his mobile from his pocket, checking for signal strength, then dialled Louisa's number. It rang once before her anxious voice answered.

"Jeremy! What's going on?"

"We're on our way to Truro with Martin and Evan. Chippy Miller's going to be stopping to pick you up and run you over there," the aide explained.

"Why? What's happened, Jeremy?"

"Martin's dislocated his shoulder. It's not serious, but of course it's painful. I'm not sure if they'll find more damage has been done and feel surgery is needed, or if it'll be a simple matter of reduction at this point," the aide said.

There was a moment of silence on the other end of the line before Louisa spoke. "I understand. I'd like to talk to Martin for a minute, though."

Jeremy looked down at the semi-conscious doctor. "He and Evan are very cold, Louisa. It's made him pretty groggy. He'll be more coherent when you see him at the hospital. I need to ring off and call Ed Christianson. He's going to want to know about the shoulder injury ... he might actually want to come in right away to take a look at it."

"Erm, yeah ... yeah. I see Chippy coming up the hill now," Louisa said as she peered out the windows in the lounge. "Poppy's here ... trying to keep me sane," she said with a small smile. "I'll ask her to stay with James."

"Good. Try not to worry, Louisa."

"Well, that's not going to happen, now is it Jeremy?" she said.

"Yeah, sorry. I'll see you in a bit, then."

"Oh, Jeremy! Could you tell Martin ... tell him I didn't mean it? He'll know what I'm talking about."

"Yep, I will."

The aide rang off and then put a call in to Ed Christianson, Martin's surgeon, before returning his attention to his patients.

Joe Penhale made the trip to the Royal Cornwall in record time. There was little traffic on the A-39 at five o'clock in the morning, and they sailed down the roadway at top speed. The constable had radioed ahead, so hospital staff were standing by when they arrived.

A nurse pressed her hand to Jeremy's chest as he tried to follow the gurneys into the ED treatment room. "I'm sorry, sir. You'll need to stay in the reception area. The doctor will come out and—"

Jeremy turned to the side and slipped by her. "Dr. Ellingham's my patient, and I go with him," he replied with finality. He pulled back his shoulders and continued on into the room.

Chapter 4

Jeremy stood, arms crossed over his chest, as he watched the accident and emergency staff work on Martin and Evan. The treatment room was the epitome of organised chaos, and the aide strained to catch any information audible over the cacophony of voices, beeps and alarms, and the clatter of instruments.

The doctor, who appeared to be the consultant in charge, eyed him questioningly before refocusing his attention on the younger of the two patients in the treatment room.

A young man in scrubs was attempting to get an IV started in the back of Martin's hand, botching the job several times over before Jeremy pulled on a pair of gloves and stepped in.

"Here, let me do it. You're making a dog's dinner of that," he grumbled.

The scrubs-clad man pulled the IV set out of the aide's reach, raising an eyebrow at him. "And you are?"

"Astonished by your complete inability to perform the most basic medical procedure. Look at the haematoma you've raised on this patient!" Jeremy said.

"How's he doing?" Ed Christianson's booming voice rang out as he strode into the room, going immediately to Martin's side. The doctor who had been working with Evan hurried over to bring him up to speed.

Jeremy tried once more to take the catheter from the hands of the young man who had been bungling the job, and once again his attempts were thwarted. He turned and pulled a new set from a supply cart and quickly tore open the plastic bag.

"I'm sorry, Mr. Christianson. This bloke seems be under the impression he has some sort of hospital privileges here. The charge nurse tried to keep him out, but he pushed past her," the young man explained, giving the aide an icy stare. "Should I call security?"

Jeremy tuned him out, focusing on getting the catheter inserted into Martin's constricted vein.

"That *bloke* is Dr. Ellingham's health aide, Dr. Carson," Ed said. He gave a nod in Jeremy's direction before turning to the consultant in charge. "Tell me what we're dealing with."

"Hypothermia. Core temp was eighty-eight degrees on arrival. As you can see, the temps down to eighty-seven point three now."

He turned and wagged a finger at the neighbouring table. "The little lad over there was at eighty-seven point six when he was brought in, but his temp's up to ninety-one point four. And the dysrhythmia that was noted upon arrival seems to have righted itself."

Ed pulled the stethoscope from around his neck and placed it on Martin's chest. He drew his brows together and straightened back up. "I'm not hearing the rales you mentioned on the phone, Portman. Are sure about that?"

"There are crackles when he's on his left side ... in the dependent lung. I couldn't hear anything when he was on his back, but his breathing was very shallow on the way in here," Jeremy explained.

"It's still very shallow. Help me turn him, please,"

The aide adjusted the warming blanket as his patient was rolled to the side.

"Yep, I hear 'em, too," the surgeon said, glancing up at the aide. "Nice catch, Mr. Portman."

He called out to a nurse on the other side of the room. "Sullivan! Can you get a central line in this patient and start extracorporeal rewarming?"

"Yes, sir." The woman pulled a drawer open and removed a blue pack, sealed in plastic.

Jeremy sidled up to the surgeon and spoke softly. "In no way do I mean to be questioning your judgement. I am curious, though; extracorporeal warming seems rather aggressive," he said, watching as the nurse threaded a catheter into his patient's jugular vein.

Mr. Christianson wrapped his stethoscope around his hand and crammed it into his pocket. "I want to get the glucose he needs into him, but I don't want to exacerbate the existing pleural effusion by rewarming with warm saline. It poses a serious risk to a patient with pneumonia if they get overloaded with fluids. And it's easily done using saline.

"We can also get his core temperature up quickly with the extracorporeal rewarming. We'll get him started on antibiotics right away and get a chest CT once he's stable." Ed began to inspect Martin's injured limbs. "How the bloody hell did something like this happen?"

"I'm not real sure. The kid over there is Dr. Ellingham's ... special project, I guess you'd say. The family are Martin's patients, and the boy was being abused by the alcoholic father. The kid fell through the cracks in the Children's Services system, and Martin was keeping an eye on him.

"Louisa called me ... said Martin had gone out to the family's farm and that he needed me out there. I was a half hour away, and by the time I arrived the father was dead—an apparent fall. And neither Martin nor the boy could be found. That's the abbreviated version. Do you want more details?"

Ed screwed up his face and shook his head. "That's enough for now." He blew out a long breath as he rubbed his palm over his head. "Okay, we'll get him warm and stable, then get him down to radiology.

"There are some loose pins that we'll have to tighten. And I may as well pull the pins we were planning to remove next week. And that shoulder will need to be taken care of, obviously. But the likelihood of pneumonia is of greatest concern to me at the moment."

Jeremy glanced over at the doctor working on Evan. "Would you mind taking a look at the boy? I know Martin would appreciate it."

The surgeon hesitated. "He's not my patient. I don't want to step on Dr. Hitchen's toes. But if he's okay with it ... I can do that." He walked over to the child's side and exchanged words with the consultant.

As the A&E staff worked to stabilise both of their patients, the sounds and smells of the treatment room began to permeate Martin's thoughts.

Something wasn't right. He couldn't hear the wind or the rain any longer. *Maybe the storm has passed.*

A loud metallic clattering caused him to startle, sending his pulse bounding as a burst of adrenaline flooded his body.

"I'm sorry, Mr. Christianson. I lost my grip," a muffled voice said as the frenetic beeping of an alarm sounded somewhere in the distance.

He tried to calm himself by inhaling deeply, but it was difficult to pull air into his lungs. *It's the boy ... his weight on my chest,* he thought before realising that the small mass he had been cradling for the last several hours was no longer lying against him. He tried in vain to reach out to search for the child, but his arms refused to move.

The background sounds faded once again, becoming a soft ringing in his ears. And the events of the last hours replayed in his head, his wife's last words taunting him. He was cold, confused, and in pain. And the thought of returning to a home devoid of the love and companionship of his wife and son was unbearable.

But he remembered Louisa's words to him shortly after his return home from hospital—her promise that she would never leave him and that they would work through their difficulties together.

And he had promised to trust her. He needed to tell her that. That regardless of her threat to take James and leave, he knew she wouldn't because she had made him that promise.

He tried to pull himself to a sitting position, the movement sending an intense jolt across his shoulder and down his arm.

He looked around wildly as he gasped for air and pulled at the oxygen mask on his face. The pain in his arm was excruciating, and he began to pull at what he perceived to be the source of his agony, the metal hardware penetrating his flesh.

Jeremy grabbed on to Martin's left hand as he tried to break through his clouded consciousness. "You need to lie still, Martin! You're at hospital. Evan, too."

Martin gave his aide a feeble shove. "Get off ... me," he said, his voice barely audible. "It ... hurts. Get it ... off."

Ed hurried back, quickly scanning the blue numbers on the machines as Jeremy wrestled their patient back down on to the table. He filled a syringe with morphine and injected it into the catheter in his wrist.

His struggle continued. "I need—to get—up."

Jeremy pushed against his chest. "No, no, no. You don't need to get up. Evan's right over here. He's being well cared for."

The curtain between the two treatment areas rustled as the aide pushed it aside. "See, he's right there. Lie back down, mate."

Martin tried to roll from the table, and Ed Christianson leaned over him, his face stern. "Martin, you have to lie still! If there's something you need, tell me, and I'll see if I can help you out. But no—more—*moving!*"

"I n-need to ... to tell Louisa ... tell her I trust her."

"She asked me to give you a message," Jeremy said as he repositioned the warming blanket. "She said to tell you she didn't mean it."

Martin looked up at the young man with confusion on his face. He squeezed his eyes shut, dropping back on to the table before exhaustion and morphine overwhelmed him, and he drifted back to sleep.

A young blonde-haired woman stepped into the treatment room and glanced around before her gaze settled on Ed. "Mr. Christianson, Dr. Ellingham's wife is here. Should I bring her on back?"

"Ah, no. Mr. Portman, could you go out and fill her in on what's happened. I'll let you make the call on whether or not she should come back right now."

Jeremy gave the surgeon a nod before leaving the room.

Louisa got up quickly when she saw the young man coming towards her. She met him in the middle of the waiting area, her hands tucked securely under her arms. "I want to see him, Jeremy." She shot a black look at the young receptionist. "That girl over there told me I had to wait."

"That's standard procedure. Let's go and have a seat. I'll tell you what's going on." The aide took hold of her arm and led her to a far corner of the room.

They settled into chairs near the entryway as the automatic doors hissed open and a cold gust of air whipped into the room.

Jeremy leaned forward, resting his elbows on his knees. "Martin and Evan are both hypothermic. Evan's temperature has come up a bit ... a very good sign. He hasn't regained consciousness yet, but the most dangerous period has passed for him.

"He has a cut on the bottom of his foot that's been treated, but he'll need to keep off of it for a couple of days."

Louisa toyed with the hem of her coat and worried her lip. "And Martin?"

"He's still pretty cold. But they've started what's called extracorporeal warming." The aide placed his fingers on the side of his neck. "They've put a catheter in his jugular vein. His blood passes through tubing that runs through a balloon containing heated saline. A machine keeps the blood circulating and monitors the temperature. This technique should warm him up quite quickly."

"And he's going to be fine, then?"

"Well, he has some bumps and scrapes. And the shoulder issue will need to be taken care of. Ed wants to wait until he's more stable before reducing the dislocation.

"Martin's body ... his larger mass ... was slower to cool down than Evan's, and it'll be slower to warm back up again. So, we'll have to be patient. It could be another hour or two before his temperature is back up to normal.

"The problem of greatest concern at the moment is that he has some fluid build-up in his left lung. They'll get him down to radiology as soon as he's stable, but it's likely pneumonia.

"Mr. Christianson opted to use the extracorporeal rewarming to avoid overloading him with fluids ... aggravating the pleural effusion ... erm, the fluid that he already has in his lungs."

"May I see him now?" Louisa asked as she got to her feet.

Jeremy remained planted in his chair. "Just a couple more things to discuss. Then yes, you can see him.

"Both Martin and Evan are getting warm humidified oxygen and glucose. Martin's been in and out of consciousness and not making a whole lot of sense when he's awake. We should see pretty rapid improvement, though.

"And I did get your message passed on to him. Although, I can't guarantee he comprehended any of it," the aide said, giving her a small smile.

"I appreciate that, Jeremy. But may I *please* see him now?" Louisa asked, twisting her purse strap in her hands.

The aide slapped his palms down on his thighs and got up from his seat. "Let's go."

Louisa gave Ed a worried smile as she approached the table where her husband lay, unmoving.

"Well, here we are ... meeting in this room again, Louisa. Maybe you need to keep this guy locked in the house," the surgeon said, patting her arm.

"Hmm. I kind of tried that. It didn't go over very well. How's he doing?" she asked, leaning down to place a kiss on her husband's forehead.

"We're seeing fairly rapid improvement in his overall condition," Ed said as he jotted notes into a chart. "We'll watch him here a while longer, then move him to a room."

"So ... he's going to be okay?"

"I think so. I have concerns about the noise we hear in his lungs. We'll know more about that once we can get some pictures."

The surgeon snapped the cover shut on the patient notes and laid it down on the supply cart. "The little guy over there is coming around nicely," he said, gesturing with his biro. "He hasn't woken up yet, but his temperature's up five degrees. He'd probably be awake now if he wasn't exhausted."

Louisa glanced over at the little boy, then at her husband's aide. "Jeremy, what should we do about Evan? The hospital can call Children's Services but ... I mean, we're not sure he even knows about his father. It would probably be best if Martin gave him that news."

She looked down at her husband and caressed his cheek. "He seems to understand the little boy. I have no clue really as to what went on out there. What do you think Martin would want us to do?"

The aide dropped into a chair. "I don't know for sure. Maybe have Joe Penhale go out to the farm ... see if the kid's mum and sister have come home. Otherwise, I don't know. But I *do* know that Martin wouldn't want the boy turned over to the Social Services people in Wadebridge."

By seven o'clock Thursday morning, Martin's temperature was back up to a normal ninety-eight point six degrees. Louisa had yet to see him open his eyes when they moved him to a room upstairs.

She had nodded off in a chair by his bed, but was roused from her slumber by the clattering of the food service staff, delivering breakfast to patients' rooms. When she opened her eyes, Martin's gaze was fixed on her. "Well, hello," she said, giving him a smile.

He stared at her for a moment before quickly turning his head away.

She had seen that look in his eyes before, and it had always been when she'd hurt him in some way. Most notably, the night of her friend Holly's concert, and more recently, when she told him she was taking James and going to Spain. It was a look of hurt and confusion.

She stood up and leaned over him, placing a kiss on his cheek. "How are you feeling?"

Despite the morphine he was receiving, shooting pain continued to radiate from Martin's shoulder, it hurt to breathe, and he had a pounding headache.

But the physical pain paled in comparison to the heartache that came from his surety that his wife intended to leave him. That she didn't mean what she had told him weeks earlier—that she would never leave him again.

"Martin?" Louisa asked again. "How are you feeling?"

He turned and looked at her. "Why are you here?" he rasped. The residual laryngitis that he had the day before had flared into a painfully raw throat, allowing him little more than a whisper.

Louisa cocked her head at him and brushed her fingers through his hair. "Martin, I asked Jeremy to pass a message on for me ... about what I said ... that I didn't mean it. Do remember him telling you that?"

"Yes," he rasped. He lifted his head from his pillow, his face taut. "Why do you do that ... say things you don't mean?" he asked as a shiver ran through him.

The door swung open, and a nurse breezed into the room. "Well, good morning, Dr. Ellingham! We've been waiting on pins and needles for you to wake up," she said as she injected another dose of morphine into his IV.

Louisa returned to her chair and watched him. His responses to the questions directed at him by the nurse were sluggish and apathetic.

The woman adjusted the warming blanket covering him and then left the room.

"How's the boy?" Martin asked as soon as the door swung shut.

"He's fine. He's in a room in paediatrics, awake and wanting to see you," Louisa said. Moving back to the bed, she took her husband's hand. "I'm very sorry I said what I did, Martin."

He looked at her incredulously before pulling away from her and flopping his arm across his face.

She rested her hand on his chest and sighed. "Martin, I *am* sorry ... *very, very* sorry."

He pulled his arm down and forced words out through his inflamed airway. "I trusted you, Louisa. You *promised!* You said we'd work through our problems together."

Finally, the penny dropped and Louisa realised she and her husband had been talking at cross purposes. "Oh, Martin! That's not what—"

The door opened again, and Ed Christianson sauntered into the room, picking up the patient notes that hung on the footboard.

"Well, let's get you downstairs ... get some pictures. How's the pain?" the surgeon asked as he walked to the head of the bed.

"Tolerable," Martin grunted.

"What hurts the most?"

He shook his head, looking up at his doctor with tired eyes. "The shoulder and head. And it hurts to breathe."

"What do you mean, your head hurts?"

Martin groaned aloud at the thought of what had transpired in the farmhouse hours earlier. "Hanley swung a bottle at me ... caught the side of my head."

"Where? Show me," Ed said, pulling his torch from his breast pocket.

Raising his good arm up, Martin touched his fingers to an area just above his left ear.

The surgeon scrutinised the injury, hissing air from his nose. "We'll add that to the list for the folks in radiology. Anything else you need to make me aware of?"

"No," Martin said irritably before his heavy eyelids submitted to his fatigue.

Mr. Christianson stopped back shortly after Martin had returned from the CT lab.

"You do have fluid in that left lung, Martin. We're already hitting you with antibiotics. The rapid strep test on your throat was positive. I'm almost certain we're dealing with a streptococcal pneumonia as well, so we should see rapid improvement with both of those issues."

"What about his head?" Louisa asked nervously.

"There's a simple linear fracture, but no sign of brain injury. Just a jolly good head thumping, it seems. We'll keep an eye on things, though."

His fingers ticked a metallic rhythm against the bed rail. "The shoulder gets a bit more complicated. We have a decision to make there.

"I think it would be ill-advised to postpone surgery any longer."

The surgeon pulled a chair up next to the bed and took a seat. "I spoke with Will Simpson, up at Imperial. He feels we should go ahead and have our top ortho man go in now and get it taken care of before any more damage is done. It's up to you though."

Martin grimaced at the thought of another setback. He lay, eyes closed, for several moments before nodding his head. "Fine, let's go ahead and do it."

Ed worked his palms over his knees and got to his feet. "You know this means a couple more weeks of relying on Portman to chauffeur you around, don't you?"

"Yes! I'm aware of that!" Martin hissed back.

Louisa put her hand on his thigh. "Try not to think of this as going backwards, Mar—"

He slapped her hand away and, grimacing, sat up in the bed. "Don't tell me what to think!" he rasped. He pressed the heel of his hand to his forehead as his jaw clenched. "God, this is so confusing!"

"Knock, knock!" Carole Parsons' voice singsonged as she and her husband Chris stepped in the door. Chris was Martin's oldest friend from medical school and Carole and Louisa had developed a strong bond during Martin's weeks in hospital.

They joined Ed and Louisa at his bedside, immediately sensing the tension in the room.

"Is this a bad time?" Chris asked, his gaze darting between the surgeon and the patient.

"Actually, could I have a few minutes alone with my husband?" Louisa said. "Maybe give us ten minutes."

"Erm, sure ... sure." Ed got to his feet and slid his chair back against the wall. "Martin, I'll stop back and we'll discuss the details of the shoulder procedure ... the timing and all."

"Thank you, Ed," Louisa said, giving him an apologetic smile.

"Maybe we'll run and get a cup of coffee. We'll be back in just a bit," Carole said as she and Chris stepped back out into the hallway.

Louisa waited for the door to shut and then pulled a chair over, sitting down by the bed. "Martin, I think we've had a *very* big misunderstanding. When Jeremy gave you my message, that I didn't mean it, you thought I was referring to the promise I made to you a while back, hmm?"

He lifted his head, his brow furrowed. "Is that *not* what you meant?"

"No, Martin. I was referring to what I said last night. About not being here when you got back from the Hanley's. The promise I made to you, to never leave ... I meant every single word of that."

He dropped back on to the bed, clutching at his right arm. After studying his wife's face for several moments, he answered, "I see."

"I'm glad. You had me worried. I thought you might not forgive me for what I said before you left last night."

"Mm."

She leaned forward and took his hand. "Is that a, you're-right-I-don't-forgive-you, mm, or a the-misunderstanding-is-over, mm?"

"The second one." He breathed out a heavy sigh. "I'm sorry I didn't trust you."

Louisa got up from her chair and leaned over, pressing her cheek to his. "It's all right, Martin. It'll take some time. We'll both just keep working at it."

Chapter 5

Joe Penhale glanced in his rear-view mirror at the little terrier sitting on the jump seat behind him. "What do you s'pose we oughta do about Buddy?" he asked, his eyes darting briefly towards Al.

"What'd you mean? Shouldn't we just drop 'im back at the farm?"

Joe gave a shrug of his shoulders. "Just doesn't seem right to dump him off ... him bein' a hero and all. It's awful cold for the little guy."

"Then why don't you take 'im, Joe? Yer always tellin' everbody how Buddy's gonna bring your department into the twenty-first century. Wouldn't think you'd wanna have yer torchbearer sleepin' rough."

The constable breathed out a theatrical sigh. "I *would* take him, Al, but unfortunately, an officer of the law has to be available at a moment's notice. Buddy's proven himself to be a valuable member of the Portwenn police force. Wouldn't want to have some ... mis-*fortune* befall our champion tracker while he was left alone, would we?"

Al lifted his chin into the air and jutted out his lower lip. "It's not like you'd be leavin' a baby home alone, though, is it?"

"Still ... don't wanna take any unnecessary chances."

Al rubbed his hand over his closely cropped hair. "Well, I s'pose I could take 'im. Just till the storm's over. But, *technically*, I'm not s'posed ta have a pet in my flat, so he can't stay."

The dog whined softly and then turned several times before settling in for a nap.

The two men rode in awkward silence until they pulled up in front of Chippy Miller's, where Al's cobbled up old car sat parked on the rock lane.

"Come on, Buddy," he said as he pushed the door of the Land Rover open. "Let's go see if we can find somethin' a local hero might like for dinner."

He peered back into the vehicle. "Oh, and Joe … finding the doc and the boy today … that was brilliant," he said, tipping his thumb up at him.

The constable cocked his head to the side with an aw-shucks expression on his face. "It was all in the line of duty, Al."

Martin's general condition continued to improve overall, and the extracorporeal warming was discontinued shortly after he was moved to his hospital room. By mid-morning, however, his temperature had risen past what is considered normal to a level indicative of a brewing infection.

Louisa was thankful for the company of the Parsons as she sat by her husband's side. Especially for Chris's reasoned voice and reassurances that things weren't going to spiral out of control.

Warren Buck, the surgeon recommended by Will Simpson and Ed Christianson, had stopped in late in the morning to discuss the procedure to fix Martin's shoulder.

"I'll do a Laterjet procedure. That involves moving a section of your husband's coracoid process and the attached muscle to the front of the glenoid." He walked over to Louisa and put his fingers on her shoulder. "The coracoid process is a projection just inside the shoulder joint. By re-attaching a piece of it to the front of the socket, we form a barrier that prevents further dislocations. I'll clean up any loose bony fragments, tidy up in there, and then tighten things up."

"How long will he have to stay in hospital?" Louisa asked as she moved to her husband's side and took hold of his hand.

"Patients can usually leave within a few hours of the procedure. Of course, Ed Christianson may want to hang on to him longer than that because of the pneumonia issue."

The surgeon picked up the patient chart from the end of the bed and penned in his notes. "We're tentatively scheduled to do this early tomorrow morning, Martin, but it's dependent on how you seem to be progressing overall. Christianson will make the final call.

"For now though, we need to get that shoulder back in place. There's a lot of oedema and spasming, so I don't want to try to do this without sedation."

Martin gave the man a nod of his head before closing his eyes and drifting back to sleep.

The wind-driven rain had pelted the windows in the hospital room all morning, but shortly after lunch the storm passed. The sky cleared, and if it weren't for the tree branches on the ground below and the vivid memories left of the events of the previous night, it would be hard to know that the storm had even occurred.

"Louisa, you really need to go and get something to eat," Carole whispered as Martin slept that afternoon. "I haven't seen you eat anything all day."

"I don't have much of an appetite," she said, gently repositioning the cold packs encasing her husband's now-reduced shoulder.

"Nevertheless, James needs his mum healthy, and you'll be of no use to Martin if you allow yourself to get run down and sick. Chris can stay with him ... let you know if any problems arise."

She raised an eyebrow at her distracted husband. "Right?" She reached her foot out and nudged his leg.

His head popped up from behind the medical journal he was reading. "What's that?"

"You can stay with Martin while I take Louisa to get something to eat, right?"

"Sure, sure. I'll call if we need you back here for anything." He gave his wife a smile before his focus shifted back to his article about the predictions for the cold and flu season.

Night had fallen by the time the two women headed back from the canteen. The lights of the city twinkled against a black backdrop as they moved through the skywalk.

"Oh, how peaceful it looks out there now. Such a contrast to last night." Louisa stopped to take in the view. "I wonder what it was like for them."

Carole leaned her arms on the handrail and peered down at the stream of people on the sidewalk below. "Martin and Evan, you mean?"

"Mm-hmm. Must've been miserable ... terrifying. I just can't imagine."

Carole took hold of Louisa's arm and tugged her forward. "Let's not dwell on it. It won't help anything. We'd better get back to that man of yours."

"Do you mind if we stop by to check up on Evan first?" Louisa asked as they neared an intersecting corridor. "I know Martin's concerned about him."

"Not at all." Carole veered left towards the set of doors leading to the children's ward. "I can't wait to meet this young man. He must be quite something to be able to hold sway over the fearsome Martin Ellingham."

"Yes, well ... it might be best if my fearsome man remained unaware of just how much power Evan wields."

Louisa approached the reception desk and spoke to a young nurse who was just checking in for the evening shift, explaining her relationship to the patient she was wanting to visit.

"Let me see," she said as she flipped through the log book. "He's in the second room down, on the right. I'll let you through the security doors."

"Thank you."

They followed the nurse down the corridor. "You sure it won't upset him to have a stranger showing up to visit him?" Carole asked.

"Evan *can* be a bit wary of strangers. And he's usually pretty quiet at school. But he knows Martin and me quite well, so I suspect he'll be all right."

They stopped in front of another set of double doors, and the nurse slid the card hanging from her neck through the I.D. machine before pushing into the room. "There you are. Visiting hours will be over in"—she turned her wrist and glanced at her watch—"less than an hour. So, you won't have long I'm afraid," she said before turning to leave.

Louisa scanned the room, looking for the child's face amongst the beds lining the wall. "I don't see him."

"Maybe we were given the wrong room." Carole dug through her purse before pulling out a tissue.

Louisa approached a middle-aged man in a short, white coat. "Excuse me. I'm looking for Evan Hanley. He would have been admitted this morning—hypothermia and a cut on his foot."

"Ah. I'm Dr. Johnson. He's right over—"

He glanced around the room before hurrying to the desk, Carole and Louisa following close behind.

"Where's Evan Hanley?" he asked as his gaze darted up and down the corridor.

"He should be in the ward, Doctor."

"Well, he's not. Find out if a family member picked him up. And call security. He wasn't to be discharged before I signed off on it!"

Dr. Johnson turned to Louisa and Carole, holding his palms up in front of him. "We'll find him. I'm sure there's a perfectly logical explanation for this."

"You've got to be kidding! You've lost a child?" Louisa said.

The man stuffed his hands into the pockets of his coat. "I doubt that very much. We have strict security measures in place. If he did wander off, he couldn't have gone far. A child wouldn't be able to reach the buttons for the automatic doors leading to the main corridor."

"Do you think his mum may have come and collected him?" Carole asked as she exchanged a nervous glance with Louisa. "Chris said there was someone here from Children's Services earlier today. Maybe they tracked down a family member."

"I haven't signed off on his discharge papers," Dr. Johnson said. "If someone picked him up, I had no knowledge of it. I'll get the staff started on a search of the ward. It may be that something frightened him and he's hiding somewhere."

"Oh, poor Evan." Louisa's concern was obvious as she patted her palms together and furrowed her brow. "I need to get back to my husband. Can you call me just as soon as you find the boy?" she said, pulling a notepad from her purse before jotting her name and mobile number down on a sheet of paper. She ripped it off and handed it to the doctor.

"I'll be happy to do that, Mrs—" He glanced down at the note in his hand. "Ah, you're Dr. Ellingham's wife."

"Yes, I am. I guess I'll have to wait to hear back from you, then."

He put his hand on her shoulder and led her to the main doors. "Someone will call you the moment we've located him. But as I said, there's probably a logical explanation."

The two women turned into the corridor leading to Martin's room.

"This is what I've been afraid of, Carole," Louisa said as she nibbled at a fingernail. "Martin's gotten himself so emotionally invested in this child. How's he going to react if the boy's mother has come and taken him off somewhere. It'll tear Martin up, not knowing if the child's being neglected or abused."

"Let's cross that bridge when—or *if*—we come to it." Carole pushed the door to the hospital room open, and they slipped inside quietly.

The lights were dimmed and Chris was slumped down in the chair where they had left him, his head tipped back, arms folded across his chest, and his copy of *The Lancet* on the floor beside him.

Louisa went quietly to Martin's bedside and leaned over to kiss his forehead. "He's still very hot," she said softly, pulling up a chair and taking a seat. She worked her hand under the covers searching for his hand, and her breath caught in her throat.

"Carole!" she whispered stridently. "Come here!"

Louisa slowly lifted the blanket, revealing a small form curled up on the bed next to her husband.

"So, *this* is Evan?" Carole asked as she leaned over to get a look at the boy's face.

"Mm-hmm." Louisa tucked the blankets back in around him. "I'd better have someone notify them in paediatrics that they can call off the search. I'll be back," she said.

Carole went to Chris's side and jostled him awake.

Giving a sudden snort, he rubbed his palm over his eyes and looked around, orientating himself to his surroundings. "Mm, sorry. Must've drifted off for a few minutes," he said as he tried to massage the blood back into his hand.

"Some guardian you turned out to be, Chris Parsons!" she hissed at him.

He straightened himself in his chair. "Something happen?" he asked, now wide-eyed.

"No, nothing much," Carole whispered. "A child disappeared from the paediatric ward, came in here and managed to climb into bed with your patient, and *you* were completely oblivious to it all," she huffed.

"What?" Chris sprang from his chair and lifted the blanket. "Ah. That's Evan, I suppose."

"Yes, Christopher. That's Evan." Carole rolled her eyes at him.

The door to the room opened and Dr. Johnson hurried in with Louisa following close behind.

"Excuse me. I'd like to check on my patient," he said, slipping past the Parsons before giving the child a quick once over.

Chris looked over at his wife. "In my defence, I was the only one watching in here *and* I had my eyes—closed."

"Yes ... and your point is?" she asked, her fingers tapping impatiently against the bedrail.

"My point is that they probably have a half dozen people over in paediatrics, and the kid got by *them!*"

Dr. Johnson reached down and slipped his arms under the boy. "Well, regardless of how he managed to make his way down here, I should get him back to his own bed."

Evan woke with a start, looking fearfully up at the four sets of eyes focused on him.

"What say we get you back to your own room, Evan?" the doctor said softly.

"Nooo! I wanna stay here with Dr. Ellig-am!" The child began to push furiously against the man's chest.

Martin was roused from his sleep by the boy's frantic voice and looked quickly around him. "What the bloody hell is going on?" he rasped.

"It seems your fidus Achates slipped out of the paediatrics unit and managed to find his way here," Dr. Johnson said.

He set Evan down on the bed, and the boy slid back against Martin. "I don't wanna be in that other place, Dr. Ellig-am. He watches me there. I wanna stay here with you."

Louisa came around the bed and leaned over, caressing his back. "Evan, Dr. Johnson isn't really *watching* you. He's just trying to take care of you."

Evan began to shed silent tears. "Do you understand, Dr. Ellig-am?" he whispered.

Martin looked back at the boy, the panicked expression on the child's face causing his own eyes to tear. "Erm ... could you leave us be for a bit?" he asked as he tried to prop himself up on his elbow.

"Five minutes enough time, Mart?" Chris asked as he moved towards the hallway.

Martin breathed out a heavy sigh. "Yeah."

He waited for the door to close before turning to Evan. "It was very wrong for you to go off the way you did. It wasn't safe for you to do that, and you had a lot of people worried. Not to mention that you shouldn't be walking around on that foot!" Air hissed from his nose as he tried to blink the fatigue from his eyes. "Okay, tell me what this is about."

Evan turned away from Martin and dangled his feet over the side of the bed. "It's *about* his eyes. He keeps lookin' at me."

"Who keeps looking at you?" Martin grimaced as he shifted, causing muscles to spasm around his shoulder.

Leaning forward, the child flopped his arms over the bed rail and groaned. "*You* know. He looks at me with his *angry* eyes. Like he did after he fell down the stairs."

Martin let himself fall back on to his pillow. "Evan, your father wasn't angry with you, he was—"

The seven-year-old whirled around. "He *was* too angry! He gets angry when I run away from him. And now he keeps watching me with his angry eyes!"

Rolling on to his stomach, Evan pulled his feet under him before burying his face in Martin's chest. "He can't see me here. *That's* why I wanna stay. Can I? Please?" he asked, peering up shyly.

Martin cleared his throat, wincing when the mannerism set off painful nerve signals in his inflamed pharynx. "Evan, do you remember what happened to your father?"

"Uh-huh. He fell down the stairs. His eyes looked very angry. *Can* I stay here, Dr. Ellig-am?"

Martin tried to put his thoughts together despite the pain in his shoulder and the throbbing in his head. The fact that Jim Hanley had died the night before would have to be made clear to the boy, but he decided now was not the time to try to have such a difficult conversation. He would be better able to explain it all to the child when his head wasn't muddled by pain and the effects of morphine.

"I'll see what I can do, Evan. But I can't make any promises. There are rules that have to be followed."

Louisa and the Parsons came back into the room, and he clenched his jaw, pushing himself to a sitting position.

"Evan, do you mind if I take a look at your wound?" he asked.

"Uh-uh." The boy flopped back, holding his foot up to be examined.

Martin looked up at his wife, gesturing. "Could you uncover that for me, please?"

"I think I can manage that little bit of doctoring. What do you think, Evan?" she asked as she unwrapped the elastic bandage from the child's foot.

"I think you did that really good, Mrs. Ellig-am. She could take care of you, too. Couldn't she Dr. Ellig-am?"

Martin and Louisa's eyes met, and she gave him a smile, brushing his cheek with the backs of her fingers.

"Mm. They did a jolly good job on these sutures," he said as he inspected the wound.

The boy pulled his foot up and peered closely at the stitches lined up in a neat row. "I think that doctor didn't want to have to pay you hell, that's why."

"What's that?" Martin asked, cocking his head as the creases in his brow deepened.

"That lady told that to the doctor. She didn't think I was listenin', but I gots really good ears. She told him he'd have to pay you hell if he didn't do a right proper job. So, does he gots ta pay you, Dr. Ellig-am?"

Chris pulled up a chair and sat down, giving his friend a roguish grin. "Yeah, Mart, does Johnson gots to pay you hell?"

"Chris!" Carole hissed at him, boxing his ear.

"Why does everyone think I'm so bloody difficult?" Martin squeaked out defensively.

Evan got up on his knees and whispered loudly into his ear. "Remember what you said! Bloody isn't proper, and it might 'fend somebody!"

Martin pulled his head away from the steamy breath and glanced abashedly at his wife and his friends.

Folding his hands behind his head, Chris leaned back in his chair and put his feet up on the edge of the bed.

Louisa sat down next to the boy and put her hand on his back. "Can you take a seat Evan so that we can have a little talk?"

Evan dropped down on to his bum, jostling the bed and causing Martin to groan. "*Careful,*" he said as he held a hand against his shoulder.

"Sorry, Dr. Ellig-am."

"Evan, why don't you tell me how you managed to get to Dr. Ellingham's room," Louisa said, giving him an encouraging nod.

Evan screwed up his face and cocked his head. "Well, my dad drank too much and then he got angry. And I got scared, so I called Dr. Ellig-am. Then he came to my house and then ... hmm." He scratched at his head. "We played a game, I think. But Dr. Ellig-am isn't very good at paying attention."

Whirling his head around, the child peered up at him. "But that's okay 'cause it was still fun. Yer just not good at games, are you?"

Martin huffed out a breath. "Just tell us how you got from your bed in the children's ward to my room."

"Oh. I sat in the bottom of the trolley they bring the food on, and the man pushed me down the hall. Piece of pi—" His eyes darted up. "I didn't say the word."

"I never said you did! Just tell us how you found my room!" Martin rasped out, his impatience now showing as fever, pain and fatigue began to get the better of him.

Evan's eyes welled with tears as he looked back at the doctor, and Louisa stepped in quickly to reassure the boy.

"Evan, Dr. Ellingham is getting very tired and he hurts. Let's just focus on how you found his room. Once you've explained it to us we can let him get some sleep, hmm?" she said giving him a smile.

The little boy wiped his eyes and smiled back at her. Then, taking in a breath, he continued. "The dinner man didn't even notice me. That's funny, innit?"

"Yes, that *is* funny," Louisa said, giving a disapproving shake of her head towards the other mother in the room.

The boy pulled the blanket up behind his back and let himself fall forward on to the bed. "So, then I saw a sign that had an orthro on it. When the man stopped, I got off the trolley, and found Dr. Ellig-am. Mine's a pint! Lucky yer room's at the end, or I would'a had to open lots of doors to find ya. Huh, Dr. Ellig-am?"

Louisa cocked her head at him "But how did you know Dr. Ellingham was in orthopaedics?"

"'Cause the nurse said she was glad she worked at Patrick's 'cause Dr. Ellig-am was in orthro something."

Martin gave a grunt and pulled at the blanket, trying to reclaim it from the boy. "It's paediatrics, not Patrick's. And orth-*o* not orth-*ro*, Evan."

The boy sat up and gave a shrug of his shoulders. "Whatever. Bet you were surprised ta see me, though, weren't ya, Dr. Ellig-am? Did ya think I'd be able ta find you like that?"

"No, Evan, I didn't. You surprised us all." Martin pressed his hand to his forehead, looking up at his wife with bloodshot eyes. "Could you and Carole take the boy down to the canteen for a hot chocolate or something? I need to have a word with Chris."

"Sure. Let's go, young man," Louisa said as she leaned over to pick the boy up.

"Stop at the desk and get a wheelchair. He's too heavy for you to be carrying."

Louisa turned and gave him a smile. "Yep."

He watched as the trio left the room and then turned to Chris, giving him a scowl. "Wipe that smug grin off your face!"

Chris pulled his hands from behind his head and planted his feet on the floor. "Sorry, mate. You've got to admit, the kid is entertaining," he said with a chuckle.

Martin turned to his left and struggled to lay back on his pillow without jarring his painful shoulder. Chris hurried around the bed to lend a hand.

"Thank you," Martin said, lying perfectly still, waiting for the spasms to ease.

"So, what is it you wanted to discuss?" Chris asked as he pulled up a chair and sat down.

"The boy. He doesn't want to go back to paediatrics. I don't ... I don't think he should, either."

"What do you mean?"

Martin rubbed at his eyes and heaved a heavy sigh. "When I arrived at the Hanley house, the father and the boy were upstairs. Hanley was bladdered. He had a hold on the boy. He was hurting him."

"Yeah, I spoke with Johnson. He said there was evidence of abuse."

"Mm." Martin closed his eyes for a moment and then explained. "Evan slipped away and ran to me. I sent him downstairs, then tried to talk Hanley into having a lie down ... sleeping it off. I was afraid for his safety as well as his son's. I'd already stitched the man's head up after another drinking episode. And he was reeling last night."

Martin reached out for the glass of water on the table next to the bed and took a few painful swallows. "Long story short, Hanley took a header and hit a table upended at the bottom of the stairs. He was killed instantly.

"The boy was within feet of where the man landed. He crouched down by his father. I think he knew he was dead. The look on his face was—"

Martin swallowed hard and shook his head. "I could see how it was affecting him, but he bolted from the house before I could get to him to—to try to console him."

Martin turned to Chris. "He wants to stay here tonight. He thinks his father's watching him—angry with him. He probably blames himself for what happened."

"I understand." Chris leaned forward, resting his forearms on his thighs. "I'll talk with the people down in paediatrics ... see if we can come up with a solution. But I don't think it's safe for him to be flopping around next to you, Mart."

"You brought a bed in here before ... for Louisa. Can we do that again?"

"I'll see what I can do, mate. Maybe they'd discharge him, and let him stay with us. I'll go have a word with Johnson," Chris said before heading for the door. "You try to get some sleep."

Chapter 6

"Oh come on, Johnson. The kid's going to find his way back down there anyway. You know that, don't you?"

Chris Parsons had spent the last ten minutes trying to persuade the recalcitrant paediatrician to relinquish Evan Hanley to the care of another patient, an unconventional step for the hospital to take, to be sure.

"As I keep saying, we have nurses who are trained to care for the needs of children. Now that we're aware of the boy's issues, we can better manage him."

Chris glanced up and down the corridor before leaning towards the man. "Look, I don't want to betray any confidences, but let's just say that Ellingham understands the boy in a way that none of your nurses can. The boy knows it. He feels safe when he's with Martin."

Johnson screwed up his face, turning away from the pleading eyes of his colleague. "I don't know. Do you have any idea the trouble I could be in if something were to happen to the kid because of this?"

"Well if you're suggesting that something inappropriate could go on, you couldn't be more wrong."

"Of course not. But what if he loses his temper with him? He *has* earned his reputation."

"Well, you're just going to have to trust me, aren't you? Martin Ellingham, bad as his bark is, would never do anything to hurt Evan Hanley. I can guarantee that if you insist on keeping him here, the boy will make another gallant attempt at escape, and quite likely succeed. He's safe with Martin, and I'll take full responsibility if anything should go wrong, which it won't."

The doctor crammed his hands into the pockets of his coat as air hissed from his nose. "All right. But I want him back down here first thing in the morning."

By the time Chris reached Martin's room, Louisa, Carole, and Evan had returned from the canteen. Martin looked up at him, expectantly, when he came through the door, and he gave him a grin and a nod of his head.

"Evan, how would you like to spend the night here ... with Dr. Ellingham?"

The child stopped toying with the wheelchair he was sitting in and looked up at Chris, giving him a nod of his head. "I know lotsa games we could play, Dr. Ellig-am."

Louisa knelt down in front of the boy. "Evan, if you stay, you must let my husband get plenty of rest. He needs lots and lots of sleep to get well. Can you help him with that?"

Evan stared down at his lap, picking at a hangnail on his thumb. "I can try."

The door opened and two young women wheeled a bed into the room. "Where would you like this, Dr. Parsons?" one of them asked.

"Just put it next to Dr. Ellingham's bed. I'll take it from there." Chris butted the empty bed up against Martin's and set the brakes on the wheels as the women headed out into the hallway.

"Well, I should get going. My taxi will be here in ten minutes," Louisa said.

Evan watched with rapt attention as she leaned over to place a kiss on her husband's cheek. Martin squirmed under the boy's gaze.

"I love you," he whispered. "Tell James ... tell him I miss him."

"I love you, too," she whispered back. "And I will."

"I'll walk you down" Carole said as she followed her to the door. "Shall I wait for you in the lobby, Chris?"

"Ah, yeah. That'd be fine. I'll get these two settled and be right along."

"Now don't say I never do you any favours, mate," Chris said, setting Evan down on the bed.

"I didn't!" Martin answered defensively. "I appreciate *very much* all that you've done for Louisa and me! I thought I'd made that clear."

"It's just an expression, Mart." Chris pulled the blankets back and slapped his hand down on the mattress. "Lay on down here, Evan, and I'll tuck you in."

"Do I hafta? Maybe we could play a game before we go to bed, huh, Dr. Ellig-am?"

"No, no, no. It's not a sleepover, Evan." Chris lifted him up and tossed him on to the mattress, prompting a giggle from the child.

Popping back up on his knees, Evan's eyes widened "Then can we have a midnight feast?"

"A midnight feast? What in the world is that?" Martin asked, curling his lip.

The boy shrugged his shoulders. "I don't know. But it gots ta be good or Lydia Bigelow wouldn't keep bangin' on about havin' em."

"Who's Lydia Bigelow?" Chris asked, prompting a grimace and a groan from his friend.

"Oh, she's in my class. She sits in front of me."

"Not your girlfriend then?" Chris said, casting a glance towards Martin, who was rapidly losing his patience.

"He's seven years old, Chris. You don't seriously think he's carrying on with the child, do you?"

"Oh, she's too big ta carry anywhere. And she's kind of a smelly little thing," Evan said, leaning his forearms on the bed rail as he peered up at the doctor. "She chuffs," he whispered, loudly.

Martin wrinkled up his nose. "It's probably all those midnight feasts. Eating too late in the day causes indigestion and adds greatly to a person's daily caloric intake. Not to mention problems with gastroesophageal reflux and a disrupted sleep pattern."

"Seriously, Martin, you're straining that throat just to give us a dietary lecture?" Chris said as he leaned back against the wall, his arms folded across his chest.

Martin glanced at the clock on the wall. "Don't you have a wife waiting in the lobby?"

"As a matter of fact, I do. Evan, do you think you can handle Dr. Ellingham on your own until morning?"

The boy's eyes darted between the two men. "I don't think I can handle him. He's pretty big. But maybe we could finish our game, huh, Dr. Ellig—"

"You're in hospital to get well, Evan," Chris said as he laid the boy back on the bed again and tucked the blankets in around his chin. "That means sleep. And Dr. Ellingham has surgery in the morning, so he needs his rest as well."

He walked around the bed and headed for the door before turning and grinning at his friend. "I could tuck you in too, if you like."

"Go home and eat your dinner, Chris," Martin rasped. "And turn off the light on your way out the door."

Chris gave Evan a wink and a smile before flipping the switch and closing the door behind him.

The room was quiet, aside from a soft hiss as air blew through the vent in the ceiling. Martin lay for some time, awaiting the expected chatter from his young charge.

He turned his head slowly so as to not attract the boy's attention, squinting at the dark form in the other bed.

Sensing no movement, he closed his eyes and had just begun to drift off when the child's voice broke the silence.

"Dr. Ellig-am, I can't get to sleep. Maybe if we played our game all the thinkin' would tire me out."

Martin groaned internally as he pried his eyes back open. "Evan, I really don't feel well, I'm tired, and it hurts to talk, so just ... be quiet. Close your eyes and think about ... think about that ridiculous dog you like so much ... Tomato."

"That's a good one, Dr. Ellig-am," Evan said as he bounced back up on his knees. "That would be funny, a dog called Tomato." He leaned over the bedrail and peered into Martin's face. "I gots a really good idea. I think of an animal, and you hafta ask questions to figure out what it is. Miss Soames plays this with us sometimes when it's raining and we can't go outside."

Martin put his hand over his eyes and took in a slow, deep, breath. "I tell you what, you lie back down. *I'll* think of an animal ... *one* animal ... and you ask the questions. But then you have to be quiet and go to sleep, is that understood?"

"Got it!" The little boy dropped on to his back and pulled his feet under the blanket, settling in for the game.

"Are you ready, Dr. Ellig-am?"

"I've thought of an animal ... yes."

"Does this animal live in a zoo?"

"Well, strictly speaking, Evan, any animal could live in a zoo ... or aquarium."

"What about *un*-strippedly speaking?"

"No."

"Does it have hair?"

"Yes."

"Does it gots a beard?"

Martin hesitated. "Yes, I suppose you *could* say it has a beard."

"Hmm, does it live at the North Pole?"

"No."

Evan got up and peered over the bed rail again. "Are you sure? 'Cause I thought you might be thinkin' of Father Christmas."

"No, of course not," Martin said shortly, his irritation building. "I'm thinking of an *animal*, Evan."

"Well, strippedly speaking, Father Christmas *is* an animal."

"Oh, for goodness' sake! It has four legs. Some live in the wild. Some on farms, and—"

"Do they live in China?"

Martin hissed out a breath and rubbed at his eyes. "Yes, I believe they do have some in China."

"Are you thinkin' of a yak?"

"No." Martin pulled his hand behind his head and looked over at the boy. "I don't think yaks have beards."

Now that his eyes had adjusted to the darkened room, Martin could see the concentrated scowl on the child's face.

"All right, I want to get this nonsense over with so I can go to sleep. So, I'll give you another clue. Certain species of this animal live in the wild, but other species live on farms ... and we get milk from them. Milk that we use to make cheese."

"Ahhh! Yer thinkin' of a sheep!"

"Nooo! Sheep don't have beards! We get milk from them, Evan, milk that we make cheese from ... *goat* cheese."

Evan stared down at the doctor before answering, warily. "Is it a ... cow?"

There was a pause before Martin gave a small groan. "All right, I see what you're up to. You're stalling so you won't have to go to sleep, aren't you?"

The boy pulled his fist up and dropped his chin into his hand. "I'm *not* tired. I've been sleepin' *all—day.*"

"Well—I *am*—tired. I'm very tired, so you're just going to have to lie down and be quiet."

Evan slipped his small body back under the blanket for a third time and lay quietly, counting the ticks as the second hand on the wall clock moved around the dial.

It wasn't long before he heard the slow, steady, sound of the doctor's somnial breathing pattern, and he moved to the edge of the bed, snaking his hand under the rail and walking his fingers towards him until they made contact with the warmth of his arm.

The boy's tentative touch nudged Martin into a subtle awareness of his presence, and he stirred slightly.

"Dr. Ellig-am ... are you sleeping?" the child whispered as he wiggled his fingers against him.

His eyes opened reluctantly and groaned softly. "You're supposed to be quiet, Evan."

"It's a goat, right?"

"Yes ... it's a goat."

The ticks of the clock replaced conversation for a moment as the boy's contact with his surly friend continued.

Then the child's brittle voice broke the silence once again. "Father Christmas won't bring me anything this year, will he?"

"Why do you say that?"

"'Cause, he never comes. I tried *really* hard this year, and I thought maybe he'd come, but I know he won't come now."

Martin's thoughts flitted briefly to his own memories of a childhood devoid of the pleasures enjoyed by other children.

"Well, there really isn't such a person as—" Something kept the words he intended to say from spilling from his mouth. "Why do you think Father Christmas won't come?"

"'Cause I ran away. He'll tell Father Christmas what I did, and he won't come." The child's breaths grew ragged as his fingers began to tremble.

"Evan, come over here," Martin said as he patted his hand on the mattress next to him.

The boy sat up in his bed and looked over at him uncertainly. "Your friend said I had to stay here 'cause I could hurt you. I think I better stay here."

"Come on over; it's all right."

The child scrambled around the bed rail and crawled up next to him, pulling the covers over his head as a shiver ran through him.

"Evan, none of what happened last night was your fault. It was entirely your father's own lookout. He was wrong to drink. He knew that drinking made him mean and that he shouldn't do it. But your father had something called alcoholism. Alcohol ... things with alcohol in them ... like whiskey and beer ... it caused his brain to not work properly. That's why he would get so angry with you. There was nothing you could do to keep him from getting angry."

"I shouldn't have run. His eyes are very scary when he's angry, but I'm not s'posed to run away. He's really angry at me now, Dr. Ellig-am. He'll find me, he always finds me! Please, can I stay with you?"

Martin wrapped his left arm around the small shape under the covers and pulled him in closer. "You're perfectly safe here, Evan. But ... well, it's—it's important that you understand your father will never be able to hurt you again.

"And he didn't fall down the stairs because he was chasing you. He lost his balance and fell. And his eyes weren't angry when you saw him. He was ... well, he hit his head very hard when he fell. It caused his brain to stop sending signals telling his heart to beat ... for his lungs to keep pumping air in and out of his body."

The doctor's arm tightened around the boy. "Your father died last night, Evan. It may have appeared that he was looking at you, but he wasn't even seeing anything at that point. He was dead, and that's just how people's eyes look after they die."

The child was silent for a while before his hand crept up on Martin's chest. "Can you come alive again after you die?"

"No. Not when your brain has been injured as severely as your father's was. Your father is gone and will never come back. I'm very sorry."

The boy took in a deep breath, and Martin felt his body relax.

"I'm sorry that I made you sick. And that they hafta fix your arm," he said, his breaths short and uneven.

"Evan, you didn't make me sick. I wasn't feeling very well before, and the cold and rain ... getting run down ... it kept my body from being able to fight off an infection."

Evan pulled the blanket from over his head and peered up at Martin. "I tried not to run away ... you told me to stop ... I heard you say, stop!" He drew in several gasps of air and clung tightly to the doctor. "I *wanted* to stop, but my feet wouldn't stay still! I tried to make 'em quit mov—"

"Shh, shh, shh, shh, shh! That wasn't your fault either, Evan. When we're really frightened, there's a part of our brain, called the amygdala, that takes over. It's a bit like the thinking part of our brain doesn't get a say in things when that happens. The doing, or reacting, part of our brain fires up and runs the show.

"Sometimes we can't control that. Sometimes our brains get us ready to fight off something dangerous … or, as happened to you, run away from it." Martin gave a soft grunt. "Sometimes we freeze and can't do anything."

Evan tapped his fingertips on Martin's chest and settled his head on to his good shoulder. "Does Father Christmas not come 'cause he doesn't like me?"

Memories of his own disappointing Christmas mornings flitted through Martin's head. "I think he just doesn't know about you. It's rather hard to find your house, you know."

"Huh. I bet you're right! *That* would explain it!"

"Do you think you can get to sleep now?" he asked as the little boy's jaw stretched into a yawn.

"Mm-hmm."

"You better get in your own bed, though. That old Dr. Parsons will be grousing at you in the morning if he finds you over here," Martin said, pulling the blanket back and shooing the child away with his hand.

Evan scurried back to his bed and pulled the covers over himself.

"G'night, Dr. Ellig-am," he whispered.

"Goodnight, Evan."

Martin closed his eyes and fell asleep quickly as the little boy's hand came to rest on his arm.

Chapter 7

Louisa returned to Truro long before the sun had dragged itself over Cornwall's cold horizon, making a stop first at the Parsons' to leave James in Carole's care.

"His sippy cup is in the bag, as well as some strawberries and yogurt. Oh, and hummus and carrot sticks. Otherwise, he'll pretty much eat whatever you're eating. But don't let him get hold of porridge or you'll be sorry. And if he doesn't like what you're—"

"Louisa, don't worry!" Carole took the child from his mother's arms. "James and I will get along just fine, won't we, precious boy?"

"Mum-Mum-Mum," James babbled as he pulled at her beaded necklace before bringing it to his mouth.

Louisa tipped her head to the side and handed her son his favourite toy of late, the squishy rubber ball that his father used to strengthen his grip. "I don't know whether to be jealous or relieved that he calls you mum."

"Oh, don't be silly. You know who your mummy is, don't you, James Henry?"

Chris picked up his car keys, and Louisa worked the buttons of her coat back through the buttonholes. "I could hardly blame him for being confused. I think he's logged more hours with you than he has with me over the last three months."

"Well, this is just a small bump in the road. I love taking care of James. And, I must say, I think he rather likes spending time here."

Louisa smiled as Carole set the boy down, his miniature trainers tapping against the hardwood floor as he toddled into the living room.

"I'll let you know as soon as Martin's out of surgery!" Louisa called out as her friend disappeared around the corner, trying to keep up with the child.

Chris and Louisa arrived at Martin's room a short time later. Chris began to chuckle softly as they approached the bed.

Martin lay on his left side, his right arm secured to his front to immobilise his shoulder, and Evan lay curled up against him.

Louisa gave him a warning look and a firm poke with her elbow before leaning over to place a kiss on her husband's head. Her cool fingers against his warm cheek nudged him towards consciousness, and he took in a slow, deep breath.

"Martin," she said softly. "Time to wake up."

Her words penetrated but his eyelids were heavy, and he lingered a few moments before allowing the harsh morning light to invade his senses. Her scent was different ... medicinal. Not like the light and flowery perfume that she was partial to.

She spoke to him again, more insistent this time, "Martin ... you need to wake up. Ed will be here soon."

He felt the weight of her hand on the side of his head as her fingers toyed with his ear, and he forced his heavy lids to open. The red rays of sunshine filtering in over the window sill blinded him temporarily, and he squinted to make out his wife's face in front of him.

"Geesh!" he squeaked as he pulled away, recoiling at the unexpected visage of the child.

Rolling on to his back, he gazed up, attempting to decipher the expression in his wife's eyes as they sparkled back at him.

"Good morning," he said, trying to pull his hand up to stroke her cheek before discovering his arm pinned to the mattress by the weight of his young charge.

"Did you sleep well?" Chris asked, standing behind Louisa with his arms folded across his chest.

Martin yanked his trapped appendage away quickly and tried to sit up when he saw the smirk bedecking his friend's face. "Fine. Just fine," he said, wiping the drool from his mouth.

Evan began to stir, stretching and yawning. He blinked his eyes at Chris before pulling his knees under him and scrambling back to his own bed.

"Dr. Ellig-am was havin' a bad dream, and I was just tryin' ta be helpful. I was really, really careful," the boy said. "Please don't grouse at me."

Chris walked over and sat down on the edge of the child's bed. "I'm not going to grouse at you, Evan. Looks to me like you did a fine job of watching out for my friend."

The child's fearful aspect relaxed into a timid smile before he turned his attention to Martin. "See Dr. Ellig-am, I told ya she wouldn't leave you here by yourself."

"What?"

Evan flopped on to his stomach and propped his chin in his hand. "You probably don't remember, but you were havin' a bad dream last night about Mrs. Ellig—"

"Okay, Evan," Louisa said, cutting the boy off before he could cause her husband any further embarrassment. "We better get some breakfast for you. You must be starving."

"I'll see if I can chase up someone from food service," Chris said as he headed towards the door.

The boy pushed himself up on straightened arms. "Maybe me and Old Doc Parsons could go to the canteen. They got lots'a different things there."

"Old Doc Parsons?" Chris grumbled. "Where did *that* come from?"

Evan sat up and swung his legs over the edge of the bed, pointing a finger. "That's what Dr. Ellig-am calls you."

"Is that right?" Chris peered down at his friend, his eyes narrowed.

"I do not!" Martin rasped.

"Well, strippedly speaking, he calls you Old *Doctor* Parsons. 'Cept that sounds so starchy. So I thought Old *Doc* Parsons would be better."

Taking note of the daggers being shot at her husband, Louisa stepped in. "I think just plain Dr. Parsons would be fine, Evan."

"It's no bother!" the boy said. "I think he looks more like an Old Doc Parsons than a Plain Doctor Parsons, anyways. Can we go get bekfrast now?"

"I'll buy," Martin said quickly, eager to appease his friend. "Louisa, could you bring me my wallet?"

Louisa retrieved the bag she had brought with her, rummaging around before producing the requested item.

Martin pulled out a twenty pound note and handed it to Chris. "That should more than cover it."

Chris snatched the bill from his friend's hand. "Oh, that doesn't *begin* to cover it, mate." He hoisted the child into his arms and walked out the door.

"Hmm," Louisa said as she watched the door swing shut. "So ... how did you do last night?" she asked as she dropped on to the bed and took hold of her husband's hand.

Martin breathed out a heavy sigh and closed his eyes. "I've made a real hash of it."

"With Evan, you mean?"

"Of course, with Evan!" he snapped. "I don't know what's going to happen to the boy! His mother left ... took his sister with her and left Evan there to fend for himself with an abusive father. By definition, that in and of itself is serious neglect of a child! Children's Services, *if* they follow protocols, won't allow the mother custody. And God knows what other irresponsible *dipsomaniacs* the authorities might shake from that family tree!" he sputtered.

"Martin, *calm—down*. We don't know. Maybe Evan has a kindly aunt and uncle who will take him in."

He hissed out a breath and shook his head at her. "People like the Hanleys don't come from well adjusted families, Louisa."

Louisa leaned forward and wrapped her arms around him. "Well, at this moment, I'm worried about you. Let's just get you through this surgery, shall we?"

"Mm." Martin pulled back and looked at her intently for several seconds before working his hand up under her ponytail and kissing her.

"That was lovely, Martin," Louisa said breathlessly when he finally released her.

"Louisa ... of all the things I'm grateful for, you're my most treasured thing." He caressed her cheek with the backs of his fingers. "Thank you for not leaving."

She tipped forward until their foreheads were touching. "I meant what I said, Martin. I'm not going anywhere."

They turned as the soft whoosh of the door signalled Ed Christianson's arrival. "Good morning, all. How are you feeling, Martin?"

"Much better than twenty-four hours ago."

Louisa moved back as the surgeon stepped up to the bed and pulled his stethoscope from around his neck. "Take some deep breaths for me."

Martin inhaled, the air moving through his chest triggering a coughing spell.

Ed moved his instrument around on his patient's back and chest, his brow furrowed.

"How does he sound?" Louisa asked anxiously, worrying her lower lip.

"Can you lay down for me ... on your left side?" Ed said as he came around and pushed the extra bed out of the way before lowering Martin's bed rail. "Another deep breath."

"Well?" Louisa asked again.

"I'm not hearing any rales today, and the fever's come down. I'll have someone come by and take you to the CT lab ... get some pictures, but I think we're probably good to go on fixing that shoulder today."

He put his hands on his hips and looked at the other doctor sympathetically. "I'm sorry to have to take away your driving privileges so soon after getting them back."

Martin gave a resigned shrug. "It'll shorten the process at the other end of all of this, I suppose."

"Yep, won't be quite as uncomfortable either when Will does his reconstructive work up in London."

Ed picked up the chart on the end of the bed and scribbled in some notes. "I'll pull the pins that we weren't able to get to last time ... two in the femur, one in the right tibia, and that second-most distal pin in the arm. And I'll tighten any you loosened on your yomp across Bodmin Moor. Then I'll turn you over to Warren Buck. Let him work his magic with that shoulder.

"He'll probably be in theatre for about an hour and a half, Louisa. If all goes according to plan you should have him back by early-afternoon at the latest."

"Thank you, Ed," she replied.

When Evan and Chris returned to the room, Martin was in radiology.

The boy's gaze darted around the room. "Where's Dr. Ellig-am?"

"They took him down to radiology, Evan. He'll be back in a few minutes," Louisa said.

Chris set him down on the bed. He quickly slid to the floor before limping to the door, struggling to pull it open. "I gotta find him!"

Hurrying over, Chris gathered the boy up and carried him back to the bed. "Evan, Dr. Ellingham will be back in just a bit. He went to have some pictures taken of his lungs."

"Why don't we see what we can find on the television, hmm." Louisa sat down on the bed next to him and handed him the remote control.

Evan flipped through the channels until he landed on a station airing a programme about the marine life of Cornwall. He sat rapt for several minutes before the door opened and Martin was wheeled into the room.

"Hi, Dr. Ellig-am! Why are you in that wheelchair?" he asked, slipping back off the bed and hurrying to Martin's side.

"Because the—bumptious—staff at this hospital seem to think I'm incapable of taking a—"

"Martin," Louisa hissed, pre-empting his frustration-induced tirade. She turned a smiling face to the boy. "I think, Evan, that the people here are just concerned about Dr. Ellingham losing his balance. He doesn't have his crutch with him."

The boy leaned his forearms on the armrest of the chair while his healthy foot searched blindly for a toehold. "Can I see your pictures?"

"Come here, Evan," Chris said hoisting the boy up yet again before pulling the computer monitor out away from the wall. "I can bring them up on the screen if you'd like to take a look."

Martin stood, grimacing as he placed weight on his fractured legs, stressed by the harrowing trek across the moor. Louisa hurried over and he rested a hand on her shoulder to support himself as he made his way back to his bed.

"Good morning, Dr. Ellingham!" a nurse said, breezing into the room and quickly taking control. Martin glanced over at the woman, recognising her from his previous stay at the Royal Cornwall.

"Look at you, up on your feet and walking. And making a proper job of it from the looks of things!"

"Mm, yes," he grunted back as he swung his legs up on the bed.

"I'm here to get you prepped and ready for theatre." She turned and spread her arms out, herding Chris, Evan and Louisa towards the door.

"I need the rest of you to give us a bit of privacy. You can come back when I'm finished with him," she said, giving Louisa a smile and tapping her finger to Evan's nose.

"But I need to stay with Dr. Ellig-am!" the child protested, wriggling in Chris's arms in an attempt to free himself.

"We'll come back in just a few minutes," Louisa said, giving him a reassuring nod as they entered the corridor. Martin could hear the boy's strident protests fade as they moved away from the room, and he breathed out a heavy sigh.

"You have an admirer I see," the nurse said as she unfastened the abduction sling from around Martin's waist.

She leaned him forward and pulled the straps away before removing the brace.

"He's a patient ... neglected by the mother and abused by the father."

"Oh, bless him! Poor little thing. Well, you can do more for that little man than you know." She tugged at the ties on his hospital gown and pulled it over his arms. "Okay, lie on back there, Dr. Ellingham, and we'll get you all smooth as a baby's bum under that arm," she said as she unrolled a towel, revealing an assortment of swabs, disinfectants and a razor.

Louisa had only a few minutes with her husband before he was wheeled off to surgery. Chris gave Evan time to say goodbye. Then he whisked him down to the canteen for a cup of hot chocolate before returning him to paediatrics.

"Well, how did that go?" Louisa asked when he returned to the room.

"About as you would imagine—tears ... clinging. So, what's Mart thinking about all of this?"

Louisa fiddled with her fingernails, avoiding eye contact with him. "Louisa...?"

"I heard you, Chris. I just don't know what to tell you because we haven't discussed it much. I guess I'm hoping the problem will resolve itself ... you know. A relative will step forward or something."

Chris fidgeted in his chair, hesitating before speaking again. "You know it's not in Martin's nature to leave this kid to fend for himself in the system, don't you? The subject of taking him in may come up. How would you feel about that?"

Louisa got up abruptly and walked to the table by the bed, filling a glass with water. "It worries me. It sounds awful, Chris, but I'm not sure I want that. I mean, we've just gotten Martin to a point physically where I'm not terrified every time he gets sick ... to where there's light at the end of the tunnel."

Chris tipped his head and peered at her over the top of his glasses, and Louisa tossed her handbag on to the bed. "Okay, so maybe I do still worry a bit when he gets sick. He's still really vulnerable. And Martin has his own son who needs him ... who needs his attention. I'm afraid that Evan would take attention away from James."

"Hey, I can understand your concerns," he said. "There's a lot that would have to be taken into consideration. It might be wise for you to be thinking this through, though, in case the issue is raised at some point."

"Yeah." Louisa set her glass down with a thud and headed for the door. "I need to get some air. I'll be back in a while."

Chapter 8

Louisa walked through the hospital corridors, her head clearer after a stroll in the brisk, late-fall air.

"Louisa!" Jeremy Portman called out.

She whirled around at the sound of his rapidly approaching footsteps, a chill running through her. "Jeremy! What's wrong? Did something happen?"

"Martin's fine," he said as he trotted to a stop. Well, I haven't heard anything yet, actually."

He took her arm and led her to a quiet alcove. "I just spoke with someone from Children's Services. They've tracked down Evan's mother. She and the daughter are living up in Manchester."

"And she's coming down?"

"No. It seems there was no love lost between her and her husband."

"But ... Evan. She certainly can't expect the child to take a train all the way up there on his own!" Her fist clenched around her purse strap at the thought of her husband, as a boy even younger than Evan, making the convoluted journey to boarding school on his own.

"The mum wants to terminate her parental rights to the boy."

Louisa stared at him, her mouth agape. "But she has Evan's sister. She wants her daughter but not her son?"

"According to the police officer who went to the woman's apartment, she says she doesn't have the means to care for two children. I suspect it's a moot point anyway.

With the history of neglect, I can't imagine she'd be allowed custody."

Louisa leaned back against the wall and took in a deep breath. "What about other relatives?"

"They're looking into it. The boy's paternal grandparents are deceased, and Mrs. Hanley's a product of the foster care system. So, it may take a bit of time to locate any existing family."

"I see. Well, what happens to Ev—" Louisa glanced down before pulling her vibrating mobile from her purse. "Excuse me, Jeremy," she said as she stepped away from him to take the call.

The aide walked across the corridor to the large observation windows on the opposite side and took a seat in the chairs clustered together in the corner. He had an unsettled feeling in his stomach, thinking about Martin and how he was going to handle the situation with the child, in both the most literal sense of the word as well as emotionally.

The clicking of Louisa's platform heels against the polished floor prodded him from his moment of reflection.

"Martin's out of surgery," she said. "Everything went fine, and he'll be back in his room in about a half hour."

"That's good news. You want to go grab a cuppa while we're waiting? We can talk on the way."

Louisa and Jeremy had returned to Martin's room shortly before two orderlies wheeled him in, groggy but awake. His shoulder was wrapped in a bulky bandage, and the entire area was packed in ice. His forearm was braced firmly to his front to immobilise the shoulder joint.

"Hi," Louisa said as she leaned over and pressed her lips to his forehead. "How are you feeling? Does it hurt?"

"A little ... woozy. But it doesn't hurt. They use ... they used a nerve block so it's ... numb," he said as he tried to focus his eyes on her.

"I'm glad it's over. Another hurdle cleared, hmm?"

"Mm."

Martin's eyes drifted shut again, and Louisa settled into a chair next to the bed to begin her now familiar post-operative vigil.

It was almost half three when he groaned softly and his eyes fluttered open. He had slept off the effects of the anaesthesia, but the nerve block had begun to wear off as well, leaving him in pain.

"I'll get a nurse ... see if they can give you something, hmm?" Louisa said, forcing a small smile. "Someone brought in some sparkling water and crackers a while ago ... if you want it." She rolled the tray table closer to the bedside, unscrewed the water bottle and pulled open the plastic wrapper enclosing the crackers.

"Would you call Ed ... ask him when I can leave?" He felt around for the remote control and then raised the head of the bed.

"Oh, Martin, I don't really think—"

"Louisa ... just call Ed," he said through clenched teeth.

Louisa eyed him for a moment before stepping into the hallway.

Martin laid his head back and closed his eyes, trying not to think about his increasing discomfort. He dozed off once more before being awakened by the whoosh of the door opening.

"Oh, gawd," he groaned softly when he saw Bert Large, his aunt Ruth's assistant's father, standing in the doorway. A little less than a week before, he had brought the man back from the edge of death after he suffered a myocardial infarction.

"Well, hello there, Doc. My boy said you were here. I thought since we're practically neighbours it would be rather ... *uncharitable*, shall we say, for me to not pay you a visit. Are you up to a little chat with an old friend?"

"Not really, Bert." Martin looked into the hallway before the door swung shut, hoping to see his wife returning to spare him the need to entertain the portly restaurateur and village philosopher.

Bert shuffled over to the bed, the sash on his dressing gown hanging ineffectually at his sides as he pulled a chair up and plopped into it, landing with a grunt and a wheeze.

"I won't stay long then. You do look a bit peaky, if you don't mind my sayin'.

"How bout this—you and me in hospital together. Quite a lucky coincidence. Why, one might even say providential."

"More like an unfortunate happenstance, I would think," Martin grumbled.

"Oh, don't be like that, Doc. You gotta look on the bright side. Why, the way I see it, fate had a hand in this. It was meant to be."

"Really?" Martin said, his tone laced with sarcasm. "Then fate has a twisted sense of humour."

"Okay, okay. I see yer point. But try ta see *my* point. This gives us a chance to really get ta know each other."

Bert shifted in his chair, the one-size-fits-all hospital gown inching higher on the portly man's thighs, causing Martin to avert his eyes.

"I, er ... hope to be going home today, Bert."

"Aww, that's a shame. Here I thought maybe we could have some time to chat."

"*Chat?* What on earth for?"

"Well, you and me ... we both had one'a them near-dead experiences, you know. And I been wonderin', Doc ... did your life flash before your eyes?"

Martin grimaced at the man's question and the pain that was now shooting through his shoulder. *"What?"*

"Well, I'm not tryin' ta be a nosy parker. It's just that when you have one a them near-dead experiences, I thought your life was supposed to flash before yer eyes, and my life didn't flash before my eyes."

Martin shook his head. "And?"

"Well, it's worrisome, Doc! Maybe it's like a bad omen or somethin'. Do you think it could mean I got some redeemin' ta do?"

"Quite possibly." Martin sighed heavily and let his eyes drift shut. "Is there a specific purpose for this visit, Bert?"

"Oh, sure ... sure. I'm gettin' to that." Bert's gaze darted towards the door then back to the doctor. "I been doin' some thinkin', Doc ... 'bout our relationship and all."

Martin screwed up his face. "I didn't realise we had a relationship."

"Oh, not like *that!* Although there might'a been a time when folks wondered about you. But then you and Louiser had yer little lad, and that put those rumours to rest right quick, didn't it?"

Martin reached his hand up and rubbed at the throbbing that had begun in his temples. "Bert ... get to the point!"

"Right. Right you are, Doc. See, it's like this ... this whole heart attack thing. It's made me realise I need to face up to some things. I haven't been able to admit this to anyone before, Doc. Not even Al.

"My Jenny left me. She went off to Woking ... ta fill in temporarily at the chemist there. She was just s'posed ta be there for a week, but she kept givin' me one reason or a'tother for not comin' home. I s'pose I knew deep down that I'd lost her. Just didn't wanna admit it."

Bert worked his plump fingers over his knees. "I finally just came right out and put it to her ... made 'er come clean with me. She'd found someone else, Doc. The restaurant hasn't been doin' so good, and I reckon she found some bloke up there who could support her, proper like. I was just satisfyin' a need for her until what she really wanted come along, if you know what I mean.

"It's hard to admit she never really loved me," Bert continued. "To know she didn't want me ... to have *other* people know she didn't want me. You can understand that, can't you, Doc?"

Martin swallowed, trying to relieve the constriction in his throat. "Yeah, I can, Bert."

"Knew you would. But thing is, I got a chance at a new life now, thanks to you, Doc. I think I was scared to admit it before, but Jenny's gone and my little boy's growin' up. One day he's gonna settle down and start a family ... have his own young ones to occupy his time."

Bert reached over to the tray table and helped himself to Martin's package of crackers.

"Al and your Morwenna ... now there's a lovely girl ... there's somethin' up there, Doc."

The man wagged his finger in the air as a small shower of cracker crumbs dribbled down his front. "A father can sense these things, you know. I need to let him go ... find my own way so he can find his."

"Look, I appreciate that this is a difficult time for you Bert," Martin said, wincing as a deep pinching pain intensified in his shoulder. "But I still don't know what point you're trying to make."

"Right you are. I'm gettin' to it. So, my point *is* ... you've been a good doc. Always there, day and night, whenever someone needs a doc. And I been carryin' around a weight ... a load'a guilt, and I wanna make amends.

"It's hard to move on when you got somethin' hangin' over you like that. It's kind'a like when you feel a cold comin' on but it never quite gets there, and it just niggles at you til you can't hardly —"

"Bert—*the point!*" Martin snapped as his pain was becoming impossible to ignore.

"Oh, sure ... sure, Doc. It's about the monkey tricks at The Crab that day ... with the ketchup. You remember that, Doc?"

That was a day Martin would never be able to forget. Shortly after his arrival in the village, a disgruntled colleague spilled the beans to some of the locals about his haemophobia. Bert was the instigator of a publicly humiliating prank, played on the doctor at the village pub.

Martin glowered at him. "What about it, Bert?"

"Well, I can't speak for the other lads, but ... well, we can let bygones be bygones, can't we, Doc? Forgive and forget, eh" he chuckled.

Martin stared at the man for a moment before tipping his head back and peering down at him imperiously. "No."

Bert's brow furrowed as he pulled his chin in sharply. *"No?"*

"No. I'm sorry to hear about your personal problems, Bert. But don't come in here asking me to forget about that. Now if you don't mind."

Bert heaved himself from the chair and walked towards the door, where Louisa had been standing, long enough to catch the restaurateur's mea culpa of sorts.

"Excuse me," the portly man said as he squeezed past her and out into the corridor.

She stepped into the room, and Martin laid his head back on his pillow to await the impending rebuke.

She sat down in the chair, still warm from its previous occupant. "Couldn't you have forgiven poor Bert?"

"Louisa, don't start," he said, putting a hand to the side of his head. "What did Ed have to say?"

Taking note of the dark circles under her husband's eyes, she decided to let the Bert Large matter drop for the time being. "Sorry, but he wants you to stay at least one more night. He's concerned about the pneumonia ... wants to be sure it's under control before you go home. How's Bert doing ... with his heart and all?"

Martin gave his head a lethargic shake. "I didn't get a chance to ask. He kept prattling on. I suppose you heard. That woman ... his fiancée, left him."

"Jenny left? Oh, poor Bert! I should go see him," Louisa said, getting to her feet.

"Best not. He hasn't told anyone yet, not even Al. I'm not sure you're supposed to know."

"Mm, I see. But he told *you*?"

"Yes. How's Evan?"

Louisa sat back down, taking his hand. "Chris and I just got done talking to a woman with Children's Services. They're going to line up a foster family for him. Just until they can find a relative who'll take him."

"Louisa." He took in a deep breath. "Louisa, that would be the worst thing that could happen to Evan right now."

"I know what you're thinking, Martin. But *you* need to get well. They'll find a nice family for him to stay with, I'm sure." Her head nodded encouragingly, but the accompanying smile was drawn taut with apprehension.

"But even if there was a guarantee of that, it's still not what the boy *needs*."

Louisa got to her feet and took her husband's head in her hands, looking into his eyes. "You can go see him.

Maybe spend some time with him before he goes to a permanent home. But right now, my concern is for you."

Martin's chest tightened and his heart raced as he pulled his head away. "I'll be fine. But a nice family ... that's not enough! Evan's not someone's pet that can be—can be rehomed!"

"I know that, Martin." She sat back and crossed her arms in front of her, huffing out a breath. "You want to see about letting him stay with us for a while ... that's what you're saying?"

He redirected his gaze to the view out his window. "Yes."

"Just till they get things sorted with his relatives, right?"

He hesitated. "At this point, yes." His heart slowed as he sensed his wife's weakening resolve.

"If we do this, Martin Ellingham—and that's a big *if* because the possibility hasn't even been raised with Children's Services. But *if* we do this, you have to promise me that your health will come first. And Evan would have to understand that, too."

"I think that can be managed," he said, turning his head to give her a small smile.

Louisa's face softened. "All right, I'll go see if I can find the man I talked to earlier," she said as she leaned over to kiss his cheek.

A nurse pushed through the door, and Louisa moved out of the way. "I'll be back in a bit," she said as she ducked into the corridor.

The nurse unscrewed the cap on the catheter in Martin's wrist. "Mr. Christianson wants to see if we can take the edge off the pain you're having, Dr. Ellingham."

"Well it took you long enough. I hope you didn't have to pull yourself away from your afternoon tea and crumpets," he snapped as Chris Parsons entered the room.

"Ah, Martin, charming the hospital staff again, I see." Chris gave the nurse a wink and thanked her before she hurried out the door.

"Exercising those people skills?" he said, giving his friend a smirk.

"Oh, bugger off, Chris."

He pulled a chair up next to the bed and took a seat. "What's going on, Mart?"

Martin mumbled unintelligibly before giving him a sheepish look. "I'm sorry; that was uncalled for."

"Martin, the shoulder's just a small setback ... not even a setback. It's progress really. It would need to be done at some point anyway. The schedule was just moved along a bit."

"I know that. I just want to get out of here. It ... it makes me edgy being here."

"I see." He watched as Martin's fingers twitched at his side. "Well, I just stopped in to say hello ... see if there was anything you needed. I'll let you get some rest."

"Mm. Thank you, Chris."

"No problem, mate."

Picking up the remote control, Martin lowered the head of his bed down and closed his eyes, the sedating effect of the pain medication overtaking him.

When he woke nearly an hour later, Louisa was sitting at his side. She looked up from the book she was reading when she noticed him trying to sit up.

He pulled at the blankets covering his legs.

"Here, let me help," she said as she got up from her chair. "Are you hot?"

"No, I need to use the lavatory." He swung his legs over the edge of the mattress and got to his feet, swaying slightly as his head began to spin.

Pushing him back on to the bed, she cocked her head at him. "Are you okay? Should I get a nurse?"

He closed his eyes for a few moments, waiting for the rocking sensation to ease. "Just stood up too fast, I think," he said as his wife's worried face stared back at him. "I'm better now."

He took several steps before he was restrained by the IV tethering him to the bed. "Oh ... could you help me?"

She removed the tubing from the catheter in his wrist before he walked stiffly into the lavatory and pulled the door shut behind him. He emerged several minutes later and walked towards the bed, his gait precarious.

"Careful there, Doc. You should have let Louiser give you a hand in there."

Martin turned to see Joe Penhale seated near the window.

A rosy hue spread across the policeman's face. "I didn't mean—I wasn't suggestin' that she actually give you a—I'm sure what you were doin' in there was perfectly natural." Joe put his hands up in front of him. "Let me rephrase that—if you were to have been doin'—that—there'd be nothin—"

"Penhale, gawd! I had to pee!" Martin snapped as he reached out to steady himself on the tray table. "Where's Louisa?"

"I asked her to step out, Do-*c*. We need to have a little ... man to man, as it were. About the events of the other nigh-*t*. I need to take your statement so I can file my report"

"I see." Martin worked his way back on to the bed before wrestling, single-handedly, with the blankets as they caught on his fixators.

He looked up at the constable. "Could you help me here?" he said indignantly.

"Oh, sure. All you gotta do is ask." Joe hurried over and straightened the covers. "Can't say that I envy you, Doc. That looks awful painful," he said, wrinkling his nose.

"What do you need to know, Penhale?"

"Louiser said you got a phone call from the Hanley boy...let's start there," the policeman said, taking a seat.

"Evan called and said his father had been drinking. I went out to the farm and found Jim Hanley upstairs with the boy. Hanley was choking him. I pried the man's hands away from the boy and told him to go downstairs while I dealt with his father."

"Did Mr. Hanley exchange any words with you?"

"He was singing when I first arrived, his words were slurred, and he was quite obviously inebriated."

"Can you remember *what* he was singin'?"

"I don't know. Does it matter?"

Joe gave a shrug of his shoulders. "I 'spose not. Just curious." He gave Martin a lopsided grin. "Rumour has it, he has quite a nice baritone voice."

Martin hissed a breath through his nose. "I tried to talk Hanley into having a lie down ... sleeping it off. But he came at me. He swung a bottle and hit me in the head before he lost his balance and tumbled down the steps. When I got to him, he was already dead. His pupils were blown, and I couldn't find a pulse. I suspect a massive cerebral haemorrhage."

"Hmph, excellent doctoring skills there, Doc. The coroner says it *was* a cerebral haemorrhage that did him in."

Martin closed his eyes as the constable scratched the details into his notebook. There were a few moments in his life that would qualify as more calamitous than the night at the Hanley farm, but none were etched in his memory quite as vividly.

"Did you attempt CPR?" Joe asked.

"Of course not! The man was clearly dead!"

Penhale raised a hand up in front of him. "No need to get yerself all worked up, Doc. That can't be a good thing in your condition." He narrowed his eyes and pursed his lips. "So, that's a negative then?"

Martin took a moment to shoot the constable a warning look. "No. I did *not* administer CPR. Now move on, Penhale."

"Right you are, Do-*c*. Now for the other little matter ... did you or did you not chase Evan Hanley out into that storm?"

"*Absolutely not!* The boy was frightened when he saw his father dead. He ran off and wouldn't stop when I called him ... he was traumatised. When I finally caught up with him, I couldn't see well enough in the blowing rain to be able to find my way back to the house.

"The boy's core body temperature was dropping rapidly. I carried him as far as I could, but I could feel my legs giving out. I didn't want him to be hurt if I fell, so he had to walk. I just couldn't carry him any farther. The best I could do was find a place that was somewhat dry and sheltered."

The constable added additional words to his notebook and then got to his feet. "I believe that's all I'll be needing for now. I don't foresee any formal charges being filed in this case," he said, snapping his notebook shut with a flourish. "But don't leave town. Leastwise not till you've been cleared by the boys in Exeter."

"What do you mean, don't leave town? I didn't do anything wrong!"

"I prefer to keep an open mind about these things," Joe said. "That and I've always wanted to say that. Just never had a perp to say it to."

"You still don't," Martin's jaw flexed as he glared at him.

"Well, *technically* ... no, probably not."

The door to the room opened and Louisa stuck her head in. "Can we come in now, Joe? Martin has another visitor."

Joe tipped his head down and peered up at her. "Well, I'm not a visitor ... as such. Although we did visit, didn't we, Doc?"

Martin rolled his eyes at the policeman before craning his neck to see around him. "Come on in."

Louisa walked to her husband's side, followed by a gentleman unfamiliar to Martin. Bringing up the rear was a distraught Evan Hanley being carried by Chris Parsons.

Joe put his hand on Martin's injured shoulder. "It might be best to keep what happened the other night on a need-to-know basis," he murmured.

"Stop that!" Martin snapped as he winced and brushed the constable's hand away.

"I'd like to thank you officer, for your assistance in this matter," the unidentified gentleman said as he extended his hand to Joe. "Officer Penhale was very persuasive in his arguments in favour of what's been discussed."

"Yes, thank you, Joe," Louisa said.

"All in the line of duty." He hoisted his tool belt and moved towards the corridor before turning towards Martin. "I'll be in tou-*ch*."

"Yes, I'm sure you will."

"Martin, this is Roger Delaney," Louisa said. "He's with Children's—"

"I wanna get down," Evan interjected, pushing with all his might against Chris's chest. He set the boy on the extra bed and he quickly slipped to the floor before climbing up to lay next to Martin, his wet sniffles interspersed with ragged breaths.

"What's going on?" Martin asked, his eyes darting from the child to his wife.

"He doesn't seem to think much of our paediatrics wing," Chris said.

Roger Delaney crouched down by the bed, at eye level with the child. "Evan, *now* can you tell us what upsets you so much about being in the other hospital room? You have all the other children with you and very kind doctors and nurses. I would think you'd like it there."

Evan squeezed his eyes shut and pulled Martin's arm around him. "His eyes can find me there," he said softly.

"Whose eyes, Evan?" the social worker asked.

"My dad's ... his angry eyes."

"I see." Roger caressed the boy's back and spoke softly. "Evan, I need to make a decision about who it would be best to leave you with until we get things figured out with your family. I have several very nice mums and dads who would enjoy having you spend some time with them. How does that sound to you?"

The boy peered up at Martin, his eyes pleading. "I want to stay with you, Dr. Ellig-am," he whispered, his words punctuated by small gasps.

Mr. Delaney pulled himself erect and tousled the child's hair. "I think that could be arranged, Evan. But I need to be sure that you understand something. Dr. Ellingham won't have the energy to do much with you until he's healthy again. You need to do your best to make sure he gets enough sleep. Can you manage that?"

Evan sat up on the bed, nodding his head vigorously. "I promise!"

The social worker pulled a clipboard from his satchel and turned to Louisa. "This has been approved by my superiors, but there are a few bits and bobs that need to be taken care of. I have some forms for you and your husband to fill out."

"Mart, when you get done with that, Ed's agreed to release you into my custody for the night. A neighbour gave Carole some reach-me-downs. She'll be here in a bit with some clothes and a coat for Evan. Then we can go."

The furrows in Martin's brow eased, and he looked down, giving the boy a small smile and a nod of his head.

Chapter 9

The tantalising aroma of pot roast, now cooked to perfection, welcomed them when they arrived at the Parsons' home. Having eaten nothing more than a single bowl of soup in the previous forty-eight hours, Martin wouldn't have hesitated to sit down to a large plate of the flavourful but high fat entree. However, Carole Parsons was the consummate hostess and had a filet of cod ready to put under the broiler for her more health-conscious guest.

"Go ahead and have a seat at the table everyone. Chris, could you get the salad out of the refrigerator, please?" Carole said. She pulled a clay roaster from the cooker and set it in the middle of the table before slipping the fish into the oven.

Chris set Evan down on the floor, and the child moved quickly to Martin's side.

Martin glanced down when he felt the boy's fingers spider up his hand and latch on to his wrist.

Louisa sat her son in the high chair Chris had pulled from retirement when she and James stayed with them after Martin's accident. The toddler immediately began slapping his hands down on the tray in front of him, demanding his dinner.

"Evan, would you like to come and sit by James?" Louisa asked in an attempt to entice the child from behind her husband's legs. "Dr. Ellingham can sit on the other side of you maybe ... hmm, Martin?"

"Mm, yes." Martin pulled himself free of the child's grasp and made his way around the table. Evan followed so closely behind him that when Martin stopped momentarily to shift his crutch, he bumped into the backs of his legs.

The movement jarred his shoulder and Martin clenched his jaw against the pain it caused, fighting his reflex to snap at the child.

He dropped into his chair as Carole slid a plate with a large serving of steaming fish and roasted vegetables in front of him. "There you go, Martin, healthy as you please."

"Yes, thank you." He sat, tucking into the meal as his young charge watched him closely.

Spearing a chunk of roasted carrot, he popped it into his mouth, savouring the enhanced natural sweetness encouraged by the cooking method. Evan grimaced, then followed suit, gagging twice before managing to force the vegetable down his gullet.

The boy sat glumly, his elbow perched on the table and his chin in his hand. "How come you like that stuff, Dr. Ellig-am?" he asked as he reached over and poked his fork into a chunk of rutabaga on Martin's plate.

"Hey, hey, hey! Get *out* of my dinner," he said sharply.

Evan pulled his hand back and looked up at Martin, his eyes becoming red-rimmed and watery.

Louisa tipped her head down, narrowing her eyes at her husband, and he softened his tone. "That's impolite, Evan. And I'm not sure why I like vegetables. I ate a lot of vegetables when I visited my aunt for the summer when I was young. That could have something to do with it."

"Well, I *don't* like 'em," the child stated definitively as he pushed them to the side of his plate. He drew a line of demarcation through the gravy with his finger before cleaning the digit off in his mouth.

Louisa eyed her husband and gave her head a subtle shake when he opened his mouth to chastise the boy for his poor table manners. "Let it go," she mouthed silently.

"Mm." He wagged a finger at the boy's plate. "Eat your beef."

While Martin's attention was focused on his own plate, Carole watched with amusement as his young charge stealthily slipped pieces of cooked root vegetables under the high chair tray to James. The younger child gave the boy a gleeful smile with each transfer of the comestibles before happily gobbling them down.

"Anybody fancy a bit of dessert?" Carole asked as she began to clear the plates from the table.

Scrutinising Evan's plate, Martin gave him a small approving smile, and a stiff, "Well done, Evan."

Ice cream with strawberries was served for dessert, a course which Evan seemed to have no trouble getting down. "Can I have another bowl?" he asked, peering up at Martin.

"You did a good job of cleaning your plate, so yes you may. But you need to ask Mrs. Parsons ... and remember to use your manners or she'll tell you no."

Carole watched the child as he sat, staring at his lap, trying to avoid eye contact with her. He swung his feet back and forth under the table before finally peering up shyly at her. "Can I have another bowl of ice cream ... please?"

"*May* I have another bowl of ice cream," Martin corrected as Carole pulled the freezer door open.

"You have ta say please or she won't give you any!" the boy whispered loudly.

"No, I mean—"

"Just say it, Dr. Ellig-am!" Evan watched worriedly as Carole slipped his refilled bowl in front of him and replaced the lid on the carton. "Quick!"

A simpering Chris leaned back in his chair, taking it all in. "What's the magic word, Mart?"

"I don't want any bloody—" Martin blurted out. "Oh, never mind."

The freezer door closed, sealing away the frozen confection.

Evan's shoulders drooped as he eyed the doctor with a reproachful expression on his face.

"Now you *definitely* won't get any ice cream," he said, shaking his head slowly. "I keep tellin' ya ... you shouldn't say bloody."

"Mm, mm, mm. I wish I could be a fly on the wall in *your* house, Louisa," Carole said. "Life in Portwenn could get *very* interesting."

"Oh, it's already interesting. We gots a Christmas Market at the school next week, don't we, Mrs. Ellig-am," Evan slurred, his tongue numbed by the frozen dessert in his mouth.

"Yes, we do, Evan. In fact, I may put you to work helping me with some of the decorations," Louisa said as she wiped strawberry juice from her son's face. James stretched himself over the side of his high chair, grabbing at Evan's hair with sticky fingers. "Oh, dear," Louisa said as she quickly wiped the smaller child's hands before getting a wet piece of kitchen roll and cleaning the sugary residue from the older boy's head.

Carole began to pick up the dirty dishes from the table and carry them to the sink.

"I can help you, Mrs. Parsons," Evan said as he scrambled down from his chair.

"No, no, no, no, no. You need to stay off that foot." Martin snapped his fingers and pointed to the child's recently vacated perch.

He gave a small sigh, and then climbed back up on his chair.

Carole wiped the crumbs from the table and gave him a warm smile.

"I've got an idea!" the boy said, pulling his shoulders back as his mood brightened suddenly. "You could come to our Christmas Market, Mrs. Parsons! You can even bring Old Doc Parsons if you want!"

Evan whirled around and looked at Louisa. "That'd be okay, wouldn't it, Mrs. Ellig-am?"

"That would be just fine, Evan, and it's very thoughtful of you to invite them. But it *is* a busy time of the year. The Parsons may have other plans."

"It's Friday night. Can you come, or do you gots other plans?" the seven-year-old asked, looking hopefully at Carole.

"Well actually, *I'm* free. But I don't know about the Old Doc." She stepped over and patted her husband's cheek. "Do you have plans on Friday evening, darling?"

"I think I can make room in my schedule," he said, giving Martin a black look before smiling up at his wife. "And I think Martin might like to take us all out for dinner. He has a debt to pay off ... for my new moniker."

Martin threw his head back and rolled his eyes, finishing the gesture off with a scowl at his friend.

"I was wondering if you men would mind if I took Louisa to the shops this evening," Carole said as she folded the tea towel and hung it over the handle of the cooker. "There are a lot of Christmas sales going on right now, and I have some boxes I need to tick off my gift list."

"Oh, I don't know Carole. This might not be the best night for it," Louisa said, glancing over at her husband.

"It's fine ... you go," Martin said.

Chair legs screeched against the floor as Chris pushed himself away from the table. "Maybe Evan can help me put the Christmas lights up outside while you're gone."

"No, no, no, no, no. He has to stay off that foot!"

"I'll bring a chair out, and he can be my sidewalk superintendent, then, Mart."

"That's brilliant, Old Doc Parsons!" Evan pulled his knees under him and leaned across the table. "What does a sidewalk super attendant do?"

"You tell me everything I'm doing wrong, Evan. Let me get your coat and we'll go get started."

Chris settled Martin on the sofa with the remote control for the television and a stack of medical journals on the coffee table, and then started his evening antibiotic infusion.

The house quickly grew quiet as Martin was left alone inside. Slipping off his shoes, he tried to get comfortable. He picked up a journal and made it through the first few paragraphs before sleep overtook him and the periodical slid to the floor.

He was awakened sometime later by the clatter of plastic building blocks being dumped on the floor.

"Mm. Did you get done with the lights already?" he asked Evan as he tried to sit himself up, a groan escaping as his stiffened shoulder complained.

The boy crawled over and put his hands on his back, giving him a well-intentioned, but ineffectual push. Martin gritted his teeth as the heels of the child's small hands dug into his ribs.

"Thank you, Evan," he said as the boy gave him a self-satisfied grin.

Evan straightened up and brushed his hands together. "Whew, you're pretty heavy!"

"Mm, yes. So ... *did* you get done with the lights?"

"Uh-uh." He grunted as he dropped down on to the floor. "Old Doc Parsons carried me in 'cause I was gettin' cold. He gots a few more to put up, then he's gonna let me turn 'em all on."

"I see." Martin picked up another journal from the table and began to peruse it while Evan set the blocks out end-to-end across the family room floor.

Martin peered over the top of the magazine, watching the boy surreptitiously. "Aren't you supposed to snap those together, not just lay them out like that?"

Evan inspected the block in his hand then looked up at Martin. "They don't gots any snaps." He set the scrutinised block down next to another. "I'm making a train."

"Bring two of those here, and I'll show you what I mean."

The boy crawled quickly to the sofa and handed a red and a blue block to the doctor.

"See ... these projections fit into the holes on the bottom of the other block." Martin explained as the two pieces clicked together. "You can make buildings or towers, whatever you want."

"Wow! You know lots about a lot of stuff!"

"Mm."

Martin watched the boy, perplexed by the seemingly bright child's lack of knowledge. "Don't you have these at home, Evan?"

Keeping his eyes on his lap, he shrugged his shoulders. "I gots *lots* of other toys."

Martin returned his focus to his journal and was soon absorbed in an article on the lowered incidence of congenital heart defects in infants born to mothers with healthy diets.

The background noise that began a short time later started off almost imperceptibly soft, but rapidly grew into a cacophony of disconnected tones and erratic rhythm.

Martin grimaced as his young charge's hammering on the keys of the nearby baby grand grated at his nerves.

"Evan! Stop pounding on that piano! You're making a godawful noise!"

The boy spun around on the bench. "It's not noise, Dr. Ellig-am. It's a song I made up for you."

Martin sighed heavily when he saw that for the second time in as many hours, he had hurt the boy's feelings.

He pulled himself to his feet before working his way across the room. He dropped stiffly on to the bench beside the child. "I'll tell you what; I'll teach you to play something. What song would you like to learn?"

Evan stared out the large windows overlooking the wooded backyard, the fairy lights on the small artificial trees that Chris had set out illuminating the scene. "'Jingle Bells'. Can you teach me that one?"

"Move over," Martin said, pulling the boy up close. "Get yourself centred in front of the keyboard. Then play the white key just to the right of the group of two black keys … the group in the middle of the keyboard."

Evan pressed the E above middle C. "Now what?"

"What do you think comes next?"

"Speech me. I don't gots a piano at home, Dr. Ellig-am."

Martin tipped his head back and peered down at him. "Sing the song for me."

"Jingle bells, jingle bells, jingle all the—!"

"Okay, okay. That's enough." What the child lacked for in intonation, he made up for in volume, and Martin struggled to keep his thoughts to himself.

"Listen to the notes. Does the second note go up or down, or does it stay the same?"

Evan sang the first several measures through again, blissfully softly the second time. "It stays the same. And so do a bunch of the next ones."

"Right, now go ahead and play them. Then think about where the next note goes."

Evan played a series of seven E's on the keyboard, singing along. Then he played the next note higher, an F. "That doesn't go right with my singin', though."

"No, it doesn't. You have to skip a white key ... go up to the next note."

Martin and his young charge worked through the piece together until Evan could confidently play through the refrain. "Huh! I know a song!"

"Yes, you do. Jolly good job, Evan."

Martin glanced over his shoulder towards the doorway before wagging his finger at the keyboard. "Now play it again, and I'll play with you."

As Evan played the melody, Martin joined in with the bass clef chords. The little boy stopped abruptly and gasped. "That's beautiful, Dr. Ellig-am! We go really good together!"

"Mm, yes. I think you'd make a fine musician." The child's exuberance and joy at his own sense of accomplishment brought a wisp of a smile to the doctor's face.

The two pianists played through the song in its entirety several times, oblivious to the small crowd that had gathered to listen, surreptitiously, from the doorway.

Their audience erupted in applause after their final run-through, and Louisa walked to Martin's side. He squirmed uncomfortably on the bench as Evan stood up next to him, a proud grin spreading ear-to-ear across his face. "Did ya like it?"

"I loved it, Evan!" Louisa said, impulsively wrapping her arms around both her husband and the boy.

"Careful! Careful!" Martin yelped as he reached up to his shoulder, protectively.

She put her hand over her mouth. "Oh, sorry! Are you okay?"

"Yeah, are you okay?" Evan asked, leaning over and peering into his face.

"I'm ... fine." Martin caught his breath as the pain eased in his shoulder. "It's getting late. You'd better be getting off to bed," Martin said, trying to deflect the attention focused on him.

"But I gots to finish being Old Doc Parsons' super attendant! I need ta turn on the lights!"

Carole lifted the boy from the bench and carried him towards the kitchen. "Let's all go out and watch you do your job, then we'll have some hot chocolate and a biscuit before bed."

It was almost nine o'clock before Evan and James Henry were finally bathed and in their pyjamas, tucked in on the living room sofa on either side of Martin while he read them a bedtime story.

The Parsons' son, Dan, was away on a weekend band trip, so Chris laid Evan, lulled to sleep by the story, on the bed in the vacated room. He pulled the blankets up under the boy's chin before turning the light off and closing the door.

James slept in the cot in the spare room, next to Martin and Louisa.

It wasn't home, but as Martin lay next to his wife in the Parsons' spare bedroom that night, he thought about the many things that had happened that day which he would need to add to his *grateful list*.

Louisa leaned forward, rubbing her nose against his. "I'm going to sleep much better tonight, having you next to me."

"Mm, yes. Me, too." Martin could just make out the glistening of her eyes in the darkened room and he reached his good hand up to stroke her cheek. "I love you, Louisa," he said as he pulled her to him to kiss her.

"I love you, too, Martin."

Chapter 10

Martin had collapsed into bed Friday night, falling asleep quickly, likely a positive side effect of the higher morphine dose that Ed Christianson had prescribed.

Louisa, however, lay awake, her anxieties about the uncertain nature of Evan's situation getting the better of her. She tried to leave her worries for the morning, focusing instead on the eerie, but strangely soothing, breathy, tenor call of an owl in the trees outside their window, but she was shaken abruptly from that meditation by cries coming from down the hall. Jumping from the bed, her jostling woke her sleeping husband.

"What is it?" he said, trying to orient himself in place and time.

"Evan ... I'll see to him. You wait here," she whispered as she pulled her dressing gown around her and hurried out the door.

Martin struggled to sit up, his head spinning as he pulled himself erect. He swung his legs over the side of the bed and sat, torn between his natural inclination to heed the boy's calls for help and his sense of responsibility to his wife and son, which demanded he not chance further injury by getting up before his head had cleared.

He heard muffled sobs as Louisa made her way back down the hallway with the boy.

"See, Dr. Ellingham's right here, Evan," Louisa said softly, sitting down next to her husband with the child wrapped in a blanket.

"He's wet the bed," she whispered in his ear. "I picked up some clothes for him when Carole and I were out. I'll go and get some clean underpants and pyjamas from the bag."

Louisa disappeared back through the door, leaving Evan on the bed next to her husband.

"Did you have a bad dream?" Martin asked as the little boy rubbed at his eyes and pulled in a ragged breath.

He shook his head. "It wasn't a dream. He's out there." The child tucked his head against the doctor and pointed to the window. "He's laughing at me."

The owl outside exhaled its quavering call once again.

"Ah, I see. Evan, that's an owl calling ... not your father. It's probably a male owl calling for its mate."

"Are you sure?"

"Positive. You're perfectly safe." Martin felt around for his crutch before pulling himself from the bed. "Let's go wash you off and get some dry things on you." He jerked his head towards the hallway. "Come on; up you get."

By the time Martin and Evan had finished in the bathroom, Louisa had returned with the new clothes.

"Well, I think it would be best if you crawled in with us tonight, Evan."

"Louisa, I really don't think—"

"Martin ... shush. We'll figure this out, just not at one o'clock in the morning, hmm?"

"Mm, yes."

The Ellingham family slept undisturbed the rest of the night. Martin woke to sunshine streaming in the window and the smell of bangers frying in the kitchen.

He lay on his left side with his wife's warmth curled against his back, mulling over how best to handle the situation with their temporary family member. James made soft happy chortles in his cot as he played quietly with a board book and his green frog puppet.

Evan was, for all intents and purposes, an orphan. Applying pure rational thought to the problem, the solution seemed obvious. Allow a seasoned foster family to take the boy in and raise him, as opposed to a doctor with a busy medical practice to run and a wife already struggling to keep up with the demands placed on her.

But this was a rare occasion when logic wasn't guiding Martin Ellingham's thinking. There was something compelling him to hang on to the boy. To protect him and give him what he knew he needed.

But to ask that of Louisa, already burdened with a convalescing husband, seemed to him rather selfish.

Louisa took in a slow deep breath and her hand, which had been resting on his hip, shifted around to the front. Her breaths were soft and even against his neck, and he found images of her naked figure nudging their way into his consciousness, turning his thoughts to more carnal matters.

He glanced at the clock. Another twelve hours, at least, before James and Evan would be off to sleep again, allowing him an opportunity to act on his impulses.

He breathed out a heavy sigh. "Good morning, he whispered."

"Penny for them?" Louisa murmured as she nuzzled her nose into his neck.

Martin wrestled himself on to his back and gazed at her, brushing his fingers through the uncontrolled wisps of hair ornamenting her face. "I really can't say … not in mixed company," he said, giving a nod towards the two children.

"Hmm, now you've made me curious. Evan's still asleep, and James isn't going to repeat it. Tell me," she prodded, teasingly.

"Best not. I have it on good authority that Evan gots really good ears."

"I *do* gots really good ears," the boy said, popping up behind Louisa.

Martin jumped, shaking the bed. "Gawd!"

Louisa tried to suppress a giggle as she caressed his chest. His heart pounded against her hand.

"You okay?" she asked as his exhalation rushed past her.

"Fine. Just fine," he answered irritably. "I'm afraid Carole's earlier prediction for our domestic life may prove accurate, though."

She kissed him on the forehead. "Hmm, yes. It *could* get interesting."

Evan directed questions in rapid-fire succession at Martin as they drove to Portwenn later that morning. All questions either related directly to Christmas or led to a question about the holiday.

"Are all children his age so obsessed with these ridiculous traditions?" Martin muttered between periods of interrogation.

"It's an exciting time for children, Martin!" Louisa undertoned. "Just try not to spoil it for him."

"I'm not trying to spoil it! I just don't understand. It's a holiday ... just like any other holiday." He glanced over at her taut face and hesitated before adding, "Although, people seem to outdo themselves when it comes to eating and drinking to excess. And, of course, they feel compelled to indulge their greedy children's desires."

Louisa bit at her cheek, trying to tamp down her irritation until they could have a more private conversation.

She took note of his strained affect. Christmas did not evoke the same romantic sentiments for Martin that it did for most people, but given what she had learned in recent months of his upbringing, perhaps it was a subject that needed to be revisited.

Reaching her hand out, she caressed his thigh. "We can discuss it after the boys are in bed. But for now, just try to be positive."

"Yes ... I am!" he hissed back.

They stopped in Wadebridge and picked up takeaway sandwiches before continuing on the road that carried them past the old St. Endellion church. Evan peered out, craning his neck until the structure was no longer in sight. "Does that church have the windows with the pictures?" he asked as he settled back into his seat.

Louisa peered into the rear-view mirror. "Do you mean stained glass windows, Evan?"

"I don't know if they're stained, but some churches have windows with coloured pictures ... and they light up."

"I see what you mean. No, I don't think St. Endellion has coloured windows. Not very many of the really old churches do."

"Oh." The child slumped into his seat, gazing out at the scenery passing them by.

They passed Trevathen Farm and wound their way down into the village, the sea fog thickening as they drew closer to the water.

Louisa carried Evan into the surgery, set him down on a kitchen chair, and then went back out for James.

"Louisa ... about Christmas," Martin said as he stood next to the car, waiting as she gathered together the assortment of books and small toys scattered about on the back seat of the Lexus. "I don't mean to be difficult. It's just that ... well, I might need some help with the subject."

"Christmas, you mean?"

"Mm."

Shifting her son on her hip, she rested her hand against her husband's cheek. "Don't worry about it. I have an idea for a little project that you and Evan can work on together."

Martin watched her as she walked towards the back of the house, an uneasy feeling settling in his stomach. "What do you mean? What kind of project?" He started after her. "Louisa!"

Louisa set James down on the kitchen floor as Martin came through the door.

"Louisa, what did you mean ... a project? What do you have in mind?" he asked warily.

"Have a seat, Martin." She pulled two spiral bound notebooks from her work satchel and handed one to him and one to Evan.

"Evan, I have some homework for you to do."

The seven-year-old stared down at the notebook that had been thrust into his hands. Then he looked up at the headmistress, warily. "But I already gots plenty of homework from Miss Soames."

"Maybe that wasn't the best choice of word. I'd like you to come up with a list of ten things that we should incorporate into our Christmas celebration this year."

"What's that mean?"

"I want you to come up with some things that we could do to make Christmas more meaningful ... really special."

She turned to her husband as he dropped into a chair, his shoulders slumping. "Martin, you have all day tomorrow to work on this because you're supposed to be resting anyway. And Evan, you can use the library at school on Monday. I need to stay late to prepare for the Christmas market. That would be an ideal time for you to do a bit of research. Maybe find out what a traditional English Christmas is like."

"Louisa, I really don't think this is necessary. Can't we just go over to Wadebridge tomorrow, pick up one of those trees they sell at Tesco's ... those plastic trees ... put some lights on it and call it Christmas," Martin said.

"I think we're s'posed ta cut down a tree in the woods, Dr. Ellig-am. And then we tie it behind a horse and have 'im drag it home for us. I saw that in a book." Evan's enthusiasm for Louisa's project grew even faster than Martin's aversion for it. He pulled his feet under him and bounced up and down on his chair.

"We don't have a horse, Evan," Martin grumbled, giving the notebook a shove to the side.

The little boy's face sank before brightening again. "Ethel Macready gots horses. Maybe you could rent one from her!"

Louisa stood grinning at her husband. "Yes! And maybe Dr. Ellingham could find some sleigh bells to tie around its neck ... make it truly festive!"

"Oh, don't be ridiculous!" He pushed his chair back and began to get to his feet.

"All right, all right. I was only joking, Martin," Louisa said as she pulled up a chair and sat down beside him. "How about if we compromise, Evan. Maybe we could have Al Large take you to the woods on the farm, and you can cut down a tree. Then he can bring it back to the surgery on the top of his car."

"Then can we decorate it?"

"Well, it wouldn't be a Christmas tree without decorations, would it?"

James crawled over and pulled himself up by his father's chair and smiled up at him. Martin reached down and hooked his elbow under his young son's bum and lifted him to his lap.

Louisa watched nervously, her hands poised in front of the child, ready to head off a potential injury.

"I think while you're doing your homework, Evan, you should also work on a Christmas list." Louisa pulled the child's notepad across the table and wrote in large print across the top of the second page, *Evan's Wish List.* "There, make a list of what toys you might want this year."

Martin watched her, giving her a roll of his eyes. "Why does everything have to be about toys? What's wrong with getting books for Christmas? Or something sensible ... useful?"

"What, like socks ... or ties you mean?" she asked, tipping her head down and peering up at him.

Evan stretched across the table, leaning on his forearms. "That would be a silly thing to put on my list, Dr. Ellig-am! How can I play with a tie?"

Martin hissed a breath of air through his nose. "Louisa, take James, I need to use the lavatory."

She lifted her son from her husband's lap and he pushed himself up from the table, grumbling as he limped off under the stairs.

The following days were busy and progressed quickly. By Tuesday, Martin was feeling much stronger and his strep symptoms had cleared. As they sat eating dinner that evening, Louisa broached the subject of Martin and Evan's homework assignment.

"Are you getting close to having your ten items yet?" she asked as she dropped a spoonful of steamed broccoli on to the boy's plate.

Evan pinched his nose shut and waved off the offensive fumes emanating from the vegetable. "I got lots of ideas on *my* list, but I don't think Dr. Ellig-am gots any on his."

"Martin?" Louisa stared at her husband, her fork poised in the air.

He threw his head back. "I've been very busy, Louisa. You should all do whatever you like ... to celebrate. I'm fine with whatever you want to do. Just let me know what you need me to pick up at the shops ... what you need help with."

Louisa huffed out a breath. "All right then, Evan, why don't you go get your list, and we can go over it while we eat our dinner."

The boy scrambled down from his chair and dashed over to the coat rack by the back door, unzipping his backpack and pulling the notepad from the centre pocket.

"This is it!" he said, slapping it down on the table next to Louisa.

"Hmm." She scanned the sheet of paper in front of her, nodding her head and mumbling the occasional, "Excellent idea."

She gave the boy a smile and tousled his hair. "You've done very well, Evan. I really like many of these suggestions. There are a couple of them, however, that might not be the easiest to pull off living in Cornwall."

Evan slid from his chair and pushed in under her arm. "Which ones won't work?" he asked as he lifted her hand from the sheet of paper.

"Well, the feeding a reindeer a carrot and building a snowman are the most obvious. We don't have reindeer, and we rarely have any snow, especially enough to build a snowman with."

Evan plopped into his chair. "Those were my favourites," he said glumly.

"But visiting Father Christmas, hanging up Christmas stockings, decorating a Christmas tree, a Christmas feast ... many of these are very good suggestions that I think we could make work! Don't you, Martin?" Louisa handed the pad across the table to her husband, accompanied by a warning look.

Martin read through the list, tipping his head and quirking his mouth. "Yes, I would say there are a few of these we could accommodate."

Evan slipped back to the floor and hopped excitedly from foot to foot. "Can we work on 'em together, Dr. Ellig-am?"

Louise watched him, her gaze imperious as he quickly averted his eyes from her.

"Mm, yes. I can help you with some of these. We may need some assistance with others, though."

By half past eight, Louisa had both boys bathed and in their pyjamas. They sat nestled in next to Martin on the sofa as he pulled a book from the tall stack of Christmas stories Evan had brought home from the school library.

"This is called *Father Christmas*, Martin said, clearing his throat in preparation for the telling of the tale.

He opened the cover of the book and furrowed his brow. "Where are the words?"

"Yer s'posed ta make 'em up."

"What do you mean, *make 'em up?*"

"You gots ta use your 'magination with this one," Evan explained, wiggling himself in closer to the doctor.

"Gawd," he mumbled. "Well, it looks like this pensioner's sleeping ... dreaming about lying on a beach somewhere." He wagged a finger at the page. "He's exposing himself to ultra-violet rays, which could easily lead to the development of a melanoma, by the way."

Evan tapped his toes together and poked his finger at the book. "Yer s'posed ta just read, Dr. Ellig-am."

Martin pulled in his chin and turned the page. "Then his alarm clock rings. He shuts it off and tries to go back to sleep. When he wakes up, he looks at the calendar and sees it's Christmas Eve. Which apparently makes him angry, for some reason. *Blooming Christmas, here again."*

Evan reached over and flipped the page, wrinkling his nose up at Martin. "It's not very good so far, is it? Maybe it's just the way yer tellin' it."

"Well, I don't have much to work with here, do I?" Martin exclaimed defensively.

Evan gave a shrug of his shoulders. "Maybe it gets better."

"Mm, yes." Martin glanced down at his son, whose small body had grown heavy against him. The toddler lay with his head in his father's lap as he brushed a corner of his blanket against his cheek.

He cleared his throat before continuing with the story. *"Get off my slippers, dog,* the man says. *Blooming snow.* Then he goes downstairs and makes some porridge"

He turned the page. "Oh, for goodness' sake. That's unnecessary," Martin groused as he sneered at the small drawing of the grumpy man in the tale, now seated on the toilet. *"I hate winter!"*

"The grouchy guy is s'posed to be Father Christmas?" Evan erupted, dumbfounded.

"Hmph, I guess so." Martin flipped through several pages of similar curmudgeonings by the old man in the story and glanced down at the boy, his expression downcast.

"I don't like him, then!" Evan crossed his arms in front of him. "He gots angry eyes."

Martin snapped the book shut. "I've had enough of that one," he said giving it a toss on to the coffee table.

"Is Father Christmas really like that?" the seven-year-old asked, smacking his fist down on the throw pillow beside him.

Taking in a deep breath, Martin peered down at him. "I think Father Christmas is different to everyone."

He wagged a finger at the book as it lay, rejected, on the table. "This author obviously thinks he's a cantankerous man who hates his job. But I'm sure not *everyone* sees him that way."

Evan tipped his head back and smiled up at Martin. "That's kinda' like you then, isn't it Dr. Ellig-am. Lots'a people think *you're* cantankersis, but yer not really ... are ya?"

Martin stared off across the room for a moment before giving the boy a small smile. "No, I'm not ... really."

"Well, if Father Christmas is like you, then I *still* like 'im!" He patted Martin's knee before sliding off the front of the sofa cushion to head for the stairs.

"Goodnight, Dr. Ellig-am."

"Goodnight, Evan." Martin looked down at his small son, sound asleep, and he lifted him to his lap.

Chapter 11

As the day of the Christmas Market approached, the level of excitement continued to build inside the walls of the small surgery.

Louisa's fussing over every detail of the upcoming event, and Evan's fixation on the holiday itself, had left Martin feeling short-tempered. Social events of any kind underscored his challenges and called attention to what he knew his wife considered a weakness in his constitution. And Christmas was *the* social event of the year.

He found himself secluded in his consulting room, studying a surgical video Thursday evening, seeking refuge from the constant bombardment of the giddy voices coming through the radio in the kitchen. Voices singing nonsensical lyrics about bionic Santa Clauses; a young woman trying to use her feminine wiles to extract fur coats, diamond rings and real estate from the old man in red; and the song that finally drove him to seclusion—"Have A Cheeky Christmas".

He attempted to focus his thoughts on the steps involved in the delicate operation being conducted on his laptop screen. There was a soft tapping on the door, and he clicked the pause button before lifting his eyes from the procedure. "Come!"

"Everything okay in here?" Louisa asked as she stepped into the room, taking a seat in the chair on the opposite side of the desk.

Martin pulled up his lower lip as he tipped his head. "I just wanted to get a little work done."

Louisa sat staring at him. The moment was painfully reminiscent of another time she had tried to have a conversation with her husband in that room. "Martin, please. Please don't shut me out."

He hesitated and then slowly closed the cover on his computer, folding his hands in his lap. "You told me once that I deliberately stand outside the crowd then wonder why I feel isolated. It's not like that—deliberate. You're right. I'm different from you and James ... and Evan. I just can't feel what you and Evan do about all the holiday ... fuss and bother. I'm sorry. I'm trying, but it all feels—" his brows pulled together— "it feels dishonest, somehow, to pretend to be enjoying it."

Getting up from her chair, Louisa walked behind him and wrapped her arms gently around his shoulders. "Do you have *any* fond memories at all, Martin? Christmas memories?"

"I was either in hiding at home ... trying to remain unseen while my mother hosted her parties, or I was at boarding school."

"Didn't they celebrate at all at the school?"

"The only other students there were the two Indian boys. Christmas was as foreign a concept to them as it was to me. I *am* sorry, Louisa. I know it's a special time for you ... and Evan. He's quite obviously taken with it all."

"Hmm, yes ... he is. Speaking of which, I left him in the kitchen making Christmas ornaments with James. I better go and check on them." Louisa walked to the door and then paused, looking back at him. "Care to join us ... maybe create a memory?"

Martin breathed out a heavy sigh. "Would I be spoiling things if we didn't have that godawful music playing?"

A smile spread across her face as she shook her head. "Wouldn't spoil it in the least."

"All right, I'll be right there."

When Martin entered the kitchen a few minutes later, he found the room strewn with round, coloured paper cut-outs, which had been decorated with glue and glitter.

"Would you like to make one?" Louisa asked, holding out a red piece of construction paper and a pair of scissors.

He put his hand up in front of him. "No, thank you. I'll just help with the—mess," he said before pulling several sheets from the kitchen roll and running them under the faucet.

Once the ornaments had been laid out to dry and the children had been bathed and deemed free of glue and glitter, Louisa tucked them into their beds. James in his cot and Evan in the small bed on the opposite end of the room.

Martin had already dozed off when his wife came to bed later that night. He was roused by the soft undulations of the mattress when she joined him, spooning up against his back and nestling her nose into the crook of his neck.

"Did you remember to lock the doors?" he asked as her breath blew warm and moist against his skin.

"Yes, Martin." Her hand caressed his hip and thigh before repeating its manoeuvres from the morning at the Parsons'. She heard him pull in a breath as her hand slid forward and a knowing smile tugged at the corners of her mouth.

"Now ... the door's locked and no really good ears are listening," she said as her fingers teased. "Care to share what you were thinking the other day?"

He rolled on to his back and gazed up at her. "I was thinking about you. You lying on our bed. The way you look after we make love."

"Why, Dr. Ellingham, I'm surprised you allow such romantic notions to occupy space in that brain of yours!"

"I am a man, Louisa."

"Mmm, yes, that you are." She rolled away from him momentarily and flipped the switch on the table lamp before returning to his side to embrace him. "So, how *do* I look after we make love?"

Martin brushed his fingers against her cheek. "Radiant. But more importantly, happy. You look happy."

Louisa raked her fingernails lightly back and forth across his bare belly. "Would you feel up to making me happy tonight?" she said as her hand crept lower.

"Mm. I'd like to, but ... well, I'm a bit constrained, don't you think?"

Her fingers inched their way under the waistband of his boxers. "We'll just have to be creative then, won't we."

Martin raised his hips from the bed as his wife freed him of the encumbrance. Then she pulled her nightdress over her head, letting it drop to the floor.

Leaning over him, she pressed her lips to the small incision in his neck where the catheter had been placed to warm his body just days before. She moved to his injured shoulder before laying a trail of kisses down his torso, settling just below his waist.

"Are you ready?" she asked.

Her voice was soothing, like velvet to his ears, but her touch ignited a desire that had been smouldering for days.

A soft moan escaped his mouth as she enveloped him in her warmth, and he reached up and pulled her to his chest.

"Careful of your shoulder," she whispered.

"Oh, Louisa." His words poured out on a breath. "God, I've been wanting—"

A scream cut through the air, yanking Martin from his hormone-induced trance.

Louisa pulled her nightdress back over her head and wrapped her dressing gown around her. Heading for the door, she flipped the lock and pulled it open.

Evan spilled in at her feet, scrambling on to the bed and diving under the covers before burrowing in next to Martin.

The child lay, trembling against him while Martin lay motionless. "Louisa, I don't have any—er, I'm not—altogether!" he whispered stridently.

She hurried over and gathered the boy into her arms. "Shh, shh, shh. My goodness, what's the matter, Evan?"

"He found me! He's outside the window!"

James Henry, rudely awakened by the commotion, began to wail.

"I'm sorry, Martin. You're going to have to deal with it," Louisa clipped. "I need to tend to James. Evan's frightened and it's dark. He won't notice anything," she whispered as she pulled the covers back and set the boy down next to him.

"Oh, gawd," Martin mumbled as his wife disappeared out the door. He cleared his throat. "Why do you think your father's found you, Evan?"

The seven-year-old worked his way back against him, curling up in a ball. "He shined his torch on me. He was watching me with his angry eyes."

Aside from the first night that Evan had been in their home, he had slept through the night. Martin and Louisa had hoped that the boy's terrors had passed.

"Remember, your father died, Evan. He can't find you anymore."

Martin winced as he rolled on to his shoulder to reach out for the blanket, pulling it up over the now-shivering child.

"But I *s-saw* him, Dr. Ellig-am!"

Martin rested his hand on his arm. "You're safe now, Evan."

The boy spent the remainder of the night in Martin and Louisa's bed. Something Martin was adamant would not become a habit. But any attempt at a discussion regarding the topic would have to wait.

The air was filled Friday morning with excitement about the evening's festivities. Louisa hammered out the final plans with Poppy over her morning cup of coffee, as Martin and Jeremy discussed a trip to Wadebridge to consult with a physiotherapist about his shoulder.

"So, Poppy, you'll walk Evan home from school and get him ready for the concert?" Louisa asked, as she picked up her purse and satchel from the coatrack.

"Yeah, don't worry about it, Mrs. Ellingham. I'll make sure he's there plenty early." The childminder dropped a few more pieces of cereal into the bowl on James's high chair tray.

"Evan, we better get a move on or we'll be late for school." Louisa gave her husband a small wave before dashing out the door.

The boy snatched his backpack from its hook and began to follow after her before turning back, giving a tug on Martin's sleeve.

He leaned over, expecting one of the boy's usual clandestine bits of information. Instead, Evan gave Martin a kiss on the cheek before skipping off to catch up with Louisa.

He glanced up at his assistant who sat watching with an amused grin on his face. "Oh, stop it," Martin grumbled before returning his attention to his breakfast.

The chaotic start to the day progressed to a frenzied afternoon. Martin and Jeremy had just returned from Wadebridge when the kitchen door flew open, banging against the wall as Evan barrelled through the room and under the stairs.

Martin stared wide-eyed at Poppy as she came through the door with James in the pushchair.

"He's a little excited about tonight," she explained, pulling up her shoulders.

A freshly bathed and coiffed seven-year-old thundered back down the stairs fifteen minutes later, his eyes darting around the kitchen. "Where's Dr. Ellig-am?" he asked Jeremy.

The aide turned his attention from the espresso machine, giving a slow whistle, grinning at the little boy. "Wow, you look right smart, Evan!"

"I know. Where's Dr. Ellig-am?" he asked breathlessly.

Jeremy took a sip from his cup and wagged a finger towards the hall. "He's in his—"

"Kay!" He gots ta tie my tie!"

Jeremy chuckled as the child sprinted back under the stairs.

Martin was on the phone with the lab in Truro when the door flew open.

"I need ya—"

Slapping his hand over the receiver, the doctor's eyes snapped as he bellowed, "What do you think you're doing? Knock before you—!" A wave of emotion came over Martin as the blood rushed from his head. "I'll—I'll call you back," he said into the phone before slamming it down on his desk.

Evan, stood trembling as Martin got to his feet. Then he turned and ran from the room.

Martin smacked the heel of his hand to his forehead, groaning internally, before trailing after the boy.

The door to the nursery was closed, and Martin could hear crying when he approached. He tapped softly and waited for an answer. Silence.

"Evan," he said softly as he opened the door. The child lay on his bed, curled up in a ball.

The doctor dropped on to the mattress and wrapping his arm around him, pulled the child into his lap. "Evan, we need to talk about this."

The seven-year-old peeked up at him before again burying his face in his sleeve

"I'm very sorry I yelled at you. I, erm—" Martin swallowed hard and took in a deep breath. "Evan, can you keep a secret if I tell you something I don't want other people to know?"

Evan pulled his head up. "I'm good at keeping secrets. Remember the mobile you gave me? I didn't tell anybody."

"Yes, you did a good job with that. But this is very private information ... something very few people know about. Can I trust you with that kind of information?"

"I won't tell, Dr. Ellig-am. I promise." The boy sucked in a slow ragged breath and stared up at Martin intently.

"My parents were quite like yours, Evan. When you came into my office without knocking ... well I yelled at you without thinking. I yelled at you the same way that my father yelled at me when I was a boy, and that upsets me very much.

"It scared me when he did it, the same way I scared you a little while ago. I don't want to be like my father in any way. Well, except that he was a gifted surgeon. But he was really quite an awful man, otherwise. And he was not a nice father."

"Then why did you yell ... if ya don't wanna be like him?"

Martin cocked his head and gave it a shake. "I'm not sure. I suppose we learn things from our parents—good *and* bad. It can be hard to *un*-learn those things. But I'm trying, Evan. I'm really, *really* trying."

Evan sat silent, tracing his finger along the strap on Martin's sling.

"I promise to do my very best to never let it happen again."

The boy looked up at him, a glimmer of a smile creeping on to his face. "I believe you, Dr. Ellig-am. You'll get it all sorted ... eventually."

"Mm. Thank you, Evan. I hope so. Now hop on down and we'll go wash your face off and get a clean shirt on you."

The child slid from the bed and peered up at the doctor. "Oh, and why I came into your office was 'cause I don't know how ta tie a tie."

"Mm. I see," he said, tugging at his ear. "Well, I'll teach you. But we better hurry up or you'll be late."

Chris and Carole Parsons greeted Martin and Jeremy when they arrived at the school that evening.

"Glad to see you didn't do something idiotic, like walking over here from the surgery," Chris said as he sidled up next to his friend.

"I *could* have," Martin replied defensively.

Jeremy gave Chris a roll of his eyes before the three men joined Louisa, Carole, Poppy, and James in the second row of chairs that had been set up for the audience.

The festivities began with carols being sung by the children. Evan, being one of the smallest, was positioned in the front row, and he gave Martin and Louisa a shy wave. James, sitting on his father's lap, gave the older boy a wonky grin and stretched his arm out as his fingers opened and closed in reply.

"That's Evan, isn't it James!" Louisa said before placing a kiss on her son's head.

The din of voices in the room dwindled to a murmur as Pippa Woodley, the music teacher, stepped on to the stage, and then quieted altogether as the teacher raised her hands to direct her choristers.

Martin felt an unexpected sense of pride in his charge as he watched him belt out the refrain of "Jingle Bells", about twenty cents flat, but sung with great flare and volume. James bounced on his father's knee as he tugged at his ear, a mannerism he seemed to have adopted from Martin.

Once the business end of the evening was said and done, the children were free to indulge in the many biscuits and fruits that had been provided by the parents and to look through the items available for purchase at the market.

Martin stood next to his wife while she chatted with Chris and Carole. He watched as Evan picked up a plastic black and white beaded necklace, fondling it.

"Excuse me, I'll be right back," he said to Chris before picking his way through the crowd to make his way to the gift tables.

"Hi, Dr. Ellig-am!" Evan said, latching on to his hand.

"Hello, Evan. I got distracted before you left the house tonight. I intended to give you a bit of spending money ... in case you saw something you wanted to buy." He pulled his hand free from the boy and reached into his back pocket for his wallet, pulling out a five-pound note. "I think I can trust you to spend it wisely."

Evan's face lit up as he fingered the piece of paper. "Wow!" he whispered. He looked up at Martin. "Thanks, Dr. Ellig-am. I know just what I'm gonna spend it on." He raced back to the beaded necklace he'd been admiring and pulled it from the table before heading towards the cashier.

"That was nice of you," Louisa said when her husband returned. She glanced around them before reaching up to give him a kiss on the cheek.

"Mm. I think you'll have at least one gift under the tree this year."

"I'll try to act surprised."

"Doc! Doc! We need you over here!" Joe Penhale yelled out over the noise of the crowd.

Martin screwed up his face. "Typical! Why can't these people ever have a medical crisis during surgery hours?" he grumbled as he pushed his way through the sea of villagers. "Out of the way!"

He began to assess the situation as he neared a body lying face up on the floor.

"What's happened?" he asked the trembling, petite brunette hovering over the victim.

"We were just visitin', Doc ... havin' some nibbles. Next thing ya know ... well, here we are. Went down like a sack of potatoes! Do somethin', Doc!"

Martin cringed at the shrill voice and glanced over, taking note of the thick head of shaking, curly locks and the teary eyes. "All right, calm down! It's a little premature to be getting yourself all worked up. I haven't even examined the patient yet."

He hesitated before lowering himself to the floor.

"Here, let me give you a hand, Doc," P.C. Penhale said as he stepped forward, taking the doctor's crutch in one hand and grabbing on to his good arm with the other.

Groaning as his knees hit the wood planks, Martin went to work, quickly examining the victim.

"I'll call for an ambulance," Joe said, taking his mobile from his jacket pocket.

"No, give me a minute." Martin pulled the victim's eyelids open, one at a time, giving a soft grunt.

Chris and Jeremy slipped in and crouched down beside him. "What's going on?" Chris asked.

"I'm not sure yet. It may be something as simple as a syncopal episode. It *is* warm in here. Jeremy, do you have your backpack in the car?"

"Yeah, I'll get it." The aide hurried off as Martin pressed his fingers to his patient's neck. His medical eyes scanned over the inert form laid out in front of him.

The heavy boots and canvas work jacket suggested the victim was likely a farmer, as did the unmanicured and stained fingernails. However, these two details seemed incongruous to the clean-shaven appearance of the victim's face.

"Oh, dear! Francis, what's wrong!" Martin whirled around at the sound of his wife's voice.

"I don't know, Louiser. We was just havin' a nice chat ... enjoyin' the evenin' and—boom!"

Louisa had James in one arm, the other was wrapped around the distraught spouse's shoulders.

Martin gave a sharp slap to his patient's face then leaned forward, "Hello! Can you hear me?"

"I'll go get a cold cloth, Mart," Chris said as he got to his feet and headed for the lavatory.

Martin attempted again to rouse the victim, "Hello! Hello—you! Can you hear me?" He looked up at the many faces huddled around the scene. "Name—anybody know this person's name?"

"Miller," Peter Teague grunted.

"Mr. Miller, can you hear me? Mr. Miller, wake up!"

Joe Penhale tapped Martin on the shoulder. "It's missus, not mister, Doc."

Martin looked over his shoulder at the victim's spouse, still being consoled by Louisa. Not *her*, you idiot—*him!*" he snapped, wagging his finger at his patient.

Louisa leaned over, "That *is* Mrs. Miller, Martin. Francis is her husband."

"*Now* who's the idiot, eh, Doc?" Penhale said, giving Martin a crooked grin.

"Oh, gawd," he muttered.

Chris trotted up with a wet towel, handing it off to his friend.

Martin slapped it on to his patient's forehead. "Mrs. Miller! Wake up!"

Jeremy pushed in through the crowd. "Here Martin," he said, pressing a small packet into his boss's hand.

"Smelling salts? What else do you have in that bag?"

"Never know what *you're* going to get up to. Have to be prepared," the aide said, giving him a puckish grin.

Martin grunted back before waving the pungent packet under his patient's nose. The woman's eyes popped open as she took in a mighty breath. "Good lord, what are you tryin' ta do to me?" she said, batting at Martin's hand. "Get away from me, you stupid git!"

"Mrs. Miller, you've fainted. I need to examine you to be sure you haven't injured yourself in the fall."

The woman pushed herself to a sitting position, and Martin looked her over carefully, noting a sizeable haematoma on the back of her head.

"I need you to go to hospital for a scan, Mrs. Miller. I believe this was nothing more than a syncopal episode, but I'd like to rule out any possibility of a head injury. P.C. Penhale will call for an ambulance."

"Gotcha, Doc," Joe said, giving his fingers a snap as he whipped his mobile from his pocket once again.

Jeremy reached his hand down and pulled the doctor to his feet. "You okay?" he asked as he looked him up and down.

"I'm fine."

Evan wound his way through the forest of legs and emerged in the clearing created around Mrs. Miller. "Did ya fix 'er, Dr. Ellig-am?" he asked as he pulled at Martin's hand.

He placed a broad palm on the boy's head. "Maybe P.C. Penhale could take you outside to watch for the ambulance," he said, eyeing Joe.

The constable shoved his mobile back in his pocket. "Can do, Doc. Come on, Evan," he said, hoisting his toolbelt before taking the child's hand.

The crowd that had gathered to watch the drama unfold dispersed quickly, and interest shifted back to the gift tables and the buffet of sweets.

"Well, another calamity dealt with by Doc Martin," Chris said as the ambulance attendants wheeled Mrs. Miller off on a gurney.

"Yeah." Martin grunted. "Say, Chris ... I was wondering if you could do something for me. I'd like to get my hands on some tickets for the festival in Truro ... the one with the reindeer ... and the artificial snow. I called over to the events office, but they said they're sold out. Do you by chance have a connection?"

"Evan?" Chris asked as he gave his friend a grin.

"Mm. And I'd appreciate if you could just answer my question without any smart remarks."

Chris jerked his head to the side. "Come on, I want to introduce you to a friend of mine."

Martin followed him across the room to where Carole stood visiting with a distinguished white-haired gentleman and an attractive woman of roughly the same age.

"Martin, I'd like you to meet Carl Joseph, the mayor of Truro. And this is his wife, Marian."

Martin extended his hand, "Martin Ellingham."

"Carl and Marian's grandchildren go to school here," Chris said.

Marian fondled her cup of punch and nodded her head. "Yes, we had a very nice visit with your wife earlier."

"Martin has a bit of a dilemma that I think you might be able to help him with, Carl," Chris said. "He's needing some tickets for the Winter Wonderland event on Boscawen Street."

"I think I could scrape some up. How many would you like?"

"Four...if you can spare them."

Carl jerked his head towards Chris. "I'll give them to Parsons ... he can get them to you I would imagine."

"I think that should work." Martin shifted uncomfortably, clearing his throat. "Er ... would there be any chance of a visitor feeding a reindeer?"

"Oh, Martin, for little Evan ... of course! How sweet of you!" Carole gushed.

"Mm, yes." A tell-tale warmth crept up Martin's neck. "So, about the reindeer?"

"What is it that you want to feed to the reindeer, Mart?" Chris asked, putting a hand on his shoulder.

Carole gave her husband a black look, accompanied by a sharp jab with her elbow.

"Well, you called him sweet!" Chris hissed back. He turned back to his friend, "So, Mart?"

Martin whipped his head around, his eyes fiery. "A carrot! Now be quiet!"

Carl rubbed his palm across his face, trying to cover his uncontrollable smirk. "I think that could be arranged, Martin."

"Thank you. I appreciate it ... very much." He turned to the mayor's wife. "It was a pleasure to meet you, Mrs. Joseph."

"Marian ... please," the woman said, placing a hand on his arm.

Martin pulled in his chin and pushed past his friend on his way to locate his family.

"Martin!" his aunt Ruth called out when she saw her nephew pass by the treats tables.

"Oh, gawd, what now," he muttered "Hello Ruth, I'm in a hurry."

"As am I. I just wanted to extend an invitation to you and the family. If you'd like slightly larger accommodations for your yuletide festivities, the B&B is available."

"I thought you and Al were going to be doing a booming holiday business. Isn't that what the ballyhoo a couple of weeks ago was all about?"

Ruth rolled her eyes at him. "It didn't pan out the way we'd hoped, Martin. You could just say thank you for the kind offer, and leave it at that."

"Yes, thank you. I'll discuss it with Louisa and let you know."

"Good. And, how are you? Recovering from your recent adventure?"

"I'm fine."

"Good, glad to hear it. Well, I need to run. Tell Louisa I'll be in touch with her about holiday plans," she said as she hurried off.

"Are you ready to go?" Martin asked when he joined Louisa, Evan and James at the gift table.

"I am. Where are Chris and Carole? Don't you have a debt to pay off?"

"Ohh, certainly Chris wasn't serious about that. It's going on eight o'clock!"

"Well past your carbohydrate curfew, I know. But I'm afraid he's coming to collect," Louisa said, giving her head a nod in the Parsons' direction.

Evan darted across the wood floor, intercepting them. "Hi, Old Doc Parsons! Did ya see me sing?"

"I did, Evan. Quite an impressive performance, young man!"

"Thanks! I sang as loud as I could."

"Yep, like I said, quite impressive. You must have worked up an appetite," Chris said as Martin and Louisa approached.

"Yeah! I'm starvin'!"

"Well, I think Old Doc Ellingham wanted to take us all out for dinner. Isn't that right, Mart?"

"Oh, he's just plain Dr. Ellig-am. He gots way too much hair to be an Old Doc."

"You're a clever boy, Evan. Let's go get that dinner, shall we?" Martin said, giving his friend a smirk.

Chapter 12

Evan sat quietly as they drove down Fore Street to the parking area at the bottom of the hill. Louisa shifted the car into park, and Martin pulled himself from the front seat before opening the back door, waiting for the boy to jump out.

"Come on, Evan, it's getting late. And I thought you were hungry!" the doctor said. "Hurry up there." A cold gust of wind blew off the frigid Atlantic waters, sending a shiver through him.

"I was just tryin' ta remember something to have for our Christmas feast. I have ta think really hard if I wanna remember something," he said as he slid to the ground.

"Why don't you just write it down? Then you won't have to remember it. You'll have one less detail cluttering up your hippocampus."

Martin began to move towards the restaurant, and Evan took two long leaps to catch up to him.

"I *couldn't* write it down 'cause I don't gots nothin' ta write with. And my list is in my shoe anyway, and I don't want to take my shoe off 'cause then my foot will get cold."

The doctor stopped and looked down at him, pulling in his chin and furrowing his brow. "Why on earth is your list in your shoe? That doesn't seem like a very sensible place to keep it."

He waited as the child crouched down to tie the shoe in question, taking extra time to poke a finger in along his foot to drive the list to a safer location.

"It *is* sensible 'cause it won't fit in my trousers. The pockets are too small," he said, demonstrating by trying to force his fist into the new khaki's Louisa had bought him in Truro.

"I see."

Evan took several steps before his attention was again diverted, this time by a dead crab lying on the concrete slipway. He crouched down, unable to resist the temptation to give it a wary poke with his finger.

Martin screwed up his face. "Oh, gawd. Get away from that! It probably harbours all manner of bacteria."

"Don't worry, Dr. Ellig-am, I'm *used* to all mannered bacteria. I've been workin' on my balloon system."

"Your *immune* system." Martin reached down and gave several sharp tugs on the boy's jacket then moved towards The Mote as he saw his wife and son disappear inside. "Come on. If we don't hurry up, this dinner is going to turn into a midnight feast."

Buddy, the little brown and white terrier who tormented Martin by following his every movement in the village, raced up to them and danced around their legs.

Evan dropped to his knees, and the animal jumped up to lick at his face.

"Eww," the doctor said, his face contorting once again. "Come on, Evan. You need to go wash thoroughly before you eat your dinner."

The restaurant was bustling, with several large tables filled with employees who were taking part in an office Christmas party. "Oh, gawd," Martin groaned as a jovial rendition of "Here We Come A Wassailing" broke out amongst them.

Swags of silver and gold glittering garland periodically brushed the top of his head as he made his way towards the table in the back corner where his wife and son were already perusing menus with the Parsons.

"Where's Evan going?" Louisa asked as she watched the boy dash away.

"To wash. He's been handling that disgusting dog of Ruth's. Not to mention a putrescent crab carcass."

"That disgusting dog did save your life, Martin. You could be a bit more tolerant of him." She narrowed her eyes at him as she reached for her water glass.

"I'm sorry?" he said, slipping past James, seated at the end of the table in a high chair.

"I assumed Joe Penhale would have told you the story several times over by now ... about Buddy's heroics the other night."

"I haven't the foggiest idea what you're talking about."

Louisa huffed. "Al Large brought him out to the Hanley's with him. Buddy sniffed around, then bolted out of the house. It was Joe who had the wherewithal to notice ... figure out that he had picked up your scent. He realised Buddy might be able to find you so he followed after him."

"Really?"

"Yes, Martin ... really. Joe and Buddy were heroes."

"I see." Martin sat, staring blankly at the floor for several moments before his attention shifted as he sensed a small wave of energy barrelling towards him.

"I gots all the mannered bacteria off, Dr. Ellig-am!" Evan said as he shoved his hands under Martin's nose. "Do they smell good enough to eat, now?"

Martin jerked his head back before taking hold of the child's wrist and giving the hand a thorough inspection. "Yep ... they're good enough to eat *with*, now. And, Evan, this isn't an appropriate place to be running. You could cause an accident. You should try to be on your best behaviour when we take you out to eat."

"Kay. I wasn't tryin' ta be unappropriate, I was just tryin' ta be quick." The boy gave a grunt as he squeezed behind Martin's chair and plopped down next to him.

Their waitress, a girl Martin recognised as a former member of the flock of teenaged girls that patrolled the village, came and took their orders, bringing with her a small container of crayons and two colouring books which she handed to the boys.

"Evan, I was wondering how that list is coming along," Louisa said as the waitress moved away.

"Which one? I've been workin' on 'em both."

"Well, let's start with the things you'd like to do to celebrate the holidays."

Evan pulled his foot up and tugged at his shoe, retrieving his notes. Martin wrinkled his nose as the child opened up the sweat-dampened pieces of paper and smoothed them out on the table top.

"Should I tell you, or do you just want ta read 'em?"

Louisa pulled the plastic wrapper off a package of soda crackers and handed them to her son. "Why don't you tell us all. I'm sure Dr. and Mrs. Parsons would like to hear it as well."

Chris leaned forward on the table. "Most definitely. I'd love to hear about all of these projects you have in mind for my best mate," he said as he flicked a wadded-up straw wrapper at Martin.

"That's unappropriate, Old Doc Parsons," Evan said, picking the projectile up from Martin's plate and setting it down carefully next to Chris's fork. "You should be on your best behaviour when Dr. Ellig-am takes you out to eat."

Martin looked down at the boy, his cheeks nudging up as he suppressed a smile. "Okay, let's hear the list."

Evan wriggled around in his chair, pulling his knees under him before he began to speak, his tone slightly ostentatious.

"Number one—" He looked up. "Just 'cause it says number one doesn't mean it's my favourite. I just needed to make sure I gots ten of these.

"Number one—buy presents. Number two—hang up Christmas stockings." His hands dropped to his sides, his eyes flitting nervously before he leaned over. "I don't gots a Christmas stocking!" he whispered in Martin's ear.

Martin cleared his throat and whispered back, "Don't worry about it, we'll get you one."

The boy's face brightened, and he pulled his list back up in front of him. "Number three—cut down a Christmas tree. Number four—" The boy's hands dropped to his sides again. "Four and five we can't do 'cause we don't have reindeers or snow in Cornwall, but I left 'em on just 'cause— 'cause they're my favourites.

"Number six—have a Christmas feast. Number seven—" Evan pulled the paper up to his face, peering at it closely.

"Can you read this?" he asked, shoving the paper under Martin's nose.

"Looks like hanj a miz-a ... and I think that last word is tow. Did you mean hang a mistletoe, Evan?"

"That's it! Good job, Dr. Ellig-am! I thought since you and Mrs. Ellig-am like ta kiss ... and yer s'posed ta kiss under a mistletoe," the boy explained, "I thought we should hang some up, then you'd have a good excuse."

"That's a lovely idea, Evan," Carole said as she pinched her husband's thigh under the table, pre-empting any teasing remarks to his friend.

"Just keep reading, Evan." Martin reached for his glass of water as he felt a sudden flushing in his face.

"Number eight—go to a church to see the baby saver and the coloured windows. Number nine—bake a fruitcake and bring it to Mr. Moysey. Number—"

"Wait a minute, Evan," Martin said, craning his neck to see the boy's list. "What's a baby saver."

Evan gave a shrug of his shoulders. "Speech me. But a lady came to our house once and said that they have a real live one at her church at Christmastime. Can we go see one?"

Martin looked at his wife, bewildered.

"Maybe we can discuss that one at home, Evan," Louisa suggested, returning her husband's look of bewilderment.

"Kay, number nine—no I did that one. Number ten—write a letter to Father Christmas."

Evan sat down on his chair. "That's all I gots."

"Very well done, Evan. Thank you," Louisa said, hurriedly clearing the baby toys from the table as the waitress approached with their meals.

It was well past the children's bedtime when they finished dinner and arrived back at the surgery.

"I think we should skip the bath tonight and just get these two off to bed," Martin said softly as he pulled the jacket from his small son, slumbering in his car seat. "Hopefully, we'll all get a better night's sleep tonight."

"Uh-uh-uh. Hope's good for breakfast, but bad for supper, Martin," Louisa replied in a whisper, wagging a finger at him.

"I think in this situation it's, hope's good for supper, but bad for breakfast."

"Hmm, yes." She slipped Evan's arms from the sleeves of his coat then picked the sleeping child up and headed for the stairs. "I'll be back for James."

Over the course of the next several days, the nocturnal routine in the Ellingham home became a literal nightmare for Evan and a figurative one for Martin and Louisa. The boy either woke them or interrupted romantic intentions at least once every night, sure that his father had discovered his whereabouts and was shining a torch on him through the window.

By Monday night, Martin's desperation for a decent night's sleep pushed him to take extreme measures. He inflated the air bed that Louisa had purchased at Tesco's and made a nest for Evan on the floor in the nursery. Then he climbed into the small twin bed in the room.

He tossed and turned as the old mattress sank under his weight, putting pressure on his shoulder as he tried to lay on his back. Fatigue had finally won out over discomfort, and he had just drifted off to sleep when he was awakened yet again by cries from the boy.

"Shh, shh, shh, shh, shh," he said as the child dove into bed with him. "It's all right, Evan."

"He's out there, Dr. Ellig-am. I just saw him! He shined his torch in here!"

"Evan, there's no one out there." Martin had repeated the same words to the boy more times than he could count, but it seemed to do nothing to alleviate his fears.

The beam from the headlights of a passing car flashed across the window pane and the boy threw his arms around him suddenly, pulling his feet into his lap and burying his face in his shoulder. Martin clenched his jaw against the pain when the child's head thudded against him.

"See! I told you!" Evan said, tightening his grip.

James woke at the disturbance in the room and began to wail. "Mum-mum-mum!"

Louisa hurried into the room, and the toddler quieted quickly as she pulled him from the cot. "Same thing?" she asked as she sat down in the rocker.

"Mm, yes. I think I may know what the problem is, though," Martin turned his attention to his charge. "Evan, those are headlights shining on the window. It's not your father."

Evan took in several ragged breaths and wiped his tears away with his palms. "Are you for positive?"

"Yes, I'm positive. I've lived here for years. Those are just headlights from the cars that go up and down the hill."

Martin looked over at his wife, her smile breaking through the grey shades of the dimly lit room. "Could you hang a blanket over the window after you lay James back down?" he asked as he shifted, trying to ease the pressure that Evan's heels were placing on the still-sensitive wound in his thigh.

Evan crawled off his guardian's lap and lay down on the bed, fatigue replacing his fear.

Martin felt his own bed calling, and he looked down at the boy. "Can you sleep now ... if we cover up that window, Evan?"

The child hesitated then gave him an uncertain nod. "I can try."

"We'll keep your door open and our door open, Evan. We're just a call away, hmm?" Louisa said as she laid James down in his cot. The toddler stretched, pulling his blanket to his cheek. "Good night, James Henry," she whispered, transferring a kiss from her lips to his head with her fingertips.

A heaviness settled in Martin's chest when he saw Evan's wide-eyed hopefulness dissolve into disappointment as Louisa moved out the door and across the landing, taking with her his opportunity for affection.

The future for the child was far from determined. But Martin realised at that moment that Louisa, too, would need to accept Evan as a member of the family before his hopes could be realised, and they could make the current situation a permanent one.

Before he rose from the bed, he placed his fingers against Evan's forehead and allowed them to brush along the boy's cheek. Then, he walked towards the landing, stopping at his son's cot to repeat the gesture. "Mrs. Ellingham has gone for something to cover that window. I'll see you in the morning."

"G'night, Dr. Ellig-am."

"Goodnight, Evan."

When Martin's alarm woke him the following morning, he breathed out a sigh and dared to feel hopeful.

"Good morning," Louisa said as she traced her fingertip along a sleep wrinkle on his face.

"Morning. How did you sleep?"

"Better than you I suspect. How are all the aches and pains this morning?" She wedged an elbow under her and peered down at him.

"Mm ... I thought we weren't going to discuss that. It doesn't change anything you know."

She sat up and pulled her knees to her chest, flipping her hair back over her shoulders. "I'll try not to bring it up too often, but I ask because I worry ... I care."

Martin's eyes drifted shut reflexively as his wife leaned down and pressed her lips to his. "That was nice," he said as he studied her face. She gave him the special smile that always seemed to reassure him that his existence in her life was welcomed.

"Do you have plans tomorrow?" he asked, as he swung his legs over the side of the bed.

"I thought I'd make that fruitcake with Evan. I need to pick up a few supplies though. Which reminds me ... do you have any rum in that little stash of yours?"

"I believe so. Why?"

She cocked her head at him, her hand drawing a slow circle through the air. "The fruitcake, Martin. A proper fruitcake should be soaked in rum, don't you think?"

"The key ingredients in fruitcake are rum, sugar and butter. I don't think there's any making it proper," he said as he pulled himself to his feet.

"Oh, Martin, a little fruitcake never hurt anyone. And besides, it's tradition."

"Yes." He stared down at her, a breath filling his chest reflexively. He blinked his eyes as he refocused his thoughts. "Erm, I'd like to make a trip to Truro tomorrow ... maybe go out for dinner in the evening."

"Oh, that would be lovely! I'll see if Poppy's available to watch the boys."

"We need to take the boys with us," Martin said before quickly ducking into the bathroom.

"Why? Martin? Martin!" James let out a howl and Louisa rolled from the bed. Her questions would have to wait for another time.

Chapter 13

By the time Louisa had James dressed and ready to start the day, Martin had finished in the bathroom and was pulling his trousers and shirt from the wardrobe.

"Poppy should be here in about fifteen minutes," she said as she stood in the doorway, bouncing her son on her hip. "She's going to help out with James while Evan and I work on some Christmas preparations."

"I see," Martin said, giving an upward tug on his zip before reaching for his shirt. "I don't believe I mentioned ... Ruth offered us the use of the B&B for Christmas Day."

"Oh, how thoughtful!"

"Mm, yes. But Joan's house, though?" he said, cocking his head. "It seems a bit out of proportion for the four of us, don't you think? Why can't we just stay here?"

His head shot up and his suddenly anxious gaze darted towards his wife. "Oh, gawd," he groaned. "Ruth and you have some sort of a ridiculous production planned, don't you?"

Louisa brushed at a non-existent bit of lint on James Henry's hoodie. "Oh, for goodness' sake, Martin, don't be silly. Ruth and I have made no *production* plans whatsoever."

"Mm, I see." His shoulders relaxed and he picked up his shirt, letting his injured arm hang limply at his side as he slipped the right sleeve over it.

Louisa watched, feeling a great deal of pride in him for his tenacity. "You're getting pretty good at that." She hurried over and pulled his shirt up over his back.

Taking advantage of the opportunity, James grabbed at his father's ear. "Da-ee!" he squealed as he latched on.

"Ow!" Martin quickly shoved his left arm through his shirt sleeve before reaching up to rub at the sting left behind by his son's well-intentioned assault.

"Oh, dear. You're bleeding," Louisa said as she hurried to the bathroom and returned with a tissue. "Looks like James could do with a nail trim."

"Yes," he grumbled as he snatched the tissue from his wife's hand and blotted at the scratches.

She tipped her head to the side. "You mentioned going to Truro tomorrow. Do you have something special planned?"

James let out an impatient mewl and began to squirm in his mother's arms.

"He's hungry," Martin said, waggling a finger at the child. "Why don't you carry him downstairs and put him in his high chair. I'll come down and feed him his breakfast while you take your shower." He kept his focus on his left hand as he painstakingly worked the last button on his shirt through the buttonhole.

"Yes, but can we talk abou—"

Their son let out a howl, kicking his feet. And Martin jabbed a finger towards the stairs. "Louisa ... James!"

He picked up his crutch and made his way towards the landing, stopping in the doorway to look back at her. "Chop-chop, I have a busy schedule this morning."

Louisa huffed out an exasperated breath and followed after him.

Setting her son in the high chair, she stood, hand on her hip, waiting for her husband to turn from his espresso machine.

"You maybe should hurry it along. You don't have a lot of time to get a shower in," he said, giving a nod towards the stairs. He set a plastic bowl on the table and removed the banana he had wedged in his sling.

Louisa glanced up at the clock. "Yes, Mar-tin." She walked off, shaking her head.

Her husband had piqued her curiosity, and Louisa's frustration at having it left unsatisfied was obvious when she came back downstairs a short time later.

Her ponytail flicked back and forth as she glanced from Poppy to Jeremy. "Where did Martin go?"

There was a gentle mechanical hum as her husband's assistant filled his cup with coffee. He turned around, giving her a smile.

"Morning, Louisa. He and Evan headed off to his consulting room already," he explained. "The Miller twins are coming in this morning. Martin said he wanted to review the notes sent over from Truro."

A bowl clinked sharply against another as she snatched it from the cupboard. "I think he's avoiding me," she said as she stared absently out the window at a colourful male blue tit foraging in the leaf litter on the ground.

"Why would he be avoi—" Poppy glanced up at her. "Sorry, Mrs. Ellingham. It's none of my business."

Louisa turned and gave the girl a wave of her hand. "Oh, it's all right, Poppy. He just has me curious about something, and I was hoping to get some information out of him ... 'bout a trip he wants to make to Truro tomorrow."

Poppy wiped a dribble of milk from James's chin before scooping a spoonful of porridge into his mouth. "A Christmas surprise, maybe?"

"Mm, that really wouldn't be Martin. I guess we'll find out tomorrow, hmm James?" Louisa leaned over and kissed her son's head before taking a seat. "How are the two of you?"

Jeremy set his coffee cup on the table and slipped in by his girlfriend. "I'm good. Still trying to make my bachelor pad look like something other than a—well, a bachelor pad. Gotta get Poppy to add a feminine touch," Jeremy said, giving her a gentle nudge with his elbow.

Poppy dipped her head and shifted in her chair. "Mum and me have been sewing doll clothes for my sister's girls ... a Christmas gift," she said. "We stayed up late last night tryin' to get it done. Mum says, nothing's so fatiguing as an uncompleted task."

"How nice, Poppy! Handmade gifts are so special ... my favourite, actually," Louisa said as Evan dragged into the room, his hands crammed into his pockets.

Jeremy pulled the chair next to him away from the table, and the boy threw himself into it.

"What's up Evan? You look bluer than Mrs. Tishell's wardrobe," the aide said.

"Dr. Ellig-am told me I was askin' too many questions and ta go away," he said, sagging into his seat like a well-loved rag doll.

Jeremy gave the boy's shoulder a playful punch. "He has reading he needs to do before his patients start coming today, Evan. He just needs a bit of quiet."

Evan swung his feet back and forth and smacked his fist on the armrest of his chair.

Louisa went to her satchel and retrieved a notepad and pencil, laying them in front of the boy. "You can help me, Evan. We need to make a shopping list," she said before lifting her son from the high chair. "Poppy's going to watch James this morning so that *we* can go buy our supplies."

Evan's face brightened, and he pulled himself erect. "For the Christmas feast?"

"No, for Mr. Moysey's fruitcake. You need to complete your menu for the Christmas feast before we do our shopping for that."

"Can we make two fruitcakes? I wanna give one to Dr. Ellig-am."

"I'm sure Dr. Ellingham would appreciate the thought, Evan, but he prefers fruits and vegetables to sweets."

Evan slapped his hands down on the table. "But how can I make fruits and vegetables? You said handmade gifts are the best, and I want to get him the best Christmas present he ever got!"

Louisa smiled across at the boy. "Hmm, that's a tall order. What I meant, Evan, is that handmade gifts often show the person receiving the gift just how much we care about them. They require a bit more thought and effort. But I'm sure Dr. Ellingham will love anything you give him because it's from you, and you're special to him."

The boy stared back at her for a few moments before his eyes began to tear. Then he scrambled down from his chair and ran from the room.

"Oh, dear." Louisa got up quickly and walked around the table. "Poppy, could you take James? I'd better go see what that's all about."

She found the boy in the nursery sitting on the little spare bed, his elbows on his knees and his chin in his hands.

"Evan, did I say something to upset you?" Louisa asked as she sat down next to him.

"I don't *want* to be special. I don't know how!" He flopped back on to his pillow and pulled his hand over his face. "It's too *hard* to be special, Mrs. Ellig-am! I'll bollocks it up!"

"What do you mean, bollocks it up?"

"I don't know how to *do* special! I'll do something wrong and it will *all* be spoilt!" the child explained as his arms gestured expansively.

Louisa cupped the boy's chin in her hand and peered down at him. Evan Hanley, you're special to Dr. Ellingham because he understands you and he likes the person you are. And what you do or don't do won't change that."

Louisa brushed a tear from the boy's cheek with her thumb. "You know, I can't think of a single other person on this earth who Dr. Ellingham understands as well as he does you."

Evan pushed himself up and gave her a scowl. "He *gots* ta understand *you!*"

"I'm afraid I *confuse* him more than anything," she giggled. "But he loves me anyway, believe it or not."

"Oh, I believe it 'cause he's always kissin' you."

"Yes, I think it's a pretty positive indicator if you get a kiss from Dr. Ellingham."

Evan's gaze drifted as he stared, unfocused, across the room. He returned to the edge of the bed and dangled his feet over the side. "I still don't think I want to be special though. It takes too much 'sponsibility."

Louisa got up from the bed and took the boy by the hand. "Well, I think that horse is already out of the barn, so let's not worry about it anymore. Shall we go finish that list and get those groceries now?" she said as she took his hand.

Louisa stuck her head in the door of her husband's consulting room before heading out for the market. Evan skipped on ahead, stopping at Morwenna's desk to say hello.

"Martin, Evan and I are going out to buy our groceries. Anything you want me to pick up while I'm out?"

His chair squeaked in protest as he leaned back, watching as his charge toyed with the bobble-head snowman on his receptionist's desk.

"Erm ... yes, actually," he said as he pulled himself forward and jotted a short list on to his notepad before ripping it off and handing it to his wife.

"Carrots, charcoal, and protein shakes?" Louisa raised a wrinkled brow. "Why?"

"I'm getting low. There are only four left in the refrigerator."

"That one I could figure out on my own, Martin. What are you going to do with the other two items?"

"They're for a ... project," he mumbled. He snatched a patient file from the corner of his desk and began to study it, glancing surreptitiously at his wife.

"I see." Louisa folded the list in half and tucked it into her coat pocket, deciding not to press the issue any further.

"We need to have a little chat about Evan, Martin."

"Louisa, this isn't—"

"Yes, I know. I don't mean at this very moment. It's just that I said something to him a little while ago that upset him, and I'm not sure what to make of his response. We'll talk about it later, hmm?"

"Why, what did you—"

She leaned down and silenced him with a kiss. "Like you said, this isn't a good time. I won't see you until this afternoon. Evan and I have a working lunch planned. We need to come up with a menu for his Christmas feast."

"I see." He peered out into the reception room again. "Do you have Evan's wish list?"

Louisa pulled open her leather bag and unzipped an inside pocket. "There's not much on it, I'm afraid. I don't think he holds out much hope for Father Christmas."

"Mm, yes." Martin glanced down at the piece of paper. "That's a ridiculous story, you know. And what message is it sending?"

"Father Christmas? It's just for fun, Martin! You take it too seriously, I think."

"Hmph," he grunted, slapping the patient file down on the desk. "If you're going to be out, I may ask Jeremy to drive me down to Hayle. There's a decent toy shop there, I understand. I thought I'd see if I can find a couple of these things on Evan's wish list."

"That'd be great. Although you don't really need to go all the way to Hayle for crayons and a colouring book," she said as she leaned over and kissed his cheek. "See you later then?"

"Yes, good."

Martin's quiet schedule, filled with re-checks and vaccinations, was abruptly interrupted mid-morning when Chippy and Irene Miller stepped into the surgery with their unhappy new-born twins.

It didn't take Jeremy long to determine the likely cause for the infants' irritability. He wagged a finger at the privacy screen as he finished examining the baby boy.

"Mrs. Miller, step behind the divider. I'll be with you in a moment!" he yelled over the din. "Mr. Miller ... stay right there and wait!" he added as he came back through the entryway with the male child in hand. "Morwenna, I need you to babysit whilst I check Mrs. Miller over!" He thrust the screaming infant into the young woman's arms and turned to walk away.

"This isn't in my job description!" she protested, staring down helplessly at the flailing, red-faced bundle.

"Take it up with Dr. Ellingham!"

Jeremy emerged from the make-shift examination room a short time later and jotted notes into Irene Miller's file.

"I need to consult with the doctor! I'll be back in a minute!" he said, giving Chippy a reassuring smile.

"Eh?" The fisherman cocked his head, turning his ear toward the young assistant.

"Sit—there!" Jeremy gestured to the chairs just inside the door, then hurried off.

He nearly collided with Poppy as she came through under the stairs. "Sorry. Didn't see you coming!" he said as he brushed his hand across her cheek.

"It's okay!" Her face flushed when she noticed Morwenna's eyes on them. "James woke up from his nap—the noise, you know! I have to—" She waved a hand towards the steps before rushing off, and Jeremy slipped through to the consulting room.

"Both babies appear to have oral thrush," the aide explained to Martin as he handed several files to him. "No signs of infection otherwise. Normal temp, normal nodes."

"And the parents?"

"Vitals are all normal. Aside from an infection in Mrs. Miller that appears to be in hand, no history of recent illness either."

"All right, give me a minute," Martin said as he sank back into his chair to review his assistant's findings.

Poppy came down the stairs with a wailing James in her arms just as Martin emerged from his consulting room.

He looked around, wide-eyed. The Miller infants' newborn cries, with a timber of bleating lambs, blended with the wails of the toddler, creating a cacophony not unlike what he remembered from his childhood stays at Auntie Joan's.

"Good, God! It sounds like a barnyard in here! Poppy … to the kitchen. Mr. and Mrs. Miller, come through, please!"

The harried parents moved through the reception room, casting apologetic glances towards the patients waiting in chairs.

Martin swung the door shut behind him then looked from one infant to the other before stepping towards the exam couch. "Pick a baby and bring it over here!" he said as he pulled his stethoscope from the table by the wall.

"They're nursin' all the time, Doc! Do you s'pose Irene's milk's run out?" Chippy asked as he laid his daughter down.

"No, not likely!" Martin inserted the earpieces of the stethoscope into his ears. He screwed up his face as he strained to hear the child's heartbeat and lung sounds before continuing on with a complete physical examination.

"All right, next baby!"

Irene laid her infant son on the couch and watched, worriedly, as the doctor repeated the exam.

"Mrs. Miller, have you been having any sensitivity of the areolas … the darkened area around your nipples?" he asked.

"Blimey, Doc! Not in mixed company!" Chippy squawked.

"Oh, for goodness' sake. It's a perfectly natural process!" Martin gave Chippy a shake of his head. "Mrs. Miller, have you or have you not had any soreness or redness?"

"They've been nursin' all the time, Doc. So yeah, I've been sore! And some crackin' too! I tried cabbage leaves, but it didn't make no difference!"

"Well, of course it didn't. It's a ridiculous folk remedy," Martin muttered pocketing his stethoscope. "It's thrush!"

Irene tipped her head and cupped her hand behind her ear. "What's that, Doc?"

"Thrush!"

"No, I *never* rush 'em. I give 'em all the time they need. It makes fer sore nipples though!"

"That has nothing to do with it! It's thr— Oh for goodness' sake!" Martin gave the couple a scowl and pulled the door open.

"Jeremy! Morwenna!" he barked. "Come in here!"

"Whatcha need, Doc?" Morwenna asked as she and the aide entered the room.

"You—take that one!" the doctor said to his assistant as he jabbed a finger towards the child in Chippy's arms. "Morwenna—take that one!" He herded them out the door and swung it shut.

Breathing out a heavy sigh, he pressed his fingers to the bridge of his nose. "Mr. and Mrs. Miller, your twins have thrush. That's what the white patches are on their tongues.

"It's not serious, but their mouths are sore and it's hindering feeding. They're not suckling properly or long enough to get an adequate amount of milk. That's why they're always hungry."

He limped behind his desk and dropped into the chair before pulling a pad down to his lap. "I'm writing out a prescription for Nystatin. It's a liquid that you'll apply to their tongues with an eyedropper—one millilitre four times a day," he said as he scratched his signature on to the pad.

"I'll need to examine you as well, Mrs. Miller. I see from the notes sent over from Truro that you received a course of antibiotics for a postpartum infection that you developed. It's not uncommon to develop thrush whilst on antibiotics. The infants would have picked it up from you during nursing."

"I made my babies sick?" Irene said as she slumped in her chair.

"There's nothing you could have done to prevent this. And as I said, it's not serious. Pick up some Calpol from Mrs. Tishell. That will ease the discomfort and the infants should be able to feed more comfortably and effectively.

"If you don't see significant improvement in a couple of days, or if either of them runs a fever, let me know right away. If you do have nipple thrush, Mrs. Miller, I'll prescribe a cream that you'll apply after each feeding. Then wipe off any residue immediately before the next feed."

The doctor pulled in his chin before grunting softly. "Mm." He put his good hand on the desktop and pushed himself to his feet. "Now, if you'll wait outside Mr. Miller, I'll examine your wife."

A deafening silence filled the little surgery as soon as the Miller's stepped out on to the terrace and pulled the door shut behind them.

Martin rubbed a large palm across his forehead, trying to ease the pounding that continued after the wails of the infants had quieted. He went back to his consulting room and dropped into his chair, laying his head on his desk.

Chapter 14

It was after one o'clock before Martin and Jeremy had finished seeing patients and were on their way to Hayle.

"What is it you're looking for?" the aide asked as they approached the village.

"I'm not sure. The boy made a list, but there are only three items on it. One of which is out of the question."

"So ... how's he doing? Settling into the routine?"

"Ohh ... I don't know. He wakes up every night crying. Although, we may have had a bit of a breakthrough last night. We'll see how he does tonight."

Jeremy glanced over as his boss rubbed at his tired eyes. "It's come at about the bloody worst time for you though, hasn't it?"

"What has?" Martin snapped.

"The boy ... this whole mess with Evan Hanley."

Shoulders drooping and sighing heavily, Martin turned his gaze to the old quarry passing them by. "It's a jolly good *cock-up* is what it is."

The engine of the Lexus purred softly, and the tyres hummed in harmony, underscoring the uncomfortable silence that filled the car.

A variety of scenarios filled Martin's head as he thought back on the decisions he had made the night of Evan Hanley's frantic phone call, and guilt churned uneasily in his stomach.

"You're doing the right thing, Martin," Jeremy said as he veered off the A-30 on to the tarmac road leading into the town of Hayle. "Taking care of the boy, I mean."

A CORNWALL CHRISTMAS 171

"I'm afraid I completely buggered things up that night, Jeremy. If I had waited for you ... I don't know. All I can do now is set things right the best I can."

The aide opened his mouth to deliver his opinion on the matter, but thought better of it when he caught the pained expression on his employer's face.

He turned his attention to the expansive vista opening up ahead, feeling blessed to live life amongst such stunning landscapes.

The area boasted some of the most beautiful and pristine beaches on the North Coast, and the tide had receded, unveiling them in all their golden splendour. Hayle had become a tourist draw in recent decades, favoured by surfers, families seeking a reprieve from the noise and pollution of the cities, and twitchers attempting to tick boxes on their life lists.

They rounded the turn from Fore Street on to Carnsew Road before pulling into a parking space alongside the unassuming storefronts.

Blewitt's Toy Shop carried many traditional toys in addition to the ubiquitous toys inspired by animated cinema. Martin perused the shop, trying to remember what toys he would include on the annual Christmas list he was required to draw up during the first three years in boarding school.

He gravitated towards the electric train sets, high up on the shelf and well out of way of small, curious hands.

He had seen a train set on display once in a shop in Delabole. It was a hot summer day, and he and Uncle Phil had been harvesting potatoes all afternoon. They delivered their haul to the distributor in the village. Then Phil Norton had taken his young nephew into a small cafe on High Street to get a milkshake.

A narrow shelf ran around the perimeter of the shop, and a small gauge train traversed the track laid out along it. His milkshake sat, forgotten on the table, as he stood on a chair watching the pistons push and pull the connecting rods attached to the wheels on the engines.

The little train clacked a hypnotic rhythm as it made its way around the circuit, a seemingly futile journey, as the little toy soon found its destination to be its beginning once again.

He had thought the little machine to be almost as grand as the internal workings of his grandfather's watch. He hoped against hope that his parents might one day relent, and a train set might appear under the perfectly adorned tree in the family's front room on Christmas morning. But as with most of his childhood wishes, it was never realised.

Martin had never included that coveted item in the teacher-mandated Christmas list that would be mailed to his parents. If he didn't include it, he could explain the toy's absence as merely a memory lapse on his parents' part, not a reflection of his own unworthiness.

And he had harboured a secret hope that there *was* actually a Father Christmas and that one year the kindly old man would deem his behaviour meritable of the longed-for toy.

"Thinking of getting him a train set?" Jeremy asked, startling him from his ruminations.

"Yes—no—erm, I'm not sure," he faltered. "I need to do some more looking." He ducked his head and wandered over to the building blocks.

There he found a confusing array of sets. Blocks for building spaceships—complete with missile launchers and droids, farm sets, even robotics sets. All of the sets were made up of many specialised parts. Tiny parts that could easily be lost on the floor, only to be found later by a toddler—a definite choking hazard for James.

His gaze finally landed on a large plastic bucket filled with an assortment of snap-together pieces; larger sized bricks, windows, and doors for adding to buildings. He picked it up and moved on to the books.

Jeremy followed along behind, retrieving things that Martin's bad shoulder wouldn't allow him to pull from the shelf.

"I'm not sure how much more we can pack in here, mate," the aide said as he rearranged the items yet again in order to accommodate another toy. You want me to go get another trolley?"

Martin glanced at his watch. "No, I think this is all I'm going to buy."

"I never would have guessed that *you* could take so long in a toy store," the aide said, giving him a lopsided grin.

"Mm, sorry. I hope this hasn't kept you from something."

"Nope. Just surprised is all."

The two men loaded Martin's purchases into the Lexus and Jeremy pressed the button on the keychain, closing the boot lid before glancing down at his watch. "Half three—you need your afternoon snack. I know a place that has the best buttys in Cornwall."

They worked their way back up Fore Street before the aide turned and crossed the Copperhouse Pool, an estuary that filled twice a day when tidal waters pushed into the village. He pulled up in front of one of the centuries-old buildings, so common in Cornwall, and parked the car.

"Oh, very funny, Jeremy!" Martin said as he read the sign over the door—The Bucket of Blood Inn.

The haemophobia that had hit him, out of the blue, and had forced him from his position as chief of vascular surgery at a prestigious London hospital had been an ever-present source of humiliation for him.

"If you find my—*difficulties*—so amusing, then why are you even—!"

"Relax, mate, that's not why I brought you here. I'll never make a joke out of that, Martin."

He nodded his head slowly at the doctor. "We still friends then?"

Martin screwed up one side of his mouth as a hiss of breath left his nose. "Yeah. I just—sorry."

Jeremy shrugged his shoulders. "Hey, I get it. They *do* have seriously good sandwiches, though. And you need to feed those healing bones of yours."

They wound their way through the establishment, surprisingly busy given the time of day, and found a table in a quiet corner.

Martin perused the menu in silence, casting an occasional annoyed glance as his aide drummed a rhythmic riff on the table with his fingertips.

"Will you stop that!" he snipped as he reached for his water.

"Mm, sorry." The young man straightened in his chair and looked around the room, his eyes drawn to the large coastal scene which had been painted on one wall. "They have great steaks here … if you were the sort of bloke who enjoyed a rare slab of beef now and then, that is."

He dumped the utensils from his napkin on to the table and placed it on his lap. "That's not where the name comes from though. Legend says that a landlord—a long time back—went to the well on the property to get a bucket of water. But when he pulled it up, the bucket was filled with blood. Turns out they found the body of a mutilated smuggler in the bottom of the well."

Martin wrinkled up his nose and set his glass down on the table with a thud. "I hope they've managed to tap into an alternate water supply since then," he said, dabbing at his mouth with his napkin.

Jeremy closed his menu and set it to the side, then looked uncertainly at his boss. "Martin, I er ... I just want to say that, about what happened at the Hanley's ... you did the right thing. God only knows what could have happened if you'd waited for me.

"I would have been disappointed in you if you'd acted any differently than you did. The kid needed your help. Think about what would have likely occurred if you'd waited around. Think about how important it'll be in the boy's recovery from all of this, to know that you came as soon as you knew he was in trouble ... to know he can count on you." Jeremy fidgeted with his silverware, then peered up. *"You did—the right—thing."*

"Mm," Martin grunted as he pulled in his chin and returned his attention to the menu. "What do you recommend ... other than steak?"

The purchased items were left in the trunk of the Lexus when they arrived back at the surgery.

"Louisa will have to bring them into the house later ... after the boys are in bed," Martin said as they walked around the side of the building towards the back door.

"Should be a memorable Christmas for the little guy, Martin."

Martin pushed into the kitchen and glanced back at him. "I hope so. It may be the only one he gets."

Jeremy cocked his head. "What do you mean by that?"

Martin took the car keys from his assistant's hand and dropped them into the basket on the counter.

"He hasn't experienced a typical Christmas—all the carryings-on that seems to be expected this time of year. I don't know where Evan may end up. Perhaps if he gets a taste of it this year— Well, perhaps it won't be so—so difficult later."

"Ah." Jeremy hesitated just long enough for an uncomfortable silence to settle in the room. "Well, I better go. Poppy's coming over for dinner tonight."

"Mm, yes. See you tomorrow," Martin said, giving a self-conscious tug on his ear as he headed off under the stairs.

James and Evan played on the floor after dinner that evening as Martin and Louisa cleared the dishes from the table. Louisa moved behind her husband as he reached to set the now-clean teacups on the shelf over the built-in buffet, wrapping her arms around him. "The shoulder feeling any better?" she asked.

"It's improving." He wriggled in her grasp until they were face to face, and then tipped his head down to kiss her.

His lips felt especially warm and soft against hers, and Louisa's tongue detected the vestiges of the peach compote which had added the sweet finish to their evening meal.

Martin felt a familiar tingle in his groin. Their newly acquired lodger had been very effective at thwarting any amorous advances by either of them since he arrived, and it now took very little encouragement from his wife to provoke a reaction.

He pushed her back as he sucked in a slow breath through clenched teeth. "Erm, you said earlier that we needed to talk—about Evan."

Louisa craned her neck to see around the corner. The two boys appeared to be absorbed in their play with James's alphabet blocks.

She kept a vigilant eye on them as she whispered furtively. "I happened to mention to Evan that he was spe—" Her gaze darted to her husband's face, "You *do* think he's special, don't you?"

Martin tipped his head at her as his right eye crinkled slightly. "Well, you'd know better than I would about his academic limitations, but *I've* seen no evidence of a disability. Quite the contrary."

Louisa stared back at him. "Not—that kind of special, Martin. I *mean*, you're very fond of him, aren't you?"

He stared absently for a moment before turning a furrowed brow towards her. "Yes."

She gave him a soft smile. "Well, it seemed to upset him very much when I suggested it. I tried to talk with him about it. He said he didn't *want* to be special. He was very adamant about it in fact—said he'd spoil it.

"You seem to understand him better than I do. It might help if you talked to him."

"Oh, I see," Martin replied with a half-grimace.

Louisa picked the damp tea towel up from the table and folded it neatly before hanging it on the back of a chair. "I was thinking ... maybe you two could have a little chat while I give James his bath."

Martin glanced over at his young charge and hissed out a breath. "Yes."

Louisa walked into the lounge and lifted her son from the scattering of wooden blocks on the floor. "Sorry, Evan, but it's time for James to have a bath and go to bed. Why don't you put the toys away, then go upstairs and get your pyjamas on."

Martin stepped down from the kitchen and walked to his wife's side. "Goodnight, James. Sleep well," he said as he pressed his fingers to the child's forehead.

"I'll be down in a bit ... give you some time to take care of things?" She raised her eyebrows and rolled her eyes in the seven-year-old's direction before moving towards the steps.

Martin dropped on to the sofa before focusing his attention on the most current issue of the *BMJ*.

The wooden blocks clacked together as the boy dropped them into a cloth bag. He pulled the drawstring shut before setting it in the playpen and heading for the stairs.

Lowering his magazine, Martin called out to the boy. "Once you have your pyjamas on, Evan, why don't you pick a bedtime story and bring it back downstairs with you."

"Really?"

"Yes, but be quick about it, or I may just change my mind."

The corners of Martin's mouth inched ever so slightly north on his face as he listened to the rapid patter of feet ascending the steps before resonating through the plaster ceiling overhead.

When the boy returned, he climbed up on to the sofa and nestled in next to his guardian, depositing the book in his lap.

It made no difference to Evan that the nonsensical words in the story were read by Martin like the rattling off of patient notes, with periodic adjournments for medical clarifications.

"That's ridiculous. It's impossible for someone's head to be screwed on too tight. One's head isn't screwed on in the first place. It's attached to the spinal column by tendons, ligaments and muscles which all work together to support the weight of the head and allow you to turn your head from side to side," the doctor explained, tipping his head back and tracing a finger along the sternocleidomastoid muscle in his own neck. "There are, of course, other purposes that the neck serves. Such as—"

Evan patted him on the leg, then tapped a finger on the whimsical, sombre-faced, green character in the book.

"Mm, yes," Martin grunted as he refocused his attention. *"It could be, perhaps, that his shoes were too tight,"* he read. "Now that *is* a possibility. Impractical footwear can lead to a number of—"

"Dr. Ellig-am—" The boy tapped at the book again and breathed out a heavy sigh.

Martin screwed up his face then continued on, *"But I think that the most likely reason of all, may have been that his heart was two sizes too small."*

Evan was prepared this time and slapped a small hand across Martin's mouth, earning him a stern scowl. "You're s'posed ta just read the story without all the talking. You keep goin' off the road, and then I forget what the story was about in the first place!"

Martin removed the child's hand from his face and pulled his handkerchief from his back pocket, wiping his mouth. "When was the last time you washed those hands?"

Evan worked his tongue in his cheek as he looked thoughtfully at the ceiling. "Hmm—remember when you told me ta wash the mannered bacteria off?"

"You haven't washed since *then?*"

"Well, I do take a bath, you know."

"Right. But you should wash your hands before every meal!" Martin huffed impatiently, giving the child a second scowl.

The boy peered up at him warily. "Are you cross at me, Dr. Ellig-am?"

"No. But for goodness' sake, common sense would dictate that you at least wash before meals. Don't you think?"

Evan gave a shrug of his shoulders as he slumped into the cushions. "I was just tryin' ta save on soap."

Martin watched the boy bat away tears, and his voice softened. "Evan, just because someone who cares about you gets annoyed or frustrated ... or even angry with you—it doesn't mean that you're not still special to them."

Evan glanced at Martin out of the corner of his eye. "My mum and dad decided I wasn't special to *them* anymore. I was too bothersome. I spoilt it."

Martin tossed the book on to the coffee table and put his arm around the boy, pulling him in close.

"Evan, it would never be your fault if your mother and father didn't think you were special. I don't know what sort of parent your dad might have been if it hadn't been for his drinking, but I can tell you that some parents are just unable to love their children."

"Can you love James?"

"I *do* love James—very, very much. And there's nothing that he could do to make me stop loving him ... or to make me love him more."

Evan picked nervously at a hangnail on his thumb, and Martin fought the temptation to reprimand him. He instead reached for the boy's hand and covered it with his own.

"My mum doesn't like boys," Evan said softly. "She likes girls better 'cause they don't get all dirty and they're not bothersome. And she says boys grow up ta be men."

He tipped his head back and looked up at the doctor. "Do you not mind that I'm a bothersome little bugger?"

"Evan," Martin said with a heavy sigh. "When I told you to leave my office this morning, it was because I needed to get my work done before my patients arrived, and your questions were preventing me from doing that.

"But just because I sent you out of the room does *not* mean that I like you any less. And to be clear, you are *not* a bothersome little bugger. But there may be times that you'll have to save your questions for later."

The child stared at him for a moment before a smile spread across his face. "Kay. Can we finish the story now?"

By the time the grouchy Christmas tale had come to an end, James Henry was fast asleep, and Louisa was in the bathroom getting ready for bed.

Evan stared up at Martin as he tucked the covers in around his neck. He watched him wide-eyed for a few moments before asking timidly, "Do you *really* think I'm special, Dr. Ellig-am? That's what Mrs. Ellig-am says."

Martin rubbed a hand across the back of his neck before giving the boy a nod. "Yes, Evan, I do think you're special. Now close your eyes and go to sleep."

Martin stood up and limped towards the doorway, stopping and turning when he heard the child whisper again. "Dr. Ellig-am—I think you're special, too."

"Mm, thank you," Martin replied awkwardly. "Goodnight, Evan."

"G'night."

Louisa was in bed when Martin entered their room. She pushed her elbow under her and said softly, "Martin, lock the door behind you. We have some unfinished business to take care of."

"Mm, yes," he answered huskily, his pulse quickening as he slid the latch and hurried towards the bathroom. "I'll just go—be back in a minute."

An amused smile spread across Louisa's face when she detected the urgency in her husband's voice.

She pulled the blankets back when he returned to the bedroom, giving him the merest glimpse of her bare skin in doing so. "May as well take those boxers off now, hmm?

Save me the trouble." She reached playfully for his waistband as he stood by the bed.

"Ah, yes—rationalising—time," he said, the words catching in his throat as her fingers worked their way south. He pulled at the elastic, slipping the undergarment over the fixator penetrating his right thigh, then dropped on to the bed.

Louisa pulled her knees under her and pushed him back on to his pillow before pressing her lips to the sensitive skin on his belly. Then she slid the boxers from his legs and deposited them on the floor.

Martin's good hand skimmed across her flank as she lay down alongside him. Her hips pressed against his, and he was unable to contain the soft, throaty, growl that worked it's way up from his chest.

As her arm reached over him to turn out the light, his fingers raced to her breast. Words floated from his mouth on a warm breath of air, "Oh, Louisa. You are so beautiful."

She glanced down at his face before flipping the switch, the hormone induced sparkle in his eyes enhanced by the soft glow of the incandescent lamp. Pressing her forehead to his she gazed down at him. "I love you very much, Martin."

"I love you, too, Louisa."

The lamp switch clicked, darkening the room. Any pain in his shoulder was suppressed by the flood of endorphins generated as his wife moved languidly, and Martin clung to her tightly while the tension that had been building in him for too many days was finally released.

Louisa rolled off and nestled against him. "Are you okay?" she asked as she covered his shoulder with her palm.

The room was silent, but for the steady tick of the mantel clock. Then he breathed out a rumbled sigh. "Yes. I'm fine—good."

Chapter 15

Martin threw his arm over his head, trying to shut out the piercing beep of the alarm clock Wednesday morning. He stabbed at empty air several times before his hand landed on its target, silencing the strident reveille.

He stifled a groan as he forced his weary body out on to the cold floor. Then, placing his good hand against the wall, he wrestled his feet into his slippers before pulling his dressing gown from its assigned place on the chair.

"How many times were you up last night?" Louisa forced out through desiccated vocal cords.

"Three," Martin grunted back. "I'm going to take a shower. You go back to sleep."

Having an explanation for the light shining in the window seemed to have alleviated Evan's very defined fear that his father had discovered his whereabouts, but he had been awakened repeatedly, pursued in his sleep by a featureless entity. Martin had stayed with him each time until he fell back to sleep, and each time his vigil by the boy's bedside had grown longer.

He was sitting on the edge of the bed fighting his stiffened limbs in order to reach his feet and don his socks when his wife emerged from the bathroom a while later. He snuck glances at her as she fished around in her lingerie drawer for clean knickers and a bra before dropping her towel to the floor. He would need to watch the time while they were in Truro if they were to get home early enough for either of them to have the energy for a repeat of the previous night's activities.

"Martin?"

His wife's voice pulled him from his carnal musing and he quickly averted his lustful gaze.

"What?" he asked with feigned innocence as he grabbed for a shoe on the floor.

She tipped her head down and peered up at him. "I *said* ... I'm concerned about how little sleep you're getting ... just getting over pneumonia and your shoulder healing and all. Why don't you let me get up with Evan tonight."

"Hopefully, neither of us will need to get up with Evan tonight."

"Hmm, possibly." Louisa dropped down on the bed next to him and pulled a pair of jeans over her legs. "He's very fortunate to have you, Martin. There are very few people who could understand him the way you seem to be able to. And having this time with you will certainly ease his transition to a foster or adoptive family, don't you think?"

Martin sat silent for several seconds before picking up his crutch and pulling himself to his feet. "Mm, I'll be in the kitchen."

Although Louisa had to be at the school for a couple of hours most days, the holiday break allowed her much more time at home, and the Christmas preparations had begun in earnest.

Martin found himself being hurried through his breakfast by his wife and young charge who had pressing matters to attend to in the kitchen.

Evan whisked his guardian's plate out from under his hand as soon as the last piece of toast was lifted from its surface. And his coffee cup, which Martin had intended to refill before retreating to his consulting room for the morning, disappeared before he could tip the last drops down his throat.

He pulled a replacement cup from the shelf over the buffet and stood in front of his espresso machine filling it with the hot brew.

"We got lots ta do today, Dr. Ellig-am," Evan said, looking up as Martin towered over him. He hesitated, scuffing his trainer against the floor before adding a wary, "And yer kinda in the way."

The child picked up the doctor's latest copy of the BMJ from the table and returned it to the bin for a second time.

"Hey, hey, hey, hey, hey! I'm not done with that!" Martin protested as he set his cup on the table and went to retrieve the journal. He turned from the bin to see his freshly poured cup of espresso being dumped into the kitchen sink.

Louisa took the cup from Evan's hand, refilled it and held it out to her husband. "Sorry, Martin, maybe you'd be more comfortable on the sofa, hmm?"

"Oh, for goodness' sake," he muttered, slapping the magazine into his sling and taking the cup from his wife. "I may as well go get some work done. Let me know if I should plan to eat out for lunch." He walked off mumbling before ducking his head under the stairs.

"Do you think Dr. Ellig-am's angry?" Evan asked, leaning against James's high chair.

"Oh, he'll get over it, Evan, don't worry," Louisa said as she wiped the breakfast crumbs from the table.

The boy threw his arm around James Henry, "We got lots a work ta do before we get yer dad ta like Christmas. Huh, James Henry?"

James slapped a playful hand against the seven-year-old's cheek and chortled when the boy jumped back quickly and ran off, cowering behind the sofa.

"Evan? James was just playing." Louisa walked briskly into the lounge and reached for the boy before he bolted for the stairs.

She hurried back to the kitchen and pulled her son from the high chair. "Let's go find your daddy, James."

Louisa rapped on the door of the consulting room and, not waiting for an answer, pushed through.

Martin grimaced. *"What is it?"* he said as he looked up from the notes on his desk.

He stared back at his wife and his defensive posture dissolved into tenderness. "Louisa? Come in," he said, his words coming out with the quasi-sigh-like quality that she so loved.

"Sorry to disturb you, but I think you need to check on Evan right away. James slapped his face—just like James does. But it seemed to scare him."

Martin got to his feet and moved past his wife. "Is he still in the house?"

"Well, yes. He ran upstairs." Louisa replied as her husband traversed the reception room and ascended the steps.

"Evan?" Martin stood in the doorway of the nursery where he could see the little boy's fingers protruding from the shadows under the bed. "Evan, it's all right, you can come out now."

The child inched forward and peered out cautiously before scrambling quickly to him, wrapping his arms around his legs.

"Evan, what's wrong?" Martin asked, reaching for the boy's hand before leading him back to take a seat on the bed.

"I don't wanna talk about it," he forced out between ragged breaths.

"I see." Martin's thoughts rushed back to his own moments of unexplained feelings of terror and helplessness. To the complete inability to defend himself when bullied by the bigger boys at school or the boys that gathered at the park near his parents' home in Kensington.

This reaction had eased after he reached his full adult height. He was now bigger than most men, but a fear still lay just under the surface—a fear of unidentifiable emotions commandeering a rational and controlled response.

He cleared his throat. "It may have *felt* real Evan, but your father is dead. What happened in the past … it won't happen again."

The boy tipped his head back and his round eyes shimmered with leftover tears. Martin reached around to his back pocket, pulling out his handkerchief before dabbing at his face. "Shall we go back downstairs … see what Mrs. Ellingham and James have gotten up to?"

Evan laid his head in the doctor's lap and pulled his arm over his face. "I'm a-barrassed. What if they laugh at me?"

Martin's hand hovered for a few seconds before he let it come to rest on the boy's head. "James's brain hasn't developed enough for him to understand what happened, Evan. And Mrs. Ellingham is just concerned. She won't laugh," he said as he nudged the boy from his lap and got to his feet. "But you better prepare yourself, you'll probably get a hug."

Louisa had an array of cooking utensils, bakeware and ingredients laid out on the table when Martin and Evan returned to the kitchen.

"Oh, Evan," she said sympathetically as she crouched down. "Are you all right?"

"Yes." The boy stepped towards her, opened his arms and turned his head to the side. "Kay, I'm prepared," he said, standing stiffly with his eyes squeezed shut.

Louisa cocked her head at her husband.

"He—er, he may be expecting a hug," Martin said, wincing before averting his eyes.

After his sleepless night, Martin was thankful for the pedestrian start to his day. Lorna Gillet, his last patient for the morning, had just left his consulting room when Morwenna stuck her head in the doorway.

"Doc, there's a guy here … says he's with Children's Services," she said as she peered in at him with gaudy plastic parrots swinging from her earlobes.

"Ah … right. I'll be out in a minute," Martin answered as he slipped the patient notes he had been reviewing into their proper sleeve before quickly tidying his desk. "And Morwenna … could you let Louisa know he's here as well. He may want to see the boy."

"Will do, Doc."

Martin leaned back in his chair, peering out his door at the same man who had stopped in his hospital room a week and a half earlier. He pulled himself to his feet and limped towards the reception room.

"Mr. Dolan," he said, reaching out with his good hand.

"It's Delaney—Roger Delaney," the man replied, returning the gesture before doffing his hat and scarf. "I'm glad to see you up on your feet."

"Mm, yes. Come on back, please." Martin led the way to his office, a disquiet building in him over the nature of the man's unannounced visit. "Please … take a seat. Would you like a cup of tea … or coffee?"

"A cup of tea would be good. There's a chill in the air today, eh?" Mr. Delaney lowered himself into the chair by the desk and set his briefcase on the floor.

"Yes. Yes, it's quite—chilly," Martin replied awkwardly, grimacing at his own social ineptitude as well as the heavy scent of cologne emanating from the man. He stepped back into the hallway. "Morwenna, could you bring in a pot of tea, please ... and some milk and sugar as well."

Morwenna stared back at him, her brows pulling together. "Tea? Are you sure, Doc? 'Cause I don't wanna bring it in there only ta have you yell at—"

"Morwenna—tea—now!" he hissed before returning to the consulting room.

"What can I help you with, Mr. Delaney?" he asked as he dropped heavily into his chair and pulled himself forward.

"I just wanted to make you aware that a Public Health Funeral has been arranged for Jim Hanley. The Cornwall Council will handle all the expenses in this case as, thus far, no relatives have been located who are willing to accept responsibility for the body. I understand that you were informed that Mr. Hanley's remains have been cremated."

"That's correct." Martin shifted nervously in his chair, his left hand gripping the armrest.

Mr. Delaney lifted his briefcase from the floor and laid it on his lap. "I'll leave the pertinent details here with you in case the son would like to be in attendance at the memorial service," the man said as the latches snapped open. He took a sheet of paper from the case and laid it on the desk.

Martin pulled it towards him, scanning over the date and location. "I'm very uncertain about how best to handle this with the boy—Evan."

"How does he seem to be doing?" Roger asked as he snapped the latches shut and set his briefcase back on the floor. "This is a tumultuous time for him. But does he seem to understand what's happened ... that his father has died?"

There was a knock on the door and Morwenna stepped in. "Sorry to interrupt, I have your tea and biscuits. She set the tray in the middle of the desk and then straightened herself, her hands folded in front of her. "Will there be anything else, Dr. Ellingham?" she asked.

Martin cocked his head, his receptionist's sudden formal air perplexing him. "No, that's all, Morwenna. Erm, thank you." He watched as the door closed behind her then turned his attention back to the child advocate.

"I'm sorry, Mr. Delaney. Please ... help yourself," he said, gesturing towards the tray of refreshments as he cleared his throat.

"As to what Evan understands, my wife and I have talked with him, reassured him repeatedly. He was quite obviously traumatised by his father, and he's been having difficulty dealing with that. He fears that his father will find him. I believe he understands that his father has died, but I'm not sure he truly believes it's an irreversible condition."

"Is he exhibiting any outward signs of distress or have there been changes in his performance at school?" the man asked as his spoon clinked against the side of his teacup.

"Until today, just a night-time problem. Imagining things that aren't there, nightmares, that sort of thing. But there was an incident this morning. I'm not sure if it would be considered a flashback, but the boy suddenly ran off and hid under his bed."

Martin picked up a paper clip from his desktop and tapped it on the armrest. "Have you, er ... been able to locate any family? Anyone who would be a willing and suitable guardian?"

"No, I'm afraid not. And I seriously doubt that we will. Mrs. Hanley is an only child, given up to foster care by her mother when she was eight.

"Mr. Hanley has two surviving siblings. A married sister with stage four lung cancer. And a brother, never married, who's just been released on parole. Neither sibling is willing or suitable."

Mr. Delaney paused, then stared, pointedly, at Martin. "I realise this was a temporary commitment on your part, Dr. Ellingham, but might you and your wife consider keeping the boy a bit longer. It would be in Evan's best interests to not disrupt his life any more than necessary at the moment. We can move him on after things have settled down a bit."

"I *will* need to discuss it with my wife, obviously. But, move him on? Are you saying that the boy will be shuffled to another set of caregivers in the future or will you be looking for adoptive parents?"

"Adoption by loving parents who are a good match for the child is what we strive for, but unfortunately that's not the outcome for many of the children in our system."

Martin breathed out a heavy sigh. "I assumed as much. If we should decide to make a longer commitment to the boy, I would have to insist that we be allowed to consult with a child psychologist ... the sooner the better."

Mr. Delaney gave the doctor a nod of his head. "Excellent. There would be no objections to that. We would need to be kept apprised of the child's progress, of course—the name of his therapist and such."

"That's fine. Would you like to visit with Evan while you're here?" the doctor asked as he got to his feet.

"As a matter of fact, I would."

Martin pulled the door open and led the advocate under the stairs and into the kitchen where Louisa and Evan were mixing batter for Mr. Moysey's fruitcake.

"Hello, Evan," Roger said as he walked over and stood next to the boy.

Evan glanced up at the man before jumping off the stool he was standing on and latching on to Martin's wrist. "Come here and look at what we're makin' Dr. Ellig-am! It's for Mr. Moysey. Do you think this will cheer him up? It's a fruitcake."

"I'm not sure what can cheer Mr. Moysey up, Evan, but it won't hurt to try." Martin peered into the bowl of batter then glanced up at his wife. "Louisa, do you remember Mr. Delaney?"

"Yes, yes! Hello, Mr. Delaney," she said as she quickly wiped her flour-covered hands on her apron before extending her arm.

"Who's Mr. Moysey, Evan?" Roger asked as he crouched down to talk to the boy.

"He's Dr. Ellig-am's friend. He's kinda grouchy so I'm going to spread him with some holiday cheer. It's on my list."

"Oh? What list is that?"

"My list of ten things ta do for Christmas. One thing yer s'posed ta do is ta spread good cheer, and I think Mr. Moysey needs some."

Mr. Delaney straightened himself back up and tousled the boy's hair. "That's a very kind thing to do, Evan."

He watched for a few minutes as the boy dumped the candied fruit, nuts, and peel into the batter and Louisa helped him to stir it in. "Well, I better be on my way. I have a stop to make in Wadebridge yet today. Give me a ring once you and your wife have had a chance to talk things over, Dr. Ellingham."

Martin followed the man back under the stairs and saw him to the door.

When he turned, his receptionist's gaze was fixed on him.

"What was that all about?" he asked as he picked up the mail from her desk and began to sort through the stack of envelopes.

Morwenna watched him, wide-eyed and guileless. "Don't know whatcha mean, Doc."

"The professional bit in there with Mr. Donovan."

Morwenna folded her arms across her chest and leaned back in her chair, narrowing her eyes at him. "His name's Mr. Delaney. And I was *tryin'* ta be helpful ... ta make you look respectable. Not that you'd notice. You seemed nervous about it, and I just wanted the meeting ta go well for you."

"I see."

Martin tossed the junk mail in the bin and set the rest of the envelopes down on the desk, giving them several taps with his fingers as he squirmed under the receptionist's gaze. "Erm, I appreciate that, Morwenna."

She stared back at him for a moment. "Thanks, Doc. So ... is Evan gonna stay with you and Louisa then?"

Huffing out a breath, he threw his head back and limped off towards his consulting room. "Pull the files for tomorrow, then go home, Morwenna."

He returned to his office, finishing up the patient notes still on his desk before looking up at the clock. He slipped Lorna Gillet's records into the last empty sleeve and pushed himself to his feet, stretching his stiffened body and rubbing at his tired eyes.

The aroma of ginger and cinnamon had found its way under his closed door, beckoning him to the kitchen where he was greeted by a scene of domestic chaos.

James was in his high chair, chewing on a small, brown, cut-out biscuit, the still soft white icing having already been deposited on his nose and cheeks.

The kitchen was strewn with recipe books, measuring cups and spoons, and the staples needed by any baker worth his or her salt.

A white mound accumulated on the floor like sand in an hourglass as the bag of sugar, lying on its side on the table above, slowly released its contents, the granules creeping over the table's edge.

Aside from a clean shadow on the stone flooring under his son's high chair, the grey slate was dusted with flour, some areas heavier than others. Bits of brown dough had escaped the bowl and rolling surface and were in imminent danger of being ground into the soles of shoes.

Martin stood, eyes blinking slowly in wonderment at the unholy state of his once pristine kitchen. "Good Lord! What have you been doing?"

"We're making gingerbread men, Martin," Louisa stated matter-of-factly as she turned to flash him a smile.

"Dr. Ellig-am! I made you a special one ... come look!" Evan said excitedly as he ran to the array of miniature figures lying supine on the counter.

Martin looked down at his feet and wrinkled up his face. "I don't want to get my shoes dirty."

"That's okay, I'll bring it over there!" the boy said as he gently picked up a biscuit and carried it across the room with all the solemnity of a funeral procession. "See, he gots all his insides! There's the heart, the stomach ... and the lungs are right here." His finger poked at the white icing outline. "And I put a brain in his head!"

Evan pulled his index finger to his mouth and licked off the residue left from the hapless little man's lungs, and then wiped the wet finger off on his apron. "It's for you!"

he said, tugging at Martin's hand before depositing the biscuit into his palm.

"Mm. I see. Thank you, Evan. It's quite anatomically accurate," he said with a slight air of pride in the boy. "Maybe I'll save it for later." Martin glanced at his watch. "We should leave around three o'clock, Louisa. Are you going to be ready to go?"

"We're almost done here, then we'll tidy things a bit."

"Ah." Martin surveyed the disaster area once more before retreated to his consulting room to work on Ruth's clock. His relatively immobile shoulder allowed him to do little more than inspect the parts and sort out those in need of repair. He had also found that the cleaning of the tiny gears was a manageable task if he rested the pieces in his lap.

There was a soft tapping on his door a short time later, and Evan poked his head into the room.

"Can I see what yer doin'?"

"Mm, yes. Come on in, Evan."

"Are you fixin' something again?" the boy asked as he leaned his forearms on to the desk and inspected the small brass parts.

"It's my aunt's grandfather clock. It needed to be cleaned and repaired. It's very old."

"Seems like everything gots ta get cleaned and repaired when it gets old."

"Many things do, yes."

"So ... do you gotta fix yer aunt sometimes?" Evan asked as he came around and climbed on to the back of Martin's desk chair, peering over his shoulder at the piece in his lap.

"Yes. Sometimes she comes to see me with a medical complaint. Is that what you're wondering?"

"Uh-huh."

Martin returned the small gear to the tray on his desktop and swivelled around, knocking the young child off balance. Evan jumped off the base of the chair and stood, staring intently at the doctor as he clasped his hands behind his back. "Your aunt gots ta be pretty old."

"Mm, don't tell her that or you'll get yourself into trouble." Martin said raising an eyebrow at him.

"How can telling the truth get you into trouble?"

"Mm, it makes no sense, I know. But you'll save yourself a lot of headaches if you can figure out when to keep your mouth shut."

"Yer not real good at that, are ya."

Louisa precluded her husband's retort to the boy when she stuck her head into the room. "Martin, James is waking up from his nap. I'll go change his nappy, and then we can go if you like."

"Yes. Evan, you better use the lavatory before we leave," he said, pushing himself to his feet. "It's a long drive to Truro."

The boy darted in behind him and slipped into the chair before launching himself with a push from the desk.

Martin peered down at him, his fingernail clicking against his watch face. "And you need to get a move on."

They arrived at the Parsons' shortly after four o'clock. Louisa, having all but given up trying to extract information from her tight-lipped husband, was anxious for a moment alone with her friend.

"So, I expect you're about to burst with excitement, aren't you, Evan!" Carole said as she crouched down to speak with the boy at eye level.

"I haven't told them yet that we're—going out for dinner. So he hasn't had a chance to—burst," Martin said as he leaned over to whisper in Chris's ear. "There's a bag in the boot of my car. Get it and put it in yours. They don't know what's up yet."

"Right." Chris looked over at Louisa and gave her a wink, eliciting a perplexed cock of her head.

"Do I gots time for the blocks?" Evan asked, giving a tug on Martin's hand.

"James should have a nappy change if we're going out, Martin. Carole, could you help me?"

"With a nappy change?"

"Mm-hmm. It'll just take a minute," Louisa said, giving her friend a jerk of her head.

"But *do* I gots time for the blocks?" Evan asked, a bit more stridently as he saw his opportunity slipping away.

"They're still in the basket by the fireplace, Evan. It's fine with me if it's okay with Dr. Ellingham," Carole called out over her shoulder.

Martin glanced at his watch and hissed a breath through his nose. "You only have a few minutes, and you must pick them up before we leave."

"So, what's going on? Martin's been very cagey about this trip over here today," Louisa said as she pulled the tabs open on her son's soiled nappy.

Carole crossed her arms in front of her. "Well, Louisa, if it's supposed to be a surprise then *I'm* sure not going to be the one to let the cat out of the bag."

James Henry reached out and grabbed the small plastic container of dry cereal from the nappy bag and Louisa intercepted it as the boy pulled at the lid. "You need to be patient, James. Save your appetite for dinner," she said before burying it deeper in the bag.

"Martin doesn't *do* surprises, Carole," she said, her mild annoyance with her friend's uncooperative attitude on display.

"Maybe it's not a surprise, maybe he's just embarrassed to admit to doing some—" Carole glanced at her watch. "Maybe we should just go before I let something slip."

Louisa picked up her son and flung the nappy bag over her shoulder before giving a huff and walking off down the hall, her ponytail whipping to the side.

Chris circled the city's business district a short time later looking for a parking space, a rare commodity in the area. He pulled into the car park next to the Methodist church, within reasonable walking distance of their final destination.

"I thought we could get some dinner at the Lemon Tree Cafe, then walk down to Boscawen Street to see the decorations," he said as he shifted the car into park.

"Let me get the meter, Chris," Martin said as he stepped from the vehicle. "Evan, do you want to put the money in?" he asked as he pushed the door shut behind the boy.

"What do I gotta do?" he asked as he picked the coins from his guardian's palm.

Martin wagged a finger at the device. "Just drop them in this little slot here, one at a time."

As Evan tipped his head back to peer up at the machine his eyes grew large and his mouth dropped open in wonderment at the beautiful sight in front of him.

Chapter 16

The spires on the century-old cathedral stretched to the heavens, the setting sun casting a warm glow on the exterior of the structure.

Evan sucked in an audible breath. "Whoa! *That's* a big church!"

"Mm, it's Truro Cathedral. It was built more than a hundred years ago," Martin said as he rapped his knuckles on the parking meter to get the boy's attention.

"I bet those staples go all the way up to the stars!"

"You mean steeples. And strictly speaking, those are spires not steeples. And they're only two-hundred and fifty feet high. The nearest star is more than twenty-four trillion miles away." Martin gave a tug on the hood of the boy's jacket and tapped again on the parking meter.

"Actually, Mart, the Sun is the nearest star," Chris said as he pulled his glasses down and peered closely at the key fob before locking the car.

Martin screwed up his face at his friend. "Well, obviously! You know what I meant. And *you* should get your eyes examined. Why aren't you wearing your contacts? Is there a problem?"

"No. Oh, I almost forgot." He unlocked the vehicle and reached behind the backseat for the bag Martin had brought with him.

Giving a snap of his fingers, Martin again tried to attract the child's attention. "The meter, Evan ... are you going to put the money in, or should I?"

"I can do it; I can do it. Don't get your knickers in a twist."

"*Excuse me?*"

The boy looked back at him, worriedly. "I bet that was 'fensive, wasn't it?"

"Yes, it was quite cheeky as a matter of fact. Now feed the meter," Martin grumbled.

The coins jingled their way through the device and Evan watched as the purchased time displayed in the small window. "There, proper job," he said, brushing his hands together. "So a hundred years. That's pretty old. Is that why it doesn't got coloured windows?"

"No, it *has* stained glass windows, you just can't see the colour because there's not enough light shining through them from the inside." Martin gave another tug on the child's jacket. "Come on, we need to hurry or we'll be too late."

Louisa wrestled with the nappy bag while trying to shift her ever growing son to the opposite hip.

"Here, let me carry him," Chris said as he handed Martin's bag to his wife and took James from Louisa's arms. "Gawd, he's getting to be a load!"

"Mm, thirty pounds," she said as she quickened her pace to keep up with her husband.

They crossed Union Place and headed towards the majestic church. Evan clung tightly to Martin's wrist despite the fact that he was yanked forward with each swing of his crutch.

"Where are we going, Dr. Ellig-am?" the boy asked, letting go long enough to leapfrog his way across the stepping stones running between the buildings.

"You keep going on about wanting to see coloured windows. So, we're going to see coloured windows."

The child came to a stop and turned to look at him. "Really?"

"Yes, really. But if we don't hurry up it's going to get too dark."

Evan's gaping mouth spread into a broad smile as he reached again for Martin's wrist.

Voices reverberated off the granite walls as they entered the nave, the arched ceilings peaking high overhead. Martin, his legs aching after the walk, lowered himself into the nearest pew and watched as his young charge's eyes scanned the immense room. The boy was drawn to a large circular window, suspended like a lapis lazuli pendant under one of the elegant stone arches.

Louisa and the Parsons wandered through the sanctuary, stopping to read the plaques and look at displays as Martin began to grow concerned by Evan's behaviour.

The child seemed mesmerised by the glass artwork. When he dropped down and stretched himself out on the floor, Martin got to his feet and limped over to him, the pain in his legs rapidly intensifying.

"Are you all right?" he asked as he cocked his head at the boy.

He smiled up at him. "I just wanted ta see 'em all at the same time."

Martin took in a deep breath and blew it out slowly, then cleared his throat as he became aware of the gawping onlookers.

Dusk was fleeting during the Cornish winter, and the colours in the magnificent windows were dulling quickly to grey. "Okay Evan, we better be going," he said, giving the child a jerk of his head.

As they sidled up next to Louisa, Martin leaned over and whispered in her ear and then turned to his young charge, "I'll be right back, Evan. You wait here with Mrs. Ellingham.

He headed towards the gift shop, returning later with a bag in his hand.

"Whatcha got, Dr. Ellig-am?" Evan asked as he bounced along beside the doctor.

"Don't be so nosy. And watch where you're going."

Before they exited the church, Evan emitted a loud "*HUH!*", giving James an impish grin as it echoed off the walls. The toddler listened to the sound and quickly duplicated the older boy's "*HUH!*" before bursting into a fit of giggles.

Martin glanced back at the stern looks coming from the congregants, there to commune with their God, and hurried his family out of the building.

He pulled his wife aside and said in an undertone, "Did you, er ... happen to bring any of my morphine with you?"

"Yes, it's in my purse. I left it under the seat in Chris's car though ... one less thing to juggle with James and the nappy bag."

Martin blew out a hiss of air and swallowed hard. "Let's go back that way on our way to the restaurant."

"Maybe we should just head on home, Martin," she said, her concern growing as quickly as the strain apparent on her husband's face.

Giving her a vigorous shake of his head, he pushed her forward. "No, there's something else I want to do. I'll be fine if I can take the edge off the pain."

Louisa looked at him uncertainly and then turned to their friends. "Silly me, I forgot my purse in your car. Could we stop and pick it up before going to eat?"

"Sure, we can cut through on Wilkes Walk," Chris said, moving James to his other arm.

Louisa glanced over at her husband as he shifted his weight uncomfortably, his seven-year-old charge hanging from his arm. "Evan, I miss having a man to hold hands with," she said. "Why don't you walk with me for a while."

Martin's pace had slowed as they made their way towards the Parsons' vehicle and the relief he needed. Louisa pulled a small bottle from her leather bag and dumped two pills into her husband's hand before passing him James's sippy cup.

"Seriously?" he asked as he scowled down at the slotted lid.

"Sorry, I'll take it off. You should keep some morphine with you, you know Martin," she softly chastised.

"Louisa, don't—"

"Everything okay, Mart?" Chris asked as he came around the back of the vehicle.

Martin handed the cup back to his wife before moving past his friend. "Fine. We should get going."

Louisa gave Chris a surreptitious shake of her head before he turned and hurried to catch up to Martin.

Evan kept himself sandwiched between the two doctors as they headed across the parking lot, but stopped in his tracks as they came around the side of the Methodist church. In the middle of the lawn, a live nativity was being re-enacted, complete with a donkey, a small assemblage of sheep, a Jersey cow, and a llama, which had been accessorised with a burlap covered faux camel's hump.

"What ... the world?" Evan exclaimed as he stared at the unlikely sight.

"Oh, I forgot they do this every year," Carole said as she and Louisa brought up the rear. "It's a fundraising event for the children's hospice. Let's go and see if you can pet the animals, Evan." She took the boy by the hand and headed towards a man who appeared to be involved with the event.

"Oh, I don't think *this* is a good idea." Martin grimaced as the boy ran his hands across a sheep's woolly back. "It's not a petting zoo. He could be bitten. That animal's mouth harbours any number of pathogens that could lead to a nasty infection," he said before starting after the child.

"Mart," Chris said grabbing hold of his shirt sleeve. "Let the kid pet the animals."

"We're on our way to eat dinner, Chris. He's going to smell like a barnyard!"

"Relax about the bacteria. You were surrounded by cows, sheep and chickens every summer as a kid and you survived. I think Evan's immune system can take a few minutes of it."

Martin gave his friend a grunt before turning around to see his young charge sitting atop the donkey. "Oh, gawd. Look what he's doing now." He limped over, intending to pull the child from the animal before something disastrous could happen. But the joyous expression on the boy's face stopped him.

Louisa stretched up to reach her husband's ear. "Just let him enjoy it, Martin," she said softly.

"Yes." He wrinkled up his face as Evan leaned forward and wrapped his arms around the donkey's neck before burying his face in its mane. "Oh, gawd," he grumbled again, throwing his head back.

The man in charge lifted the child back to the ground and he ran excitedly to his guardian. "Dr. Ellig-am, did ya see me? I got ta sit on that donkey!"

Martin cleared his throat and gave the boy a nod. "Yes, I saw you, Evan. Very good. Shall we go eat dinner, now?"

"No! I gots ta see if they have a baby saver!" he said before dashing off to speak to the man in charge.

The Ellinghams and the Parsons followed after him.

"Do you gots a baby saver at this church?" the child asked as he stared up at the man.

The fellow looked to Martin and Louisa with a furrowed brow. "Not sure what he means, folks."

"We aren't either, I'm afraid," Louisa said as she crouched down. "Evan, what do you mean by baby saver?"

Evan gave a shrug of his shoulders. "Speech me. But the lady from St. Kew's said they have a donkey and a cow and a baby saver at Christmas. Do *you* gots a baby saver?" he asked the man again.

"Ahh ... I think you mean a baby *Saviour*," he explained. He picked up the baby, which was bundled in a blanket and sleeping on the lap of a woman dressed as the Virgin Mary, then lowered him down for Evan to see. "This is my son. He's playing the part of Jesus this year."

Evan stared at the infant for several seconds then threw his arms out to his sides. "You mean it's just a plain old *baby*?" he moaned. "That lady made it sound like something really, really special! That's just a stupid baby! A plain ol' stupid baby!"

He stomped off towards Martin, feeling he'd been played the fool.

"I'm sorry, I think we've had a bit of a misunderstanding here. I'm sure he didn't mean to be rude," Louisa said as she pulled a five pound note from her purse and deposited it into the collection can sitting prominently on a table. "And I'm quite sure your baby's not—stupid. Thank you for letting him see the animals."

She gave the man an anaemic smile before hurrying off to catch up to her husband. "Well, that was embarrassing," she said as she took his hand.

"They're bound to have dissatisfied customers when they practice false advertising, Louisa," Martin grumbled.

"*They* didn't do anything wrong Mar-tin."

"Well I hope you're not suggesting it was the boy's fault! You didn't make things any better!" he hissed into her ear.

Evan stopped in front of them, his shoulders slumping. "I wanna go home," he said, as his lip quivered.

Louisa crouched down beside him. "Evan, we're going to have a nice dinner with the Parsons and then go to look at the Christmas decorations. I'm sure you don't want to miss that." She reached out and tried to take hold of the child's hands but he pulled them up, burying them in his armpits.

"I just wanna go home."

Martin breathed out a heavy sigh. "Why don't you all go on ahead. Evan and I'll be there shortly."

"Want us to order a hot chocolate for you, Evan?" Chris asked as he tousled the boy's hair.

Evan stood, mum, shaking his head.

"Go on, Chris. We'll be along in a bit," Martin said, giving him a nod of his head. "And go ahead and order that hot chocolate."

Martin walked the boy over to a bench at a nearby bus stop and lowered himself down. "Are you disappointed that the baby saver wasn't as grand as you had hoped it would be?"

"Kinda," Evan said, kicking his toe against the pavement.

"Is there something else?"

He stuffed his hands into his pockets and shrugged his shoulders. "You and Mrs. Ellig-am were fighting ... about me. I told you I'd spoil it."

Martin squeezed his eyes shut as the child's words hit him like a punch to his solar plexus.

"I'm very sorry that you heard that."

"I keep tellin' ya, I gots really good ears."

Martin pulled in his chin and gave a grunt. "Yes, you do. And yes, your behaviour was perhaps not what most people would consider to be proper. That's something Mrs. Ellingham and I can straighten you out on later.

"But, Evan, a child is *not* responsible for the difficulties between two adults. Adults should be grown up enough to work out their differences. Your mother's running off was her own lookout, and your father's drinking was *his* own lookout, not yours. A child should not be held responsible for their parents' failures."

"But will Mrs. Ellig-am run off if *she* gets cross at me?"

Martin hesitated. "First of all, she's not cross at *you*—er, *with* you. I seem to have a way of frustrating her. But she's not cross.

"And to answer your question ... she's promised me that she'll never leave. And I trust her. We had a difference of opinion a while ago, and we should have waited to discuss it in private. Where we *would* work it out, by the way. But I—I apologise, Evan."

"That means you're sorry, right?"

"Mm, yes." He stifled a groan as he pulled himself to his feet. "Come on, your hot chocolate's getting cold."

By the time the bill had been settled at The Lemon Tree and the Ellinghams and the Parsons had made their way to Boscawen Street, the crowds had begun to gather.

Shoppers hurried in and out of stores as carollers, dressed in Victorian attire, worked their way up and down the street. White lights outlined the store fronts, and swags of greenery, bejewelled with tiny fairy lights, stretched across the street at every intersection.

A large facade of Santa's Workshop had been erected in the middle of the business district, and Chris and Martin steered their group in that direction.

"Wow, what's that?" Evan asked as the structure loomed ever larger.

"Well, let's go see, shall we?" Martin said as he tugged his crutch and the accompanying small load forward.

Evan froze in place as they came through the doorway. A gentle current of air, cooled as it passed over piles of man-made snow, hit their faces. On one corner of the intersection, snowballs were being tossed back and forth. On the other side, a small army of white soldiers was sprouting up from the ground.

The boy's eyes, filled with awe, drifted up to meet Martin's. "Are we gonna make a snowman?" he whispered—as if speaking them aloud might break the spell.

"If you still want to ... yes."

Several young women dressed as elves, complete with pointed ears and pointy-toed shoes, were collecting tickets for the event. Chris reached inside his coat and relinquished those that he had purchased as well as the four that the mayor had dropped off for Martin.

One of the women handed a shovel to Carole and two sets of cardboard reindeer antlers to Louisa, which she promptly perched on the heads of the two boys.

"Martin, was this your idea?" Louisa asked as her eyes scanned the wintery scene in front of them.

"Of course not. I would assume the council organised a committee and they—"

"No! To come here. Was this your idea?"

He squirmed under his wife's adoring gaze and mumbled, "The boy wanted to build a snowman, so we're going to build a snowman."

Louisa fought her impulse to throw her arms around him and kiss him, instead opting to reach out and caress his arm.

"What was that you were saying about Martin not doing surprises?" Carole asked as the two men and the boys headed off towards the machine that was generating the ice crystals.

"Well, obviously, I don't know my husband as well as I thought I did. Come on, let's go watch. This should be interesting," Louisa said as she gave a tug on her friend's arm.

Chapter 17

Martin headed to an area just outside the crowd, wincing and grumbling as an errant snowball hit him in the thigh.

"You okay, Mart?" Chris asked as he brushed the residue from his friend's trousers and fixator."

"I'm fine. Idiots. They should be careful where they're hurling those things; there are children around."

Evan gambolled about, fascinated by the impressions his feet left on the ground. He saw his guardian come to a stop next to a pile of fabricated snow and ran to catch up.

Martin pulled two pairs of mittens from the bag that Chris held in his hand. "Better put these on," he said giving the larger pair to Evan and James's smaller pair to Louisa.

"I don't know how ta build a snowman, Dr. Ellig-am," the seven-year-old said as he scanned his surroundings.

"I've not made one before either, Evan. But I believe the standard procedure is to roll the snow into balls. I'm just not sure there's enough snow to do that."

He scrutinised a three-foot-high pile next to him as he tugged at his ear. "How about we have Dr. Parsons scoop more snow on to this pile here and we'll start from there."

"That's a great idea! Come on, Old Doc. I'll help ya!" the boy said, pulling on Chris's sleeve.

"Here, Louisa, let me help," Carole said as she took the tiny mittens and slipped them over James's chubby hands. Louisa set her son down and he toddled off towards his older playmate.

Taking the shovel from his wife, Chris pushed it along the pavement, creating a harsh grating sound as it scraped the tarmac and sending a frightened James Henry running to his father.

Martin leaned down and rubbed his son's back. After a few reassuring words, the child felt confident enough to venture off again.

Once Chris had nearly filled the shovel with snow, he called to the seven-year-old. "Okay, you drag it over to your pile, Evan. He tipped the handle down and the boy took hold of it, grunting as he hauled it to their work area. Chris dumped the scoop of snow on to the existing pile before going back for another load.

Martin stood watch, contributing suggestions as he deemed necessary. "Lift with your legs, Chris. If you strain that back of yours again, we'll have to get a couple of those pointy-eared females to cart you back to your car."

"Maybe Mrs. Parsons could give him a piggyback ride," Evan said as he jumped between two puddles that had formed from the melting snow.

Chris stopped to give his friend a black look, then handed the shovel to Evan to haul back to the pile.

"I think you need a bit more on the east side Chris," Martin said. "One more scoop should do it Then we can start shaping this into something a bit more recognisable."

James was wary of the snow. He almost immediately took a tumble into it, getting it on his face and bursting into tears.

Martin sought out a nearby bench where he consoled the boy. He pulled his handkerchief from his pocket and wiped the tears and melted snow from his son's face. After a few minutes of clinging to his father's leg, James pattered back over and flopped into an icy pile, giggles bubbling from his mouth as the older boy scooped snow on top of him.

"Come on, Evan, you're falling down on the job," Chris said as he waited for the boy to haul another shovel load.

"Comin' Old Doc!" Evan shouted as he raced across an icy patch. The child's feet flew out from under him, and he came down hard on the pavement. There was a brief moment of silence before he let out a wail.

Martin hurried to his side and, holding on to his crutch, dropped to one knee. He sat the boy up and peeled the child's hands away from his face. "All right, let me see," he said, peering down at the bloodied nose and mouth, forcing back the reflex that was threatening to bring up his recently consumed dinner.

He pulled his already damp handkerchief from his back pocket and wiped the worst of the blood away. "Louisa, do you have a clean towel in the nappy bag?"

"Yes—yes. I think so," she said as she dug around briefly.

"Shh-shh-shh-shh-shh. You'll be all right, Evan," Martin said as his wife handed him a small tea towel. The boy's sobs continued as Martin quickly scanned the rest of his body before returning his attention to the most obvious damage.

"Well, you're going to have a sore mouth for a few days. Let me check your teeth," he said as he gently pulled the youngster's lips back before running a finger along his incisors and cuspids, feeling for chips in the enamel.

"You've loosened a couple of your front teeth, but they should tighten back up. I don't see that any lasting harm has been done. It's going to make eating difficult for a while, though."

Evan's sobs exploded into wails again, and Martin wrapped his good arm around him, pulling him to his chest. "Shh, you'll be all right."

"But Dr. Ellig-am, I won't be able ta eat the Christmas feast!"

"Well, let's wait and see. You might very well be just fine by then. It's more than a week away. But if not, we'll put your Christmas dinner through the blender."

He patted the child's back and released him from his embrace. "Right now though, we better get some ice on that. Then you have a snowman to finish," he said, giving the child a poke in the stomach and setting the cardboard antlers back on his head.

Louisa stood, arms wrapped around herself, watching the interaction between her normally gruff husband and the child. An uneasy feeling came over her as it became apparent that Martin's feelings for Evan ran much deeper than she had realised.

"Well, if you were going to take a tumble, you picked a good spot to do it, Evan," Martin said as he folded snow inside the towel and held it to the boy's face. "Plenty of ice."

He then turned to his own problem. He was on his knees on the hard pavement. His legs were tired, painful, and now wet, cold, and stiff. "How 'bout if I just stay here on the ground with you for a while, and we can work together to finish this snowman," he said to the boy, dropping to his backside next to the snow pile.

Evan blinked back the last of his tears and nodded his head.

Martin sat on the slush covered street, his legs straddling the pile as they fashioned it into a classic three-tiered snowman shape. He flexed his limbs, hoping the muscles would loosen after a bit, allowing him to get back up. "Oh gawd," he mumbled as the frigid snow melt began to soak through his trousers.

"He looks a little lumpy, don't you think?" Evan said as he scratched at his head with a mittened hand.

"I wouldn't worry about it," the doctor said. "I understand it's a benign condition in snowmen."

James ran over and flopped against his father, clutching his shirt in his small fists as he rested his head against his shoulder.

"What are we gonna use for his face?" Evan asked through the makeshift cold pack.

"I came prepared for that. Chris ... the bag?" Martin said as he crammed his frozen left hand under his arm to warm it.

Chris handed the sack to Evan, and the child upended it, shaking the contents out on to the ground. "Wow, you thought of everything, Dr. Ellig-am."

The charcoal eyes and mouth, and the carrot nose were added to the head. Then the charcoal buttons down the front, the bottom-most button being added by James—with some gentle assistance from his father.

Evan took a step back, admiring their work. "What'll we use for his arms? A snowman gots ta have arms."

"The spoons—that's what they're for," Martin said as he blew warm air into his hand.

Evan dropped his cold pack into Martin's lap then picked up two wooden kitchen spoons and jabbed them into the sides.

"Oh, that's adorable! Did you paint the mittens on the bowls of the spoons, Martin?" Carole asked as she leaned over to pick up James Henry.

"God, no. Jeremy did that." Martin pushed himself back from the frozen sculpture and began to contemplate his situation. His still inflexible legs were not going to allow for even a graceless escape from his current position.

The bench he'd been sitting on was about ten feet away, not far at all if he were walking the distance, but a long way to scoot on one's bum.

"Let me get another pair of hands, Mart. We'll get you up off the ground," Chris said as he started off in search of assistance.

"Chris, just help me— Oh, for goodness' sake," Martin grumbled as he watched his friend walk away. Wrinkling up his face, he began to push himself in the direction of the bench.

"I can help you, Dr. Ellig-am," Evan said, stepping forward and working his small fingers under his arms.

"You're too small, Evan. Take the towel and go sit down—ice that face of yours," he snapped.

The boy's shoulders slumped as the doctor passed him the cold pack.

Martin had worked himself to within four feet of the bench when Chris returned with help. He groaned as he looked up into the face of none other than Father Christmas himself. "Oh, brilliant. Just *brilliant*, Chris. Did you inform the media as well?"

"Didn't think of it, mate."

"Ho! Ho! Ho! Let's see if we can't get you back on your feet, eh young man?" Father Christmas boomed.

"I can manage!" Martin snapped as he brushed the jolly man's hand away.

"Better be on your best behaviour, Mart. Unless you want to get coal in your stocking," Chris said with a smirk.

Directing a severe scowl at his friend, Martin set his jaw and gave himself two final mighty shoves with his left arm and his legs, propelling himself to within reach of his objective. As he pulled his arm back to leverage his body from the ground, he felt himself being quickly lifted into the air and deposited on to the bench.

"A little elf told me you'd gotten yourself into a bit of trouble," Father Christmas said with a hearty chuckle, bending down and pulling open the Velcro closures on the doctor's trousers.

"What the bloody hell do you think you're doing? Bugger off!" Martin batted at the red, velvet-clad arm, shooting visual daggers at the man.

Evan leaned over and breathed a moist warning into his guardian's ear. "Now you've really done it, Dr. Ellig-am! You said *two* 'fensive things—and to Father Christmas, too!"

Louisa could see the frustration and embarrassment growing in her husband and was about to intervene when Martin leaned forward, scrutinising the man in red.

His anger evolved into confusion as the eyes began to look familiar.

Santa straightened himself to his full height and peered down at him imperiously. "Where's your coat? Good, God! You're just getting over pneumonia!"

Martin stared back at him, his brows drawn tightly together. "I get hot. *Not* that it's any of your business!"

"Relax, I just want to take a look at your pins while I'm here," Father Christmas said as he tugged again at the Velcro.

Chris watched with amusement as his friend screwed up his face.

"Oh, very clever, Chris! Why didn't you tell me it was—" He gave Evan a sideways glance, then wagged a finger at Ed Christianson. "Why didn't you tell me— *Father Christmas*—had a medical degree?"

"Gee, I don't know, Mart. Why did you tag me with my new moniker?"

"I didn't!"

"Okay, settle down," Ed said, eyeing the two like a headmaster refereeing a feud between school boys. "Chris says you're having pain in your legs."

"Oh, for heaven's sake! I've just been on my feet a lot."

"Well, I'm here. I might just as well take a look." He gave a tug on his red velvet trousers and knelt down, checking the wounds where his patient's pins had been removed a week and a half earlier before checking for any hardware which could have loosened. "All looks good, Martin. Just a lot of oedema. You need to get those feet up and ice the legs when you get home—understood?"

"*Yes*. What are you doing here anyway?"

Ed glanced over at the seven-year-old who was now watching him intently. "Just stopped to say hello to the boys and girls. Then I need to get on back to the North Pole. I have a lot of work to do before Christmas Eve, you know."

"I see."

Martin had put a lot of thought into how best to handle the tale of Father Christmas with his young charge. It was not as simple as it would be with James.

He and Louisa were in agreement that their son would learn about the story of Father Christmas as just that, a story. If James wished to pretend it to be true, he could.

But Evan already believed in the benevolent character, and the boy was doubtful that his name would be on the man's list of children to be visited on Christmas Eve.

Martin had managed to defer any serious discussions about Father Christmas up to now, but he hadn't realised the character was scheduled to make an appearance at the Winter Festival. He wouldn't be able to put it off any longer.

Ed took a seat on the opposite side of Martin's young charge and crossed his legs. "I believe your name is Evan, isn't it?"

The boy shimmied away from him and nestled against his guardian.

Leaning forward and resting his forearms on his thighs, Ed inspected the boy's recent wounds. "What happened to your face? You been in the wars with that snowman over there?"

Evan's hand slipped under Martin's arm as he peered up warily at the bearded man. "Kids aren't s'posed ta talk to strangers, you know," he said, his brow creasing.

"Yes, I do know. And that's a good rule to follow. But I'm not really a stranger, am I? I come to your house every Christmas."

Martin grimaced and gave the surgeon a shake of his head.

Evan's feet began to swing under him as he leaned into Martin. "Uh-uh. You never do. Dr. Ellig-am thinks you never came to my house 'cause you didn't know about me— 'cause my house was too hard ta find. But you *do* know about me 'cause you just said my name. And George Fletcher says your sleigh gots TGS, so you can find anybody. So how come you never came?"

Ed looked over at Martin, a growing concern registering on his face.

Martin reached down and slapped the closures shut on his trousers. "Let's talk about this when we get home tonight, Evan. I think we can make some sense of it all. But for now, it's okay to talk to this man. He's my friend, Ed."

"Father Christmas's name is Ed? I thought it was Santa."

"No, this is Mr. Christianson, my surgeon. His first name is Ed. He's just dressed as Father Christmas. Might be best if you kept that bit of information to yourself, though."

"That's kinda dodgy, Mr. Christianson," Evan said, shooting the man a disapproving glance. "It's not nice to try ta fool people."

"Thank you, Ed, for all your help," Louisa said, looking rather chagrined as she stepped in and took the boy by the hand, leading him over to the snowman. "Let's get one more picture, Evan. Then we better get you home to bed."

"Er, we have another stop to make, but we need to get a move on," Martin informed her before turning to his surgeon. "Thank you, Ed. I do appreciate your assistance."

"No problem, Martin. Have a Happy Christmas."

By the time they had walked back to the Parsons' SUV and driven over to the carpark where the reindeer were awaiting their big entry ahead of Santa's sleigh, James had fallen asleep and Evan was getting drowsy, leaning heavily against Carole.

The animals were still in the temporary pen that had been erected on the pavement, a thick bedding of straw laid down under them.

Chris turned when he heard Martin take in a gasp of air as he forced his stiffened limbs from the vehicle. "I can do this Martin. Why don't you just sit tight," he said as he stepped out into the chilly night air.

"No. I'm fine. I want to do this." Martin went to the back of the vehicle and removed a small bag that had been stashed behind the seat before pulling Evan's door open.

"Okay, let's go tick off another of the boxes on that list of yours," he said as he waited for the sleepy child to slide off the seat and on to the ground.

Evan rubbed at his eyes and looked around, his gaze settling on the antlered beasts in front of him. "Those—those are reindeers!"

"Yes they are. And if I remember correctly, you, for some unimaginable reason, want to feed one," Martin said, handing the child the bag as they headed towards the pen.

Even peered into the sack and gave his guardian a small smile before his face became suddenly serious. "They won't bite me, will they?"

"Nah, they won't bite ya, lad," a short, stocky gentleman wearing canvas coveralls and wellies said as they approached. "Me and the wife 'ave been hand feedin' 'em since they was calves. I'd trust them afore I'd trust a chicken."

Martin introduced himself to the man. "I, er ... appreciate your willingness to help the boy out, Mr. Ferris."

"Taint no problem. Come on over 'ere, Evan. Whatcha got in yer bag fer 'em?"

"Carrots. Dr. Ellig-am gots a whole bunch of 'em here," the boy said as he held the striped, plastic sack up for the man to see.

"You know the way to a reindeer's heart, that's fer sure. Carrots is like candy to 'em. Pull one on outta there Evan. See if Clyde 'ere wants one."

"He gots a name?" the boy asked as he yanked an orange titbit from the bag.

"Had ta have somethin' ta put on the marriage licence, eh?" Mr. Ferris gave the child a wink and tousled his hair.

"Clyde's got a *wife?*"

"You bet 'e does. That'd be Sally over there."

"Oh, gawd," Martin groaned as an image came to mind of Clive and Sally Tishell, smiling at him with cardboard antlers atop their heads.

"Them two's pretty near inseparable." Sleigh bells jingled as Mr. Ferris slipped a harness over the head of one of the does.

Evan giggled as Clyde extended his lips to pull at the carrot. "What does Sally do when her husband's gotta pull the sleigh?"

"*Sally* wears the pants in that family, Evan. Clyde stays at 'ome. 'E's bone idle, that one. 'Cept durin' the rut. Ol' Clyde goes all out durin'—"

"Ohh, no-no-no-no-no!" Martin exclaimed. "I'm not going to try to explain *that* tonight, as well. Let's move this conversation on to something else."

He wrinkled up his nose as the reindeer left a trail of viscous saliva on his young charge's hand.

"How come *Sally* pulls the sleigh?"

"Take a look at ol' Clyde's head. You see any antlers?"

"Uh-uh. What happened to 'em?"

"The blokes lose 'em in late autumn. The gals keep 'em til spring. Wouldn't be quite fittin' ta 'ave Father Christmas bein' pulled 'ouse to 'ouse by a bunch of antlerless reindeer, now would it?"

Evan's brows pulled together. "So all of Santa's reindeers are—*girls?*"

"'Fraid so, little lad."

Sally pushed past Clyde and worked her nose into Evan's bag of carrots, pulling the last of them into her mouth.

"Well, that's that then." Martin said, taking the empty bag from the child's hand and shoving it into his pocket. "We should be going. What do you say to Mr. Ferris, Evan?"

"Thanks for lettin' me feed your reindeer, Mr. Ferris. You got some really nice ones."

"It was my pleasure, boy. You folks have a Happy Christmas."

Both boys were sound asleep by the time they arrived back at the Parsons. Chris shifted Evan into the Lexus and Louisa held James as Carole moved his car seat.

"Well, you have a wonderful Christmas," Louisa said. "Do you have big plans?"

"It's actually going to be a quiet one. Chris's mum and dad are going to Paris, and my side's getting together at my parents'. Chris has to work on Boxing Day, so we decided to stay home this year.

"Dan's going to be in London with a school group, so ... should be romantic," Carole said as she raised her eyebrows at her husband.

Louisa held back her suggestion that the Parsons join them on Christmas Day, opting instead to wait and discuss it with Martin first. "Well, again ... have a wonderful holiday and thank you so much for all your help today."

"Oh, this was fun! I bet those two little ones sleep well tonight."

Martin gave a grunt and ducked into the car.

"Evan's been getting up a lot in the night ... wearing Martin out a bit," Louisa explained.

"Well, better luck tonight."

Once they had cleared the traffic near the city, Louisa reached over and took her husband's hand. "Martin."

He lifted his head from the headrest and turned to look at her. "Hmm?"

"Martin, what you did for Evan today was ... and don't take this the wrong way, but it was very, very sweet of you. He has memories that'll last him a lifetime."

"I hope so," he said, pulling in his chin. "I'm going to need to straighten out this whole Father Christmas mess, you know."

"Oh, Martin, just let him enjoy the magic of it for a while. Children *love* Father Christmas."

"Mm." He laid his head back again and closed his eyes.

Chapter 18

Martin's hand became heavy in hers, and his breaths deepened as the miles passed them by. She glanced over at him, slumped against the window in his seat, and despite the wonderful evening they had together, her heart felt strangely heavy.

As they came around one of the turns on the road leading into Portwenn, Louisa swerved suddenly to avoid a large box in the middle of the lane.

Martin's head thunked against the window. He grunted softly, and began to stir.

"Sorry 'bout that. There was something in the road back there," she explained.

Pulling up his arm, he looked down at his watch. *Half past eight.* "The boys are wet and dirty. They should have baths before bed, don't you think?"

"Yeah. I'll get James bathed first thing." She hesitated and then glanced in the rear-view mirror at the slumbering seven-year-old. "Martin ... I think we need to talk about—" She jerked her head in the boy's direction.

"Problem?" he asked.

"Not a *problem* really. I just think it would be good to be sure we're both thinking along the same lines."

"Ah."

He looked out at the harbour as the car climbed Roscarrock hill, the moonlit vista widening as they neared the surgery.

His wife shifted the gearbox into park, and as he pushed his door open, a cold damp wind rushed in from the sea, sending a shiver through him.

Nerve endings in his legs sent pain signals racing to his brain as he shifted his weight from the seat, momentarily taking his breath away. He waited for his body to adjust to the sensation before pulling the back door open and unbuckling his charge's seatbelt. "We're home, Evan. Time to wake up."

The boy blinked sleepy eyes at his guardian and then moved quickly to the centre of the seat. "I don't *wanna* go home!"

"We're at the surgery, Evan ... my house. Come on out." Another shiver ran through him as the wind penetrated his damp clothing. "Come on. Hurry up, I'm getting cold."

Evan slid across the seat and dropped to the ground, latching on to Martin's wrist as they made their way around the back of the house.

The air still smelled of spices when they pushed through the door and into the warmth of the kitchen, and the seven-year-old went immediately to the counter to assure himself that all was well with his little platoon of gingerbread men.

"Do you want one before bed?" Louisa asked as she pulled the door open on the refrigerator and removed the jug of milk.

"Yeah. Can Dr. Ellig-am have one too?" Evan turned to Martin. "You could eat the special one I made you," he said through tentative tender, lips.

Martin pulled out a chair and sank into it heavily. "No thank you, Evan."

"Here's a glass of milk for each of you. I need to go bathe James. Then it'll be your turn, young man," Louisa said as she tapped a finger on the child's head and walked off under the stairs.

The boy leaned his forearms on the table and pulled his feet up behind him, dangling against the edge as he peered at Martin through narrowed eyes. "I think you look hungry. I'll go get your biscuit," he said decisively before dropping back to the floor and racing towards the hallway.

"Evan, come back here!"

The child's wet trainers squeaked against the slate as he stood in front of the doctor, his hands folded behind his back.

"You need to take those shoes off before you track up the surgery. Then ... well, I suppose you can get one of those biscuits from the counter for me."

Evan dropped down on to his bum and tugged as the soaked trainers resisted his efforts.

"You should untie your shoes before you take them off, you know," Martin admonished.

Pulling at one of the wet laces, the seven-year-old immediately transformed the bow into a knot.

The doctor snapped his fingers. "Here, give me your foot."

Lying back on the floor with his foot propped on his guardian's knee, Evan stared up at him while the knot was picked loose and the shoe was pulled from his foot. "I had a lot of fun today, Dr. Ellig-am."

"Good. Now the other one." Another snap of the fingers.

"What was *your* favourite part?" the child asked.

Martin pulled the wet socks from the boy's feet and warmed his cold toes in his hands as he thought through the question. "I've always liked Truro Cathedral ... the rose windows. They remind me of a kaleidoscope my aunt Joan would let me play with when I spent summers with her."

Martin inspected the nearly healed cut on the bottom of the child's foot and gave it a pat. "We better wash, then eat those biscuits. It's already past your bedtime."

Martin turned the handle on the tap and pumped soap on to his young charge's hands. "Make sure you get around your fingernails. God knows what organisms lurk in reindeer effluvium."

"My favourite part was after I fell."

"After you fell?" Martin said, handing the boy a paper towel.

Evan dried his hands, then selected two gingerbread men and laid one in front of his guardian before taking a seat next to him. He gave a shrug of his shoulders. "I liked the hug."

Martin reached for his glass, trying to swallow back the painful constriction in his throat with a gulp of milk.

"Break a piece off and dip it into your glass," he said, taking notice of the discomfort the boy was having while trying to eat his biscuit.

Crumbs sprinkled down on to the table top as a small, brown arm was snapped off. Then the seven-year-old dunked the titbit into his milk. He slipped the softened bite into his mouth and gave the doctor a lopsided grin.

"Better?" he asked, an eyebrow raised.

"Yep."

By the time Martin and Evan finished with their snack, Louisa had fished James Henry from the bath water. "All right, your turn Evan," she said as she wrapped her son in a towel.

Martin leaned over and flipped the trip lever on the drain, allowing the water to be released. "We need to clean up that face," he said as he worked the older boy's hoodie over his head, careful to avoid bumping his mouth.

"You're not going to be down on those knees anymore today, Martin," Louisa said, lowering her brow at him. "I'll take care of Evan's bath."

"*Uh-uh!* Yer a girl! *And* yer Mrs. Ellig-am!" the boy screeched in alarm. "That wouldn't be—"

The boy hesitated as he searched for a word he could get out through his painful lips. "That wouldn't be—not 'fensive."

"I'll ... sit on the edge of the tub or something," Martin said as the child's pleading eyes fixed on him. He flipped the trip lever back down and started to run a fresh bath. "Could you bring several face cloths and a towel?"

"Martin, I don't think—"

"Louisa, just bring me what I need."

She gave him a scowl before going to the laundry cupboard, returning with the requested items.

"You *will* be careful, won't you?" she asked, eyeing him anxiously.

"We survived a night on the moor. I think we can manage fifteen minutes in the bathtub, don't you, Evan?"

The boy tried to restrain a smile, and a small snort erupted from his nose.

"All right, I get the message. I'll leave you two to it, then," Louisa said as she began to pull the door shut behind her. "I'll be just across the hall if you need me."

"Yes." Martin leaned over to shut off the tap. "Dip your fingers in there, is it the right temperature?"

Evan leaned forward and swam his fingers through the water. "I don't know if it's the right temperature, but it feels good."

"Okay, pull off those trousers and pants, then get in and lie down," the doctor said, turning away to give him privacy.

He handed a face cloth back to the boy. "Cover up your—bits—with that."

A small stream of water skittered across the floor tiles as the child splashed down into the tub.

"Are you ready?" Martin asked.

"For what?"

"For me to turn around. Do you have your bits covered?"

"Yeah."

Martin lowered himself on to the lid of the toilet and then shifted himself to the side of the tub before rolling up his sleeves.

"I'm going to put a wet washcloth on your face, Evan ... soak that dried blood off of there."

The child pulled a hand up to wipe the renegade drops of water from his eyes, revealing both the yellowing bruises left by Jim Hanley as well as the accumulation of dirt in the creases around his armpit. It had been some time since the child had received the attention of a caring adult.

Martin reached for the bottle of bath soap and applied it to a third cloth. "Okay, you hold that wet flannel on your face and sit up. You're going to get a proper scrubbing tonight."

Evan sat quietly as the face cloth worked its magic.

"All right, I think you're pretty clean, but I need to wash the bits."

"Kay, but don't look."

The doctor finished the job quickly and returned the shroud to its assigned location. "Okay, all done. Let's see how that face is looking." He peeled the wet cloth away and inspected the damage carefully.

"Well, it's not pretty, but faces heal quickly due to the plentiful blood supply to the head and neck. We'll keep icing that. I'm guessing you'll be in fine form by Christmas Day."

Squirting a generous amount of shampoo into his hand, Martin lathered the boy's hair. Then rinsed it, taking note of a bit of eczema on his scalp. Yet another potential sign of neglect.

"I think we're done." He shifted back to the toilet lid before pulling himself to his feet with his crutch. "I'll leave your towel here. You wrap yourself up and I'll go get your pyjamas."

Pulling the bathroom door shut behind him, Martin leaned back against the bedroom wall and took in a deep breath as he wiped at his eyes.

"You okay?" his wife's concerned voice asked.

His head shot up. "Mm. I need to fetch his things." He moved past their bed and squeezed by Louisa as she stood in the doorway.

James was sleeping soundly when a pyjama-clad Evan crawled into bed, and he and Martin spoke in hushed voices.

"Evan, I was wondering... how do you feel about Father Christmas?" Martin asked as he pulled the blankets up and tucked them under the boy's chin.

"You mean the real one or the Ed one?"

"The Father Christmas who you think has forgotten you every Christmas."

Evan shook his head slowly. "He didn't forget, Dr. Ellig-am. I told ya that. I think he doesn't come 'cause I always spoil it."

Martin rubbed a palm across his face, trying to pull together words that might alleviate the child's sense of guilt. "Evan, do you trust me?"

"You never lie, Dr. Ellig-am."

"Well, that's not entirely correct. When I told you I thought Father Christmas never came to your house because he didn't know about you ... that wasn't an honest answer. I just didn't know how much I should tell you at that time.

"But I think you need to know the truth about Father Christmas and why he never paid you a visit ... so you don't continue to blame yourself."

Martin now had the boy's rapt attention, and he stared back uncomfortably at his clear blue eyes. "Well, maybe we should begin with the people who were in costumes outside the church."

"With all the animals?"

"Mm. They were there because many people believe that a very long time ago, a baby was born. A baby that was sent to save the world. And because the baby was sent to save the world, he's called the Saviour."

"What can a *baby* save the world from?" Evan asked, sitting himself up and crawling into his guardian's lap.

"Ow!" Martin rubbed at his thigh as he shifted the child to a more comfortable location. "That's a much more involved discussion that I don't want to get started on tonight. But let's just say that the day the baby ... the Saviour ... was born—Christmas Day—is a very special day to many people, and they like to re-enact that day by dressing like the people who were there when it happened.

"They include the animals that may have been there at the time as well. That's why the woman from St. Kew's was so enthusiastic when she told you about having a baby Saviour ... or saver."

"So, when I called the man's baby stupid, I said something special was stupid?"

"Yes. But you didn't understand that at the time, so I think we can give you a pass. But I suppose in general—

just to be on the safe side—it would be best if you refrained from name calling."

"Sorry, Dr. Ellig-am," Evan said as he slumped into Martin's chest. "So which of the people does Father Christmas dress like?"

"What people?"

"When that special baby was born."

"Father Christmas isn't trying to dress like any of those people. And I really don't know why he dresses in that ridiculous outfit."

Martin's eyes drifted shut momentarily, his head nodding, before he brought his hand up and rubbed it across his face. "We're getting off track here Evan. My point is that people were very excited about this baby when it was born and they brought the baby gifts. This is why we give gifts to others at Christmastime. And the story of Father Christmas grew from that idea of giving to others."

Evan sat quietly for several moments then asked, "So Father Christmas started by bringing gifts to that baby?"

Martin blew out a hiss of air and scratched his head. "No, Father Christmas is a character who represents a-a feeling—an attitude that many people embrace at Christmastime. He's not a real person, Evan. He's a spirit of—generosity, I guess you could say."

"But if he's not really a person, then how come grown-ups tell kids he is?"

"It's very confusing, I know. And I'm sorry about that. I think that for many children it's enjoyable to believe in Father Christmas—it's exciting. Those children grow up, have their own children, and want to share that experience, I suppose."

"But the kids at school get presents from Father Christmas, so he *gots* to be a real person."

"Those presents come from their parents, Evan. But some parents either don't have the means—the money to buy presents—or they choose not to, as was the case with my parents.

"I'm not sure which was the case with your parents, but either way, it was *not* because you weren't a good child. You're a very fine boy, Evan.

"I'm telling you the truth about Father Christmas because I think it's very important that you understand why he never came to your house. That it has nothing to do with whether you were naughty or nice. That you *didn't* spoil anything. And you need to be able to trust me if you're going to feel safe with me. It was time for you to know the truth, and I'm very sorry if you're disappointed."

"The kids at school think Father Christmas is real. It's fun for them."

"Yes, for many children it is. And for that reason, it would be best to not discuss what we've talked about with any of the students at the school. But for some children, the story can hurt—very much."

Evan sat so still for so long that Martin had begun to think he had fallen asleep, but then he stirred.

"It still hurts a little," he said suddenly. "But it doesn't hurt as much as it did." He crawled from Martin's lap and pushed his feet under the blankets. "Dr. Ellig-am ... can I have another hug?"

Martin ducked his head and cleared his throat. Then, he leaned over and wrapped his good arm around the boy's small body.

"Goodnight, Evan," he said as he pulled himself to his feet and crossed the room to his son's cot, laying a broad hand on the toddler's fuzzy head.

He paused in the doorway when Evan called out, "Dr. Ellig-am ... they're called genitals, not bits. Just thought you'd like ta know."

"Mm, yes. Thank you, Evan. Goodnight."

"G'night, Dr. Ellig-am."

Martin was spent. He moved back across the landing to their bedroom and pulled a fresh vest and boxers from the dresser before continuing on to the bathroom. When he emerged fifteen minutes later his wife was in her pyjamas, sitting in bed, scribbling into a notepad. She hurriedly slipped it into the drawer on her bedside table and turned the blankets back for her husband.

"Lie down and get comfortable, Martin," she said as she picked up her pot of cocoa butter. "I want to work on those legs, then I'll go down and get the cold packs."

"That really isn't necessary. But the ice would be good."

"Just hush and lie down. We need to talk anyway," Louisa said as she pushed her husband back on to his pillow.

The wind whistled softly through the draughty old windows, pushing a ripple of cool air across Martin's legs. His wife's warm hands felt comforting as she began to work the circular massage motions around his fixators.

"How did Evan's bath go?"

"Fine. He was overdue for a jolly good scrubbing though. You, er ... said you wanted to talk about him. Is there a problem?"

She dipped her fingers into the pot of cream again and smoothed the cocoa butter on to her hands. "Not a problem, as such. I am wondering what you think may happen with him ... when Children's Services will figure out what to do with him."

Martin winced at his wife's words and turned his head away. "That Dunwich fellow who came by—"

"Delaney, Martin. *Delaney.*"

"Yes. He wasn't just making a social call. He wanted to let me know about the arrangements for Evan's father's funeral."

"Oh, gawd," she moaned. "I hadn't thought about that. I don't want to have to pay my respects to that man."

"You don't have to. And I don't think Evan should either. I've given it some thought ... I'll go. That way if the boy has any questions, I can answer them."

Louisa patted her husband's hip before giving him a gentle nudge. "Turn over and I'll work on the other side."

Martin rolled to his left before settling in on his belly. "He, er ... he asked if we might consider keeping Evan for a while ... to avoid a disruption at a traumatic time."

Louisa's movements were suspended and Martin heard her huff out a breath. "How long is he thinking?"

"He didn't say."

"And ... what did you tell him?"

"I said that we'd discuss it and I'd get back to him."

"Oh, Martin. I don't know. I mean, through the holidays, yes. But ... well, we do have our own child who needs us. And you're still recovering—surgeries ahead of you yet—physical therapy. Not to mention what you're trying to work through with Dr. Newell and the difficulties the two of us have had."

Martin worked his way on to his back again and stared up at her. "I know you're concerned. But we can make a real difference, Louisa. When I was a surgeon, I made a difference. I saved lives—so frequently it became routine. I know that this is different, but we can save Evan's life, in a sense."

Louisa screwed the lid back on the pot of cream and returned it to the table top. "I'm going to go get the cold packs ... be right back."

A wave of nausea came over Martin as he lay with his eyes closed ... thoughts of Evan being shuffled from one foster home to the next going through his head. The boy would, in all likelihood, end up going down the same dismal road as his parents.

"Here we go," Louisa said cheerfully. She tucked the assortment of pillows that sat on the chair under her husband's legs before laying the cold packs on top of them. "You want an extra blanket? I can get the duvet out of the cupboard if you like."

"I'm fine, Louisa."

She looked at him—at his pained expression. "I do understand your feelings, you know. I'm just—"

"No! You obviously do not or you wouldn't be so anxious to be rid of the boy!"

"I'm *not* anxious to be rid of him, Martin. But we have to be realistic. Look at you! Your legs are swollen, you're in pain—exhausted. You can't do it all, Martin, and I *will* not stand by and watch you kill yourself trying!"

"Ohh, now you're exaggerating. Having a seven-year-old boy in the house isn't going to be the end of me."

Louisa pushed her pillow back against the headboard and nestled into it, her arms folded across her chest. Neither of them spoke for several painfully silent minutes.

Martin ran his palm over his face and then turned to her. "I would appreciate it very much if you would agree to having Evan here a while longer."

Louisa's face softened and she reached out, stroking her husband's cheek. "Let me sleep on it, hmm?"

He gave her a tired nod. "Yes."

Chapter 19

Louisa grabbed hold of her husband's vest, restraining him as she sat herself up in the bed. "You stay here. I'll go this time," she said as she swung her legs over the side and reached for her dressing gown.

Martin lay, staring at the grey ceiling as he strained to make out what was being said across the hall. The fresh air and excitement had not had the sedating effect on Evan that they had hoped for, and once again the child's whimpers and nocturnal distress had roused them from their sleep.

The only upside of the regularity of these occurrences was James Henry's seeming adaptation to the nightly commotion. Though Martin and Louisa's sleep was interrupted with equal regularity to the seven-year-old's, the toddler rarely stirred.

Martin's eyes had just drifted shut again when a sudden shaking of the bed jolted him back to wakefulness. He groaned as Evan landed heavily on him, the boy's fists clutching on to his vest.

"Sorry, I couldn't stop him." Louisa said softly. "He's upset ... and he needs fresh pyjamas. I'll put the clean ones here. If you can help him change, I'll take care of the sheets."

"Mm, yes." The boy lay mum as Martin rubbed his palm over his shoulder. When he heard the harsh shudders ease into deep breaths and felt the child loosen his grip on his shirt, he asked, "Do you want to talk about it?"

Evan's fingers inched along his guardian's arm before coming to rest on his hand. "You took me home. You took me to my house and you left me there 'cause— 'cause I spoiled it. I was too much trouble." The boy sucked in a ragged breath. "No one was there and I was all alone."

Martin pulled his hand out from under the small weight and brushed it across the boy's head. "It was a dream, Evan. I haven't left you alone."

He pulled his knees under him and wrapped his arms around his guardian's neck.

"We better fix you up with some dry pyjamas, then tuck you back into bed," the doctor said, returning the hug with a mannered pat on the boy's back.

Martin pulled himself free of the child's grasp and stepped out on to the cold floor. He flipped the light switch in the bathroom, slapping a hand to his eyes before pulling the face cloth, still damp from its previous use, from the side of the tub. After running it under the hot tap, he returned to the bedroom. "Up you get Evan. Let's take care of things so you can get back to sleep."

Evan crawled to the edge of the mattress before cascading to the floor. He stood with his arm pulled up over his face.

The doctor sighed and reached back, turning off the bathroom light. "Okay, off with the wet ones."

Evan pulled his other arm up and pressed the heels of his hands to his eyes, the filtered moonlight giving him away. Martin leaned over and pushed the boy's bottoms and pants down to his knees. "You'll need to take it from there. I'm having difficulty bending my legs."

The child wriggled free of the encumbrances, keeping his face well concealed.

"This happens to all children at one time or another, Evan. It's all right." Martin leaned down again and wiped the urine from the child's skin with the face cloth. "I need to rinse this and hang it up. You put the dry things on," he said, tugging the boy's hand from his face before pressing the clean pyjamas into it.

"I can tuck him back in," Louisa said as they met on the landing a few minutes later.

Martin glanced down as Evan's fingers tightened around his wrist. "It's fine; I'll do it. It'll just take a few minutes. You go back to sleep."

Louisa reached up and stroked her thumb across her husband's cheek before returning to their bedroom.

Martin pulled the covers back and Evan dove under his arm, nestling into the fresh bedding.

"Will you stay 'til I fall asleep?" the boy asked, his dewy eyes glistening in the bit of light seeping in the blanket covered window.

"Yes. Evan ... your dream. I'm sure it was frightening being left alone, but try to remember that what you dream is *not* real. I promise you that I'll make sure that you're taken care of. That *is* real. Now, close your eyes and go back to sleep."

Martin had returned to his own bed once Evan had dropped off and was awakened five hours later by the gleeful giggles of children, drifting up from downstairs.

He glanced at the clock and pulled himself quickly from the bed, hurrying to the shower while grumbling about his wife's recent tendency to turn his alarm off when she deemed his sleep insufficient.

As he entered the kitchen a while later, his wife looked up and flashed him a smile. "Good morning!" she said before taking note of his stormy expression. She got up from the table and turned towards the counter, reaching into the cupboard. "Cup of coffee?"

"Louisa, you are aware that I'm a doctor with a full schedule of patients this morning, aren't you? That I need to have time to read through patient notes before I actually see those patients? That I might possibly want time to eat breakfast before I start my day? How am I to do all that if you turn off my alarm and let me sleep until all hours of the morning?"

She glanced into the lounge at the two small boys playing on the floor and then lowered her head, peering at him through narrowed eyes.

"Yes, Martin. I *am* aware that you're a doctor, *and* that you have patients to see this morning. But I heard Mrs. Bollard leave a message on the answer phone. She's not coming in.

I checked your appointment book, saw she would have been your first patient and decided to let you sleep a bit longer. And it's not all hours of the morning, it's half eight."

She huffed out a breath. "Now ... would you or would you not like a cup of coffee?"

Martin dropped his gaze to the floor and cleared his throat softly. "I see. Erm, yes. A cup of coffee would be—good."

The threatening storm had dissipated and Louisa set a cup of espresso on the table as her husband took a seat. "I heard you in the shower so I got your breakfast ready," she said as she plated up an ample serving of scrambled eggs and toast, setting it in front of him before going to the refrigerator to retrieve the orange marmalade.

"Thank you," he said softly. "I had a discussion with Evan last night—about the baby saver and the Father Christmas confusion."

Louisa set the jam jar on the table and took a seat. "What did you say?"

"I—told him the truth. He need—"

"Ohh, Martin! You didn't!" she whispered stridently.

He gave his head a shake as he tipped his nose into the air. "He needed to know, Louisa. He was blaming himself for never having had Christmas at his house. He thought Father Christmas didn't come because he had spoiled it."

Louisa flicked her ponytail and crossed her arms in front of her. "But did you really have to take the fun out of it, Martin?"

"*Fun?* Louisa, there's nothing fun about being the only child at school to not get anything for Christmas!" he hissed, glancing over his shoulder at the two children in the lounge.

She pushed her chair back and began to pull things from the table, dishes clattering as they dropped heavily into the sink.

Martin took in a calming breath as he waited for his wife to reclaim her seat and then asked, "Have you, er ... given any more thought to what we discussed last night?"

Louisa shook her head slowly. "Martin, I've been thinking about it all morning and—" She looked up at him before quickly averting her eyes from his beseeching gaze. "I just think that—I just can't agree to something when I think it could have an adverse effect on your recovery, Martin. I'm sorry."

Martin laid his fork down and pushed himself away from the table before limping off under the stairs.

The door to the consulting room slammed shut and Louisa breathed out a heavy sigh. Then, picking up her husband's untouched breakfast, she set it on the ground outside the back door. Buddy, curled up by the potting bench, hurried over to indulge himself as Louisa ran her hand over his head.

She returned to the kitchen to clear the breakfast dishes from the table. The decisive conclusion that she had reached earlier in the morning began to lean towards uncertainty as she stared blindly out the window, thinking about the look of desperation she had seen on her husband's face.

Her train of thought was broken by the sound of Aunt Ruth's voice.

"Good morning."

"Ruth, hello!" she said, picking up a plate next to the sink and setting it in the dishwasher. "Take your coat off and stay a while."

"That phrase always seems to put me on the defensive for some reason. Too many years in the company of psychopaths, I suppose," the woman said as she lowered herself into a chair.

Martin's elderly psychiatrist aunt had spent most of her adult life working with the criminally insane at England's infamous Broadmoor Hospital.

"Tea?" Louisa offered.

"Yes, please." Ruth pulled the basket from the centre of the table and began to sort through the tea bags. "I just thought I'd stop by to see how my nephew's doing."

Louisa placed a cup in front of her and filled it with hot water before refilling her own. "He's doing surprisingly well actually. Despite the fact that he's not been getting a lot of sleep."

Ruth sat up a little straighter. "Oh? Not the nightmares again, I hope."

"Well, as a matter of fact, yes ... in a way." The younger woman gave a discreet nod towards their little lodger.

"We had a discussion last night. Martin would like to extend the current arrangements a while longer, but ... well, I just don't think it's a good idea Ruth. Martin's getting worn out, and it's too much stress on him right now."

Ruth eyed her nephew's wife, shifting in her chair. "I see. So, you think the current situation is stressing him?"

Louisa stirred a splash of milk into her tea. "He's trying to do too much. Keeping up with patients, being a father, a husband, *and* taking on this added responsibility."

"Does Martin feel he's under too much stress?"

"You know Martin, he doesn't recognise stress. He just keeps putting one foot in front of the other. Only now this—this current situation, as you put it, has become almost all consuming to him. He seems so driven to do all he can, and the stress is beginning to show."

Ruth tapped her fingers on the table top and watched as Evan stacked wooden blocks into a tower before James Henry knocked it down. "Perhaps the two of you could visit with Barrett Newell. It might very well prove useful in this circumstance."

"Hmm, possibly. Martin does listen to him. He's a doctor; he might be able to get through to him—help him to see that he can't take this on right now."

Ruth eyed Louisa briefly then stirred another spoonful of sugar into her tea. "Yes, that's *exactly* what I was thinking."

As the two women chatted, Martin pored over patient notes in his consulting room, trying to ignore the tempest inside him. The silence in the room was broken by two firm raps on the door. "Come!" he called out.

"Morning, boss," Jeremy said as he stepped into the room. The young man walked over and took a seat, dropping his backpack on to the floor. "How did the big outing go last night. The boy have a good time?"

Martin tapped a set of notes down into its sleeve and laid it on a pile on the corner of his desk. "It went well ... for the most part. And yes, he had a good time."

Jeremy tipped back in his chair and cocked his head at him. "You look tired. Are you getting enough sleep?"

Martin grabbed on to his crutch and pulled himself to his feet. "Don't *you* start in, Jeremy."

"It was just a question, mate."

Pulling the flaps back on a box of supplies from Mrs. Tishell, Martin began to shelve the vials and packets inside. "Erm, I suppose you need to know—I used sixty milligrams of Toradol last night, and again at eight this morning."

Jeremy leaned over and unzipped his backpack before pulling out his notepad. "You overdo it last night?"

"Mm." He limped back to his desk and jotted notes on to a pad before tearing it off and stuffing it into his pocket.

"I was informed by Chris Parsons that they've seen an increase in influenza A cases. A surge in numbers is expected after the holidays, so be extra vigilant in your screenings. It's bound to make it this way eventually."

"Yep, I'll keep my eyes skinned." The aide zipped his backpack shut and walked to the exam couch. "Okay, let's take a look."

"I'm fine, Jeremy."

"That may be, but you're not seeing patients until I check you over."

Martin rolled his eyes upward and blew out a hiss of air, before conceding defeat and taking a seat on the table.

"Uh-uh. Don't sit—down to your boxers. I'm going to grab a cup of coffee—give you some time to undress," he said as he headed towards the door.

Martin threw his head to the side and wrinkled up his face. "Ohh, is that really necessary?"

Jeremy snapped his fingers at him. "Down to the boxers. I'll be back in a minute."

Louisa gave the young man a smile as he entered the kitchen, and Evan hurried over to greet him. "Hi there, Mr. Portman!"

"Hi, Evan. I heard *you* had a good time last night."

"Uh-huh. We saw lots of stuff. The coloured windows, and the baby's donkey. And I got ta sit on it, too.

"And we made a snowman and saw Father Christmas. Did you know he's not real? Dr. Ellig-am said two 'fensive words to him, but it doesn't matter 'cause he's just Ed.

"And we saw the reindeers that pull Santa's sleigh and—" The boy squeezed one eye shut and scratched at his head. "Hmm, if Father Christmas is pretend, then does that mean that reindeers aren't real either?"

"No, they're real. But they don't live around here," the aide said, leaning over to inspect the little boy's face. "What happened there?"

Evan touched his mouth, gingerly. "I fell when we were makin' our snowman. But Dr. Ellig-am says I'll be in fine form for the Christmas Feast."

Louisa moved towards the doorway. "Jeremy, could you watch the boys—just for a few minutes? I need to have a word with Martin."

Evan tugged at the aide's shirt sleeve as Jeremy glanced quickly at his boss's wife. "Yeah, that's fine," he said before returning his attention to the boy.

Making her way under the stairs, Louisa knocked softly on the consulting room door before pushing through. "What's going on? Is something wrong?" she asked as she scanned her scantily clad husband.

"Jeremy's just being overly conscientious."

She tipped her head down and squinted her eyes at him. "Hmm. No secrets, right?"

Martin screwed up his face. "I've had some pain—which is to be expected after a strenuous day. I used some Toradol, *which* I told my punctilious health aide about by the way."

"But you forgot to mention it to your punctilious wife," Louisa said softly as she stepped closer.

"Yes."

"May I ask why?"

Martin reached for his vest. "If Jeremy's not going to come back to perform this examination I may as well get dressed."

Louisa pulled the shirt from his reach and held it behind her back. "He's watching the boys while I have a word with you. Now, answer my question, Martin. Why did you not tell me about using the Toradol?"

"May I please have my vest? I'm at a distinct disadvantage here," he said as he tried to reach behind her.

Taking another step forward, she held the shirt out to him and waited as he slipped it on. Then she gave him what he had come to know as her don't-mess-with-me look.

"I didn't want to give you another reason to say no to keeping Evan with us."

"I see." Her arms slipped around his chest. "You have an appointment with Dr. Newell tomorrow. Maybe he could see us together ... help us get this sorted, hmm?"

Martin cocked his head at her. "So you're not saying no?"

"I'm *saying* ... let's work this through with Dr. Newell ... not bring it up again until then."

"Ah ... yes."

"Good. I better get back to the boys," she said as she pressed her forehead to his. "I'll send your punctilious aide in so that he can complete his overly conscientious examination."

Martin took his wife's chin in his hand and kissed her.

As the couple worked out their temporary truce, Jeremy had given each of the boys a glass of milk. Then he tried to entertain the toddler with toys on the floor while answering a peppering of questions from the seven-year-old.

"But do the girls *really* wear the pants in the family?" Evan asked.

James Henry toddled from the lounge to the step up into the kitchen before dropping to his knees and crawling over to the aide.

"Jebby, Jebby," the seventeen-month-old said as he patted Jeremy's leg.

"So *do* the girls wear pants?" the seven-year-old persisted.

"Hey, little man! How are you?" The young man scooped the toddler up and tossed him into the air, eliciting a delighted squeal from the littlest Ellingham.

"Mr. Portman, I *asked* ya something!" Evan screamed as he stomped his feet on the floor.

"Evan Hanley! That is *not* acceptable behaviour. It's very rude," Louisa said as she entered the kitchen in time to witness the child's tantrum. "Go up to your room and calm yourself down. I'll be along in a minute to discuss this."

He gave a final stomp of his foot, and Louisa snapped her fingers, pointing towards the stairs. Evan batted back tears as he stormed off with clenched fists.

"Sorry about that, Jeremy. Here, let me take James. You go check on Martin," she said as she pulled her son from his arms.

"It's okay. The poor kid's been through a lot." Jeremy held his palm up and the toddler slapped his hand against it, giving him a gap-toothed grin. "Good luck with the talk."

"Yeah." Louisa said as she stepped down into the lounge. "Good luck with Martin's exam. Let me know if you find anything."

Evan lay curled up on his bed facing the wall when Louisa and James came into the nursery. Louisa set her son in his cot, handing him his stuffed bear and then sat down next to the older boy. "Evan, we need to talk about what happened downstairs. Can you turn around so that I can see you?"

He rolled over slowly, his hands pressed to his eyes as he pulled in ragged breaths.

"Evan, why did you yell at Mr. Portman the way you did?"

"I'm sorry. I won't do it again. I *promise*!"

Louisa got up and went across the hall, returning with a box of tissues. "Here, sit up and blow your nose—dry those tears. Then I expect an answer to my question."

Evan peered out from under a fist before pulling a tissue from the box and clearing the mucous from his airway. "I promise, I won't do it again."

"I hope not. Evan, I won't tolerate that kind of behaviour in my house."

"I'm really sorry, Mrs. Ellig-am. Please don't—don't—" The boy rolled over, facing the wall again as his sobs resumed.

Louisa pulled him to her lap and wrapped her arms around him. "Can you tell me what's wrong, Evan?"

"I'm scared you'll go away! You'll go away 'cause of me. And something bad could happen to Dr. Ellig-am 'cause you aren't here to take care of him!"

"Evan, look at me," Louisa said as she took hold of the child's chin and tipped his head back. "I am never going to leave Dr. Ellingham. I will never leave my family. I promise."

The boy took in a long, ragged breath and nodded his head.

Louisa sat for a few moments, his words resurrecting her own childhood feelings of abandonment. And she realised that it wasn't only her husband who could understand the boy.

Chapter 20

Despite the tense start to the day, the morning had passed uneventfully. Martin straightened his leg and tapped his wife's foot as she sat on the opposite side of the table at lunch, eliciting a startled smile from her.

He kept his eyes focused on the sandwich he was constructing, peering up briefly to gauge her reaction. His cheeks nudged up slightly before he returned his attention to his meal.

The quiet in the room was broken by a knock on the door. "I'll get that," Louisa said, pushing her chair away from the table.

A waft of cool salt air moved into the kitchen as she pulled the door open. "Al! What a nice surprise! Come on in, we're just finishing eating."

"Hullo, everbody," the younger Large said as he pulled a spare chair away from the wall and took a seat. It's a beauty of a day out there so thought I'd check out the woods next to the farm. Maybe scare up a Christmas tree. Anybody here fancy comin' along?"

Evan scrambled from his chair. "I do! I do!" he said as he jumped up and down. "Can I, Dr. Ellig-am?"

Martin tipped his head down and furrowed his brow. "Yes, I think I can trust Al to not lose you along the way somewhere."

The young man leaned back in his chair and folded his hands behind his head. "Maybe I better tie you to my belt, eh, Evan?"

Evan's smile hardened into a scowl. "I don't *like* being tied up. You can get your own stupid tree," he said as fell back into his chair.

"Evan! We had a talk about this once before today. I think you owe Mr. Large an apology!" Louisa said, ignoring her husband's almost imperceptible shake of his head.

Martin cleared his throat and got to his feet. Then he took his young charge by the wrist and led him down the hall.

He dropped into the chair behind his desk and gestured for the boy to come closer. "Evan, do you want to tell me why Mr. Large's comment upset you?"

Evan gave a shrug of his shoulders and scuffed his foot on the carpet. "I just don't like bein' tied up, and if that's what I gotta do to go on a Christmas tree hunt, then I don't wanna do it!"

"What do you mean, tied up?"

The boy crossed his arms tightly across his chest. "I just don't wanna do it. Do I gots ta do it, Dr. Ellig-am?"

Martin hesitated then opted to not press the boy for further details. "Well, Mr. Large wasn't serious when he made his comment. It was a joke. At least I think it was a joke.

"But I'm sure he wasn't serious. I've known Al a long time. If you'd still like to go with him, I can assure you that he would never do anything to hurt you."

"I made Mrs. Ellig-am angry again, didn't I?"

Martin grimaced and tipped his head to the side, "Maybe a bit. What do you mean, again?"

"I yelled at Mr. Portman. But he wouldn't *listen* to me and I got fust-rated!" The child planted his fists on his hips and huffed, "How come grown-ups can not listen, but kids got to?"

The doctor hesitated. "I suppose—perhaps if you haven't learned the social niceties by the time you get to be an adult, everyone's given up on you. Or they just don't care anymore.

"But you're still a child and you're learning. And I won't give up on you because—because I *do* care. So, I want you to go back out and apologise to Mr. Large. I suspect he might still be willing to take you along to chase up a Christmas tree."

Evan flashed Martin a smile then ran towards the door before stopping and returning to throw his arms around his neck. "Thanks Dr. Ellig-am."

"You're welcome, Evan. If you ever want to talk—about the tying up thing—that would be fine."

"Kay."

By the time apologies were made and Evan and Al were headed out on the hunt, it was time for James's nap. Martin rocked the boy and read to him until he fell asleep, and then his mother laid him in his cot.

"Martin, you look knackered. Go and have a lie-down," Louisa said steering him across the landing towards the bedroom.

He turned and pulled in his chin, peering up at her with one eyebrow raised. "You could join me."

"Then you wouldn't get any sleep, would you," she said as she pushed him back on to the bed. She lifted his feet on to the mattress and pulled off his shoes, examining them before setting them down next to the chair. "You're going to need a new pair. Between the hike on the moor and the festival last night you've kind of done this pair in."

"I might be able to get my black shoes on now."

"Hmm, not very stylish with brown trousers though. And you *need* to keep these feet up so that the swelling will go down again," she said, her face tightening as she wrapped her hands around his oedematous ankles. "We could go see what they have in Wadebridge tomorrow."

"That would be good. I could get a haircut as well."

"Mm, I suppose you are overdo. She brushed her fingers across his cheek as she leaned down to kiss him. "Get some rest now."

"Yes."

Louisa was in the kitchen working on a shopping list a short while later when she heard the familiar thunk of Martin's head connecting with their bedroom door frame. The sound was followed closely by a sharply uttered expletive.

She hurried through the lounge and was met at the bottom of the stairs by her scowly-faced husband.

"I thought you were going to try to get some sleep! It's only been—" She turned and looked at the clock on the mantel. "It's only been fifteen minutes, Martin."

"Mm, I know!" He held a hand to his forehead as he passed by her and headed towards the kitchen. "That—that—that *cackle* of hyenas who terrorise the village is camped out on our doorstep again!" he spluttered. "Why do they have to be so loud?"

"Oh, those girls move on eventually. They're teenagers. It's best to ignore them."

"Hmph. I don't know how I can be expected to do that when they keep waking me up."

He went to the refrigerator and pulled a cold pack from the freezer, holding it to the noticeable swelling above his right eye as he took a seat at the kitchen table.

"Here, let me see," Louisa said as she pulled the pack away, sucking in a small breath. "Oh, dear, that's nasty."

"Mm, yes."

"Maybe I should call Jeremy. Isn't headache a sign of a concussion?"

"*No!* I mean, yes—but no, it's not. I mean this headache is not. I woke up with it."

"I see. You sure you're okay? You look a little pale." She set a glass of water in front of him.

"I'm fine."

Returning to the table, Louisa sat down to finish her list.

"What are you doing," Martin asked, watching her from under the blue pack pressed to his brow.

"Oh, just some items that I need to pick up so that Evan and I can work on his Christmas Feast."

"I see." He reached out and pulled the paper from under his wife's hand. "Ohhh, really?"

"What?"

He wrinkled up his nose. "Sausage, bacon, cream, sugar? Just what do you have in mind, a mass cardiac event?"

"It's a traditional English Christmas Feast, Martin. And there are healthy things on this list as well."

He pulled the piece of paper back across the table and scanned it. "Brussels sprouts, cranberries and chestnuts?"

Giving him a shrug of her shoulders, she tipped her head down, peering up at him warily. "We'll have potatoes, too."

"Gawd," he groaned.

"Martin, Evan's researched this very thoroughly and he's come up with a menu. You should be proud of him. He spent the better part of two hours searching the internet for information about Christmas traditions. *And he was reading at the school library before the break started.*"

Martin breathed out a heavy sigh. "Yes."

Al and Evan stopped and picked Morwenna up before heading out of the village. Evan sat, sandwiched between the two adults, as they made their way through the narrow lanes that led to the farm.

Al regaled the boy with tales, passed on by Joan and Ruth, of Martin's summers spent helping Joan and Phil with the farming chores. Gravel crunched under the tyres as they pulled into the yard, and the boy stretched up, anxious to get a look at the home, which by now had been elevated to almost mythical status.

"I'm gonna go get a Thermos of hot chocolate to take along," Morwenna said as she headed towards the house.

"Come on, Evan. We need ta go get a saw from the barn. Then we'll go track down that elusive creature—*the Christmas tree,*" he said with hushed, drawn out theatrics.

The boy giggled and ran on ahead as Al hurried to keep up with him.

The old barn door creaked as it was pulled open. "Gonna hafta oil those hinges," the young man said as he squinted his unaccustomed eyes in the dimly lit interior.

"Wow! I bet Dr. Ellig-am had lots of places ta hide in here." Evan slowly turned, enthralled by the menagerie of old gardening tools, butter churns, milk cans and boxes of retained treasures.

Despite the fact that the old structure had not housed animals of any sort for more than two decades, the air still smelled of cow manure, hay, and the mustiness that comes with age. And specks of dust, no doubt many that were floating around when Martin was a boy, hovered in a shaft of sunlight coming in the high window.

The boy was drawn to the tall ladder leading up to the hayloft, and he stroked his hand over the boot-worn tread boards. "Did Dr. Ellig-am climb this when he was little?"

Al gave the child a grin. "Was the doc ever little?"

"Well, he had ta be 'cause you can't be born your grown-up size. See, babies start out in their mum's stomachs, then they come out somehow. Then they keep getting bigger until they stop growing. That's how you know they're all growed up. Dr. Ellig-am wouldn't of ever fit in his mum's stomach the size he is now."

Al scratched at his chin. "No, I s'pose yer right."

"Besides that, she never could've swallowed him."

"*Swallowed* him?"

"Ta get him in her stomach."

"Mum's don't *swallow* babies, Evan."

The boy dropped his hands to his sides and cocked his head at the young man. "Then how *do* they get in there?"

Al gulped and licked his lips, which had suddenly gone dry. "Tell ya what, why don't you take that up with the doc. He'd do a better job explainin' it."

"How come you talk like that Mr. Large. Do you gots marshmallows in your mouth?"

"No. No marshmallows. I just mumble." The young man cleared his throat then jabbed a finger skyward. "You wanna climb the ladder?"

Having successfully deflected the conversation away from the origin of babies and his verbal idiosyncrasy, Al gave the boy a tour of the hayloft before they picked up a saw and headed back to the car.

They crept through on the rutted dirt lane that led to the woods. Then the young man brought the car to a stop. "This looks like prime Christmas tree habitat to me, Evan. What'd you think?"

"I'd like it here if *I* was a Christmas tree."

Morwenna pushed her door open and stepped out. "Okay, out you get little man."

The boy scrambled from the car and ran for the woods.

"Whoa, whoa, whoa, Evan! You gotta stay next ta me!" Al shouted as he ran to catch up to his little liability.

He reached down and took hold of the boy's hand. "The doc would have my head if anything happened to you, so ya gotta stay right by me, understood?"

Evan furrowed his brow at him and nodded.

The young man scanned the area before moving into the woods. "Okay, keep yer eyes open. That perfect tree can be hard ta spot."

"What does it look like?" the boy asked as he stopped suddenly to pick up a rock. "Is this a diamond?"

Al took it and held it up to the light. "Nope, it's quartz, I think. It's a nice one though."

Evan tossed the rock to the ground and then stooped to pick it up again, pushing it into his pocket. "So, what *does* the perfect tree look like?"

"Well, it's gotta be green to start with," Morwenna said, earning her scowls from the male members of the search party.

"Obviously." Al stopped and looked around before heading off towards a copse of evergreens. "You wanna watch for a tree that's just the right size and has lots'a branches for hangin' things on." He let go of the boy's hand to circle a possible candidate.

"That one looks mean," the child said as he eyed it, askance.

"Mean?"

"Yeah, it gots those hangy-downy branches that look like they're gonna grab you."

"Hmph. Best to avoid that one then, eh?" Al reached out and tousled the child's hair, giving a jerk of his head before moving off towards another grouping of trees.

"Now *there's* a friendly lookin' tree! Just tall enough but not too tall. None a them hangy-downy branches. And it's green to boot!" he said, giving Morwenna a grin.

"And it gots lots of places to hang stuff! Can I cut it down?" Evan asked, his excitement irrepressible as he leapt up and down, shaking his fists.

Al held a palm out in front of him and lowered his voice. "Just settle down there. We gotta give 'er one final inspection first, Evan."

He circled the tree, bending down periodically to peer up into its branches.

"Whatcha lookin' for?" Evan whispered over his shoulder.

"It has ta have that special Christmassy vibe, ya know," Al whispered back. He stood up suddenly. "Yep, *this* is the one—fer sure."

He began pushing the dead leaves and sticks away from the base of the evergreen. "We need to make room ta work, first of all."

Evan joined in, kicking enthusiastically but ineffectively at the debris, the lion's share of the twigs and decaying matter escaping the path of his small foot.

"Okay, that oughta do 'er," Al announced as he got down on his knees and beckoned the child over with a wave of his arm.

Evan scrambled down next to him. "You can be my assistant, kay?" he said as he patted the young man's arm.

"You got it, mate. Morwenna—saw," he said with great gravity in his voice as he held out his hand.

"Yes sir!" Morwenna juggled the Thermos and the bag of biscuits she had brought along and handed Al the tool.

"Grab on to the handle right here and we'll make our first cut," he told the boy. Evan gripped on to the saw and Al slipped his hand in next to the boy's smaller one.

Bits of bark and sawdust dropped to the ground as they worked the blade back and forth.

"Okay, I think that's deep enough on this side. Now we need ta go over to the other side and make the final cut."

The young man and the boy got to their feet and Evan gave his arm a shake. "Whew! That's hard work!" He leaned over and took in a deep breath. "It smells good."

"Yeah, kinda piny-like, eh?" Al said, giving a tug on the boy's jacket before moving to the other side of the tree.

They repeated the previous procedure, with Al doing the real work as the child began to flag. "Give it a little tug your way Morwenner, we've almost got it," the young man said as the pine listed slightly.

"Okay, Evan—she's all yours." Al moved back and pulled himself to his feet, his hands raised and ready lest the tree begin to fall towards the child.

Evan grunted as the saw lurched back and forth, bending periodically as the blade would bind against the wood.

"Keep 'er up, mate! Yer almost there!" Al said when Evan stopped and heaved out a breath.

The seven-year-old shook his arm one more time before resuming the final sawing motions.

"Timber!" Morwenna yelled as there was a cracking sound before the pine hit the ground.

Evan jumped up and looked at Al in disbelief. "I did it! I did it—I did it!"

"Yeah, you did. And I'd say that effort deserves a reward. Should we have some hot chocolate and biscuits?"

Morwenna sat down on a large log, patting the seat beside her. "Come on over here, Evan."

The trio munched on Hobnobs and drank hot chocolate as they relaxed in the quiet of the wood before it was time to drag the tree back to the car.

Al pulled a long piece of rope from Morwenna's bag, tying the centre of the length to the trunk of the tree and one end around his own waist before turning to the boy. "Okay, Evan. We gotta work together to pull it outta here. Lift up yer jacket and I'll tie this end around you."

The boy stood, eyeing the young man for several moments. Then he hiked up his coat.

The sky had turned a soft pink by the time they arrived back at the house with their quarry, and the air had grown cold.

Evan held the door open as Al and Morwenna lugged the tree into the large living room before securing it in a stand.

"We better give it some water, Evan. You want ta do the honours?" Al asked as the little boy followed him to the kitchen."

"Why do ya gotta give it water?"

"So it doesn't dry out. If it dries out, all the needles will fall off—*and* it's a fire hazard."

They returned to the living room with a pitcher filled with water and Evan scrutinised the tree. "Do I have ta get the whole thing wet? I don't think I can reach the top."

"No-no-no. You dump the water in the stand and the tree sucks it up."

Evan looked up at Al, a dubious expression on his face. "But it doesn't got its roots anymore."

"Yep, funny thing that. It can suck up the water without its roots."

"Huh."

Martin was reading on the sofa, his legs propped up and iced, when the hunting party returned to the surgery. Evan barrelled past Louisa and landed next to him.

"Hi, Dr. Ellig-am! We had fun!"

"Did you find what you were looking for?" he asked as he reached out to pull the cold packs from his legs.

"Uh-huh. We found a good one! And I found somethin' for *you*," he said, reaching into his pocket. "It's a rock."

Martin took the object, now sticky with pine tar, from his charge's hand. "Mm, it's quartz—cairngorm. It's found in the mountains of Scotland. Where was this?"

"Just layin' on the ground. Do ya like it?"

"I do," Martin nodded. "I just wonder how it ended up at Joan's farm." He turned the piece over, tipping it into the light and then got up from the sofa.

"Where are ya goin'?" Evan asked as he trotted along behind.

"I want to look at it with my loupe."

"Loop of what?"

"I'll show you."

Martin dropped into his desk chair and pulled a hinged box from a bottom drawer. "This is a loupe," he said as he held it out for the boy to see.

"It's a magnifying glass that fits in your eye socket. I use it when I'm working with small clock parts. There are some marks on this rock I want to get a better look at."

He pulled his desk lamp closer and inserted the instrument, peering closely at the stone. "Yep, this has been worked ... grooves carved into it."

"What's a groob?"

"A *groove*. Like a deep scratch."

"How did the groobs get in there?" Evan asked as his feet sought a toe hold on the desk chair.

"Come around to the other side, and I'll lift you up so you can see."

Evan hurried around and Martin hooked an arm around his waist before pulling him to his lap.

"Here, hold this up to your eye and look through it."

His cheeks raised up as the boy's face lit up.

"I can see 'em! Where did those come from?"

"I'm not sure what this particular stone was used for. But many years ago, it was common for cairngorms to be used in jewellery. The Druids believed the stone was special. That it could protect the owner from harm. That idea's been scientifically disproven, of course."

"What are Druids?"

"They were a group of people who lived around here a very long time ago. Cairngorm is still used in jewellery, but not as a talisman—er, a stone that provides safety or brings good luck. It's just decorative."

Martin took the loupe from the boy's hand and reinserted it, examining the rock again. "The grooves are quite worn so I would guess this stone was worked a very long time ago."

"By a Druid?" Evan asked as his eyes grew wide.

"Possibly. Perhaps to ornament a sword or, as I said, for a piece of jewellery."

"A sword!"

"That's just a possibility."

Evan took the rock from Martin's hand and peered at it closely. "Bugger, it doesn't gots any blood on it," he said dejectedly.

"Well, that would have been thousands of years ago. The rain would have washed it off by now. It's still possible it was in a sword handle—used in a battle perhaps," Martin said as he lifted the boy to the floor.

"I gotta tell Mr. Large!"

The corners of Martin's mouth tugged up slightly as he listened to the fading footsteps and the excited chatter in the kitchen.

He slipped the loupe back into the box and was leaning over to put it back in the drawer when he heard his wife's soft voice.

"Well, you certainly made that little boy's day."

"Mm. It's an exciting discovery."

She slipped behind the chair and wrapped her arms around her husband's neck. "So, do you really think it was used in jewellery? Or a sword, which Evan is convinced is the case."

"There's likely no way of knowing. I do know one thing though. I probably won't get my rock back."

Chapter 21

"You think it's a bad sign—Dr. Newell scheduling us for a double session?" Louisa asked as they neared Truro on Friday afternoon.

Martin cocked his head and pulled up his chin. "I would imagine he wanted to allow enough time to get all our questions answered. Try not to read too much into it, Louisa."

Her gaze was drawn to her husband's fingers which had been drumming on his leg for the last five minutes. His palm flattened when he noticed her, and he cleared his throat before asking, "Poppy can stay late, then? We'll stop at the barbers in Wadebridge on the way home?"

"Yes, Martin. I won't take you back to Portwenn without a haircut." Louisa gripped the steering wheel a little tighter and took in a breath. "Erm, there's something that I've been wanting to discuss with you about Christmas ... and Evan's big plans."

"You're referring to the Christmas Feast, I hope."

"Well, yes. There are a few people he would like to invite."

Martin dropped his chin to his chest as he released a low groan.

"Hear me out, please," Louisa said as she put a hand on his leg. "Ruth will be there, of course, but he'd like to ask Jeremy and Poppy to join us as well ... and the Parsons. He doesn't think it would be good for Old Doc to be lonely on Christmas Day."

"I see. I'd be all right with that, I suppose. Although, I'm quite sure that Old Doc had no intentions of being *lonely*. I think he may already have"—he cleared his throat— "activities planned for the two of them."

Louisa gave her husband an impish smile. "Oh? Did he elaborate?"

"*No*, thank God." Martin answered, wrinkling up his nose.

She cast a furtive glance in his direction and stroked her fingers along his thigh. "And ... he'd also like to include Al and Morwenna. He's taken quite a liking to Al since their outing yesterday."

Martin rubbed a hand across his forehead before letting it drop to his lap. "Fine. But I doubt that Al will want to leave his fath—" Martin whirled his head around, grimacing at his wife before throwing his head back. "Oh, please don't tell me we'll have to put up with Bert all day!"

"No Martin, you're the only one who has to *put up* with him. The rest of us will delight in his company."

"Gawd, I knew you and Ruth had some kind of production planned!"

"That's not the way it happened, Martin. Not at all. There are other reasons for celebrating at the farm."

"Well, that puts my mind at ease," he grumbled.

Louisa was regretting having brought up the subject of the holiday guests as her husband grew more sullen and irritable as they neared the Royal Cornwall campus.

"Try to relax," she told him, caressing his knee as they sat in Dr. Newell's office.

A door could be heard opening and Louisa gave his leg a final squeeze.

"Martin ... Louisa, how are you?" Barrett Newell asked as he entered the waiting area.

Louisa stood up, picking her purse up from the sofa. "Good, and you?"

"I'm just fine, thank you. Come on back and we'll get started."

Martin gave his wife an anxious grimace, and she returned it with a self-assured smile.

The psychiatrist closed the door behind them. Dropping into his chair, he rolled it up to his desk, flipping open the two files in front of him. "Well, Martin brought me up to speed on the basics when he called yesterday. Evan's history—what's transpired since the night his father died. I thought perhaps we could begin by discussing how the Ellingham household has fared with this new and unexpected development. Louisa ... would you like to get us started?"

"Well, *James* loves having Evan around," she said, giving her husband a confident nod. "I think he finds him to be an endless source of amusement really."

She ran her hand across her thigh, smoothing out her skirt. "He won't remember any of it, of course, but he's enjoying it all the same. Evan builds towers with James's blocks, and James knocks them down. That sort of thing. It's good fun for both boys."

Dr. Newell smiled as he rocked back in his chair, resting his elbows on the armrests. "So, I can safely assume then that James, at least, is comfortable with the current situation?"

Louisa batted a wisp of hair away from her face as she laughed nervously. "Well, he *is* still just a baby really ... not hardly old enough to weigh in on the issue."

"Of course. And how would you weigh in on the issue, Louisa? Any thoughts—concerns?"

"Well, I'm very happy that we can be here for Evan—to help him through a difficult time—until other more suitable, *permanent* arrangements can be made. But—well, this has been wearing on Martin. Evan's become quite attached to him, and he's rather demanding of his time and attention."

Martin, who had been sitting silent and unfocused, turned suddenly. "No, he's not! I mean, of course in the night—with the nightmares, perhaps he is. But overall, he's been no more demanding than James."

"Well, you have to admit, Martin, you're not getting a lot of sleep these days."

"I'm a doctor, I'm used to having my sleep disrupted."

Louisa crossed her legs and laced her fingers together over her knee. "I do worry about Martin. Evan wakes up at least once every night. Sometimes it's nightmares, but a lot of the time he just wants Martin. He's Evan's source of security, I think."

She turned to her husband. "You haven't had more than one good night's sleep since Evan arrived, Martin, and it shows. I'm concerned."

"Martin, how do you feel you're bearing up under these new demands?" the psychiatrist asked.

"I'm fine."

Dr. Newell took note of his patient's nervously tapping fingers. "Do you think Louisa's exaggerating when she describes this new nightly routine?"

Squirming in his chair, Martin glanced over at his wife. "She's accurate in her description of the *routine*, but as I said, I'm a doctor. I used to be a surgeon. This is nothing new to me."

"Yes, but Martin, you're also recovering from very serious injuries, and you're immunocompromised," Louisa said, resting her hand on her husband's arm. "You need to be getting enough rest."

Martin pulled his arm out from under her and rubbed his hand over the back of his neck. "Have I been ill since Evan arrived? Have I suffered any setbacks—taken any falls?"

Louisa huffed out a breath as her ponytail flicked once behind her.

"You mentioned, Martin, that you and your wife have come to an impasse, of sorts, about what the next step should be with this child. You'd like him to stay a while longer ... let things settle down a bit before any further action is taken?"

Martin folded his hands on his lap and straightened himself in his chair, an action Louisa knew signalled his transition into professional mode.

"That's correct. I believe that to move him on to a new set of caregivers at this time could have a devastating effect."

"To be clear, Dr. Newell, I have no objection to keeping Evan with us through the holidays," Louisa explained. "In fact, he has quite a festive day planned for all of us."

The therapist came around and took a seat on the front of his desk. "Martin, Louisa's concerns *are* valid. You had a very close call and your health is still fragile."

Martin glanced up at the doctor. Then giving a huff, he pushed himself from his chair, wandering to the window.

"Remember also, that fatigue could make a recurrence of your depression more likely."

Emboldened, Louisa nodded her head at the man. "That's an excellent point—one I hadn't considered."

Martin's fists clenched as the psychiatrist kept his focus fixed on him. "That said, I do think that your assessment of Evan's needs is accurate. I suspect that once the excitement and distraction of the holidays is over, the real impact of his father's death and those hours on the moor will hit him. That will likely be a crucial adjustment period for the boy."

Louisa's face tightened as she sat back in her chair. "Even so, I *have* to consider Martin's health," she said before turning to her husband. "And—well, I'm sorry, Martin, you are my first priority, and I really believe that to extend Evan's stay would be too fatiguing and stressful for you."

Martin turned to face her, his fingers twitching at his sides. "Those things we can work through. I can stop seeing patients for the time being if that would make a difference to you."

"That doesn't take care of the problems with him at night though, does it, Martin?" she argued back.

"Louisa … if Evan stays, I intend to get him in to see a therapist. That issue may resolve itself. If nothing else—"

"What?"

"Well, he could sleep with us, I suppose."

"Oh, Martin." Louisa tipped her head to the side as she gazed up at him sympathetically.

He looked over at the doctor. "He's done nothing wrong the entire week he's spent with us. Aside from a couple of understandable expressions of frustration, that is. He tries to do as we ask. He apologises profusely when he *does* do something wrong. What's it going to do to him if we take him over to Wadebridge after Christmas and say—Here, *you* take him. He's too much of a disruption in our lives? That he's too demanding—*needy*—wetting the bed. That we were happier before he arrived."

"I think you're being a bit dramatic, Martin," Louisa said.

"No! I'm *not!*"

Louisa opened her mouth to speak, but Dr. Newell held a hand up to stop her. "Let's let Martin finish that thought. Please ... continue, Martin."

He rubbed his hand roughly over his head and hissed out a breath. "That's the message he's going to get. That he's too much trouble. That he's in the way—spoilt things again."

Dr. Newell pushed himself from the desk and walked back to his chair.

"Louisa, I'm curious. What message were you left with when your mother ran off on you and your father?"

She twisted her purse strap in her hand. "Well, it was a different situation, of course. But I was hurt that she had to get away from Dad and me to be happy."

"And as a child, why did you think she couldn't be happy living under the same roof with you and your father?"

"Well, she's always had a bit of wanderlust. Maybe more than a bit. And I'm sure staying home with a child all the time—not the most exciting way to spend your day—made her even keener to get away."

"Do you feel any sense of responsibility for your mother's abandonment of you and your father?"

Louisa pulled up her lower lip and shook her head slowly as she thought over the man's question. "It was her choice. Neither Dad nor I wanted her to leave. I tried to get her to stay, but she said she just wasn't cut out to be a mum—that it wasn't what she had envisioned for her life—that she felt like she was being suffocated being stuck in the back of beyond.

"She made a clean break of it, and the last I saw of her, she seemed quite happy with her chosen lifestyle. I may have been more child than someone like my mother could handle."

"Why do you say that? Were you a troublesome child?"

Louisa shook her head at the man. "I'm not sure I know what you're getting at. I thought we were talking about Evan—and Martin."

The psychiatrist steepled his fingers, tapping them against his lips. "I just want to make sure that both you and Martin are considering all the factors that might affect this decision that you're confronted with. Why do you say you may have been more child than your mother could handle, Louisa?"

She brushed a wisp of hair forcefully out of her face. "I may have been a bit—troublesome—at times. My mother would have used the word obstinate. But I would say I was more like some of my strong-willed students. I didn't like being told what to do or how to do it."

"Do you think that your strong-willed temperament may have been a factor in your mother's leaving you?"

Louisa's brow lowered as she sat for several seconds before answering. "No, I can't imagine leaving James if he turns out to be a bit headstrong. That would be quite—narcissistic—and inexcusable really."

"That sounds like your mother," Martin grumbled.

"Mar-tin," Louisa hissed as she shot her husband a black look and huffed out a breath.

Dr. Newell rephrased his question. "But you and your mother are different people. Do you think the stubborn streak you had as a child contributed to your mother's decision to leave?"

Louisa fidgeted, picking at her fingernails before looking up at the doctor. "I thought that at one time. I know better now—that I'm a mum. But when I was growing up, I think I felt that if I hadn't been so bloody bull-headed, as Mum used to say, she wouldn't have left us."

"How about your father? How did he deal with having a strong-willed child?"

"He had his moments of frustration, but I tried very hard to be more compliant after Mum left ... didn't want to rock the boat, you know," she explained, her hand circling in the air.

"What did you think might happen if you—rocked the boat?"

Louisa tugged at the hem of her skirt as she tried to blink back tears.

Martin swallowed hard as he watched his wife. He reached into his back pocket and pulled out his handkerchief, slipping it into her hand before taking a seat next to her.

She wiped the moisture from her cheeks and pulled her shoulders back. "There was a period of time where I think Dad was having thoughts of leaving. He never would have gone off and left me alone ... at least I don't think he would have. But I tried to just do as he said—tried to put up a good front so he'd be happy in Portwenn."

The psychiatrist's chair gave a resentful squeak as he shifted his weight and pulled his ankle up over his knee. "Given your own childhood experiences, Louisa, you bring a unique understanding to the situation with Evan. I would imagine there have been times when he misses his mum, the first female influence in his life."

Louisa shook her head. "He's never mentioned her."

"Does that strike you as odd in any way?"

"No, it's easier to not think about her. I mean—I would imagine easier anyway."

The therapist cleared his throat before redirecting the conversation. "If I'm understanding correctly, what Martin is asking for is a temporary extension of Evan's stay in your home. Is that what you understand his request to be, Louisa?"

"Yes, it is. But—well, if we extend Evan's stay, then what? Will we revisit the issue all over again in a few weeks—months? It'll be harder for Martin to let him go the longer he's in our home. And it'll be harder for Evan to leave."

"And harder for you to tell Martin no the next time?" Dr. Newell said softly.

Louisa glanced up at him, nodding her head. "I'm not sure I *could* tell him no the next time."

"And the alternative would be to either give Evan a permanent foster home—or adoption."

Louisa sat mum for a few moments, her focus on her lap, before looking over at Martin. "It's not what I expected for our future. I pictured this idyllic little family. You—me—and James. Possibly even another child. Except I had in mind starting from scratch," she said, giving him a weak smile.

"Evan wasn't in the picture. It's hard to accept that—well, everything would be different, wouldn't it?"

Martin grasped for words. "I didn't realise—y-y-you had this all planned out."

"I'm sure it sounds rather ridiculous to you, but I had this image in my head of how things would be, and Evan would completely change that picture.

"But it's not only adjusting to the idea of a different future. I just don't know if, given our track record so far … well, if our marriage could stand up to the challenges that could come with a boy like Evan.

"He comes with some very unpleasant baggage. Are you really willing to take that risk? Perhaps sacrifice a healthy home life for James in order to give someone else's child a better chance in life?"

A look of uncertainty spread across Martin's face and his jaw clenched. "I don't know what to do," he said. "I-I— I can't just go off and leave Evan. But I can't abandon you and James either."

"Why would you need to abandon your family, Martin?" Dr. Newell asked as he crossed one leg over the other.

Martin scowled at him. "Louisa isn't going to be happy. Evan will see that—see how she looks at him. You can see what effect that kind of environment had on me." He rubbed at his eyes. "And Louisa's right. I'd be risking a healthy home life for James."

He shook his head and wiped his palms on his trousers. "But I can't leave him."

Louisa reached out and pulled his hand from his thigh. "Children's Services will find a loving family for him, don't you think?"

"*No*! He's seven years old! No one wants to adopt a seven-year-old child!" He licked his suddenly dry lips as his breaths quickened. "You don't understand," he said, his voice quavering.

Dr. Newell leaned forward, resting his arms on his thighs as his biro spun in his fingers. "What is it that Louisa doesn't understand, Martin?"

He got up again from his chair. "That I need to do this. I *have* to take care of the boy. I can't just—j-j-just cast him aside because life was happier—*simpler* before he came to stay. I need to do this."

"What do you mean by that Martin ... that you *need* to do this."

"Well, I-I—I have a duty of care."

"Martin, I'd like you to take a moment and think about this. See if you can't uncover what it is that makes you feel such a strong need to help Evan."

"I just told you. I have a duty of care to the boy. I'm a doctor, and I have a duty of care."

Dr. Newell rocked slowly in his chair as he toyed with the wedding band on his finger. "I do understand that you would feel a sense of professional responsibility. The boy did come to you first as a patient. What I want you to think about, though, is whether there's something beyond the obligation that you have as a physician."

Martin looked over at his wife, grimacing as he gave her a slight shake of his head.

"Try, Martin," she said softly.

He bit at his lip as he stared past the doctor for several moments before taking in a sharp breath and pulling his hand up over his eyes.

"Nobody helped him then, but I can help him now. I couldn't then, but I can now," he said before turning to his wife. "I can't let it happen again. I can do something this time and to ask me to go through all that again, Louisa—I can't do it."

Louisa's ponytail swished back and forth gently as she stared back at him apologetically.

Martin sighed heavily as he sat back down next to her.

"You're right. I'm afraid I *don't* understand, Martin," she said as she took hold of his hand.

Dr. Newell came around and reclaimed his position on the corner of the desk. "It's not just Evan that you're trying to save, is it, Martin?"

Martin's mouth opened and closed several times as he shook his head and uncertainty creased his brow.

"Do you see yourself in Evan? Your seven-year-old self?" the doctor asked.

Louisa caressed her husband's moist palm with her thumb as she waited for his response.

"I suppose I do," he finally answered. His gaze met the therapist's. "This has all been self-serving? I haven't been trying to help Evan? I've been trying to—to work through some sort of unresolved issues of my own?"

"Your fundamental motivation *is* for Evan, Martin. He's benefited greatly from all that you've done to help him. But it's a symbiotic relationship.

"By helping this boy through this devastating period in his young life, you're beginning to recognise what you, as a seven-year-old, so desperately needed but didn't receive.

"You can identify with Evan. You've experienced what it's like to be unwanted—to live in fear—to feel so overwhelmingly alone in the world—helpless.

"But in giving Evan what he needs, you're also giving the very vulnerable seven-year-old in you what he needed forty years ago."

Louisa stared at the floor in front of her as the significance of the therapist's words hit her.

"The two of you have a hard decision to make. What you decide will be life changing any way you slice it. So, take your time with this. There's no rush at this point. I would recommend you think of this as a time to gather information and to share concerns that each of you may have.

"Martin, you mentioned that if you and Louisa do decide to extend Evan's time with you, that you would like for him to see a therapist. I can give you the name of a very fine child psychologist. It might be helpful for you both to visit with her before you make a final decision—get questions answered. I'm sure she'll want to visit with Evan as well."

Louisa drew in a deep breath. "Thank you, Dr. Newell. We'll talk it over. But you're right, it is a big decision."

The therapist got up from his chair and came around to the front of his desk. "I do want to mention one other thing that you should keep in mind as you deliberate about this.

"If you should decide to make the current situation long-term, don't expect that you'll feel the same sort of bond with Evan that you do with James, your biological child. Some people do, others don't. The important thing will be that you treat both of the boys in the same manner—not show a preference for one over the other. But don't let a fear that you won't feel the same way about Evan that you do about James worry you."

The man moved towards the door as Louisa and Martin got to their feet. "I'll be out of the office until after the holidays, but if either of you have need of me before then, leave a voicemail message, and I'll get back to you."

Stopping at the reception desk, Dr. Newell picked up a business card and handed it to Martin. "You may opt for a different therapist, of course, but Abby Peterson is quite skilled at helping children work through post-trauma issues."

"Mm, thank you. I'll call her Monday morning," he said as he slipped the card into his wallet.

Neither Martin nor Louisa spoke until after they turned on to the A-39. Martin glanced over at her before reaching a hand out to caress her thigh. "I'm sorry for all of this. I didn't know when I gave Evan that mobile that we'd end up in this place as a result of it."

"Oh, Martin, don't apologise," Louisa said, placing her hand on his. "It scares me to think what might have happened to Evan if he hadn't been able to call you that night.

"And this isn't an altogether bad place to end up anyway. To say we have a lot to work out is an understatement, but don't give up on me just yet," she said, giving him a smile.

Chapter 22

The wind had come up, and it had begun to rain as Martin and Louisa entered the town of Wadebridge. By the time they left the barber's a half hour later, the air had turned frigid. Another winter storm was bearing down on the Cornish coast.

"You go on ahead," Martin shouted over the gust driven rain pelting the shop windows. "I'm slowing you down." He readjusted his crutch under his arm, ducking his head as he forced his stiff legs to propel him into the storm. "I'll be there in a minute."

Louisa hesitated and then dashed for the car. Wiping the raindrops from her face, she glanced into the rear-view mirror in time to see her husband disappear under a small green awning that she had passed moments earlier.

Oh, Martin, what are you up to now? she thought, trying to tamp down her growing impatience. She was getting anxious to get back to Portwenn to see how Poppy and Jeremy had fared with the added responsibility of a seven-year-old.

She started the engine and the interior of the vehicle warmed quickly. Her thoughts turned to their earlier session with Dr. Newell and the painful memories which had been resurrected. She had spent her adult life trying to be the antithesis of her mother.

She pictured her idyllic little family in her head. Martin was never going to be that husband—father—loved pillar of the community.

A smile spread across her face as she realised, *that* Martin would bore her to tears. That Martin was romantically demonstrative, always showering her with gifts and endearments; a playful and fun-loving parent; and never knew a stranger, adored by all.

But her real-life Martin was; romantically awkward and shy, bringing her flowers on one single occasion and recoiling at the idea of public displays of affection; stiff and formal with their son, preferring to share a medical journal article or surgical video to picking up a toy; and gruff, often rude, and disinterested in the goings-on in the village, unless it pertained to the health of the community.

But her real Martin was also a committed and loving husband, devoted father, and he was well-respected for his skills as a doctor. Her real Martin wasn't ideal, he was extraordinary.

She was shaken from her musings by sound of the passenger side door opening, and her husband fell into the seat.

"Martin, you must be freezing! You're soaked to the skin!"

He reached behind him and pulled his handkerchief from his back pocket, wiping his head and face. "I'm fine."

"You really should wear a coat, you know."

He gave his head a vigorous shake. "It's restrictive. And like I keep saying, I get hot. It takes a lot of energy to move around right now, Louisa."

Her gaze met his, causing her breath to catch in her throat. Reaching up, she placed a lingering kiss on his lips.

"What did you get?" she asked softly as her hand brushed against the bag on his lap.

"Oh. Sorry, it's not for you," he said refocusing his attention on the bag in his hand as he tried to get his wits about him. "It's on Evan's list, and I told him I'd get him one."

Louisa took the bag and reached in, pulling out two very traditional Christmas stockings made from red gingham fabric.

"Oh, Martin! And they even had them with the boy's names stitched on them!"

"No. That's what took so long. I had that added. They have a machine that does it there in the store. Mm." He took the gifts from his wife's hands and stuffed them quickly back into the bag.

She reached up again, kissing him a second time. "They'll be so excited to hang them up."

"Well, James isn't likely to remember any of it."

"Yes, I *do* realise that." She placed her hands on his cheeks and studied his face. "You are an extraordinary man, Martin."

His brows drew together as he cocked his head at her. "It really wasn't difficult. I just picked the stockings that I wanted and told the woman what to stitch on them. And then of course I, ah"—Louisa silenced him with another kiss— "I paid for them."

"Let's go home," she whispered.

Poppy was emptying the dishwasher and James Henry was gnawing on a piece of Melba toast in his high chair when Martin and Louisa entered the back door. Martin slipped into the pantry and stashed his purchase on the shelf above the washer and dryer before returning to the kitchen to greet his son with a caress across the top of his head.

Evan was wrestling with Jeremy on the floor in the lounge. Martin screwed up his face at them. "What on earth are you doing?"

"Sorry, Martin," the aide said as he peered up at his boss.

The boy squirmed out of Jeremy's grasp, making a mad dash for the kitchen. "Hi, Dr. Ellig-am! We were just playing old 'lympic games— 'cept they didn't wear clothes back then. But Mr. Portman says that would be unappropriate now." The child narrowed his eyes at the doctor. "Hey, you got a haircut, didn't ya!"

Martin pulled in his chin and gave him a grunt. "I did. You could do with a trim too, you know. Perhaps we should make a trip to Wadebridge next week."

"Just you and me?" the boy asked hopefully.

"If I'm cleared to drive, yes. Otherwise we'll get—your opponent—to chauffeur us over there."

Martin headed down the hall, and Evan trotted along beside him, keeping up a steady stream of chatter. "Can we pick up some of the stuff for the Christmas Feast while we're there? We got lots a stuff we need—ta do all the cookin' with, you know."

Martin stopped and eyed the boy. "What kind of— stuff?"

"Mrs. Ellig-am's making a list."

"Ah, yes. I think I've seen that list." Rounding the railing, the doctor headed up the stairs.

"So, can we?"

They came to a stop in the bedroom doorway and Martin huffed out a breath. "Can we what?"

"Can we pick up the stuff?"

"Get the list made up by the time we go, and yes, we can pick up the stuff. Now if you'll excuse me, Evan, I need to use the lavatory."

"You don't need an excuse ta use the lavatory, Dr. Ellig-am. You just go when you gotta go."

Martin stared down at the child. "It's an expression. And it means I don't want you following me into the bathroom," he said impatiently. "Why don't you wait downstairs."

Evan grabbed on to the door jamb and swung himself back and forth. "That's okay, I'll just wait here."

"Oh, for goodness' sake," he grumbled as he made his way across the room.

When he re-emerged a short time later, Evan had planted himself on the top step. The boy jumped up and grabbed on to his wrist before hopping down the steps behind him. He let go as they neared the bottom, stopping on the fourth step up. "Watch this, Dr. Ellig-am!" he said before leaping past Martin to the slate floor below.

Martin caught himself on the railing, just avoiding tripping over the boy. "Evan! Be careful!"

"Oh, I am. I never go higher than four steps. I can jump a long way. What did ya think?"

"I think you need to come down those steps in a civilised manner if you don't want to end up with a broken neck."

"Oh, I won't break my neck. I gots my lucky rock, remember?" Evan pulled the piece of smoky quartz from his pocket and held it up as evidence.

"Evan, I didn't mean to give you the impression that your rock will bring you good luck. And it *definitely* won't keep you from breaking your neck jumping off those stairs."

Evan examined the rock in his hand before looking up at Martin. "Well, I'll try not ta do anything to break my neck ... just in case. But the *Druids* thought it was lucky."

Martin threw his head back. "Oh, good grief," he said as he walked off under the stairs.

"Oh, good grief, what?" Louisa asked, intercepting him in the doorway and wrapping her arms around his neck.

"I may have inadvertently given someone the idea that the rock he found at the farm is some sort of—medieval lucky rabbit's foot," he groaned.

"Oh, I see. Well, I wouldn't worry about it Martin. Children love to pretend things are magical at his age," she murmured into his ear.

"Hmph. Well I better make sure he's clear on the pretending bit."

She brushed her thumb over his cheek and then slipped past him. "Evan, could I see you for a minute?" she asked as she led the child back under the stairs.

Evan watched her warily, keeping one eye on Martin as he moved about the kitchen. "Are you cross at me about something?" he asked, a tremor in his voice.

"No, Evan." Louisa crouched down in front of him and took his hands in hers. "I'm not cross at all. I just wanted to tell you that this might be a good time to ask Jeremy and Poppy if they'd like to join us on Christmas Day."

A small smile eased its way on to the child's face. "Dr. Ellig-am won't mind?"

"Nope. We talked about it in the car today. In fact, you can call the Parsons and Al and Morwenna later and invite them, too."

"Thanks, Mrs. Ellig-am!" the boy said as he wrapped his arms around her neck and squeezed on to her tightly before running back to the kitchen.

Martin turned to look as Evan's trainers slapped against the slate flooring before he came to a stop in front of the aide. "Mr. Portman! Do you wanna eat the Christmas Feast with us? Mrs. Ellig-am said it's okay!"

"Well thanks for the invitation, little mate, but I already promised Poppy I'd spend the day with her."

"Oh, you can bring her along. You two go together so I figured she'd come anyway. And she's pretty nice—for a girl."

Martin watched as the child jumped from one foot to the other, awaiting the young man's answer.

Jeremy cocked his head and raised an eyebrow at the childminder. "Yeah, that would be great, Evan," he said after getting an affirming nod from his girlfriend.

"Yes!" The little boy grinned up at his guardian and gave his fist a firm pump.

Martin's eyes crinkled at the child's enthusiastic response, and he felt an unfamiliar lightness in his chest.

It was late by the time the Ellingham home had calmed down enough for the bedtime routine to commence.

James had been bathed and Louisa nestled him into the crook of his father's arm before getting Evan started with his bath.

The toddler's eyelids were heavy as Martin gazed down at him, and it took only minutes of listening to his father's resonant voice, reading of the latest news in vascular surgery, before he had drifted off to sleep.

Martin laid his head back and closed his eyes, his thoughts focused completely on the soft scent of baby shampoo and the warmth and weight of his son's body as it pressed against him.

He had spent decades of his life virtually bereft of human physical contact, and he was suddenly overwhelmed to now experience it with this small person who shared his own genetic material.

He was startled from his reverie by his wife's hands on his face.

"Martin, are you all right?" she asked as she leaned over him, her face filled with concern as she brushed the moisture from his cheeks.

Heat flashed up his neck when he realised he had been caught in a very affecting moment. Clearing his throat, he pulled a hand to his face, rubbing at his eyes. "I'm fine. You can put James to bed now, though."

Louisa lifted the boy from his father's arms and gave her husband a final questioning look. "Hmm," she said as she turned towards the steps. "You'll come up and tuck Evan in for the night?"

"Yes, I'll be right there."

Martin clenched his teeth against the pain that still wracked his bones every time he got to his feet. He went to the kitchen, filling a glass from the tap and sipping at it as he stared out at the black night.

If Evan became a permanent fixture in their family, would he be able to show the boy the same kind of affection that he shared with James Henry? Dr. Newell's words echoed in his head. *The important thing will be that you treat both of the boys in the same manner—not show a preference for one over the other.*

He felt confident that he could be impartial when it came to discipline, but would Evan be able to tell that his bond with James was nonpareil?

He took another sip from the glass before dumping the remainder down the drain and heading for the stairs.

"Hi, Dr. Ellig-am. I got a book all picked out," Evan said, moving over as Martin entered the room and lowered himself on to the mattress. "It's about the heart. And it shows all the blood vessels, too," he explained to the doctor as he flipped the cover open.

"See, that's the aorta right there." A small finger traced its way down the chest and belly of the gender-neutral figure on the page.

"I'm not sure this is appropriate bedtime reading material. Maybe we should save this one ... read it during the day," Martin suggested.

"Why, what's wrong with it?" the boy asked as he sat up in the bed, his curiosity now piqued.

"There's nothing wrong with it. I just don't think a book like this would help you to fall asleep. Maybe the one about the rabbit who ends up with indigestion after eating too much would be a better choice. I think it's on the shelf over there," Martin said, wagging a finger towards the collection of storybooks on the wall.

"But those are *baby* stories!" the boy whined.

James let out a soft whimper, stirring in his cot, and Martin shushed the older boy. "You need to keep your voice down, Evan."

"I wanna know where blood comes from!" he whispered stridently.

"All right, all right. Give me the book." Martin flipped the cover open again. "This is way too long to read tonight. How 'bout we just talk ... I'll answer your questions."

"'Kay. So, where *does* it come from?"

"It's a rather complicated process. Different organs in the body work together, each contributing different ingredients to make the blood. But the bone marrow is responsible for much of the formation of new blood cells."

"What's bone mallow?"

"Bone *marrow*. It's the soft material inside some of the large bones."

Evan rubbed at his head and pulled his brows together. "All the bones I've seen are empty."

"Mm. It's only found in the bones of living things, or sometimes you can see it in the bones of meats that we eat. A ham bone—beef shanks—any of the larger meat bones."

"What does it look like?"

"It's sort of a soft, spongy material."

"Oh, *that's* how come it gots that name."

"No, it doesn't have anything to do with marsh—"

"So, when something dies, it doesn't gots it anymore?"

Martin hesitated, becoming uncomfortable about the turn the conversation seemed to be taking. "No. It doesn't *have* it anymore."

He flipped the cover of the book shut and laid it on the table next to the bed. "I think we should find a story on James's shelf to read."

"But Dr. Ellig-am, if you don't got bone mallow then your body can't make blood, right?"

"That's correct." Martin struggled to his feet and walked across the room, picking up the first book his hand landed on. "This is a good moral story—*The Tortoise And The Hare.*"

"Lydia Bigelow's mum says you almost died 'cause you ran out of blood. Did your bone mallow leak out where the bones broke apart, so then your body couldn't make any more blood?"

Martin breathed out a heavy sigh and returned to the bed. "You better move out of the way, I don't want to sit on you," he said as he lowered himself down next to the boy.

"Evan, my bone marrow didn't leak out, but I did lose a lot of blood from a number of cuts that I sustained. I lost blood much faster than my body could manufacture new blood.

"But the doctors at the hospital gave me blood that had been donated by healthy people. If they hadn't done that, then yes, I would have died. Our blood is very important."

Evan rose up on his knees and put his arm around Martin's shoulder. "I'm sure glad they had all that leftover blood laying around."

"It wasn't just lay—" Martin glanced down at his watch before grumbling softly. "We'll take that up another time, I guess. There's something else I want to discuss with you tonight—about that rock of yours."

"My lucky Druid rock?"

"Well, it's not lucky. The *Druids* thought it was lucky, but we know now that's not true. But if you want to believe ... er, *pretend* it to be lucky that's fine. You must understand, however, that the rock will *not* protect you from harm if you do something dangerous. Do you understand what I'm saying?"

The boy dropped back on his heels and peered thoughtfully up at the doctor. "You're saying that my lucky rock is just for protecting me from pretend things?"

"Well ... *yeess*. I suppose that's one way to look at it. But do you understand that you can't go across the street out here and jump off the cliff, expecting that rock to keep you from getting hurt? That you need to be careful with your body?"

"I won't do anything like that. I promise."

"Good. Well, it's late. You need to get to sleep."

Martin winced as Evan wrapped his arms around him in a hug before placing a kiss on his cheek.

"G'night, Dr. Ellig-am."

"Goodnight, Evan." He cleared his throat and got to his feet before tucking the blankets in under the child's chin.

"Dr. Ellig-am."

"Yes?"

"You should be careful with *your* body, too."

"I try to be, Evan."

"But you weren't that night you had your crash. Lydia Bigelow's mum says you were drinking. You said that makes your brain not work right. Will you promise you won't drink anymore?"

Martin hissed a breath from his nose before forcing his rapidly stiffening limbs to bend one more time.

"Evan, I wasn't drinking that night."

"But Lydia Bigelow's mum said—"

"Lydia Bigelow's mum says way too much. So, does Lydia Bigelow for that matter. A lorry driver fell asleep while he was driving and he crossed into my lane. He ran into my car."

"Oh." Evan worried the satin edge of the blanket with his fingertips and stared up at the doctor.

Martin rubbed a hand over his tired eyes. "Was there something else bothering you?"

The child's lower lip quivered as he asked warily, "When *you* drink, do you get angry?"

"Evan, most people don't have any problems when they drink. Mrs. Ellingham likes to have a glass of wine now and then, but she just has one glass. It's when people drink too much that it becomes a problem."

"Will *you* promise not to drink too much though?"

"I don't drink alcohol, so you don't need to worry about that."

The child gave Martin a broad grin, flipped over on his stomach, and reached under his pillow, pulling out his lucky rock. "G'night, Dr. Ellig-am."

"Mm, goodnight, Evan." Martin reached a tentative hand out, stroked his palm over the child's head, and then got to his feet before repeating the gesture with his son.

Chapter 23

"All quiet in there?" Louisa asked when Martin finally limped into the kitchen from under the stairs.

"Well, let's wait and see. James is asleep, but Evan was full of questions tonight, so he didn't really get a bedtime story."

Turning from the sink, Louisa leaned back against the counter as she dried her hands on the tea towel. "What sort of questions?"

"Mostly about bone marrow—and blood."

Louisa grimaced and side-stepped her husband, draping the towel over the hook on the end of the counter. "Not an ideal topic to discuss with a seven-year-old at bedtime, Martin."

He reached behind his wife to pick up the tea kettle. The handle on the tap squeaked softly before water splashed into it.

"I realise that, Louisa. I tried to steer him away from the subject, but the boy was persistent." The kettle now full, Martin returned it to its base before plugging it in and flipping the switch.

His fingers drummed on the counter as he gazed absently out the window. "Who's this Lydia Bungalow girl Evan keeps going on about?"

"*Bigelow*. Her mum helps out in the cafeteria at the school," she said, pulling a teacup from the cupboard and tapping it against her husband's stomach. "Her father's Adrian Bigelow." He has the farm supply store over in Pendoggett."

Martin wrinkled his nose and his hand squeezed tightly around the cup as the man's name triggered less than pleasant memories of another Adrian—his disgruntled former pupil and colleague who had informed the village of his blood sensitivity and made his ensuing years in 'the village of the damned' all the more difficult.

"Don't make that face; he's a very nice man," Louisa said, her lips taut.

Martin shook himself from his musings. "I didn't say he wasn't." The teapot began to hiss its readiness, and he pulled it from its base. "Are you having tea?"

"Yes ... Mar-tin," she clipped as she pulled the cup back from his hand and set it down next to her own on the table. "Well then what was the face all about?"

"Would you like milk in your tea tonight?" he asked, attempting to change the subject as he moved towards the refrigerator at the opposite end of the kitchen.

"Yes, please. But answer my question. What do you have against Adrian?"

His face contorted once again, and Louisa hissed a breath from her nose. "Mar-*tin*."

Pulling out his chair and taking a seat, he peered up at his wife as she splashed milk into her cup. "I don't know Adrian Bigelow. I'm just reminded of that annoying prat, Adrian Pitts, at Royal Cornwall. He did that Cronk boy's splenectomy several years ago."

"Oh, I see. Well ... maybe you should try to let that go. It *was* a long time ago."

"Not as long as you might think," Martin said, tapping his spoon against the rim of his cup, a bit more firmly than necessary.

Louisa eyeballed him. They sat for several minutes, sipping at their Earl Grey as they listened to the waves crashing against the harbour walls.

"So, this Lydia Bigelow ... is there some reason her name keeps popping up?" he finally said.

Louisa looked up at her husband, giving him a wry smile. "She *is* a cute little girl. I suspect Evan rather fancies her."

"He's seven years old!"

"Still ... I've seen him making moon eyes at her when I've filled in for Trisha, the year twos' teacher, when she's been sick."

He shook his head as he blinked slowly. "But ... he said she smells. He said that she ... chuffs."

Louisa got up from her chair and came around the table, leaning over her husband from behind. "The course of true love never ran smoothly, Martin," she said, pressing her cheek to his. "You, of all people, should know that."

She ran her fingertips suggestively along his jawline then stepped towards the hallway. "Are you ready for bed?"

"Mm ... yes." He tipped his cup back, drank down the last bit of tea, and then put the two teacups in the dishwasher before hurrying after his wife.

When Martin finished in the bathroom a short time later, Louisa was lying in the bed on her side. She had freed her chestnut locks from their usual constraints, and they cascaded gently over her bare shoulder, which peeked out from under the duvet.

He gazed at her for several moments as she lay with her eyes closed, his shoulders rising as a deep breath filled his lungs before being slowly released in an inaudible sigh.

Louisa opened her eyes and smiled up at him. She was past being unsettled by her husband's sometimes peculiar ways, especially when it came to the more intimate aspects of their relationship. She had come to appreciate what had at one time felt like leering for what it really was—adoration.

"Don't you think you should come to bed? You're going to get a chill," she said as she pulled the covers back for him.

"Mm ... yes," he answered, giving his head an almost imperceptible shake. He pulled off his dressing gown and laid it neatly on the chair before sliding in next to her.

"Mmm, this is nice," Louisa said as she stretched herself out against the length of his bare body, pulling her arms in as he embraced her. A gust of wind rattled the windows of the old structure as she moved closer, and his grasp tightened.

He caressed her arm before his palm settled against her cheek. "You look especially beautiful tonight."

"Thank you, Martin," she said, giving him a shy smile.

Rolling towards her, Martin's lips, warm and yielding, met hers as his hands ran lightly over her skin, sending a tingle through her.

She pulled back from him slightly, examining the red incision line across the front of his shoulder. "Does it hurt anymore?" she asked before placing gentle kisses across the area.

"No, not a lot," he answered distractedly before leaning forward once again, this time trailing kisses down her neck and across her clavicle.

The heady male scent and fragrance of aftershave lotion that emanated from his warm mass, as well as his obvious arousal, fanned the flames of her own desire, and she slipped a leg over his hip, pulling him to her.

"Oh, Louisa," he breathed out. A soft growl slipped from his lips as his arms constricted around her. "I love—"

His endearment was cut short by the sound of pattering feet, and his wife quickly pulled away from him.

"Dr. Ellig-am!" Evan's voice called out as he rattled the latch on the door, struggling to get in. "Dr. Ellig-am!"

"Bloody hell!" Martin hissed through clenched teeth.

"I'll get him back to his room, you put some clothes on," Louisa got up from the bed, and wrapping her dressing gown around herself, hurried to the door.

Martin flopped back, pulling his hand up over his face to stifle a groan. "Gawd."

He forced himself from their cosy nest and worked a tee shirt over his right arm before slipping it over his head, all the while, listening to the boy pleading with his wife to let him into the room.

"He'll be out in a minute, Evan. Let's tuck you back in while we wait for him," he heard her say as their voices faded away across the hall.

After slipping a pair of boxers on, Martin grabbed his dressing gown and lumbered towards the nursery.

When he saw him in the doorway, Evan leapt from the bed and pushed past Louisa. He pulled frantically at his guardian, trying to climb into his arms.

Martin leaned over and hooked his left arm under the boy's backside, hoisting him into the air.

"Martin, be careful!" Louisa whispered, hurrying towards them.

"I've got him, Louisa," he said, giving a jerk of his head. "Let's go to our room to talk about this before we wake James."

The child clung to him as they crossed the landing, his arms locked around his neck and his legs wrapped tightly around his waist. Martin moved towards the bed, and Louisa held on to his arm as he lowered himself down.

Evan's body trembled as wheezy gasps for air were interspersed with uncontrollable sobs and coughing fits.

"Shh, shh, shh, shh, shh. It was just a bad dream," Martin said as he patted his back. "Louisa, go down to my supply cabinet and get an albuterol inhaler? They're on the top shelf on the left side."

"Yeah—yeah. Is the key in the same place you kept it before?"

"Yep. Be quick about it please. And bring my stethoscope as well."

Louisa dashed out the door and Martin turned his attention to the child. "Try to slow your breathing down, Evan. You're safe now."

Martin felt the boy's body relax slightly and he loosened his grip. "Can you tell me what it was about?"

The seven-year-old pulled back and looked at Martin, shaking his head. "I don't—wanna—say it."

Louisa hurried back into the bedroom and held out a small box.

"Can you open it?" Martin asked.

"Yeah, sorry." She peeled the top back and handed her husband the small canister inside.

He tipped it into the light, double checking the label and then shook it, squeezing the mechanism several times before the audible puff of air confirmed its readiness. He placed a hand on the back of the child's head and worked the inhaler into his mouth. "Deep breath." *Puff.* "Another one." *Puff.*

He waited until the wheeze in the boy's airway quieted and then inserted his stethoscope into his ears. "Breathe in for me," he said as he placed the diaphragm on to Evan's chest. "There, that's better."

Louisa went to the bathroom and returned with a wet flannel. "Let's wipe that face, Evan. Then maybe you can talk about your dream ... it might help," she said, giving him an encouraging nod.

Evan took in ragged breaths as Louisa wiped away the tears and mucus.

"Okay, try to calm down," she said softly. "This must have been a *very* frightening dream. But it wasn't real. And it does usually help to tell someone else about it ... makes it not so scary."

The boy glanced up at his guardian before his face crumpled and he began to cry again. "If I say it, it m-might really happen!"

"Evan, look at me," Martin said softly.

The boy pulled back slowly and peered up at him.

"I told you the truth about Father Christmas because I want you to be able to trust me. And you can trust me now when I say that it's safe to tell us about your dream. Nothing bad will happen."

The boy turned his gaze to his lap, picking vigorously at his fingernails. "It was about my dad ... and you."

He leaned forward, resting his forehead against Martin's chest. "He was hitting you with that bottle and you were bleeding ... *a lot*. All your blood ran out. I tried to scoop it up and put it back in the hole in your head where it was coming out, but he grabbed me and wouldn't let me go and—and—" The boy began to sob again. "You—you went away, and I was all by myself with him again!"

A wave of nausea washed over Martin as he was suddenly back in his parent's house, watching Auntie Joan walking away, leaving him alone with a mother and father who loathed him and blamed him for his grandfather's death. His arms tightened around the boy as he swallowed back the saliva that flooded his mouth.

Louisa watched her husband, his distraught face illuminated by the light from the bathroom.

He closed his eyes and sat quietly for several seconds. Then he took in a deep breath before bending his head down to kiss the top of the child's head. "I'm still here and you're still here. You're not alone," he said hoarsely. "Your father died Evan, and there's no way that he can ever come back to life."

Martin sat with the boy until his shuddering had stopped and his body had grown heavy in his arms. Then Louisa picked him up and returned him to his bed.

When she came back to the bedroom, Martin was gone. "Martin?" she called softly from the top of the stairs. Hearing water running, she followed the sound to the kitchen where she found him leaning over the sink, splashing water on his face.

"You okay?" she asked.

He glanced back at her and turned off the tap.

"Here," she said as she pulled the tea towel from the end of the counter.

He stood hunched over, his elbows resting on the edge of the sink as he reached a blind hand out for the towel before pressing it to his face.

Louisa caressed his back and then tugged him upright, watching as he wiped away the remaining moisture, noting his red-rimmed eyes. Reaching up, she gently touched the side of his head where Jim Hanley's whiskey bottle had made contact. "I'm so sorry you had to experience that."

"Mm. It didn't occur to me that Evan had seen it. I'll need to be sure to mention it to that Gabby Peterman woman ... the child psychologist. It's obviously contributed to his trauma."

A small smile floated across Louisa's lips. "I believe it's Abby Peterson, Martin."

He gave a shrug of his shoulders.

"I think you should talk with Dr. Newell as well."

Martin shook his head. "That would be inappropriate. He'd be crossing a professional boundary if he were to interject himself into another doctor-patient relationship. He'll want to let the psychologist handle Evan."

Louisa threaded her arms under his, clasping her hands behind his back. "I meant *you*—talk about you. That was a pretty strong reaction you had. Understandable though—you were attacked by the man."

Martin's eyes darted as he wriggled from her grasp. "I'm fine about that." He limped to the buffet and pulled down a glass before returning to the sink.

Louisa took a step to the side, and her husband turned on the tap, filling his glass with water before guzzling most of it. He dumped the rest into the sink and set the glass down on the counter with a sharp thunk. Then, pressing his hands to his eyes, he breathed out a long sigh. "What he said—what Evan said about being left alone with his fath—"

Martin's words caught in his throat and Louisa took a step forward, embracing him. "I see," she said softly as she pressed her ear to his chest. "It struck the chord a little too hard?"

"Mm." He lowered his arms, placing one hand on his wife's back as the other cradled her head.

"Let's go to bed," she whispered.

They woke the next morning to a cold day, but the rain had stopped and the clouds were beginning to clear. Martin lay alone, listening to the voices in the kitchen. Catching the occasional word or two, but mostly just appreciating the presence of his family in a house that had at one time felt very lonely. There was a thundering of footsteps on the stairs, before the bed shook as Evan leapt on to the mattress.

"Hi, Dr. Ellig-am!" the boy said as he leaned over on his forearms to peer into his face. "Mrs. Ellig-am said I could wake you up. We're havin' pancakes for breakfast! Not the

Pancake Day kind'a pancakes, the American kind. Mrs. Ellig-am is putting oats in 'em ta make 'em less objectional to you."

Rubbing at his eyes, Martin sat himself up and yawned before swinging his legs over the side of the bed. Evan jumped down and took hold of his hand, tugging on him as he got to his feet. "Come on, Dr. Ellig-am! Shift your arse; we got lots ta do today!"

The doctor pulled away and narrowed his eyes at the boy.

The child slapped a hand to his mouth and stood, stock-still, watching Martin's stony face. "Sorry, I said a 'fensive word again, didn't I."

"Of course, you did! Give this some thought, Evan. How *should* you have worded that?"

Evan rolled his eyes to the ceiling as he pondered the question and then turned a wary gaze towards Martin. "*Hurry up* your arse, we got lots ta do today?"

"*Noo!* There's nothing wrong with saying shift!"

Evan looked up at the doctor and cocked his head. "Then why do we get 'tention if we say piece of shift?"

The doctor let himself drop to the bed, eyeing the boy incredulously. "I thought you had really good ears."

He rubbed a hand over the back of his neck. "Think about what you said to me—shift your arse, we've got a lot to do today. If shift isn't an offensive word, which word do you think *is* offensive?"

The child mouthed his words and then shrugged his shoulders. "Arse?"

"*Yes.* It would have been politer to say, we need to hurry, we have a lot to do today."

"Sorry, Dr. Ellig-am."

Evan leaned back against the bed and dropped his hands to his sides, a hangdog expression on his face.

Martin breathed out a heavy sigh. "All right ... let's get the piece of shift bit sorted before you get yourself into trouble with it somehow. Have a seat up here," he said, patting the mattress next to him before reaching into the drawer of his bedside table and pulling out a pad of paper and a Biro.

"This is the word you used." Martin scrawled the letters S-H-I-F-T on to the paper. "*Shift*—it means to move something. It has other meanings, but that's all you need to know for the purpose of this conversation."

He ripped the sheet of paper from the pad and handed it to the boy. "Now, the other word—*S-H-I-T*—there's no *f* in that word. That word means the same thing as faeces and, therefore, it would be an offensive name to call someone or something, wouldn't it?"

"I don't know. What's a faeces?"

"Oh, for goodness' sake," Martin grumbled. "That disgusting smelling stuff that comes out of your—your *bottom* when you use the toilet!" he snapped.

Evan's mouth dropped open as the penny dropped. "Oh, now I see!"

Martin drew an *x* across the second printed word, tore off the second sheet of paper and passed it to the child. "Shift is an acceptable word, the other isn't. Understood?"

"Yes, sir."

"Good. Now, you better hurry up, I think you said we got lots ta do today, didn't you?"

The child gave the doctor a smile before skipping from the room.

Chapter 24

"Good morning," Louisa said when her husband entered the kitchen a short time later. "Coffee?"

He pulled a chair out from the table and took a seat. "Yes ... please."

Hearing his father's voice, James toddled towards the kitchen from the lounge. He dropped to his knees and crawled across the slate to Martin's side, latching on to his trousers and pulling himself to his feet. "Da-ee—up," he said, patting his leg.

"Good morning, James." He turned his hand over and James smacked his palm against his father's, giggling at the resultant sound.

Louisa set a cup in front of her husband and lifted her son on to his lap. "Now you're happy, aren't you!" she said liltingly as she brushed her thumb across the child's cheek. "We're having oatmeal pancakes with peaches and creme fraiche. Should I scramble some eggs for you, too?"

"Yes, that would be good. Thank you." He took an apple from the bowl on the table before passing it to his son. James wrinkled up his nose and gave his father a grin as he brought the pome to his mouth.

Martin's lip curled as his wife slipped a plate of pancakes in front of him. "This isn't a very healthy way to start the day."

"Oh, stop it Martin," she scolded. "I bought the creme fraiche that has those healthy little bugs in it. The ones that aid in digestion. And I hardly put any sugar on the peaches."

"Why did you put sugar on the peaches at all? Peaches are naturally high in sucrose. To add sugar is completely un—"

"Hush up and eat your breakfast, Martin. The boys *loved* it."

"Yes, I'm sure they did." He gave his plate another sneer before picking up his fork.

"Martin, erm ... Evan has a little activity planned for us today," Louisa said as she cracked an egg into a bowl.

His head shot up, and he looked back at her, wincing. "Ohh, it's not something with glue, is it? I really don't li—"

"Martin—shush. There's no glue involved."

Evan jumped up from his play in the lounge and ran to the kitchen. "Yeah, Dr. Ellig-am, we're gonna go decorate the Christmas tree I found with Mr. Large!" he said, slinging an arm up over Martin's shoulders.

"Poppy and Mr. Portman helped me make popcorn and cranberry strings yesterday, and we got all the ordaments that me and James made with Mrs. Ellig-am."

"We *have* all the or-*na*-ments that James and *I* made, Evan," the boy's guardian corrected.

The child rubbed his palms together, bouncing excitedly. "Yeah, you can bring those ones, too!"

He cocked his head at the boy as his brow furrowed. Then he rubbed his eyes before giving his wife a half-grimace. "You don't really think I'd add to the festive atmosphere, do you?"

Louisa slipped another plate in front of him and leaned over to place a kiss on his cheek. "I think that it wouldn't be the same for any of us without you. Besides, we need *someone* to put the star on the top of the tree."

Martin blew out a hiss of air and stabbed his fork into his eggs.

It was mid-afternoon when Ruth came through the back door, carrying a large insulated jug in one hand and a plastic bag in the other.

"Hello, Ruth!" Louisa said, giving the elderly woman a hug. "We're about ready to leave—just waiting on Martin. He said he had some work to do in his office, but I suspect he's stalling."

Ruth pulled a chair away from the table and took a seat. "He's not overly enthusiastic about our foray into Dickensian tradition, I take it?"

"Well, it's difficult for him. His memories of Christmas aren't the brightest."

"No, I suppose not," Ruth said as she folded her hands on the table. "Margaret always had a beautifully appointed home, but I doubt very much that Martin was allowed into those rooms, let alone to touch anything.

"And beyond that dreadful Christmas after my father died, Martin didn't come home for the holidays. Probably just as well."

"Well, Evan and I are determined to give him some happy memories this year," Louisa said surreptitiously, keeping a watchful eye on the hallway. "Cuppa while you're waiting, Ruth?"

"Yes, please. Well, I've put the wheels in motion on my end of things. Everything should be in order by Christmas Eve."

"Oh, that'll be perfect Ruth. Thank you so much. It really is a wonderful gift."

"We shall see. You do realise this could blow up in our faces, don't you?"

Louisa worried her lip as she set two cups on the table and filled them with hot water. "Mm, I do. Let's hope for a Christmas miracle."

The old woman's gaze was drawn for a moment to the children in the lounge. "Any word from the authorities about—" she asked, gesturing with her teacup towards the orphaned child.

"The child advocate spoke with Martin. They asked us to consider extending the current arrangements," the younger woman responded, her brow furrowed.

"*Oh*, I see. And you're not comfortable with that, I take it?"

Louisa took a seat across from her, glancing towards the consulting room. "I'm worried about Martin—*and*—" she said softly, giving her head a jerk towards the lounge. "I've never seen Martin the way he is with Ev— Er, this particular individual."

She ran a thumb and forefinger up and down her cup handle, breathing out a heavy sigh. "And *he's* becoming very attached to Martin. We have the name of a child psychologist, though. Martin's going to call first thing Monday morning to set up an appointment."

"Good. It's a very big decision any way you look at it."

Louisa leaned forward, speaking in a hushed tone. "What do *you* think, Ruth. Is this a good idea? Good for Martin—us?"

Ruth peered up at her nephew's wife. "I suspect that Martin may be able to work through some of his own issues as he helps the child, but that's not really Martin's intention, is it? Or is something else worrying you?"

"Well, it will mean a major change. And not just in our daily routine. Our family is James, Martin, you and me. I'm having trouble getting my head around anything different."

"Well, this is, of course, your decision. And one I don't envy, by the way," she said, waving a bony finger at Louisa.

"But most of us don't adjust to major changes overnight. Don't expect that if you do decide to extend his stay."

Ruth hesitated. "Look, Joan told me enough about Martin's and your history to know that my nephew's somewhat eccentric approach to wooing the opposite sex didn't sit well with you.

"And that he was hurt deeply when his rather bumbling attempts at romance went awry. I would imagine *you* were hurt as well. Especially if it was difficult for you to see his attempts for the genuine displays of affection that I'm sure they were."

Louisa ran a finger around the rim of her teacup. "Yeah, well, I wasn't always fair with Martin. I loved that he was different from any other man I'd ever met, but I expected him, in some ways, to be just *like* every other man I had ever met."

"But there must have been something about Martin that kept you interested, despite his frequent faux pas," the old woman said as she stirred another spoonful of sugar into her tea. "Something in his character that helped you to see beyond the difficulties between the two of you.

"Do you feel anything towards that young man over there? Anything that you could build on—help you to see beyond the challenges that will inevitably lie ahead in *that* potential relationship?"

Louisa glanced over at the two little boys. "It's just hard, Ruth. It sounds ridiculous, I know. But it feels like I'm being unfaithful to James when I do have moments with—" she said, giving a nod towards the lounge.

"That's interesting." The elderly woman stared absently out the window. "I had a friend who shared that same sense of ... guilt, if you will, before her second child was born. All of her time and attention had been devoted to her eldest child, and when she found herself pregnant, she felt as if she was taking something away from her first-born."

Louisa pulled in her chin and furrowed her brow at her. "Are you saying I'd be having the same conflicted feelings if Martin and I had another child of our own?"

"I'm merely relating a story, dear. You take from it what you will." Ruth leaned forward and lowered her voice. "But if you don't have feelings for that child, then perhaps it would be best to hope for another family who *could* love him in the way that all children deserve to be loved."

Louisa shook her head. "But what about Martin? This could be beneficial for him."

"You know as well as I do that Martin would *never* use that child for his own benefit. He would only make this situation permanent if he thought it best for the child. And it would be like living his childhood all over again if he knew that you harboured any resentment towards the boy.

"Yes, it would be painful for him to let the child go, be prepared for that. But it would be much worse for him to have you unhappy and the boy aware that he's not wanted. This *must* be something that's right for all involved. I am in no way handing down judgement here. I'm just saying you need to think this through carefully."

"I will, Ruth," Louisa said with a resigned sigh.

"Good."

The sun had begun to drop behind the trees when the Ellingham family arrived at the farm later that afternoon. Evan hopped his way from the car to the house, trying to keep his footsteps on top of Martin's shadow as it stretched out across the brown lawn.

"Brrr! It's cold out there today," Louisa said as she hurried through the door. "Martin, would you get a fire going in the fireplace?"

"Yes. I think I can manage that," he said as he pulled a lighter from the bag of bits and bobs that his wife had carried in and headed for the large living room.

"Don't forget the damper!" she called after him, alluding to the moment that set off a chain reaction of unfortunate events on their wedding night.

He re-emerged, ducking his head as he came through the doorway before focusing a glassy stare on her.

Louisa made a grab for James Henry as he toddled quickly towards the steps, hoisting him to her hip. "I'm just teasing you, Martin," she said, stroking her hand across his cheek as she passed by. "But ... you kind of did forget to open the damper."

Martin pursed his lips as his jaws clenched. "No, I did not! That was *not* my fault!" he stated emphatically. "That damper was already open; the chimney was blocked."

He hissed out a breath and turned quickly, his head cracking against the door casing. "Ow!" he yelped as he doubled over, slapping a hand to his forehead.

A startled James burst into tears, distressed by his father's outburst. Louisa pulled his head to her breast and cooed softly to him.

Evan pulled a chair over to the refrigerator and opened the freezer compartment, grabbing for a bag of peas.

He leapt to the floor and ran to Martin's side. "Here Dr. Ellig-am, put this on it. I read in a book that vegetables are good for things like that."

Martin reached for the bag as he wiped at the tears that stung his eyes. "Thank you, Evan."

"You better sit down for a bit, Martin. That *was* quite a bump," Ruth said as she took hold of his elbow and tried to lead him to a chair.

"I'm fine," he growled back, pulling his arm away. "I'll go see if I can manage to light a fire without burning the house down."

Ruth cocked her head at Louisa. "Well, we're off to a brilliant start."

"Yeah, sorry. That was my fault," she said. "I'll let him cool off a bit, then go and have a word with him."

Evan followed after Martin. "Can I help?" he asked, watching as he piled logs into the firebox.

The doctor turned a weary visage towards the little boy as he pressed the bag of vegetables to his head. He was prepared to dismiss him to another room, but the child's eager eyes softened his mood, and he wagged a finger at the woodpile in the corner. "Why don't you bring a couple of those logs over here."

"Kay."

Martin pulled up a stool and sat down before working kindling in around the existing wood in the fireplace.

He took an additional log from the boy and laid it on top. "Get some more of those sticks from that basket over there ... put them in around the bigger pieces of wood."

Evan worked quietly until the pile was declared ready for lighting.

Martin picked up the lighter from a nearby table, glancing over at the seven-year-old. "Do you want to do this?"

Evan's eyes grew round. "Can I really?"

"Yes, but you have to make me a promise first."

"Kay."

Martin's cheeks nudged upwards as the boy pulled his hands behind his back, attempting to contain his excitement as he bounced on his toes. "You must *only* do this when an adult gives you permission. And an adult must be right next to you when you do it. Fire can be a very dangerous thing, and it's not for playing around with. Got it?"

"Got it! Now can I?" he said, reaching his hand out.

Martin released the child safety switch before the lighter clicked and a small flame appeared at the end of it. "Okay, I'll hold the button down and you light the kindling ... er, the little sticks."

Evan wrapped his hands around Martin's and guided the flame to the tinder, his face lighting up as the twigs ignited.

Martin looked down at the seven-year-old's hands. They weren't much bigger than James Henry's hands. Granted, James had inherited his father's solid paws, but Evan was unusually small for his age. *I need to get him in to see a paediatrician ... get a thorough physical done,* he thought.

"That's the way, now light the other sticks." Martin glanced to the side as he saw movement from the corner of his eye.

"How are you men doing in here?" Louisa asked as she watched the flames begin to dance in front of her.

Martin looked up and gave her a grunt before turning his attention back to the job at hand. "There, I think that's got it, Evan," he said as he pulled his hand back away from the fire that was beginning to crackle and pop. He reached over and tugged at the fireplace screen, giving the boy an approving nod. "Well done."

"Thanks, Dr. Ellig-am. I never got ta do *that* before."

The boy's brows drew together as he peered closely at him. "How's your head?" he asked, pulling Martin's hand and the bag of peas away. "You gots a bruise ... but I think you'll live."

"Good to know," he said, getting to his feet.

"Martin, could I have a word?" Louisa asked. "Evan, I think Aunt Ruth is ready for your help in the kitchen."

"Okay!" the child said before dashing off.

Martin tipped his head back and looked down at his wife. "Problem?" he asked aggrievedly.

"Yes, Martin, there is a problem. I said something I shouldn't have, and I think I may have caused hurt feelings in the process. I made you an object of ridicule earlier, and I owe you an apology."

He turned away from her as he rubbed at a bit of soot on his palm. "I just wasn't aware that you blame—"

He huffed out a breath and shook his head. "I wasn't aware that you still think about that night—that fiasco."

"Well, of course I think about it. It *was* our wedding day. A rather auspicious occasion, don't you think?"

"Gawd," he mumbled as he pulled a poker from the stand on the hearth. He yanked the screen back roughly and jabbed at the logs, sending sparks flying.

"Careful, Martin. You don't want to—"

"Louisa, don't say it!" He dropped the poker back into the stand, iron clanking harshly against iron.

"Mm, sorry." She wrapped her arms around him from behind, clasping her hands across his belly. "This is nice," she said as she pressed her cheek to his back.

"Louisa, I'm sorry—about the honeymoon."

"I'm sorry I brought it up. It *was* a rather unforgettable experience, though, wasn't it?" she added, hoping to lighten the mood.

"Yes. Yes, it was. I'll go see if Ruth needs some help," he said, pushing her hands away before quickly hurrying off towards the kitchen.

Louisa dropped heavily into a chair and slapped a hand to her head. *Stupid, stupid, stupid, Louisa!* she muttered.

"Anything I can do?" Martin asked as he entered the kitchen and tossed the now thawed peas into the bin.

Ruth pointed to a chair as she balanced James on her hip. "Yes, you can sit down and let me look at your head ... assess the situation."

"It's not necessary, the situation's already been assessed. It appears I'll live."

The elderly woman gave her nephew a crooked grin. "Good to hear." She gestured towards a chair. "Have a seat. I need you to hold your son."

Martin pulled a chair away from the table and dropped into it.

Ruth settled James Henry on to his father's lap, then she narrowed her eyes at her nephew. "You know, Martin, your wife and your shadow over there have worked very hard to make this Christmas a special one," she murmured furtively. "It would behove you to try to enjoy it. Or to at least make a gallant attempt at feigned appreciation."

"Yes, I know. I know."

Chapter 25

"So, what would you like me to do?" Martin sat, looking around the room, wondering at the array of garland, boxes of lights, and ornaments of various sorts and sizes strewn around on the floor. Evan stood on a chair in front of the counter as Ruth poured amber liquid into glasses.

"When I'm finished here," Ruth replied, I'll take the baby, and you can take those fairy lights and old ornaments and put them in the other room. Evan's preparing some very festive looking hors d'oeuvres, and I've prepared the wassail ... using apple juice in place of cider, of course."

"I see," he said, craning his neck to peer around the boy to the platter that he was filling with skewered foods of some sort.

Ruth set a glass in front of him. "Try that ... tell me what you think."

Martin took a sip and gave a soft grunt. "Hmph."

"I see. Your waxing lyrical may go to my head," Ruth said dryly.

James Henry reached a hand towards his father's glass, wiggling his fingers.

"Are you thirsty, James?" he asked softly, bringing the glass to his son's mouth. "This is a treat, so don't get used to it."

The boy sucked at the rim, sending a trickle of warm sticky liquid dribbling down the backside of the tumbler and on to the table. Martin grabbed for a napkin, trying to stop the trickle from making its way towards his trousers. "Oh, gawd."

"Here, Martin, let me take him. You get things under control there. Then take those boxes in to Louisa," Ruth said as she pulled James from his lap.

Martin took a few more swipes at his leg with the napkin before getting to his feet and loading up his arms with lights and ornaments.

Louisa was adding water to the Christmas tree stand when he limped into the living room.

"Where do you want these?" he asked as he stood awkwardly.

She stretched up and gave him a kiss before taking the boxes from his hands, setting them on the floor. "If you can help me put the lights on, then we'll be ready to hang the garland and decorations when Ruth and the boys come in."

Picking a box up, she slapped it against his stomach. "Here, you get started while I go put this away," she said, hurrying off with the watering can.

Looking from the lights in his hand to the tree, a warm flush of embarrassment spread up his neck. He set them on a nearby table and took a seat on the sofa.

"Everything okay?" Louisa asked when she returned from the kitchen.

"Fine. I just think this is something that you and Ruth would be better at. I'm not very good with this sort of thing."

Coming up behind him, she wrapped her arms around his neck. "I'd rather do it with you."

"Louisa." he sighed and shook his head.

"What is it, Martin?" she murmured, nuzzling her nose into his neck. Her soft breath against his skin sent a small shiver through him.

He pushed her arms away and struggled to get to his feet. "*I* don't know what I'm supposed to do here!"

"What? With the lights on the tree?"

"Of course, with the lights on the tree!" He turned and looked at her, shaking his head. "Why do you ask me to do these things that you know I'm rubbish at ... or clueless about, in this case. If you're trying to humiliate me, your tactics are working."

Louisa tipped her head down and peered up at him. "Martin ... it's just a Christmas tree. It's not that hard."

"My point exactly! It's not that hard—for *you!* And for just about every other Englishman, it's not hard. But I could be a bloody head-hunter from Papua New Guinea for all I know about decorating a Christmas tree!"

He snatched the box from the table and waved it in the air. "How, *exactly*, am I supposed to do this? Do I stick them on there going up and down? Do I go around and around with them? Or maybe I just—go with the flow—take them out of the box and throw them on there," he said, gesticulating wildly. "Stick them on wherever they happen to land."

Louisa glared at him, her hands perched on her hips. "You could have just asked how to do it, you know, Martin."

Tapping his fingers on the side of the box, Martin took in a deep breath and then shifted his gaze to the floor. "Yes, I could have. But—well—yes, I could have."

Taking the lights from him, Louisa pulled them from the box. "Here, first you have to untangle them. You do this one and I'll work on another one. Then I'll show you what to do next."

"Mm, yes."

He held the tangled mass up in front of him, looking for a loose end to start with. "You know, if these had been put away properly the last time they were used, we wouldn't be having to do this."

"They're some that Joan had used. Maybe she was in a hurry when she was putting things away. She *was* a very busy woman, hmm?"

Martin glanced up at her with a wistful expression on his face before refocusing his attention on the ball of wires and bulbs.

Although the dexterity in his injured hand had improved, it required a great deal of concentration to get his fingers to perform many tasks, and the muscles in his arm tired quickly. He took a break from the tedious process, trying to shake out a cramp that had set in.

"You, okay?" Louisa asked as she straightened out another loop in her strand of lights.

"It's like trying to untangle a bowl of cold spaghetti with a tyre lever," he grumbled.

"Just leave it if it's too hard. I can get it when I finish with this one," she said, giving him a sympathetic smile.

He hissed out a breath and returned to the task.

A patter of footsteps grew louder as Evan ran in from the kitchen. "Hi Dr. Ellig-am! Whatcha doin'?"

"I'm making a hash of untangling these Christmas lights is what I'm doing." He jerked at his arm, trying to free the wire that had gotten hung up on his fixators.

"Stop wigglin' around and I'll get it off ya," the boy said, grabbing on to the doctor's arm with one hand as he uncoiled the strand of lights with the other. "There, that's got it."

Evan took a step back, studying Martin's deeply furrowed brow. "Yer not havin' much fun, are you Dr. Ellig-am?"

"I'm trying, Evan," he said with a sigh.

The child took the mass of lights from his guardian's hands and then gave a tug on his shirt sleeve. "I'm good at untangling stuff," he said into Martin's ear. "You want *me* ta do this while you go show Mrs. Ellig-am the mistletoe?" The boy wiggled his eyebrows and gave the doctor a cheesy grin.

Martin stared down at him. "Now you're being cheeky. Why don't you just help me get this mess sorted, then we'll get the lights on the tree."

"Nicely done, men!" Louisa said as she came over to inspect her husband's progress a short time later. "Bring that string on over and I'll show you how to fasten them on."

She took the male end of the strand of lights and plugged it into a socket next to the tree, lighting up the white bulbs and eliciting an enthusiastic response from Evan.

"Hey, they work!"

"Yes, they do. So now we start at the bottom and work our way up and around. Martin, if you can hold the lights, I'll fasten them on."

"Yes." Martin watched his wife as she worked, sneaking the occasional peek at her upturned bum as she circled the tree slowly.

"Martin," Louisa said, giving a gentle pull on the strand in her husband's hand. "Pay attention."

"Yes, I am."

"To the *lights.*" She tipped her head back and gave him a beguiling grin.

"Mm." He tugged at a reddening ear and averted his gaze.

"That looks really good already, Mrs. Ellig-am," Evan said as he sat perched on the sofa watching them work.

"Good! I think we're ready for another string, Evan. Can you bring one over?"

"Yep." The boy said as he jumped to the floor.

He dragged the second set of lights across the floor, handing the plug to Louisa, and Martin bent down to gather the rest of the strand into an organised handful.

By the time Ruth came in with refreshments, the tree was ablaze with warm white light.

"Your son has gone down for his nap," she announced as she set a tray of glasses on the dining table.

"Oh, thank you, Ruth," Louisa said, pulling the lid off a box of old ornaments, gently fingering the coloured glass baubles. "These are absolutely beautiful! Were they Joan's?"

Ruth walked over and looked over the younger woman's shoulder. "Oh! Here I thought Mother had thrown those out when we were children. They were my absolute favourite. I always thought they looked like raindrops."

"'Cept those ones are all different colours," Evan said as he folded himself over the back of the sofa, swinging his feet up behind him.

"Yes, well, when I was a girl, I thought they must have fallen from a rainbow. Seemed a perfectly logical explanation to a five-year-old."

Evan's head shot up and he eyed Ruth dubiously. "You're just tryin' to wind me up, aren't you, Dr. Ellig-am."

"Well, they didn't actually fall from a rainbow, Evan. That's just what I thought when I was five."

"*That's* the windin' up part. You're too old to have been five!" the boy said, a giggle forcing its way through his nose.

Ruth gave her nephew a black look. *"Mar-tin?"*

"Why are you looking at me like that? I have nothing to do with it!"

Evan pulled his feet over his head, somersaulted over the back of the sofa, and sat looking smugly at Ruth. "He's right. He didn't tell me nothin'. I figured that out all by myself."

The elderly woman folded her arms across her chest and narrowed her eyes at the child. "Oh, I see. Well, I have a document to prove otherwise, young man."

She pointed a finger at Martin. "What about my nephew over there? Do you think *he's* too old to have been five?"

"Uh-uh. *He* knows how to play games, so he *gots* to have been a kid."

Louisa and Ruth shot each other startled glances as Martin's ears reddened again.

He tipped his head to the side and rubbed his palm across the back of his neck. "Why don't you show us what you have in the other boxes, Ruth."

"Don't try to change the subject, Martin. Things are just getting interesting," the old woman said. She turned back to the boy. "We'd like to hear a bit more about these games that the other Dr. Ellingham plays, Evan."

Martin threw his head back. "Ohhh, for goodness' sake! We played a game when we were freezing out on the moor ... just to keep our—the boy's mind off the cold."

"*And*—don't forget about the game we played at the hospital," Evan added as he flopped back on the sofa.

Louisa took pity on her husband as he fidgeted under his aunt's scrutinising gaze, stepping in to try to divert the conversation.

"Well, I think that's very nice that Dr. Ellingham is willing to do things like that with you, Evan."

"Yeah, but sometimes he has trouble with his paying attention."

"Yes, he does," she said. "But I suppose that's true of all of us at one time or another. Hmm, Martin?"

He huffed out a breath. "I thought we came here to decorate a Christmas tree."

"Yes, Dr. Ellingham's right. Let's have a snack. Then we'll hang the ornaments on the tree." Louisa headed for the kitchen stopping briefly to gesture to the child. "Come on, Evan. You can bring your special treat in."

The seven-year-old leapt from the sofa and darted past Louisa. They emerged from the kitchen a few minutes later with Louisa carrying a tray of cheese sandwiches and Evan, walking backwards, concealing a tray in his hands.

Martin walked towards the table as Evan turned and set the tray down with a flourish.

"Ta-da!" the boy said, a grin spreading ear to ear.

Louisa watched her husband's face. His eyes began to sparkle, and she knew that Evan had hit the mark with his contribution to their light repast.

"It's that green fellow—from that book of yours," Martin said as he wagged a finger at the tray of appetisers. "The grouchy one."

"Yep!" the boy said as he picked up a skewer and held it out. "See—the white ball on his Santa hat is one of those teensy marshmallows. I stuck that on the stick first, then I stuck the strawberry on with the pointy end up. And guess what the fuzz on the bottom of his hat is."

Martin brought the titbit up closer to his face. "Hmm ... looks like a slice of banana."

"That's 'cause it *is* a slice of banana! And the grape is his head. Do you like it?" Evan asked as he eyed his guardian closely.

A small dimple appeared on the doctor's right cheek. "I do like it, Evan. Very much. It's very clever. Nicely done."

The boy turned a beaming face to Louisa. "He likes it!" he whispered loudly.

Louisa leaned over and took the child's face in her hands, giving him a spontaneous kiss on his forehead. "Yes, he does like it. And it was all your idea."

Evan pulled his face back, his eyes scanning hers. "Were you just bein' polite, Mrs. Ellig-am, or did you kiss me 'cause you like me?"

"That was definitely a kiss because I like you, Evan," she replied before adding a kiss to his cheek. "Now, let's eat. Then we need to get that tree decorated!"

They were less than forty-eight hours away from the winter solstice, and in Cornwall that meant there was just under nine and a half hours of sunlight in a day.

Aunt Ruth flipped the switch on the wall, and the ceiling lights illuminated the darkening room. Louisa retrieved the lighter from where Martin had left it on the table near the fireplace and lit the candles she had scattered about near the Christmas tree.

Martin watched her, his head listing ever farther to the right as he struggled to make sense of her actions.

She picked her mobile up from where she had left it laying by the tray of sandwiches. And then she tapped away on the screen.

The sentimental sound of Johnny Mathis, singing of chestnuts roasting on an open fire, emanated from a small speaker on a table in the corner of the room.

He screwed up his face. "Louisa, do we have to—"

"Relax, Martin; I'm being selective. There will be no small rodents breaking into song today," she said as she walked over and patted his cheek.

"Mm, yes."

She put a hand on the seven-year-old's head and tipped his face towards hers. "Go fetch your bag of popcorn and cranberry strings and we'll hang those on the tree first."

The boy's face lit up as he dashed off towards the kitchen, returning seconds later with a brown paper bag. "I gots 'em, Mrs. Ellig-am. Should I put 'em on?"

"Well, if we want them to look their most beautiful, we need to start at the top and spiral them around the tree. Martin, could you get us started?"

He pulled in his chin before taking hold of the end of the first strand as the child eagerly yanked it from the bag. The boy seemed unconcerned by the bits of popcorn being shed on to the floor.

Opening his mouth to administer an admonishment regarding the child's carelessness, Martin was brought up short by his wife's elbow as it hit him sharply in the ribs. He winced as he whipped his head to the side, giving her a questioning glare. She stretched up on tip-toe. "It doesn't matter, Martin. We'll clean up later. He's having fun," she whispered into his ear.

He gave an acknowledging grunt as he watched the popcorn and cranberries process from the bag like a length of small intestine being removed from an abdominal cavity.

Evan picked up the bag, upending it to spill the last of the garland on to the floor. "That's the whole lot," he said as he wiped his hands on his trousers.

Louisa grabbed a napkin and brushed the crumbs from the boy's fingers. "Well done, Evan. Now we need Dr. Ellingham to fasten his end on the top of the tree," she said as she joined a wire hanger to the garland.

Ruth pulled a dining room chair over to where she could observe the activity, setting her glass of warm wassail down on a small table next to her.

"Are you gonna be our sidewalk super attendant, Dr. Ellig-am?" Evan asked her.

Ruth gave the boy a crooked smile. "That sounds like the perfect job for me, Evan."

"Is this where you want it?" Martin asked as he waited, the wire hanger poised over a branch.

Louisa moved up behind him, resting her hands on his waist. "What do you think, Evan? Does that look about right?"

The seven-year-old cocked his head and squinted his eyes. "Maybe that little branch up a little more would be better."

Martin raised his hand up and began to fasten it on to another branch.

"No, not that one," the child said, jabbing a finger at the tree. The one with the one long needle stickin' out."

Martin groaned softly. "What long needle sticking out? They all look the same to me."

Evan slipped in between Martin and the tree, peering up. "No, you gots the branch that looks like a stretched-out porcupine. I mean the other one. The one that's about as tall as a baby snake and as long as a baby snake."

Martin lowered his arm and huffed out a breath. "It's a pine tree Evan, not a reptile."

The boy giggled. "I know that, Dr. Ellig-am. It just *looks* like a baby snake. Now you better hurry up or we'll be here all day."

The doctor cast a sharp glance at the boy before moving his hand up slightly.

"Stop, Dr. Ellig-am! That's the one! That's the one!"

"All right, settle down." Martin hooked the wire over the branch and then turned his head to look at his wife.

She pressed her lips to his shoulder and squeezed her arms around his middle, causing him to tense and pull in a small gasp. "Sorry," she said. "Did that hurt?"

"A bit. It's all right now, though." He looked down at her and she loosened her grip as she shifted to his front.

"This is very nice," she said, leaning forward to place a kiss on his chest.

"If you wanna kiss her on the mouth, there's some mistletoe hangin' in the doorway, Dr. Ellig-am." Evan's said. "I hanged it up just for you."

"Mm, yes." Martin pulled back from his wife and cleared his throat. "We better hurry up or we'll be at this all day."

"I'll catch him under the mistletoe later—don't worry," Louisa whispered to the disappointed child.

"Let's get this lovely garland on," she said. "Then we can hang the ornaments. I think what might work best is for you to carry the string around behind Dr. Ellingham as he moves around the tree, Evan. Can you do that?"

"Sure, I can!" The boy leaned over, scrambling along the floor to pick up the line of popcorn and cranberries. "'Kay, I'm ready," he said as he straightened himself, watching Martin expectantly.

Louisa followed along with the two male members of the team, instructing her husband on the proper placement of the ornamentation.

Martin glanced down and grimaced at the occasional crisp, popping sound of a cranberry as it fell victim to the seven-year-old's feet, and his wife shot him a warning look.

"I know, I know. He's having fun," Martin whispered to his wife. "But you do realise, don't you, that we can't expect Ruth to clean up the mess. And I can't very well get down on my hands and knees to do it. That leaves—"

"Yes, Martin, I know. Please stop worrying about the mess. I spend half my days at the school cleaning up messes."

By the time the final foot of garland had been affixed to the tree, James Henry's protestations at being left alone in his cot in the kitchen could be heard over the rich orchestral rendition of Tchaikovsky's Nutcracker Ballet.

When Louisa returned with the boy, he was rubbing at tired eyes and confused by his unfamiliar surroundings.

Martin sat down on the sofa, elevating his aching legs. "Here, I can take him," he said, reaching out for him. The boy buried his face in his father's chest when Louisa set him on his lap.

"How 'bout the rest of us finish up with this decorating, hmm?" Louisa said, tousling the seven-year-old's hair.

"Come on, Dr. Ellig-am," Evan said, taking Aunt Ruth by the hand and helping her to her feet. "I'll let you put on your favourite ones."

"Thank you, Evan. That's very chivalrous," the elderly woman said as she walked to the tree.

"Here, Ruth." Louisa handed her an azure blue teardrop-shaped ornament. "You may have the honour of hanging the first one."

Martin watched as his aunt reached up and hooked the wire over a needle-clad branch, the image strangely familiar. "Did Grandfather Ellingham decorate a tree at Christmastime, Ruth?"

"Yes, he did. One of the few traditions he carried on with after Mother died."

"Hmph," Martin grunted, pulling up his chin. "I think I remember that."

"Well, perhaps you have a positive memory after all." The old woman walked behind the sofa, patting her nephew's shoulder as she passed by.

She went to the box on the table and pulled out a yellow-green, glass teardrop. "This one was my absolute favourite, Evan," she said as she lowered it for the boy to see. "It reminded me of the new grass that comes up in the spring."

She shook a wire hanger free of the others and slipped it on to the ornament. Then she reached for a branch before hesitating, holding it out to the seven-year-old. "Here, Evan, why don't you hang it this year."

He looked up at her excitedly and reached out, before quickly pulling his hands behind his back. "No, I think you better do it."

"I really don't mind," the old woman reassured him.

Louisa leaned down. "I think Dr. Ellingham must really like you, Evan, to want to share her special ornament with you."

"But I don't *wanna* hang it up, Mrs. Ellig-am!" he whispered back.

Deciding against pursuing the matter further for the moment, Louisa gave Ruth a shrug of her shoulders. "Thank you, Ruth, but you go ahead."

Louisa, Ruth and Evan worked their way through the box of teardrop ornaments as Martin sat watching. "That's the last of those," Louisa said as she put the lid back on the box. She set the empty box aside and opened the next one in the stack.

Evan peered over the side, his eyes lighting up as the red and white striped, glass candy canes were revealed. "Those look like the real ones, 'cept the real ones don't gots the little hangers on the top."

"Oh, these are so sweet!" Louisa laid one in her palm and showed it to her husband. "Don't they look just like something Joan would have?"

"Mm, yes. Her dietary habits were appalling," he answered dryly.

Louisa pulled the ornament back and gave him a visual reprimand, provoking a cock of his head and a raised eyebrow in return.

"What?"

"Oh, *Martin!*" she hissed. She reached to pick her son up from his lap. "All right, get up," she said, extending her hand. "*You* need to get in the Christmas spirit."

He screwed up his face and then swung his feet to the floor. Picking up his crutch, he pulled himself up with it as his wife held on under his arm.

He was nearly upright when his right knee buckled under him, sending him plonking heavily back on to the sofa, his wife and son being dragged down with him. Louisa let out a startled shriek, and James Henry erupted into a fit of laughter as he struggled to right himself.

"*That's* the spirit, Dr. Ellig-am!" Evan said, jumping on to the sofa next to him.

Turning a rapidly warming face towards his wife, Martin pulled in his chin. "Mm, sorry."

"Are you okay?" Louisa asked, putting her hand over her mouth to stifle a giggle.

He cleared his throat and got to his feet. "I'm—fine."

"Here, Martin, you hang the next one," Ruth said, hurriedly slipping a hanger on to a glass candy cane before her nephew could escape to the kitchen.

He eyed the tree dubiously. "Where should I put it?"

Evan jumped from the sofa and raced to his side. "I think you should hang yours up at the top 'cause no one else can reach up there, Dr. Ellig-am."

"That's an excellent suggestion, Evan," Louisa said as she pulled another box from the stack of ornaments. "Oh, Joan's written *for Martin* on this one."

He came over and peered over her shoulder. "Mm, just set it aside. I'll open it at home."

"But it might be Christmas ornaments. I think you—"

"Just set it aside, Louisa!" he snapped back. "We don't need to deal with that now!"

Louisa stared back at him for a moment before reluctantly laying the box on an end table.

Evan walked back to the sofa and pushed himself back into the cushions.

"Could you go to the kitchen please, Evan"—Ruth said, taking note of the child's sudden change in affect—"and bring the ornaments that you and James made for the tree?"

The boy slid from the seat and plodded towards the kitchen.

"You better go and have a private word with that young man, Martin. Set things right again," the elderly woman said, eyeing her nephew imperiously.

"I'm sorry?"

"I believe your little row with your wife has resulted in a moment of Weltschmerz for the child."

Martin cocked his head at her. "What row?"

"Oh, don't be obtuse," Ruth said impatiently. "Your cross words a moment ago ... it was distressing to him."

"That's ridiculous," he scoffed.

"Mar-tin." The elderly woman pressed her hand to his back and wagged a bony finger in the child's direction. "Go."

He threw his head back and huffed out a breath. "Fine!" he hissed before moving off.

Louisa raised her eyebrows at Ruth, shaking her head.

He stopped for a moment in the kitchen doorway, then he went to the sink and filled a glass with water.

The seven-year-old sat with his hands on the table in front of him, his chin resting on his fists.

"Evan ... is there a problem?" he asked before taking a sip.

The boy shrugged his shoulders but remained mum.

Taking a seat next to him, Martin rested his arm across the back of the child's chair. "Did it upset you that I was short with Mrs. Ellingham?"

Another shrug of the shoulders was followed by a moist sniff. "You need ta say yer sorry for bein' all shirty else she's gonna leave, Dr. Ellig-am," the child said, turning a teary face towards him.

Martin breathed out a heavy sigh. "I see. Evan, Mrs. Ellingham won't leave just because we had a disagreement."

"You didn't *have* a disagreement. *You* got all shirty with her. That makes mums leave."

Martin pulled his arm from the back of the chair and spun it around so the boy was facing him. "I suppose I could have been politer—yes, you're right. But Mrs. Ellingham is aware that I can be—gruff and-and—"

"Rude?" The child sniffled and wiped the back of his hand across his nose.

Martin grimaced, pulling his handkerchief from his back pocket before pressing it to the boy's face. "Blow."

Evan sucked in a deep breath before exhaling forcefully as he threw his head forward, sending mucous hurtling through his nostrils and under the bottom edge of the handkerchief.

Screwing up his face, Martin wiped his hand and huffed out a breath. "I miss my aunt Joan very much. My mother didn't—"

He dropped his head to the side as he quirked the left corner of his mouth. "My mother didn't have much of an interest in being my mother, but my Auntie Joan"— the words caught in his throat— "she did. I didn't *mean* to be rude, Evan.

"But—well, I do know that it comes out that way at times, and I'm sorry for that. I also know that Mrs. Ellingham won't leave. She promised me she wouldn't ever do that, and I trust her."

Evan stared at his feet as they swung vigorously to and fro under the chair. He peered up at his guardian. "Can you still tell 'er yer sorry ... just ta be on the safe side?"

Martin pursed his lips as air hissed from his nose. Then he got to his feet and went to the doorway. "Louisa," he called. "May I have a word with you?"

The seven-year-old waited expectantly as the sound of footsteps grew louder.

"What is it, Martin?" she asked as she peered around him at the child.

"I, er—I'd like to apologise for being—for being all—shirty. About the box from Joan."

Louisa gave her awkward man a soft smile. "Thank you, Martin. I accept your apology."

Evan leapt from his chair and hurried over to give a tug on the doctor's sleeve. Martin leaned over, and the boy breathed warm, moist words into his ear.

Giving a roll of his eyes, he straightening himself before taking his wife's chin in his hand. Then, tipping his head down, he placed a lingering kiss on her lips, bringing a broad smile to Evan's face.

"I'm assuming from that smug look on your face that my apology was satisfactory?" Martin asked him.

The seven-year-old tipped his head to the side. "Yeah, that was pretty good," he said before slipping past them and darting towards the living room.

"That *was* pretty good," Louisa said. "Almost worth you getting all shirty with me. But ... if you'd like to make it better than satisfactory, we *are* still under the mistletoe." She gave him a coy smile and tipped her head back as he pulled her closer, pressing his lips to hers.

It was late by the time the tree had been trimmed, Ruth had been dropped off at her cottage, and the Ellingham family had returned to the surgery.

"I'll get something together for supper if you like," Martin said as he set the bag of leftover speared Grinch heads on the counter.

"Thank you, Martin. I'll take James up and give him a bath, then get Evan started with his." She turned to the seven-year-old and waved him towards the steps. "Come on up, young man. You can get some pyjamas together, and then when I get done bathing James, it'll be your turn."

"Kay," the boy said before running ahead, his feet pattering on the stairs.

Martin limped down the hall towards his consulting room with the box from Joan under his arm. He set it on his desk and began to pull the flaps open and then hesitated before slipping it into a bottom drawer.

He returned to the kitchen and rummaged through the refrigerator, finally pulling a carton of eggs from the shelf.

Deciding on scrambled eggs for dinner, he cracked them into the bowl. Then pulling the wire whisk from the utensil drawer he beat the yolks and whites together.

His right arm tired quickly, and he began to lose both the strength and control needed for the job. Shaking the cramp from his arm, he retrieved the bottle of milk from the refrigerator and set it on the counter. Then he scooped up the empty egg shells and pulled the cabinet door open to access the trash bin.

"Oh, God!" The odour of a forgotten fish carcass hit his nose. He yanked the bin from the cupboard and lifted out the liner, attempting to keep it at arm's length as he limped towards the back door.

A gust blew in off the harbour as he turned the knob, wrenching the door from his hand and pushing a waft of stench into his face. His stomach churned as he turned to get himself upwind of the rotting trash while he wrested the lid from the outdoor bin.

Throwing the bag of rubbish into the can, he pulled a handkerchief from his back pocket, covering his nose.

"Martin, why is the door hanging open? It's freezing in here!" Louisa said as she stuck her head through the door.

Slapping the lid back on, he whirled around, his brow pulled down. "I was trying to get this bag of-of—*detritus*—disposed of as it should have been yesterday!"

"Well stop dithering! You're going to catch your death!"

He blinked back at her. "I'm not *dithering!* I couldn't get the lid off the bloody bin!"

He grumbled under his breath as he pushed past her, heading for the sink. "You should take the trash out immediately if you've thrown raw fish into the bin, Louisa," his said as he vigorously scrubbed his hands.

"Sorry, I forgot. The appointment with Dr. Newell yesterday and everything, you know."

He gave an annoyed grunt as he reached for the tea towel.

"Why don't you let me finish up here. You go see how Evan's coming in the bath, hmm," she said, kissing him and patting his bum. "Then we'll eat and get the boys off to bed ... maybe go to bed a bit early ourselves?" She gave him a look that brought a warmth to his ears.

"Mm, yes."

Martin spent the remainder of the evening watching the clock as his thoughts flitted from parental and household duties to a recurrent image of his wife's upturned bum circling the Christmas tree.

With both boys tucked in for the night, he pulled the door shut to the nursery and locked their own bedroom door behind him before completing his nightly ablutions in record time.

Louisa breathed out a long sigh when he slipped in next to her, his mass radiating an immediate warmth as he embraced her. "This is very nice," she said, pressing against him.

"Yes—it is." The words rumbled from his chest.

"I know that today wasn't altogether enjoyable for you, Martin," she said as her fingernails raked lightly across his back. "But I really hope that it'll provide you with at least *some* positive memories for future Christmases."

Martin swallowed hard and tightened his grasp on her. "I'll definitely have one positive memory," he said before reaching back to turn out the light.

Chapter 26

"Martin," Louisa said softly as she tried to jostle her husband awake the next morning. *"Martin."*

"Hmm?"

"I think you should check on Evan. He didn't wake us up at all last night."

Martin lay for a few moments as his wife's words began to sink in, and then he sat up abruptly and threw the blankets aside. Sucking in a breath as his feet hit the icy cold floor, he pulled his dressing gown from its assigned place on the chair. "I'll be back in a minute."

James's soft chortles could be heard as he traversed the landing, followed by the sound of a rattle making contact with the floor. "Uh-oh!" the toddler said.

Martin glanced first at the seven-year-old, still asleep in his bed, then he greeted his son. "Good morning, James," he said, reaching into the cot and extracting the baby. "Did you sleep well?"

James batted at his father's face before latching on to his ears and pulling his head to his own.

Louisa would not yet allow her husband to carry their son for fear he could lose his balance or have a leg give out. But he had been able to get away with cradling the child in his arms while stationary.

"Everything okay in here?" Louisa asked as she slipped in next to him.

"All appears to be perfectly normal ... aside from the fact that we were able to sleep through the night."

Martin stared blankly for a moment before quickly passing his son to Louisa. "Perhaps he's ill. I better check on him."

Before Louisa could open her mouth, James was in her arms and Martin was at Evan's bedside. The child lay, curled into a ball on his side, with all but his face covered by the thick duvet.

The doctor pressed the backs of his fingers to the boy's forehead. "Hmm, he could be a bit feverish."

"Or he could just be warm because he's buried himself in blankets. Let him sleep, Martin. He hasn't had a good night's rest since he arrived," Louisa said, giving a tug on his arm.

Martin hesitated, staring down at him, cocking his head as he detected movement under the covers.

"Martin! Just leave him be!" Louisa whispered, pulling at his sleeve.

He tugged his arm from her grasp and reached down, pulling the duvet back. Louisa slapped a hand to her mouth as her husband blurted out, "Oh, gawd! What's *that* doing in here?"

Evan began to stir, bringing up the arm which had been wrapped around Joan's little brown and white terrier. He rubbed at his eyes and gave his guardian a smile. "G'morning, Dr. Ellig-am."

"Good morning," Martin answered gruffly. "What exactly is that?"

The boy looked down at Buddy and screwed up one side of his face. "Well, I don't know *exactly*. But he gots the sticky-up hair on the top of his head so—maybe he's a poodle?"

"I *mean*, where did it come from?"

"I think ... from France."

"I know poodles come from France, for goodness' sake!" Martin waggled his finger at the little animal. "Where did that particular dog come from? How did it end up in your bed?"

Evan swung his legs over the mattress and Buddy leapt into his lap. "Oh, there's a perfectly logical 'splanation about that."

The child patted Buddy's head, inciting him to jump up and slather mucilaginous kisses on to the boy's face. Evan fell back on to the bed, giggling.

Martin folded his arms across his chest and stared down at the boy. "I'm waiting to hear your logical explanation, Evan."

"Oh." The boy wriggled out from under the little dog and reached under his pillow. "Remember my lucky rock?" he asked as he held it out at arm's length.

"I remember your rock, yes."

"Well, see ... every night before I went to sleep, I rubbed my lucky rock, and then I wished for a colouring book and a box of crayons. And then I wished *two* times for a dog that's not pretend. I woke up in the night and there he was—under my bed! Bob's your uncle!" the child explained, his hands unfolding in the air.

"He's that dog that was outside that place we ate at after the Christmas Market. Mrs. Ellig-am calls him Buddy. You must not remember him."

Martin whipped his head to the side. "Oh, I remember him." He took a step forward, snapping his fingers. "Out! Out you get!"

Buddy flattened himself on the mattress, laying his chin on his front paws.

There was another snap of the fingers and a more adamant, "Out!"

The little canine whined softly and peered up at the doctor through a fringe of unkempt hair.

"Martin—a word, please," Louisa said as she gave a tug on his sleeve.

He huffed out a breath and turned to follow her.

"Problem?" he asked as she whirled around on the landing.

"Yes, Martin. There is a problem!" she hissed. "You can't just throw that little dog out!"

"Why not?" he asked, as he looked back at her guilelessly. "I always have before."

Louisa's ponytail flicked a warning. "Because, Mar-tin, Buddy is responsible for finding you and Evan when you were freezing to death on the moor! And it could be very upsetting to Evan to have Buddy taken away now that he thinks he's his dog."

"I'll explain the situation to him, then. It's simply not possible. There are certain health standards to be maintained in a doctor's surgery," he replied, his tone resolute as he headed back across the landing. "He'll understand."

Martin returned to the nursery and picked the terrier up from the bed, holding him out like the rotten fish the night before. "I'll be back in a minute, Evan, and we'll discuss this."

Evan got up on his knees, peering around the corner. "Are you gonna feed him his breakfast, Dr. Ellig-am?" he called out.

"Stay put, I'll be right back!" he yelled as he continued past his wife, stuffing the animal under his arm before heading down the stairs.

"Oh, *Martin!*" Louisa hissed, her ponytail flailing as she followed after him.

Setting the little terrier down on the floor, Martin flipped the latch on the kitchen door. Then he snapped his fingers, herding him on to the back terrace. "Out!"

He turned around to face his wife's icy gaze. "Louisa, we can't tell the boy that he can have that dog."

"Then just what do you plan to tell him, Martin?"

"I'll simply explain that it's not feasible to keep a dog in a doctor's surgery. Evan's future's uncertain. We can't very well be telling him he can have a pet when we don't even know where he'll be two weeks from now!"

He went to the sink and scrubbed his hands before pouring himself a glass of water. "How did that creature get into the house, anyway?"

"I don't know, Martin. Maybe he came in with all that cold air you let in last night," Louisa said as she turned and headed for the stairs. "I'll let Evan know that you'll be along shortly."

Air hissed from the doctor's nose as he set his glass down on the counter. He gazed out the window at the barren winter landscape. The moving form of the little terrier caught his eye as he worked his way under the potting bench, seeking refuge from the cold wind and the heavy mist which had begun to fall.

A wave of guilt passed over him as he remembered the bone-chilling cold that night on the moor just two weeks before. He pressed his fingertips to his temples then headed off to set things straight with his young charge.

Evan's head shot up from the book he was reading when he heard his guardian enter the bedroom. "Hi, Dr. Ellig-am! I stayed put, just like you said."

"I see that," Martin answered, taking a seat on the bed. "Evan, we need to talk about the dog. It's just not feasible to keep an animal in our house."

The smile evaporated from the child's face as he cocked his head at the doctor. "But he's mine, Dr. Ellig-am! Remember my lucky rock?"

"That is *not* a lucky rock, Evan. It's just a rock. And that dog doesn't belong to you, I'm afraid."

"Who does he belong to then?"

Louisa cast a warning glance over her shoulder as she pulled a sock over her son's foot.

"As far as I know, he doesn't belong to anyone," Martin said, clearing his throat. "He was my aunt's dog at one time, but after she died, he—"

"Dr. Ellig-am died!"

"No, no, no, no, no. The other aunt … my aunt Joan."

"But if he doesn't gots anyone who wants him, don't you think it's our 'sponsibility to want him?"

"It's not that simple, Evan. I have my patients to consider. Dogs can carry disease. And some of my—"

"No, they don't."

"Well, actually, they do. They're host to any number of parasites which can transmit disease, as well as fungal and bacterial—"

"We can wash off all the mannered bacteria! And you can give him his shots so that he doesn't get rabies. And I know you can figure out a way to get him to stop transmittin' stuff. Most of the other kids at school have pets, and they don't get sick, so their parents must've figured it out. And you're *way* smarter than them, so I know you can if you really want to."

"It's not that simple, Evan. I have patients who are allergic to dogs. It could trigger symptoms in them to have—"

"But he can stay in me and James's room. Then they wouldn't get their symptoms triggered."

Martin let out a long breath. "Evan, we don't know how long you'll be—"

"Martin, maybe this isn't the time to discuss the future. Hmm?" Louisa said.

He gave her a scowl. "Yes." Rubbing a large palm over his face he looked down at the child. "I don't think it would be fair to let that dog get used to living in our home, only to have to adjust to living on the streets again later, do you?"

"But you don't gots ta worry 'bout that 'cause he *won't* have to adjust. He can just stay living here."

Louisa leaned back against the changing table with James in her arms and raised her eyebrows at him.

Martin sighed. The tide of public opinion had turned against him, and to continue to argue his case would be like trying to empty the harbour with an eyedropper.

"All right, here's what we'll do, Evan. I'll get some wood and nails, and you and I'll build the dog a house out on the back terrace. He can live out there—keep you company while you're here. But he can't live inside the house, understood?"

Evan pushed his lower lip out in a pout and folded his arms in front of him. "He's gonna think we don't want him."

"He's a dog, Evan. I highly doubt he has the intellectual capacity to—"

"Martin."

He glanced up at his wife and clamped his mouth shut.

"Evan, you and Dr. Ellingham can build Buddy a lovely house so that he *will* know that you want him. And we can put food and water out for him—maybe make him some doggie biscuits for Christmas even."

The seven-year-old's face lit up again. "Yeah, and we could hang a Christmas stocking for him!"

"Ohh, no. I'm not going on a hunt for—"

"You can stop at that little shop near the barbers when you take Evan for a haircut, Martin," Louisa said, her eyes snapping. "Yes?"

"Yes." Martin got to his feet and walked towards the landing, tugging at his ear. "Evan, get dressed and we'll eat breakfast. Then we'll see if we can scare up some wood."

Martin groaned as he crawled into bed that night. He had spent the better part of the day helping Evan cobble together a crude representation of a dog house with wood he'd harvested from several old crates that were in the shed behind the surgery. His arm ached from swinging the hammer, and, after being on his feet the better part of the day, his legs were now throbbing.

He lay, the cracks in the ceiling a reminder of yet another project that needed his attention. He listened as his wife set the lock on the front door and watched for her form to appear in the doorway.

"I brought some ice packs," she said as she entered the room. "Thought you might be needing them."

"Mm, thank you." He pushed himself into a sitting position as his wife adjusted his pillow behind him.

"You made that little boy very happy today, you know," she said, leaning over to place a kiss on his forehead.

He peered up at her, hesitating before saying, "This is going to make it more difficult when he has to leave. You know that, don't you?"

Louisa picked up the extra pillows scattered about the room and tucked them in around his arm and legs before wedging the cold packs in against them. "Let's just take it a day at a time, hmm?"

Martin gave her a scowl. "I don't think that's a luxury we can afford, Louisa. The boy's already feeling insecure ... not knowing who'll be here for him tomorrow. I think we need to be giving his future—our future—serious consideration."

"I'm working on it, Martin," she said as she brushed her fingers across his cheek. "I'll be back in a minute."

The hum of an electric toothbrush could be heard, followed by the sound of running water, before the bathroom door opened and Louisa re-entered the room. "Thoroughly chilled, now?" she asked as she began to remove the blue packs.

Martin rubbed at his eyes, which had drifted shut. "Mm, yes. I think it's adequate."

"Good, I'll run these back down to the freezer and be back up. Don't go anywhere." She patted his cheek and hurried towards the stairs.

When she returned, she picked up the pot of cocoa butter from her bedside table. "Okay, off with the vest and I'll see what I can do about those aches and pains."

"That's really not necessary, Louisa. I just want to go to bed."

"And that's what we're doing. Now, vest off— chop, chop," she said as she circled her hand in the air.

Martin huffed out a breath before pulling his left arm and his head from the garment. He worked it over the fixators on the opposite arm and then acquiesced to his wife's wishes, shifting himself down, manoeuvring his way around the cumbersome hardware on his limbs.

"Maybe we should each make a list of the pros and cons of extending Evan's time here ... help us to look at this decision objectively," Louisa said as her hands caressed his shoulders.

Reaching an arm out and pulling open the drawer on the table next to him, Martin removed a pad of paper. "I've been thinking about that. I'll leave it here and you can read through it sometime."

Louisa reached for the notepad. "I can look at it now."

Martin slapped his hand down in front of hers. "Look at it another time; it's getting late." He slipped it back into the drawer and slammed it shut. "You know where to find it."

A faint smile spread across Louisa's face as she returned to massaging the tension from her husband's muscles.

There was a time when his actions would have upset her. But whether it was recognising it for what it likely was, a sudden display of insecurity on his part, or her own current confidence in their relationship, she found him strangely charming at that moment.

She leaned over to nuzzle her nose behind his ear. Her hands slid down his back and under the waistband of his boxers.

"What are you doing?"

"Just trying to loosen you up a bit."

"Mm, I see," he said, clearing his throat.

She smiled, smugly as she worked her way down his legs. "Okay, roll over, and I'll do the other side," she said, giving him a gentle nudge.

Dipping her fingers into the jar again, she straddled him while working her palms across his chest. "I've been wanting to tell you, Martin ... you've been really wonderful with Evan."

"He's a patient—I have a duty of care."

Louisa's motions ceased momentarily as she watched him before shifting her caresses to his shoulders. "Mmm, you *are* tense," she said as she allowed her hands to slide down his arms. "Understandable ... considering the day you had."

Martin gulped as she stared down at him, her gaze penetrating. "I'm not tense," he said, huskily. "Likely just a normal contraction of muscle tissue in response to the earlier icing of the oedematous tissue."

She cocked her head at him. *Hmm, guess I have shy Martin in my bed tonight,* she thought as her fingers kneaded their way around the fixator pins in his right arm.

He cleared his throat again and continued, "At cold temperatures, oxygen is more tightly bound to the haemoglobin and doesn't release very easily."

He closed his eyes and took in a breath as his wife's lips fluttered against his neck before settling in the hollow of his throat.

She sat back up, dragging her fingernails lightly across his skin.

He swallowed hard. "This slower rate"—another clearing of the throat—"rate of release leads to a lower amount of"—another gasp—"of oxygen available to the muscles, making..." Martin pulled her to him, lifting his head to bury his face in her neck. "You are so very beautiful," he whispered.

Louisa pulled back and stared into his eyes. The softness, the love that she saw in them, overwhelmed her and she began to cry.

Martin felt his gut tighten as his singular emotion—love, mixed suddenly with fear and confusion.

He began replaying his own words in his head. What had he said—done—this time to upset her. He cupped her cheek in his hand as he brushed at her tears with his thumb. "I'm sorry, Louisa. I don't know what I did to upset you, but whatever it was, it was unintentional."

She looked down at him and took his hands in hers, bringing them to her lips. "You did nothing wrong. I'm just very happy. Very, very happy."

He gave her a sideways glance. "You don't look happy."

Slipping in alongside him, Louisa gave him a reassuring smile. "I promise you, I *am* happy. I never thought we'd be sharing a moment like this together. We went through some dark times, and I nearly threw this all away."

"Ah."

"It *does* scare me to think of how close we came to losing it all. Does it scare you?"

His brows drew together. "Well, I try not to dwell on those things."

"But trying is very different than actually succeeding, isn't it?"

"Yes. Yes, it is." He pulled a hand up to brush the wisps of hair from her eyes.

Louisa worried her lip as she studied his face. "I'm just so afraid of doing something that could put us back in that dark place, Martin."

He shook his head as he wrapped his arm around her, eliciting a short yelp as a fixator pin poked her side.

"Mm, sorry," he said, readjusting the position of his arm. "Louisa, do you trust me? Trust that I won't let things go again—deteriorate to the point they did?"

There was an interminably long period of silence in the room, the only sound the whispered beat of winter mist as it blew against the window.

"Louisa?"

"I heard you, Martin. I'm just not sure how to answer that. I do trust you. I trust you completely to do anything in your power to make sure it doesn't happen again. But if all the responsibilities, pressures—all the stuff you're dealing with—if it overwhelms you again— Well, I just don't know how much power *you* have over that."

"Ah." He lay stroking his fingers up and down her back as he mulled over what she had said, his touch sending a shiver through her. "Perhaps you could make a list for me—of things I can do—or say to reassure you?"

She pulled her head back and kissed him gently on the lips. "That's very thoughtful of you, Martin. But for the moment, I think that I'd find it most reassuring if you made love to me."

Chapter 27

Martin groaned and wrapped his pillow around his head, trying to block out the high-pitched admonitions of his alarm on Monday morning. A call out at two a.m., thrown in with a trip into the nursery after another of Evan's nightmares, had left little time for sleep.

"What was the emergency last night?" Louisa asked, her voice thick, as she watched her husband hoist himself from the bed.

An unintentional groan slipped from his mouth. "I *thought*, judging by the breath sounds that I heard over the phone, that it was a recurrence of the patient's hypersensitivity pneumonitis. It turned out to be a suspected case of pemphigus vulgaris," he growled.

Louisa wrinkled up her nose as she got to her feet and pulled her dressing gown over her shoulders. "Sounds nasty—whatever it is."

He brushed past her and moved into the bathroom. "It's a chronic blistering condition, and it *is* nasty if one actually has it. But it's a far cry from the athlete's foot it turned out to be."

He picked his toothbrush up from the shelf and laid down a strip of toothpaste along the bristles before pressing the switch on the handle.

"Well, I suppose it *can* be frightening to wake up ill in the middle of the night."

The whirring of the toothbrush came to a stop, and Martin stepped out of the bathroom. He stared at her, blinking several times. "Did you miss the part about athlete's foot?" he mumbled through a mouthful of foam.

Louisa dropped back down on the bed, running her fingers through sleep tangled hair. "I'm just saying, maybe this person overreacted. Maybe they—and I know you can't discuss your patients," she said, her hands held up in front of her. "Well, I can't imagine someone would intentionally call you out in the wee hours for something as trivial as *athlete's foot*."

"Oh? The man thinks nothing of wasting my time during surgery hours. And he didn't just waste *my* time. I had to call Jeremy to pick me up and take me over there! Two people had their sleep disrupted just to appease his hypochondriacal tendencies." White foam spattered from his mouth as he gesticulated with the inert toothbrush.

"Oh, dear. Malcolm Raynor." Louisa got up and followed her husband into the bathroom, wrapping her arms around him from behind as he spit into the sink.

"Mm." He reached for the towel and wiped his face dry, taking note of the darkening circles under the eyes of the visage in the mirror. He turned in his wife's grasp and rested his chin heavily on her head.

"Must be frustrating to not have the energy you used to, hmm?" she said.

He sighed. "It's not quite four months. We have to remember that."

She reached down, patting him on the backside. "*You* have to remember that. I just have to look at you."

Martin straightened back up. "Mm, I should move things along. I have patient notes to go through this morning."

"I'll go down and make your breakfast then. You can go through your notes while you eat."

He watched as her image grew smaller in the mirror before pulling out his razor and shaving gel, applying it to his cheeks.

His mind drifted to their conversation the night before, and a glimmer of a smile passed across his face. The administering of the requested reassurances had certainly been pleasurable.

It was nearing nine o'clock by the time Martin had eaten breakfast and prepared for his patients. He sequestered himself in his consulting room and pulled Abby Peterson's business card from his wallet.

Having spoken with Dr. Newell, the therapist had been anticipating his call. Feeling some sense of urgency to begin her work with Evan, the boy's first session had been scheduled for Wednesday afternoon. But she would meet with Martin and Louisa in just a few hours to gather information on the child and the circumstances surrounding the current situation.

Martin twisted the phone cord around his fingers as he attempted to explain himself to the woman. "We—er, I should say my wife and I see things from different perspectives in regard to extending the child's stay with us. It could prove beneficial to have an independent voice in making the decision."

He picked up his biro and scribbled absent-mindedly on a set of patient notes. "Up to this point, the boy has been primarily my responsibility. I'm realising that will have to change if he's to be with us for an extended period of time. And I suppose—I suppose I could use a bit of—" He took in a slow breath. "—a bit of help in having that discussion with my wife."

The biro swung back and forth in his fingers as he listened to the voice on the other end of the line. "Yes. Yes, I agree. He's been having frequent nightmares and I think it's important to deal with whatever issues may be triggering them. I don't want him to have to go through—" Martin grimaced at his inability to admit to his own difficulties. "I don't—" He tossed the biro down on his desktop, pressing his fingers to his eyes. "Well, I—I appreciate you working us in so quickly."

The phone cord found its way back around his fingers as he sat, nodding his head. "Mm, yes. We'll see you at three o'clock."

He hung up the phone and stared out the window. He would need to plan ahead, carefully framing the conversation he knew he needed to have with the boy. He certainly couldn't surprise him with a visit to a child psychologist as he had with the trip to Truro for the Winter Festival.

He laid his head down on his desk for a few moments, only to be startled from sleep a half hour later when his receptionist walked into the room.

"Sorry, Doc. Didn't mean to disturb your lie-down," she whispered. "But then, maybe your desk isn't the best place for that. You should go upstairs and have a proper rest."

"I'm fine Morwenna. What did you need?" he asked, rubbing a hand roughly over his face.

"Just thought you might want ta know—that Dr. Lippolis fella from over in Wadebridge called. He wanted ta know if you were gonna be around this morning. He didn't sound exactly friendly."

Martin groaned and squeezed a palm around his forehead, his knuckles whitening.

The receptionist took another step forward as a concerned expression spread across her face. "Don't worry about it. I'll get rid of 'im, Doc—tell 'im you got called out or something."

"No, no, no, no, no. If I'm with a patient, wait until I'm done. Then send him in."

Morwenna gave him a shrug of her shoulders. "If you say so."

She hesitated, spinning the large, heart-shaped ring bedecking her finger.

The doctor pulled a set of patient notes from its sleeve and began to study it before glancing back up at her. "What is it?"

She shook her head. "It's nothin', Doc." The red chunk of plastic made several more rotations. "Well—yes, there *is* something.

"I just want you ta know that the villagers appreciate havin' a good doctor—a really great doctor. Well, most of 'em anyway. But there's lots of 'em that are worried about you. You know ... tryin' ta do too much."

Martin leaned back in his chair and stared blankly past her for several moments.

"Doc...you all right?"

His gaze shifted, and he made eye contact with her. "I'm fine, Morwenna. I, er—I'm just tired."

"Right then. I'll send Dr. Lippolis back when he gets here." The young woman turned and headed back to the reception room.

"Morwenna!" Martin called out.

The rattle of the young woman's jewellery grew louder as she returned. "Yeah, Doc?"

"Can you give me a bit of warning before you send him back?"

"Yeah, sure thing."

Lorna Gillett was the first patient to be seen. Her regular, doctor-imposed blood donations had brought her ferritin levels down, but Martin had concerns about her atypical blood glucose levels.

"Have you seen any improvement in the joint pain since we reinitiated the phlebotomy?" Martin asked as he shined his ophthalmoscope into his patient's eyes.

"Hardly have any at all anymore, Doc. I swear, you're a miracle worker."

Martin gave a grunt and laid the instrument down on his medical cart before picking up his otoscope. "Turn your head, please."

Brushing the woman's thick mane of red hair aside, he inserted the specula into her left ear then the right. "Your left ear's inflamed—any pain?"

Lorna gave a shrug. "Yeah, sometimes more than others. I had a cold a month or so back. Just thought it was one of those *give-it-a-little-more-time* kind of things, you know."

"Mm, I don't think so. I suspect you have a bit of otitis," he said as he released the plastic dilator from the otoscope, allowing it to fall into the waste bin. "I'll write you a prescription for an antibiotic. We'll get the phlebotomy taken care of, give it a couple of weeks, check your ferritin levels again, and take it from there."

"Thanks, Doc. What about the other thing—the blood sugar thing. Should I be worried about that?"

Martin tipped his head to the side as he palpated the front of the woman's neck. "It's something that needs to be monitored. There's a slight possibility that your pancreas may have been compromised by the haemochromatosis. If that's the case, you could develop diabetes. It's not something that should cause you an undue amount of worry, however."

Lorna sighed and tipped her head, giving him a soft grin. "I'll try to only worry an *appropriate* amount then."

Martin stared back at her, pulling his eyebrows together. "Mm."

Chippy and Irene Miller were seated in the reception room when Lorna walked through the door a while later. The unusually loud hum of conversation drew Martin from the consulting room to investigate the commotion.

It seemed half the village had congregated at the surgery to get a first look at the Miller babies. Chippy and Irene were book ended by Bert Large and a woman Martin only knew as the woman who took over the operation of the green grocers when the previous owner moved away.

Bert wiggled a pudgy finger under the bald-headed infant's chin. "Oh, you're a fine little lad, aren't you!" He said in the hyper-inflective voice used by adults when attempting to communicate with babies.

"How 'bout colic? They been havin' any trouble with colic? 'Cause if they *have*, I got an old family recipe that can help with that."

"Oh, gawd," Martin groaned. "Bert, unless you've acquired a medical degree since your recent hospitalisation, I would greatly appreciate it if you'd peddle your snake oil elsewhere."

Bert pulled in his chin and glared back at the doctor, sour-faced. "That's the thanks I get for tryin' to be of use to my community. "

"If you want to be of use, Bert, move it on. And take this gaggle of baby gawpers with you," Martin grumbled.

"And after I went outta my way ta make you my special soup," the portly restaurateur said. "Which reminds me—how's that goin, Doc? Keepin' the lead in that pencil okay, or could you use another batch?"

"*Bert!* For God's sake!"

Martin's ears burned as twitters rippled through the room.

"Look, Doc, I'm just sayin', if yer havin' any trouble in that department—which would be expected after what you been through, by the way—you just let me know. I'd be happy ta make up another batch. Gotta keep that sweet Louiser happy in the bed—"

"Bert, get—*out!*"

Martin waved a hand towards the consulting room. "Mr. and Mrs. Miller, come through. Morwenna, get rid of Bert. And all those without appointments." Martin shook his head as he stepped through into his consulting room. "Gawd."

The Miller twins slept peacefully in their parent's arms, only waking when they were laid on the examination table. The thrush which had made them so miserable two weeks earlier had cleared, and they had gained a healthy amount of weight.

Martin gazed down at the nappy-clad child lying on the table as he listened to the typically rapid thrumming of its heart. The baby boy's bald head and bright eyes brought back a flood of memories. He covered the child's chest with a broad palm, relishing in the sensation of the warm, velvety skin against his hand.

Chippy gave him a knowing smile. "Nothin' like it, eh, Doc?"

Martin gave his head a small shake and cleared his throat. "I think I'm done here, Mr. Miller. You can get your son dressed now."

He slid behind his desk and pulled out the single cards contained in the sleeves laying in front of him, scribbling notes into them. "Well, your children appear to be on the expected developmental track. I'll need to see them again in a month for the necessary jabs, but they appear to be thriving, healthy infants. You're doing a fine job with them," he said, the right corner of his mouth inching north.

He glanced down again at the name on the card in his left hand—Miller, Chloe Irene. "Chloe ... that's nice," he said, unthinking.

"Named her after her mum," Chippy said. "The other one's Dylan. Named 'im after *you*, Doc ... look." The fisherman beamed proudly as he poked a finger at the card in Martin's right hand. "Thought we'd call 'im D.D. for short."

Martin furrowed his brow as he glanced down at the heading on the patient notes—Miller—Dylan Doc. He fought to suppress an amused smile. "I'm honoured."

"Well, if it weren't for you, there's no tellin' what might a happened that night. I coulda lost all three of 'em. It's our way of sayin' thank you, Doc," Chippy said.

Irene got to her feet, slinging the nappy bag over her shoulder as she looked down lovingly at the baby boy in her arms. "I just hope we can bring 'im up ta make you proud, Doc."

Martin cleared his throat again and headed for the door, pulling it open. "Well, I'd say you're off to a very good start."

As Chippy and Irene left the building, Jeremy came through from the lounge.

"I thought I'd run down to the chemist for some supplies while we have a break in the action. That okay with you?"

"That's fine, Jeremy," Martin said as he flipped through the patient files before returning the babies' notes to the file cabinet next to the receptionist's desk.

"I'll be back in a few minutes," the young man said before excusing himself, slipping past a man coming in the door.

The light airy sensation that the doctor had been left with after the Miller's visit condensed heavily into his chest as he turned his attention away from the file cabinet.

A burly, black-haired gentleman sporting a rumpled shirt and garishly coloured tie glared back at him. "Ellingham," he greeted Martin curtly. "Might you be able to spare a moment of your valuable time?"

Martin glanced at his wide-eyed receptionist and then tucked in his chin before giving a nod towards the consulting room. He ducked under the doorway, followed closely by Alex Lippolis who ducked a bit farther.

"I'm on a tight schedule so we'll have to make this ..." The receptionist listened as her boss's voice faded away behind the door.

"Have a seat," Martin said, waving his hand at the extra chair on the opposite side of his desk.

Lippolis hiked up his trousers and sat down "I had a call from Gordon Black with the review board the other day. I understand you have something to do with that," the dark-haired doctor said.

"I spoke with Chris Parsons, yes."

Lippolis rested his elbows on the armrests of his chair, folding his hands in front of his face. "*That* was a mistake, Ellingham. You called on two separate occasions, accusing me of failing to properly care for your patients. *Evidently* I didn't make myself clear during those conversations."

Martin swallowed hard as the other doctor glowered back at him, but he kept a steely gaze fixed on the man. "You made yourself perfectly clear. You refused to admit to the obvious mishandling of either of those cases. I had no recourse but to pursue further action."

"I *warned* you, Ellingham." The man leaned forward on the desk, a thunderous expression on his face. "I run a clean practice. You're not immune to the occasional oversight yourself."

Martin erupted. "Oversight! Are you bloody joking? My haemochromatosis case now faces the possibility of a lifetime of insulin injections and the constant worry about her blood sugar levels because of your—*oversight!*" he spat.

"And you completely missed an advanced case of gestational diabetes! Even ignoring the National Health Service guidelines regarding the administering of the second trimester glucose tolerance test!

"That *oversight* nearly resulted in the death of a mother and both of her unborn children! It nearly left a man with no family whatsoever! That's not an *oversight*, it borders on medical malfeasance!"

In the reception room, Morwenna listened to the growing rancour and hesitated for a few moments before picking up the phone. A crash could be heard, causing her to jump as she tapped her fingers nervously against the receiver. "Come on, Joe!" she whispered as she waited anxiously for the police constable to answer his mobile.

Martin's attention shifted to the photo of his wife and son, which now lay under broken glass on the floor. "I think you better go," he said through clenched teeth. *"Now."*

Dr. Lippolis rose from his chair and slapped his hands down on his colleague's desk. "Damn you, Ellingham! You're trying to ruin my career, aren't you!"

He tipped his head back and peered down at Martin imperiously. "Ah, I see," he said, shaking a finger in the air, "*You* want my job!"

"That's ridiculous!" A familiar odour wafted towards him and Martin wrinkled up his nose. He took in a calming breath and stared back at the figure towering over him.

"You're drunk, Alex," he said. "I think you should just sit down and cool off. We can discuss this when you're sober." He tried to project an air of confidence as he felt the cooling sensation of perspiration breaking out across his forehead and upper lip.

The other physician's expression grew thunderous as his olive complexion reddened. He reached a long arm out, jabbing a finger into Martin's chest. "I'm *not* drunk. Don't you dare call Parsons accusing me of *that,* too!" he hissed.

Martin blinked reflexively as a heavy spray of the man's saliva hit his face. Lippolis pulled back, wiping his mouth on his sleeve. Then he straightened himself before walking around to the other side of the desk.

Martin struggled to his feet and took a step back, putting a palm up in front of him. "All right, Alex. Maybe we should j-just let this matter rest for a few days until—"

Dr. Lippolis grabbed hold of the front of Martin's shirt and pushed him back forcefully, sending him to the floor.

The latch rattled as the door to the room was forced open suddenly, slamming back against the wall behind it.

"Police! Stop right there—don't move a muscle!" an authoritative voice warned.

Martin looked around Alex Lippolis' broad silhouette to see Joe Penhale coming up behind the out-of-control doctor.

"Get your hands behind your head—now!" the constable commanded.

Alex pulled his hands behind him, slowly. "Oh God," he groaned.

Joe yanked his handcuffs from his tool belt, slapping them on to the doctor's left wrist, then the right.

Martin lay, unsure of what to do as he watched the normally inept policeman take charge of the situation.

Morwenna's strident voice could be heard coming from the other room, and Jeremy appeared in the doorway. "What the hell? Martin, are you okay?" he asked, dropping down beside him.

"Yes." He eyed his attacker's trembling left leg. "He's not though," he said, wagging a finger at Lippolis. "Help me up."

The aide hoisted his friend to his feet, and Martin gestured towards the exam couch. "Get up there, I need to take a look at you," he ordered the other doctor.

"I'm fine," he snarled back.

"Quite obviously *not!* Now shut up and get on the couch."

Joe put a hand on Martin's arm and said in an undertone, "I need to process the suspect first, Doc."

"No, you don't. You need to take those handcuffs off so I can examine my patient."

"*Well*, technically, he's not a patient. He's a suspect in an attempted homicide."

Martin held back biting words, huffing out a breath. "I believe Dr. Lippolis may be ill, Penhale. Take the cuffs off so that I can check him over. If I determine he's intoxicated, I'll turn him over to you. Agreed?"

Joe's head dropped to the side. "That would be a serious violation of standard police protocols."

"I could care less about your police protocols!"

"I'm not sure I approve of your attitude, Doc. However, I suppose I could overlook normal procedure this one time—considering our professional relationship and all—if the suspect agrees to—"

"Oh, for goodness' sake! Just get those stupid handcuffs off, Penhale!" Martin said, throwing his head back.

"They're *not* stupid," Joe muttered, and not for the first time in their 'professional relationship'.

Pulling a syringe and a tourniquet from his medical cart, Martin handed them to his assistant. Jeremy swabbed the man's arm and drew up a vial of blood.

"I'm assuming you'll need this when you file your report," Martin said, hesitantly handing it to the constable before swallowing the flood of saliva that had filled his mouth. "I trust you can get it to the lab for analysis without losing it along the way?"

"Gee, thanks, Doc," Joe grinned. "Your confidence means a lot."

Martin closed his eyes and took in a breath, trying to rein in his temper. "You're welcome, Penhale."

He turned to his patient. "Can you behave in a civil manner long enough for me to conduct this examination privately, or do I need to have my bodyguard standing by?"

Lippolis pressed his hands to his head as he stared back at Joe's self-satisfied grin. "I'm all right now."

"Jeremy, you can stay. Penhale, wait out in the reception room. Be ready in case I need you again. And, er ... you handled things well a minute ago—very professionally. Thank you."

The policeman gave a tug on his tool belt. "All in the line of duty, Doc." He donned a serious expression, shifting his gaze back to Lippolis. "One false move and—" He shook his fist at the man before leaving the office.

Martin waited until the door closed and then turned to the visiting doctor. "This is Jeremy Portman, my assistant. Jeremy—Alex Lippolis. We're all medical professionals here. What's said behind that door, stays behind that door. Now, what the *hell* was that all about?"

Dr. Lippolis slumped over, his face in his hands.

"Alex ... do you have Parkinson's disease?"

The doctor lifted his head and looked at Martin, teary-eyed. "For about two years now."

"And you've been self-medicating—hiding it so you could keep practicing?"

"Yes. Idiotic, I know."

Martin nodded vigorously. "Yes, it *was* idiotic. You put both your professional reputation and, more importantly, the health of your patients at risk. Not to mention your own health!

"What you've done violates the Hippocratic oath! You've committed clinical negligence—several times over as a matter of fact! Not to mention the God-knows-how-many civil laws you've broken! *And*—in all probability—criminal laws!"

He whipped his head to the side as he worked up a head of steam. "For God's sake! The barber-surgeons of the middle-ages would have had your head for what you've done! To take such a cavalier attitude towards the oath you took when you became a doctor flies in the face of the most basic—medical ethical principles! Good, God! What were you *thinking?*"

Alex sat staring blindly in front of him. "I don't know," he said, his voice barely audible. "I guess I thought I could handle things on my own." He looked up at Martin. "I was going to stop practising if it began to affect my performance as a physician."

Martin screwed up his face. "Oh, for goodness' sake!"

He yanked a pair of exam gloves from the box on his medical cart and worked them on to his hands. "That didn't work out the way you planned, did it?" he grumbled, peering up at his colleague.

Air hissed from his nose. "Well, it's a fine mess now. But first things first. We need to get your medications sorted so that you're not—coming at people. Then we'll get you to a competent—and *objective*—neurology specialist. Once all that's been taken care of, we'll deal with the legal ramifications."

Martin gave his colleague a thorough physical examination before asking Jeremy to step out of the room. He returned to his desk. "Have a seat, Alex," he said, gesturing with his fountain pen. He sat back in his chair, eyeing the man icily. "I assume you've been using L-dopa to control your symptoms?"

"Yes."

"I suspect that what I thought was alcohol on your breath was actually digestive alcohol vapours coming up with your medication-induced gastric reflux."

He sighed and stared back at the man. "You have to report this to the investigative board immediately. And I mean by-the-end-of-the-day immediately. Call Chris Parsons. If you don't, *I* will. You can't treat another patient. Not unless you get the board's approval first."

"They'll have my licence, you know that," Dr. Lippolis said.

"Yes, almost certainly. And *rightly so.*" Martin scratched at his head as his eyes settled on the man's twitching left hand. "I'd be willing to go with you—when you appear in front of the board."

The ailing doctor's head shot up. "Would you be willing to speak on my behalf?"

Martin pushed himself back away from his desk. "Of course not!" He wiped a palm over his face. "I *will*, however, go with you if you like—just so you don't have to face this alone. But I *cannot* and *will* not make any excuses for you."

"I'm sorry, it was unfair of me to ask that of you."

"Yes, it was."

Dr. Lippolis stared absently out the window then turned to Martin. "God, I'm glad this is out in the open."

"What about your family—your wife. I assume she knows ... about the Parkinson's?"

"No. That's why I did it. She's been battling breast cancer. I was afraid the stress of my illness could compromise her chances of a good outcome."

"I see." Martin got up from his chair and Dr. Lippolis followed him to the door.

"I'm sorry about this, Ellingham," Alex said.

"I'm sorry about the Parkinson's—and your wife." Martin returned to his desk and sank into his chair. *He should have told her.* He let his head drop back and closed his eyes.

Chapter 28

The disruption caused by Alex Lippolis' visit to the surgery had put Martin behind schedule. He was finishing up with patient notes when his receptionist walked in, dropping the day's mail on to his desk.

"Shouldn't you be eatin' your lunch? Your aunt said yer s'posed ta be gettin' an adequate number of calories and—"

"Be quiet, Morwenna," Martin said, casting an annoyed glance in her direction.

"I'm just sayin', you shouldn't be skippin' meals. You need the protein—and the calcium. And yer always tellin' your patients it's not good ta—"

Martin's face filled with furrows as he looked up at her. "Morwenna! It's none of your business!"

"*Fine*, just tryin' to be helpful."

"If you really want to be helpful, tell Louisa I'm running behind schedule and not to wait on me for lunch."

"I shall do that right away," she said with roll of her eyes. "But you *are* remembering yer not s'posed to be workin' more than—"

"Morwenna!"

The young woman dropped her hands to her sides, slapping them against her hips. "I'm just tryin' ta keep you out of trouble you know."

Martin's head flew up, his eyes fiery. "Well, stop—trying!"

Morwenna huffed out a breath before turning to walk down the hall, her bangles rattling softly.

Evan and James were playing under a makeshift tent in the lounge when the receptionist came through the doorway. The toddler let out a loud squeal as he crawled out from under the shelter—a purple blanket which had been fastened with clothespins to the backs of four kitchen chairs.

Evan emerged closely behind him, a steady *chh-chh-chh* sound coming from his mouth.

"What are you two little men up to?" Morwenna asked as she stepped down from the kitchen.

The seven-year-old looked up. "We're a train!" he said, butting James in the backside with his head.

The toddler squealed again and giggled as he scrambled forward.

"I'm the engine, and James is the caboose." Evan came to a stop, pulling one of his hands off the floor and poking a finger towards the opening under the blanket. "That's the roundhouse, and under the kitchen table's the station."

James came around the tent and ran headlong into the older boy, triggering another fit of giggles as Evan fell theatrically to his side.

Morwenna turned towards the kitchen where Louisa was putting the ingredients for sandwiches on the table. "The doc said to tell you ta go ahead and eat without him. He's still workin' at his desk."

Louisa glanced at her watch then threw the tea towel down on the counter. "That man! It's after one o'clock!"

"Don't be too angry with 'im. He *does* have a pretty good excuse today."

"What excuse?" Louisa opened the refrigerator and pulled the bottle of milk from the door.

"That Lippolis guy from over in Wadebridge—the doctor fellow. He came in. He was in a right bate. Yelling, knockin' stuff off the doc's desk.

"Made me as jittery as a lobster sittin' by a stew pot, so I called Joe Penhale. I'm surprised you didn't hear all the commotion."

Louisa shook her head. "I took the boys to the school with me for a couple of hours. What do you mean in a bate?"

"He was furious!"

"Furious, how?"

"Knocked-the-doc-to-the-ground furious. Joe-slapped-the-cuffs-on-'im furious."

"*What?*" Louisa squeaked out before rushing towards the hall. She stopped and whirled around in the doorway. "Get the boys started eating, hmm, Morwenna?"

"Yeah, okay. But, you don't need ta wor—"

Morwenna threw up her hands as her boss's wife disappeared into the consulting room. "Typical. *Why* doesn't anybody listen to me?" she muttered. Then she turned to the little boys. "All right you two, bring the train into the station, it's time for lunch."

"Martin, are you alright?" Louisa asked as she charged through the consulting room door.

He looked up from his work, his biro poised in mid-air. "I'm fine. Didn't Morwenna tell you I was running behind?"

"*Yes,* she told me. She also told me you'd been attacked by the GP from Wadebridge!"

"Ohh," he groaned. He eyed his wife as she worried her lip. "Strictly speaking, I wasn't attacked. Why does she have to be so theatrical all the time?"

Louisa stood, tipping her head to one side then the other as she searched for any visible damage to her husband. "Well, maybe she didn't say that in so many words. But she said you'd been knocked to the floor. That sounds like an attack to me. Especially in your condition! You could have been seriously hurt, Martin!"

"Louisa—calm—down. I'm fine. Yes, I fell. But no damage was done." He pulled in his chin and turned his gaze back to the work in front of him. "Except maybe to my ego ... and possibly my superhero status."

Louisa cocked her head again. "Hmm?"

"It's something Jeremy said once," Martin explained.

"Oh, I see. Well, what *did* happen?"

He hesitated, grimacing. "I can't say, he's technically a patient ... as of today."

"A patient?"

"Yes. And as I said, I really can't say any more! I need to finish these patient notes before we leave for Truro so—"

"Truro?"

Martin's chin dropped to his chest. "I forgot to tell you. I called the therapist that Barrett Newell recommended. She wants to meet with the two of us at three o'clock this afternoon ... with Evan on Wednesday. I called Ruth. She can watch the boys."

Louisa's hands rose to her hips. "Oh, I see. You remembered to call Ruth, but you forgot to tell *me*?"

"I'm sorry. I just ... I'm sorry."

Louisa took note of the fatigue on her husband's face and tried to tamp back her annoyance at his atypical memory lapse.

"Well, I guess I'd better hurry up then," she said, glancing at her watch. "I need to change and get things ready for Ruth." She took a step towards the door then turned and peered down at him through narrowed eyes. We have less than an hour you know. And *you* need to eat."

"*Yes!* I'm trying to hurry."

They were running ten minutes behind schedule by the time they were in the Lexus and making their way down Roscarrock Hill. Martin squirmed and groused about everything from the temperature inside the car to the bits of paper littering the roadway.

"Just settle in—try to relax," Louisa said. She patted his thigh, causing him to jump as his already taut muscles twitched.

He pulled his arm up, glancing conspicuously at his watch one more time. His wife's laissez faire attitude towards timeliness was a trait that he struggled to tolerate on a good day, but the unfortunate incident with the errant GP and the uncertainty about their upcoming appointment had made him tense.

Being where you were supposed to be, when you were supposed to be there had been literally beaten into him as a boy, and the stress that he felt at that moment was dangerously close to bubbling over into a row-causing, caustic remark.

Louisa reached back into her purse on the floor behind her and pulled out a plastic bag, handing it to him. "Here, I brought your lunch. Now just try to relax and ... *eat*."

Martin shot her a dark look before ripping the plastic closure apart, pulling out a rather compacted sandwich.

"You put mayonnaise on this," he said, wrinkling up his nose as he peered under a slice of bread.

"That's right, and you *are* going to eat it, Mar-tin. You haven't been taking in enough calories lately, and you've been missing meals. A few extra calories will do you good."

"Yes, but mayonnaise is full of saturated fat. And you'd be shocked, if you looked at the nutritional information, at how much sodium is in just one tablespoon of the stuff."

"We already get more sodium than we need in the bread and cheese that you put on here. Not to mention the pre-packaged turkey breast, which is appallingly high in sodium.

"You may not realise it, but there's even salt in this slice of tomato and the—"

"Martin."

"I'm just saying, Louisa, that the sodium contained in that tablespoon of mayonnaise tips this sandwich into unhealthy territory."

He lifted his chin and gave her a sharp nod, certain that he had convincingly made his case.

She looked over at him with narrowed eyes. "Live dangerously this time—eat the stupid sandwich, Martin."

He dipped his head and, curling up his lip, reluctantly took a bite.

Abby Peterson's office was located next to the children's wing on the second floor of the main hospital building in the Royal Cornwall complex. They were greeted by a bubbly, grey-haired woman when they entered the waiting area.

"You must be the Ellinghams," she said as she stooped over to pluck a large stuffed rabbit from one of the chairs.

"Yes, we are," Louisa said, giving the woman a broad smile and extending her hand. "And you must be Dr. Peterson."

"Oh, my goodness, no. I'm the receptionist, Jean Teague. Dr. Peterson will be with you in a minute. She had to take a phone call. Please, take a seat."

The woman tossed the furry animal into a toybox in the corner of the room and proceeded to collect the blocks strewn across a play table, shovelling them into a brightly coloured bag. "May I bring you a cup of tea?"

"I'm fine, thank you," Louisa said as she scanned the room.

"How about you, doctor?"

Martin swallowed, attempting to clear the oily residue left behind by the mayonnaise from his mouth. "Yes, please. White—no sugar."

"You make yourselves comfortable. I'll be back in a tick with your tea, Dr. Ellingham."

Martin paced the room, inspecting everything from the pictures on the walls to the cleanliness of the carpet.

Louisa slipped behind a low table, covered by a neatly arranged assortment of children's periodicals as well as magazines for more mature readers. She dropped into a chair and patted the seat next to her.

"Come and sit down, Martin. You're making *me* nervous, too."

He whipped his head around. "I'm not nervous."

"Hmm. Well, just come and sit down anyway."

Jean returned to the room, and after pushing the magazines to the side, she set a cup down on the table in front of Martin.

"There you go, doctor. I have some paperwork for you to fill out. Just basic contact information. You can leave it on the counter over there when it's completed. Otherwise, please make yourselves at home. Dr. Peterson will be out shortly."

She gave them a smile and handed Louisa a clipboard with a pencil attached to it before bustling back down the hall.

"She seems nice," Louisa said as she began to fill in the requested information.

"Mm," Martin grunted. He swished hot tea around in his mouth, again trying to rid himself of the last vestiges of his lunch.

The pencil scratched harshly against the hard surface, creating a tap every time Louisa dotted an *I* or crossed a *T,* and Martin glanced over with a scowl. "Can you do that more quietly? It's giving me a headache."

She paused, then laid the pencil on the clipboard and handed it to him. "You fill it out. Then you can be as quiet as you like."

He rubbed a hand across his forehead. "I'm sorry. I suppose maybe I *am* a bit nervous."

She leaned over and kissed his cheek. "It'll be just fine. But I have a question. How are we supposed to fill in this section about Evan? We don't even know when his birthday is."

"The fifteenth of May, 2009," Martin answered. He pulled a small piece of paper from his shirt pocket, handing it to his wife. "This is the information from his medical file."

"Oh, good." She pulled the clipboard from her husband's hands, then scratched and tapped the new information on to the sheet.

There was a soft rattle as a door opened somewhere at the other end of the office before a woman with wavy, light brown hair walked towards them.

"Hello! Dr. and Mrs. Ellingham ... it's a pleasure to meet you. I'm Abby Peterson," she said, extending her hand as Martin and Louisa got to their feet. Please, come on back."

Louisa laid the clipboard on the counter, and they followed the psychologist down the hall.

The usual weather related pleasantries were exchanged between Dr. Peterson and Louisa while Martin looked about the room.

The walls were painted yellow. Bright enough to give the space the illusion of warmth, but soft enough to have a calming effect.

A row of windows, about four feet off the floor and draped with fabric festooned with jungle animals, ran the length of one wall.

The lower third of another wall was lined with row upon row of shallow shelves which held hundreds of plastic and metal cast representations of plants, animals, male and female characters, and many of the trappings of human existence.

In one corner sat something similar to a coat rack. The vertical piece was studded with wooden dowels which held sundry of animal puppets and the odd human representation.

And nearby, a child-sized wooden trestle table, with a top built more like a shallow box than a customary table top, held fine, clean sand.

The psychologist pulled a chair over next to the sofa, one of the several adult-sized pieces of furniture in the room, and waved a hand. "Please, make yourselves comfortable."

She sat down across from them, and her gaze drifted uncontrollably to Martin's injured arm. He shifted uncomfortably and pulled the arm up, letting it rest, concealed behind his wife.

"I'm sorry, Dr. Ellingham. I didn't mean to stare. I've read about the external fixation devices used with some fractures. I'd just not seen anything like it up close before. I find the method to be quite fascinating."

Martin gave the woman a soft grunt of acknowledgement.

Abby cleared her throat and looked down at the file in her lap for a moment before returning her focus to her clients. "Well, Dr. Newell filled me in very briefly concerning your situation, but I'd like to hear a bit more about Evan's background. How long have you known the boy?"

Martin quickly launched into a synopsis of the child's clinical history.

"I first saw him in August. Records left by my predecessor indicated that he had given the boy the immunizations required before starting school. He had also treated the child for tonsillitis and otitis on single occasions. Aside from those two entries, there was nothing remarkable," he said as he moved his arm to his lap, relieving the stress on his surgically traumatised shoulder.

He continued, "As I said, I first saw the child as a patient four months ago. I diagnosed asthma and pneumonia. I also noted circumferential bruising to his wrist as I was conducting the physical examination.

"The father was an alcoholic and known to experience rages when intoxicated, so the bruises concerned me. But the child refused to admit to any sort of abuse at that time.

"However, on a call to the family home a week later, I found him with an injured arm. X-rays confirmed a radial and ulnar fracture, occurring in tandem with new circumferential bruising. The boy admitted to me at that time that he had received the injuries from his father. I took him to hospital and contacted Children's Services."

Dr. Peterson nodded her head. "And is that when you were given temporary custody of the child?"

"Mm. No. I was ... out of touch with the boy for a period of—"

"Martin was in an automobile accident in early September," Louisa interjected. "He spent five weeks in hospital and another six weeks recovering at home before returning to seeing patients."

She shifted, giving a tug on the hem of her fitted skirt. "I'm the head teacher at Portwenn Primary, so, of course, I know Evan as a student. But it was in the middle of November that Martin really got involved with the boy's difficulties at home."

"I see." Dr. Peterson listened, taking notes periodically as the Ellinghams outlined the progression of events that led to the boy living under their roof.

"Martin, please tell me about the night that Mr. Hanley died. I'm particularly interested in what Evan may have seen or heard," Dr. Peterson said. "Did he actually witness his father's death or was he in another room when this occurred?"

Martin sat stiffly as he related the moments when Jim Hanley's body tumbled down the stairs towards his son. He blinked, attempting to contain the tears that were gathering in his eyes.

"I felt for the man's pulse, and—and I turned away for a moment. When I looked up, Evan was right there, crouched beside his father.

"I could tell by the look in his eyes that—" His voice seized up as the same emotions he felt the day his grandfather died washed over him.

Clearing his throat, he tried to continue. "I could see the fear in—" He glanced over at Louisa. She gave him an encouraging nod, and he took in a deep breath.

"The man was quite obviously dead. Blown pupils—a deep gash in his head—blood leaking from the nose and mouth. Evan"—he cleared his throat again— "the look on his face was—"

He sucked in a ragged breath. "I'm sorry, can you give me a minute?"

"Of course," Dr. Peterson said. "Could I get either of you a glass of water?"

Louisa sat, wanting nothing more at that moment than to console her husband. "Yes, please. Maybe a glass for each of us?"

"Certainly. I'll be back in a few minutes."

The sound of Dr. Peterson's heels clicking against the floor grew softer. Louisa linked her arm in her husband's, and she leaned against him, caressing his chest with her free hand.

Her hand rose and fell over his deep inhalation, and when she looked up at him, his eyes were closed and his jaw set.

"I'm so sorry, Martin. I had no idea it was that bad that night."

She hesitated and then nestled in closer. "Have you talked to Dr. Newell about it? That's a pretty horrible thing to witness. Maybe you need—"

"No." He shook his head. "You don't understand. What I saw that night with Mr. Hanley ... it pales in comparison to what I saw as a surgeon. It's...it was Evan's reaction. I knew exactly what he was feeling. I was—"

The faint sound of clicking heels brought the private conversation to an abrupt halt. Louisa pulled her arm away and straightened herself, reaching over to give her husband's hand one last reassuring squeeze.

Dr. Peterson re-entered the room and set a tray holding three glasses and a pitcher of water on the table.

"Thank you for waiting," she said as she filled the glasses. "Martin, you were describing the night that Evan's father died. Has the boy discussed the incident since it happened?"

"We've had a number of conversations. He was afraid that his father was watching him. He seemed very focused on the man's eyes and how they looked after he died. He interpreted the fixed gaze as an indication that his father was angry with him ... that he blamed him for his fall down the stairs."

"And were you able to reassure him?"

"The subject hasn't come up in the last week or so. He's still having persistent nightmares, however." He shifted his weight as he rubbed at his aching right thigh.

The psychologist's sympathetic expression caused him to avert his eyes. "As for how effective I've been at reassuring him," he continued, "he seems reassured for a short time, but those fears that his father is watching him—with angry eyes as Evan puts it—they keep cropping back up.

"Perhaps it's a good sign that he hasn't mentioned it in the last week, but—but I suspect we're not done with that. He seems to understand that his father has died, but I get the feeling he doesn't accept that it's an irreversible condition."

Abby picked the file up from the table and scratched some notes into it before eyeing Martin intently. "Dr. Ellingham, as a former vascular surgeon, I would imagine that you're accustomed to the sort of graphic image you would have seen the night of Mr. Hanley's death."

The ever-present furrow between Martin's brows deepened. "I'm not sure that a person ever gets used to watching someone die in a violent manner, Dr. Peterson."

"No ... no. I didn't mean to minimise what you witnessed that night or as a surgeon. I was wondering about your strong reaction as you were relating the story earlier." She hesitated. "Have you had a similar experience to Evan's?"

Martin stared at her, unflinching. "I'm a doctor. I used to be a surgeon. I've watched many people die."

"I see." The therapist set the file back down on the coffee table and leaned forward, her elbows on her knees.

"Is the current situation with Evan in your home just for the short term, or have you been thinking of making the arrangements permanent?"

Louisa glanced over at her husband. Martin sat silent, his jaw still tense. She tapped her fingertips together in her lap and looked at the psychologist. "We've discussed the possibility of extending Evan's stay. It's a difficult decision ... where to go from here. I worry about whether or not what we see in him now is what we can really expect. And if issues crop up, how Evan's behaviour could affect our own son. And I worry about Martin. Whether or not he can handle taking something like this on right now."

"Those are all legitimate concerns, Mrs. Ellingham, and it's wise to come into this with your eyes wide open. I can tell you that there will be inevitable bumps in the road.

"Some children have a great deal of difficulty and require ongoing therapy. Some move in and out of therapy as their needs change. There are specific developmental stages when problems are more likely to surface, but if you're aware of that, we can intervene quickly and help him through those more challenging times, should the need arise."

Louisa tipped her head and narrowed her eyes. "Just what do you mean by challenging. This is the part that really makes me apprehensive."

"Well first, let me preface this by saying that all children go through stages that are particularly trying for parents, regardless of their background. Although, some seem to navigate those transitions much more smoothly than others. A child's personality greatly influences how resilient they are to life's insults."

Dr. Peterson straightened in her chair. "How would you describe Evan's temperament?"

Louisa broke into a grin. "He's a very sunny little boy. He can be rather shy around strangers ... unless he's with Martin or me. But he warms up to most people quickly."

Louisa crossed her legs and laced her fingers together over her knee as she stared out the row of windows. "You almost *feel* Evan's presence before you know he's in the room, if you know what I mean."

The therapist laughed, nodding her head. "I *do* know what you mean. I have one of those at my house."

Louisa's smile faded as her voice took on a more serious tone. "About the challenges you mentioned, what exactly do you mean by that?"

"Whether you choose to adopt or choose to make Evan a permanent part of your family as a foster child, he may tend to be more rebellious than your biological child," the psychologist explained.

"He may use the fact that you're not his biological parents as justification for not obeying you for instance. Push the boundaries a bit farther.

"You may need to be extra vigilant about being consistent with your discipline—very clear about your expectations regarding his behaviour. And be firm ... but fair."

"Hmm, I see." Louisa twisted her wedding band back and forth on her finger.

Martin tried to shift his legs as his left calf began to cramp. The fixators banged against the edge of the coffee table, causing him to wince. He got to his feet to try to ease the spasm.

"He hasn't shown any sign of missing his family. Is that something we should worry about? Is it normal?" he asked.

"There's a range of normal, Dr. Ellingham. But at the moment Evan is distracted by the newness of everything. I would expect that there will come a time when the losses that he's suffered will hit him.

"He may grieve the loss of not just his father, but his mother and sister as well. His father died—in his mind, abandoned him.

"But his mother rejected him and took his sister away from him. Rejection can be terribly damaging to a child. More damaging even than abandonment.

"He may act out at times, through oppositional behaviour or withdrawal for instance. Those would be times when a mental health professional could be called upon."

Louisa shook her head. "This all sounds so frightening."

"Mrs. Ellingham, I know that I'm painting a rather stark picture. I just want you to be aware of the range of behaviours that can be seen in children who share similar histories to Evan's. You've said that he has a very sunny disposition. That will be of great help to him along the way and likely lessen the chances of difficulties.

"And bear in mind, if and when the squalls hit, you don't have to try to get through them on your own. There are people who have trained long and hard so that they can be of help to you."

Louisa bit at her lip. "Hmm, I just don't know. This has all been exhausting and stressful for Mar—"

"It hasn't been stressful!" Martin said, whirling his head to look at her. "I mean, yes, I suppose it has. But not for the reasons you think."

"Perhaps it would be helpful for your wife if you could be more specific, Dr. Ellingham. In what way *has* this experience been stressful?"

Martin looked incredulously from Louisa to the therapist and back again. "Well, the not knowing what's going to happen to the boy! There's been an *enormous* question mark hanging over the child's head for more than a month now!" he said, wincing as he waved his hands in the air. "The knowing that I can help him, but my hands are tied. *That's* stressful."

"But Martin, you've done so much for him already!" Louisa said.

He shook his head and rubbed a hand over the back of his neck. "The boy needs more than that. He needs to feel secure, and I'm not sure there's a bloody thing I can do about it. I feel—I feel stuck. Completely useless. *That's* why I'm stressed. Not because of what I'm doing for the boy, but because of what I'm *unable* to do for the boy. It's like my grandfather all ov—"

He quieted and returned to the sofa.

The psychologist folded her hands in her lap and looked at him pointedly. "Dr. Ellingham, I don't mean to pry, but it could facilitate my work with Evan if I knew that your own background gives you a unique understanding of the boy.

"If I were teaching piano to a musician's child, my approach would be different than it would be for a child of parents with no musical background whatsoever. I can assure you, everything said in this room is confidential."

Martin glanced over at Louisa, and she reached out, lacing her fingers with his.

Air hissed from his nose. "I—watched my grandfather die. So yes, I do understand what it was like for Evan that night."

The therapist leaned forward, resting her arms on her thighs. "I see. And abuse, both physical and emotional ... do you understand Evan in that regard as well?"

"Yes." Martin kept his gaze focused on his lap, his palm reddening as he dug his thumb into it. "The outcome doesn't have to be the same for Evan though, does it? It doesn't have to affect him the same way?"

"The same way? Do you mean the same way that your childhood experiences affected you?"

He brought his head up and gave her a warning look. "Yes."

"And what effect did your childhood have on you?"

A flicker of alarm passed across Martin's face. He hesitated, then straightened himself and jutted out his chin. "I'm *wondering*—if intervention *now* can help the boy to develop into a normal—fully functioning—*adult*?" he said through clenched teeth.

"I'm sorry. I didn't mean to put you on the spot," the psychologist said. "I just wasn't sure if there was something specific that you might be referring to. But in answer to your question, I do believe we can greatly increase Evan's chances of having a healthy emotional life, yes."

"Good." Martin cleared his throat and brushed at his trousers. "I haven't yet discussed Wednesday's appointment with him. Do you have any advice in regard to preparing him for the visit? What should I tell him to expect?"

"I would recommend you focus on the activities that we'll do together. The idea of talking to a stranger can be scary to a child, so a lot of the communication is done through creative activities.

"Play is the language of children, and most of my work with Evan will be done through play. Children are more relaxed when they're distracted by play, and they often express themselves through play. The activities that we'll do together have been developed to encourage openness."

The therapist briefly described some of the methods that she would be using with the boy and showed Martin and Louisa a number of examples of drawings done by children she had treated in the past.

Louisa heard her husband take in a breath and release it heavily. She gave him a nervous smile, then turned to the psychologist. "Martin still has a long way to go in his recovery, and he's supposed to be getting rest, eating well, and avoiding exposure to contagious illnesses.

"I've already seen him allowing the first two to slide and with an additional child in the house, this one exposed to illnesses at school—well, I'm very concerned about how having Evan in our home, long term, could affect Martin."

She turned to her husband. "Martin, before I'll even entertain the idea of a long-term arrangement with Evan, you have to promise me that we'll share the duties more equally than they have been up to this point. Let me take some of the load off of you. You just can't keep doing it all."

Martin felt the therapist's eyes on them and began to fidget. "Erm, perhaps we should discuss this on the way home, Louisa." He turned his gaze to Dr. Peterson. "I think we can navigate our way through this issue on our own—now that it's been raised."

"That's fine. I'm glad to see that you're thinking this through carefully. I'm really looking forward to meeting your little ray of sunshine," she said as she got up from her chair and made her way towards the door. "Please feel free to call if either of you have any other questions or concerns."

Martin filled his lungs with air as they exited the waiting area and stepped into the hospital corridor. "God, I'm glad that's over," he said.

"Dr. Peterson seems very nice and very competent. But I'm glad it's over, too." She stretched up and placed a kiss on her husband's lips. "Ready to go home?"

"Mm, no. I want to stop by Warren Buck's office ... see if I can drive yet."

"Martin, don't rush things."

"I'm *not*. He won't clear me if he has any qualms about it."

"Hmm."

By the time Martin had received Mr. Buck's blessing to get back behind the wheel and they were on the A-39, the sun had dropped below the horizon.

"So ... you want to finish our discussion about Evan?" Louisa asked as she reached over and brushed her fingers across her husband's cheek.

"Mm, yes. About sharing the duties more evenly you mean?"

"Yes, that's what I mean. The getting up at night with him is wearing you down. You can't deny that."

Martin's hands clenched around the steering wheel. "Yes. Perhaps I'll have to be firm with him about that ... limit the number of times I'll come into his room."

Louisa tipped her head down and peered up at him. "Or maybe firmer about making him try to get back to sleep on his own?"

"I've been giving that some consideration ... trying to remember what was helpful to me when I was young."

Reaching out, she rested a hand on his thigh. "After nightmares?"

"Mm. I'd read my copy of Gray's Anatomy under the covers ... with a torch."

Louisa's lips pulled into a smile. "Why does that not surprise me?"

"Mm, yes." Martin squirmed under his wife's intense gaze. "I thought that I might try giving him a torch tonight—leave a stack of books by his bed."

"It's certainly worth a try." Louisa hesitated before quietly suggesting, "We *could* try allowing Buddy to sleep with him."

Martin gave her an incredulous glance. "Absolutely not! Especially not in James's room. Evan has likely built up some tolerance, given his exposure to that dog he pretends is his. But James's immune system—"

"Could use a bit of building up, Martin."

"No. I'll give him a torch tonight. I'm confident that will do the trick."

"Oh, Martin," Louisa sighed. "Well, if it doesn't—do the trick, I will be the one getting up with him. Got it?"

Martin dropped his head to the side. "Louisa, I'm—I'm having difficulty with this. I took this on myself and I should see it through myself. I'd feel guilty having you burdened with something you didn't sign on for."

"I didn't exactly *sign on* for James."

"My point exactly! You have no idea how guilty I felt. Watching you go through the pregnancy—not helping out."

"Well, *you* didn't sign on for that either. And I didn't really give you a chance to help out, hmm?"

"Mm. Still, I'll get up with Evan."

Louisa crossed her arms in front of her, turning to face her side window. "Then I won't be giving any more thought to Evan's permanence in our home."

"Louisa—please don't."

"Martin, you made me a promise when you were in hospital. You said that if Evan came to stay with us, your health would come first. Are you going to renege on our agreement?"

He huffed out a breath. "I don't renege."

"All right, then. You do whatever it is you're going to do with the torch. But if Evan still gets up, I go tuck him back in."

Martin ducked his head. "Yes."

Chapter 29

"What's that for, Dr. Ellig-am? You gonna look at my throat?" Evan asked as Martin came into the nursery Monday night, a torch tucked under his arm and a stack of books in his hand.

"Of course not. Don't you think this one's a bit overqualified for the job?" He set the light down on the bedside table. "The beam needs to be more focused. You'd have to have a really big mouth for a torch like that one to be effective."

Evan sat up in the bed. "Oh, you mean like Lydia Bigelow's mum?"

Martin dropped down next to him, shaking his head. "No, no, no, no, no. I never said Lydia Bigelow's mum has a big mouth, Evan. I only said she says too much."

The child tipped his head to the side. "What's the difference?"

"One is a generalisation and not polite; the other is a statement of fact."

"Oh. So, what's the torch for then?"

"Hopefully, it's going to help us all get some sleep tonight. If you wake up in the night, Evan, I want you to use this torch and look at a book. See if you can get yourself back to sleep before you come into our room."

"Naa, that's okay. The old system works just fine for me."

"The *old system* may work fine for you, but I'm not finding it ideal. You need to try this. It worked for me when I was your age. Just take the torch and a book under the covers and read for a while. You'll probably get sleepy again."

"But what if I'm really scared? Can I come get you?"

"I don't ever want you to think you can't come in and wake Mrs. Ellingham or me up if you really need us, but I want you to try to get yourself back to sleep. We can always talk about the dreams in the morning if you like."

Evan flopped back on the bed. "This is a stupid idea."

Martin gave the boy a scowl. "It's *my* idea!"

"Still a stupid idea," he grumbled as he sat back up and punched his pillow.

Air hissed from Martin's nose. "Okay, let's do the bedtime story so you can get off to sleep. Lay down there."

Louisa glanced up from her book when Martin came down the stairs a few minutes later. "They both all settled for the night?"

"Yes. For the time being anyway. We'll see how it goes." A soft groan slipped out as he stepped up into the kitchen.

"Think the torch will work?"

"Quite possibly not; it's a stupid idea it seems."

"Oh, dear."

"Would you like a cup of tea?" he asked, pulling the tea kettle from its base and filling it with water.

"Could you bring me a glass of wine?"

"Mm. I don't understand why the boy thinks it's a stupid idea. He hasn't even given it a chance."

His footsteps falling heavily, the right more heavily than the left, he crossed the kitchen, pulling the corkscrew from the drawer in the buffet. He stood tapping it against his palm as he stared absently down the hall.

Louisa laid her book down and walked into the kitchen. "What's wrong, Martin?" she asked, taking the corkscrew from his hand and picking the wine bottle up from the counter.

"He *actually* said it was a stupid idea."

Louisa filled a wine glass, then walked over to her husband, putting her arm around his waist. "It was bound to happen sometime," she said, stretching up to kiss his cheek.

"Mm, it's not that. I've had stupid ideas before. But I really thought he'd like the idea of the torch."

"I was referring to being knocked off the pedestal that little boy's had you on." She thrust her glass into his hand. "Here, you take my wine in with you ... go put your feet up. I'll bring your tea. I don't really trust you to be walking around with hot beverages."

Martin grumbled under his breath as he made his way to the sofa.

"Stings a bit, doesn't it?" Louisa said as she set a steaming mug down on the coffee table in front of him.

"I just don't understand why he think's it's a stupid idea. I thought it would be fun for him ... crawling under the blankets ... all by himself with a good book."

"I think you may have just diagnosed the problem, Dr. Ellig-am."

"I don't follow."

"All by himself." Louisa patted him on the leg. "No Dr. Ellig-am under there with the flashlight."

"Mm, I see."

Louisa lifted her husband's arm and nestled in under his shoulder. "Martin."

"Hmm?"

"Are you going to tell Chris about what Alex Lippolis did?"

"I'll talk to him tomorrow. Hopefully Alex will have spoken to him on his own. If not ... yes, I'll have to tell him."

"*Good.* I can't believe he did that! He could have really hurt you, Martin." Louisa took hold of his hand and pressed it to her lips.

"Ah ... that."

"Yes, of course that. What did you *think* I was talking about?"

"Mm, nothing."

Martin picked up a medical journal, and Louisa returned to her novel, opening to the dog-eared page.

They sat quietly for some time before Martin drank down the last of his tea, glanced over at her, and cleared his throat. "Erm, Louisa ... what Alex did ... it was inappropriate, but—"

"*Inappropriate!* Martin, the man pushed a colleague on to the floor! An injured colleague no less! Need I remind you that you're recovering from a horrible accident? That fall could have resulted in a serious injury ... a major setback for you? Or worse!"

"Louisa, I certainly don't need any reminders about my current physical condition. I can't say very much about what happened, but ... well, perhaps you'd feel better about it if you knew that a health issue contributed to Alex's atypical behaviour."

"Oh." She stared absently for a moment. "Well, I don't think I feel any better about it, but maybe I can be more forgiving."

"Good. Are you ready to go to bed?"

"I am ... it's been a long day."

The only sound in their darkened bedroom that night was the steady ticking of the mantel clock and the occasional scratching of a gull's feet on the slate roof overhead. Martin and Louisa had been sleeping for a full four-and-a-half blissful, undisturbed hours when Martin was awakened by a tugging on his vest and his young charge's voice.

"Dr. Ellig-am," the boy whispered. "Dr. Ellig-am, I need your help."

Martin sat up and rubbed his eyes. "What is it, Evan?"

"I had a bad dream."

"Did you try reading for a while?"

"Uh-uh."

"Well, go back to your bed, get your light and a book, and read. Then if you really can't get back to sleep, I'll come—er, Mrs. Ellingham will come and sit with you for a bit."

"I don't think that's gonna work very good 'cause—"

"Evan, don't say it's a stupid idea until you've tried it," Martin whispered. "Now go back to bed."

The child's shadowy figure flapped its arms in frustration. "But I don't know how ta turn the torch on!"

"Oh, I see. Well, give it to me, and I'll show you."

"That's not gonna work either 'cause it's by my bed."

Martin glanced over at his wife, sound asleep and oblivious to the goings-on next to her.

"Okay, I'll come show you, but then you have to try to get yourself back to sleep."

The two made their way back to the nursery, and Evan crawled back under the covers.

Martin groped around in the dark and found the switch on the torch. "Can you feel that little bump there?" he said as he ran the child's finger over the button.

"Yeah."

"You just push that when you want to turn the torch on and off." Martin pressed the switch and a beam of light illuminated the ceiling. "See—there you go. Now pull the covers over your head and read your book."

"Thanks, Dr. Ellig-am."

"Mm, yes." Martin grunted and turned to limp back across the hall before slipping carefully back into bed next to his wife.

He had just drifted back to sleep when a bright light jarred him from his slumber. He slapped a hand to his eyes and sat up abruptly, his heart pounding. "What is it now, Evan?" he hissed, peering between his fingers.

"I can't get it to shut off."

"What's going on, Martin?" Louisa mumbled as she rose up on her elbow.

"Mm, just a bit of a mechanical glitch. Go back to sleep." He turned his attention back to the boy. "Here, Evan ... feel that bump right here?" He guided the boy's fingers to the switch again.

"Yeah."

"Just push on that until it clicks and the light goes out. You just do the same thing as when you turn it on."

There was a succession of small grunts and gasps as the child tried without success to get the torch to turn off. "I don't gots enough muscles for it."

"Oh, never mind. I'll shut it off for now, and we'll work on the problem tomorrow."

"'Kay."

The switch clicked. "Goodnight, Evan," Martin said, dropping back on to his pillow.

"But, Dr. Ellig-am, it's too dark now; I don't wanna walk back by myself."

He began to sit himself up only to be yanked back down by the back of his vest.

Louisa leaned over him. "Remember what I said, Martin."

He watched her form as it glided across the room and out the door with the boy.

As had been promised, Tuesday was men's day out for Martin and Evan, and Evan could only have been more excited if it were Christmas.

The boy waited in the reception room with his coat and mittens on as Martin finished with his final patient of the morning, Robin Thornton, the local automotive mechanic who had been suffering from a cough and chest pain.

The door to the consulting room opened, and Evan jumped down from his chair. "Is it time ta go now, Dr. Ellig-am?" The boy trailed behind him as he headed towards Morwenna's desk.

"I'm almost done, Evan. Morwenna, could you call over to Truro and set up an echocardiogram for Mr. Thornton?"

"Sure, Doc."

He turned back towards the hallway, his charge shadowing him closely. "And don't let them put you off until next week. I want him in there today or tomorrow," he said over his shoulder.

Ducking through the doorways, he stepped back into his exam room. Robin watched in amusement as Martin moved about, seemingly unaware of the child behind him.

"I want to switch you to an inhaled cholinergic, Mr. Thornton," Martin said, dropping into his chair. "We'll see how you do with that. If needs be, I can step you up to an inhaled corticosteroid.

"I'm also sending you over to Truro for an echocardiogram ... just to rule out any possible cardiac issues."

Evan pulled his mittens from his now-sweaty hands and laid them down. He leaned against the dresser behind his guardian's chair and pressed his palms on to its surface, watching as the moist handprints left behind evaporated away.

He laid his head on his forearms and stared at the Buddha statue that adorned the piece of furniture. His small fingers walked their way up the figure's rotund belly before inspecting the left nostril, poking a forefinger into one gold nostril, twisting it back and forth.

"You think there's something wrong with my heart, then?" the mechanic asked, his body stiffening in his seat.

"Just a precaution...given your age and that fact that you're having some chest pain. It's a common symptom with respiratory disease. The connective tissue in the rib cage can become inflamed when you're labouring to breathe."

Martin jotted some notes on to the man's patient card and slipped it back into its sleeve. Then he scribbled out a prescription and ripped the sheet of paper from the pad, sliding it across his desk.

Mr. Thornton picked up the script and got up from his chair before heading to the door. Martin, tailed closely by the seven-year-old, followed behind him.

"Morwenna, were you able to get that echo scheduled?" he asked.

"Tomorrow morning at ten," she said, handing the patient another piece of paper. "They want you there at half past nine though, Mr. Thornton."

"Why didn't they just say half nine then?" he grumbled.

"Just ta make your life interesting, I s'pose." Morwenna gave him a forced smile.

The door to the surgery closed behind the man as Jeremy came through the entryway from the lounge. "That's the last of 'em, boss," the young man said.

Martin glanced around the room, his brow furrowing before he looked at his aide. "Could you take care of any loose ends, Jeremy? I have another commitment this afternoon."

"Sure. I'll see you tomorrow."

Making his way to the kitchen, Martin glanced around the room before passing through the lounge to the stairway. "Louisa!" he called out. *"Louisa!"*

"What is it, Martin?" she asked as she headed down the steps with James Henry perched on her hip.

"Where's Evan? We're supposed to go over to Wadebridge today."

Feeling a sharp tug on the back of his shirt, he spun around. "Oh, there you are. Are you ready to go?"

The boy grinned at him and bounced on his toes. "Yeah, I've been waitin' for ya."

"Evan, don't forget your mittens," Louisa said as she squeezed past her husband.

The seven-year-old darted off to the exam room and returned with a pair of bright red mittens in hand. "Okay, I'm ready."

The first stop was the pub that Martin and Jeremy frequented on their many trips to the physical therapy centre.

They placed their orders at the counter and went to find a booth. Martin took a seat, forcing his stiffened limbs under the table. Evan pulled off his coat and threw it on the bench on the opposite side before sliding in beside him.

"Why don't we go over this list of yours while we wait for our sandwiches," Martin said.

Evan jumped back off the bench and fished around in his coat pocket, returning to his seat with a rather worn and smudgy piece of paper. "This is a really good idea, Dr. Ellig-am."

"Mm, yes. I do manage something a bit cleverer on occasion."

The boy slapped the list on to the table, making a great display of smoothing out the wrinkles. "There she is," he said with a flourish of his hand.

"Ah." Martin picked up the list and began to scrutinise it. "Good grief, this is worse than I thought it would be!"

"Too s'pensive?" Evan asked with a look of concern on his face.

"No. But we're going to give Bert Large another heart attack feeding him all of this."

"Oh, Mrs. Ellig-am said to tell you she gots a *special* menu for Mr. Large."

Martin looked down at the boy, his eyebrows raised. "Oh. That was good planning on her part."

"Yeah, she said she didn't want ta give you any s'cusives for not gettin' the stuff on the list."

A young woman stopped at the table and slid a plate in front of Martin before giving Evan a smile. "I'm assumin' you're the one who requested the peanut butter and jelly sandwich with lots of ketchup and mustard?"

He grinned up at her. "It's my favourite."

"Maybe you'll let your dad try a bite," she said, setting the plate down and tousling his hair.

"He's *not* my dad," he said, giving her a scowl before turning a smiling face to Martin. "*He's* my best friend."

"I see. Well, you two enjoy."

The boy bit into his unconventional sandwich, looking as happy as a clam at high tide.

The trip to the barbers was a potential stumbling block to a happy afternoon. Evan's mother had always cut his hair, and according to Louisa, she would allow it to get quite long before shearing it off very short. This resulted in taunts from the other children at school. As a result, Evan's expectations for the outcome were no different this time around.

Martin held tightly to his hand as they entered the shop. He spoke with a man named Jerry, pulling a folded sheet of paper from his pocket and handing it to him. "These are my wife's specifications."

Jerry looked over Louisa's notes and smiled before jerking his head towards a chair. "Okay lad, up you get. We'll have you lookin' right smart before you can say Jack Robinson."

Martin stood nearby for a while as the barber snipped at the child's shaggy head. Once Jerry seemed to have the boy engaged in light-hearted banter, he stepped towards them.

"Evan, I'm going to run next door for a minute. I'll be right back."

The seven-year-old slid from the chair and ran to him, latching on to his wrist. "No! You can't leave me here all by myself!"

Martin leaned over. "I'm not leaving you here by yourself. This man's been cutting my hair for the last five years. He'll take good care of you. And I'm just going to the shop next door to order a Christmas stocking," he said softly. "I'll be back in no more than five minutes."

"How long is five minutes?"

"I tell you what ... you take my watch. I'll be back before this little hand goes all the way around five times," he said, removing the timepiece from his wrist.

Evan's shoulders drooped as he walked back to the chair. "Just don't forget about me!" he yelled as the doctor walked out the door.

When Martin returned a few minutes later, Evan jumped down and ran to his side. "Can we go now?" he asked between sniffles.

"Are you done with him, Jerry?"

The barber walked over and ran a comb through the boy's hair, creating a jaunty flip over his forehead. "Now I'm done with 'im."

"Can we go then, Dr. Ellig-am?"

"Yes. I just need to pay the man." He gave the boy the once-over, jutting out his chin. "You better watch out. That Bungalow girl's going to be after you when she sees you looking so handsome."

"*Bigelow*, Dr. Ellig-am."

"Mm, yes."

Evan peered up at him worriedly before his face relaxed. "I'll just be sure I mess things up good before I go to school," he said, taking in a ragged breath.

By the time they had picked up the now embroidered stocking, Evan had calmed down and was looking forward to their next stop—Lidl's grocery.

Martin peered at him in the Lexus' rear-view mirror. "Evan, do you remember how I promised to always be truthful with you?"

"Yep. And you came back, *just* like you said you would."

"That's right. Sometimes I'll need to leave you on your own for a bit. But I'll only leave you if I think you're safe on your own. Or I'll leave you with people who I trust."

"'Kay. Can we go get the stuff now?"

"Yes."

The trip to the market went smoothly, aside from a small bump in the road when Martin tried to persuade Evan to opt for healthier ingredient options.

The boy rolled his eyes at him. "Mrs. Ellig-am *said* you'd do this."

"I'm not saying that you can't make these things. But there are ways to adjust a recipe so that it's lower in fat and unhealthy calories. How 'bout you substitute low sodium chicken broth for the cream in the mashed potatoes."

"She said you'd use that *word*, too."

"What word."

"That one you just said. And she said to tell you—" He crossed his arms over his chest and tipped his head down, peering up at Martin with narrowed eyes, his lips taut and his voice as high as he could make it. "Absolutely no *sup-stutions*, Mar-tin!"

The doctor pulled in his chin and tugged the list from the child's hand. "What's next?"

The shopping trolley was full by the time they had located all the items that Evan and Louisa deemed necessary for a proper Christmas Feast.

"Well, I think we've about bought out the store," Martin said. "There shouldn't be any complaints about our purchases. I want to pick up a torch that those fingers of yours can operate, then we can pay for all of this and load it up."

It was almost three o'clock by the time Martin set the last bag in the boot and closed the lid. "That's it. Now we just need to unload it at the farm." He glanced down at his watch. "If we're lucky, we might even have time to squeeze in a snack before dinner."

"Oh, we're not done *yet*. We still gots ta get the Christmas goose."

"The Christmas goose! I just unloaded a fifteen-pound ham into the boot!"

"Yeah, we needed *that*, too."

Martin huffed out a breath. "Okay, let's go get it then," he said, starting back towards the market.

"No, Dr. Ellig-am! They don't gots 'em in there. We have ta go to an upholstery farm to get a goose."

Martin turned and screwed up his face. "A *what?*"

"An upholstery farm. You know ... where they gots chickens and turkeys and gooses and stuff."

"You mean a *poultry* farm?"

"*Noo!* An *upholstery* farm." Evan's tongue worked its way out the side of his mouth as he dug in his pocket, pulling out a wadded-up piece of paper. "This is the place Mr. Large told me about. I wrote it down so I wouldn't forget."

Martin held out his hand and the boy dropped the wad into his palm. He picked apart the tangled mass and squinted his eyes as he tried to decipher the scrawled, phonetically spelled words. *DrEWS UPOLDsTrEE FrAM*.

"What does that say?" he asked his charge.

Evan pulled the sheet from his guardian's fingers and peered at it. "Yep. See, I told ya. It say's Drew's *Upholstery Farm* ... just like Mr. Large said."

"Gawd," Martin moaned softly. "Okay, where is this place?"

Evan scratched at his eyebrow. "In Bude. I'm *pretty* sure."

"*Bude!*" Shaking his head, Martin pulled his mobile from his pocket and did a search. "I see a Drustrup *Poultry Farm*."

"That's it!" Evan said, jumping up and down. "Can we go?"

The doctor rubbed a hand over his face. "All right, get in the car."

The afternoon light was beginning to fade as they pulled into the driveway leading to the neatly kept farm. Chickens ran about in a large pen, their nervous clucking crescendoing to a frenetic chorus as Martin and Evan got out of the car and walked towards the house.

A tall lanky man, clad in denim trousers and a plaid flannel shirt, stepped out on to the porch.

"Nigel Drustrup. How can I 'elp you?" he asked as he strode towards them, stooping to scoop up a wayward hen before dropping it back into the pen. "A bit'a the wanderlust that one 'as, she does."

The man handed the doctor a sheet of paper and he glanced down at the price list. "Ah. Thank you."

"Why don't you tell him what you want, Evan."

The boy looked around at the small flocks of geese and white Pekin ducks foraging for small insects and bits of green grass peeking through the brown winter lawn.

"Which ones are the Christmas gooses? That what I want."

"Well, lad, we're fresh outta geese for this season. We sell out of 'em by the end of November, I'm afraid."

"Oh, *no!* Now what are we gonna do, Dr. Ellig-am?"

"We have plenty of ham, Evan."

"But that's *not* the same thing! Why can't we have one of those white ones over there?" the boy said, poking a finger at a small group of Emdens.

"Them are all too old," the farmer said. "You'd be chewin' til Easter if you tried to roast one'a them. Like I said, all this year's geese are sold.

"We do got a few nice ducks all dressed and ready for trussin' though. A couple of them is almos' the same as a Christmas goose. Some folks prefer 'em for the Christmas Feast, actually."

Martin raised his eyebrows at the boy.

Evan eyed the man suspiciously. "Do they gots a place where we can stick our chestnuts?"

The farmer's gaze darted towards Martin. "He bein' cheeky wit' me?"

"I believe he's referring to stuffing them."

"Oh, then you bet they 'ave. Stuff up right nice in fact. Better 'an any goose. A goose 'as too much fat for stuffin' really."

Evan scuffed at the rock drive with his trainer and jammed his fists on his hips. "Well, if *that's* all ya gots, then you should give us a special deal."

The farmer's gaze returned to Martin.

"Yep, now he's being cheeky." The doctor held the sheet of paper out to the boy. "These are the man's prices, Evan. They seem reasonable to me. How 'bout it? Do you want a couple of ducks or not?"

"Yeah, it's better than nothin'."

The farmer gave a nod of his head. "Good 'nuff. Come on, we'll go get 'em then."

They followed the farmer into a low white outbuilding. The large door swung slowly on it's hinges, stirring the chilly air enough to send a shiver through Martin.

Nigel flipped a switch and the spartanly furnished room was illuminated. It was empty, aside from two old wooden desks and several shelves of books about all things related to poultry and poultry husbandry.

Mr. Drustrup pulled the latch on a heavy metal door to a refrigerated room and disappeared, returning shortly with a dressed duck encased in clear plastic in each hand. The latch on the door clanked sharply as it snapped back into place.

"Here you are, mates."

Evan threw up his hands. "But I thought you were gonna cut off their heads first!"

"Their 'eads *is* off, boy," the farmer said.

"But I wanted ta *see* it! I wanted ta see its eyes!" Evan slapped his hands against his thighs as his face reddened and tears gathered before spilling on to his cheeks.

Martin cleared his throat. "Mr. Drustrup, could I have a moment with the boy?"

"Sure nuff. I'll jus' go put these birds in yer car." The barn door closed behind him.

"Evan, what's this all about? Did you even *want* a Christmas goose?"

"Yes, but ... I *wanted* to see."

"What did you want to see?"

"I wanted to see how it looked ... if it looked the same after it died."

"Ah, I see."

Martin pressed his lips together as he thought through how to handle the situation. "Okay. Let me talk with Mr. Drustrup a minute. You wait here."

Evan waited as his guardian stepped outside. He returned with the farmer several minutes later. The man carried a plastic-wrapped parcel in his hand.

"Mr. Drustrup has the head from a duck he butchered earlier today. He'll show it to you if you'd like to see it," Martin said, resting his hand on the seven-year-old's shoulder.

Evan grabbed on to his wrist. "I wanna see it."

Nigel opened the plastic and held the contents out in front of him.

The child stared at the body part for several seconds before reaching a tentative hand out, stroking a finger over the feathers on the bird's head before cautiously touching the glazed eye.

Martin watched uneasily, hoping this hadn't been one of his more stupid ideas.

Evan's shoulders began to shudder before he turned suddenly and grabbed on to the doctor's shirt, attempting to climb into his arms.

"Mr. Drustrup, could you lift him up for me, please?"

Nigel lay the duck head on the floor and hoisted the boy into the air. Evan grabbed on around the doctor's neck and buried his face in his shoulder before letting his tears flow freely.

"Your father's dead, Evan. He won't ever be alive again." Martin said quietly.

He held the boy tightly until his crying had stopped. "Can I put you down now?" he asked.

"Uh-huh."

Mr. Drustrup took the child from the doctor's arms and set him on the floor. Evan shuddered as he wiped his sleeve across his nose.

Screwing up his face, Martin pulled his handkerchief from his pocket, wiping at the shiny trail left behind on the child's coat.

"Are you ready to go home ... to the surgery now?"

"No. We gots ta go to Dr. Ellig-am's farm first so we can drop everything off."

The farmer put his hand on the boy's head. "Be sure you get them birds in the refrigerator soon as you get 'ome. Won't stay very fresh if you ferget 'em in the car."

"Oh, we won't forget 'em," Evan said. "We can't have a real Christmas Feast without 'em."

Martin pulled up his arm and checked the time. It was now almost five o'clock. "Mr. Drustrup, thank you for your help ... with everything," he said taking his wallet from his pocket before handing him a ten and fifty-pound note.

"Glad ta do it'. Hope for the best for the lad there. Maybe you'll bring 'im back for a goose next year."

"Mm," he grunted back before leading Evan to the car.

Martin was tired and aching by the time he pulled the Lexus into the parking place by the surgery. Evan ran ahead of him, charging through the back door, anxious to share the details of his adventure with Louisa.

"*Well*, I was beginning to think I should send PC Penhale out to find you two! What took so long?"

Evan regaled Louisa with the details of their afternoon as she finished putting dinner on the table.

The child's chattering continued throughout the meal, and the barrage of information didn't stop until he had been excused from the table.

The rest of the evening passed quickly and by the time the children were bathed and ready for bed, the seven-year-old's eyes were getting heavy.

Martin read Evan and James a story before tucking them in for the night, setting the new torch on the table before turning out the light.

Shortly after midnight, he was again jolted into semi-wakefulness by a blinding light. He sat up abruptly, colliding sharply with the metal torch aimed at his face. "Ow!" he yelped, slapping a hand to the bridge of his nose. "Bloody hell!"

"Mar-tin!" Louisa hissed as she bolted upright. "Watch your language!"

"It hurts, Louisa!" he squeaked back.

"I don't care. Bite your tongue if you have to when you're around the boys!"

He pulled his head away as her breath blew sharply into his ear with each syllable.

"What *is* it, Evan?" he growled.

The boy climbed up on the bed and laid a book in his lap, poking a finger at the page. "I was just wonderin'—*what's* that word?"

Louisa erupted in a fit of giggles as she swung her legs over the bed. "You go back to sleep my genius husband. I'll see you in the morning." She planted a kiss on his forehead before she took the boy's hand and led him from the room.

Chapter 30

Martin scowled at the miserable looking reflection in the mirror. The bruised and abraded nose, a product of his collision with the torch the night before, called attention to the darkening circles under his eyes, giving him the appearance of some poor sod who hadn't fared well in the wars.

He grunted at himself before leaning over the sink to splash cold water on his face. As it softened, he wiped at the bit of dried blood which had oozed from the scrape.

"Here you go," Louisa said as she pressed a towel into her husband's groping hand. "How did you sleep?"

Martin stood back up as he blotted his face dry. "Not very well. I lay awake most of the night waiting for the next disruption."

Taking hold of his vest, she peered up at him. "Oh, Martin! That must have hurt!" she said, gingerly touching the darkening area on his face.

"I *did* mention that last night, Louisa."

"I know you did. I guess I thought you were just being a baby about it."

He glanced down at the external fixators holding his fractured body together and blinked back at her. "Really?"

She winced. "Sorry, I wasn't thinking very clearly, maybe."

He reached over and turned the handle on the shower tap.

"When are you going to talk with Evan about this afternoon's appointment?" Louisa asked as she picked up her toothbrush from the shelf next to the sink.

"This morning. I've been thinking it through," he said, slipping off his dressing gown and stepping under the water. "I need to get the words straight in my head."

"You'll do just fine. He seems to love anything you do with him." Returning to the bedroom, she laid out her clothes on the bed as the toothbrush whirred away.

"Martin, I've been think—" She tipped her head back to prevent toothpaste foam from dripping down her chin and hurried back to spit into the sink. "I've been thinking a lot about Evan's difficulties at night ... the bedwetting and the nightmares.

"I know you're opposed to the idea, but let's face it, the only really good night's sleep any of us has had, aside from James, was the night that Buddy sneaked into—"

Martin pushed the shower door aside and wagged his finger at her. "No, Louisa. Don't even bring it up. I don't want to have to share my house with a dog."

"Well, your torch idea hasn't been a brilliant success, has it?"

He pulled in his chin. "I'm still working the bugs out of the system."

"Well, you better exterminate them soon."

Delivering a dark look, he rolled the shower door closed again.

Louisa bent over the sink to wash her face before patting it dry as she watched her husband fight his uncooperative limbs.

Picking up the bottle of shampoo, he squeezed a puddle into his right hand before setting the container back on the shelf. Then, he transferred the shampoo to his left hand and awkwardly worked it into his hair.

She sighed, slipping her dressing gown off and rolling the glass door to the side. "Can I give you a hand with that?" she asked as she poured a puddle of shampoo on to her palm.

A wave of heat spread up Martin's neck and cheeks as Joe Penhale's bumbling words to him the last time he was in hospital came to mind. He swallowed as his wife reached up. Her fingers worked their way through his hair as her breasts brushed against his skin. Reaching reflexively, he grabbed on to her waist to steady himself.

"I think that'll do. Tip your head back and we'll rinse," she said.

The water rained down, washing the lather from his head. She wiped a rogue bit from his brow before stretching up to kiss him.

Pulling her in close, he wrapped his arms around her back, keeping his left arm positioned under the right to protect her from the protruding pins.

Her scent rose on the clouds of steam which drifted up from the floor, and he nuzzled his face into her neck to capture it before it mingled with the scent of his soap. "This is a nice way to start the day," he said, his voice a half-step lower than normal.

"Mmm. It is, isn't it." She pressed her cheek to his wet head as her hands glided down to the small of his back. "I don't s'pose it'd go over well if you just...closed up shop?"

His wife's words jarred him back to the reality of the work day, and he straightened himself. "No, I *don't* think it would go over well." His eyes sparkled as his mouth conveyed not a smile per se, but rather an expression of contentment. "Perhaps later?"

She patted her hand on his chest. "We can only hope."

Martin stepped from the shower, leaving Louisa to finish her preparations for the day. Wrapping a towel around his waist, he picked up the tea towel he used to wipe down his fixators and returned to their room to dry the devices. He had just dropped on to the bed when he heard the slapping of bare feet against the wood floor in the hall.

"Hi, Dr. Ellig-am!" Evan said as he bounced on to the mattress and buried himself under the blankets.

"Mm, good morning." Martin's modest nature caused him to quickly pull Louisa's jeans over the towel around his lap. "Erm, you're up awfully early. It's not even seven o'clock yet."

"Yeah. I can't get my brain to stop thinkin' about Christmas. It's just two more days. Did you know that?"

"Yes, I was aware of it."

"So, that means it's the day after tomorrow. That sounds even closer, don't you think?"

"Mm, I suppose it does."

"What do you think Father Christmas is doing on the day before the day before Christmas? Think he's still making toys, or do you think he's sleepin' so he's all rested up for bringing all the presents?"

Glancing over at him, Martin cocked his head. "Do you remember what I told you about Father Christmas?"

"Yeah, I remember. I'm just pretendin' about it. But I think I might get a present this year 'cause Mrs. Ellig-am asked me what I wanted, and nobody ever asked me that before."

"I see." Martin ran the towel over his head and smoothed out his hair with his fingers. "Evan, we're going to take a little trip over to Truro this afternoon."

The boy bounced up on his knees and crawled across the bed, sitting down next to his guardian. "Wow, two trips in a row! What are we gonna do on this one?"

"We're, ah ... we're going to see someone I know. Her name is Dr. Peterson...Abby Peterson."

Evan eyed him warily. "Will it hurt?"

"No. She's a different sort of doctor. She's going to help you with your nightmares. We'll go over today so that you can meet her. And I know she's looking forward to meeting *you* ... getting to know you."

Evan looked at Martin askance and shook his head. "No, I don't think so. You do a good job with my nightmares. I think I'll stick with you."

"You know, Evan, I've—I've had some trouble with nightmares, too. But I found a doctor who's been able to help me a lot."

The boy jumped down on to the floor. "I've got an idea. How 'bout we both go to *your* doctor ... together. That would be fun, don't you think?"

"My doctor is trained to help adults, Evan. Dr. Peterson is trained to help children. She's quite nice, and she has a very nice office ... a lot of toys to play with ... even a sandpit. You'll be playing a lot of games ... drawing pictures ... things that you really like to do."

The child stood quietly for several moments before he began to cry. "Can I at least stay until after the Christmas Feast?"

Martin shook his head. "Evan, I'm not *leaving* you with her. We'll come back home ... come back here after we visit Dr. Peterson. You'll still stay with us. I'll just take you to see her sometimes. Then I'll bring you right back home with me."

"Promise?"

"I promise. Maybe we'll stop by Old Doc Parson's office when we finish up at Dr. Peterson's. You can say hello." He patted his hand against the boy's back as his crying diminished to sniffles.

Evan glanced down, picking up a leg of Louisa's jeans while furrowing his brow at the doctor. "These are Mrs. Ellig-am's trousers you know."

"Yes, I realise that. Why don't you go get dressed. And pull the door shut behind you."

"'Kay. See ya."

Martin cringed as the door slammed behind him, rattling the windows.

The morning progressed uneventfully for the most part. Martin treated an eclectic mix of maladies and medical concerns ranging from dermatological conditions to cardiac ailments.

The more mundane cases bookended an only slightly more interesting laceration to a farmer's hand. Jeremy had been summoned to the consulting room to suture it before the doctor dressed the wound and sent the man on his way.

Louisa and the boys were eating lunch when Martin came through under the stairs.

"Mm, sorry," she said, dabbing at a drip of broth that was threatening to escape down her chin. "James and Evan were getting hungry, so we started without you."

"That's fine." He went to the cooker and poked at the pot of broth with the ladle. Although Poppy was no cuisinier, her cooking was definitely more satisfying than those served by his wife recently.

Her time spent on Christmas preparations as well as her need to keep up with work at the school left her little time for the more pedestrian domestic duties.

I'll stop and pick up a sandwich on the way to Truro, he thought. He took a demitasse cup from the cupboard. *I'll just say I'm not terribly hungry at the moment.* He glanced down again at the soup as the smell made its way to his nose. *It really wouldn't be a lie.*

"Here, let me get that for you, Martin," Louisa said as she hurried over and slipped in front of him. "Oh, for goodness' sake, you need to eat more than that!"

She snatched the diminutive receptacle from his hand, replacing it with a deep soup bowl. "Go sit down. I don't want you carrying this back to the table; you could burn yourself."

Martin turned away from the cooker, screwing up his face. "I think I can manage to bring my own dinner to the table," he muttered under his breath.

He took a seat next to Evan. The little boy batted at the greyish-green orbs floating on the surface of the nearly colourless broth in his bowl.

Louisa set an ample serving down in front of her husband, giving him a smile. "As Bert would say—*enjoy!*"

"Mm, yes." He glanced over at the seven-year-old, sitting with his head propped in his hand as he stared forlornly at his lunch. If misery loves company, Martin and Evan were perfect companions.

"So, Evan, are you excited about your trip over to Truro with Dr. Ellingham?" Louisa asked.

The boy's feet began to swing under the table. "I've been thinkin' about that. Maybe it's not such a good idea. That lady might tell people about me."

"Dr. Peterson isn't allowed to talk to anyone about her patients, Evan. There are laws that doctors have to abide by. I can't even talk to Mrs. Ellingham about my patients," Martin explained. He put a spoonful of broth into his mouth, making a gallant attempt to not pull a face as he chewed the overcooked, tasteless, chunks of vegetables.

"But she might forget about the laws and tell somebody by mistake. And anyway, you don't want to have another accident before you're all healed up from the last one, do you?" He peered up at Martin, his eyebrows raised.

"I'll drive carefully. Now eat your lunch."

Martin and Evan left Portwenn early enough to stop at the sandwich shop in Wadebridge. "We should pick up a snack ... something to hold you over until supper," he told the boy.

They ate their sandwiches as they drove and arrived in Truro five minutes ahead of schedule.

Martin held on to his charge's hand as he limped towards the main building on the Royal Cornwall campus. Their pace slowed gradually until they finally reached the automatic doors. They stepped through into the hospital atmosphere, with its medicinal smells, echoing voices, and metallic clatterings.

Evan began to pull back against his guardian's grasp. "I don't *like* this place, Dr. Ellig-am!"

Martin stopped and leaned down. "We're not staying here, Evan. We'll go back to Portwenn in a couple of hours. We'll have dinner with Mrs. Ellingham and James. Then you'll have your bath and I'll read you a bedtime story. You and James will go to bed in your own room. But first, we're going to see Dr. Peterson."

"But I don't *want* to tell her about my dreams! I don't know her!"

Martin glanced around him, grimacing at the staring onlookers. "Evan, do you remember when you came to see me at my surgery a long time ago? When you were sick and having trouble breathing."

"Yeah," he said, rubbing at his eyes with his free fist.

"You didn't know me then, but we became friends, didn't we?"

"Yeah."

"Dr. Peterson wants to be your friend, too."

"But what if she tells people about them!"

"Evan, I know you trust me, and I trust Dr. Peterson. She won't tell *anyone* about your nightmares."

"But ... do I gotta tell her about the other thing?"

Martin stared blankly at him before raising his eyebrows and tipping his head back. "Ah, you mean the wetting the bed?" he whispered in the boy's ear.

"Uh-huh."

"A lot of children have that trouble, Evan. But you don't need to tell her about that unless you want to. No one's going to force you to talk about anything, not even the bad dreams, if you don't want to talk about it." Martin pointed his finger at the lifts. "Come on, you can push the buttons."

"Well, hello, Dr. Ellingham. How are you today?" Jean Teague asked when they came in the door.

"I'm fine. He is, too," Martin said, wagging a finger at the boy. "We have a two o'clock appointment with Dr. Peterson."

Jean brushed off Martin's abrupt manner and came around from behind her desk to introduce herself. "So, you must be Evan, then?" she asked as she leaned down to speak to him.

Evan stepped behind Martin's legs, peering around as he clutched on to his wrist with his left hand and his trousers with the right.

"My name is Mrs. Teague." Wrinkles creased her cheeks as she began to point out the toy areas in the waiting room.

The child tugged on Martin's sleeve and he bent down. "What is it, Evan?"

"I wanna go home!" he whispered.

The doctor took hold of his wrist and walked over to take a seat. "Come on, sit down," he said, laying his crutch on the floor and patting the chair next to him.

Evan looked up at him teary eyed. "Are you sure you're not gonna leave?"

"I promised you I wouldn't, didn't I?"

"Yeah. But can you promise again?"

Martin breathed out a small sigh. "I promise I won't leave. You're going to visit with Dr. Peterson, and then we'll go see Dr. Parsons before we head back to Portwenn."

Evan sat slumped in his chair as Martin picked up a magazine, flipping through it aimlessly. A door could be heard opening and the boy startled, grabbing for his guardian's shirt sleeve.

"It's okay," Martin said softly.

"Hello, Dr. Ellingham," the therapist said as she approached.

Martin gave her a nod of his head, "Dr. Peterson." He picked up his crutch as he got to his feet, and the seven-year-old jumped down before darting behind his legs. "Evan, this is Dr. Peterson."

Abby crouched down. "Hello, Evan," she said, her dimples sandwiching a broad smile. "I'm really looking forward to spending time with you."

Martin kept gentle tension on the child's arm, but he had one arm securely wrapped around his guardian's right leg, and he wasn't budging from his shelter.

The psychologist straightened back up. "Come on back and I'll show you my office. I think you'll like all the toys we can play with." She held her hand out to the boy, but he kept both of his firmly attached to Martin.

Abby moved on ahead of them as the doctor struggled to untangle his young charge from his legs before following her down the hall. "It'll be fine, Evan, he said, giving him a small nod and a smile."

Chapter 31

"This is where we'll be spending our time together, Evan. Let me show you around," the therapist said as she walked to the sand table. "This is my sandpit. We won't play with it today, but sometimes when you come to see me, we'll use it with these little figures over here," she said, gesturing expansively towards the rack-lined wall.

Martin felt the child's grip on his leg relax as he ventured forward to peer at the assortment of small metal vehicles clustered on one shelf. His eyes followed along a line of miniature people and animals before he reached tentatively for a reddish-brown, shaggy dog before he pulled back.

"It's all right, you may touch them if you like, Evan," the therapist said as she picked up the small replica the boy had been admiring and held it out to him.

Evan took it from her fingers and showed it to Martin. "Guess who that looks like."

Martin grunted and leaned down, his eyes narrowing as he peered closely at the object. "Mm, I don't know. Maybe a bit like Mr. Portman."

A snort of air escaped the boy's nose, and he slapped a hand to his mouth. "Mr. Portman's not a dog, Dr. Elligam. I *meant* ... what *animal* does it look like?"

"Ah. You mean Miss Peacock's dog?"

"Miss *Bab*-cock."

"Mm, yes ... the vegetable dog."

"Can you tell me about this ... vegetable dog, Evan?" the therapist said as she crouched down in front of him.

He took a step back, bumping up against Martin's leg. "He's not *made* out of vegetables, he just likes to dig 'em up, so Miss Babcock named him Potato. He's an Iris shredder."

"Oh, I see." She stood up and began to amble towards the puppet rack. "Is Miss Babcock your teacher?"

Evan grasped on to his guardian's wrist again as he followed after her. "She's just my friend. She's old."

"Well, Potato sounds like quite a special dog."

"He is, but he's kinda' slobbery."

"Some dogs are like that," she said with a chuckle. "Evan, this is my puppet rack. Would you like to pick a puppet to play with while you're here? Maybe you could pick one for me as well."

The boy released his grip on Martin's wrist and circled around, scanning over the assortment before finally settling on an orca whale and a round human figure with a puffy white hat.

"You can have the man," he said, thrusting it at her.

"Oh, I like this one. Thank you, Evan."

She led them to a small, round table and pulled out a child-sized chair. "Let's sit down and see what kind of story we can make up about our puppets."

Glancing over at his guardian, the boy slipped into the chair, and the therapist sat down beside him.

Lowering her voice, Dr. Peterson flapped the hands on her figure. "My name is Mr. Rutledge. What's your name?"

Evan cocked his head at her. "He doesn't gots a name 'cause he's a whale."

"Silly me, of course. Where do you live Mr. Whale?"

"In the ocean. In really deep water. 'Cept when I'm hunting for my dinner," Evan said, adopting an artificially low voice appropriate for a whale. "I like to eat seals and walruses and stuff for my dinner. And I gots ta go close to land to find 'em."

"Do you eat fish?"

"I eat all kinds of fish. I love fish!" the boy said, slipping into the game.

"How about your friend there, Mr. Whale? Abner over there." The therapist had "Mr. Rutledge" pat Evan's free hand.

"Oh, his name's not Abner, it's Evan. He only likes fish if it's the with-the-chips kind."

Martin scratched at his head as he stood next to his charge. The nonsense games that women seemed to favour when interacting with children puzzled him. He shifted his weight from his more painful left leg as he wondered how long the game could go on.

Evan squinted his eyes at the puppet on the therapist's hand. "You look like you eat *a lot* of fish."

"I actually like bangers and mash better than fish," she said in an undertone, leaning the small man towards her patient.

"That's why you're so fat, I bet."

"Yes, I could stand to lose a few pounds, eh?"

"You should eat more fish."

The banter between puppets continued for several more minutes before 'Mr. Rutledge' suggested they take a break and do a bit of drawing.

Martin couldn't tolerate being on his feet any longer and moved towards the adult-sized chairs on the opposite side of the room. "I need to go sit down, Evan. I'll be right over here."

The boy turned and called out, "No! You need to stay here where I can see you!"

"I'm going to be right over here. You can see me."

Evan gave Martin a scowl and moved his chair around the table so that he was facing him.

Abby placed a sheet of white paper in front of the boy and set a box of crayons in the centre of the table.

"I'd like you to draw a picture for me, Evan. In your picture, I'd like you to include a house, a tree, and a person. And I want you to draw them as well as you can," she explained, pushing the crayons to within the boy's reach.

"I'm going to draw the same thing, and when we get all done, we can tell each other about our drawings."

"Can I use any of these colours, or do I gots ta use certain ones?"

"Any colours are fine."

The therapist picked up a crayon and began to sketch on her sheet of paper.

Evan dug around in the box. "Do you gots Inch Worm Green?"

The therapist moved the box towards her and pulled out a crayon. "There you go. That's one of my favourite colours."

Evan tugged it from her fingers. "I better use it first. Just in case you use it all up."

They worked quietly. Evan glanced up frequently to assure himself of his guardian's presence, but he returned his attention immediately to his artwork.

"There, I think I'm done," he declared, pushing the sheet of paper towards Dr. Peterson.

"Oh, that's very nice, Evan," she said as she scanned the drawing.

"Did you get yours done yet?" he asked, pulling his knees under him and leaning across the table.

"I have one more thing to add," she said, holding a finger up in front of her as she picked up a yellow crayon and drew a circle at the top of her picture.

"Oh, no! I didn't put a sun on mine." The boy's head dropped into his hand.

"That's okay, Evan. There's no right way to draw your picture. If you really want to add a sun you can, but you don't have to."

He pulled the sheet of paper back and studied it. "I think I like mine without a sun."

The therapist slid her chair over next to him and laid the two drawings side by side.

"Your picture gots a lot more colouring," the seven-year-old said.

"I like to colour. Evan, can you tell me about your picture?"

"It gots a person and a house and a tree, just like you said."

"You did a very nice job. Can you tell me about the house? Does somebody live there?"

Evan looked at the therapist questioningly. "Houses always gots someone living in them." He hesitated. "Well, almost always. My house has people in it."

"Can you tell me about the people who live there?"

The boy tapped his finger on the drawing. "You can't see 'em 'cause of the cover on the window, but they're talking and havin' their dinner."

"What are they talking about?"

"Just regular stuff. They're askin' the boy what he did at school and stuff ... those things parents are *s'posed* ta talk to kids about." He leaned forward a bit more. "Are there people in your house?"

"Yes, there's a mum and a dad. And they have two children."

"Are the parents nice?"

"Yes, they love their children very much."

"How do you know? What are they doing?"

"The children are playing, and the mum is making cookies. What should we imagine the dad is doing?"

"Maybe he's fixin' things!"

"Some dads are very good at fixing things, aren't they?"

"Dr. Ellig-am's *really* good at fixin' things."

"There are many kinds of houses. We drew two different kinds. See how our windows are different sizes? Can you tell me about the windows on your house?"

"They're little windows," the boy said, scratching a fingernail across a thick area of green on the roof before wiping the crayon off on to his pants.

"Why did you choose to put *little* windows in your house?"

Evan reached over to Dr. Peterson's drawing and looked at it before putting it back down. "You shouldn't make your windows so big. It's easier to get the covers over them if they're little."

"Oh, do you think they need covers?"

"Sure, they do. If they don't gots covers, people can see in."

"That's very true. I like your person. Is it a boy or a girl?"

"Boys don't wear dresses, Dr. Peterson," Evan said with a giggle.

"Silly me, I didn't notice the dress. Can you tell me about the girl ... how old she is?"

"I'm not sure. But she's littler than me. She gots ta stay outside though 'cause she was bothersome."

"I see. That's a shame; she must be lonely."

Evan watched the therapist warily before jumping from his chair and running over to Martin. "Remember, you promised," he whispered.

"I remember. I'm not going anywhere." Martin cleared his throat and ducked his head when he saw the therapist watching him with a smile on her face. "But you better get back over there and finish telling Dr. Peterson about your picture."

Evan hesitated and then returned to his chair. "Who's your person?" he asked.

"That's my little boy. His name is Charlie."

"Does he gots red hair like that?"

Dr. Peterson picked up a brown crayon and coloured over the figure's bright red head. "I made it a bit too red, maybe. This is more like it."

"Does he like to climb trees?"

"We don't have any trees around our house, so he hasn't really had a chance to try it. Do you like to climb trees?"

"Yeah. Miss Babcock has a good tree for climbing."

"Tell me about the tree you drew in your picture. What kind of tree is it?"

"It's a friendly tree. Friendly trees got the branches that go up on the ends, so they don't drop you."

"I never thought about that, but I bet you're right! Is there the other kind of tree then ... unfriendly trees?"

Evan glanced over at Martin, who sat listening to the conversation before turning his attention back to the therapist. "They're scary. I go way around 'em."

"I don't know very much about trees, Evan. Can you tell me what they look like?"

"Oh, you'll know 'em if you see 'em. They gots the hangy-downy branches that look like this—"

The little boy stood up and stretched his arms out in front of him, bent his fingers in a talon-like manner, and donned an angry face, baring his teeth. Dr. Peterson pulled back in mock fear and put her hand to her chest. "Oh, my goodness. That is a frightening tree!"

Satisfied that he had made his point, Evan climbed back up on his chair.

"It's a very tall straight tree," the therapist said, tracing her finger down the linear truck. "Is it very old?"

"It's about as old as Miss Babcock."

"How old is Miss Babcock do you think?"

"Hmm, I think about a hundred years old or something."

"I see. One hundred—that's a lot of years."

"Yeah. She says she gots a wrinkle to prove every one of 'em. And I believe it!"

Dr. Peterson picked up Evan's drawing and held it up, admiringly. "Well, I'm going to put your picture in a special file, Evan. I'll keep it in a safe place so that we can get it out and look at it whenever we want. You did a very fine job."

The boy gave her a timid smile and glanced over at Martin. "Can I go sit with Dr. Ellig-am now?"

"You know, Evan, I believe Mrs. Teague has a special snack planned for you. Are you hungry?"

"Can Dr. Ellig-am have a snack, too?"

"I need to talk with Dr. Ellingham in here for just a few minutes. But he could have a snack when we're done talking."

The therapist got up and reached out for the boy's hand. After a nod from Martin, he accepted it and walked with her to the waiting area.

She returned to the room a short time later and closed the door behind her before picking Evan's drawing up from the table.

"Well, he's a charming little boy, Dr. Ellingham," she said as she took a seat across from him. "We do have some things to work on though."

"Mm, he hasn't had a good start in life," Martin said straightening himself.

"The drawing that we did actually revealed a few things about Evan. Let me show you," she said as she laid the picture down on the coffee table.

"Some proponents of this assessment activity read far more into it than I tend to. However, it has proven to be a very useful tool for me in determining where a child may really be struggling."

The psychologist tapped a manicured finger on one of the boy's small windows. "Evan drew all of his windows completely covered by curtains. And I'm sure you heard his answer to my question about the windows being so small."

Martin worked his hand over his knee. "He's had nightmares about his father looking in his bedroom window at him, so we covered it with a blanket."

"I see. The small windows can be indicative of a reluctance to be open about feelings, but in Evan's case it may have more to do with his needing that sense of security that covered windows provide."

There was a rattle on the doorknob, and Evan's strident voice could be heard. Martin made a move to get up, but the therapist held up a hand to stop him.

"Mrs. Teague will get him busy with something. She's a wonder with children," she said as Martin settled back on the sofa.

Dr. Peterson continued. "That need for security was again expressed with the drawing of the tree. Evan focused on the safety that those sturdy, upturned branches provide when he's climbing a *friendly* tree, but he was very graphic in his description of *unfriendly* trees.

"A child like Evan will have learned to be hypervigilant around an abusive parent, and that same response is triggered when he sees things which are suggestive of those negative images from home ... an unfriendly tree, for instance. That hypervigilance may be reflected in an inability to trust others as well, which would make it difficult for him to form friendships—relationships."

The therapist drew Martin's attention to the paper again, tracing a finger along the trunk of the tree. "Evan's picture has no ground line that one would expect to see. The tree's trunk doesn't widen into a sturdy base which is rooted into the soil. And the house and the person in his picture seem to be floating in the air. This child really feels very little sense of security."

Abby folded her hands in front of her. "Evan very clearly feels secure when he's with you ... or knows where you are. But he doesn't have a sense that the security is permanent.

"Children can't thrive unless they feel secure, and it appears the boy's tenuous situation at home has had an adverse effect. His drawing is at a level that one might expect from a child of five rather than a seven-year-old."

Martin gave the woman a scowl and pursed his lips. "I disagree. He's quite intelligent and very resourceful."

"Yes, he clearly is. I'm saying that Evan is *emotionally* immature. But in a secure and nurturing environment, he will catch up to his peers."

"What do you mean ... emotionally immature?"

"He likely has difficulty forming friendships with children his own age. He may gravitate towards children younger than himself.

"Intellectually, he *is* a very clever little lad. But the domestic stress and traumas have prevented him from maturing emotionally—socially—making friends. Does he have many friends at school?"

Martin spread his hands in front of him. "I have no idea. My wife could speak to that."

He stared off absently, then back at the psychologist. "Why? Does he need to have friends?"

"We're social creatures, Dr. Ellingham. One doesn't need to be a social butterfly, but a child who grows up in an environment devoid of human relationships will struggle in adulthood. So, in answer to your question ... yes, Evan needs to have friends. But one or two close friends is all that's necessary."

"Mm."

"Before we wrap things up, I really want to talk about Evan's person. He drew a house with a boy, inside, who has the attention of his parents. Standing outside the house, he drew a girl who has been shunned ... rejected by her parents.

"Evan was sent a very strong message when his mother not only rejected him, but rejected him and *kept* his sister.

"If neither he nor his sister had been wanted it would have been damaging, but his mother kept her daughter. For his mind to make sense of what's happened, Evan likely feels that there must be something wrong or bad about him personally. This is certainly an issue that I'll be exploring further with him. It's entirely possibly that he harbours resentment towards his sister."

"Well, don't you think that would be *understandable?*" Martin snapped.

Dr. Peterson hesitated, taken aback by the vehemence in his voice. "It *is* perfectly understandable. It's not healthy, however.

"Evan is bound to feel some anger over what's happened to him, and he needs to express that anger. But it needs to be directed in the right place. It will be of no benefit to him to get that anger and frustration out if he doesn't understand who the legitimate target of that anger and frustration is.

"The anger may come out in an inappropriate manner or he may turn it on himself. This is why it's important that we help him work through it."

Rubbing a hand over his face, Martin nodded his head. "Right."

The psychologist reached out and picked up the drawing, leaning forward with her arms on her knees. "Your wife's assessment of Evan's disposition was spot on.

"He *is* a very sunny little boy despite his experiences up to this point. A naturally introverted child would not have fared as well as Evan has. They probably would have shut down by this point."

"Yes." Martin said, squirming on the sofa before clearing his throat. "Do you feel the emotional—er, social effects are reversible?"

The psychologist got to her feet and took a step towards the door. "I'm optimistic. If given the proper environment, I believe Evan still has the ability to thrive. He will, of course, always be affected by the traumatic experiences he's had, but I think we can lessen the negative consequences and teach him how to deal with the lasting effects."

"Mm."

Evan ran towards the hall when he heard the door open, and he grabbed on to Martin's wrist. "Can we go see Old Doc Parsons now?"

"Yes, I think we're done here," he said, glancing over at the therapist for confirmation.

"Yes, we are done, Evan. You did a very fine job today. I think next week we'll spend some time at the sand table."

"Can I choose again?"

"Yes, you may choose again," Dr. Peterson said, placing a hand on his head.

Martin and Evan made their way towards the lifts which took them back to the first floor. Chris's office wasn't far from the main entrance, and once Martin had pointed it out to him, Evan ran on ahead, rapping lightly on the door.

Chris's voice could be heard inside. "Come in!"

Evan fumbled with the latch before struggling with the heavy door. When Chris pulled it open from the inside, the boy fell through into his legs. "Hi, Old Doc!"

"Well, this is a surprise!" Chris said as he lifted the child into the air. "Did you walk all the way over from Portwenn, or do you have wings hidden in these armpits?" He wiggled a finger under the boy's arm.

"I don't got wings, Old Doc!" Evan squealed and giggled as he pulled his arm down against his body.

Martin was lagging behind, his fatigue beginning to get the better of him. "Got a few minutes?" he asked as Chris held the door for him.

"Yeah ... yeah. It's kind of slow actually. What are you two doing over here?"

"We—er, Evan had a doctor's appointment."

"Oh?" Chris cocked his head and raised an eyebrow. "Everything okay?"

"I'm not sick or nothin', Old Doc. I just drew pictures with Dr. Peterson. And we played with the puppets."

Chris nodded his head as he set the child on the floor. "I see. Abby Peterson?"

"Mm," Martin grunted, tucking his chin. "First visit."

"Are you still comin' to the Christmas Feast?" Evan asked as he poked at a pendulum toy on Chris's desk.

"We wouldn't miss it. Mrs. Parsons is going to come over tomorrow and help you and Mrs. Ellingham do some of the baking. I'll come over when I get done with my work here at the hospital."

"I hope we didn't spoil any plans you may have had," Martin said, dropping heavily on to the sofa. He pulled his feet up, trying to conceal a grimace.

"I'm actually looking forward to spending a night alone with Carole in the house where we first—"

"*And* we better be going," Martin said as he swung his feet back to the floor with another grimace.

"No, no, no. I was going to say *kissed,* mate. Geesh! I have raised a kid of my own, you know."

"Mm, yes." Martin brushed at his trousers. "I didn't think Auntie Joan was ever going to stop with the smirks and snickers every time your name came up in a conversation."

"Hey, how were we to know the walls were so thin?" Chris said, his voice lowered as he gave the seven-year-old a sideways glance.

Martin threw his head back and groaned. "Oh brilliant, just brilliant, Chris."

"Old Doc *is* brilliant, isn't he, Dr. Ellig-am?" Evan said, plopping down next to Martin and patting his leg. "Almost as smart as you, huh?"

"Yeah, too smart for his own good, evidently. Now I'm going to be fielding questions about the inferior construction of my aunt's house."

"Sorry, Mart. It was really nice of Ruth to offer us the use of the place."

"Mm, it's a big house. You better bring your torch so you don't get lost if you have to get up to pee in the night."

Chris laughed. "Or drag Carole back to the bedroom if she gets lost. Are you coming out to the farm tomorrow?"

"I'll see what time it is when I finish up with patients."

Chris's eyes narrowed. "What do you mean by that? You're only supposed to be working two hours a day."

"I still have paperwork I need to do, Chris." Martin leaned his head back against the wall and closed his eyes for a few moments. "Have you heard anything about the Wadebridge situation?"

"We're trying to line up a locum until we can fill the position. Patients will have to go up to Bude or down to Newquay until then."

Martin rubbed a hand across his face and pulled his head up. "I better warn Jeremy to be extra vigilant. We're going to have every influenza infected sluggard within a fifteen-mile radius of Portwenn trying to pass themselves off as healthy because they can't be bothered to drive any farther for treatment."

He reached for his crutch and pulled himself to his feet.

"We should be on our way. We just stopped in to say hello." Martin said before giving the boy a wave of his hand. "Come on, Evan."

"Bye, Old Doc."

"Bye, Evan ... bye Mart. We'll see you tomorrow."

Evan took hold of his guardian's wrist as they walked through the corridor towards the doors. "I like Old Doc Parsons. I'm glad he's your friend," he said.

"Yes. I am too, Evan." A faint smile crossed Martin's face.

Chapter 32

The usual rush hour traffic had combined with holiday travellers and the dark of night to create stressful driving conditions as Martin and Evan made their way back west towards Portwenn.

Martin kept both hands firmly on the steering wheel, trying to ignore the surge of adrenaline that coursed through him every time headlights flashed in his eyes.

He glanced into the back seat. *Good, at least the questions won't be flying for the next half hour*, he thought when he saw that the boy had dropped off to sleep.

He returned his attention to the highway. He drew in a deep breath, filling his lungs with air as he tried to loosen the growing constriction in his chest.

As they neared the town of Wadebridge, the sense of anxiety that Martin had been feeling intensified. He shook his head and focused on the road in front of him. A transport lorry flew past them from the opposite direction, its draught buffeting the much smaller Lexus.

Martin glanced down at the fuel gauge. He would need to make a petrol stop at the service station on the edge of town.

Another lorry passed them by, and he berated himself as his hands grew moist. **Gawd,** *pull yourself together. Be logical. The odds of another accident here are negligible.*

The Lexus moved around a curve in the road and the bridge loomed in front of him. He squinted as the lights from an oncoming lorry shone in his eyes, blinding him for a moment, and his hands began to tremble uncontrollably.

He pulled off on to the side of the road, shifting the car into park. Leaning back against the headrest, he tried unsuccessfully to ignore the roiling in his stomach and the muffled hiss which had begun in his ears. He grabbed for the door handle, and shoving it open, he vomited into the grass.

Evan stirred in the back seat. "Are we home?" he asked, stretching up to see out the window.

Martin pulled his handkerchief from his back pocket and wiped his mouth. "No...not yet."

Another vehicle approached, its headlights illuminating the interior of the Lexus.

"You look all peaky, Dr. Ellig-am. Are ya sick?"

"No, of course not," he snapped before taking in a deep breath and shifting the car into drive. He waited for a string of cars and lorries to pass by before continuing on across the bridge, and turning into the service station parking lot. "I need petrol, Evan. Sit tight there."

The cold night air whistled in his ears as the fuel pump hummed. The nausea had eased, but his mouth tasted sour and his lips had gone dry.

The pump clunked off, and he returned the nozzle to its hanger before walking to the passenger side of the vehicle to open the back door. "I need a bottle of water, Evan. I don't want to leave you out here alone, so come on," he said, giving his head a jerk.

"Dr. Ellig-am, I need ta pee," the boy said as they stepped inside the building.

Martin looked to the left and then the right before spotting the sign for the toilets. While Evan used the urinal, Martin splashed cold water on his face and patted it dry with paper towelling.

He leaned against the wall as the seven-year-old repeatedly pushed the pump on the soap dispenser. Martin interjected when the soap began to overflow the child's cupped hand. "Whoa, whoa, whoa. That's more than enough, Evan."

"I just wanna be sure to kill all those mannered bacterias."

Martin sighed and rolled his eyes as Evan clapped his hands under the water, sending soap bubbles into the air before stabbing at them with a single pointed finger.

He reached over and yanked a strip of towelling from the dispenser, shoving it towards the boy. "That's more than enough washing. Now dry your hands so we can get going," he said sharply.

The child looked at him warily. "Are you cross at me, Dr. Ellig-am?"

"No, I'm not cross. I'm just—" He huffed and wagged a finger at him. "Just finish drying your hands and we'll get on home."

Martin paid for the petrol, a bottle of milk for Evan, and a bottle of water for himself before they got back into the Lexus.

Louisa looked up from the pot on the hob when they came through the back door. Evan pulled off his shoes and coat, setting the shoes by the door and flipping the coat over a peg on the coat rack before running into the lounge to play with James Henry.

Martin went to his wife's side and inspected the sauce that was simmering away. It emitted steam, laced with the scent of garlic, basil and oregano.

"We're having spaghetti marinara," she said, stretching up to kiss him. How did it go?"

"Fine. It went fine. It'll take some time for him to be comfortable with her, but ... it went fine."

Louisa turned and wrapped her arms around him before pulling back. "Oh, for goodness' sake, Martin!

You're all sweaty! What in the world were you two *doing* at Dr. Peterson's?"

"We can discuss it later. I'm going to shower," he said brusquely before pulling away from her and limping off under the stairs.

The evening passed quietly once the dinner clean-up had been completed. Martin sat on the sofa with James in his lap and Evan wedged under his arm as he read through a small stack of books that the older boy had retrieved from the nursery.

By the time the freshly bathed children had been tucked in for the night, the panic that Martin had experienced on the trip home had eased into a disconcerting edginess, accompanied by a fine trembling in his hands.

He sat down on the sofa, put his feet up on the pillows atop the coffee table and picked up a medical journal. The pop of a wine cork as it was freed from its bottle distracted him, and he glanced over at his wife.

She sensed his gaze on her and looked up from the glass sitting on the counter. "Want some?" she asked teasingly, holding the bottle up in front of her.

Martin hesitated before pulling in his chin. He gave her a sheepish sideways glance. "Would you mind bringing me some of that malt that's in the pantry?"

She cocked her head at him before pulling a tumbler from the cupboard.

"You okay?" she asked, as she walked into the lounge and held out the glass of amber liquid.

"Mm, just a bit tense." His hand shook noticeably as he reached for the Scotch.

Louisa nestled in next to him, her glass of wine in hand. "Tense ... about?"

Martin took a big swig of Scotch from his glass, giving a shudder and screwing up his face before setting it down on the end table with a clunk. "I had a-a bit of difficulty on the trip back from Truro."

Louisa's eyes darted over his face. "What happened, Martin?"

"It was a panic attack, I suppose ... before crossing the bridge. I had to pull to the side of the road until the traffic cleared before I—" He threw a hand up. "I was afraid to cross the bloody bridge."

He leaned back and closed his eyes, his chin trembling.

Setting her glass down on the coffee table, Louisa moved closer, laying her head against his chest. "Martin, you went through a horrifying ordeal. It's still fresh in your mind. I'm sure this will improve with time."

"Mm." He sat silent and motionless for a number of minutes until the inebriating effects of the alcohol began to kick in. He opened his eyes and pressed his lips to her head. "Would you mind going upstairs with me?"

Louisa got to her feet and took his hand as he rose unsteadily to his feet.

"You really are a lightweight, hmm?" she said as she picked up his glass, almost as full of Scotch as when she had presented it to him.

He winced. "Sorry."

"No need to apologise. As long as you don't fall asleep this time."

Martin watched his wife's swaying form as she set the two glasses on the counter. She looked back at him coyly before heading for the stairs. He locked the doors and turned out the lights before following after her.

When he reached their bedroom, he stood in the doorway, watching surreptitiously as she pulled off her jeans before going into the bathroom to brush her teeth.

As she leaned over the sink to wash her face, he slipped in behind her, his hands seeking out bare skin.

"Hello," she said as she turned to him, her voice soft and sultry.

He leaned down, and tipping her head back, he brushed his lips against hers before trailing kisses down her neck.

She returned his kiss, allowing it to deepen as she tasted the smoky-sweet Scotch on his breath. The buttons on his shirt were slipped through the buttonholes and she tugged impatiently at his shirttails.

"Oh, Louisa," he whispered as he brushed her hair from her shoulder and nuzzled into her, inhaling deeply. His hands slipped under her jumper, caressing her back and pulling her to him.

"Martin, I think we should move this to the bedroom, don't you?" She pushed forward, gently, nudging him towards the door.

He took a step back and she slipped past him, stopping by the bed to remove her top.

"Louisa, wait." He took a step towards her. "May I?" he asked, taking hold of the bottom edge of her jumper.

She raised her arms over her head and he pulled it slowly upwards. His eyes darkened as they drank her in, and the garment dropped to the floor.

The sensual dance between them took a pragmatic pause as Louisa helped him to work his clothing over the hardware affixed to his frame.

"There, that's better," she said, dispensing with the last article of his clothing and flipping the lock on their door before crawling into the bed.

Martin lifted his legs on to the mattress and rolled over to face her.

"Now, where were we?" Louisa said as she propped herself up on her elbow.

"I believe I had removed your jumper." Martin pulled the covers back and ran his fingertips across her shoulder and down her arm. "I was studying your—"

He stopped and cleared his throat. "I believe I was studying your, erm ... form." His fingers made their way back up her arm before following along the curve of her breast. "You are the loveliest thing, Louisa," he whispered hoarsely before rolling forward to kiss her.

She leaned into him and wrapped a leg over his hips as she hugged him tightly.

As they held each other, Martin felt his body begin to relax and the emotional edginess ease—as if the pressure that he had been feeling building up in him was being absorbed by her.

He inhaled deeply. "Oh, Louisa," he said, the words tumbling out softly as he released the breath. "I—"

"Dr. Ellig-am! There's someone in my room!" Evan voice called out as he turned the doorknob back and forth.

Martin pulled away from his wife and punched his pillow with his good hand. "Bugger!" he hissed. The rattling doorknob had become a very effective, but unwelcome antidote to his wife's beguiling advances.

Louisa jumped from the bed. "You—*stay*," she said, snapping her fingers at him as she reached for her dressing gown. "I'll be *right* back, and we can finish what we started."

Martin pulled his arm under his head and watched her disappear into the darkened hallway. Then he sighed and dropped back on to his pillow to await her return.

"What is it, Evan?" Louisa asked, taking the child by the hand.

"There was a loud noise in my room. I think there's someone in there!" he said as he clung to her arm.

Louisa leaned down and picked the child up, carrying him back to the nursery. "What kind of noise was it, Evan?"

"It was a someone-scary's-in-my-room noise—a bang noise."

Louisa pulled the blankets back on the boy's bed and he crawled under the covers. As she stepped forward to tuck him in, her foot knocked against something, sending it skittering across the floor.

"Here's your scary someone, Evan. It's your torch. How did it get on the floor, for goodness' sake?"

Evan wiped at the tears on his cheeks and took the light from her hand. "I don't know. Maybe it fell out of my bed."

"You should put it on the table when you're done with it, Evan. Then it won't end up on the floor." She took the light from the boy and slid the switch to the "on" position. "Well, no harm done; it still works, right?"

"Thanks, Mrs. Ellig-am," the child said, taking the torch and testing it himself, turning it off and on several times.

"All right, you need to go back to sleep now." She hesitated a moment before leaning over to kiss the boy's forehead. Then she crossed the landing and returned to their bedroom.

Closing the door behind her, she turned the lock before doffing her dressing gown and slipping back into bed next to her husband. "He's all settled again," she said as she leaned over and pressed her forehead to his. "Martin." She jostled him. *"Mar-tin?"*

He pulled in a snuffled breath as his head turned away from her, unconsciously.

Louisa breathed out a resigned sigh and got up to unlock the door. Then she lay back down, pulling the blankets under her chin and closing her eyes.

The clock read 3:45 a.m. when Martin was awakened by the all-too-familiar tugging on his sleeve. "What is it?" he asked.

"My torch won't turn on, Dr. Ellig-am." The boy pressed the button several times to demonstrate. "See."

"Yes. Yes, I see," he whispered. He glanced over at his wife, sound asleep beside him, before forcing his torpid muscles to pull him from the bed.

Herding the boy into the hallway, he pulled the bedroom door shut behind him before flipping the switch on the wall. "Here, let me look at it."

Evan held the torch up, and Martin inspected it with squinted eyes.

"It worked really good before I went ta sleep, but then when I woke up it had gone off," the child said. "Maybe you should tell those people at the market they gots ta make you a refund."

Martin grunted and wiped a palm over his face. He shook the thing several times before again trying the switch.

"Think it gots a bad bulb?"

"Well, it shouldn't. I just bought it." He narrowed his eyes at the boy. "What do you mean when you say it worked when you went to sleep, but it had gone off when you woke up?"

"Oh, that means the 'lectricity in the batteries went into the bulb, and it made that little wire inside the glass bubble light up. Kinda' like magic don't you think?"

"No, no, no, no, no. I know how a torch *works*. I'm asking— did you fall asleep with the torch on, and then it was off when you woke up."

"That's *'zactly* what happened! Think you need to make a refund?"

"No, I think I need to put some new batteries in the thing. And you need to be sure you turn it off *before* you fall asleep. You've run the batteries down."

Martin glanced towards the stairs, reluctant to attempt the descent while half awake. "Evan, can you go down to the pantry for me?"

The boy's eyes darted between the steps and his guardian. "It's dark, Dr. Ellig-am."

"You know where the light switches are. The fresh batteries are in the drawer next to the washing machine. I'll wait right here. All you need to do is call for me if you need my help."

Martin opened the torch and took out one of the spent batteries. "You need to get three of them, and they should all be this size. It doesn't matter what colour they are," he said, handing the samples to the boy.

"'Kay. I'll be right back."

Martin waited, finally calling softly to him. "Evan, are you coming?"

He listened to the slap of his charge's bare feet against the floor before he appeared at the bottom of the steps.

"Got 'em!" he said as he scrambled up the stairs.

"Good job, Evan." Martin slid the new batteries into the torch and turned it on.

"It works!" Evan reached a hand up for the light before returning happily to the nursery.

Martin followed behind, leaning over to pull the blankets up. The child wrinkled up his nose. "You should make a refund for your apple juice, Dr. Ellig-am. It tastes funny."

"What apple juice?"

"The apple juice on the counter. I was thirsty, but I couldn't reach the water handle, so I was gonna drink the rest of your apple juice." He wrinkled his nose again. "It was gross."

Martin's breath caught in his throat. "Open your mouth, Evan."

He leaned down and sniffed at the boy's breath. "How much of that ... *apple juice* did you drink?"

"I didn't drink any. Remember, I told you it was gross. I spit it out in the sink."

"You're sure you didn't swallow any of it?"

"Uh-huh. I think you should get a different brand next time. Want me ta help you pick some out?"

"I think I can manage."

Martin got up and limped across the landing, returning with a cup of water. "Here you go," he said, handing it to the boy. "In future, it would be wise to give any food or drinks you see lying around a miss. You'd hate to get your hands on any more bad apple juice."

Evan gulped down the water. "Ahh! That's better."

"Yeah, I bet. Goodnight, Evan."

"G'night Dr. Ellig-am."

Martin tossed and turned in the bed for the next several hours, his sleep disrupted repeatedly by a series of dreams, all with a similar theme—an enormous, dark mass descending on him, leaving him with a distressing sense of foreboding. He woke with a start, shortly after 7:00 a.m., pushing back against the mass as his eyes shot open.

"Sorry, Martin. Did I hurt you?" Louisa asked. She stared down at him worriedly, as she lifted her weight from his chest.

He blinked the sleep from his eyes as his galloping heart began to slow. He rubbed at them and shook his head. "No. You, erm ... startled me," he said, clearing his throat.

She reached a hand under his vest. "You did it again."

"I did what again?"

"You fell asleep on me again. I was quite disappointed."

"Mm, sorry." His arm tightened around her back as he pulled her close.

"It's Christmas Eve," she said.

He tipped his chin to his chest, looking down at her as the parallel furrows between his eyebrows deepened. "Strictly speaking, it's not Christmas Eve. The word eve is a reference to the period of time after sundown, so Christmas Eve won't begin un—"

"Mar-tin!" Louisa's hand smacked against his stomach.

He grimaced and sucked in a breath. "Ow! That *did*—hurt!"

She sat up quickly. "I'm *sorry*," she said as she pulled up his vest to examine him for any possible damage. Leaning forward, she trailed kisses down the vertical scar transecting his belly. "You okay?"

"I'm fine. Happy Christmas—Eve."

Her eyes sparkled back at him and she stretched up to give him a lingering kiss. "Happy Christmas Eve, Martin."

"What time is Carole meeting you at the farm?"

"Sometime between nine and nine-thirty. So, I better get a move on."

"I believe Evan would say, 'You better shift your arse.'"

"*What?*"

"Don't worry; he's been set straight."

"Hmm, I hope so. I'd hate to have that be James's first sentence."

The kitchen was abuzz with activity when Martin came down for breakfast a while later, but he didn't ask about the goings-on for fear he might actually get an answer.

He watched from the corner of his eye as he ate his breakfast, and then rinsed his dishes and added them to the dishwasher.

Louisa and the boys left with Ruth, and Martin made his way under the stairs to review patient notes. The morning dragged, with a schedule made up of blood pressure and blood glucose checks interspersed with vaccinations and repeat prescription consultations.

"That's the last of 'em, Doc," Morwenna said when he came through to the reception room.

"Mm, yes." He turned and ducked back across the hall before returning with an envelope in his hand. "Happy Christmas, Morwenna," he said, holding it out at arm's length.

He pulled his hands behind his back and cleared his throat. "I'd like to say thank you—for all that you do ordinarily, but also for all that you've done to help out over the last four months. It hasn't gone unnoticed."

Morwenna pulled the greeting card from the envelope, a smile spreading across her face when she saw the sizable bonus inside. "Thanks, Doc. That's really nice. Really, really nice."

"Mm. Well, we'll see you tomorrow for this big Christmas Feast. See what you can do to get Bert to fill up on vegetables and fruit beforehand. I don't want to be responsible for another cardiac event."

"I'll pass the message on ta Al. And I'll do what I can."

Martin pulled in his chin and headed back to his consulting room.

He was putting the finishing touches on the last of the patient notes when Jeremy rapped on the door jamb. "You about ready to wrap it up for the day?"

"Mm, yes. Erm, why don't you come in and sit down, Jeremy."

The young man stepped into the room before dropping into the chair opposite his boss.

The side drawer screeched softly as Martin pulled it open, taking out another envelope, identical to the one he had just presented to his receptionist. "Happy Christmas," he said as he slid it across the desk.

The young man removed the card and a bank cheque fell out into his lap. He picked it up, his brow creasing as he read it. Swallowing hard, he looked up at the doctor. "Martin—I—I do really appreciate the gesture, but—well, I'd feel really uncomfortable accepting this."

Martin cocked his head at him. "Why?"

"You're being very generous."

"I'm not being generous," he bristled. "You've been an exemplary employee. It seems a bonus is deserved."

"Yeah, but I haven't been *this* exemplary," he said, jabbing a finger at the piece of paper. "It's—well, it's too much."

"*It's too much?* What's that supposed to mean?"

"It means I'd feel guilty accepting it."

Martin screwed up his reddening face. "Well, you'd be an *idiot,* then, because *I'm* your boss, and *I* feel it's commensurate with the experience and dedication you've brought to the job!

"You've gone above and beyond what was expected, and I'm *trying* to show my appreciation! Besides that, you're my friend! So, say thank you, and take the bloody money!"

Jeremy tipped his head down as he fingered the cheque. "Thanks, mate. I do appreciate it."

Martin huffed out a breath. "Well, thank goodness we have that sorted." He gave his assistant a small smile. "And ... you're welcome."

Chapter 33

"How come yer doin' that?" Evan asked as he watched the kitchen activities from his perch on the counter. "Are those the ones we're not s'posed ta eat?"

Carole picked up another chestnut and cut an *X* into the skin. "No, the cut helps the skins to loosen when we roast them. We need to peel the skin off before we put the chestnuts in the stuffing."

"Here, Evan, you can break these green beans into pieces for me while you're sitting there," Louisa said, setting a bowl of the washed vegetables next to him. "You can put the pieces in here." An additional ceramic bowl clinked against the countertop.

"I'm good at breakin' stuff," he said as he turned sideways, pulling a knee up. "My mum says *that's* what I'm good for." The broad grin he gave her collapsed quickly before his gaze shifted to his lap.

She wrapped her arms around him and rested her cheek on his head. "You missing your mum, Evan?"

He swiped an arm across his face before snapping a bean in half.

Giving him a squeeze, Louisa kissed his head. "You're good for a great many things, Evan."

A heavy hush hung in the air before Carole said, "How 'bout we have some music while we work?"

"That's an excellent idea." Louisa went to the dining room, returning with the set of speakers, and soon the silence was replaced by the festive tunes of the holiday season.

"So, how do you think Martin's doing these days? Is he feeling any better?" Carole asked as she opened the door of the cooker. The sweet, nutty aroma of roasting chestnuts wafted out.

"Oh, that smells wonderful!" Louisa said, inhaling deeply before returning to the celery she was chopping. "In answer to your question ... it's kind of hard to tell with Martin. He doesn't want me to ask him about pain, and except for his worst days, he *acts* as if nothing's happened. But I know he hurts."

"How 'bout the practice? Is that going all right? He still just working the two hours a day?"

Louisa turned. "Are you gathering information for your husband?"

She winced and pulled up her shoulders. "Sorry ... he's concerned."

"Well, you can report back that, for the most part, he's been sticking with the agreed upon patient hours."

"The operative words being, *for the most part*," Ruth said wryly as she moved to Carole's side to watch her peel the skins from the chestnuts.

Louisa raised her eyebrows and stared pointedly at the elderly woman. "He has patient notes ... paperwork that he needs to take care of," she said defensively.

Ruth shifted James Henry to her other hip. "No one has *that* much paperwork, dear. Does he have some kind of project going?"

"Ruth, I'm not privy to what Martin does behind his closed consulting room door."

"I do appreciate the need for doctor-patient confidentiality. I was just curious if he might be writing again—rediscovering his scholarly side."

"I really don't know what he's been busy with Ruth."

"Well, I hope he hasn't been working himself too hard. But my real concern is that he's not been eating as well as he had been. And, of course, that he's exhausted."

"Well *none* of us would be sleeping well if we were in Martin's shoes," Louisa said, poking at the air with a chef's knife.

Evan's head popped up from his work. "He gots big shoes, but I don't think even *James* could sleep in 'em, Mrs. Ellig-am."

A grin spread across her face. "That's just a saying, Evan. What I mean is, none of us would be sleeping well if we had those fixators fastened to us."

"Then that's what you should say 'cause then it wouldn't be so confusin'."

"I'll try to remember that, Evan." She turned to Carole. "I know he's uncomfortable. And I also know that he's doing his best, so I'd appreciate it if you would pass that on to your dear husband along with the other details which have been shared."

"Don't worry. I'll go easy on him. Maybe it's good that he's had a distraction," Carole said, jerking her head towards the bean-breaker sitting on the counter.

Louisa answered with a nod. "He has certainly been kept busy." She pushed the celery from the cutting board into a skillet with melted butter before starting in on chopping an onion.

"Now *that's* a proper job!" the seven-year-old said, holding the bowl out in front of him.

"All done?" Carole took it from the boy, setting it on the table before lifting him to the floor. "Nicely done, Evan." She looked down at the tiny bits of green beans and smiled. "They're even the perfect size for James Henry."

By mid afternoon, the ducks from Drustrup's had been cleaned, and all the food preparation that could be done ahead of time had been completed. The readied starters, vegetables, stuffing, assorted sauces, and desserts had been stashed in the back entryway to keep them cold.

"Oh, thank goodness, they're finally here," Ruth said, looking out the window at the white lorry which had pulled into the driveway.

Evan ran to the door. "I gotta go tell Dr. Ellig-am that our ducks had guts in 'em!"

"It's not Dr. Ellingham, Evan. It's delivery men," Louisa said as she took the boy by the shoulders and turned him back towards the kitchen. "It's a special present that Ruth is giving to Dr. Ellingham. And we don't want to spoil the surprise, so we need to keep it a secret."

The child pulled his hands behind his back as he bounced on his toes. "I'm a really good secret keeper! Remember my mobile?"

"Yes, you did a wonderful job keeping that a secret. We'll let Ruth tell her nephew about this surprise, though. Hmm?"

"'Kay."

It was shortly after four-thirty when Martin ducked through the low kitchen doorway. He stared in wide-eyed astonishment at the array of food set out on the kitchen table.

"Good, God! You don't seriously think we need all this for a Christmas Feast, do you?"

"Oh, we need *far* more than this for a Christmas Feast, Martin," Carole said as she slipped behind him with a plate of cheeses and sausage, stretching up to kiss him on the cheek as she walked by. "This is just for our little gathering tonight. And—hello to you, too."

"Mm, sorry. Hello."

Evan ran into the kitchen from the dining room. "Hi, Dr. Ellig-am! I've been waitin' for ya," he said, latching on to his wrist.

"Hello, Evan." He wagged a finger at the array of food. "Did you do all this?"

"Mrs. Ellig-am and Mrs. Parsons helped. And those ducks we got had guts in 'em. You wanna see? I saved 'em for you," he said before his head whipped around towards the door as another vehicle pulled into the driveway. He ran to the entryway and peered out the window. "It's Old Doc!" he said before bolting outside.

Martin turned to Louisa. "Where's James?"

"Nap. He should be up soon, though."

"Mm."

He stood in front of the sink, sipping at a glass of water as he watched his friend scoop the seven-year-old up and spin him around.

Louisa approached him from the side and slipped an arm around his waist. She hadn't missed the conflicting emotions registered on his face.

Dust was stomped noisily from shoes before Evan and Chris came through the door from the entryway.

"Happy Christmas Eve!" Chris said as he set two champagne bottles on the counter.

"Oh, it's not Christmas Eve yet, Old Doc. Strippedly speaking, eve is after the sun goes down, and it's not even dark yet."

"Hmm, I wonder where that little nugget of information came from?" Louisa said, narrowing her eyes at her husband.

"Why are you looking at me like that?"

"Well, it does sound like something I've heard before, Martin."

"That's 'cause Miss Soames says it. You probably heard it from her," Evan said as he rested his chin on the table, eyeing the biscuits arrayed on a tray.

Martin pulled up his chin, giving her a look of righteous indignation, and she stretched up to kiss his cheek before whispering an apology into his ear.

James Henry's unhappy pleas for attention, coming through the baby monitor, signalled the end to his nap, and Louisa hurried off to collect him.

"Hey, Evan, would you help me carry our bags in from the car?" Chris asked.

"Sure! I like helping."

Chris leaned over as he passed his wife. "Bring in the presents while I have him upstairs."

"Got it!" she whispered back.

"I'm going to go in and put my feet up," Martin said, jabbing a thumb towards the dining room. He took a step towards the doorway and Carole hurried to step in front of him.

"I, erm ... I need your help with something out here, Martin."

He huffed out a breath. "I'm really tired, Carole."

"It'll just take a few minutes."

"Yes," he said, screwing up his face.

She glanced around, looking for something to busy him with until Ruth was ready for them in the other room. Pulling a tray from the cupboard she shoved it into his hands. "I don't think these biscuits look very attractive on that tray. Could you just ... arrange them on this one instead?"

"Seriously?"

"Yes, Martin ... seriously. And don't ask questions," she told him as she pulled a chair out from the table. "Sit down there. I need to go bring in some gifts for the boys."

He scratched his head and dropped into the seat.

Louisa returned with James and carried him over to see his father.

"How are you, James?" he said, brushing his fingers across the boy's cheek.

"Didn't like waking up in a strange room, so he's a little grumpy at the moment." She pointed a finger at the tray of biscuits. "Why are you doing that? I *just* got done arranging those."

"I don't know why I'm doing it, Louisa. Carole seemed to find the other tray to be insufficient, and I'm doing the best I can here. Don't put me in the middle of it."

Ruth entered the kitchen, giving Louisa a surreptitious nod of her head before turning to her nephew. "*Martin!* ... hello. When did you arrive."

"Just a bit ago. Where have you been?"

"I was, er ... having a lie down. That's where I was. I was tired, so I was having a lie down on the sofa."

"Why? Are you unwell?"

"Of course not."

He set the freshly arranged platter of biscuits on the table and got to his feet, dodging Carole as she slipped between them with bags in each hand.

"You're not feverish, are you?" he asked, reaching up to press his fingers to the elderly woman's forehead. "Influenza's been making the rounds."

"Oh, stop it, Martin! I'm not ill," she said as she batted his hand away.

"You don't ordinarily need a rest in the middle of the—"

"Martin, did you finish with those biscuits?" Carole interjected as she came back into the room.

"Mm, yes." He gave his aunt a final scrutinising look before walking to the sink with the rejected tray.

Footsteps could be heard on the stairs, and Evan leapt over the bottom two steps into the kitchen, followed quickly by Chris.

"Well, it looks like we're all here now. Shall we fill up our plates and take this party to the dining room?" Ruth said.

Louisa put her hand on her husband's arm. "Martin, I brought some of your shakes ... they're in the refrigerator. You should have one of those, hmm?"

Giving her a scowl he pulled a can from the refrigerator and turned for the dining room.

Carole intercepted him. "Where are you going, Martin? You need to fill up your plate."

He pointed a finger at the can in his hand. "I'm just going to set this down in the other room. I'll come back for my plate."

She snatched the shake from his hand. "I'll do that for you. You go get something to eat."

He watched as she hurried off into the dining room before joining the queue which had formed at the table.

By the time he had filled his plate, the others were gathered around the Christmas tree, and traditional carols were playing through the speakers sitting on a far table.

Louisa, with James balanced on a hip, came over when she saw him enter the room. "Ruth has something for you," she said.

He glanced over at his aunt who stood in the opposite corner of the room next to a baby grand piano. Ribbon was wrapped around it from four sides, meeting at the centre of the rear lid in a large bow.

"It's a gift ... from Ruth," Louisa said, tipping her head to peer up at him.

He blinked back at her, swallowing hard. "Excuse me," he said before slowly walking from the room.

Louisa looked worriedly at Ruth.

"Let me take James. You go," Carole said as she took the toddler from her arms.

Martin stepped outside, the hinges complaining as the door closed behind him. He filled his lungs with cold air and tried to tamp back his hurt and anger.

The hinges squeaked again, and he clenched his jaw, ready to lash out at the unfortunate soul he heard approaching behind him.

He recoiled when his wife's fingers touched his arm. "How *could* you, Louisa?" he said, keeping his gaze fixed in front of him. "I told you that in *confidence*. I *trusted* you."

"Martin, I don't know what you're talking about. Does this have something to do with Ruth's gift?"

"Joan was the only person I'd ever discussed that with up until a few weeks ago. And she only knew that Edith had publicly announced her rejection of my proposal. Do you have any idea how difficult it was for me to share all that with you? *Do you?*"

"I'm not following. What does what you told me have to do with Ruth's gift?"

His head tipped to the side. "The piano—isn't that—I mean—" He heaved out a breath as his shoulders slumped. "You didn't tell her."

"Of course not. As you said, you told me that in confidence. I'll *never* break that confidence."

"Well, then why the piano?"

"Evan was going on to Ruth about how you taught him to play, and she thought that maybe if you had a place where you could get away ... play on your own ... well, she thought you might pick it up again. The house is empty a lot of the time, so you could be by yourself. She thought it would be therapeutic."

"I see." He turned and looked at her sheepishly. "I'm ... I'm sorry."

Louisa tucked her hands under her armpits as a shiver rippled through her.

"Come here," Martin said softly as he opened his arms to her. "I've embarrassed myself—again," he groaned as his grasp on her tightened. "You're cold; we better go inside."

The creaking of the door hinges alerted Evan to Martin and Louisa's return, and he ran to the kitchen to meet them, jumping up and down excitedly. "Old Doc and Mrs. Parsons brought presents, and one's for *me*! Can I open it?" he asked as the flip of hair over his forehead bounced up and down.

"That was very nice of them," Louisa said. "Did the Parsons say that you could open it now?"

"Old Doc said I could open it if it's okay with you. So, can I?"

"Did you finish eating?"

"Yep. 'Cept for the biscuits. Do I gotta eat biscuits before I open it?"

"No, you don't *have* to eat biscuits first. But let me get my mobile so I can get some pictures."

Evan darted back into the dining room and Martin followed after.

The fire Chris had started in the fireplace crackled and popped, adding to the ambience being created by the candles that were scattered about. He looked around, wondering how many bronchial irritants were being emitted by the lit paraffin.

Evan and James were sat on the floor in front of the Christmas tree, with brightly coloured packages in their laps. James picked at a corner of the wrapping paper with a fingernail. And Evan looked up at his guardian with a smile that appeared to nearly kiss his ears.

"Okay, I'm ready," Louisa said as she sat down on a footstool and lined up her shot.

"Can I go?" Evan asked, his fingers twitching.

"Yep, you can go," Chris said.

For a child who could hardly wait for the moment, he removed the gaily coloured wrapping with painstaking precision. When the covering was finally lifted off, he held up the plastic package inside—three pairs of socks, adorned with sea creatures. "I gots new socks!" he said excitedly as he ran to Martin. "Look Dr. Ellig-am, they gots whales and seahorses and starfish and—" He grunted, trying to pull the plastic packaging apart. "Can you get it?"

"Mm. Hand it here," Martin said before the boy shoved it towards him.

He pulled at the plastic and grimaced as pain shot through his injured arm. "You better take it over to Dr. Parsons," he said, returning the socks to the child.

Evan dashed over to Chris, and he pulled the wrapper apart.

Evan removed the brightly coloured socks and sat down on the floor to replace his plain white socks with the new ones. He stretched his legs out in front of him and admired the new look. "Thanks, Old Doc! Thanks, Mrs. Parsons!"

James had been captivated by the older boy's actions, but now returned his attention to his picking at the wrapping on his gift.

Evan scrambled over to watch as the bow was pulled from the paper.

"Maybe it would help if you could tear a bit of the paper for him, Evan," Carole said.

The seven-year-old pulled up a flap that the toddler could grasp on to and he shook the present back and forth. Another package of socks dropped to the floor.

"James gots socks just like mine!"

Chris held out his hand. "Here, Evan. I'll open it."

Carole picked James up and removed his socks from his feet before replacing them with a new pair. When she set the boy down on the floor, he crawled back to reclaim his bow.

He sat, spraddle-legged as he toyed with the sticky decoration, and Evan butted his feet up to the toddler's. "Look, we go together now," he said.

"Yes, you do, Evan." Carole gathered together the already forgotten wrapping.

Martin glanced over at Louisa as she cleared her throat and got up from the footstool before moving to the sofa.

"Erm, Ruth ... could I have a word, please?" Martin said.

The elderly woman followed her nephew to the kitchen. "I'm sorry, Martin," she said as she entered the room. "I didn't mean to put you on the spot the way I did."

"Mm, no. I need to apologise. There was a bit of a misunderstanding ... between Louisa and me." He fidgeted, poking at a frosting coated snowman on the biscuit tray. "I ... I appreciate the gesture."

"It's not a gesture, Martin. It's a gift. I know you didn't receive a lot of encouragement as a child, but I can encourage you now. I spoke with Carole Parsons, and she discouraged me from buying a piano for your lounge at the surgery."

"Mm, yes. That would be a wasted investment. The salt air that close to the harbour would rust the strings in no time at all. Not to mention the damage the humid conditions would have on the soundboard. This is a logical solution."

"Well, I'm not saying you have to play it, but I understand from Carole that you play quite well."

Martin moved to the sink and filled a glass with water. "*Played.* That was a very long time ago," he said as he stared absently at the dark window.

"Well, I'm an old woman, and I'm running out of things to spend my money on. So, the instrument is here if you should decide to take it up again."

He turned and Ruth took his injured arm gently between her hands. "It could prove very beneficial."

"Mm, yes," he said, tucking his chin.

It was shortly after eight that evening when the Ellinghams arrived back at the surgery. James and Evan had been bathed and sat nestled with Martin on the sofa while Louisa tidied the bathroom.

Martin pulled a book out from under his BMJ laying on the coffee table. "I've been informed by a credible source that this is a special story," he said, clearing his throat. "Presumably one that is typically read on Christmas Eve. Seems appropriate for the occasion, don't you think?" he asked, his eyes darting between the two boys.

James gave his father a gap-toothed smile and patted at his cheek.

"Sounds 'propriate to me," Evan said. "At least if that means it's a good one ta read tonight. 'Cause it *is* the night before Christmas."

"Yes, it is." Martin flipped the book open to the first page. *"Twas the night before Christmas and—"*

"What's a 'twas, Dr. Ellig-am?" Evan asked.

"It's a contraction—erm, a joining of two words. In this case, it and was to make 'twas."

He shifted his son's weight from the tender area in his thigh to higher up on his lap, and then continued. *"Twas the night before Christmas, when all through the house, not a creature was stirring, not even a mouse. The stockings were hung by the chimney with—"*

Evan jumped to the floor. "Oh, no! We didn't hang up the stockings yet!"

Martin screwed up his face and patted the cushion next to him. "We'll get them taken care of in a bit. Just sit down now and listen to the story."

The seven-year-old gave his guardian a dubious look before climbing back up on his perch.

"So, the stockings are hanging, and now it looks like the children are all tucked into bed, hoping Father Christmas will be coming soon." He glanced over at his charge. "Remember, this is just a story."

"I won't forget, Dr. Ellig-am!" Evan said, throwing his head back.

"Mm, yes." Martin cleared his throat again. *"The children were nestled all snug in their beds, while visions of sugar*—oh, now that's just ridiculous. Sugar-plums dancing in their heads? Does this—" Martin flipped the book closed and peered at the cover. "Does this Moore fellow even know what a sugar-plum is?"

Evan patted a hand on Martin's knee. "It's just for pretend, Dr. Ellig-am." He opened the book back up and tapped a finger on the page. "We were right there."

"The sugar-plums were dancing in their heads. And mama in her kerchief and I in my cap, had just settled our brains for a long winter's nap." Martin shook his head. "That should prove challenging with those sugar-plums dancing around in them."

Evan turned to look at him. "In what?"

"In their brains. They just said— Mm, never mind." Martin rubbed a palm across his forehead. *"When out on the lawn there arose such a clatter, I sprang from my bed to see what was the matter."*

Evan moved in closer to Martin and wedged himself under his arm.

"*Away to the window I flew like a flash, tore open the shutters and threw up the sash.*"

The seven-year-old slapped his hands over his eyes. "Stop reading! Stop reading! It might be someone scary out there, Dr. Ellig-am!"

"It's no one scary, Evan. It's just Father Christmas."

The boy turned his head, slowly uncovering his eyes, and James slapped his hands over his own eyes, pulling them away before erupting in juicy giggles. Evan repeated the action, engaging in a game of peek-a-boo with the toddler.

"All right, all right. Are we going to finish this story or not?"

"I think I've had enough of it. Can we hang up our stockings now?" Evan said, sliding from the sofa.

Martin sighed and snapped the book shut. "I'm not sure what Mrs. Ellingham's done with them."

"Mrs. Ellingham's left them right where Dr. Ellingham put them," Louisa said as she came down the stairs. "Are you all done with the story?"

"As done as we're going to get with it, I think."

Louisa went to the pantry and reached up on the top shelf, pulling down two bags. One from each of her husband's forays into the Wadebridge gift shop.

"I had Mr. Large stop by and put some hooks in the mantel so you have something to hang them on," she said as she pulled the two red gingham stockings from the bag. "Here you go, Evan."

The boy held it up in front of him, tracing over the letters with his finger. "It gots my name on it!" he whispered. "Does that mean I get ta keep it?"

"Yes, it's yours to keep. Dr. Ellingham bought that for you," Louisa said.

He walked over and crawled up on the sofa, wrapping his arms around Martin's neck before giving him a kiss on the cheek. "Thanks Dr. Ellig-am."

Martin looked up at his wife, his face warming. "Well ... yes."

Louisa mouthed the words *you're welcome*.

"You're welcome, Evan," he added, patting the child on the back.

Evan slipped the loop on his stocking over a hook before doing the same with James's stocking.

"What's in the other bag?" he asked.

"Dr. Ellingham picked one up for someone else as well." Louisa pulled the third stocking from the bag. She stared at it incredulously before casting a disbelieving glance at her husband, huffing out a breath. "Oh, Martin."

"You did want the animal's name on there, didn't you?" he asked nervously.

"Yes, I did. But look at it, Mar-tin."

He pushed himself up from the sofa and walked to her side, pulling the stocking from her hands to inspect it. "What's wrong with *this?*"

She took it back and held it up in front of her before turning it one hundred and eighty degrees.

He cocked his head and raised his eyebrows. "Problem?"

"This *isn't* the—*animal's*—name."

"I believe it was his name when Joan had him."

"Martin, it's *Buddy*, not Butty."

He blinked his eyes at her. "Well, that makes absolutely no sense. The name in and of itself implies that the creature is someone's friend, which is highly unlikely considering its usual habit is to vagrantly loiter on either our doorstep or at the sandwich shop. Where it feeds on day old butties which have been tossed in the rubbish bins, by the way. *Hence* the name—Butty."

Martin, certain that he had made his case, returned to the sofa, took a seat, and began to peruse his medical journal, pouting aggrievedly.

Evan took the stocking from Louisa's hands and hung it over the third hook, and then took a step back to admire the Yuletide display. "Well, *I* like it," he said. "Dr. Ellig-am musta thought about Buddy really hard ta come up with that one, and I think that means he likes him."

Martin rolled his eyes, and Louisa tipped her head down, trying to hide her smile.

With the children nestled snug in their beds, Louisa rejoined her husband downstairs a short time later. She poured a glass of wine for herself and a glass of single malt before taking a seat next to him on the sofa.

"Louisa, I had the Scotch last night to steady my nerves. I don't want to make it a habit," he said as she set the glass in his hand.

"I don't want you to make it a habit either, but I really enjoyed the way our evening was playing out last night. Maybe we could give it another go?"

He watched her for a moment, her eyes sparkling back at him, before lifting the glass to his lips. Then, he got to his feet and offered his hand to her. "Would you mind going upstairs with me?"

Louisa stood up and kissed him as her fingers worked the top buttons of his shirt. "Maybe I'll get my Christmas wish tonight," she said, giving him a coy smile.

"Mm, yes." He swallowed hard. "I'll just ... go lock up." He watched her swaying form as she headed for the stairs.

Picking up the two glasses, he took them to the kitchen where he dumped what remained down the drain. Then he went to the door and turned the lock.

As he reached for the switch to turn off the outside light, he glimpsed Joan's little brown and white terrier, sitting outside, blinking his eyes at him.

His hand hovered over the lock for a moment before turning it again and pulling the door open. "All right, come on," he said gruffly, giving a jerk of his head.

Buddy gave him a final blink of his eyes before darting past him and up the stairs, making a right turn into the nursery.

Martin followed as far as the landing. Then he made a left turn into their bedroom. His wife would get her Christmas wish tonight ... if he had anything to do with it.

Chapter 34

"Dr. Ellig-am. Dr. Ellig-am, are you awake?"

Martin pried his eyes open and stared up at the shadowy figure hovering over him. "What is it, Evan?"

"It's Christmas. You wanna get up so you don't miss any of it?"

He groaned as he rolled to his side to peer at the clock. "Gawd, it's not even six-thirty yet! The sun doesn't come up for another two hours, Evan," he whispered.

"But the paper just came. Don't you wanna get up and read it before the news gets old?"

Louisa rolled over, her arm flopping over her husband's chest with a hollow thump. "What is it, Martin?"

"Mm, sorry to wake you. It's seems it's Christmas morning ... barely."

She pushed herself up in the bed and rubbed at her eyes. "Happy Christmas, Evan," she said, her voice still thick with sleep.

"Happy Christmas! You wanna get up and start celebratin'?"

"In a minute, Evan." Louisa leaned over her husband and pressed her lips to his, allowing them to linger. "Happy Christmas, Martin."

His eyes met hers momentarily before darting towards the child who stood by their bed watching them.

"Erm ... Evan's waiting," he said before clearing his throat as he tried to wriggle out from under her.

"Oh, you can keep kissin' her as long as you want, Dr. Ellig-am. I don't mind waiting." The child gave him an encouraging nod.

"I think we're done now, Evan. Thank you, though," Louisa said. "Why don't you go put your robe and slippers on."

Martin swung his legs over the side of the bed and wiped a palm across his face.

"Are you gettin' up?" the little boy asked hopefully.

"Well, I'm certainly not getting any sleep as it is, so I may just as well, don't you think?" Martin grumbled.

He stood up, putting a hand against the wall to steady himself as he worked his feet into his slippers. Giggles could be heard coming from the nursery. Martin sighed. "I can get him. You rest a bit if you like."

"No, that's okay. I'll get him. I want to wish him a Happy Christmas," Louisa said as she got out of bed and slipped on her dressing gown before venturing across the hall.

She slapped a hand to her mouth when she turned on the light in the nursery. James sat in his cot, grasping on to the ears of his stuffed rabbit as Buddy tugged on the tail from the other side of the rail. Another stream of chortles erupted from the toddler's mouth as the little terrier gave a shake of his head and a playful growl.

"What's going on in there!" Martin called from their bedroom doorway.

Louisa took a step back and smiled at him innocently. "Nothing, Martin. I've got James, you just go ahead and … do whatever you were going to do."

She redirected her attention to the perceived problem at hand. "How did *you* get in here again!" she whispered as she gathered the little dog into her arms before peering around the door jamb.

Evan came across the landing. "Buddy slept with me last night. Do you s'pose Father Christmas let 'im in?"

Louisa glanced at the closed bathroom door. "I doubt that. But it might be best if we didn't discuss this around Dr. Ellingham, hmm?"

"Why 'cause?"

"Because, he doesn't want Buddy in the house. We don't want to spoil Christmas for him by getting his day off to a bad start, do we?"

"Uh-uh."

"I'm going to run down and put Buddy outside. You stay here; I'll be right back."

Martin came out of the bathroom a short while later and walked across to the nursery. He glanced around the room before peering under the bed.

"Whatcha lookin' for, Dr. Ellig-am?" Evan asked as he took his robe and slippers from the wardrobe.

He straightened himself quickly, shaking his head. "Nothing ... nothing."

By the time Louisa returned, Martin had picked James up from his cot and was talking to him softly.

"Where have you been?" he asked as she stepped into the room.

"Mm, just got a glass of water." She glanced over at the seven-year-old as he sat on the floor pulling on his slippers and gave him a barely perceptible shake of her head. He returned her gesture with a giggle, stifled quickly with a hand over his mouth.

"James must be teething again," Martin said. "That'll have to go in the wash; it's covered in drool." He held the dog-slobbered rabbit out to his wife, screwing up his face.

She took the rabbit by the ears, holding it in her fingertips. "Mm, yes it will."

"Do you think Father Christmas came, Dr. Ellig-am?" Evan said as he quickly pulled the sash of his robe around him.

Martin passed James to Louisa. "Well, let's go see. Could just be he managed to find you this year."

The boy flashed his guardian a smile before darting from the room.

Martin had just made it to the top of the stairs when he heard excited shouts from below. "He came! He came, Dr. Ellig-am! He came!"

Evan appeared at the bottom of the steps. "Hurry up! He came!" He ran back and forth between the lounge and the entryway as he waited impatiently for his guardian to reach the first floor.

Latching on to Martin's wrist, he kept a steady tension as he urged him towards the stockings suspended from the mantle. "Can I look?" he asked.

"I think we better wait for Mrs. Ellingham. She's likely to want pictures." His eyes scanned the room, looking for any sign of the terrier he had let in the night before. His brow crinkled before he shifted his attention back to his charge. "How 'bout we go start some breakfast?"

Evan took a last longing look at the barely visible somethings peeking out over the top of the cuff before following him to the kitchen.

"Pull a chair over here, Evan. You can cook the porridge this morning." Martin reached down into the cupboard and pulled out a pot, setting it on the counter. "Have you measured out ingredients before?"

"I dunno. What's a 'gredient?"

"In this case, the in-gre-di-ents would be the water and the oats."

Evan squinted his eyes for a moment, and then shook his head. "Nope, I never measured *them*."

"Well, have you ever used a measuring cup?" he asked as he pulled it from the shelf.

"Uh-uh."

He set the cup down on the counter. "You need four and a half cups of water."

"How much is four and a half?"

Holding the cup up in front of the boy, he pointed to the one cup mark. "See that top red line?"

"Uh-huh."

"Fill it to that line four times. Then fill it to this line in the middle once."

Evan reached out and turned on the tap. Water ran up and over the sides of the cup. "Oh, no! I gots too much!"

Martin dropped two slices of bread into the toaster before returning to the boy's side. "Just dump a little out, then set it down on the counter. Get down so you can eyeball it straight on."

He waited, throwing his head back as the child dumped and refilled the cup for the fourth time before finally getting it right.

"Perfect!" Evan said as he straightened up.

"Okay, good job. Now you need to do that three more times."

Returning to his breakfast preparations, Martin set out bowls, plates, and utensils before going to the refrigerator for the bottle of milk and the orange marmalade.

"How are you coming there?" he asked as he came back to check on the boy.

Evan turned a teary face to him. "I don't know how many I gots left."

"You needed three more, Evan."

"I *know!* But I don't remember how many I put in there already!"

Martin gave him several pats on the back. "Shh, shh, shh, shh, shh. Just a minute."

He went to the table, and after casting a furtive glance towards the hall and lounge, he lifted the lid on the sugar bowl.

"Okay, here's what you're going to do."

He dumped the water from the pot and set it back on the counter with a clunk. Then he lined up four sugar cubes in front of the seven-year-old. "Every time you pour a cup of water in here, you're going to eat one of these," he explained, wagging a finger at the queue of cubes. "Once they're all gone, you know you have four cups of water measured out."

Evan wiped his face with the back of his hand. Martin pulled a sheet from the kitchen roll before dabbing at the boy's cheeks.

"Thanks for not gettin' cross 'cause I spoilt it," the child said, taking in a ragged breath.

"You didn't spoil it, Evan, you're learning," Martin said softly before narrowing his eyes. "But this"—he circled a finger over the sparkly cubes—"is a special thing because it's Christmas. Don't get used to it. Got it?"

The boy gave him a toothy grin. "Got it."

By the time Louisa came downstairs with James, Martin and Evan had finished their breakfast preparations.

"Sorry to take so long. I decided to give James a bath so he'd be fresh for the big celebration. Thanks for waiting for us," she said.

"Can we look in our stockings now?" Evan said, pulling his arms behind him as he struggled to keep his feet planted on the floor.

Louisa tousled the boy's hair. "Yes, you may look now." She took James to the lounge, setting him on the floor in front of the coffee table before pulling her mobile from her pocket.

Evan struggled with his stocking, unable to hoist it from the hook. "It's too heavy, Dr. Ellig-am."

Martin lifted it up, handing it to the boy before getting James's stocking and setting it on the floor in front of him.

The two boys sat side by side as Martin and Louisa watched from the sofa. Louisa snapped a picture each time a treasure was pulled from its festive container.

In the top of each stocking was a small, gift-wrapped package. "You'll want to take that with you to the farm today, Evan," Martin explained. "But, you can open it here if you like."

Louisa's eyes darted questioningly between her husband and the gaily wrapped parcel in the seven-year-old's hands.

Evan carefully peeled the paper away, revealing a small cardboard box labelled 'pessary rings'.

Martin glanced over at his wife, and she furrowed her brow at him. "Perhaps you'd like to help James with his," he said, clearing his throat.

The paper was quickly ripped away from the toddler's package, revealing a box identical to Evan's. "You gave the boys *pessary rings?*" Louisa asked incredulously.

"Of course not. I just used the boxes; they were the right size." He took the box from his wife and pulled the top off before removing a brightly coloured train engine Christmas ornament.

"Oh, Martin. May I see it?"

"Mm, yes."

"This is *beautifully* crafted," Louisa said as she turned it over in her hands. "There's a date painted on the bottom ... 1969."

Evan pulled at the lid to his box before gazing, open-mouthed, at the delicate hand-blown ornament inside.

"That one's quite fragile, Evan, so be careful," Martin cautioned.

The boy lifted it from the box by the attached azure blue ribbon, holding it up in front of him. "It looks like those round windows at the big church!"

"Mm, yes." Martin got to his feet and walked down the hall to his consulting room, returning with a folded sheet of paper. "They're from Joan, actually," he said as he handed it to Louisa.

She gave the little train engine back to him and unfolded the paper.

My Dear Marty,

My intention is to give you this box at Christmastime, as you prepare to celebrate your first holiday as a father. But lest life intervene in any way and prevent me from passing it on personally, I want to leave you with some sort of an explanation as to its contents.

Every year, after you started coming to spend summers here at the farm, I tried to convince my stubborn brother to allow you to stay the holidays with your Uncle Phil and me. And every year, your father refused my request. The man's a bloody idiot! I'm sorry, Marty, but there it is.

Knowing the inevitable answer didn't keep me from trying, however. And every year, on the outside chance that your father would change his mind, I prepared for your arrival—baking and decorating so that the house would be ready for you.

*And every year, I bought a special ornament, hoping that we could begin a family tradition. That you would run downstairs on Christmas morning, knowing you would find a special ornament, selected just for you, in your Christmas stocking. You would hang it on the tree. Before, of course, turning your attention immediately to the gifts **under** the tree.*

I had hoped that we might have at least one Christmas that we could spend together as a family. But life isn't always fair. It doesn't always give us what we want ... or what we deserve. Does it, Marty?

Phil and I took turns hanging each year's ornament in your stead. I've dated each one. Some are particularly symbolic, and I hope that your happy memories will have held strong enough for you to understand their significance.

Some are merely ornaments that I thought you would find particularly interesting or beautiful. You always did have a refined appreciation for beauty.

I have always loved you, Martin. I couldn't love you more if I had given birth to you myself. The love you've shown me in return, through hugs and kisses when you were small, to your attentiveness to my financial, physical, and emotional well-being as a grown man, has given me hope that one day you'll be able to fully share that very special side of yourself with someone else.

This seems an appropriate time to remind you of your impending fatherhood and the woman who's carrying your child. You love her dearly; I know that Martin. I also know how deeply you've been hurt in the past and what a risk you'd be taking to share your feelings with her. But you'll never know what could have been if you can't bring yourself to take that risk.

Your aunt Ruth is fond of saying, we're the authors of our lives. My wish for you is that one day you will come to realise that you deserve to have the family that you've been wanting for so many years. That you'll write your own story, and it will include that family.

The affection-starved little boy who showed up on my doorstep every summer has grown into a very fine man. Perhaps you and Louisa will find some way to reconcile your differences. And together with your child, you will become the family you've longed for. Perhaps you will have a family who loves and cherishes the very fine man that you are.

Maybe you'll be able to create your own traditions with the son or daughter who will be arriving soon—carry on the tradition begun by Phil and me in your absence.

It's a bit difficult for me to picture you decorating a Christmas tree, but if you do choose to make use of these ornaments, perhaps you'll think of me when you hang them.

Happy Christmas, Marty.

Love,

Auntie Joan

Louisa wiped the tears from her cheeks, got up, and wrapped her arms around her husband. "Oh, Martin," she whispered. "What a special gift."

"Mm ... yes." He inhaled deeply as he pulled his wife tighter. "The engine is from the year Uncle Phil and I stopped at a cafe that used to be in Delabole. They had an electric train running along a shelf near the ceiling. I enjoyed watching it. Phil took me back there several more times that summer. It was the last summer they were in business."

"And the one you gave to Evan?"

"As Evan said ... it looks like the rose windows in Truro Cathedral. That was the summer of 1968."

"Where should I put my ordament, Dr. Ellig-am?" Evan said as he tugged on Martin's sleeve. "I don't want it ta get smushed."

"Mm, I'll take it. You can hang it on the tree when we get to the farm."

"Kay. Can I get the rest of the stuff outta my stocking now?"

"Yes, you *may*."

James had crawled away from his stocking to investigate the wrapping paper which had been removed from the older boy's box and now had it torn into several pieces. Evan picked a small, saliva-soaked piece from the toddler's chin before gathering the rest of the bits, taking them to the bin.

"Thank you, Evan. That was very thoughtful," Louisa said as she sat down on the sofa with her mobile in hand.

The boy dropped back to the floor and removed a fuzzy set of reindeer antlers which were attached to a headband. He looked at it, his eyes widening. "Oh, wow! They must be just-growed antlers 'cause they gots the fuzz on 'em!" He examined the headband and gave Louisa a scowl. "What's this thing for?"

Louisa laid her phone on the table. "Come here. It goes on like this," she said before perching the antlers atop the child's head.

"I gotta go see!" He dashed off towards the lavatory under the stairs.

His footsteps thundered back through the hall before he emerged with a grin on his face. "I look like Clyde!"

"Clyde?" Martin tipped the boys head back, scrutinising him. "Clyde who?"

"Just plain ol' Clyde. Remember ... Clyde and Sally."

"It's *Clive*, Evan ... not Clyde." Louisa said before snapping a photo of her son sporting his own pair of antlers.

Martin slipped the ornaments back in the pessary ring boxes and set them on the mantle. "No, he's right, Louisa...it's Clyde."

"Martin, check your patient notes ... it's *Clive*."

"Oh, Clyde's not Dr. Ellig-am's patient. Clyde needs a ven-trarian, not a people doctor.

"Clyde's a reindeer. So is Sally," Martin informed her.

"Oh, I *see*."

James had pulled a chunky plastic dumper truck from his stocking and ran it back and forth on the carpet beside him.

Picking up his own stocking, Evan upended it, the contents spilling out on to the floor. "Wow! I gots an orange! And an apple and bubble gum!"

Martin looked at his wife. "Louisa, I don't—"

She pulled her index finger to her lips. "Shush, it's sugarless, Martin."

"Mm, yes."

"And I gots a ... I gots an *airplane!*" The seven-year-old jumped up from the floor and ran to his guardian. "Thank you, Dr. Ellig-am!" he said as he threw his arms around his neck.

"That's actually from Mrs. Ellingham."

The boy veered right and embraced Louisa tightly. "Thanks, Mrs. Ellig-am. And this one really flies, too!"

"You're welcome, Evan. I'm sure Dr. Ellingham would enjoy helping you put that together. Then the two of you could take it up to Rosstree Field to fly it. You'd enjoy that, wouldn't you, Martin?"

He looked over at her with an anxious expression on his face. "I, er ... yes."

James crawled over next to the older boy, digging through the contents on the floor.

"Here, James," Louisa said, gathering her son up and returning him to his own stocking. "Those belong to Evan. These are yours." She dumped out an assortment of finger puppets, toys, and small packages of teething biscuits.

"What are these?" Evan asked her, holding up a package in each hand.

"That's bubble-gum scented soap, and those are tattoos."

"What are tattoos?"

"It's like a picture that you can stick on your skin," Louisa said as she picked up her mobile and snapped a picture of the boy.

"Oh, like the men gots at the pub my da—" He climbed on to the sofa and worked his way under Martin's arm before returning his attention to his gifts. He turned the package over. "Wow. There's even a spider. Can I stick one on now?"

Louisa gave her husband a small nod. "Sure. Why don't you have Dr. Ellingham help you."

Evan handed Martin the package, and he scanned the instructions. Then he pushed himself up from the sofa and headed towards the hallway. "Come through," he said, waiting as Evan passed him, giving him a wary eye.

"Whatcha gonna do, Dr. Ellig-am?"

"If you want this procedure to be conducted properly, you need to come back to my exam room."

The child whirled and looked at Louisa.

"It's okay, Evan. I think it's a completely painless procedure."

Martin followed the boy down the hall and into the consulting room before hooking his left arm around him and hoisting him on to the couch. He took a step back, scanning under his desk and the couch, cocking his head."

"Whatcha lookin' for, Dr. Ellig-am?"

"Mm, nothing—nothing."

He went to his medical cart and pulled out an alcohol soaked disinfecting pad. "Where are we going to put this thing?" he asked the boy.

"I think it should go right here where everybody can see it," the child said, pointing to the back of his hand. "Remember, I want the spider one."

Martin swabbed the area before pulling out another drawer on his medical cart, removing a small sponge. He went to the sink and ran it under the tap before squeezing it out.

"Okay, it says we need to peel off that clear plastic that's covering the design. Can you manage that?"

Evan picked at the film, his tongue working its way out between his lips. "There, that gots it."

Pressing the design to the child's hand, Martin blotted it with the sponge before slowly peeling away the backing."

"Brilliant!" the seven-year-old said as he admired the tattoo.

When the two returned to the kitchen a few minutes later, James was in his high chair, munching on cereal bits.

"Can I dump the oats in the pot now, Dr. Ellig-am?" Evan asked as he reclaimed his position on the chair by the counter.

"Nope. We need to get the water boiling first," he said, moving the pot to the hob and turning the knob to high. "You can push the lever down on the toaster though."

Martin winced as the boy dragged the chair across the floor, the legs screeching against the slate. The bread disappeared into the appliance before the shrill screech rippled through the air again as the chair was dragged back to the stove.

Evan looked out the window over the sink, spotting Buddy, his head peeking out of the doghouse. The animal's mop of hair fluttered in the breeze. The dog saw the boy and got to his feet, wagging his feathered tail.

The child leapt from his perch. "We forgot *Buddy's* stocking!" Evan said, leaping from his perch.

He ran to the fireplace and lifted it from its hook before carrying it to the kitchen. After pushing the bowls to the centre of the table, he dumped out the bags of treats and hand baked dog biscuits. A small green ball bounced on to the floor and rolled across the room.

"Where did that come from," Louisa asked as it passed her by.

"I saw it at the Christmas Market and gots it for him. He needs a toy," Evan said.

"That was very thoughtful, Evan. I'm sure he'll love it." She looked up from the banana she was slicing into James's plastic bowl. "I bet he'd like a bit of a treat right now, don't you think? Get his Christmas morning off to a cracking start?"

Martin turned. "Erm, I'm not sure that's a good idea."

Louisa dropped her hands to the table. "Oh, Martin, please don't start policing Buddy's diet, too."

"I'm not. It's just that his exact location may be a bit—indefinite—at the moment. I mean, there's no telling where he may have wandered off to."

"Oh, I can tell ya. He's wandered off to his doghouse," the seven-year-old said.

Martin whirled back around and peered out the window, furrowing his brow at the little terrier.

"I'll give 'im one of the biscuits we made," Evan said before tearing the zip bag open and removing a treat. He hurried to the door, pulling it open, and the terrier darted inside. Making a beeline for the doctor, he jumped up, resting his forepaws against his legs.

"Oh, get off!"

"Calm down, Martin. We'll get him back outside. Just let the boys give him his Christmas treats first," Louisa said as she lifted her son from his high chair.

She pulled another biscuit from the bag before crouching down next to Evan. "Here you go, Buddy. Happy Christmas!" she said, holding it out to him.

"Hey, he likes 'em!" Evan grinned broadly as the little canine crunched eagerly on the hand baked treat.

"I'm gonna get 'im another one," he said, dashing back to the table.

Louisa ran her hand over Buddy's head. "Bring one for James, too," she said.

Evan handed her a chunk of dog biscuit before getting down on his haunches next to the toddler.

Louisa set her son on the floor before extending his arm and putting a treat into his plump palm. The terrier nuzzled furiously, trying to get to the morsel as the toddler's fingers closed reflexively around it. James burst into a fit of giggles as the wet tongue drilled its way to the buried treasure.

Martin stood watching, his brow creasing at the thought of the innumerable pathogens now covering his son's hand.

His eyes shifted from the slobbery fingers to the gleeful smiles on the boys' faces. His cheeks nudged up ever so slightly before he refocused his attention on the potential health hazard to the children.

"Their hands will need a jolly good scrubbing before they come to the table, Louisa," he admonished.

"*Yes*, Martin," she said, pushing herself up from the floor. "Dr. Ellingham's been very tolerant, but we shouldn't push our luck, Evan. We better put him back outside."

"Aww, but poor Buddy ... he's gonna feel like nobody wants him. He's gonna be sad that he has ta be all by himself for Christmas."

Martin threw his head back. "Oh, for goodness' sake," he grumbled before lifting the lid on the heating water.

"Are you going to want to cook the porridge or not, Evan?" he said, his patience with the quasi-Dickensian scene wearing thin.

"Yeah, I can do it!" the boy said, running back to climb up on his chair.

"No, no, no, no, no. Go wash those hands first."

"Be right back." Evan jumped to the floor and took off down the hall.

Louisa closed the door behind the little terrier and took James to the sink to wash his hands. "Thanks for letting the boys do that," she said before reaching up to kiss his cheek.

"Mm, well ... yes," he mumbled back.

James Henry was returned to his high chair and given his bowl of sliced banana.

"Now, where were we?" Louisa asked as she took hold of her husband's sleeves and turned him around, backing him up to the counter.

He gave her a small smile. "I believe you were expressing your appreciation."

"Ah, yes." She stretched up again and slipped her hand behind his head, pulling him towards her, kissing him as she pressed against him. Her kiss deepened and Martin's hands slid down her sides and over her hips.

"I should'a hanged the mistletoe up here instead of at the farm. It would'a been a lot more useful," Evan said as he emerged from the hallway.

"Geesh!" Martin jumped and Louisa took a step back as he slapped a hand to his chest. "For goodness' sake, Evan. Don't sneak up on us like that," he said breathlessly.

The boy flipped a plastic bag on to the kitchen table. "Oh, I wasn't sneakin'. You just weren't payin' attention again."

Martin rolled his eyes. "Come over here if you're going to cook the porridge."

The Ellinghams sat finishing their breakfast a short time later. Evan got down from his chair and dug around in his bag. "I gots some presents for you," he said as he handed Louisa a small parcel.

"Why, thank you, Evan," she said as she took it and began to peel the gift wrapping away.

"I even made the paper."

"I see that! It's lovely." The paper fell away from the contents, and Louisa stared down at a folded-up strip of garishly coloured fabric with baubles of various sorts glued to it. She cocked her head.

"It's a hair tying thing—like that brown one you always have holding your ponytail. 'Cept this one's more beautiful," he explained, bouncing on his toes.

"It's so colourful, Evan!"

"Yeah, and it's handmade 'cause you said those are the best kinds. I got a tie at the Christmas Market to make it out of. Bet'cha didn't even know that it used ta be a tie."

"No, I never would have guessed!"

Evan stood watching her for a few moments before saying, "Aren't ya gonna put it on?"

Martin raised an eyebrow at her from across the table, and she shot him a dark look.

Giving the boy an awkward smile, she pulled her hands behind her and tied the new accessory to the base of her ponytail. "There, how does it look?" she asked, her gaze meeting her husband's.

His eyes moistened as he answered hoarsely, "Very nice. It's very, very nice."

The seven-year-old reached back into his bag and pulled out a rolled-up sheet of paper with a ribbon tied around it. "This is for James, but *you* better open it so it doesn't get all banana-y," he said, handing it to Martin.

Martin pulled the ribbon off and the sheet of paper sprang open, revealing a colourful drawing of two figures standing by a tower of square objects.

"That's me," Evan said as he tapped on the taller of the two figures. "And the little one is James. And we're makin' a block tower. Maybe we can hang it by his cot, so he can see it when he wakes up in the morning."

Martin placed a palm on the boy's head. "That's very nice. I'm sure James will appreciate it."

"And I saved the best for last," Evan said as he dumped the last parcel out on to the table. "This one's for you, Dr. Ellig-am."

Martin furrowed his brow, wondering what had become of the purchase he'd watched the boy make for Louisa at the Christmas Market.

"Open it," Evan said as he bounced excitedly.

Martin removed the paper from the package, taking note of the painstakingly drawn tiny Christmas trees, snowmen and stick reindeer. Inside the wrapping, he found the black and white beaded necklace. He lifted it up, holding it out in front of him.

"It's for hangin' on the mirror in your car. See, it gots a piano ordament on it ... that hangs on the bottom. And that's you and me sittin' there."

Suspended from the beads, attached with a loop of yarn and adhesive tape, was a rather crude rendering of a black grand piano, drawn on black construction paper and ornamented with two glued on short-haired figures on a bench. The entire paper decoration had been laboriously covered in transparent adhesive tape.

Louisa held her breath, certain that her husband would never want such a thing so prominently displayed in his immaculate Lexus.

"Do you like it?" the boy asked, hesitantly.

Martin nodded his head as he batted tears from his eyes. "This is the nicest gift anyone's ever given me, Evan. I like it very much." He leaned over and hugged the boy. "Thank you."

"You're welcome, Dr. Ellig-am. Can we go to the Christmas Feast now?"

Louisa glanced at her watch. "Yes, we can, Evan. Go upstairs and get dressed. I've laid some clothes out for you." She gave her husband a smile and an incredulous shake of her head before getting up to clear the dishes.

Chapter 35

It was almost 10:00 a.m. when the Lexus rolled through the dips in the lane leading to the farm. Louisa kept her head turned towards her side window, struggling to not laugh at the improbable juxtaposition of the black and white beads hanging from the rear-view mirror of the posh vehicle.

The moment Martin shifted the gearbox into park, the seven-year-old pushed his door open and ran for the house.

"Evan!" Martin called out. "Come back here and help carry some things in." He reached into the cubby in his door and pulled out a manila envelope, tucking it under his arm.

The boy's feet skidded on the gravel as he came to a stop, triggering a whirr of chaffinch wings as a startled flock erupted from the tall grass near the barn.

"What do ya want me ta carry, Mrs. Ellig-am?" he said as he returned to the car.

Louisa handed him a bag with several of Martin's protein shakes and another bag containing two small bottles of milk. "Will you take those in and put them in the refrigerator for me?" she asked before she pulled James from his car seat.

"Sure. Then I gotta tell Old Doc about my Christmas stocking." He turned and raced for the house.

When they entered the kitchen, Carole was wrapping miniature sausages with strips of bacon and Chris was chopping apples for the stuffing.

"Happy Christmas!" Carole said, greeting them with her greasy hands held out to her sides as she applied kisses to cheeks.

"Happy Christmas!" Louisa set James Henry on the counter and tugged his cap from his head, static sending his fine, blonde hair in all directions.

"Gosh, it already smells wonderful in here." She removed the boy's coat before running her palm over his head to tame the wispy fly-aways. "What's in the cooker?"

"It's a cranberry crisp. Thought it might be a pud that Martin can tolerate."

"That wasn't necessary," he said, blinking his eyes at her.

"I know it wasn't *necessary*, Martin. I wanted to do it."

"Mm, I see" He set the two small pessary ring boxes and the manila envelope on top of the refrigerator before moving to the counter to inspect his friend's apple-cutting operation. "You should keep your fingertips tucked back when you do that, you know."

Chris huffed out a breath and stood with the knife poised in the air for a moment. "You *always* do this."

Martin turned and leaned back against the counter, folding his arms in front of him. "I just have no desire to be reattaching any of your body parts."

The other doctor gave him a black look and returned to his task with vigour.

Carole shook her head at the two men, and then turned to Louisa. "When are the others arriving?"

"Poppy, Jeremy, and Ruth are supposed to get here shortly before noon. I thought it'd be best if we didn't have too many people underfoot while we're trying to prepare dinner—mainly Bert—so I told Al and Morwenna to arrive around twelve-thirty." She turned on the light in the cooker and leaned over to peek in the door. "Ooh, that looks delicious!"

"Bugger!" Chris yelped, pulling his hand up.

Martin jerked his head to the side as his face blanched. "Ohh! Nicely done, Chris. I *told* you." He grabbed on to his friend's hand and pulled him to the sink.

"Oh, dear." Louisa speered between the two men as her husband attended to his friend. "Will it need stitches?"

"Of course not, just some antiseptic and a plaster."

"I'll get them from the lavatory," she said before hurrying off, returning shortly with the small packet and a bottle in hand.

Martin swallowed and closed his eyes for a moment before taking in a deep breath. "Could you hand me a paper towel?"

"Yeah ... yeah." Louisa returned with the requested item and gave it to her husband before patting a hand on the victim's back. "Chris, I'm *so* sorry. And on Christmas Day, too."

Martin threw his head back. "Oh, for heaven's sake, it's a superficial wound. And if he'd listened to my advice in the first place, it never would have happened."

Chris donned his most wounded expression. "And after *all* I've done for you, mate."

"Chris ... *really?*" Martin said, holding his friend's finger up in front of him.

The emergency attended to, Carole returned to her sausage wrapping. "So, Evan, have you had a good Christmas so far?"

"Yeah! I even got a stocking! I hanged it up last night, and it was all filled up this morning. I got bubble gum and an apple and an orange, and I gots this tattoo ... it's a spider," he said, shoving his hand in front of her.

"Oh, my! That looks like the real thing."

"Yeah, I know. That's 'cause *Dr. Ellig-am* preformed the procedure. He's a really good doctor. And guess what else ... I gots an airplane. That's from Mrs. Ellig-am, and it really flies! Well, it will once me and Dr. Ellig-am put it together."

"So, Father Christmas managed to find you there at the surgery, eh?" Chris said as he added the chopped apple to the bowl of stuffing which had been prepared the day before.

"Yep. And he brought stuff for James and Buddy, too. Whatcha doin' there, Old Doc?" he asked as he rested his arm on the countertop and poked a finger at one of the ducks.

"I'm going to dress these birds of yours."

"Is that 'cause they don't got their feathers anymore?"

Martin gave the boy a scowl. "It's ... *because* they don't *have* their feathers anymore."

"That's what I figured. So, then do you gots ta undress 'em again before we eat 'em?"

Martin huffed out a breath.

Chris scratched at an eyebrow as he looked up at his increasingly irritable friend. "Dressing a duck is the same as stuffing it, Evan. You want to help me with that?"

"Yeah!" Evan pulled a stool over next to him.

"You better go wash first," Martin said.

The boy dashed out of the kitchen, returning quickly, wiping his hands dry on his trousers.

By the time the poultry carcasses had been stuffed, Carole and Louisa had disappeared into the living room to prepare the table for the eleven expected diners, plus James in his high chair.

"There, that should do it, Evan," Chris said before going to the sink to wash the greasy residue from his hands.

"As soon as Carole's dessert comes out of the cooker, we can get these guys roasting."

Martin wagged a finger at the poultry. "Don't those—*guys*—need to be laced shut first?"

Chris shook his head. "I don't think we have the string or the metal skewer things. Can't the stuffing just sit in there?"

"I suppose it could. It's going to be a bit on the dry side though, don't you think?"

"Hmm, you might be right." Chris hoisted Evan up to the sink, soaping his hands. "Maybe Al has some fishing line out in the barn," he said. He set the boy on the floor and dropped the tea towel over his head.

Martin held up his hand. "No, no, no, no, no. Fishing line will melt."

"Well, what are we gonna do then?" Evan looked anxiously from one doctor to the next.

"Not to worry. I have an idea." Martin limped off through the little back entryway, returning a short time later carrying his medical bag. He set it on the kitchen table and opened it up, removing two sealed packets of suture material from a small drawer. "3-0 cotton," he said, handing one packet to his friend.

Chris gave him a sharp nod. "Brilliant, mate. Do you have a couple of forceps and needle holders in there by chance?"

Martin pulled open another drawer and removed the requested surgical instruments, handing one set to his friend before passing him a pair of surgical gloves.

Chris shoved a platter containing one of the ducks to the side. "You stitch that one up, and I'll do the other one."

Martin looked over at the seven-year-old. "Evan, would you like to close?"

"You mean tie it shut?"

"Well, this would be a modified version, but yes."

"I'm really good at tying my shoes now." The boy's cheeks glowed a warm pink in the light streaming in the window.

"Mm, I'm not sure that skill will prove terribly useful here. I think you're up to the job, though. Pull that stool over a bit more. We need to give Dr. Parsons a wide berth. He can be a bit dangerous with a needle and thread."

Chris's intense concentration on the task in front of him was broken. He straightened himself and glowered at his friend. "That was *not* my fault! The old bugger slapped my hand. Your arm just happened to—be in the way of the needle."

The boy looked up at his guardian, wide-eyed.

"A medical school mishap," he explained.

"What's a mishap?"

Chris took a step to the side and put his arm around his shoulders, turning him around. "That's a *mis*-take that can *hap*-pen ... mis - hap. And the *mistake* was made by the titanium-clad wise guy over there when he *happened* to inadequately control the belligerent patient I was stitching up."

"For the *record* ... you called him a gin-soused old git and he threw a wobbler," Martin said. "*That's* why he got away from me." He tipped his head down, peering over at Chris out of the corner of his eye.

Evan stood stock still, his rapidly blinking eyes focused on the larger of the two verbal sparrers.

Martin jabbed at the duck with his forceps as his indignant expression softened. Then he raised an eyebrow and pressed his lips together in a restrained grin, which together with Chris's snort, quickly alleviated the seven-year-old's anxiety.

"This patient should be much more compliant, Evan," Martin said. "But we'd better hurry up, or this duck won't be done in time for the Christmas Feast."

He slipped a pair of sloppily fitting surgical gloves over the child's hands before working a pair over his own. Then he handed the child the scissor-like needle holder. "Take that in your right hand and the forceps in your left." Reaching for the small packet containing the pre-threaded needle, he tried unsuccessfully to tear the end off. He shook the cramp from his right arm before grasping the item in his teeth and ripping it open.

"Still having some difficulty with that hand, mate?" Chris asked.

Martin gave him a quick glance and a grunt of acknowledgement before returning his attention to his charge, showing him how to use the needle holder. "Let's stitch the neck cavity shut first."

Placing his hands over the boy's fine-boned fingers, Martin took Evan through the basic process of suturing a laceration closed.

Chris watched over Martin's shoulder as Evan snipped the tails on the last suture, brushed off his hands and jumped from his chair.

"What do ya think, Old Doc?" he asked, his fists wedged on his hips.

"I think Dr. Frankenstein himself would be impressed. Nice work, Evan," he said as he transferred the birds to a roasting rack.

The timer beeped and Chris removed Carole's cranberry crisp from the cooker before sliding the two ducks in to replace it. "Now we wait," he said.

"What are we gonna do while we wait?" the child asked.

Louisa walked into the kitchen carrying James on her hip. "How 'bout we go relax around the Christmas tree?"

she said, giving her husband a jerk of her head before leading the way towards the living room.

Martin pulled the small boxes from the top of the refrigerator and followed after her. He scanned over the dining table as he walked by.

Place settings of Joan's white china dinnerware and silverware sat in front of each chair. And a runner of greenery ran down the centre of the bright red tablecloth, punctuated by fifteen tealight candles. He wrinkled up his face at the thought of having to sit down at a table crowded with people overindulging in the spirits and provisions of the holiday season.

Evan bounced past him, followed quickly by James, trying to keep up.

The seven-year-old stopped and looked at the tree, aglow with lights and sparkling decorations. "That's the most beautiful Christmas tree ever, don't you think, Dr. Ellig-am?"

"Yes, it's very nice, Evan. Would you like to hang your ornament?"

"Yeah. I'll find the perfect spot."

Martin slipped one of the wire hangers he had brought with him through the ribbon on the azure blue ornament before handing it to the boy.

Working her hand into her husband's, Louisa squeezed his fingers gently as they watched the little boy search for the perfect branch.

Evan looked back over his shoulder. "It gots ta be a place where it looks like it's hangin' in the air ... like the windows.

Martin released his grip on his wife's hand and stepped forward. "How about right here, Evan?" he said, pointing to a void between branches high in the tree.

"But I can't reach that one, and I wanna put it on myself."

The doctor leaned down and hooked his elbow under the boy's bum. "Hang on around my neck," he said before straightening back up. Louisa hurried forward and held on to his arm to steady him.

"There, that's the perfect spot," the child said after slipping the hanger over the sturdy branch. "It's even up by the ceiling like at the church."

Chris took Evan from his friend's arm and set him down on the floor.

After fondling the train ornament for a moment, Martin attached another hanger before surveying the tree. "Louisa, could you … help?" he asked, nodding his head towards his son who sat at his feet, playing with a bow which had been pulled from a gift.

Louisa picked the boy up and stuck the bow on the top of his head before handing him to his father. Then she wrapped her arms around his waist from behind.

He stood with his eyes closed for several moments before kissing his son's head, inhaling deeply, and hanging the little train next to Evan's ornament.

He choked back a sob and turned slightly, handing James back to his wife. "I'm going to get a drink," he said before limping off towards the kitchen.

When he returned to the living room, classic holiday tunes emanated from the speakers on the table, and James was underneath the Christmas tree, pulling the bows from the packages.

"Where did all these presents come from?" the seven-year-old asked.

"Well, maybe we should look and see." Louisa knelt down and reached for a small package, pulling open the gift tag. "What does that say?"

Evan peered over her arm. "It says ... *To Jay-mez*." He glanced up at her. "Or, maybe it's s'posed ta say James."

"Yes. It says, *To James, From the Parsons*."

"Can he open it?"

"That would be fine, Evan," Carole said as she sat the toddler down next to the older boy and put the package in his lap. "You might need to help him, though."

The wrapping was carefully loosened by the seven-year-old before being quickly dispensed with by James.

"It's a book ... about trucks!" Evan said.

Pulling a gaily wrapped rectangular package from under the tree, Carole said, "There's another present here...for you."

Evan took it from her quietly and sat, picking the paper off carefully. "It's eggs! I got eggs!" he said, holding the carton up for all to see.

Martin cocked his head and looked at his friend. "An unconventional choice, but it's not full of saturated fat and sugar like the godawful chocolate that most people feed children this time of the year."

"Hate to disappoint you, Mart. Open it up, Evan."

The child pulled the lid up on the egg carton, laying bare one dozen foil-wrapped chocolate eggs, each containing a toy surprise.

"Thanks, Old Doc! I *always* wished for one of these!" he said as he picked up an orb and gave it a shake. "Can I eat one?"

"Better wait until after the big dinner. You don't want to spoil your appetite." Chris cast an apologetic glance at his friend and shrugged his shoulders.

Louisa began to sort the remaining gifts into two piles. "Well, you and James have a lot of gifts to open before everyone else arrives, so we better keep moving," she said.

Evan stared at the assortment of packages being set in front of him. His eyes grew wide, and his lower lip began to quiver before he got to his feet and ran to Martin. He climbed into his lap and wrapped his arms around his neck.

Louisa gathered James into her arms and gave the Parsons a small jerk of her head. "Why don't we go and get some punch. Then when we come back the boys can open their gifts," she suggested.

Martin was left alone with his young charge. He waited until the child's crying had quieted before asking, "What's this all about, Evan? "

The boy pulled his face away from his guardian's shoulder and explained through ragged breaths. "You just—just—you happied me."

"Oh. You certainly don't seem happy."

"I *am* hap—happy, Dr. Ellig-am. It's must just be comin' out funny."

"I see." He pulled his handkerchief from his back pocket and wiped the child's eyes and nose. "If it's too much, Evan, you can just open what you feel like today and save some for another time. Would that be better?"

Martin grimaced as the boy nestled into his lap and let his head fall with a thud against his still tender rib cage.

"No, I wanna open 'em ... just ta see what's in 'em. But I think I'll just pretend they're mine. Just ta be on the safe side." He scrambled to the floor and ran to the kitchen leaving Martin scratching his head.

"We're all done talking, so you can stop drinkin' punch now if you want," Evan said before running back to take a seat on the floor in front of the tree.

Louisa and Carole positioned themselves to take pictures and video as Chris came into the living room carrying James.

"Here you go, Mart," he said before depositing the boy on his lap. "I'll bring his gifts over here so you can help him with them. I think Evan's going to be busy doing his own unwrapping."

"Mm," Martin pressed his fingers to his son's cheek. "How are you, James?"

The toddler flopped back, causing his father to stifle a groan as his head landed with a thump against his chest. "Da-ee!"

"Can I go?" Evan asked as he sat with a three-foot long, rectangular-shaped box poised on his lap.

"Yes, you boys may both go ahead ... open your presents."

"Who gave us 'em?"

"That one on your lap is from my aunt Ruth," Martin said. "The rest are from Mrs. Ellingham and me."

The child began to pick at the tape on his gift, and the shiny silver paper fell away. "It's a Beluga Whale!" he squealed, jumping up with the box and running to his guardian. "Can you get it outta there, Dr. Ellig-am?"

Martin scrutinised the packaging, fingering the white plastic zip ties which held the animal firmly in place. "I think you're going to need to have Dr. Parsons help you with that."

Chris went to the kitchen and returned with a scissors, snipping the ties and freeing the plush mammal before handing it to the boy.

"Wow, I'm surprised the other Dr. Ellig-am can still remember about toys."

"Mm, better not tell *her* that. She just might take that gift back," Martin said, raising an eyebrow at the child.

Evan whirled his head around as his arms tightened around the whale.

"He's not serious, Evan," Louisa assured him before giving her husband a dark look.

Martin grunted and tucked his chin.

"What does James gots there?" the seven-year-old asked as he stood up, clutching on to his new toy.

The toddler pulled the bow from the package and brought it to his mouth.

"He's not likely to open that on his own, Mart," Chris said, crossing his arms in front of him as he leaned back in his chair. "You're going to have to hel—"

"*Yes!* I realise that." Martin screwed up his face before pulling a piece of tape loose and showing James the gift peeking out from inside.

Carole repositioned herself so that she could capture the moment on video.

The toddler pulled the wrapping off and leaned forward, his moist hands squeaking as he pulled them across the clear plastic cover of the wooden train set inside.

"Well, I bet I know what the boys will be playing with this afternoon," Chris said.

Evan slipped in between the coffee table and the sofa. "That's really cool, James. Ya want me to help you put it together?" he singsonged in the voice he had grown accustomed to hearing from his head teacher.

Martin pointed a finger back at the boy's stack of presents. "You can put the train together after dinner. You have some more gifts to open right now."

The boy bounced back to his spot on the floor and slid a large snowman papered box towards himself before beginning his meticulous unwrapping. "It's another train!" he yelled as he stared at the box, and then ran for his guardian.

Chris scooped him up, preventing a painful and possibly injurious collision with his friend. He held him out and the boy wrapped his arms tightly around Martin's neck.

"Thanks, Dr. Ellig-am."

Martin sat awkwardly for several seconds as the boy retained his grip on him. He cleared his throat and patted the boy's back. "That's something we'll need to put together in the shed out back. There are too many small parts for James to get hold of in the house. And of course, it's an electrical hazard for a toddler."

Evan wiggled away from Chris and returned to the box, peering closely at the myriad pieces before pushing the toy aside. "Can James open another one now?"

Chris set another package next to his friend. "There you go, Mart."

James needed no encouragement this time, tumbling from his father's lap to tear at the paper covering the gift from his great-aunt.

"Oh, James! A boat for the bath. Won't that be *fun*?" Louisa said, snapping a photo.

Martin scrutinised the scooping and pouring capability of the brightly coloured tug. "We'll need to be sure the water's drained from that after each use. It could become a breeding ground for all manner of bacteria."

"I can wash the mannered bacterias off if you want," Evan said.

"I think it'll be just fine, Evan. But that's very nice of you to offer," Louisa said, tousling his hair. She leaned over and set another package in the boy's lap.

Evan began his methodical unwrapping.

"You know, you can just rip the paper off, Evan," Louisa said with a smile and an encouraging nod.

Martin's mouth opened and closed as he fought the urge to defend the child's gift opening technique.

The seven-year-old sat for a moment before looking up at her. "If I just rip it off, then it's all over, though."

"Hmm, that's very true. You open them however you like, then," she said before taking a seat on the end of the coffee table.

The boy peeled off the final piece of tape, shaking it from his fingers. "Blocks! It's blocks ... it's blocks, Dr. Ellig-am!"

"Mm, yes, it is."

"And they're the real snap together kind, too!" He glanced down at the reindeer-shaped gift tag before turning towards Martin with a furrowed brow. "This says it's from Father Christmas."

"All the tags say that," he answered. "If your classmates at school ask you what Father Christmas brought you, you'll be able to answer them honestly."

Evan gave him a broad smile. "That's pretty good thinkin', Dr. Ellig-am."

James unwrapped a wooden farm animal puzzle which, once opened, kept him entertained.

The seven-year-old sat with two remaining gifts on the floor in front of him, his pointer finger swinging back and forth between them as he recited an old Cornish children's rhyme.

"Ena, mena, mona, mite,
Bascalora, bora, bite,
Hugga, bucca, bau,
Eggs, butter, cheese, bread.
Stick, stock, stone dead—*OUT.*"

He shoved the loser of the rhyme to the side and grunted as he hefted the other package to his lap. The ritualistic unwrapping was then begun anew.

"It's a book! It's a book, Dr. Ellig-am! And it's about whales and sharks and shrimps and all kinds of animals that live in the ocean."

He got up from the floor and carried the book to the sofa, settling in next to his guardian with his straightened legs extended in front of him.

"There's something else in there you may want to check out," Martin said as he reached over and flipped quickly through the pages before pulling out a small folder.

"What's in it?" Evan asked as he pulled it from Martin's hand.

"Some information about Basking Sharks, some postcards, a bookmark ... and there's a certificate that says Evan Hanley has adopted a shark named Rooster."

He removed the official looking certificate and held it out to the boy. "It says, Certificate of Adoption." He reached into his pocket and pulled out a small plastic shark attached to a keychain. "This came with it."

"Cool! It's a basking shark!"

"Mm, I believe *Rooster* is as well."

The child's toes tapped together as he examined the certificate, tracing his finger over his name. He tipped his head back and grinned broadly at the doctor, the light from the Christmas tree reflecting in his eyes.

The creases around Martin's eyes deepened and his cheeks tautened before he wagged a finger at the solitary gift left lying on the floor. "Hadn't you better open the last one?"

Evan slid from the sofa and scrambled over to pick up the package. The paper rattled before falling to the floor. "It's a colouring book! And crayons! Just like I had on my list! I put it on my list and I *got* it!"

Martin stiffened and grimaced in advance of the boy's enthusiastic expression of appreciation. "Thanks, Dr. Ellig-am, this is my most favourite present," he said before pressing wet lips to his guardian's cheek.

"All the gifts are from Mrs. Ellingham as well," he told the boy softly.

Evan climbed off the sofa and went to Louisa, giving her a kiss before saying, "Thanks for all my presents, Mrs. Ellig-am."

"You're very welcome, Evan."

She embraced him firmly, and he whispered into her ear. She smiled, giving him a nod of her head. "I think this would be a perfect time. They're in my bag over there if you'd like to get them."

The boy dashed over to Louisa's handbag, which had been left on the small table next to the kitchen doorway. He pulled out two more gift-wrapped packages and raced back before handing them to Martin. "These ones are for you ... from me and James." He took a step back and pulled his hands behind him.

"Mm, I see. He glanced over at Chris and Carole, wincing at what felt like an audience as he tore the paper from the gifts inside.

A folded up white T-shirt fell away from its wrapping and he pulled it from the clear plastic bag.

"It's a basking shark on there," Evan said. "I thought you needed something ta wear with your boxers that wasn't a vest. I got it extra big so it'd fit over your fissators."

"I see," Martin said, his brows lowering as he read the caption underneath the picture. *"Misunderstood?"*

"Yeah. You know—how people think sharks are scary and grumpy and everything, but they're not. They're just being their brand ... kinda like you."

"Mm. Thank you, Evan. Thank you, James."

The seven-year-old bounced up and down on his toes, waiting as the paper was removed from the second gift.

Martin lifted the lid on the long narrow box inside, revealing a tube made of burled bubinga wood, polished to perfection.

"It's a climascope," the boy said, watching his guardian closely.

"It was Evan's idea, Martin. He said you told him the windows at the cathedral reminded you of the kaleidoscope that Joan had," Louisa said.

He swallowed and looked up at the boy. "You remembered that?"

"Yep. But this is a new kind," he explained, tapping his finger against the tube. "It gots oil in it, and those little pieces float around. It works really good, 'cause we tried it out."

Martin lifted the instrument from its packaging and put it to his eye. "It's very beautiful. Thank you."

"And it even gots a thing you can put it on when you're not using it." Evan pulled the decorative brass stand from the box and set it on the coffee table. "See, you put it on your desk."

"Hmm, I might want to find a safer place to keep it. I wouldn't want it to get broken. Maybe on the dresser behind my desk."

"So ... do ya like it?"

"I like it very much. Almost as much as the decoration for my car."

The little boy gave him a broad grin before turning his attention back to his colouring book. "Hey, this is all pictures of insides," he said as he turned the pages. "Hearts and bone mallow and everything."

"Yes, it's a Gray's Anatomy colouring book. It was one of my favourite books when I was your age. Although mine was the textbook version."

Evan looked back at him dubiously. "I think you might hafta help me 'cause I've never see'd someone's insides before."

"I'd be happy to. But you know, you don't need to know what the internal organs look like. You're going to learn that as you colour them in."

"Oh, I know. I'm just wonderin' which parts are Inchworm Green."

Chapter 36

The kitchen was alive with activity again by the time Poppy, Jeremy, and Ruth arrived at the farm.

Carole took a pair of wine glasses down from the cupboard shelf and glanced out the window. "Oh, they're here," she said.

The door to the entryway opened and Ruth stepped into the kitchen. "Happy Christmas, everyone. Season's Greetings and all that," she said dryly, slipping off her coat.

Louisa hurried over to embrace her. "Ruth! Happy Christmas!"

Glass clinked against granite as Carole hurriedly set the wine glasses down on the counter. "Here, let me help you with your coat, Ruth." Taking the garment from the elderly woman's arm, she hung it on the coat rack in the pantry.

"Happy Christmas, all," Jeremy said as he followed Poppy in the door a moment later.

Carole kissed Jeremy on the cheek before turning to his girlfriend. "And you must be Poppy. I saw you at the open house, but I didn't get a chance to introduce myself. I'm Carole Parsons ... Chris's wife. It's so nice to finally get to meet you."

"You too, Mrs. Parsons. Thanks for invitin' me to come today."

"Well, it's Martin and Louisa's do. We just came to keep Martin in line."

Jeremy peered towards the living room. "Where is Martin?"

"We chased Martin and Chris out of the kitchen a few minutes ago. I suspect you'll find them hovering around the table of starters. Go on in and join them."

"Mm, I need you to do something first, Jeremy," Louisa said as she walked over with a jar in her hand. "Can you get this lid off for me?"

The young man deposited the manila folder in his hand on top of the refrigerator before unscrewing the lid from the jar. Air hissed from the seal and the button on the top made a soft metallic ping. He held it up, inspecting the label. "Mmm, Berrio Mill—I like this honey mustard."

"So does Martin," Louisa said, taking the jar and lid from him. "I got lucky. It was the last jar on the shelf at the market the other day."

Poppy and Jeremy ventured from the kitchen and found Martin and Chris standing at the starters table, as predicted, already partaking of the offerings.

"Poppy ... Jeremy," Martin said, giving them a nod. He screwed up his face at the red and white hat perched on his assistant's head. "You look ridiculous, you know."

Jeremy gave him a grin. "Thanks, mate. That's what I was going for."

Martin blinked back at him with a furrowed brow.

"Hi'ya, Mr. Portman!" Evan said as he abandoned the structure he was building with his new blocks to join the others.

"Hi, Evan. How's your Christmas going? Did you hear any prancing little hooves on your roof last night?"

"Hooves of what?"

"You know, those reindeer that fly Father Christmas around to deliver presents."

Evan glanced over at Martin before giving a tug on Jeremy's sleeve. "Father Christmas is a fake," he whispered confidentially. "It's really a man named Ed. But it's okay if you wanna just pretend about him."

"About Ed?"

Evan let out a snort. "Course not, Mr. Portman. About *Father Christmas!*"

The aide gave him a solemn nod. "Got it."

"Evan, Jeremy and I have something for you and James," Poppy said as she handed the boy a large gift bag emblazoned with a reindeer sporting an oversized nose.

"Should I open it, or should I let James open it?"

"Oh, this one's yours. We have another one for James."

Evan set the bag on the floor and reached into it, pulling out an eighteen-inch-tall, brown, plush dog toy. He held it up in front of him, scrutinising it for a moment before a smile spread slowly across his face. "He's pretty cute."

"He's actually a puppet," Jeremy said. He crouched down, taking it from the boy and inserting his hand into the pocket in the back of its head. "Hi, Evan. My name's Wrinkles," he said as he opened and closed the dog's mouth in mock conversation.

"Is that 'cause you gots all those lines on your face?" the boy asked, sticking a finger into the folds in the plush.

"Yeah, I'm a Shar Pei."

"Oh, you're in the dog book in the library at my school." He peered up into the puppet's mouth before tentatively pinching its tongue between his thumb and forefinger.

"I can'd dalk vewy wewl wiff you 'olding my ton li tha."

Evan began to giggle and pulled the offending hand behind his back. "Sorry."

Martin's shoulders rose and fell as he watched the scene play out before turning back to the starters table to refill his plate.

The dog grabbed on to the edge of the bag with its mouth, giving it a shake. "If you look in there you'll find something else—something that pretty lady with the blonde hair over there made."

The seven-year-old reached in and pulled out a clear plastic zip bag. "What is it?"

"It's clothes ... for Wrinkles," Poppy said, opening the bag and removing several outfits, laying them out on the sofa.

"Wow, you even made him pyjamas! Thanks, Poppy!"

"You're welcome."

James crawled towards them, pushing his new tugboat along under one hand, and Poppy knelt down, tipping the second gift bag on to its side. "This is for you, James." The toddler reached into it, grabbing on to the long fuzzy mane of a lion puppet.

Evan's attention shifted quickly to the newest toy. He dropped to the floor and shoved his hand into the void in the back of the animal's head and directed his conversation to the toddler. "Hi, James. I'm a lion. You can tell that 'cause I got all the long hair around my head ... see?"

The seven-year-old brushed the tufts across the younger child's face. As the fuzzy hair tickled his nose, James pulled his head away, causing him to lose his balance and topple backwards, banging his head on the wood floor.

He let out a wail and Jeremy scooped him up, depositing him into his father's arms. He calmed quickly, and Martin pulled his handkerchief from his pocket to wipe his tears dry.

"Erm, Mart ... you might want to go check on Evan. He took off up the stairs," Chris said, taking hold of James.

Martin ran his palm over the back of his son's head a final time before turning to scale the steps.

He followed the seven-year-old's whimpers down the hall, turning into his old room. "Evan, can you come out from under the bed so I can talk to you?"

He was met with silence, broken only by the occasional ragged breath or sniffle. "Evan, James is fine. It was just a bit of a bump on the head. Come on out now."

The boy slowly wriggled out into the daylight and got to his feet. He stood with his back against the wall and an arm over his face. "I'm sorry."

"What are you sorry about?"

"I didn't mean ta do it ... ta knock James over."

"James just lost his balance. You didn't knock him over."

Evan's arm dropped to his side. Martin pulled the chair away from the desk and took a seat before waving the boy to him.

"So, you're not angry?"

"No, I'm not angry. But even if you do make me angry sometime, I won't hurt you ... touch you in that way. You don't need to hide." Martin used his now damp handkerchief to dry the boy's tears before giving him a jerk of his head. "We better get back downstairs before we miss out on any more of the Christmas celebration, don't you think?"

Evan took hold of Martin's wrist, and they headed down the hall.

Al Large's voice could be heard emanating from the kitchen as they got to the bottom of the steps. Martin groaned softly, knowing that with Al came Bert.

"All taken care of?" Chris asked, raising an eyebrow to his friend.

"I believe so." He glanced at his watch. Despite the nibbling on starters, his stomach was beginning to rumble, and the aroma filling the house had whetted his appetite.

He made his way to the kitchen and took one of his shakes from the refrigerator. "Where did Jeremy get off too?" he asked his wife.

"He and Poppy went for a walk. They'll be back in a few minutes."

"Hi'ya, Doc! Happy Christmas," Morwenna said, moving in to give him a hug.

He pulled back, eyeing her incredulously for a moment. "Mm, yes." He turned and limped back towards the living room.

"Where's your father, Al?" Ruth asked, pulling a baking sheet from the cooker before replacing it with another.

"Oh, he's comin'. He's just ... er, yep, he's comin'."

"Go on in and make yourselves comfortable," Louisa said to the young couple. "There are starters on the table and we'll be ready with the mains in just a few minutes."

"It smells incredible. Sure there's nothing I can do ta help?" Morwenna asked.

"I'm sure. We seem to exceed this kitchen's capacity for cooks with more than the three of us in here at a time. We'll call on you for clean-up, though."

"Hello, Morwenna ... Al. Good to see you again," Chris said, extending his hand when the pair entered the living room. "How's your father doing, Al?"

"Better ... yeah, lots better. Thanks for all you did for 'im that day."

"I don't know that I really did all that much. It was Martin who wouldn't give up."

Martin pulled in his chin. "I should check on the boys," he said before moving off to take a seat on the sofa.

"The doc's always been rubbish at acceptin' compliments," Al said, raising his glass of punch in Martin's direction.

A jovial burst of chuckled *ho-ho-hos* rippled through the softly playing carols and relative serenity of the room. "Happy Christmas one and all!" the plump, bearded figure exclaimed as he entered from the kitchen.

Martin turned quickly. "Oh gawd," he groaned.

Evan jumped up from the floor where he was playing with his new blocks and scrambled up next to Martin, kneeling next to him with his arms hanging over the back of the sofa.

The benevolent old man set his ratty pillowcase down on the floor and leaned over, resting his hands on his knees. "Well, hello there. Yer that Evan feller my boy's—er, my assistant's been tellin me about, eh?"

"Yeah, but you knowed that already," the seven-year-old said as his arms scissored back and forth in front of him. "I didn't know *you* were comin' today."

"Well, I wasn't plannin' on it, really. But I was in the neighbourhood, you see, and every year when I come to yer house, you're snorin' away. So, I thought to myself—why Santa, you should just stop by and say hello to that Evan lad ... meet 'im proper-like."

The boy narrowed his eyes. "We've had this discutchion before, you know."

The bewhiskered mouth pulled up like a keyhole. "I don't remember that."

"You can start forgettin' stuff when you get old, can't ya, Dr. Ellig-am?"

"Mm, yes. It's not uncommon." Martin got to his feet and walked to the window.

"Did ya come ta check on Dr. Ellig-am's fissators?"

"What's a fissa—?"

"Well, how 'bout that!" Jeremy interjected as he and Poppy came in from the kitchen. "I heard a rumour Father Christmas was here."

"Oh, this isn't Father Christmas; remember what I told ya? This is Ed."

Martin turned and furrowed his brow at the boy. "That's not Ed."

"Yes, it is."

"No. *That's* Mr. Large."

"Oh, thanks a bunch, Doc! Now you done gone and spoiled it," Bert said, ripping the hat from his head and pulling the faux beard down under his jowly chin.

"Just give 'em the gifts, Dad," Al said. "Just give 'em the gifts."

Bert pulled a package out of his make-shift Santa sack. "This one's fer you, boy," he said, handing Evan a small hold-all.

The child undid the zip and opened it up. "Wow, it's for shavin' my whiskers off! Thanks Mr. Large!"

Martin's brows pulled together as he hurried over to inspect his young charge's latest acquisition.

"Easy there, Doc. It's fake," Bert said, shaking an enthusiastic thumb in the air before reaching back into his pillowcase.

"And this one here's for young James." He handed the toddler a plastic fishing pole and a bucket of brightly coloured plastic fish. "It's for when he takes his bath, Doc."

"Mm, yes. Thank you, Bert."

The jolly man reached into his bag one last time, lifting out a jar and an envelope. "There you go, Doc. Happy Christmas," he said, handing the container to Martin. "I brought some a my soup for the big nosh up today, but this is just fer you."

He held out the envelope. "And this is from me, too. Sort'a a peace offering I guess you could say. That apology I made in hospital *was* a bit rubbish, I s'pose, an I wanna do it proper now."

Martin tipped his head back and eyed the man warily. "Go on."

"What we did to ya that day at the pub—well, what *I* did—" Bert worried his red velvet hat in his fingers. "Well, it was wrong. And I jus' wanna say—I'm sorry. I hope we can let bygones be bygones, if you know what I mean."

Martin drew in a long breath as his brows pulled together. "Yeah, I do know what you mean." He offered his hand and Bert took it as his bow mouth turned up at the corners.

"I appreciate it, Doc."

Carole, Ruth, and Louisa came in from the kitchen, setting several more bowls and platters on the table.

"I think we're ready to eat now," Carole announced.

Evan set his new shaving kit down on the coffee table and took hold of his guardian's wrist. "Come on, Dr. Elligam. You can sit by me."

Chris took a seat at one end of the table with Carole next to him. Martin set the jar on the coffee table and slipped the envelope from Bert into his shirt pocket before sitting down at the opposite end of the table. Evan climbed on to the chair to the left of him.

Louisa set James Henry's high chair between her and her husband and took a bib from the nappy bag, pulling it over her son's head. One by one, the rest of the guests filled the empty seats.

"Blimey! Our ducks look really good!" Evan said as he stood up on his chair and leaned over the table to get a closer look at the pièce de résistance, completely encircled by Carole's bacon-wrapped mini-sausages.

He reached out, and plucking a sausage from the platter, he popped it into his mouth in one piece.

"No, no, no, no, no!" Martin said, tugging at the child's shirt sleeve.

"No, no, no—no, no." James parroted from his high chair, demonstrating a clear awareness of his father's penchant for pentadic exclamations.

Martin's head snapped around. He looked wide-eyed from his son to his giggling wife before redirecting his attention to the older of the two boys.

"For goodness' sake, Evan, sit yourself back down and mind your manners."

"I was just looking at my stitchin' job. It looks pretty good, doesn't it?"

"The horizontal mattress sutures were a good choice, Mart," Chris said. "Didn't think about the shrinkage problem as the skin roasted. You and Evan had much less dehiscence in your closure than I did with my interrupted sutures."

Carole wrinkled her nose at Louisa, and Louisa returned it with a curl of her lip.

Martin straightened himself, giving his young charge a proud nod and a small smile. "Evan and I also used a deeper stitch where the wound edges were thinner ... evened out the tension, thereby limiting—"

"Oh dear, oh dear," Bert chuckled. "Listen to you, Doc. Goin' on about sewin' up our dinner like it was some poor bloke on an operatin' table. And there you were, not that long back, gettin' yerself all fussed up over a little blood in one'a *my* salads."

"That posed a serious health risk, Bert! I should have shut you down right then and—"

"Oh, for goodness' sake!" Ruth snapped. "Can we dispense with the medical repartee? I'm *hungry*."

She slapped a pair of kitchen shears down in front of her nephew. "Remove those sutures so we can eat the bloody ducks."

Al and Morwenna exchanged worried looks.

A CORNWALL CHRISTMAS 513

Jeremy got up from the table, turning the volume up on the festive tunes which had been all but obliterated by the spirited conversation. Then he returned to the table, sloshed a bit of wine into the glasses by each plate, bypassing the high chair and the seven-year-old, and lifted his own glass into the air. "Happy Christmas, everyone!"

Chapter 37

"*Hel-lo?* Anybody home?"

The nasality of the voice emanating from the kitchen alerted the dinner party to the presence of the local constable, and an instantaneous hush fell over the room.

Martin groaned and Louisa reached under the table, putting her hand on his knee. "Be nice—please," she whispered. "We're in here, Joe! Come on in!" she called out.

Giving his wife a beseeching look he hissed, "Louisa, it's *Christmas!*"

"That's right, Martin. Goodwill to men—remember?"

He groaned again as she tipped her head down, giving him the threatening smile he knew he couldn't refuse. "Yes."

The policeman appeared in the doorway with Joan's little terrier in his arms.

"Buddy!" Evan said as he slid from his chair to greet him.

Martin reached out, hooking the index finger of his left hand over the boy's collar, bringing him to a halt.

"No, no, no, no, no. Not while you're eating your dinner." He wagged a finger and wrinkled up his nose. "Penhale, take that creature out of here."

"No can do, Do-*c*. I'm afraid I found him wandering aimlessly through the streets of Portwenn this morning, looking for a meal in the rubbish bins outside the pasty shop. The law requires you to deal with this accordingly."

"Aimless wandering and rummaging through rubbish bins could hardly be considered novel behaviour for that creature. Why am I suddenly responsible for what he gets up to?"

"Because, word on the street is you have provided this—*creature*—with physical accommodation. In providing said accommodation, you have taken on legal responsibility for him, and therefore you are required to provide a safe habitat in which he will reside. The law frowns on dog owners who fail to properly care for them."

"That's *not* my dog."

Joe cocked his head and gave him a crooked grin. "Come on now, Doc. We all know about the special relationship you two have."

The doctor whipped his head to the side. "Gawd."

"You may be unaware of it, but in accordance with the Animal Welfare Act of 2006 you are required to provide said creature with, and I quote, 'a suitable diet, a suitable environment, and to ensure that said creature's needs to exhibit normal behaviour patterns are met.'"

Martin curled up his lip. "Normal behaviour patterns? Then we're back to the aimless wandering and bin rummaging, I believe. That would suggest that I *am* providing for the said creature's needs, wouldn't it?"

Joe pulled up his lower lip and tipped his head. "You got a point there, Do-*c*."

Martin glanced across the length of the table at his smirking friend and gave him a dark look.

The policeman hoisted up his tool belt and continued with his harangue. "The Animal Welfare Act of 2006 also requires you to protect him from pain, suffering, injury and disease. Is he current on his vaccinations?"

Louisa noted her husband's clenched jaw and stepped into the conversation. "To be fair, Joe, it's been less than a week since Martin and Evan built the doghouse. We haven't even had time to think about these things."

"Well, I suppose I can let it go a little longer. I have a couple of pamphlets here you might find useful, Doc. Information on responsible pet ownership—provided by our friends at the Animal Welfare Foundation," the policeman said, holding out two folded pieces of paper.

Martin snatched them from his hand. "Oh, for goodness' sake," he said, screwing up his face. "Your guide to the welfare of your pet?" He glanced at his wife in disbelief. "What makes my *pet* happy? I'm still trying to suss out what makes *you*—"

"Martin."

He laid the pamphlet down next to his plate and cleared his throat when he saw the dark look on his wife's face.

Louisa turned a tense smile towards the constable. "How 'bout you put him in an upstairs bedroom for the time being, Joe. We can figure things out later, maybe?" she said, giving the policeman an apologetic smile.

Joe gave a shrug of his shoulders and started for the stairs.

Louisa's ponytail whipped to the side as her gaze shifted abruptly towards her husband. "Martin, could I have a word with you in the kitchen?" she said as her chair legs scratched against the wood floor.

Martin cleared his throat and got to his feet, following after his wife.

"Uh-oh," he heard a small voice say behind him. "Dr. Ellig-am really did it now."

Chris tipped his head down peering up at him with a cocked head and a raised eyebrow as he walked by.

They passed through under Evan's mistletoe and Louisa whirled around, her eyes snapping. "Martin Ellingham, don't you *dare* spoil this Christmas celebration," she whispered stridently.

"Maybe I need to remind you again. That *creature*, as you call him—and Joe Penhale as well for that matter—saved"—she jabbed her finger at him and he flinched—"your"—another jab and another flinch—"life!" She jabbed, and he flinched a third time.

"Don't you think you could show them both a little kindness? Don't you think you could try to at least be civil ... hold that tongue of yours? Hmm? I mean"—she sighed—"poor Joe. He has no family around. He's all alone on a holiday that's supposed to be all about family, loving one another, and the spirit of generosity. He comes out here, *obviously* hoping for an invitation to stay for dinner by the way, and you give him a hard time."

"I'm *not* giving him a hard time!" Martin whispered back. "I just take exception to him coming into my home—Ruth's home—when we have guests, no less—accusing me of being a lawbreaker—trying to foist that little miscreant and his malefactions off on me!" he squeaked.

Louisa balled her fists at her sides as she blinked back tears. "Martin Ellingham, I've worked very hard to make this a memorable day. Evan's hardly been able to contain himself. And we're so lucky to have you still here with us to share in it. I am asking you ... please—don't—spoil it."

Air hissed from his nose and he pursed his lips before his body began to relax. He nodded. "We should get back in there."

Louisa cocked her head at him.

"I'll do my best," he said softly, brushing his fingers against her cheek.

"Thank you, Martin." She stretched up and kissed him before they returned to the table.

The jangling of Joe's toolbelt could be heard as he descended the stairs and Martin got to his feet. "Would you, er ... would you like to join us for dinner, Penhale?"

"Oh! Thanks, Doc. That's nice of you. I did have designs on a very tasty lookin' ready meal in my freezer, but I s'pose I could postpone it until tomorrow."

Jeremy got up and pulled a chair over for the policeman, and Louisa hurried to the buffet to get another place setting of china and silver.

"There you go, Joe. Have a seat," she said taking his jacket from him as he pulled it off.

"This new, Joe? It looks very nice."

"Latest official police issue as a matter of fact." He gave his fingers a snap. "That reminds me, I better get my mobile out of the pocket. Never know when a citizen will have an emergency and need to reach me."

Louisa held the coat out and the constable fished the device from the pocket.

Al pointed his fork in the air. "I been meanin' ta ask, Joe ... why weren't you answerin' yer phone the night the doc was—"

He glanced over at the seven-year-old, who sat picking at the Brussels sprouts on his plate. "You know ... the night of the storm," he said, giving a subtle nod towards the boy.

"Oh, that. Bit of an equipment malfunction, I guess you could say. You see, there was this training exercise scheduled up in Exeter, and what with a hec-tic schedule here in Portwenn and the fact that I couldn't leave the village unprotected, I was unfortunately, unable to attend."

His eyes darted around the table. "It wasn't like they had any reservations about my bein' there or anything."

"I'm sure we could have managed without you for a day, Joe," Louisa said as she added some chopped duck and some of Evan's bean bits into a plastic bowl for James. "I'm sure those training exercises are important."

"Don't wanna take any chances, Louiser. Trouble has a way of *zeroing in* on a community when it's at its most vulnerable."

The constable took a moment to take a bite of bread before continuing. "So anyways ... as you say, Louiser, those training exercises are important if I'm going to stay in top form, this one in particular. It involved the use of two of an officer's most potent deterrents to criminal activity—pepper spray and the Taser."

Martin's eyes drifted shut as he sighed heavily. "Is there a point to this, Penhale?"

"I'm gettin' to it, Doc. You see, I decided to ... re-enac-*t* the exercise on my own, just to make sure I remain current on the latest *tech*-nological advancements.

"I decided it might be best, given the tools employed, to do this particular training exercise outside. I hung my jacket on a post and I was practicing my use of the pepper spray ... improvin' my aim, you know. By the time I got done, my jacket was covered in it, naturally."

"Naturally," Martin grumbled, earning him another dark look from his wife.

"I don't get it. Why didya hang your jacket on the post?" Morwenna asked as she reached for the bowl of roasted potatoes.

"Well, I couldn't very well be sprayin' it with pepper spray while I was wearin' it, now could I? I'm not *that* stupid."

"No. I mean, why didn't you just spray the post? Might have been more of a challenge ... smaller target ta hit and all." The receptionist's bracelets clacked against the bowl as she set it down.

Joe let out a derisive snort. "You seem to be missing the bigger picture, Morwenna. An officer of the law has to be in the game, both physically *and* mentally.

"I'd be of no use to you if you were bein' mugged, and I froze because I couldn't force myself to shoot anything other than a fencepost, eh? I need that mental image to be able to act appropriately."

"So as long as she's mugged by a fencepost wearin' a police issue jacket, you've got her back ... that what yer sayin', Joe?" Al said with a grin.

Louisa glared at the young man, and he squirmed in his chair, redirecting his attention to his plate.

"That still don't explain why you weren't answerin' yer phone, though," Bert said as he speared a forkful of green beans.

"I'm gettin' to it, Bert. So anyways, I emptied my can of pepper spray and moved on to the Taser exercise."

The policeman picked up the peppermill from the middle of the table and gripped it between both hands as he pointed it at Poppy, narrowing his eyes.

"I focused on my target—slowed my breathing—and pulled the trigger. My jacket *burst* into flames."

Joe shrugged his shoulders. "It seems tasering a suspect who's been pepper sprayed can have ... *undesirable* consequences. Let's just say my mobile, which happened to be in my jacket pocket, became collateral damage."

"Gawd!" Martin muttered, jabbing at another slice of duck.

"Martin, shush!" Louisa whispered.

Chris passed his bowl to Carole. "Could you get me some more of that soup that Bert brought?"

"Sure, how much?"

"Fill it on up. That's some crackin' good soup, Bert," Chris said.

Martin and Louisa exchanged knowing glances as Carole passed her husband his brim-full bowl.

"It is mighty good, taint it?" the portly man said. "You might wanna go easy on that though, Doc. It can have a—whatcha call it—an *amnesiac* effect."

"You mean aphrodisiac effect I think, Bert," Jeremy said.

"What's that mean?" Evan asked, sitting up taller in his chair.

"It means if you eat too much of that soup you forget to eat your vegetables," Martin said, poking his fork at the untouched Brussels sprouts on the child's plate.

"No, it don't, Doc," Bert said. "I'm surprised you never heard of this one before, what with you bein' a doctor an' all." He turned to Chris. "It gives a bloke a good stiff—"

"*Bert!*" Martin erupted. "Act appropriately ... please!"

"I was just explainin' about the stiff jolt of energy that soup can pack is all, Doc," he said, pulling in his chin and donning his most aggrieved expression.

Louisa sucked in an audible breath. "Chris and Carole, did you enjoy your time here at the farm last night?"

"We did," Carole said. "We had a nice romantic walk in the moonlight. The stars were shining, the air was calm, and it was warm for a Christmas Eve in Cornwall, wasn't it?"

Louisa nodded. "It *was* a lovely night."

"That's a good thing, huh, Old Doc—it bein' warm? You didn't hafta worry so much about it gettin' cold in the house 'cause of the thin walls—like the last time you were here. And no one was around ta snicker at ya either."

Carole froze as a flush spread across her face, and Chris tugged at his collar.

"We had a very enjoyable evening. Yes, we did," the doctor said before gulping down his half-full glass of Pinot Grigio.

"And with the moon you probably didn't even need that flashlight when you dragged Mrs. Parsons to the bedroom."

Carole shrank into her chair as a whispered *"Christopher!"* hissed from the corner of her mouth.

The light danced in Martin's eyes as he looked down the table at his friend. "He gots really good ears," he said, a hint of schadenfreude detectable in his tone.

"Can I have some more Bethel ham, Dr. Ellig-am?" Evan asked.

The creases in Martin's forehead deepened as he looked down at the boy. "What's bethel ham?"

"*That's* a bethel ham," he answered, poking his fork at the platter just out of reach.

"That just a ham."

"Uh-uh. Not at Christmas. I read all about this when me and James went to the school with Mrs. Ellig-am.

"They gots a book in the library about when the baby Saviour's mum and dad had ta go away 'cause they didn't pay their taxes. When they finally got to a hotel, they counted out all their money, but they didn't have enough left. So, they found a farmer with a barn and gave him a Bethel ham and he let them stay there."

He jabbed his fork at the platter of meat in front of him again. "So, you see, *that's* why we eat Bethel ham at the Christmas Feast." He flashed his guardian a proud grin. "Can I have some more?"

"*May* I have some more." Martin picked up the boy's plate and shifted all but one of the Brussels sprouts to his own plate. "Eat that," he said, setting the lone sprout back down in front of him. "Then I'll get you some more ham."

Evan's chin dropped to his chest before he reluctantly nibbled a leaf from the vegetable, gagging once before washing it down with a gulp of milk. He flopped back in his chair, crossing his arms in front of him. "Are you sure you're really s'posed ta *eat* 'em?"

"Yes. And they're rich in the vitamins and fibre that our bodies need if we want to remain healthy."

Martin looked over at Bert's plate, raising an eyebrow. "Look at all the vegetables that Mr. Large is eating. He's supposed to be eating healthier, and I'm pleased to see he's doing a proper job of it today."

The seven-year-old eyed the restaurateur, his gaze settling on his round belly. "Dr. Ellig-am, how do babies get in their mum's stomachs?"

Martin cleared his throat and reached for his water glass. "Maybe we could discuss it another time, Evan. It wouldn't make for proper mealtime conversation."

Chris pushed his plate forward and leaned his forearms on the table. "I'd be very interested in your answer, Mart."

Evan wiggled a finger at Al. "The skinny Mr. Large is probably interested, too. I asked him before, but he didn't know. He said I should ask you."

"Oh, *did* he?" Martin sneered as he shot daggers at the young man.

Al's eyes darted back to his plate as he felt himself under the doctor's scrutiny.

"I'm a little fuzzy on the matter myself, Doc," Joe said, giving Martin a guileless grin.

"Oh, for heaven's sake! If any of you are in need of a refresher course, be in my consulting room at five o'clock. I'll bring you all up to speed on where babies come from. But right now, if you don't mind...I'd *like* to eat my dinner."

The puds were being served by the time Evan had managed to choke down his solitary Brussels sprout. He was looking rather green about the gills, prompting Martin to make another trip to the Lexus to retrieve his medical bag.

"Any pain in your abdomen ... nausea?" the doctor asked as he examined his young patient.

"I don't think so. But my stomach is squirming. I *told* ya ... it was that Brussels sprout. I think it was poisonous," Evan said as he sat on the kitchen counter. He sputtered and his tongue protruded from his mouth like a cat attempting to hack up a hairball.

Martin screwed up his face. "It wasn't poisonous."

"It sure *tasted* poisonous. Can I have my bethel ham now?" the child asked, swallowing hard and giving a shudder.

"Not until I'm sure you're not coming down with something."

Martin inserted a digital thermometer into the boy's ear as he pressed the backs of his fingers to his forehead. The instrument beeped. "Well, you're not febrile."

"I keep tellin' ya, Dr. Ellig-am, I just gots sprout bits in my teeth. It tastes icky." The boy coughed again.

"Nonsense," Martin mumbled. He hoisted the child to the floor and snapped his bag shut. "Okay, I promised you ham," he said, herding him back to the dining table with a wave of his hand.

Louisa looked at her husband worriedly as he sat back down in his chair. "Is he all right?"

"Mm, yes. His Brussels sprout was toxic, it seems."

An amused grin spread across Louisa's face.

Martin speared a slice of ham and dropped it on to the seven-year-old's plate before proceeding to cut it into bite-sized pieces.

He grimaced and dropped the knife as a jolt of nerve pain shot through his hand and arm. The knife hit the wood floor, sending a clear metallic ping pealing through the air. The utensil skittered across the floor, coming to a stop under James Henry's high chair.

Martin and Louisa bent down simultaneously, their hands touching as they reached to pick it up. Their eyes locked, and she stretched forward, pressing her lips to his.

Evan giggled. "They're kissin' again."

Martin pulled his head up sharply, colliding with the underside of the high chair tray. "Ow!" he yelped. A conspicuous flush spread up his neck as he straightened himself.

Chris grinned at him and shifted in his chair, pulling an arm up on the back rest. "You okay, Mart?"

"I'm fine." He cleared his throat and tugged at a reddened ear.

It was the middle of the afternoon before the puds had been consumed and the dishes washed. Bert tired easily, and Al and Morwenna took him home as soon as the last pot had been washed and dried.

Joe Penhale lingered for what, to Martin, seemed an interminable amount of time. But around three o'clock he made his apologies for breaking up the party before speeding off in his Land Rover to apprehend a suspect who was, allegedly, peddling his wares door to door in the village.

As soon as he had polished off the last of his Bethel ham and finished his puds, Evan pulled Martin aside and sat him down on the sofa before running to the refrigerator to retrieve a small sealed plastic container.

He enthusiastically ripped the lid from the bowl and set the container down on the coffee table in front of his guardian. Picking up his new colouring book, he wriggled himself under Martin's armpit.

"Can you read to me about my duck guts?" he asked as he dropped the book into Martin's lap.

Martin glanced quickly at the blood-rich giblets, swallowing back the saliva that filled his mouth.

The vital organs were under constant scrutiny from the seven-year-old as Martin read to him about the function of the heart and the liver.

"Ooh, brill," Jeremy said as he peered over Martin's shoulder.

Evan flipped the book shut and held it up over his head. "Yeah. And see ... it's like the one Dr. Ellig-am liked when he was a kid. 'Cept this one it's okay ta colour in."

"Yep, like I said ... pretty cool." The aide came around to the other side of the sofa.

"Where is everybody?" Martin asked, glancing behind him.

"They went to walk off some of those Christmas Feast calories." He fidgeted. "I, er ... I have something for you," he said, handing him a manila envelope.

Martin furrowed his brow as he turned the package over in his hands, and then pulled open the flap and slid out the contents. "Where did you get this?" he asked incredulously.

"An online site." The young man tipped his head down as he tried to read his friend's confused expression. "Don't you like it?"

Martin stood up, crinkling an eye. "This was supposed to be for *you*."

The aide snatched the papers and the envelope back. "Oh, bugger. *This* isn't mine!"

"Obviously. But now that I've opened it, I guess you may as well have it."

Jeremy stared at the papers and shook his head. "I don't understand. It's a letter of recommendation for medical school?"

"Mm. Three letters actually. One from Chris, one from Ed Christianson, and one from me.

"I heard from Robert Dashwood, my old tutor and a former colleague, last week. You're under no obligation of course, and you would, obviously, need to apply—jump through all the necessary hoops, so to speak. But if you're still interested, you have a place at Imperial College's School of Medicine next fall term."

Jeremy stood silently for several moments before responding. "Wow. I certainly didn't expect this," he said softly.

"I realise finances could be an issue, but I've managed to secure several scholarships for you. You would of course need to make up the difference, but with the bonus I gave you, I think it's doable."

The young man took a step forward and wrapped his arms around Martin in a bear hug.

Martin tensed, trying unsuccessfully to stifle a groan, and Jeremy pulled back quickly. "Sorry ... sorry," He gave his patient a quick visual inspection before wiping at his eyes. "You have no idea how much this means, Martin. You having this much confidence in me."

"Mm. Well you're very capable of doing this—doing it well. But again, you're under no obligation. Give it some thought, then let them know." Martin pulled in his chin and wagged his finger at the papers. "There's something else in there."

Jeremy leafed through the recommendation letters, pulling out a sheet with a prominent letterhead. "Crikey! You got the article I've been working on in the *BMJ!*"

"I submitted it ... yes. I thought it was worthy. It won't come out until the February issue though."

The aide stared at his boss, wide-eyed. "I just don't know what to say."

"Thank you is usually appropriate at a time like this."

"Well, yeah! Of course! Thank you, Martin."

Martin blew out a breath. "Well, I'm glad we got that sorted without any histrionic outbursts."

Jeremy put his hand up in front of him. "Wait right here. I do actually have something for you."

He hurried off towards the kitchen, returning seconds later with another manila envelope. "I'm almost positive I have the right one this time," he said, holding it out to his boss.

Pulling up the second flap, Martin slid a periodical from its sleeve. *The Journal of The American Medical Association?* February 25, 1939?"

"Check out page seven twenty-nine," the aide said with a nervous smile.

Martin flipped through the pages, opening to an article titled, Surgical Ligation Of A Patent Ductus Arteriosus: Report of first successful case. Authored by, Robert E. Gross, M.D.; Henry E. Ellingham, M.B., B.S., F.R.C.S.

It was Martin's turn to be at a loss for words. He passed his fingers across the page, a tangible connection to his grandfather in his hands. Sucking in a ragged breath he turned and limped from the room.

The aide put his hand on Evan's head. "I'll be back. You stay right there, got it?"

The seven-year-old glanced up from his book. "Got it," he said, giving him a wave of his hand before returning his attention to the internal organs displayed before him.

Jeremy found Martin leaning against the house, just outside the entryway. "You okay, mate?" he asked.

Martin inhaled deeply. "Yeah. I just needed some air."

The young man leaned back next to him. "Ah, nothing feels quite as nice as the warmth of the sun on your skin in the dead of winter, does it?"

The doctor's head snapped to the side as visions of his wife danced in his head. He narrowed his eyes at his aide.

The young man shook his head. *"What?"*

Martin averted his eyes. "Nothing ... nothing." He tapped his fingers against the periodical before looking at the young man askance. "You really think that, do you?"

Jeremy's brow lowered as he studied his friend's face for a few moments. "Ah, I get it. The melanoma risk ... that what you're getting at?"

"No! Of course not! It just that the feel of the sun on my skin is not at the top of my list for—" Martin cleared his throat, suddenly feeling more *normal* than he ever had before.

He raised the journal up. "This is a wonderful gift. Thank you."

Jeremy let out a whistle. "That's a relief. I thought I'd bollocksed it up for sure."

"Mm. Not at all. This is very special. And...you remembered our conversation about my grandfather and the American surgeon."

"Yeah, it was a compelling story." The young man tapped his finger on a fixator on Martin's arm. "Come on, let's go back in before you freeze your bones."

Chapter 38

The Lexus moved back through the dips in the farm lane as the Ellingham family headed out late Christmas afternoon.

Martin craned his neck, looking into the rear-view mirror at Buddy's shoe button eyes staring back at him, and a perplexing heaviness settled in his stomach with the growing realisation that he may be forced to accept the animal as a member of the family.

"You okay?" Louisa asked as she rested her hand on his thigh.

He swallowed back the lump that had worked its way into his throat. "Mm, I'm fine."

"Hmm." She tipped her head down and peered up at him, and his gaze darted towards her before refocusing on the deserted tarmac road abutting the little lane. He made a right-hand turn towards Portwenn.

"Looks like rain moving in, doesn't it," Louisa said as they came over a rise and the horizon opened up in front of them.

"Mm. The Met Office is forecasting a series of storms to move ashore over the course of the next couple of weeks."

As they descended Church Hill, haze veiled the little village, and a wall of dark clouds rolled northeast over the Atlantic waters. By the time they pulled into the parking space next to the surgery, the wind was picking up, and a heavy mist had begun to fall.

A CORNWALL CHRISTMAS 531

Martin turned off the engine and unlocked the doors. "We need you to help carry things in, Evan," he said, heading off the seven-year-old's certain hasty departure into the house.

"Sure, I'm good at helpin'," he said as his door swung open. Buddy scampered across his lap and on to the wet pavement before racing to the back of the building, his plumed tail flaring out behind him.

Walking around to the boot, Martin pulled out two plastic bags, slipping the handles over his charge's hands. The child grunted theatrically as he plodded off around the side of the house.

"Brrr, that wind is getting cold!" Louisa said, hoisting her son higher on her hip. "Sure you can handle that?" she asked as she eyed her husband. "You don't want to take a tumble on the—"

"I'm not an invalid, Louisa," he snapped back. He balanced Evan's new electric train set on the Lexus, wincing as he positioned it under his arm before limping off across the slate path.

"Here, let me help," his wife said as she pushed the kitchen door open. Martin gave the little terrier, curled up inside his doghouse, a sideways glance as he passed by.

Slipping James into his high chair, Louisa set the bag down on the table. "Oh, Martin, you're soaked. Go get out of those wet clothes before you catch your death," she said as she spread her coat out over the back of a chair to dry.

Air hissed from his nose as he pulled his son's knit cap from his head. "There's more to bring in." Taking his handkerchief from his pocket, he dabbed moisture from the boy's face.

"I think the rest can wait until later, don't you? Wait until the rain has stopped?"

Martin headed towards the door. "It's supposed to continue for several days. I may as well bring everything in now," he said, quickly slipping outside.

"Oh, *Martin!*" Louisa muttered under her breath.

Evan stood in the lounge, his fingers working nervously up and down the plastic sleeve containing his new airplane. "I can help 'im, Mrs. Ellig-am," he said softly.

Louisa gave the child a weary smile. "That's very sweet, Evan. I would appreciate that."

The seven-year-old pulled himself to his full three foot, ten-inch height and gave her a proud grin. "And I'll make sure he doesn't catch his death, too. You don't gots ta worry." He laid his airplane on the coffee table and ran to get his coat before dashing out the door.

By the time Martin and Evan had all the gifts carried into the cottage and Martin had changed into dry clothes, Louisa had an assortment of leftovers from the Christmas Feast set out on the table.

Evan watched closely as his guardian slathered orange-cranberry relish over a slice of crusty bread before laying down a thick layer of duck meat on top of it.

"Are you sure yer s'posed ta eat it like that?" the boy asked, wrinkling up his nose.

Martin capped off his sandwich with another slice of bread. "It's actually a favourite of mine," he said, pressing it down with his palm. "The cook at my boarding school always roasted a turkey for the students who didn't go home over the holidays."

"So how come you put the cranberries on there? The cook made that, too?"

"Mm, yes. And when she served up the leftover turkey on bread for supper I thought it was too dry. So, I added the relish."

The child reached for two slices of bread and followed suit. He took a wary bite, his jaws working several times as a cranberry-laced grin spread across his face. "Wow, yer even smart at sandwiches, Dr. Ellig-am!"

Louisa nudged her husband with her foot and shot him a coy smile from the opposite side of the table. "All those years at boarding school paid off after all, hmm?"

"I would think my readiness for the rigors of medical school would be more convincing evidence of the efficacy of public school than the ability to make a decent sandwich, Louisa."

"It was a joke, Martin."

He pulled in his chin. "I see," he said, returning his attention to his dinner.

A gust of wind caused the old stone cottage to groan, and Evan shot his guardian a worried look.

"It's fine," Martin said. "This building's been here for over a hundred years."

The boy settled back into his chair and resumed the eating of his sandwich.

"Well, Evan, I would say our Christmas Feast was a brilliant success, wouldn't you?" Louisa said, scooping another spoonful of peas into her son's bowl.

"Yeah, and the food was really good, too. Well ... most of it." The boy took a swig of milk before whirling his head towards Martin, his eyes wide. "Oh no! We forgot Mr. Moysey's fruit—"

"Evan! For goodness' sake, don't talk with your mouth full!" Martin barked as he wiped a spray of macerated sandwich and milk from his shirtsleeve.

The boy gulped. "But, this is important! We forgot all about Mr. Moysey," he said, teary-eyed.

Looking at his watch, Martin sighed. "Finish your dinner and I'll walk you over there."

"Martin, I don't think you—" Louisa was stopped in mid-sentence by her husband's annoyed glance. She tipped her head down and peered up at him. "You'll be careful? And bring your mobile?"

The creases in the doctor's brow evaporated as he studied his wife's worried face. "Yes." His shoulders rose and fell as he pulled in a breath. "I'll be careful."

The rain had stopped by the time Evan and Martin headed down Roscarrock Hill, but the waves being pushed ashore by the cold wind had forced more than the usual number of fishing boats into the harbour, seeking sanctuary from the churning Atlantic waters.

Evan gripped tightly to the plastic bag holding the fruitcake with one hand and grasped on to Martin's wrist with the other. "Have you ever been on a boat, Dr. Elligam?" he asked.

"Yes, a few times." The doctor stopped and flipped the boy's hood up over his head.

"What's it like? Kinda like sittin' in a tree when the wind's blowin' it around?"

"I've never been in a swaying tree, so I couldn't say one way or the other."

"But just *pretend* then." Evan released his hold on his guardian and leapt into a puddle, sending a spray of dirty water in all directions and just shy of the doctor's shoes.

"Careful! Careful!"

The seven-year-old spun around. "Oh, don't worry. I got my balance really good before I jumped. I wasn't gonna fall."

"That's not what I was worried about."

Evan reclaimed Martin's wrist. "So ... *pretend*, Dr. Elligam."

"Pretending's not an efficient use of my time."

Even with a limp, Martin's long stride tugged the boy forward, and he took several skipping steps to keep up. "Does that mean you don't gots enough of it?"

Martin stopped and looked down at the child's face, illuminated by the light at the bottom of Dolphin Street. "Enough what?"

"Time. Don't you gots enough of it, or why don't you pretend?"

"I'm a bit old to start pretending."

"You mean you haven't even *started* yet?" the child said, slapping a hand to his forehead.

Martin gestured as he started up the path. "Come on, it's getting late. We better get that cake to Mr. Moysey or we'll be waking him up."

Evan sprinted over the cobblestones and up the steps and then rapped his small knuckles against the door.

The lock rattled from the inside before the latch clicked. "What do *you* want?" Mr. Moysey growled as he glared down at him.

The boy spun around, looking for his guardian, and Martin stepped up behind him, putting his hand on his shoulder. "Go ahead and tell him why you're here, Evan."

He backed himself up against the doctor's legs. "I brought you somethin' for Christmas."

The old man gave a grunt. "Well, I suppose you can come in, then."

They stepped into the soft glow of the cottage. "I made you somethin', Mr. Moysey," the boy said, holding out the bag. "Yer one'a the things on my list, so I came to spread you with some Christmas cheer."

Mr. Moysey took the bag and reached in, pulling out a festively wrapped loaf. He tore the paper off and stared down at the unexpected gift. "Eleanor, my wife, used to make me one of these every year," he said, tears welling in his eyes. "She didn't like fruitcake, but it was a favourite of mine, so—"

Pulling his hands behind his back, Evan bounced on his toes. "So, does that mean you like it?"

"Hmph. Yes—I like it." He scratched at his scraggly beard and screwed up his mouth before finally managing a small smile. "Thank you."

"Mrs. Ellig-am did all the sharp knife stuff, but I did the measurin' and stirrin'."

Martin stepped towards the fireplace. "How's the clock working? Keeping time alright?" he asked.

"Yes. Yes, just like new actually. Thanks to all the diddling around you do with clocks—and the help you gave me."

Mr. Moysey picked a stack of old newspapers up from the seat of a chair and motioned to the doctor. "You may as well sit down."

"Mm. We can't stay long. The boy needs to be getting off to bed soon."

The man's shoulders fell. "Oh. I see."

Martin glanced over at Evan and then dropped into the chair. "Maybe we could stay for a few minutes."

The child gazed about the room at the stacks of boxes and periodicals. "Are you shiftless, Mr. Moysey?"

The old man jutted out his chin. "Of course not! And I resent the accusation, young man!"

Taking a step to the side, Evan put his hand on Martin's thigh. "Was I bein' 'fensive?" he whispered.

"I believe Mr. Moysey may have found your remark to be unwarranted ... yes," Martin said, tipping his head to the side as he scratched at an eyebrow. "Perhaps you should apologise."

"Sorry you got shirty," the seven-year-old said, scuffing a trainer on the floor. "Maybe you just don't like takin' the trash out. My mum says my dad's shiftless, 'cause he doesn't ta—" He leaned in against his guardian and his hand slid up to pat the boy's back.

"You want me ta move your newspapers away from the fireplace, Mr. Moysey?" the boy asked hesitantly, stepping towards the hearth.

The old man gave him an icy stare.

"It's just 'cause I don't want ya gettin' hurt if you make a fire. Miss Soames teached us about safety at school and yer not s'posed to put—"

"It doesn't matter. I don't use the fireplace," he responded gruffly. "There must be something blocking the flue...makes a bad smell in here."

"Maybe it's seagulls. I could come over and help ya get 'em outta there."

"What would *seagulls* be doing in my chimney?"

Evan gave a shrug of his shoulders and glanced over at Martin.

"Perhaps Father Christmas got himself stuck in there. That would explain his failure to show up at your house every year," Martin said.

Evan began to giggle, and the old man's grim face relaxed into something resembling a smile. He went to a built-in glass doored cabinet, pulling out two tumblers and a bottle, sloshing liquid into each of the glasses. "Here you go, doctor," he said, holding one out to Martin.

Martin put his hand up in front of him. "No, thank you. I don't drink."

"What d'you *mean* you don't drink?"

"Oh, that doesn't mean he doesn't drink anything. It just means he doesn't drink the stuff that gives you angry eyes," the child explained.

"Hmph. I just thought a toast might be appropriate is all."

Martin hesitated and then reached a hand out for the glass. "Happy Christmas, Mr. Moysey," he said, clinking it against the old man's before putting it to his mouth and tipping his head back.

"I think we better be getting home before Mrs. Ellingham sends out a search party." He set the glass on a side table and got to his feet.

Evan followed him to the door. "Happy Christmas, Mr. Moysey."

"Happy Christmas to you, too. And ... thank you for the fruitcake."

The seven-year-old watched his guardian warily as they made their way down the cobblestones to Middle Street. "Dr. Ellig-am, why did you drink that stuff?" he finally asked.

"I was just trying to be polite."

"How come you decided ta be polite to Mr. Moysey? You never bother with bein' polite to anybody else."

Martin stopped and looked down at him. "I'm polite!"

The boy took a seat on a bench parked outside the Slipway and rolled his eyes up at his guardian. "That's *not* what Lydia Bigelow's mum says."

"Let me guess. You got that from Lydia Bigelow herself."

"Yeah. Her mum says you're a rude bugger."

"Well, I assure you, I don't *try* to be rude."

"You mean it just comes out of your mouth that way?"

"Noo. I mean, I say what I think." He dropped on to the bench, next to the child. "I don't have a predisposition toward the convenient lie."

The seven-year-old screwed up his mouth and nodded his head. "I think that must be what happens when *I'm* bein' 'fensive."

"Mm. Quite possibly."

Evan's gaze shifted to the boats illuminated in the harbour, and he sighed heavily. "Maybe you should just pretend."

"Pretend what?"

"Pretend ta be nice."

"It's no good acting nice. You have to want to."

"*Why?*"

"*Mm, I know!* It doesn't make a lot of sense to me either. But Mrs. Ellingham seems to feel it's necessary."

The boy shifted, putting space between them. "Are you gettin' shirty 'cause you drank that stuff with Mr. Moysey?" he asked softly.

"I'm not getting shirty. And I didn't really drink it. I was just ... pretending."

"Huh. You pretended that pretty good!" Evan stood up on the bench and moved in close, slinging an arm around Martin's shoulders. "Close yer eyes, and I'll teach ya how to pretend yer in a tree."

"Evan, I don't think—"

A small hand was slapped across his eyes. "Just do it, Dr. Ellig-am. It'll be fun!"

Air hissed from the doctor's nose. "I hope you washed recently."

Evan pulled his arm up and spit on his hand before wiping it on his trousers. "There, now it's clean," he said, returning it to its previous position.

"*Gawd.*"

"Now, you just gotta think about the air comin' in and out of ya. Can you feel it?"

"Of course, I can."

"Can you feel how the air pushes you around on the bench a little ... like yer sittin' in a tree when the wind's blowing?"

Martin cleared his throat. "We should be getting ho—"

"Shush, this is important." The boy pressed his hand more tightly to his guardian's face. "Think about how you feel all move-y when the air goes in and out, and pretend yer sittin' in a tree. Can ya see the leaves wigglin' around?"

"No."

"Can ya see any birds?"

"No."

The child's hand fell away from Martin's eyes, and he flapped the arm in the air. "Well, what *can* ya see then?"

"Nothing. My eyes are closed."

"Dr. Ellig-am, you're not even *tryin'!*" He sat down and jammed his elbows into his thighs, dropping his chin into his hands.

Martin threw his head back and took in a deep breath. "All right, all right. Give me another chance."

Evan gave him a sideways glance before getting back to his feet. He repeated the previous procedure again, with only slightly less enthusiasm.

"Now *this* is the part that's hard for you 'cause you still need ta learn about pretending. Try ta make a picture in yer head of leaves wigglin' and birds hoppin' around on the branches."

Martin breathed out a resigned sigh as he struggled to conjure up pastoral images while the child's saliva-bathed hand pressed against his face.

Gradually, a forgotten childhood memory eased back into his thoughts; lying on the ground under the tall shade tree that used to stand near Auntie Joan's house; watching the squirrels as they jumped from branch to branch; imagining himself high in the tree where his parents couldn't find him, couldn't reach him to take him away from Joan and Phil.

His body relaxed and he nodded off for a moment before the sudden drop of his head and a cold blast of wind returned him to consciousness.

Evan pulled his hand away as he leaned over and peered at him. "Are you done yet?"

"I believe so," he said after clearing his throat."

"What did ya see?"

"You told me to see leaves and birds, so that's what I saw. And ... squirrels."

"Squirrels is really good, Dr. Ellig-am. They're funny."

The boy gave him a penetrating stare. "So...is it?"

"So is it what?"

"Is it like bein' on a boat?"

Martin gave his head a small shake. "Yes. Yes, I suppose it is." He got to his feet. "Come on, we better get on home."

Evan leapt from the bench and grasped on to his guardian's wrist before they ducked their heads into the mist which had begun to fall again.

Chapter 39

Louisa gave James Henry a final kiss and laid him in his cot before heading back downstairs. Picking at a fingernail, she peered out the window in the lounge, breathing a relieved sigh when Martin and Evan appeared coming up the hill.

Hurrying to the kitchen, she busied herself at the sink.

"Hi, Mrs. Ellig-am!" Evan said as the back door swung open. He flipped his coat over a peg on the wall and dropped to the floor to pull his trainers from his feet.

Louisa shut off the water and gave him a smile. "Well, I was about to send a search party out after you two."

"Huh! That's just what Dr. Ellig-am said you were gonna do."

Martin's eyes followed his wife's atypically tidy actions as she feigned composure, wiping her hands on the tea towel before folding it neatly in half and hanging it over the hook on the end of the counter.

He tipped his head to the side and tugged at his ear. "Erm, Mr. Moysey asked us to stay for a bit and I didn't want—erm, I thought I should— Well, I *am* his doctor. I thought I should ... observe him for a while. And I *did* have my mobile with me. If you were concerned you could have—"

"It's fine, Martin." Her arms coiled snugly around his waist as she laid her head against his chest.

Noticing his young charge's eyes on them, he took a step back. "Where's James?" he asked as he peered into the lounge.

"Bed."

"Bed?" He pulled up his arm and fidgeted with his watch. "It's a bit early, don't you think?"

"He was absolutely knackered, Martin. It was a big day for him."

"Mm, I see."

"Problem?" she asked, cocking her head at him.

"No ... no."

His gaze flitted towards the pile of toys the two boys had received as gifts, causing an involuntary smile to creep across his wife's face as she noted his wistful expression.

"Evan, would you like to play for a while before you need to go up to bed? Maybe Dr. Ellingham could help you pick a new toy to try out?" she said, tipping her head down and peering up at her husband.

The seven-year-old jumped down the step into the lounge and hurried to examine the collection. "We can play with something *together*, Dr. Ellig-am! You can choose."

Martin rubbed a hand over the back of his neck as the colour rose in his cheeks. "We don't have a lot of time. Why don't we open up your new train set ... just take a look."

Evan's brow furrowed as he ran a finger along the box before hoisting it up with a grunt and carrying it to the kitchen table. Martin took a seat, and the child pulled out the chair next to him.

"Made you a cup of tea," Louisa said, setting it down as she leaned over him to inspect the scene on the lid.

"Mm, thank you." Martin's gaze was drawn to the hint of cleavage exposed when his wife bent over him, and he cleared his throat self-consciously.

"I'll just leave you to it then. I'm going to go upstairs and tuck in under the covers...read for a bit." She stroked her palm against his cheek before whispering in his ear, "Don't come to bed too tired, hmm."

His eyes rolled towards his young charge whose attention was riveted on them. "Yes. I'll be along in a bit."

Evan watched her as she disappeared around the corner and then turned to his guardian. "Do you like Mrs. Ellig-am?"

"Of course, I like her. I married her, didn't I?"

"Yeah. But sometimes people who *don't* like each other get married. Maybe you *thought* you liked her when you married her, and then you changed your mind."

"I don't change my mind." He lifted the cover from the box, revealing an array of tiny parts. Picking up a small engine, he turned it over in his hands. "We'll need to pick up a sheet of plywood ... build a train table to lay the track out on."

"Do you think she likes you?"

"Mrs. Ellingham?"

"Yeah. I mean she kisses ya and everything, but how can you tell if she really likes you ... for real?"

Martin squinted his eyes at the boy. "What is it you want to know, Evan?"

"Mrs. Ellig-am likes James, doesn't she?"

"Yes. He's her son, so of course she li—" He pressed his fingers to his eyes and then set the little engine back down in the box. "Yes, she likes James very much."

The child pulled his feet under him and got up on his knees, leaning over to pluck a level crossing sign from its plastic compartment. "How can you *tell* she likes him very much?"

Martin leaned back in his chair and studied the boy. "Well, she takes care of him and wants to do what she thinks is best for him. She makes sure he's eating an optimally nutritious diet, keeps him clean and warm—safe."

"Yeah, but she does those things for all the kids at school, too. How can you tell that she thinks James is special? Or that *you're* special?"

"There's not *a* sign that says one person is special to another. It's not as obvious as that piece of plastic in your hand."

Evan narrowed his eyes at the crossing indicator and set it back in the box.

Martin hissed out a breath. "I suppose the fact that she tolerates the twenty things about me that are crap could be taken as an indication that she likes me."

"You got *twenty* crap things?"

"According to Mrs. Ellingham, yes."

The boy gave him a blank stare, and Martin screwed up his face. "Well, it stands to reason that she must like me if she puts up with all my less desirable qualities, don't you think?"

A glimmer of recognition registered in the child's eyes, and he gave his guardian a broad smile. "I think I get it now, Dr. Ellig-am. You're a good explainer."

"Good. I'm glad we got that sorted."

"But ... what are your crap things?"

Martin's elbow thunked against the table and his head dropped into his hand. He straightened himself and looked at the boy. "To start with, I'm gruff, monosyllabic, and rude."

Evan nodded his head. "Yeah, that's true. But what's manasyballic?"

"That means she thinks I don't talk enough."

"Huh. Wonder why she thinks that?"

"Mm, I know!"

"That's only three things. You gots"—the child's eyes rolled towards the ceiling as he worked his tongue in his cheek—"you got *lots* more crap things ta go. Name some more."

"Oh, good grief, Evan!"

He hissed air through his nose and screwed up his face. "I don't know—I'm not Mr. Hearts and Flowers. I make decisions without asking her first. I'm not good in social situations—insult people and don't use unnecessary societally prescribed manners. I eat fish all the time. And I lecture too much about eating unhealthy foods and the idiocy of alcohol consumption."

"That's still only eight things."

"Well, you're just going to have to figure out the remaining twelve on your own."

The boy wrinkled his brow. "What's those manners you don't do?"

The doctor huffed out a breath. "I fail to say please and thank you."

"*Ohhh.*"

The subject of the doctor's imperfections was dropped and he and Evan spent the next half hour examining the myriad of small parts in front of them.

Martin glanced over at the clock on the mantel. "We better get you off to bed, or you won't have any energy for working on this tomorrow," he said.

The boy slipped from the chair and ran to the lounge, gathering up his dog puppet and beluga whale. He looked over the pile of gifts he had received and picked up the airplane kit. "Maybe we'll play with one of my real presents tomorrow instead." Laying it back down, he dashed off up the stairs.

Thunder had begun to rumble by the time Martin joined Evan in the nursery, and flashes of lightning cast momentary shadows on the walls and ceiling. The seven-year-old glanced nervously towards the eerie contours as they appeared to loom over his bed, propelling him ever closer to his guardian sitting next to him.

Martin closed up the book of tales he had been reading from and set it on the bedside table. "Evan, I was wondering ... what did you mean when you said that you were going to pretend the presents you received were yours?"

The little boy sighed and patted his guardian's hand. "That means that you just imagine something that's not for real, remember? We practiced this earlier, you know."

"I know what pretend *means*. I'm wondering why you feel the need to pretend your gifts are real ... to pretend they're yours. They were given to you; they *are* yours."

Evan scratched at his head, reminding Martin that he needed to examine his scalp again.

"Oh, I know some of 'em are mine. It's just the ones that won't fit in my backpack that I'm pretendin' about."

"I'm sorry, I don't follow."

"Well, see ... some of 'em are too big to go in my backpack. You know, like the train set. So, I can't take 'em with me. But I can pretend it's mine for now. *Now* do ya follow?" he asked, watching the doctor intently.

The doctor swallowed. "Mm. Yes, I understand. But I'm sure we can figure something out ... a way to make sure you can keep your toys with you. I don't want you to worry about that. All right?"

Evan sat staring for a moment, and then shook his head. "I think I'll still pretend ... just ta be on the safe side."

"Suit yourself." Martin got to his feet.

Lightning flashed brightly, followed by a loud clap of thunder which rattled the bedroom window, and the seven-year-old looked up at him, wide-eyed. "Don't lock your door, okay?"

"Yep, okay," he answered, straightening the blankets and pulling them up under the child's chin. "I'll be sure it's unlocked before we go to sleep."

He touched the backs of his fingers to the boy's forehead before stepping over to repeat the gesture with his son.

Louisa looked up from her book when she noticed her husband watching her from the doorway. "Hello."

"Hello." He pulled the door shut behind him. A floorboard squeaked under his feet as he walked across the room, dropping down on to the mattress.

"How was your playtime with Evan?" she asked, slipping her bookmark between the pages before setting her novel aside.

"We weren't playing, Louisa. We were ... evaluating the situation."

"Oh. I see."

"It went fine." He reached out and tucked a stray wisp of hair behind her ear, allowing his thumb to lightly brush her cheek as he pulled his hand away.

Pulling him down on the bed, she shifted over to rest her head on his good shoulder. "I bet he's excited about his new train set, isn't he?"

"Mm. He's excited, but ... he's reluctant to think of some of his gifts as his. "

"Oh?"

"If they won't fit in his backpack, he can't take them with him. I ... I think we need to make a decision ... about Evan, Louisa."

She stroked her fingers lightly across his chest, stopping to work the top buttons open. "I've been giving it a lot of thought. I think we should tell Mr. Delaney that Evan can stay with us a while longer."

Martin lay quietly, but his shortened, more rapid breaths betrayed the stress he was feeling.

"What do you think?" she asked.

He rolled to his side to get up from the bed, but she pulled him back down.

"Don't go running off on me before you answer my question, Martin." She furrowed her brow at him. "Don't you want him to stay with us?"

"Of course, I do. But"—he rubbed the heel of his hand roughly against his forehead—"he needs a home, not just temporary accommodation. He needs to feel *secure*."

"What are you saying, Martin?"

"I'm saying, I don't want him to get used to a safe and—and—loving home if it's going to be yanked away from him. It might be better for him if he didn't get used to feeling at home here if he's going to be sent off to live in a revolving door foster care system in the end."

Louisa raised up on an elbow and cupped her hand against his cheek. "What is it that you want?" she asked softly.

"I want you to be happy. I don't want to make you unhappy—to lose you over this."

She tipped her head down, touching her forehead to his. "Martin ... what is it that you want?"

He lay with his eyes closed for several moments before taking in a deep breath.

"I want to adopt Evan."

"I see." She kissed his cheek and laid her head back on his shoulder. "We don't even know if that's a possibility ... do we?"

"I'd need to discuss it with that Dunwich fellow, but yes, I think it's a possibility. You have to want it as well though, Louisa. Evan won't be happy if he knows we don't both want him to be part of our family. And more than anything else, I want you to be happy."

Pulling herself up and straddling him, she stared down at him pointedly. "Let me make myself clear, Martin. You are *not* going to lose me over this, no matter what happens. Now, I think the best course of action is to let Mr. Delaney ... *Delaney*...know that Evan can stay with us while we sort this all out. In the meantime, we can talk with him about all of this, and ... well, I think it'd be good to talk to Dr. Newell about it a bit more as well."

Martin blinked the moisture from his eyes. "You're not completely opposed to the idea then?"

"No. I'm not completely opposed. But—and I can't believe I'm saying this to you of all people—one of us needs to be objective in making this decision. And in this instance, I think it has to be me."

"I see."

"So"—her fingers worked the remaining buttons on his shirt open, and she tugged his vest up before kissing his belly— "how's your energy level?"

"Adequate. I, erm—I should go lock up though." He swallowed hard and reached up to pull the garishly coloured ribbon from her hair.

"It was nice of you to wear this today. He'll"—he drew in a staggered breath—"he'll always remember it."

Louisa leaned over and pressed her cheek to his. "I'm so sorry, Martin. Margaret Ellingham didn't deserve a child, and you deserved so much more than what you were given for a mother."

She straightened up and crawled from the bed. "I'll just go and brush my teeth then, hmm?"

"Yes. I'll lock up and be back in a few minutes."

His gaze followed her as she went into the bathroom. Then he got up and made his way downstairs.

The walk to Mr. Moysey's earlier had left him with a hunger he knew would prove disruptive to his sleep. So, taking one of the protein shakes, that helped to feed his healing fractures, from the refrigerator, he quickly swigged it down.

The storm had strengthened, the strong gusts blowing sheets of rain against the windows, and lightning illuminated the little kitchen in strobe-like fashion. He glared at the back door as it began to rattle. Buddy scratched furiously from the outside, frightened by the sudden increase in the intensity of the gale.

Martin's eyes darted between the barrier holding back the little canine and the stairway separating him from the woman waiting for him in their bedroom.

He pressed his lips together and hissed out a breath before starting down the hall towards his consulting room. He returned with a bottle of disinfectant spray and a surgical pack which he opened, laying the contents out on the kitchen table.

After spreading the surgery drape out across the counter, he donned the plastic apron and snapped on a pair of surgical gloves. Then, he pulled the back door open and whisked the terrier from its perch on the doorstep.

Slamming the door shut against the wind, he deposited his 'patient' on the drape. Buddy's tail wagged furiously as the worst of the moisture was blotted from his coat with a wad of paper towelling.

The terrier reared up suddenly, bracing his front paws against the doctor's chest before dragging his tongue across his face. "Oh, gawd!" Martin groaned, pushing the animal away and grabbing for a sheet of kitchen roll to wipe away the offensive matter left behind.

"Stay there," he ordered, holding a hand up in front of him. He grabbed for the bottle of disinfectant and sprayed a liberal coating over Buddy's body.

"Go make yourself useful," he mumbled as he set him on the floor, shooing him towards the stairs.

Giving a self-satisfied nod, he gathered up the incriminating evidence and returned to the consulting room, concealing it in the bin.

He slipped back into the bedroom moments later, avoiding eye contact with his wife as he ducked into the bathroom.

"Everything okay?" Louisa asked when he slipped into the bed next to her. "Took you a while down there."

"Mm, fine. I, er … I was hungry so I had one of my shakes. Sorry to keep you waiting."

"Hmm, violating your carbohydrate curfew again. What am I going to do with you, Dr. Ellingham?"

"The carbohydrate load in those prescription shakes is really fairly low, Louisa. They're intended to supplement fats, minerals, vitamins, and primarily protein."

"It was a joke, Martin."

"Ah, yes." He rolled to his side and reached into his bedside table drawer, withdrawing a gift wrapped in red paper with a tatted ribbon of interlocking green wreaths. "I, er … got you something," he said as he rolled back and extended it to her, his gaze flitting shyly towards her before shifting away again.

"But … we agreed we weren't going to exchange gifts this year … all the extra expenses we've had and all."

"It's not a big thing."

She gave him a small smile and sat up in the bed.

"That's actually a hair ribbon," he said as she pulled the tatting from the gift. "Although, I don't think it's as nice as the one Evan made for you."

She held it up in front of her. "It's lovely, Martin. Thank you."

She peeled away the red paper to reveal a rectangular cloisonné box, decorated with creamy-white mother-of-pearl gardenias. "Oh, Martin," she said, her voice hushed.

"They're like the flowers I—"

"Like the gardenia you gave me! Yes, I know they are."

She lifted the lid on the box. It had been filled with sticks of rock candy which were embedded with red hearts. Underneath each heart was printed, 'Always, Martin'."

"Oh, Martin, this is jus—" She buried her face in his shoulder, unable to hold back the tears.

Martin grimaced. "I'm sorry. I should have gotten you a necklace ... or earrings. Something more—"

She cut him off, pressing her lips to his. "*This* is absolutely perfect. I couldn't love a gift more." She wiped the tears from her cheeks and began to giggle as she looked down at him. "Oh, Martin, you're completely at sixes and sevens, aren't you?"

"Well, I just thought—I mean, you told me the night we drank wine together that if I was a stick of rock I'd be—"

She silenced him with a kiss. "That was a very memorable night, wasn't it?"

"Mm, I don't actually remember much after that." He eyed her warily. "You're not upset then?"

"No, Martin. I'm not upset."

"Oh, good." He breathed out a heavy sigh before wagging a hesitant finger at the box. "It's, erm—it's hearts and flowers."

"It *is*. And it's lovely, just lovely." She brushed her fingers against his cheek before reaching into the drawer in her bedside table. "This is for you. It's just a little thing." She handed him a small gold gift bag with dark green and gold paisley printed tissue paper peeking out of the top. "Seems we both reneged on our agreement," she said as she sat back on her heels.

Martin propped himself up on his good arm and reached into the bag, pulling out a hardcover children's book.

Louisa reached over and flipped the cover open. Martin silently read his wife's neat, feminine script.

To my own very Real "Velveteen Rabbit".
Happy Christmas, my extraordinary man.
All my love, Louisa

He swallowed hard as he looked up at her briefly before his eyes darted to the side. "Mm, thank you." He set the book next to his bedside lamp and got to his feet. "I, erm ... I need to use the lavatory."

Watching his broad back as he disappeared through the bathroom doorway, Louisa knew her gift had not been well-received. Why, she was uncertain.

Martin splashed cold water on his face, trying to cool the heat of embarrassment he was feeling. Then he waited a few minutes before returning to the bed.

Louisa was sitting up, stroking her fingertips across the cool enamel inlay on her box. "Thank you very much for this, Martin. It really is beautiful."

"You're welcome."

"I'm ... sorry you didn't care for your gift," she said, waving a finger at the book.

His head whirled around. "No, no! I like the gift. It's just ... it's what you wrote."

"What's wrong with what I wrote?"

"You *did* equate me with a child's worn out, pathetic plaything. Is that how you see me? As worn out—threadbare and pitiful?"

Giving him an understanding smile, Louisa set her box aside and slid down under the blanket, nestling up to him. "I think you take a much more literal view of the story than I do. But, I do see many parallels with the kind of life you've had ... the kind of man you are.

"Maybe you should read the story again with a more figurative interpretation. I think you may better understand the meaning of my words. And I can assure you, I do *not* see you as threadbare or pitiful, Martin."

"What about pathetic?"

She reached over him and pulled open his drawer, removing his treasured, folded up "Reasons" list. He grimaced and grunted as she slapped it to his chest. "*This* is how I see you. I always will because you are *exactly* what it says on the tin—Doc Martin through and through. And a little—wear—won't change that," she said, waving a hand at his battered body.

She tossed the sheet of paper on to the table and pulled the blanket back, tugging at his vest. "Sorry about that smack. I didn't mean to hurt you," she said as she leaned over to kiss the recently assaulted area.

"Mm, it's f-fine." He sucked in a breath as her kisses moved along his abdominal scar towards the waistband of his boxers.

She reached over and switched off the lamp. "Now, let's see how much energy you saved for me."

Chapter 40

Louisa was awakened by a soft whisper in her ear.

"Mrs. Ellig-am."

She rolled away from her husband and on to her back. "What is it, Evan?" she said as she looked up at the boy in the dim early-morning light.

"We gots that problem again, Mrs. Ellig-am. You wanna get up and fix it so we don't get Dr. Ellig-am's day off to a bad start?"

Louisa slapped a hand to her face and groaned softly. "What do you mean, Evan?"

"You know ... that problem like was in me and James's room *yesterday* morning. He's there again."

Her eyes shot open, and she whipped her head around to look at her husband. Martin was sleeping soundly, oblivious to the conversation going on next to him.

She slipped from the bed and pulled on her dressing gown before putting a finger to her lips, tacitly quieting the boy as she jerked her head towards the hall.

With Evan in tow, she crept from the room, pulling the door closed behind them and crossing the hall to the nursery.

Louisa looked into the baby cot at her son who was happily entertaining himself with his new lion puppet. "Good morning, James," she said softly.

The toddler gave her a bright smile before returning his attention to his toy.

She turned towards the little white dog curled up on the bed. "Buddy, why you little— How do you suppose he keeps getting in here, Evan?"

The seven-year-old gave a shrug of his shoulders. "I dunno. Maybe there's a mouse hole somewhere."

"Hmm. That would have to be an awfully big mouse hole, don't you think?"

"Maybe Buddy just stretches himself out, long and skinny."

She gave him a smile and ruffled his hair before gathering the little terrier into her arms and heading for the stairs with Evan trailing behind her.

"It's sure good it's not all lightningy and thundery out there anymore. Buddy doesn't like it," the seven-year-old said as he hopped up the step into the kitchen.

"How do you know that?"

"'Cause ... he crawled under the covers with me last night. But I kept him from bein' scared."

"Oh, poor Buddy," Louisa said, cuddling the little canine. Her brow furrowed, and she cocked her head to the side. Burying her nose in the animal's coat, she inhaled deeply, a knowing smile creeping across her face.

The upstairs floorboards creaked, alerting her to her husband's movements.

"Why don't you fill Buddy's food dish and set it by his doghouse, Evan. Then I'll put him back outside before Dr. Ellingham comes down."

"Yeah, he might get all shirty if he finds out Buddy snucked in again."

"Hmm, I don't think you need to worry too much about that."

Upstairs, Martin was on the hunt. He had already conducted an initial search of the nursery, master bedroom, and the bathroom and had just started in on a recheck of the boys' room when his wife's voice broke the silence.

"What are you looking for?" she asked as she eyed him, bent over, peering under Evan's bed.

He straightened himself quickly, banging into the corner of the bedside table. "Ow!" he yelped as the lamp toppled to the floor.

"Uh-oh!" James pulled himself to his feet in his cot to get a better view of the action.

Louisa picked up the lamp and set it back on the table. "What are you doing, Martin?"

He rubbed a hand over the small knot developing on his head. "Nothing—nothing. I was just"—he cleared his throat and shook his head—"nothing."

"I see." She picked James up and walked over to kiss her less-than-forthcoming husband. "Well, when you get done with your *nothing*, why don't you go clean up and get dressed. I'll have breakfast waiting."

She tipped her head down, giving him a sideways glance and a small smile before turning to go back downstairs.

He leaned over to take one final look under Evan's bed and James's cot before making his way to the shower.

Louisa was putting a platter of bangers on the kitchen table, and the boys were already eating when Martin joined her in the kitchen a short time later. He glanced down at his watch and hissed air from his nose.

"What is it, Martin? Are you getting tired of eggs and sausage?"

"No. Well, yes ... but ... no, eggs are fine. I just ... well, that's a lot of eggs," he said, wagging a finger at his plate.

"Yes, it is. But you need to be taking in more calories than you have been lately, so sit down and eat."

He took a seat before pulling his arm up again, rechecking the time.

"Oh, Martin, for goodness' sake! It's Boxing Day. Can't you just try to relax for a change?"

He lowered his eyes and poked his fork at his eggs before stabbing it into a banger.

"What *is* it, Martin?"

"Al's stopping by in a little while," he mumbled. "I wanted to have the shed cleaned out before he gets here."

"Why?"

"He mentioned he had a sheet of plywood in the barn that we could have. He's dropping it off."

Louisa set a cup of coffee down in front of him. "And just what would you be doing with a sheet of plywood?" she asked as she wrapped her arms around him from behind and nuzzled her nose into his neck.

Evan eyed her closely. "So we can build a train table, Mrs. Ellig-am. We decided that last night after you went ta bed," he said.

He hesitated for a moment, and then straightened himself in his chair, pulling his shoulders back. "And we *didn't* even bother ta ask ya first."

She gave the child a sideways glance before sliding another banger from the platter and on to her husband's plate. "You still need to eat properly though, Martin. The construction will just have to wait."

"Here, you can have this back." The seven-year-old jabbed his fork into a sausage and transferred it from his plate, back to the platter in his headmistress's hands. "Sausage is filled with salt and fats and God knows what. You gots any fish, Mrs. Ellig-am?"

Louisa cocked her head and looked down at him, her brows pulling down into a vee. "No, I do *not* have any fish, young man." She set the platter down on the table with a clunk and went to take a seat.

Evan waved his fork at her. "Your arteries get all plugged up if you don't eat right, you know. And you can blow your heart up if that happens, so if you wanna live a long time you gotta eat healthy stuff. And you're already gettin' kinda old, so you're runnin' outta time ta do it."

"Is that so?" Louisa narrowed her eyes at her husband.

He blinked back at her with justifiable naivete. "Why are you looking at me like that?"

"Oh, Martin!" Her ponytail flicked to the side.

Boxing Day passed quickly, with Evan and Martin spending the daylight hours in the shed and Louisa working in the kitchen most of the day to prepare a special dinner.

By the time twilight had fallen over the little village, Martin was ravenous and Louisa was exhausted, but proud of the lovely spread she had laid out for the evening meal.

The latch rattled before the back door slammed open, hitting the wall with a bang. James whirled around in his high chair to check out the source of the noise.

"Evan Hanley!" Louisa said, pulling a hand up to her chest as she took in a startled gasp. "That is *not* how you enter this house. Go back outside and come in that door properly."

Evan threw his head back and rolled his eyes at her before retracing his steps on tip-toe. When the door opened again, Martin stepped through, followed by his young charge. The boy turned and closed the door with exaggerated assiduousness.

"Go wash your hands for supper, Evan," Martin said as he inspected the array of food on the table. "What's all this?" he asked, wagging a finger.

Louisa picked up the tea towel and wiped her hands, giving him a satisfied smile. "It's our holiday dinner."

"Holiday dinner? But we just did that yesterday. And we consumed far too many calories. Do you really think it's health—"

"It's a special holiday meal for *us*, Mar-tin. *Just us.*"

"I see. What will we feed the boys?" He reached down and brushed his fingers over his son's head as he sat, gnawing on a teething biscuit.

"*This!* This special meal is for us ... you, me, James, and Evan." She huffed out a breath.

"Ah."

He watched his wife's shoulders slump as she tossed the towel to the counter in surrender.

"It looks very nice, Louisa," he said softly. "And I'm very hungry."

Her face brightened. "Thank you, Martin."

The rubber soles of Evan's trainers squeaked against the vinyl flooring as he rounded the corner to race through under the stairs.

"No more mannered bacteria ... see," he said as he held his hands out for inspection.

"What's that on the backs of your fingers?" Martin asked.

The boy wrinkled his brow. "Oh, that's not bacteria; that's just some leftover jam from breakfast." He licked at the sticky, red residue before wiping his hand on the front of his shirt. "Got it."

"No, no, no, no, no. Go back and wash again. And do a proper job of it this time."

Evan plodded off under the stairs, and Martin took a seat at the table.

"He's been a bit ... odd today," Louisa said, nodding towards the hall as she passed a serving bowl to her husband.

Martin wrinkled up his nose at the fat laden cauliflower cheese. He glanced up at his wife before fishing out a solitary bit of the vegetable, placing it on his plate and spooning some on to Evan's. "Odd? In what way?"

"Well, for starters, he was bangin' on about how he hated flowers this morning—listing all the reasons he thought they were stupid." She took the bowl from him and handed him a plate of bacon-wrapped, roasted baby potatoes. "Don't you think that's odd?"

"He's a seven-year-old boy, Louisa. I would consider it odd if he showed much of an interest in them at all." Martin sighed as he looked down at the side dish in his hand.

Evan returned to the kitchen and climbed up on the chair next to his guardian. His eyes passed over the lovingly prepared meal before he screwed up his face and said, "What am *I* gonna eat?"

"Evan, I've gotten you started," Martin said, wagging a finger at the boy's plate. "And you have plenty of choices here. What would you like? Some salmon?" he asked as he reached for the platter.

"That's a fish, right?"

"Yes, it's a fish. Would you like some or not?"

"Yeah. But everything else looks gross."

"Evan! Where are your manners tonight?" Louisa asked, eyeing him incredulously for a moment before returning her attention to filling James's bowl.

"Oh, my manners are still here. I just decided not to use 'em. And I didn't even ask ya first."

He rested his elbow on the table and dropped his chin into his hand before reaching across with his fork to tap on the wine glass sitting next to Louisa's plate. "You *know* ... that stuff's not good for ya."

"It's just one glass, Evan. I'm sure I'll be fine. Thank you for your concern though," Louisa said, forcing a smile to her face.

Martin winced as the weight of the platter began to strain his broken arm. "Do you want the salmon or not, Evan?"

He shrugged. "I guess."

Louisa's head shot up. "Manners, young man."

Evan rolled his eyes. "I guess—*please.*" His words dripped with sarcasm.

Martin slid a piece of fish on to his plate, next to his broccoli. Setting the platter down heavily on the table, he directed a scowl at his young charge. "I *believe* Mrs. Ellingham was asking you to rephrase that answer in a polite manner," he said, his impatience with the boy registering in his raised voice.

The seven-year-old peered up at his guardian warily as his feet began to swing underneath him, and then his gaze dropped to his plate. "Yes, please."

Martin cleared his throat. "That's better. Now eat your fish."

Dinner had been finished with no further childish improprieties to ruin Louisa's attempts at a nice family meal together, and James and Evan were busy in the lounge, assembling James's new wooden train set while Martin and Louisa cleared the table.

Hurt and disappointed by the lack of enthusiasm shown for her culinary efforts, Louisa hardly spoke as her husband washed the pots and pans, handing them to her to dry.

Pulling the plug from the sink, he sighed as he watched the water swirl down the drain.

"Here," Louisa said, handing him the tea towel.

He wiped the moisture from his hands and folded the towel in half before hanging it on its assigned hook. "I'm sorry your holiday meal didn't come off as you'd hoped."

She raised her hands in the air and let them fall to her sides. "It's all right. I wasn't thinking, I guess. I think maybe I fixed the kind of holiday meal Mum would have made ... what makes it feel like the holidays to *me*.

"I mean, *really* ... I could have fixed a big platter of fried chorizo ... it would've had about as much appeal for you, hmm?"

He brushed the backs of his fingers against her cheek before wrapping his good arm around her waist and pulling her to him. "I liked the steamed broccoli and the baked salmon ... very much. Thank you for making it."

"You're welcome." She pulled back and patted a hand against his chest. "Well, I'm exhausted. I'll go run James's bath."

Martin helped Evan put the train set away while Louisa got their son ready for bed. And then he took his charge upstairs and tucked him in for the night.

As he walked out on to the landing, he glimpsed his wife in their bedroom, her hair still hanging damp around her shoulders after her shower.

He took a step back, ogling her as she picked up the trail of clothing she had left lying on the floor. Her dressing gown fell open, exposing her feminine form momentarily before she straightened up and refastened her sash.

As she glanced up at him, he quickly averted his eyes. Then he gave a tug on his ear and headed back downstairs to lock up and turn off the lights.

Passing through the lounge, he caught the scent of his wife's gardenia, which now resided in front of the window.

After flipping the deadbolt on the back door, he took a small, clear glass from a shelf in the buffet and filled it with water. Returning to the lounge, he pinched a creamy white blossom from the houseplant and floated it in the container.

Louisa was sitting, propped up against her pillow rubbing lotion on her hands when he re-entered the room. He set the vase on her bedside table before leaning over to place a kiss on her head.

"I'll go brush my teeth," he said, moving off towards the bathroom. When he returned, the lights were off and his wife had nestled herself in under the covers.

He slid into the bed, pulling the blankets up around him and rolling towards her to kiss her goodnight. His hand brushed against her bare breast. "Erm...you took your pyjamas off."

"Your astute powers of observation are one of your most beguiling qualities, Dr. Ellingham," she purred.

"Mm, yes." He cleared his throat. "I thought"—he felt the pressure of her hand against him and he swallowed hard—"I thought you were exhausted."

"I was." She pressed her lips to his and then pulled back to look at him. "It must be all those other beguiling qualities having an effect on me."

"I see." He glanced towards the nursery. "I, erm ... I should check the locks ... make sure I didn't forget one. I'll be right back," he said as he pulled himself from the bed.

Returning to the kitchen, he flipped the deadbolt, tugging the door open. Buddy darted from his doghouse and stood watching him, his black eyes shining in the incandescent light.

"Okay, come through."

The terrier darted in and ran for the stairs. Martin locked the door up tightly for a second time and turned, taking a step towards the lounge before a movement to his side caught his eye.

His wife stood, arms folded across her chest. His head tipped to the side as he gave another tug on his ear. "He, erm ... seems to facilitate the process."

Louisa walked across the room, her stern expression easing into a soft smile as she held out her hand to him and gave a nod towards the stairs. "Come on."

Chapter 41

Martin looked up from his desk when Morwenna stuck her head in the door early Wednesday morning.

"Doc, that Roger Delaney fella's here ... says he wants a word with you."

The doctor pulled his arm up and glanced at his watch. "Mm, right. Erm, send him on back. And tell Mrs. Richards it'll be a few more minutes."

"Right."

The receptionist hesitated, and Martin glanced up again, raising his eyebrows at her. "What is it?"

"I just wanted ta say that I think it'd be a shame if they sent the little guy off ta live with some total stranger, relative or not. He really likes you, ya know."

Martin stared at her for a moment before returning his eyes to the patient notes in front of him. "Just send Mr. Delaney in, Morwenna."

He listened to the young woman clatter away and grunted softly.

The latch rattled again, and the social worker came through the door.

"Mr. Delaney, good morning." Martin got to his feet and extended his left hand.

Roger settled into the chair in front of the desk and set his briefcase on the floor. "Did you have a good Christmas?" he asked.

"Yes. Yes, we did. And you?"

"It was wonderful. We go to the Scillies every year. My wife's parents have a cottage on Tresco, so the family gathers there. Lovely place, but the reception's rubbish, so I apologise for not returning your call.

"I have business in Pendoggett later this morning, so just thought I'd drop by ... bring you up to speed on the Hanley boy's situation in person."

Martin worked his jaw back and forth as he absently tapped his fingers on his desktop.

"First of all, I want to thank you and your wife for being so decent to the boy."

"Mm ... not a problem," the doctor said as his fingers tapped a little faster.

"He's been through quite a trauma, and being in a calm and loving environment for the last several weeks will, no doubt, have benefitted him greatly."

Martin's fingers stopped tapping, and he ripped a sheet of paper off his notepad, wadding it into a ball. "Well, as I said, it's not been a problem."

The Children's Services advocate picked up his briefcase and snapped the latches open before pulling out a manila file folder.

"The authorities conducted an exhaustive search for relatives who might be willing and capable custodians for the child. This wasn't an easy task, given the unique circumstances. It's not often that we encounter a situation like this.

"Mr. Hanley's parents are deceased, and there are no other living relatives who would be considered suitable caregivers—even if they had any interest in the boy ... which they don't."

The doctor's left hand worked around the ball of paper, his knuckles whitening as his anxiety and impatience grew. He nodded. "And ... "

"Well, as you know, Dr. Ellingham, Mrs. Hanley was given up to the foster care system by her mother when she was a child."

"Yes, I'm aware of that."

"The hope has been that the boy might have a maternal grandparent who would step forward to take charge of him. But the grandmother died more than ten years ago, and Mrs. Hanley was refusing to provide the authorities with the name of her—"

"Mr. Delaney, get to the point!" the doctor snapped.

The advocate jumped in his seat and stared back for a moment. "Yes. Mrs. Hanley finally confessed to the authorities, who have been following up on this in Manchester, that she was the product of an assault. The man was never identified."

The doctor relaxed back into his seat. "I see." He rubbed a hand across his forehead and looked over at Mr. Delaney contritely. "I apologise. I've been concerned for Evan and on edge about this."

"That's understandable."

"So, what happens now?"

"Well, Evan has been officially declared a ward of court. He'll live in the foster care system for the time being. If we can match him to a suitable adoptive family, we will. However, as I'm sure you know, the vast majority of people are not keen to adopt an older child. The preference is for an infant."

"Yes." Martin tossed the wad of paper on to his desk. "Would it be—I mean, my wife and I have discussed this— erm, the possibility of adopting the boy. No firm decision has been made, but we're ... interested. Do you think that would be a possibility?"

"Yes, most definitely!" Mr. Delaney said, nodding vigorously. "Fostering to adopt allows the child a smooth transition into the adoptive home. I'm assuming you and your wife would have no objections to keeping Evan with you in the interim?"

"Well, as I said, no firm decision has been made. But if we do decide to adopt, then of course the boy would be welcome to stay during the adoption process."

Mr. Delaney got to his feet. "Let me know what you decide, and I can put the wheels in motion. As you have been fostering the child already, we could expedite the process. Should take about six months before we can make it official."

The doctor pushed himself up from his desk and walked the advocate to the door. "I'll be in touch just as soon as I can give you an answer one way or the other."

Martin had a sum total of three patients that morning. One routine childhood immunization and two prescription refill checks. Two patients called in to make appointments and reported symptoms that sent up red flags, prompting Morwenna to send them on to Newquay.

And Jeremy, concerned about their possible contagiousness, stopped two patients at the front door. Despite their grousing about the inconvenience of it all, they went off to the Newquay clinic as well.

"What am I even doing here, Jeremy? A chimp with a needle and syringe could do what I did this morning," Martin said as he dropped into the chair behind his desk.

His assistant sat down on the desktop. "It was a slow day, Martin. Once we get past this influenza outbreak I won't need to be so hypervigilant."

The sound of trainers slapping against the vinyl flooring in the hall could be heard before Evan rounded the corner into the consulting room, followed closely by James.

"Hi, Dr. Ellig-am!" Evan landed with a final leap, and Martin put his hand out to guard his injured legs.

"Da-ee! Up!" James slipped in under his father's outstretched arm, scrabbling at his trousers and the fixators penetrating his legs to climb into his lap.

"*Sheesh!*" Clenching his jaws, Martin struggled to get a hand under his son's backside in an effort to relieve his pain.

"Whoa, whoa, whoa, James," Jeremy said as he hurried around to scoop the boy up. "You okay, Martin?"

He took in several deep breaths and swallowed hard before the colour began to return to his face. "Yep, I'm fine."

The toddler kicked his feet, reaching out for his father, and Martin gestured to his aide to set him in his lap.

"Morwenna said you were done already and we could come in here," Evan said as he stepped up on to the base of his guardian's chair before wrapping his arms around his neck. "If yer all done, then you can come and finish our train track, can't ya?"

"I'd like to see that, Evan," Jeremy said as he uncoiled the boy's arms and hoisted him up. "But let's give Dr. Ellingham a few minutes to recover from your greeting first. Martin, you sure you're okay, or do you want some Toradol?"

"No, I'm fine. Let's go show the man what we've done, Evan," he said before hooking his left arm around his son and lowering him to the floor. "Come on, James. You can see, too." He reached his hand out, and the toddler grasped on to his finger, giving him a broad grin.

"Hello, Jeremy. Are you staying for lunch?" Louisa asked as they came into the kitchen from under the stairs.

"No, thank you. I'm meeting Poppy at The Crab. I just wanted to see this train of Evan's before I go."

"Oh, it's Dr. Ellig-am's train, too. He's helped a lot," Evan said as he hurried to the back door.

Louisa wagged a finger at him as his hand landed on the doorknob. "Don't forget your coat, Evan."

He took a step towards the pegs behind the door, and then turned around, eyeing her for a moment. "I don't wanna wear it," he snapped before giving her a defiant look and stepping outside.

Martin pulled James's jacket from the rack and handed it to Jeremy before following after his young charge, his jaws clenching.

His raised voice could be heard delivering a sharp rebuke before the seven-year-old stepped back inside and pulled on his coat. He turned to Louisa. "Sorry I was disrespectable," he grumbled, scuffing his trainer on the slate before heading back out the door.

Louisa sighed and tossed the tea towel on the table.

"He giving you and Martin a bit of trouble lately?" Jeremy asked as he worked James's short arms into the sleeves of his coat.

"He's been giving *me* a lot of trouble lately. He'll do anything for Martin, no questions asked. But he won't do anything *I* tell him to do.

He's rude, he's constantly making disparaging remarks about girls—and trying to get him to talk to me is—is—he's worse than Martin!"

Jeremy hoisted James into his arms. "Maybe he's missing his mum."

"Mm, could be. But I'm beginning to think he just doesn't like me."

"He's pretty attached to Martin. Maybe he's jealous of the time and attention he gives you."

Louisa's face brightened. "Yeah, maybe that's it. I bet you're right, Jeremy. I hope you're right anyway. Martin and I have been considering adoption, and I'd hate to think the thing that could bugger it up is *me*."

"Nah, what's not to like about you?" The aide gave her a smile before following after his boss.

"Crikey! That looks like the real thing," Jeremy said as he squeezed into the little shed.

Evan grinned up at him from the stool he was perched on. "Yep, it's a right cracker all right. It even gots a vile duck."

"*Viaduct*, Evan," Martin said as he fitted in the final section of track.

"Yeah, that's what I said."

Martin screwed up his face and then handed the seven-year-old the tack hammer. "You want to put the connecting piece in?"

The child gave him a broad grin. "You mean I can hold the nail all by myself?"

"I think you're up to the job. Besides, I don't think my fingers can take anymore whacks with that hammer."

Evan plucked the tiny spike from his guardian's fingers and set it down into the hole in the piece of track. His tongue worked its way out the side of his mouth as he tipped his head and peered closely at his target. He choked up on the handle and swung the little tack hammer, driving in the spike that completed their circuit. "I did it, Dr. Ellig-am! And you didn't even have to hold it for me."

"Yes, you did. Well done."

The boy reached for one of the miniature engines. "Can we try her out now?"

"I need to hoover things off to be sure we don't have any debris on the track. But then you can—try her out."

Evan bounced on his stool, waiting impatiently as the appliance whined away.

"There, that ought to do it." Martin moved the vacuum cleaner back into the corner of the shed and then plugged in the transformer sending power to the rails.

"Can I put all the cars on now?" the seven-year-old asked as he held an engine in each hand.

"Yep. Make sure you have the wheels set right on the track if you don't want to derail our train."

Martin double-checked to make sure the cars were all placed properly, rolling each one back and forth several times. He set the controller in front of his young charge and showed him how to change from forward to reverse and how to control the speed.

"You ready?" he asked as he put his hand over the boy's.

"Ready."

The dial turned to the right, and the little train began to move.

"It works! It works! We did it, Dr. Ellig-am!"

Martin's left cheek pushed up ever so slightly as Evan gave him a triumphant grin. A draught pushed into the shed, and he glanced over at the door.

"Sorry to interrupt your play," Louisa said, taking note of the sparkle in her husband's eyes.

The expression skittered away as he pulled in his chin. "I wasn't playing," he mumbled. "I was just"—he wagged a finger at the train table— "helping the boy."

Louisa gave Jeremy a knowing smile before turning back to her husband. "Sorry, my mistake. But I *am* afraid I'm going to have to be the spoilsport. We need to eat so that you and Evan can get over to Truro for your appointment with Dr. Peterson."

"Dr. Ellig-am, do you think that lady will make me draw another house this time?" Evan asked as they neared the county's administrative centre a short time later.

"I don't know what you and Dr. Peterson might talk about today, but I hope you'll make an effort to be politer with her than you've been with Mrs. Ellingham lately."

Slumping into his seat, the child turned his head to stare out at the buses lined up in front of the park and ride. He pulled up a hand and scratched vigorously at his head.

Martin peered at him in the rear-view mirror, screwing up his face. "We should make a stop at Mrs. Tishell's when we get back to the village ... pick up some shampoo to clear up that eczema on your scalp. It doesn't seem to be improving with the change to your diet."

Neither of them spoke again until they had parked and were walking towards the hospital. Evan stopped and picked up a stick, poking at a dead bird lying in the grass next to the sidewalk before running to catch up to his guardian.

"Dr. Ellig-am, what's a scalp?"

"It's the skin on your head."

He latched on to Martin's wrist and trotted along next to him to keep up. "Do birds got scalps?"

"Strictly speaking, yes. But we ordinarily only use the term in reference to humans."

"So, do birds get that egg stuff on their heads?"

Martin stopped and stared down at him for a moment. "It's called *eczema*, Evan. And as far as I'm aware, birds aren't prone to developing it."

"Then how come I gots it?"

"You *have* it because you weren't being well— Well, there can be a number of different causes. But as I said, we'll stop and pick up some shampoo that should help clear it up."

Martin pulled Dr. Peterson's office door open, and Evan leapt through under his arm.

"Hi Mrs. Teague!" he said, walking over to the play table where the grey-haired woman was tidying up.

"Well, hello, Evan. Did you have a nice Christmas?"

"Yep. I got presents this year and everything."

Martin dropped into a chair and picked up a magazine as the door opened down the hall. "Hello, Evan ... Dr. Ellingham," Dr. Peterson said as she walked into the waiting area.

Evan gave her a smile, but inched over next to Martin and rested his hand on his knee.

The therapist reached out to him. "I thought we'd play with the sand today, Evan. Let's go on back."

The boy took her hand, and Martin made a move to get to his feet before she held up a palm.

"We'll be out after a little while," she said, giving him a nod of her head before leading her patient towards the hall.

Evan pulled away and ran back to Martin, crawling into the seat next to him and latching on to his arm.

Martin nodded towards the psychologist. "You need to go with Dr. Peterson, Evan. I'm going to wait here this time."

"But you need to come along ... so I can see where you are!"

Air hissed from his nose. "I'm going to stay right here. You go and—play. I'll still be sitting here when you come back."

The boy slid from the chair and dawdled back towards the psychologist. He turned around before they entered the therapy room. "Don't leave me, Dr. Ellig-am! Promise?"

"Yes, I promise."

The door clicked shut behind them, and Dr. Peterson walked to the racks of replicas on the wall. "Come on over here, Evan. You can pick some figures to play with in the sand."

Evan's gaze flitted between the door and the therapist before he made a move for the shelves.

He quickly gravitated towards the animals, plucking the shaggy dog, which he had favoured on his first visit, from the rack. "How many can I have?" he asked.

"As many as you like. You can take some now and play with them and then come back for more if you like."

Dr. Peterson pulled a small chair out from the sand table and took a seat.

A house, a whale, and a car were also selected, and the seven-year-old brought them over, depositing them into the sand.

He glanced over at the door. "I better check on Dr. Ellig-am," he said as he dashed for the door and pulled it open.

The therapist followed after, catching up to him as he climbed back up on to the sofa next to his guardian.

"Evan, we haven't finished with our sand play yet. Dr. Ellingham will be waiting here when we get done," she said, taking his hand.

He pulled away and turned towards Martin. "I don't like this anymore. Can we go home?"

"Evan, you need to go back with Dr. Peterson. I'm not going anywhere. I promise."

"Come on, Evan. We're going to go play some more. Dr. Ellingham will be waiting right here when we get done."

Martin gave him a nod, and he slipped from the sofa, casting an apprehensive glance over his shoulder as the psychologist led him back to the therapy room.

"Now what do I gotta do?" Evan asked as he dropped on to a chair.

"You go ahead and play. You can make up a story or create a scene ... whatever you like. I'd just like to watch if you don't mind."

"Does it gots ta have a house and a person and a tree?"

"Nope. You get to do whatever you want today."

Evan pushed the house down into the sand in one corner of the table and used his fingers to trace a meandering path to the opposite corner. He stepped back to the racks of figures, scanning them over before picking up a bus from amongst the vehicles.

"Did ya know I ride the bus ta school everyday?" he asked the therapist as he navigated the little toy through his roadway.

"I didn't know that. Do you enjoy riding the bus?"

Evan shrugged his shoulders. "I like it if I get to sit by the driver."

"Oh? Is the driver a friend of yours?"

He returned to the racks and picked up two more buildings, one large and one small. "He's not my friend, but he gots ta keep those big boys from bothering me 'cause it's his job."

"I see. The big boys don't bother you when you sit by the driver?"

"Uh-uh." He parked the new building in the corner where his path came to a dead end and pulled the bus up next to it. "Did you know Dr. Ellig-am's house is on a cliff?" he asked as he scraped sand into a pile and set the smaller building on top of it.

"Is that Dr. Ellingham's house there?"

"Yep." He pushed a large area of sand to the side, dropping the whale into the crater left behind. *"Pshwew!"* he said, gesturing expansively with his arms. "Whales make big splashes."

His attention returned to the bus, and he wound it through his path back to the other end of the sand table. Picking up the shaggy dog, he galloped it around. Sand began to fly as he scooped it up with the dog's feet, throwing it into a pile. "Potato's a good digger, isn't he, Dr. Peterson!"

"He certainly is." She brushed some of the thrown sand back into the box. "Is Potato a boy or a girl dog?"

"He's a boy. That's how come he digs up Miss Babcock's garden. She gets all angry and yells at him, but it's not Potato's fault. It's just his brand."

"What do you mean, Evan? Is he a special brand?"

"Uh-huh. He's an Iris shredder. That's how come he digs up her flowers. So, she shouldn't have got him, 'cause that's what he was made for."

"He was made for digging up gardens?"

"Uh-huh. *And* he's a boy."

"Do boys dig up gardens?"

"Just boy Iris shredders. Boys are bad. They do bad things."

"We all do things we shouldn't sometimes, Evan. Boys *and* girls ... even grown-ups."

"But boys are *just* bad."

"Dr. Ellingham is a boy, but you seem to like him. I'm sure *he's* done things he shouldn't have a time or two, especially when he was a child."

"Oh, he does things he's not s'posed to do all the time."

Evan went to the rack and returned with a handful of miniature people, two taller figures and two smaller figures. He dropped the two female figures into the hole excavated by the dog before covering them with sand.

"He says words he's not supposed to, but Mrs. Ellig-am still likes him." He pounded his fist down on the sand several times and looked up at her. "He gots twenty whole things that are crap about him—*twenty* things! And she *still* likes him, so he knows he's special. I don't think even *I* got *that* many crap things."

A soft smile floated across the therapist's face.

Evan ran back to the shelves and took down another tall male figure. He returned to the table and set the figure on top of the car. *"Vroom, vroom,"* he said as he inched it towards the house.

The vehicle came to a stop, and he walked the figure through the sand. "Hello, Evan," he said in the most artificially low voice he could muster. The remaining small figure was picked up. "Hi, Dr. Ellig-am. Did ya come to check on me?"

"Does Dr. Ellingham come to your house to see you when you're sick sometimes?" Dr. Peterson asked.

"Just when I broke my arm." He looked up with a broad smile. "I got ta listen to my heart with his stepascope."

"Oh, that's really interesting, isn't it!"

"Mm." The boy let the small figure fall back into the sand and picked up the other tall one. "What are you doin' 'ere?" his voice growled out. "Get away from my boy!"

The two 'men' waged a brief tussle with one another before the newest figure on scene fell to the ground and the remaining figure moved towards the 'boy'. Evan's hands moved quickly in tandem to the edge of the table where he allowed the 'man' to plunge to the floor.

The child's movements froze as he stared at the now inert form looking up at him from below. He took in a short breath and whirled around. "I want my dad!" he said as he bolted for the door.

He struggled for a moment with the knob before throwing the door open and racing down the hallway, leaping on to the sofa and into Martin's lap. He pulled himself into a ball and hid his face in his guardian's chest as he clung to his shirt.

Martin clenched his jaw and squeezed his eyes shut as the boy's weight rested on his fractured arm, now pinned between the child's knees and his lap.

He blinked back tears as he pulled his good arm up around the sobbing child's shoulders. "Shh, shh, shh, shh, shh."

Dr. Peterson joined them in the waiting area, glancing over at a mother and her children, there awaiting a session. She leaned down and spoke softly to Evan. "How 'bout we go back into the therapy room, but Dr. Ellingham can come with us this time."

Evan straightened himself, and Martin tried to stifle a yelp.

The therapist hurriedly lifted the boy up, setting him on the floor. "Are you all right, Dr. Ellingham?" she asked, looking at him askance.

"I'm fine." He held his arm to his belly as he pushed himself to his feet. "Come on, Evan."

Martin and his young charge took a seat on the sofa, and the psychologist sat down on the coffee table in front of them. "Evan, can you tell me about what you were pretending a little while ago ... right before you ran out of the room?"

The seven-year-old's feet began to pendulate underneath him as his hand crept towards Martin's leg. "I wasn't pretendin'; I was rememberin'."

"Can you tell me about what happened ... about what you were remembering?"

Evan slumped against his guardian. "I don't wanna talk about it. If I talk about it he might do something bad."

"Who might do something bad?"

The boy looked up at Martin. "Do I gots ta tell her?"

"You don't have to tell Dr. Peterson anything you're not ready to talk about, Evan. But nothing bad is going to happen," he told the child as he pulled his arm up around him.

The therapist leaned forward, resting her elbows on her knees. "If you'd like to tell me, Evan, I would be happy to listen."

He glanced up at his guardian. "He gets too rough, and it hurts when that happens. He *always* finds me."

"Are you afraid he'll find you again?"

"Uh-huh. But mostly I'm afraid he'll—" Evan turned and buried his head under Martin's arm, his hand patting against his chest.

"What are you afraid of, Evan?" Abby asked softly.

The boy sniffed and pulled back, looking up at his guardian with teary eyes. "I don't want him to find you!" he whispered stridently.

Martin swallowed hard. "Evan, your father is dead. He can't hurt you, and he can't hurt me. He can't be angry anymore."

The seven-year-old shuddered and wiped his nose on his sleeve. "He can't even be *angry* when he's dead?"

"No."

"Are you sure?"

"I'm absolutely positive." Martin pulled his handkerchief from his pocket and wiped the child's cheeks. "Blow," he said as held it to his nose.

Mucous and air burbled into the doctor's hand. His lip curled slightly before he realised he had the attention of the therapist.

Clearing his throat, he thrust the handkerchief at his charge. "Here, you can ... finish up there." He wagged a finger at the shiny residue left on the boy's upper lip.

"Evan, I think Mrs. Teague has some special holiday biscuits and milk for you," Abby said. "Why don't you go get started, and Dr. Ellingham will join you in just a minute."

"Kay." He got up on his knees and wrapped his arms around Martin's neck before slipping from the sofa to search out the receptionist.

Dr. Peterson closed the door and returned to her perch on the coffee table.

"You handled that very well," she said giving Martin a smile and a nod of her head.

"Mm. I never considered he might think his father could still be capable of thought."

"It can be difficult to predict how an individual child will process a concept as complicated as death."

"There's really nothing terribly complicated about it. Death is merely a condition where biological functions cease to sustain an organism, causing the process of decomposition to begin."

"Yes, but when you're seven years old there are a lot of grey areas."

Martin's mind drifted back to his own childhood momentarily. "Yes."

"Evan became upset today while playing with the toys in the sand." Abby got up and went to the table, retrieving the toys selected by the boy. "He was, I believe, re-enacting the night his father died."

She held out two of the miniatures. "He also chose these two figures which I believe represented his mother and sister. He buried them and packed the sand down over them."

"He doesn't talk about his mother and sister. I didn't know he thought about them."

"Well, remember that I told you rejection can be terribly damaging to a child ... painful as well. Evan received a very clear message that he's a bad child ... that boys are bad.

"I believe he's beginning to understand that doing something one shouldn't does not make one a bad person. And I give full credit to you and your wife for that.

"Keep reinforcing that idea. He's likely to have insecurities for a while, and those insecurities will likely resurface during those transitional stages we talked about at our initial meeting."

"Will he ever get past that?"

"It will depend on Evan to some extent. But how his life unfolds from this point could have a profound effect ... one way or the other."

The therapist straightened herself and folded her hands in her lap. "Have you and your wife given any more thought to adoption?"

"Yes. No definite decision has been made, but it was discussed recently. It's certainly a possibility."

"Good ... wonderful." Abby tapped her fingertips together and she took in a deep breath. "Before Evan ran from the room earlier, he looked around for you."

"Mm, yes. We've been spending a lot of time together."

"I believe there's more to it than that, Doctor. He wanted you because he was distressed. He blurted out, 'I want my dad'. He's beginning to see you as his father figure."

Martin blinked back at her and tipped his head to the side. "Oh." His brow furrowed as his gaze shifted to the floor.

"I'm telling you this, Dr. Ellingham, because it's important that you're aware of the bond that Evan has formed with you.

"We've reached a tipping point. You and your wife need to make a decision about adoption. To keep the child with you any longer could have devastating effects if it's only going to be a temporary situation. Evan will learn to fear human relationships ... be afraid to let himself get close to another person."

Martin swallowed hard. "Are you saying that if we can't commit to making him a permanent member of our family, we need to return him to Children's Services?"

"It seems counter-intuitive, I know. One would think that the more time he can spend in a loving home the bet—"

"No, I understand." He wiped a hand over his face and breathed out a heavy sigh. "We'll make the decision. If we can't ... I just want what's best for the boy."

Dr. Peterson got to her feet. "I know you do," she said, putting a hand on his arm before heading for the door.

Martin glanced into the rear-view mirror as they entered the town of Wadebridge a short time later. Then he veered right, heading towards the town centre. "How 'bout we get some ice cream before we head home, Evan?" he said as he pulled up to the Bridge Bistro.

"Really? But it gots all that fat, and it'll spoil me for dinner."

He pulled up his arm and looked at his watch. "Dinner's still two hours off. I think you'll be back in fine eating form by then. And I don't suppose a little fat will do either of us any harm."

The sun was dropping below the horizon when the Lexus pulled into the parking space by the surgery. Evan ran around to the back of the house as Martin stopped to stare across the harbour.

An almost intolerable anxiety and sense of dread had built in him on the trip home. It felt as though he was about to, once again, ruin someone's life.

He could accept that his parents' inability to feel any affection towards him was beyond his control. But the fact was, his presence had been the cause of his mother's unhappiness. The sense of guilt he felt for that was oppressive.

Louisa slipped into bed next to her husband that night very aware that something was bothering him.

She had become adept at recognising the signs that he was having pain—his stiffened gait, the occasional winces and grimaces, the difficulty with movement in general.

But it was more than that. She laid her head on his shoulder and traced lazy circles on his chest. "How did things go on your trip to Truro today?" she asked.

"Fine ... fine. Traffic was light, the weather was good."

"What about with Dr. Peterson? All okay there?"

"Yes, she seemed fine—appeared healthy."

"I wasn't enquiring about her health status, Martin. I was wondering how the therapy session had gone."

"Ah, yes. It went ... fine." He hesitated. "Have you, er ... have you given any more thought to the future?"

Louisa slipped her arm under her, propping herself up as she peered down at him. "The future?"

"Evan."

"I've been thinking about it. He's a very nice little boy ... for the most part. He's been a bit difficult lately, though. Hmm?"

"Yes. Has his behaviour been making you unhappy, Louisa?" he asked, brushing his fingers across her cheek.

"No. I'm not unhappy. It's just a bit hard on my self-esteem to think he doesn't like me."

"He likes you!" Martin wrestled himself to a sitting position. "He made you the hair ribbon, remember."

Louisa sat herself up next to him and pulled her knees to her chest. "You think he did that because he likes me?"

"I think he made it for you because he wants you to like *him*."

"He's had a funny way of trying to win me over lately."

His hand slid across the mattress towards hers. "Does he need to do that ... to win you over?"

"No, not really. I s'pose he did that a long time ago. He loves you ... adores you really. So, I love him."

"Ah, I see." Martin's brow furrowed. "But do you *like* him? Would it make you unhappy if he were around ... permanently?"

"Martin, I told you ... you're not going to lose me over this."

"*Yes.* But would it make you unhappy? Years from now, would you resent me—*him?* Would you resent him for having wasted years of your life!"

She put her hand on his arm. "Martin, calm down. I know you're anxious to make a decision on this, but we both need to be sure of ourselves. I still have concerns about how adopting Evan could affect your recov—"

"I'll try to get more sleep ... eat more. That's not what I'm concerned about. I'll heal."

"Well you may not be concerned about it, but I am. And it's more than that. You have a long way to go with Dr. Newell. I worry about how the added stress might affect your progress with him."

"I'll make an appointment with him. We can discuss it. What time is it?" He turned and peered at the clock. "It's not that late. I'll go give him a call, see if he can work in a session tomorrow."

"Martin, I think it can wait until morning. He may have gone to bed."

"He said if either of us has need of him over the holidays to give him a call ... leave a message."

Martin slipped from the bed and had reached the landing before his wife could call out. "Martin!" she undertoned, trying to avoid waking the children. "Martin!" She threw her hands up in the air before working her way back under the blankets.

She had just dozed off when he returned. He crawled in next to her, calmer but looking abashed.

"You didn't wake him, did you?"

"As I said, Louisa, I was just going to leave an answerphone message. But he was *not* asleep and he picked up. We're to meet with him at one o'clock tomorrow," he said as he lay staring at the ceiling.

Louisa got up from the bed and collected the pillows piled on a chair in the corner. After pulling the covers back and placing a kiss on each of his legs, she tucked pillows under them. "The weather's changing, hmm? Causing you problems?"

"Mm. I think we have another storm that's supposed to move in Friday."

"Your arm's really swollen tonight. I'll go get some ice."

Martin took hold of her wrist. "It's fine. Just come to bed. I ... I need to feel you right now."

Louisa paused and then went around to her side of the bed before slipping her nightdress over her head, letting it drop to the floor. Then she crawled in next to her husband and allowed him to quench his tactile thirst.

Chapter 42

"Were you able to reach Poppy?" Martin asked as espresso trickled into his cup the following morning.

"She'll be here at noon." Louisa picked up the last of the breakfast dishes and returned to the sink. "I think Jeremy's coming with her, so Evan should be happy."

Martin grunted, tucked the newspaper under his arm, and limped towards the table. "Noon? That's cutting it a little close don't you think?"

Louisa rolled her eyes as she added a plate to the dishwasher. "It'll be fine. It gives us at least ten minutes to spare."

"I'm just saying, any number of things could happen between here and there to slow us down. Traffic, farm wagons, tractors, sheep on the road. Can she come at eleven forty-five?" He dropped heavily into a chair.

"Oh, for goodness' sake, Martin! It's the A-39; there aren't going to be any sheep on the road.

"Poppy's meeting some friends from school for lunch, and she's already moved their meeting time up the way it is. I can't ask her to cancel the lunch altogether."

She swiped a hand over her forehead, brushing a wisp of hair from her face. "We'll be fine, so stop your fussing."

Martin dipped his head and glanced at her annoyedly. "Yes."

The latch rattled on the back door, and a cold blast of air blew in as Ruth stepped into the kitchen.

"Ruth, good morning!" Louisa said as she hurried over to help the elderly woman with her coat. "What brings you out and about on such a cold day?"

"I was at a book signing over at Stoneman's yesterday. I couldn't help but think of you when I saw this, Martin," she said as she set a bag down in front of him.

Pulling out a book, he screwed up his face at the sketchy reptilian image on the cover. He flipped through it, his brow furrowing before he peered up at his aunt quizzically. "You're likening me to an extinct predator? Is this some sort of retaliation for my comments about your age related—disbenefits?"

"Oh, for God's sake, Martin. Do I really need to explain the moral of a children's story to you? Read it to the child, and maybe he can shed some light on it for you."

Louisa pulled the book from under her husband's hands as he pushed himself up from the table.

"I have patients," he said, trundling off under the stairs.

Ruth's gaze followed her nephew as he moved stiffly down the hall. "Is he all right?" she asked, wagging a finger at him.

"It's been a bad couple of days." Louisa perused the new book and pulled out a chair, taking a seat across from her husband's aunt. She glanced into the lounge where the two boys were playing, and then leaned towards the elderly woman. "This is about adoption?" she whispered.

"I suppose it could be interpreted that way."

"What do you mean, *interpreted* that way?" Louisa tapped her fingers sharply against the pages. "The dinosaur raged through the village scaring everyone with his frightening roar? The little dinosaur followed the fearsome dinosaur, copying his every move? A moving tale about a young dinosaur's search for a father? Really, Ruth! This could have been written about Martin and Evan!" she hissed.

"Now, don't look at me like that, Louisa. I'm merely attempting to speed this process up a bit."

"What process?"

"Oh, for heaven's sake! This decision that the two of you keep going around the house on! At the rate you're taking it, the child will have completed his A levels before you finally put pencil to paper."

Louisa's ponytail flicked. "I'm sure you're only trying to help, Ruth, but this really is none of your business. It's a decision that Martin and I need to make together."

Ruth drummed her fingers on the table top. "Would you mind if I made myself a cup of tea?"

"Yes ... yes, where are my manners." Louisa got to her feet and took in a deep breath, attempting to collect herself as she filled the kettle and turned it on.

"I'm only concerned for my nephew, you know," the old woman said softly.

"I'm concerned for him as well, Ruth. That's what makes this so difficult." Louisa put cups on the table and passed her husband's aunt the basket of tea bags before taking her seat again.

"Are you certain there's not more to it?" Ruth asked.

"What do you mean?"

"Well, on the whole, I would say that Martin has benefited greatly from this experience. Yes, that night that Mr. Han—that unfortunate night was a close call. But he did seem to gain some confidence from that ordeal—that he's not as helpless as he—or we, rather—thought he was.

"And this is all helping him to see why he struggles with the social interactions that come so naturally to most of us.

"And physically, aside from the little adventure a few weeks ago, I can't see that his recovery has been adversely affected. If you can get him to eat more and figure out a way to resolve the night-time disruptions, I think this could be very good for him."

"Hmm. Fingers crossed, we're getting close to solving that last problem," Louisa said, glancing towards the back door.

Ruth's fingertip made several passes around the rim of her cup. "I suspect you know where Martin stands on this issue. And as far as I've been able to tell, you seem to care for the child as well.

"You need to determine the source of your reservations and make a final decision, one way or the other. If you're concerned about Martin's health, then look at what all this uncertainty is doing to him."

The old woman glanced at her watch and pushed herself away from the table. "Well, I should be going. I somehow got myself talked into doing another one of Caroline's phone-in shows."

"But didn't you want a cup of tea?"

"I think I'll give it a miss." She gave the younger woman a crooked smile as she slipped on her coat and stepped out into the brisk air.

Louisa gave her head a shake and got up to turn off the tea kettle.

Martin stood in front of the sink a few hours later, glancing at his watch. "Louisa, we really need to be going."

"Yes, yes, yes!" she said as she hastily scribbled notes on to a piece of paper. "I want to pick some items up while we're over there, and I don't want to forget anything."

She turned to their childminder. "James didn't eat a whole lot for lunch, so he might be hungry later. There's some diced chicken in the refrigerator and—"

"Louisa!" Martin said, fingering his watch. "She takes care of him five days a week, I'm sure she can manage for a few hours."

Giggles erupted from Evan as Jeremy entertained him in the lounge. His giggles blossomed into all-out laughter as the aide held him up, suspended by his ankles.

Martin looked over at them. "Oh, for goodness' sake."

Something slipped from the boy's pocket and fell to the floor with a thud. "Uh-oh! My lucky rock!" he said as he wriggled around, trying to reach it. "Gots it." He looked over at his guardian with an upside-down grin.

Martin acknowledged the child with a nod, and then rapped a knuckle against his watch face. "Louisa! I don't want to keep Dr. Newell waiting."

Her husband's voice drew Louisa's gaze from the antics in the lounge, and she hurried to grab her coat. "Thank you so much Jeremy and Poppy. We'll try to be back by half three or thereabouts," she said as they left the house.

The first half of the drive to Truro was smooth and uneventful, but as they neared Winnard's Perch, traffic began to slow.

They were about a half mile from the little resort community when the traffic ground to a halt. A herd of cows had taken up temporary residence, grazing on the tufts of green grass that grew up amongst the brown winter thatch along the verge.

Cars threaded their way through the animals, one at time, and air hissed from Martin's nose as he looked again at his watch.

"Don't you dare say it, Martin," Louisa warned as she narrowed her eyes at him.

"Well, we did ask the man to see us in the middle of his holiday. The least we could do is—"

"Do you want me to get out and shoo them aside while you drive the car through, Martin? Hmm?"

He whipped his head to the side. "*Noo*. But if we had left—"

"Martin, just drop it—and mind the cows."

He pulled in his chin and returned his eyes to the road, inching forward.

By the time they reached Dr. Newell's office it was one fifteen, and Martin, having received no apology from his wife for her dilatoriness, was sullen and chippy.

The psychiatrist had abandoned his usual suit and tie for a pair of light coloured khakis and a dark blue polo shirt. He leaned back in his chair, scratching at an eyebrow.

"I understand, from what Martin told me last night, that the two of you have reached the proverbial fork in the road. That you need to come to an agreement about whether adopting Evan is in everyone's best interests. So, let's see if we can work through this in such a way that both of you feel understood while making this decision."

He turned. "Since I had the opportunity to speak with Martin last night when he called, I'd like to get your perspective on this, Louisa. What are your thoughts?"

She tapped her fingers together in her lap. "Well, first of all, I think we're rushing into things. I mean, I realise the not knowing is stressful for Martin, but isn't it important that we're positive about any decision we make?

"We've had Evan in our care for less than a month, so do we even know him well enough to be making a decision right now? And a relative who would be willing to raise Evan may step forward. Maybe we're putting the cart before the horse."

Dr. Newell cocked his head and eyed Martin. "Is there anything you'd like to discuss with Louisa?"

Martin sighed. "I may have neglected to mention that Mr. Delansky stopped in yesterday. The authorities completed their search for any relatives, and they came up empty-handed."

Louisa shook her head. "But why didn't you tell me yesterday ... when we were discussing this?"

"I don't know." He squirmed under his wife's pointed stare. "I didn't want to pressure you."

Dr. Newell's biro tapped against his lips. "And the sense of urgency that you feel in making a decision?"

"Something happened with Dr. Peterson yesterday," Martin said, his head dropping to the side. "She told me we need to make a decision one way or the other—now. If we can't commit to giving Evan a permanent home, we need to return him to the care of Children's Services."

"Why? What did you do, Martin?" Louisa asked, her posture stiffening.

"I didn't do anything! I was waiting in the reception area—as I was *asked* to do, by the way—Evan was in with Dr. Peterson. He got upset and came running out to me.

"Dr. Peterson told me later that he had—that he had referred to me as Dad when he called out for me. She thinks it would be better for him to be moved on to foster care now before his attachment to me becomes any stronger."

A small smile came, unbidden, to Louisa's face. "He called you Dad?"

"Mm. I know!"

The therapist came around to the front of the desk and took a seat on the corner. "Martin, I realise the time you had with your aunt was fleeting, but how would you describe the relationship you had with her?"

Martin rubbed his thumb into his palm as he stared out the window. "She told me a few years ago that I was like a son to her."

Feeling his wife's hand on his knee, he glanced down.

"And your feelings towards her?"

His gaze returned to the window. "She was right when she said she'd been more of a mother to me than my own mother ever had."

"And when you thought she no longer had the time for your visits ... when all contact was cut off ... what effect did that have on you?"

Martin grimaced as he staggered to his feet. "You're the psychiatrist. Can't you figure that one out for yourself? I was afraid to trust anyone that way again ... to get close. And I'm afraid the same thing's going to happen to Evan."

He turned to his wife. "I don't know what to do, Louisa. I didn't tell you about the visit with Del Monte or what happened at Dr. Peterson's because I don't want to push you.

"And I'm afraid of the decision you're going to come to. Either way, I make someone unhappy—I ruin someone else's life." He pressed his fingers to his eyes and swallowed. "I made her unhappy and I've made you unhappy."

"I'm happy now, Martin. You make me very happy *now*," Louisa said.

"My point exactly! You're *happy* now. I can't do that to you ... to make you unhappy again. And I don't want to make Evan unhappy. But either way, I'm going to be responsible again."

Dr. Newell leaned back on his hands. "What do you mean by that, Martin—to be responsible again?"

"To be responsible for making someone unhappy—miserable! I don't want that for Evan—for him to carry that around with him all his life." He scowled at the psychiatrist. "Good God, man? Are you listening to me at all?"

"I am listening, Martin. You feel like you're between the devil and the deep blue sea. If you and Louisa decide against adoption, Evan likely ends up in the same place you were as a child—unloved and unwanted. But if you and Louisa decide in favour of adoption, you're afraid both you and Evan will be responsible for Louisa's unhappiness."

The psychiatrist noted his patient's trembling legs and gestured. "Why don't you take a seat, Martin."

He hesitated before returning to his chair.

"I can only imagine the enormity of the burden you've been carrying around," the therapist continued. "Feeling responsible for your mother's unhappiness."

He leaned forward, resting his arms on his thighs. "How long have you felt this way, Martin—that you were responsible for your mother's unhappiness?"

He blinked back at him and shook his head. "I've always been responsible. I tried to make her happy—to make her smile."

"In what way?"

"Doing as she asked, making her gifts. As I got older, trying to console her." His lip curled slightly. "Gestures of affection."

"And you couldn't make her happy?"

"No."

"What could you have done differently? Looking back on it now through your experienced adult eyes, what could you have done that *would* have made her happy?"

Martin's hands clutched at his knees as he sat, his eyes darting. "I don't know." He shook his head. "I'm rubbish at this kind of thing. I don't seem to be able to see the obvious—what people need from me to be happy."

"All right. Let's take you out of the picture again. What could James have done to make your mother happy?"

Martin focused intensely on his hands as he thought through the doctor's question. "I don't know!" he snapped. His jaws clenched as he squeezed his eyes shut, and his head pivoted side to side. "I—don't—know."

The therapist's fingers tapped against the edge of the desktop. "Martin, you're having difficulty with this question, not because you're rubbish at this, but because there is no answer to the question. We are not responsible for anybody else's happiness. That's an unfair burden to place on any human being, especially a child.

"You weren't responsible for your parent's lack of love for you, and you weren't responsible for your mother's happiness or unhappiness any more than you're responsible for *Louisa's* happiness or unhappiness.

"Your mother was responsible for her own happiness then, and Louisa is responsible for her own happiness now."

Martin's gaze swung slowly to his wife, the creases in his forehead deepening.

Louisa shifted uncomfortably in her chair. "I'm not sure what you're getting at," she said. "Are you saying that if I'm not happy, it's my own fault?"

The therapist laced his fingers together over his knee. "This isn't about assigning blame. I'm saying that our emotions are regulated by how we choose to interpret an event. How we choose to respond."

"But when Martin says nice things to me ... does nice things ... that makes me happy."

"Can you give me an example of what you mean—a nice thing he's said or done?"

Her eyes met her husband's, and she gave him a soft smile. "He gave me a gardenia plant," she said, her words causing his ears to warm.

"And how did you interpret that gesture?" Dr. Newell asked. "What sort of emotions did his gesture evoke?"

"I felt loved ... that he went into a flower shop and selected that plant for me. That's not the sort of thing Martin does, but he did it for me. And he put a lot of thought into it." She reached out and put a hand over his. "I felt loved."

"Would you say it made you happy?"

"Yes, very happy."

"What if you had interpreted his gesture differently? That he was trying to soften the blow of bad news, perhaps. Or that he had done something or maybe failed to do something, and he was trying to appease your impending disappointment in him. What sort of emotions would those interpretations evoke?"

Louisa pulled her hand away from her husband's and straightened in her chair. "I suppose anxiety, resentment ... probably anger."

"Can you give me an example of something Martin has said or done to make you unhappy?"

"Well, he can be rather insensitive."

Martin's head dropped as he brushed at his trousers.

"Can you be more specific?"

"Well, there was a time that he told me my perfume—"

"Oh gawd," he groaned as he turned towards the window.

The psychiatrist gave her a nod. "Go on Louisa."

"Well, it was our first real ... *only* real date. We'd been to an outdoor concert, and Martin had taken my hand as we were walking back to the car.

"I had this compulsion. I pulled him off the path and behind a tree. I kissed him. He kissed me back and it was wonderful. Then he made an insulting comment about my perfume ... that it smelled like urine and—"

"To be clear," Martin interjected, "I did say that it was only faint."

Louisa crossed her arms in front of her and sat, tight-lipped.

The therapist's eyes shifted between his patients. "I take it the evening came to a rather dreary end?"

"I told Martin I didn't want to see him anymore," she said.

"How did you interpret Martin's comment, Louisa?"

"It was rude ... and insensitive."

"Why do you say that it was rude and insensitive?"

She looked back at the therapist, perplexed. "He said I smelled like urine! That's hardly complimentary. I can't imagine he was enjoying"— she brushed a hand over her face— "kissing me—touching me."

Her ponytail whipped to the side and her purse strap tightened around her hand.

"And the emotions that were evoked?"

"I was angry—hurt and humiliated, of course!"

"How might you have felt about his comment if you had interpreted it differently. Perhaps assumed he was nervous or unsure of how to react to your advances?"

Louisa's fingers stroked her throat as she glanced away. "I suppose I may have felt sympathetic ... wanted to help him out ... or at least just let it go."

"Perhaps you could have even asked him why he said it. Let him know that it hurt your feelings."

"Hmm, maybe."

"Instead of ending the night with you feeling hurt and humiliated, you may have gone to bed with a better understanding of how Martin was feeling in that moment. You may have even gone to bed knowing that this wasn't an insensitive man, but rather a very sensitive man who was grasping in an unexpected moment. You may have even gone to bed—happy."

"I think I can see your point. But are you saying that the nice things that Martin says and does shouldn't make me feel happy?"

"No, not at all. What I'm saying is that what Martin says and does—how he acts—that shouldn't be the *source* of your happiness. Just the cherry on the sundae."

The doctor's chair complained as he rolled forward and rested his arms on his desk. "Let's look at your present dilemma.

"Louisa, I think Martin has been quite clear about the impossible position he feels he's found himself in. How are you feeling about the idea of adoption?"

She bit at her bottom lip and glanced quickly in her husband's direction. "Well, it would completely change the picture I had of our family."

"Describe that family for me."

She circled her hand in the air. "You know—normal."

"And adopting a child would make your family abnormal?"

"Well, it's just that Evan comes from a very dysfunctional family and—"

Martin's eyes flashed as he whirled his head around. "*You* come from a dysfunctional family! *I* come from a dysfunctional family! You want *me*. At least I think you do. Why don't you want Evan?"

"I'm not saying I don't want Evan, Martin. But adopting a child with Evan's background is a scary proposition."

"What do you find scary about it, Louisa?" the psychiatrist asked.

"It just seems like we'd be testing our marriage by bringing him into the family ... like it'd be reckless."

"What if Evan starts acting up, rebelling ... gets to be too much for one of us, and we just ... if we just give up on the marriage—leave?"

Martin shook his head. "Louisa, I could never do that. To go off and leave you to deal with things on your own. I know that's what I was going to do when I was planning to return to London, but in the end, I don't think I could have done it."

"Martin, it's not *you* I'm worried about. Well, I'm worried about you but not in that way. It's *me*. I'm worried about me doing that to you."

"Oh." Martin pulled in his chin. "You stayed with me the entire time I was in hospital ... and since. Do you really think that anything Evan could throw at us could begin to compare to that ordeal?"

He hesitated before mumbling, "Besides, you promised you wouldn't leave again and ... I trust you. I have confidence in you."

Louisa reached over and put her hand on his, squeezing his fingers. "Thank you, Martin."

"Do you have any other concerns, Louisa?" the therapist asked.

"Well, I'm very worried about the effect the added stress of an adopted child would have on Martin's recovery, both physically and emotionally."

"Louisa has a very valid point. You do still have a lot of healing to do from your injuries, Martin. And no matter what your decision is, don't let yourself get complacent about the work you still need to do in this room. You're feeling better and that's good, but you're at a precarious point in your emotional recovery.

"It's common for patients to begin to feel they don't need therapy any longer ... to try to go it alone. Don't lose your focus. You have a family who needs you healthy. That must be a priority."

The therapist walked Martin and Louisa out to the waiting area and wished them well with the decision they had to make.

Louisa reached over and took her husband's hand as the door to the office closed behind them, and they made their way towards the car in silence.

Martin eyed her anxiously as she sat next to him, worrying her lip. She looked over at him only once—to request a stop at a paper goods store so that she could pick up school supplies.

He followed her through the aisles, twice transferring items into her shopping trolley after she abstractedly laid them in a trolley of discount goods nearby.

She turned to him as they stood in the queue at the checkout. "Martin, would you mind stopping somewhere ... getting something to drink?"

"It's a little early in the day to be drinking, don't you think, Louisa?"

She tipped her head down. "A cup of tea, Martin. I just want to sit down somewhere and talk ... preferably with something hot to drink."

Giving him a roll of her eyes, she softened it with a smile when she saw the concerned expression on his face. "Don't worry," she whispered in his ear before placing a kiss on his cheek.

He handed the cashier a twenty-pound note, his face reddening as the woman gave Louisa an amused grin.

Snatching his change from her hand, he limped towards the door.

They dropped their purchases at the car and walked a distance down the block to a small cafe.

"This is nice," Louisa said as they sat in a quiet corner, waiting to be served.

"Mm."

She picked up the tent card in the middle of the table, scanning the array of hot beverages on offer before setting it back down. "Dr. Newell was helpful today."

"Was he?" Martin willed his wife to put an end to his mental agony and say what she had to say about the future for Evan.

"Well, what he said made a lot of sense."

"Ah."

"Martin, I *have* been giving a lot of thought to adoption ... more than you know. And I do have some very legitimate con—"

"Louisa, I'll make a concerted effort to eat more. I stopped with Evan in Wadebridge yesterday, and we each had a bowl of ice cream."

"And about getting enough rest ... well, if it would help the boy to sleep—you and me to sleep—"

He pinched his lips together and hissed out a breath. "Well, I suppose—I suppose that dog of Joan's can come in at night.

"But *just* at night. And *only* if it's been vaccinated and properly sanitised. I don't want to be responsible for incubating some previously eradicated, flea borne pestilence in my surgery—have it resurface to rampage, unchecked, through the village."

"That's good to know. *Although,* I was going to say that I have some legitimate concerns about the future. You know—the challenges that could come with taking in a child with Evan's history."

"Oh." He straightened the silverware on the table in front of him.

A young woman approached and set a cup of espresso down in front of him. Then she set a cup of tea and a scone with clotted cream and strawberry jam down in front of Louisa.

"Thank you," Louisa said before the waitress hurried away.

Martin wagged a finger at the traditional mid-afternoon sweet on his wife's plate. "That's not good for you, you know."

"I don't eat it everyday. I just feel like celebrating." She spooned up a large dollop of cream and held it up in front of his face. "And you better start proving to me that you're going to follow through with your promises."

He eyed her quizzically. "What are you saying, Louisa?"

"Open up, then I'll explain," she said, thrusting the spoon at him again.

Martin took the utensil, and the first Cornish clotted cream to pass his lips in decades went into his mouth. He screwed up his face and washed it down with espresso.

Louisa took hold of his hand and gave him a smile. "Martin, for the first several weeks we had Evan with us, I'd been trying to picture him as a member of our family, but I just couldn't let go of that image I already had in my head.

"But recently, when I've tried to imagine our family *without* Evan a part of it"—she shrugged her shoulders—"I can't.

"Yes, I'm concerned about what difficulties he may experience because of the start he had in life. And I'm scared to death that I'll waver on my promise to never leave you again. But Dr. Newell's right. Neither you nor James ... nor Evan ... none of you can make me happy or unhappy.

"The gardenia did make me very happy, but only because I was happy already. There was nothing you could have done during those dark times to make me happy, Martin. It wasn't your fault."

He shook his head vehemently. "No, I was withdrawn ... depressed. And I dragged you down with me."

"That may have played a role in it, but I had some of my own demons to battle. And your accident ... well, it was an experience I would never wish on anyone, but it forced me to grow up and to put things into perspective.

"I know that I can count on you, Martin. You're the one person who has never let me down. And I know that no matter what challenges may lie ahead, we'll be just fine ... if we face them together."

"I'm sorry, Louisa," Martin said, shaking a furrowed brow at her. "I still don't know what you're saying."

"I am *saying*, Martin ... that Evan would be the cherry on my already wonderful sundae. I *want* to adopt Evan."

Chapter 43

Evan sat sullenly picking at his scrambled eggs the following morning. He ran jam-stickied fingers through his hair and sniffed at them before wrinkling up his nose.

"That shampoo the lady sold us makes me stink," he grumbled as his chin dropped into his hand. "How many more times do you gots ta put it on my head?"

Martin peered at him over his newspaper. "However many times it takes to clear up your eczema—four to six weeks, I would guess."

"How many days is four to six weeks?"

Martin hissed out a breath of air and laid his paper down. "There are twenty-eight days in four weeks and forty-two days in six weeks."

The boy's shoulders slumped, and his eyes began to tear as he looked back at his guardian in disbelief. "But I'll starve before then! The smell gets all mixed up with the food smell, and it makes my stomach feel all—dodgy."

Louisa turned from the hob and slid another serving of eggs on to her husband's plate. "Oh, Evan, it's not that bad."

"No, he's right. It *is* that bad," Martin said, reaching a hand across the table to press his fingers to the boy's forehead. "Finish your breakfast, and then we'll walk down to Mrs Tishell's to see if we can find something less objectionable." He picked the paper back up and snapped it open.

The child's face brightened, and he held his fingers to his nose before tucking into his bacon.

"When are you planning to make your call?" Louisa asked.

"As soon as I finish breakfast." Martin tipped the last of his coffee into his mouth and set the cup back down on the table, looking up at her uneasily. "You haven't changed your mind, have you?"

"No, Martin, I haven't changed my mind." She returned the frying pan to the hob and took a seat across from him. "Do you have any special plans for the day, Evan?"

He gave her an indifferent stare. "No." He looked at the clock. "Do I gots time ta play with my blocks before we go, Dr. Ellig-am?"

"Yes, but you'll need to wash those hands first."

The boy slipped from his chair and headed down the hall.

"Evan," Louisa called out. Come back and excuse yourself from the table properly first, please."

He emerged in the doorway, his fists on his hips, and tipped his head down, narrowing his eyes at her. "*You* need ta start paying better attention. Didn't you hear Dr. Ellig-am tell me ta go wash my hands?" He turned and ran off under the stairs.

Martin whipped his head around and his eyes flashed. "Oh, no you don't!" he muttered as the newspaper smacked against the table and he pushed himself to his feet.

He returned a moment later with the boy in tow. "Now sit down and excuse yourself properly. Then I expect you to apologise to Mrs. Ellingham for being so cheeky with her."

Evan scuffed his trainer on the floor, and plopped into his chair. "Sorry, Dr. Ellig-am."

"Yes, well." Martin took in a calming breath as he tugged at his collar.

The child's foot tapped against the table leg. "Sorry for bein' cheeky, Mrs. Ellig-am, and can I be excused now?"

"I want you to come over here and see me first. Then, yes, you may be excused."

He looked up at his guardian. After receiving an encouraging nod, he slid from his seat and walked over to her, watching her warily. "I'm—I'm sorry I'm bad, Mrs. Ellig-am."

"Oh, Evan, you're *not* bad. What you said was disrespectful and impolite, though." She leaned forward and sniffed. "Hmm, you two are right. That shampoo definitely has to go."

"I'll go make that call," Martin said as he headed towards his consulting room.

Louisa got up and returned with a dampened piece of kitchen towel, rubbing it over the boy's head. "There, you're a little less sticky without the jam in your hair. Now go upstairs and run a comb through it," she said as she patted his bum.

Martin grabbed for his desk as the shock-like sensations that jolted through his bones caused his right leg to give. He grimaced, dropping into his chair, and laid his head down on the desktop for a few moments, waiting for the pain to ease.

Evan's trainers squeaked on the floor in the hall, before his footsteps could be heard on the stairs. Shaking his head, Martin's cheeks nudged up slightly at the thought of his young charge's need to run, bounce, skip, and leap when propelling himself from one place to the next.

He pulled a business card from his desk drawer and picked up the phone. As he informed Roger Delaney of the decision that he and Louisa had come to, Evan passed by the consulting room, catching enough of his guardian's muffled words to know that he was the topic of conversation.

He craned his neck to peer into the kitchen, checking that the coast was clear. Then, pressing his ear to the door, he strained to catch bits and bobs of Martin's end of the call.

" ... don't want him ... I don't see any point in dragging this out any longer. Whatever you can do to move ... "

He pressed his head tighter to the door.

" ... misbehaviour. I don't know if it's ... get this done as quickly as possible."

Silence.

" ... anyone else who might want him?"

Evan's heart began to pound as he tried to block out the background noise with a hand to his ear. "... talk to him today ... let him know that we're going to ..."

The desk chair squeaked as Martin got to his feet, and the boy ran off through the kitchen, dropping down next to his blocks on the floor in the lounge.

Martin was pulling patient notes from the file cabinet in the reception room when Louisa came downstairs with James in her arms, now in a fresh nappy and dressed for the day.

"Do you have many patients coming in this morning?" she asked.

"Just two."

"Two? That's it?"

"Mm. Everyone's probably at the market buying cider and crisps for their New Year's Eve house parties," he said, curling his lip as he yanked another set of notes from the drawer.

He jabbed the cardboard sleeve in the air. "Mark my words, I'll have them coming in tonight," he groused.

"There'll be the inevitable set-tos down at the pub at the very least. Not to mention the idiots who—"

"Oh, Martin. Everyone's just trying to have fun."

"Yeah, a jolly good knees-up," he sneered.

She shook her head and huffed out a breath before glancing towards the lounge. "Did you get your call made?" she said in an undertone.

"Mm. He was pleased with our decision, of course. I told him I was concerned that the uncertainty of the situation could be resulting in the boy's recent misbehaviour."

"You think that's what it is? Jeremy thought he might be jealous of the attention you give me."

"I very much doubt that. He seems disturbingly fascinated with the attention I give you."

Louisa stretched up and kissed him. "I don't think that was the kind of attention he was referring to. Maybe *time* would have been a better choice of word."

"I see."

James pulled at his father's shirt, and Martin took him from his mother's arms. "Well, I told Mr. Del Monaco that I thought we needed to move the process along as quickly as possible."

"It's Mr. Delaney, Martin—not Del Monaco. And not DeLansky or Del Monte either. You'd be wise to remember the man's name." She huffed. "Is he sure there are no other relatives lurking out there somewhere?"

"He assured me there aren't."

"When do you want to tell him?"

"Evan?"

"Yes, Martin ... Evan."

He handed James back to her and shook out his arm. "I suppose we should broach the subject with him today ...

make sure we're not getting ahead of ourselves. It's possible he won't want to be adopted."

"Martin ... seriously? Do you really think he's going to pass up the chance to be *your* son?"

He cleared his throat and tugged at his ear as a pink flush spread up his neck. "I think he needs to feel it was his choice. Maybe after dinner tonight ... after the boys' baths."

He pulled up his arm and looked at his watch. "I'd better get down to the chemists before it gets any later," he said before heading into the lounge.

"Are you ready to go, Evan?" he asked, peering down at the boy as he lay on the floor poking a finger at his blocks. He eyed the child suspiciously as he got to his feet and went to the kitchen to collect his coat. "Do you feel all right?"

Evan gave a shrug of his shoulders before shoving an arm into a sleeve. "I feel okay. I just don't know why the grown-ups get ta decide everything," he said before plodding towards the front door.

Martin grunted and followed along behind him.

They walked in silence down Roscarrock Hill, stopping once so that Martin could rest on the bench outside the pottery shop. When the cowbell on the door to Mrs. Tishell's store jangled a few minutes later, the woman's voice rang out from upstairs, "I'll be right with you!"

Evan punched his fist into a display of sponges as Martin perused the assortment of shampoos. A hollow clip-clop could be heard on the steps before the shopkeeper emerged from behind the wall.

"Dr. Ellingham! Two visits in three days. To what do I owe the pleasure?"

"Seborrheic eczema," he said brusquely. "That shampoo we picked up the other day smells disgusting."

"Oh dear, I *am* sorry."

"Do you have anything less offensive?"

"Let me just take a look. I'm sure between the two of us we can find something that would be more to your liking than what you have at home," she said, batting her moon eyes at him.

Martin took a step back as she moved towards him, encroaching on his personal space. "Yes, well ... if you could just show me what you have, I think I can make the decision on my own."

The chemist ran her fingers across her forehead, pushing back her fringe before allowing them to trail languidly along the neckline of her pale blue knit dress. "Of course, I'll just go see what I can find."

"Gawd," Martin muttered as the woman disappeared into a back room.

Evan walked over and laid his arms on the glass countertop, resting his head on his hands. "How come she looks at you that way?"

"What way?"

"Kinda like Mrs. Ellig-am does when you're not doin' any of your crap things. Does she like you?"

"Of course she likes me; she's my wife. I thought we covered this a few nights ago."

"*No.* I mean Mrs. Tishell. Does *she* like you?"

Martin pulled in his chin and wagged a finger at the row of sweets on a shelf. "Why don't you go pick out a treat."

"Really?"

"Yes, but take your time. Choose carefully because I'm not going to buy you more than one." And neither did he have any intention of explaining the odd chemist's obsession with him to a seven-year-old boy.

Mrs. Tishell emerged from the back and set four bottles on the counter. She gave the doctor a coy smile as she tugged at the bow perched just below her cervical collar. "This is what I have on offer, Dr. Ellingham."

Martin's eyes were drawn, unwillingly, to the woman's now partially bared chest. He forced his attention back to the selection of shampoos, unscrewing a lid and taking a sniff. Pulling his head back, he wrinkled his nose and replaced the cap.

"*Mmm*, this one's quite nice," Mrs. Tishell said as she thrust a bottle towards him. "What do you think ... Doctor?"

As he bent down hesitantly to inhale the scent, she leaned forward. He quickly straightened himself when the top edge of her bra came into view.

"Did you find that appealing?" she asked with another bat of her eyes.

"That was ... satisfactory. The *shampoo* ... is satisfactory." He cleared his throat and turned to his young charge. "Do you have what you want, Evan?"

The boy's hand wavered between a small package of Jelly Babies and a chocolate bar before finally snatching up the fruit flavoured candy. "This one."

"Put these on my personal account please, Mrs. Tishell."

"Certainly, Doctor."

She dropped the items into a bag and Martin snatched it from her hand. "Come on, Evan." He limped towards the door, his elbow toppling a small tower of body lotions as he went by.

Louisa wiped her hands on the tea towel and dropped it on to the table when they came in the back door a few minutes later. "Well, hello you two!" she said. "Did you get what you wanted?"

"Oh, I got *more* than I wanted," Martin mumbled as he set his purchases on the counter with a thud.

"What's that s'posed to mean?"

He glanced over at his wife's anxious expression. "Mm, nothing ... nothing."

He handed Evan his Jelly Babies, and the boy dropped the unopened package on to the table before returning to his blocks.

Martin wagged a finger at him. "He didn't say a word the entire walk home."

"Well, it can be a bit of a let-down for children once all the presents have been opened—the celebrations are over. Maybe you could help him put his aeroplane together after lunch."

"Mm, yes."

"Then you could take him up to Rosstree Field to try it out. That would cheer him up."

Martin winced. "I'm not going to be very good at this kind of thing, you know."

"You just need a little practice. Assembling a toy aeroplane should be a breeze compared to putting clocks back together, hmm?"

"Yes." He headed towards the hallway. "I have patients."

Evan seemed to grow more morose as the day wore on. The Jelly Babies, which he had picked up at Mrs. Tishell's, still sat unopened on the end of the table as they finished eating lunch.

"Why don't you get that aeroplane you got for Christmas, Evan, and we'll put it together," Martin said, putting the last of the dishes in the dishwasher.

"I already packed it." The boy stepped down into the lounge and flopped himself on to the sofa.

"Packed it? Well, go *unpack* it then."

He trudged off up the stairs, returning a short time later with the toy, still in its plastic wrapper. Slapping it down on the kitchen table, he climbed into a chair.

"Okay, let's see what we've got," Martin said as he tugged futilely at the packaging.

"Here, let me," Louisa said, taking it from his hands and pulling it open.

He looked up at her, forcing a small smile. "Mm, thank you."

Evan punched out the pieces from the sheets of balsa, and his guardian helped him to insert them into their corresponding notches. Then the propeller was slipped over the end of the stick that served as the body of the plane.

"Okay, now you need to hook the rubber band over the hooks at each end of the fuselage," Martin instructed.

"Can you do it?" Evan asked as he slumped back in his chair.

The doctor hissed out a breath and completed the final step before pushing himself to his feet. "Get your coat, and we'll go try it out."

The boy's face brightened, and he hurried over to pull his jacket from the peg behind the door.

Martin looked down wistfully at his son who sat on the slate floor playing with a set of stacking cups. Louisa wrapped her arms around him and kissed his cheek. "You'll be able to take him for walks again soon." she said, patting his bum. "Better take your crutches with you."

"Yes."

By the time they had reached the top of Roscarrock Hill, Martin's legs were weakening and he was resting most of his weight on the crutches. He lowered himself on to the bench overlooking the village, sitting for a few minutes as he watched Evan throw pebbles over the side of the cliff.

The boy giggled as a herring gull swooped down, grabbing a hurled rock from the air before deeming it inedible and letting it drop on to the ground.

He soon tired of the game and came over to sit down beside his guardian. They looked out over the water, enjoying the warmth of the winter sun and the unusually gentle breeze.

Evan jumped suddenly from his seat. "Dolphins!" he said, pointing a finger. "There's dolphins, Dr. Ellig-am!"

"Yes, I see them. Good eye, Evan."

"I never saw them for real before." He climbed back up on the bench and stood up next to the doctor, shielding the sun from his eyes. "Do you think they're lookin' for food, or where do you think they're goin'?"

The boy tottered, and Martin wrapped an arm around his legs to steady him. "I don't know. Maybe they have Brewster on their tails."

"You mean *Rooster*. Why would *he* be chasin' them?"

"Maybe he's looking for his dinner."

"But he doesn't gotta look for his dinner. I adopted him, so somebody comes and feeds him."

"That's not really what that means, Evan. The money I paid for you to adopt Rooster goes into a fund to pay for shark research. It helps to pay the salaries of the scientists who study them."

"How come they gotta study 'em?"

"To learn about them—what they need to live and reproduce—to thrive."

"Oh. I didn't know *that's* what adoption meant."

"What do you think it means?"

"You know, like you say you're gonna feed someone and take 'em to the doctor and give 'em a place to sleep and stuff."

"When people adopt a child, then yes, they're agreeing to do all of those things. But adoption means much more than that. The child who's adopted becomes a part of that family—the new mother and father's own child."

"You mean a kid can get different parents if they want?"

Martin tipped his head to the side and tugged at his ear. "Well, yes. Children can get different parents, but people adopt a child only if the child's birth parents can no longer care for them."

"So does the kid get to pick the parents *they* wanna adopt, or do the grown-ups decide?"

"Children can't adopt adults; adults adopt children."

"Oh." He slid from the bench and kicked at the ground, sending a shower of gravel flying. "Can we fly the plane now?"

"Yep ... yep." Martin pulled himself to his feet with one of the crutches.

They walked away from the cliff edge, into the grassy expanse that stretched to a nearby pasture. Martin showed his charge how to turn the propeller and wind the motor.

The glorified rubber band, used to store energy which provided power to the little plane, twisted along its length. Knots began to line up, like a strand of pearls, until they reached the front end of the fuselage.

"Okay, I think you've got it there, Evan," Martin said as he grasped on to the propeller and moved the fingers of the child's right hand under the wing. "Now take your left hand and hold on to the propeller so the rubber band doesn't unwind before you're ready to launch it."

An involuntary groan slipped from Martin's mouth as he leaned over to pluck a bit of dry grass from the ground. "We need to see which way the wind is blowing ... launch the thing *into* the wind," he said as he dropped the grass through the air.

He took hold of the boy's shoulders and turned him to face the primary school before placing his hands over his to grip the little aeroplane. "Tip the nose into the air a bit. Yep, yep, that's it. Now, let go of the propeller and give it a little push."

The child pulled his left hand away, and the miniature prop whirred. The toy wobbled through the air a few times before levelling out, carving graceful circles through the light wind pushing in off the Atlantic.

Evan stood, mesmerised, as he watched it soar freely. It climbed a bit higher with each orbit over their heads, before the propeller stopped spinning and it began its descent. A broad grin spread across his face as he turned to his guardian. "Wow! It really works, Dr. Ellig-am!"

"Mm. A simple matter of aerodynamic principles in action. It has to do with the pressure distribution caused by the airflow over the wing. The pressure on the bottom of the wing is greater than on the top of the wing. That difference causes the aeroplane to be pushed into the air."

The child gave him a blank stare, and Martin scratched at an eyebrow. "Are you familiar with Newton's law of action and reaction?"

Evan wrinkled up his face. "I gotta get my plane," he said before gambolling off.

The winding and launching of the little plane was repeated several more times, with one flight ending abruptly with a nose dive into the grass. Standing back on a fifth attempt, Martin let his young charge take his "solo flight". He watched, feeling a sense of pride in the child.

The boy sent the plane off on one flight after another, his arm finally growing tired after countless turns of the propeller. "Here, Dr. Ellig-am, you want a turn? I can't do it anymore."

Martin put a hand up in front of him and shook his head. "No, thank you."

"Come on, Dr. Ellig-am," the child whined.

"Ah, really, Evan, I don't think I'd be very good at it."

"But you showed me really good."

"I did a bit of reading about how it's done. You did the actual flying of the plane."

"Mrs. Ellig-am told us at an assembly once that you gotta have competence in yourself. So just use your competence and do it."

Martin rolled his eyes and held out his hand. "Okay, one more time, and then we better head home," he said as he leaned forward on his crutches.

It took him several tries before he was able to get his stiff and weakened right hand to perform the way he needed it to, but he finally had the rubber band wound, and he released the toy.

Whether it was a fickle wind or a thermal, an upward current of warm air, the aeroplane suddenly took off and headed out towards the open ocean.

"Oh no! My aeroplane!" Evan cried out before dashing towards the cliff edge.

"Evan, stop!" Martin yelled, starting after the boy as quickly as he could.

The child ran at full-tilt, his eyes never leaving the plane as it soared through the sky.

Panic sent adrenaline coursing through the doctor's veins as he watched helplessly, the distance between the boy and the precipitous fall to the granite boulders below closing rapidly. "*Evan Hanley! Stop right where you are!*"

The anger in his guardian's tone caused the boy to stop in his tracks and look back for a moment. Then he turned to run down Roscarrock Hill and towards the surgery.

Martin watched as the little plane dove into the water before it was engulfed by a wave, and then followed after his young charge.

"What happened?" Louisa asked when her husband entered the kitchen. "Evan's very upset."

Martin glanced around. "Where did he go?"

"Upstairs, I assume to his room. What did you say to him, Martin?"

He stared at her for a moment and sighed before continuing on under the steps.

Evan was lying face down on the bed, his head buried under his pillow, when he entered the nursery. He lowered himself down next to him and sat, silent, before saying softly, "Evan, I'm sorry I lost your plane. I'll buy you another one."

The seven-year-old flipped himself over and sucked in a ragged breath.

"Are you still angry at me?"

"I wasn't angry. I was—I was. I thought you weren't paying attention to where you were going. I thought you were going to run over the edge of the cliff. I was—"

He cleared his throat. "You scared me; I wasn't angry."

"Oh."

"Come on, you must have worked up an appetite with all that running around. Let's go have a glass of milk."

Martin spent the remainder of the afternoon in his consulting room, catching up on his bookkeeping duties. When he came out to the kitchen shortly after half five, Louisa had supper simmering on the hob.

"It smells good," he said, peering over her shoulder as his hands settled on her waist.

"Mm, it does. I got the soup Bert gave you out of the freezer."

"Ah."

She reached for an oven glove as she passed him a basket of crusty bread. "Put that on the table, will you?"

"Mm, yes."

Louisa set the pot of soup down next to a plate of sliced meats and cheeses before going into the lounge to gather up her son. "Come on, Evan. It's time to eat." She reached a hand out and tousled the seven-year-old's hair.

Martin dropped into a chair, grimacing, and his wife eyed him with a look of concern. "You better sit down on the sofa tonight and ice those legs."

"I'm fine, really. In fact, I thought ... I thought we might walk down to the Platt a little later. Take in the fireworks."

"Really?" Her brow lowered as she eyed him anxiously.

"*Fireworks!* I always wanted ta see fireworks!" Evan said. He pulled his feet under him and leaned his arms on the table. "Lydia Bigelow says her mum and dad take her every year."

Louisa gave her head a shake. "I don't know if it's a good idea, Martin. There'll be a crowd of people down there—kids running everywhere. And you've already been on your feet too much today."

He tipped his head down to hide the pained expression on his face. "I just thought you'd enjoy it."

"*I'd* enjoy it!" Evan said, bouncing in his chair.

Louisa hesitated before filling her husband's bowl with soup. "Will you call Jeremy ... see if he can walk down and back with us in case you—"

Martin slapped his spoon down on the table with a sharp thunk.

She watched him for a few seconds before saying softly, "I just worry about you."

His abstracted gaze settled on the basket of bread for a minute before his shoulders rose and fell. "Yes, I can do that."

"Thank you, Martin." She picked up the seven-year-old's bowl and had it poised, ready to fill it with soup, when her husband stopped her.

"Erm, Louisa, I'm not sure that's a good idea."

"You haven't become a believer in the powers of Bert's soup, have you?"

"Don't be ridiculous." He poked around at a prawn floating in his bowl and peered up at her shyly. "But if Lydia Bigelow's going to be there tonight, perhaps we shouldn't take chances."

Evan wrinkled up his nose. "I don't think it's a good idea even if Lydia Bigelow's *not* there tonight. I don't like that kinda soup," he said, putting an end to the discussion.

After dinner, Martin took Evan upstairs and gave him a bath, washing his hair twice to remove the last vestiges of the odour from the first shampoo.

When they returned to the lounge, Louisa situated her husband on the sofa, elevating his legs on the coffee table before surrounding them with cold packs.

"I'll be back after I have James bathed," she said, setting several periodicals on the sofa next to him and placing a kiss on his head.

He waited anxiously for her to return, glancing frequently at his charge who was working on a stylized replica of a lorry, following the directions that came with his new blocks.

When Louisa settled in next to him a short time later, she gave him a knowing smile and nodded her head towards their young charge. James pushed away from her and scrambled towards his father. "Hi, Da-ee," he said, grinning up at him with a wrinkled nose.

The corners of Martin's mouth nudged up. "Hello, James." He pulled him into his lap and cleared his throat. "Evan, Mrs. Ellingham and I have something we'd like to discuss with you. Come over here, please."

The boy sat unmoving for a moment before getting to his feet and taking a seat on the table, next to his guardian's legs. His nervous eyes flitted between Martin and Louisa.

"I spoke with Mr—" He glanced over at his wife.

"Delaney," she whispered.

"Yes, Mr. Delaney, the man who talked to you at the hospital and stopped by to check up on you a while back. Do you remember him?"

"Yeah. Can I work on my lorry again, now?" the boy asked as he got to his feet.

"No, not just yet. There's something important that we need to talk about."

Martin rubbed his hand across the back of his neck. "First of all, Mrs. Ellingham and I"—he glanced down as his son reached out for the older boy—"and James, have enjoyed having you staying with us.

"But it was meant to be a temporary arrangement. Just to give Mr. Delaney time to find a relative—an aunt, uncle ... a grandparent who you could live with until you're grown. Someone who could care for you properly."

The child picked up a medical journal and focused his attention on it. "What are they doin' in this picture?" he asked, holding the periodical up in front of his guardian's face.

"They're performing an open transmyocardial laser revascular—"

Martin hissed out a breath and tugged the journal from the boy's hands. "You need to pay attention, Evan," he said as his brow furrowed. "They've tried to find a relative who could act as your guardian, but it seems there are no relatives who would be suitable caregivers for you."

The child spun around, fixing his gaze on the stockings still hanging from the mantel, and he pressed his hands to the sides of his head.

Martin glanced over at his wife, and she gave him an encouraging nod.

"What would normally happen in a situation such as this," he continued, "is that Children's Services would try to locate foster parents who would take care of you. Or you would live in a special home with other children who have—"

Evan pushed himself from the table and raced from the room.

"Evan?" Martin called out. His shoulders sagged. "Well, I made a total cock-up of that."

"I'll go," Louisa said, patting her husband on the knee. "You rest those legs."

When she came into the nursery, Evan was shoving items into his backpack. He wiped his face on his sleeve and picked up his book about ocean animals, adding it to the rest of the items.

"What are you doing?" she asked as she dropped on to the bed.

The boy gave a shrug. "Packing my stuff."

"Are you planning to go somewhere?"

"I'm not *planning* it. Grown-ups get all those decisions."

"Oh, I see. Well, before you get too far into that, would you please come back downstairs. Dr. Ellingham was trying to talk to you, and I think he's feeling a little disappointed that you didn't want to listen to him."

Evan looked up at her. "I didn't mean ta make him disappointed. It was just gettin' too hard to wait for the words."

"Well, you didn't really give him a chance to say the words."

"That's 'cause he was takin' too *long*."

"Sometimes it takes him a while to get the words out. I think you should come back downstairs and let him finish. That would make him happy, I know."

The boy dropped his head into his hands and sat silently for a few moments before getting to his feet. "Okay."

"Don't worry, Evan. It'll be all right," Louisa said as she guided him towards the steps.

Evan reclaimed his seat on the coffee table. "Sorry I didn't listen, Dr. Ellig-am," he said.

"Mm, it's okay. I'll try to do a better job of it this time." He turned to his wife. "Louisa, could you take James?"

Wincing as his son's weight was lifted from his lap, he shifted and directed his attention to the seven-year-old. "Evan, I'm trying to tell you that you have no relatives to care for you. But ... well, we talked about what it means to adopt a child earlier today. Do you remember what I told you?"

The boy picked at a hangnail, oblivious to the blood that had begun to seep from the wound he was creating. "Yeah. The kids don't get to choose."

Martin's head tipped to the side as he raised his eyebrows. "Well, yes. But I also told you that when a child is adopted, he becomes the new parents' own child—a member of the family."

Glancing down, saliva flooded his mouth when he caught sight of the child's fresh, self-inflicted wound. He leaned forward, gently tugging the boy's hands apart to stop him from worrying his fingers.

"Evan, Mrs. Ellingham and I would like ... well, we'd like to apply to adopt you. Once we've submitted the required application papers, a judge will decide if Mrs. Ellingham and I would make suitable parents for you."

Evan stared back at him for a moment before tears began to well in his eyes and his lip began to tremble. He slid from the coffee table and scrambled into his guardian's lap, wrapping his arms around his neck.

Martin's jaw clenched as he fought to contain the expletive threatening to slip out, and he reached down to shift the boy's knobbly knee from the wound in his thigh.

Taking in a deep breath, he swallowed hard and went on. "We do, of course, want to hear what you think about all of this. I don't mean to imply that we've made the decision without you. I'm not sure how you—"

A small hand was slapped to his mouth, and Evan buried his face in his neck.

"Dr. Ellig-am, *stop—talking*," the child said, his arms tightening as he began to shudder.

Martin looked over at Louisa, his expression making it clear that he was now in over his head.

She reached out and rubbed the boy's back. "Evan, are those happy tears or sad tears?"

"Uh-huh!" he wailed before turning a blotchy face towards her. "Does this mean I *don't* gotta leave?"

"No, Evan. You don't have to leave."

"And *you* like me, too?"

"Of course I do! Did you think I didn't?"

"I couldn't tell. But Dr. Ellig-am said that if I did lots of crap things and you still liked me, that means you think I'm special.

"And I did *a lot* of crap things and you still want to adopt me, so you *must* think I'm special." He pulled in a ragged breath. "It understands a reason."

Louisa tipped her head down and narrowed her eyes at her husband. "It *understands a reason?* Does it, Martin?"

He tipped his head back and wagged his nose in the air. "Louisa, you're getting a very distorted version of the way that conversation played out. The boy asked if you liked James. I told him that you did, obviously. He then asked how I—"

Louisa silenced him with a kiss. "Martin, stop talking. We can get to the bottom of it later."

He pulled in his chin. "Yes."

Evan tipped his head back and looked at his guardian warily. "Can I still call you Dr. Ellig-am if you adopt me, or do I gots ta call you Dad?"

"You call me whichever you're comfortable with." Martin pulled his handkerchief from his pocket and wiped the child's face. "But either way, you're going to have to get used to my losing your aeroplanes if we adopt you."

The boy scratched at his head. "I can tie string on 'em so you don't lose any more."

"I'm not sure they'd fly very well if you did that. Maybe we should just stock up ... have some spares on hand in case of an emergency."

"But will you still be my parents if I don't call you Mum and Dad?"

Louisa set James on the sofa and knelt down in front of him. "Evan, before I married Dr. Ellingham, my name was Louisa Glasson. The kids at school called me Miss Glasson. Do you remember that?"

"Yeah."

"After I married Dr. Ellingham, I had my name changed to Louisa Ellingham. Now all the children call me Mrs. Ellingham, don't they?"

"Yeah."

"Changing my name didn't change me into a different person, did it?"

"Uh-uh. You're still our head teacher."

"That's right. And I still love James just as much as I did when I was Louisa Glasson. Dr. Ellingham and I will love *you* just as much, too, whether you call us Dr. and Mrs. Ellingham or you call us Mum and Dad."

Evan stared at her wide-eyed. "You'll love me if you adopt me?"

"Oh, Evan, we love you now! That's *why* we want to adopt you. But adoption is something you have to want, too. So, we want you to think about this."

"Oh, I've been thinkin' about it a long time. Well, wishing I didn't gotta leave—ever. Every night on my lucky rock I wished it. I don't gots ta think anymore. I wanna stay here. I want you to adopt me."

The boy looked at Martin, his expression serious. "So are you and Mrs. Ellig-am my mum and dad yet?"

"No. We need to fill out some paperwork, and a judge will make the decision in about six months ... about when the summer holiday starts. But until then, you'll live with us."

A smile spread from ear to ear across the seven-year-old's face. "So I don't gotta go live with someone else?"

"No, Evan. You can stay right here," Martin said.

The boy's arms tightened around his neck again before he pulled back and kissed him on the cheek. He pressed his forehead to his. "I love you, Dr. Ellig-am."

Martin patted the boy's back. "I love you, too, Evan."

Louisa wiped tears from her cheeks as she watched them, finally understanding how desperately her husband had wanted this.

The tender moment ended abruptly with a yelp from Martin as his charge pushed himself from his lap and ran towards the stairs.

"I gotta go unpack my stuff!"

Chapter 44

Louisa slid over next to her husband, sandwiching their son between them in an embrace. "You handled that very well, Martin."

"Mm. It went better than I thought it would."

She smiled at him, shaking her head slowly. "That little boy is so very lucky to have you."

"Mm. You told him you love him."

"I did ... I do. It's hard not to, isn't it?"

Martin pulled James to his lap, his arm grasping him securely. "Louisa ... if he weren't the way he is—sunny ... Well, if he were awkward or—or strange ... Could you still feel the same about him?"

Louisa sat for a moment before looking at him pointedly. "Evan is a sunny little boy, yes. But it's the kind and caring ... sensitive little boy *underneath* that sunny disposition that I love. So yes, if he were, as you put it, awkward and strange, I would most definitely still love him. I'd have to be a calculating, self-absorbed"—Louisa's jaws clenched as she spat out— "*ice-queen*, not to love him."

There was a knock on the kitchen door, and Louisa leaned forward to place a kiss on her husband's forehead before getting up to answer it.

"Hi, Louisa," Jeremy said as he and Poppy stepped into the house.

"Hello, Jeremy." She gave him a chaste kiss on his cheek before extending the same greeting to the childminder. "Hello, Poppy."

"Hi, Mrs. Ellingham."

The aide stepped down into the lounge and pulled a chair over next to the sofa, dropping into it. "You doing okay?" he asked fixing a scrutinizing gaze on his patient.

"Fine. I've just been on my feet a lot."

A thundering of footsteps was heard on the stairs, and Evan leapt down into the entryway. "Hi, Mr. Portman! Guess what! I'm gonna get adopted!"

Jeremy's head whirled towards his boss, his slack-jawed expression shifting into a smile. "You and Louisa?"

"Mm, yes. We just finished discussing it, so he's a bit—Mm."

Evan ran into the kitchen and tugged on the childminder's hand. "Poppy, did ya hear? I'm gettin' adopted!"

"I did hear that!" Poppy's eyes darted between Louisa and the boy, and Louisa gave her a shrug of her shoulders. "Sorry, I didn't think to discuss it with you first—give you a bit of warning about it all."

"That's okay." The girl knelt down and wrapped her arms around him. "That's really wonderful, Evan."

Louisa leaned over. "Evan, it's fine that you told Jeremy and Poppy your news—this is very exciting, I know. But let's wait until the judge makes his decision to tell anyone else—make it a surprise. Okay?"

"But what about Dr. Ellig-am—the other one? And Old Doc and Mrs. Parsons *gots* ta know, don't they?"

"Yes, I agree. How 'bout we have a celebration ... invite them. Then after that we can keep it a surprise?"

"Okay."

Martin glanced at his watch. "We should be going," he said as he wrestled his legs from their perch. Jeremy got up and helped him to his feet.

As had been the case all day, the air was unusually calm as they walked down the hill. The stars sparkled overhead in the cloudless sky, and Martin stopped to point the constellation Orion out to his young charge. "That red star there is Betelgeuse."

The boy giggled. "That's a funny name. Like the stuff that comes out of 'em when they get stepped on you mean?"

"Yes. It sounds strange, I know, but that's the most common way of pronouncing it."

Louisa shifted James on her hip as she tried to get a better grip on him.

"Here, let me carry him. He's getting to be a heavy load," Jeremy said as he took the boy from her arms.

"Yeah, he's going to be big like his daddy."

"Jebby—Jebby," the toddler said as he patted a hand against the aide's cheek.

As expected, a crowd had filled the Platt by the time they reached the bottom of Roscarrock Hill. And cheers could be heard coming from the pub, like raucous interludes amongst the belting out of drinking songs.

Jeremy handed James to Poppy and hoisted Evan into his arms, out from under the feet of distracted partiers.

"Mind if I buy these two a glass of punch, Martin?" Jeremy asked.

"That's fine. But no more than half a cup for James. God knows how much sugar they may have put into it." He reached behind him for his wallet.

The aide shook his head. "I've got this one," he said before heading towards the refreshment tables set up in the lifeboat house.

Martin glanced over at Louisa who was standing alongside Poppy's parents. His chest filled with air as he watched her in animated conversation.

"Evenin', Doc," Awen Teague drawled as he stepped up next to him. "Surprised ta see you 'ere. But I s'pose it taint a bad idea ... just in case someone blows off a 'and or somethin', eh?" he laughed.

Martin scowled at him and grunted. The nasal voice of the local constable could be heard over his left shoulder and he turned.

"Fancy seein' you here, Doc. You come to watch the fireworks, or are you here in your capacity as the local medi-*c*?"

"The fireworks, Penhale."

"Need a little *di*-version, do ya, Doc?"

"Yeah, something like that."

"We have quite an exemplary show on tap this year. The best yet, if I do say so myself."

Martin looked at him askance. "What do you mean—*we*?"

"Me and some of the boys—Chippy Miller ... Eddie Rix ... Peder Teague. Oh, and John's draggin' himself away from the pub for a bit ta help out, too."

"Are they properly trained and licenced?" Martin asked, suddenly on alert.

"Really, Doc, do you think I would'a let *that* little detail slip by me?"

"And you? You've had the necessary pyrotechnical training and passed the examination?"

"Well, technically—no."

"As an officer of the law, do you really think it's appropriate for you to be up on the cliff setting off rockets, then?"

Joe hoisted up his tool belt and gave the doctor a reproachful look. "Life's not all beer and skittles, Doc. I won't have time for playin' around with the fireworks. I'm there to supervise—make sure no innocent civilians wander into the laun-*ch* area."

Martin's posture relaxed. "I see."

"Good to know you're on notice, though. Ya never know when a rogue rocket might go astray—make a beeline for an innocent bystander, eh, Doc?"

He grunted and shook his head.

"Well, I'd love to continue our little cha-*t*, but duty calls, as they say."

The policeman turned, pulling his wallet from his pocket and flashing his I.D. as he wended his way through the crowd. "Clear the way folks. Urgent police matters to attend to," he said with exaggerated solemnity.

Martin looked around for his wife, finding the crowd movements had pushed them apart. He limped towards her, trying to close the distance between them, but he was stopped by a hand on his shoulder. "Never thought I'd see you at one'a these village dos, Doc."

He whipped his head to the side. "Mm—Bert. How are you keeping? You're not overdoing it, are you?"

"Oh, don't you worry about me none. I'm feelin' better than I have since I was a teenager. You should'a told me changin' my diet and gettin' a little exercise could make such a difference. I would'a done it a long time ago."

Martin rolled his eyes. "Is that right. Well, I'm glad you've seen the light," he said, trying to move away.

"Here, Doc ... just wait a minute there," Bert said, putting a hand on his arm. "Have you tried out the recipe yet?"

"What recipe?" Martin said, screwing up his face and yanking his arm away.

"*You* know." He leaned his still-jowly face towards Martin's ear. "The *recipe*—for my special soup."

The doctor gave him a blank stare, and Bert's face fell into a moue. "Don't tell me you haven't even read the note I gave you, Doc. I put my heart and soul into it!"

Martin stammered as he tried to cover for his lapse. "Oh, yes. I—I ... I, er forgot to mention that. Thank you, Bert. We actually had some of your soup for dinner tonight."

The restaurateur's dour expression brightened. "Oh great! How did it come out? As good as mine?"

"Yes. Yes, it was—as good as yours. We could hardly tell the difference, in fact."

The portly man nudged him with his elbow. "I gotta hand it to you, Doc. Excellent planning that was there. You're gonna see in the New Year in proper fashion, eh?" He gave Martin a sly grin and shook both thumbs in the air. "I'll be listenin' for the rockets to be goin' off."

"Oh for God's sake!" Martin hissed as he threw his head back and watched the man waddle off.

A loud boom echoed across the harbour, and the Platt was illuminated with the red light cast by the first explosion. He felt another hand settle on his arm and he turned to see his wife and son beside him. Louisa gave him a smile and another rocket soared into the air, opening a blossom of white across the night sky.

"Oi, Doc ... 'ere, 'ave a seat," Ewan Teague said as he tucked a chair in behind Martin's legs.

The doctor grimaced and looked uncomfortably at his wife.

"He just wants to help," she said, stretching up to reach his ear. "Go ahead and sit down. You don't want to hurt his feelings."

He cast a sheepish glance at Ewan. "Mm, thank you," he said as he lowered himself into the seat.

Another loud bang went off over their heads, the concussion reverberating between the granite cliffs, and a startled James burst into tears before his father reached for him.

Louisa settled the boy on her husband's lap and he pulled him in against his chest, covering his ear with a protective palm. The child calmed quickly and watched, wide-eyed, as the fiery streamers sprayed out against the black backdrop.

The wonderment that Martin saw in his son's eyes caused a persistent gathering of moisture in his own. Memories of the harsh admonishments that quashed his own sense of childhood awe still haunted him. He shook off the angry voices and pressed his lips to James's head.

Small arms snaked around his neck from behind, and he turned to see the same sparkle in Evan's eyes. "Wow!" the child whispered.

Martin settled in, and for the sake of the two little boys in his care, he allowed himself to be absorbed in the magic of the pyrotechnics.

The crowd lingered after the show ended, and Martin, Louisa and their small entourage threaded their way through the bodies and headed back up the hill towards the surgery.

Poppy and Jeremy said goodnight before returning to the Platt to join in with the party that would last well into the night. The Ellinghams attended to their usual bedtime routine.

Martin had just tucked Evan in when a ruckus began outside the front door. He cast an I-told-you-so look at his wife and worked his way down the steps.

Yanking the door open, he snapped, "For God's sake, what is it?"

Three teenage boys stood on the terrace, the shortest of them as white as a sheet and in tears.

"It's Jack, Doc. He's bleedin' to death. Blew his thumb off with a French banger," one of boys explained, stifling a laugh. "Prat." He reached out and snapped his injured friend's ear.

The doctor's stomach roiled when he looked down to see blood dripping on to the slate pavers just outside the door. "He didn't blow his thumb off, and he's not bleeding to death," he growled.

Louisa came down the steps and tried, unsuccessfully, to peer over her husband's shoulder. "What's going on?"

"Firecracker injury. Bring me a kitchen roll, please."

"Yeah."

She hurried back a moment later, thrusting the paper towelling towards her husband. James began to stir upstairs and she patted his shoulder. "I'll be right back."

He wrapped the paper towels around the boy's injured hand before giving a jerk of his head. "Come through."

The three teenagers followed him into the consulting room, and Martin ordered the patient on to the table. Removing the covering, he inspected the wound.

"It hurts, Doc! Help me, please!" the boy said as he squirmed in agony.

"I'm going to. How did this happen?"

"I lit a firecracker. I didn't think it was gonna—go off and I went ta pick it—"

He began to sob uncontrollably as his hand trembled from the pain.

"Pillock," the third boy said, snorting.

Martin's head snapped up, and he glared at his patient's companions. "All right! Perhaps it wasn't the smartest thing in the world to do, but you two geniuses aren't exactly distinguishing yourselves either!"

Louisa came into the room. "James is asleep again. Anything I can do to help?" she asked as she took a step towards the table.

"Oh Jack!" She slapped a hand to her mouth when she saw the damage that had been done to her former pupil.

"Louisa, go call Joe Penhale. Tell him I need him A.S.A.P."

Martin jabbed a finger at the taller of the two boys. "You—go get his parents."

Then he landed a fiery gaze on the boy who had delivered the last cutting remark. "And *you*—shut up and go sit on the steps outside—wait for P.C. Penhale."

Louisa cocked her head at him. "Martin, I don't think—"

"Louisa, just go call Penhale."

She noted her husband's steely expression and herded the two teenagers from the room, pulling the door shut behind her.

Martin turned his full attention to his patient. "You're going to be fine," he said, softening his tone.

He went to his medical cabinet and pulled open a drawer, returning with a foil pouch. "Let's lay you back before you fall over." He lowered the head end of the exam couch and helped the boy recline.

"This will help a lot," he said, donning a pair of exam gloves and attempting to pull the pouch open before reaching for his scissors. "You have second and third degree burns to your thumb and hand."

He removed a wet dressing from the pouch. "This is soaked with a gel that will pull out any residual heat. It should make you significantly more comfortable. When your parents get here and I have their approval, I'll give you something for the pain."

The door opened a while later, and Louisa stepped back into the room. "Joe's on his way."

"Thank you," Martin said as he worked the gauze around the wounded appendage.

The front door could be heard opening and closing and Louisa peered out. "It's your mum and dad, Jack."

"Would you see them in please, Louisa."

"Yeah." Giving the young man a reassuring smile, she hurried out the door.

The boy's parents stood in the reception room, their faces etched with worry.

"Mr. and Mrs. Clyde, it's nice to see you again," she said.

"Where's my son? He in there?" Mr. Clyde pushed past her.

"Yes, Martin said to go on back."

Mrs. Clyde followed after him, leaving her alone in the room. She listened to the parents' raised voices and worried her lip over what Martin may have said or done to rile them.

The front door was pushed open again and Joe Penhale rushed in. "Where's the casualty?" he asked, giving a sharp, upward tug on his tool belt.

"It's Jack Clyde. He's in with Martin. I'll go let him know—"

The latch on the exam room door rattled and Martin stepped out. "Penhale, I need you to get the Boyd boy over to Truro. I don't want to wait on an ambulance. If we move quickly on this, they may be able to save his thumb.

"Mrs. Boyd will ride along with you, and her husband will meet you there. I've given the boy something for the pain; it should keep him comfortable during the trip."

"Right, Doc ... blues and twos all the way on this one," Joe said.

Martin gave a nod towards the door. "And get the name of the idiot sitting out on the terrace. You'll want to follow up on this."

"Got it," he said. He pulled his notebook from his jacket and whipped his biro from his pocket before heading back out the door.

The strain on Martin's face was evident. Louisa put her hand on his arm as he turned to head back to the consulting room. "Are you okay?" she asked.

"Mm. I'll be finished up here soon."

She cringed at his pronounced antalgic gait before the consulting room door closed behind him.

A few minutes later, Jack Clyde and his mother were being raced to the Royal Cornwall by the constable, and Mr. Clyde was making his apologies to Martin.

"I'm sorry for the things I said in there, Doctor. I s'pose I was scared for my boy."

"It's all right—understandable. I do think chances are good your son's thumb can be saved."

"Well, thanks for all you done for 'im, Doc," the man said before hurrying off.

Martin turned and, without saying a word, headed up the steps. Moments later, Louisa heard the sound of his haemophobia-induced retching coming from the bathroom.

She went to the kitchen and filled the tea kettle with water before turning it on.

"Was it bad?" she asked when he came through under the stairs a short time later.

"Mm. He walked unsteadily over to the sink and filled a glass with water, drinking it down before standing motionless with his eyes closed.

"Martin, go sit down ... put your feet up," Louisa said as she took hold of his arm and turned him around. She held on to him until she had navigated him past the step down into the lounge, then went to the pantry and pulled his bottle of single malt from the shelf.

She set a glass of the amber liquid down on the coffee table and removed several cold packs that she had tucked under her arm.

"Let's get you more comfortable," she said as she lifted his legs on to the table and tucked pillows and the blue packs around them. "Here, sip on this."

She handed him the glass and he huffed out a breath. "Louisa, I don't really feel like—"

"Martin, shush. I'm going to get a cup of tea; I'll be right back."

When she returned a minute later, she dropped down on the sofa and nestled in under his arm.

"Wanna talk about it?" she asked.

"I really can't discuss my patients."

"Yeah, I s'pose not." Her fingers stroked his thigh. "Martin, those boys ... well, they were just being teenage boys. I know that, according to the law, they shouldn't have been mucking about with fireworks, but—"

"You think I shouldn't have reported them to Penhale, don't you?"

"Well, boys will be—"

"Yes, boys will be boys. That's a very feeble excuse for unacceptable behaviour in my opinion. That young man may never recover full use of that hand because boys were being boys."

"Well, I'm sure Jack's learned a very hard lesson tonight. I'm not sure Joe's involvement will benefit him in any way."

"I don't *want* Penhale to get involved with him. But the other two boys, quite obviously, *didn't* learn anything from it.

"If seeing their friend with his thumb blown to a nearly—*unsalvageable*—condition didn't have any impact, perhaps an ASBO will do the trick! That Clive boy needs to find a better set of friends. And I told him as much."

"I know those boys, Martin. They're really pretty good kids."

"Oh really? The same kind of *pretty good kids* who torment another child with taunts because they're not developing as quickly as the other kids, or because they're clumsy? Or lay in wait for them in the school corridors to give them a good bashing because they prefer intellectual pursuits to battering their brains with a football? Is *that* the kind of *good* kid you're referring to?"

Louisa stared at him for several moments, her brows knitting. "Martin, what brought all this on?"

He squeezed his eyes shut and pressed his fingers to the bridge of his nose. "Those boys— How can human beings be so cruel to one another?"

"I'm sorry, Martin, I'm not following."

"The Clive boy—the other two boys were taunting him while he was in pain—and scared to death, no doubt. There was no compassion in them. How could a *good* kid be so merciless in his treatment of another?"

"Oh ... I see. Poor Jack, I can understand now why you thought Joe should be involved."

Martin tipped back his glass and drew in the liquid before easing the burn left behind with a clearing of his throat.

"We better get you upstairs before you fall asleep," she said, giving him a small smile. She took his glass and set it on the table before getting to her feet and extending her hand. "Come on."

He put a palm up in front of him. "I've got it."

Louisa was in the bathroom by the time Martin had locked up the doors, turned out the lights and joined her upstairs.

He stood outside the closed bathroom door between them, remembering a morning not so long ago when that barrier had seemed impenetrable. Pulling up his arm, he looked at his watch—eleven-thirty. A half hour remained of what had been a tumultuous year. "Louisa?" he said softly.

The latch rattled and she pulled the door open. "Yes?"

He tipped his head down, peering at her shyly. "I'm sorry I got upset with you. It wasn't your fault; you didn't know what had gone on with those boys."

"It's all right. Are you feeling better now?"

He pulled her into an embrace and took in a deep breath. "Now I am."

She closed her eyes and relaxed in the security of his arms. "Martin ... erm," she glanced down, "you really need to get that recipe from Bert."

Giving a self-conscious glance at the object of her attention, he pulled away. He went to the laundry basket, digging through the clothes until he found the shirt he had been wearing on Christmas Day. Then he fished the forgotten envelope from the pocket and handed it to his wife.

She looked at him, bemused, before pulling open the flap and scanning the index card. "Squid oil? That's the secret ingredient—squid oil?"

"What?" Martin snatched the grease-stained recipe card from her hand and looked down at the restaurateur's sloppy print. "Oh gawd! We've been eating *squid oil!*"

She screwed up her face. "It does sound a bit ... less than appetising."

Taking a step towards him, she slipped her arms under his. "Well, as far as I can tell, there have been no *adverse* effects. So maybe we should just ... go with the flow?"

Martin tipped his head down, pressing his lips to hers in a passionate kiss, his hands sliding under her pyjama top. "I, er ... I'll be right back," he said as he turned and headed towards the stairs, ducking through the doorway.

"Martin, where are you going?"

"Just following through on my promise."

Moments later, she heard the kitchen door open and close, followed quickly by the sound of Buddy's footsteps as he scrambled towards the nursery.

When her husband came to bed a few minutes later, she pulled the covers back slightly more than necessary, giving him just a glimpse—for inspiration.

He slid in next to her, his hand coming to rest on the warm velvety skin of her bare hip. "We have an anniversary coming up soon," he said.

"Yes, we do. It's been quite a year, hmm?" Her fingers stroked his chest as she stared absently towards the ticking mantle clock.

"Mm. We're certainly ending it in a very different place than where we started it." He brushed her hair back from her shoulder before cupping her cheek in his hand. "I was afraid I'd lost you, Louisa."

"And I almost lost you." She leaned towards him and pressed her forehead to his. "But we hung on. We helped each other through some very difficult times, and we're much stronger for it."

Martin pushed himself up on his elbow and gazed down at her, his eyes glinting in the moonlight coming in the window. "Thank you for not giving up on me."

"Oh, Martin," she sighed, "I've made some very big mistakes. It scares me to think where we'd be now if I *had* given up on you."

"Mm, we'd have lost our synergic advantage."

"Hmm?"

"Synergy—the whole is greater than the sum of its parts. It's an expression often attributed to Aristotle and is used to describe—"

Louisa pressed a finger to his mouth. "Maybe you should just come up and show me what you mean," she murmured.

Placing a kiss on her forehead, he gave her a knowing smile and nudged her on to her back.

A series of mini-rockets went off somewhere in the village, interrupting the quiet night with crackles, whistles, and pops as Martin and Louisa saw in the New Year in proper fashion.

They were awakened a short while later, still in each other's arms, when a gust of wind slammed into the house. Martin lay looking at his wife. "You were half right," he said, his cheeks nudging up.

"About what?"

"About proving Ed wrong. The rockets—Ed said before I left hospital that there wouldn't be any harps playing or rockets going off for a while, but I'm reasonably certain I heard rockets that time." He brushed his fingers across her cheek as he swallowed. "I will *always* love you, Louisa."

She leaned towards him, pressing her forehead to his. "And I will always love you ... my extraordinary man."

Martin switched off the light. His wife's arm reached out to encircle him, and the shadow of loneliness that had pursued him through life gave ground. He lay, feeling warm and safe as the cold Atlantic wind ushered in what would be remembered for years as the big New Year's Day Storm.

Don't miss out!

Click the button below and you can sign up to receive emails whenever Kris Morris publishes a new book. There's no charge and no obligation.

Sign Me Up!

https://books2read.com/r/B-A-PAJD-GVSL

BOOKS 2 READ

Connecting independent readers to independent writers.

Also by Kris Morris

Battling Demons
Battling Demons
Fractured
Fragile
Headway
Insights
A Cornwall Christmas

About the Author

Kris Morris was born and raised in a small Iowa town. She spent her childhood barely tolerating school, hand rearing orphaned animals, and squirrel taming. At Iowa State University she studied elementary education. But after discovering a loathing for traditional pedagogy and a love for a certain tall, handsome, Upstate New Yorker, she abandoned the academic life to marry, raise two sons, and become an unconventional piano teacher. When she's not writing, Kris builds boats and marimbas with her husband, who she has captivated for thirty years with her delightful personality, quick wit, and culinary masterpieces. They now reside in Iowa and have replaced their sons with ducks.

Read more at www.ktmorris.com.

Printed in Great Britain
by Amazon